CANDIDA'S OWN
ITALIAN RENAISSANCE

CANDIDA'S OWN ITALIAN RENAISSANCE

A Sensuous Journey Through Time

BARBARA SHER TINSLEY

iUniverse

CANDIDA'S OWN ITALIAN RENAISSANCE
A SENSUOUS JOURNEY THROUGH TIME

iUniverse books may be ordered through booksellers or by contacting:

iUniverse
1663 Liberty Drive
Bloomington, IN 47403
www.iuniverse.com
1-800-Authors (1-800-288-4677)

ISBN: 978-1-4917-5936-3 (sc)
ISBN: 978-1-4917-5935-6 (e)

Library of Congress Control Number: 2015903214

Print information available on the last page.

iUniverse rev. date: 08/11/2015

CONTENTS

ACKNOWLEDGEMENTS

The author wishes to thank the post beat novelist, Lynn Rogers, for her content editing of *Candida's Own Italian Renaissance*. Her contributions on northern California 70's sub-culture and photo essay on Alviso, Candida's habitat, were very useful.

In addition, I would like to extend my gratitude to my friend, Catherine Fulde, former English teacher, for her helpful comments on earlier forms of my chapters. As always, my supportive husband, William Tinsley, listened to me read *all* the chapters in their various forms over the two year period in which this novel assumed its present shape. Many of his insights are embedded in these pages.

DEDICATION

This novel is dedicated to my beloved husband, Prof. William E. Tinsley, who took an unfailing interest in all its permutations, and made astute observations on many historical and dramatic events incorporated into the final version.

CHAPTER I

I GET THE "BOOT"

I, Candida Darroway, am looking forward to the autumn quarter, 1973, at Altamonte College, with its clear view of the Bay Bridge to Oakland. It offers the only clarity I have some days. I am thirty-two and got tenure as Associate Prof at thirty. I teach Language Arts, that is, French and Italian–that's my "bag," stodgy as it may seem. I earned a Ph.D. at Cal, where for decades academics had been defending civil rights. All I ever defended at Cal was my dissertation. It was entitled *Boccaccio: Plague of Platitudes,* my analysis of Boccaccio's rhetorical style.

Before I even started my dissertation, crowds of students surrounded Sproul Hall defending rights to help run the place. They were angry over a host of things, including 'Nam.' The War is still not over, but almost. And students still don't have much power, nor professors, for that matter.

Don Hicks, a non-academic editor from a small press in Oakland, had thought my dissertation would sell better as *Boccaccio's Bouquets.* I'd wanted to publish as soon as possible, because we were in a period of stagflation, and jobs in literature–in all fields–were scarce. Given my "desertion" by both parents after they divorced–I was fourteen then–I felt I had only myself to rely on, like many young women today. So I went along with Don's title and cover. It speeded up publication and sales. He greeted me in his cramped office behind a taco restaurant on College Avenue.

Don said, "Hi, Candida, I've got your cover under way. My designer is busy drawing male and female skeletons for it. Black, of course. There'll be skeletons wearing Renaissance hats, feathers, ruffs, whatever. They'll sniff nosegays (a plague "remedy" thought to ward off infection) and peer down or up ladies' dresses. A pair can be having sex in the left corner while another dances in the upper right. What do you think, Candida?"

"Oh, fine, Don." I thought it grotesque, but I was not in the mood to delay the publication process by arguing over the cover. I needed this publication for the job I did get at Altamonte College.

Don seemed nervous. In many ways, I was too. Not just because his stuffy little print shop office was confining. I had to find another kind of fresh air, a kindred spirit, another academic in a related field who would be my life's partner. Finding a man I could love, rely on, and reproduce with was important. I'd aim high–a job at a university, not a small liberal arts college where I had landed. I wanted academic success, but I was average in traditional ways. I wanted a family. That was because I really didn't have one, at least, not long. My parents were on the outs since I was ten. I longed to raise lovable kids in a loving home. I visit my parents, both remarried, with new sets of kids to care for, but feel like a prowler on the premises. So, my next non-scholarly objective is marriage. Even if the times they were "'A-changin,'" as Bob Dylan taught us in the sixties, I wanted to select the changes I adopted. Family *and* scholarly fame, too. I wanted it all.

"What I like about you, Candida," Don Hicks said, "is your practicality. And you're kind of pretty, though you wear dismal outfits. Why not change your palette? brighten up?"

At first I thought he meant palate, and wondered at his cheekiness.

"Maybe," he hesitated, "we could get together some week-end? Talk about your next book? Eat Chinese in the City? Drinks at a little place I know?"

He didn't name the little place. His apartment, no doubt. Because of Dad's many infidelities to Mom before their divorce, I was leery of Don and others who were attracted to me. They all had their lines. Dad probably used the same ones on the secretaries he seduced; one of whom, a ditsy creature named "Chérie," he finally married. They had two sons.

Don and I had nothing in common but his publishing my dissertation under a grotesque, sexy, cover. Was this cover another way of sending me a message?

"Actually, I've already found my intended mate," I told him. I hoped I could communicate with him between the extremes of death and love, which, for me, was clearly not possible with Don. I *was* practical.

I did need to get my private life in gear. I sometimes feel like Lily Bart in Wharton's novel, *The House of Mirth*, good, but never quite good enough. Only I am three years older than she was! I tell myself I want a loyal man, not a dull lover and assured date for a lifetime of dinners in. Rather, a caring academic with whom to balance babysitting, housework, and teaching with innovative sex that comes from absolute trust. But, aside from Tony, I have never done much to make that happen. Am I afraid to try? I don't know. At least the Pill has liberated me from making any regrettable biological errors.

"Bye, Don." I picked my purse up from the print shop floor. "Can't wait to see the final product. I owe you so much." *But not my body*, I thought. I left his place feeling relief for having dodged an unwanted date. The platitudes of Boccaccio's elites on the other hand, fascinate me. Like political speech today. Don's platitudes are not interesting, just clichés.

The cover of the book is problematic. How would I have known then that academic peers wound send hurtful notes about the bawdy skeletons when the book came out two months later? They avoided comment on the rhetorical issues I'd raised. But positive reviews were in the works, information slipped me by my major professor. It would be nice if they landed in the *PMLA* and *Renaissance Quarterly Journal*. After that, a promotion. Possibly, a prestigious job offer. Maybe I'd find my real mate on some university campus, at some academic convention.

The Feminine Mystique by Betty Friedan had appeared in 1963, the year I received my Bachelor's degree in the humanities. I didn't actually read it until I was almost done with my dissertation. Then it hit me. She was right. A woman could and should do more than raise kids in suburbia, no matter what the rest of society thought. She could do that and exercise a profession. Friedan reconfirmed my ambition to have everything.

I was now working on Boccaccio's *Filocolo*, a long vernacular prose romance, probably because there was so little of it in my life. Romance couldn't last too long. Or sexual passion long enough. This is admittedly a reflection on my boyfriend of sorts, Tony, slightly less than my age, and rather immature. He finds it hard to make up his mind about anything, though he is sweet and gentle. In bed he did what he did rather fast, then fell asleep, snoring.

3

Tony is Anthony Murphy. He lives in Gilroy, but we see each other most weekends. Last night he came up to Alviso, one of the oldest and most maligned towns in the South Bay. I rent a cottage there. Tony sleeps over on weekends. A superior engineer, he was laid off from his job ten months ago. The firm left to do business in Puerto Rico. Tony's mother was Italian, as is mine. His grandmother, Teresa, to whom I probably am closer than to Tony, raised him from the age of two. His mother had Tony at fifteen. At seventeen, she disappeared. She'd never been in touch since.

Tony has blue eyes and short, curly hair, golden. Not Black Irish in looks, or even what most people think of as Italian. He would be handsome if his shoulders were not so broad. He started lifting heavy weights when he lost his job, so now, instead of a size forty jacket, he wears a forty-six. Some shoulders. But good to cry on. Also, his stomach was beginning to bulge. He should work on his abs and forget the heavy weights. Having lost his job, and still unemployed, he is depressed. Who wouldn't be?

"Tony," I said to him last night, "can I ask you something really intimate? I haven't usually. So I hope if I do, you won't get upset. Promise you won't?"

"How can I promise if I don't know what the question is?" Tony is very logical. Not well read, but logical.

"Okay. But don't get mad."

"Do I ever get mad at you, Candida?" He sighed. No, he doesn't. He was like a big, loyal pet, not a dog; perhaps a pony, who sees me weekly, and canters after me with expectations of getting a carrot. A kiss. Sympathy. Sex. Our conversations are often about his grandmother, who is like my aunt, or even an older sister.

The trouble is that I am increasingly feeling like Tony is my brother—my younger brother. He was born in 1943, not 1941 like me. Tony and I talk about our childhoods. Not too gripping, that. We watch golden oldies on T.V. Fred Astaire and Ginger Rogers in *Top Hat; Charade*, with Cary Grant and Audrey Hepburn; *Vertigo* with Kim Novak and Jimmy Stewart. Tony's favorite old film was *An Affair to Remember*, with Deborah Kerr and Cary Grant. Cary and Jimmy were always, it seemed, twenty years older than their female partners. I wondered why young women seemed so enthralled with older men on screen? It wouldn't happen much in real life, I figured, unless the girl was subconsciously looking for a father or something. I'm certainly not. Dad is a great father to his second set of children, but too distracted now to be great for me.

Tony and I discuss his grandmother, Teresa. Tony's joblessness. Our love of all things Italian. We almost never talk of our love for each other except once, the other night.

"Tony, why do you make love to me so fast?" This was *It*. "I think our longest love making session was under ten minutes. Usually, less than five."

My bedroom clock had a large, phosphorescent face. I had started to time him, with one eye closed. We'd been making love for over two years. I knew it was bad to close one eye, because it interfered with my necessary headtrip. My body only traveled so far without my head.

"And why," I continued, "don't you talk while making love? Give me feedback? Encouragement? Ideas! And afterward. Why not hold me close for a few minutes? Sometimes you fall asleep before I can roll over, and you snore so loudly I cannot sleep. Teresa says you don't snore in Gilroy." Tony laughed.

"I don't sleep with my grandmother. How would she know?" Then he shrugged. "Its not you, Candida. You know I am very attracted. If I were not unemployed, I would no doubt propose."

No doubt, I thought. Oddly, I'm not devastated that he hasn't. It does make me glad that he finds happiness making love to me, and that I matter to someone. The big Italo-Irish lunk. They say the Irish were the Italians of northern Europe. But the Italians of southern Europe did well not to be the Irish of the South. Think how much sooner Mediterranean culture developed than Irish culture did. There had to be a reason. Last night Tony stayed awake for nearly fifteen minutes after we made love and we talked. It wasn't mad and passionate love or talk, but it was ten minutes longer than usual. I timed it. But I have to search for the right topics to keep any conversation going. I know Tony is very smart but in all the wrong things: math, science, physics, engineering. I simply cannot try to explain why French and Italian language and literature mean more to me than just a means for speaking with foreigners. Of course, to be fair I don't understand engineering, or any of the projects he finds interesting, because we have been so diversely educated. Other than that, I feel very close to him; like a brother. Perhaps because I feel Teresa is almost another mother.

I do feel loved. My problem? I don't think I really love Tony. I am just rooting for him to get out from under. No, I am generally under, but he is the underdog. I lied to Don Hicks. Tony is solid and sweet and would never intentionally desert me; but I feel he will not turn out to be my mate, because eventually, I fear I will desert him. There are many ways to desert somebody. Reliability beats romance in the short run. But does it in the long one?

The next day. I'm sitting in my office at Altamonte College up the peninsula preparing for my next class. The phone rang.

"Yes, this is Professor Darroway. Who is speaking, please? Professor Ferrell? Now? My first class starts at ten and it is already 9:15. Couldn't we do it later? No? Well, all right. Come on over. I'll be in my office until 9:50, when I leave for my ten o'clock in Old Main."

Rob (short for Robin) Ferrell teaches art history. He is a handsome, gifted, charming full professor. He has huge classes of two hundred adoring students. I had watched him striding across campus. I heard him lecture on Michelangelo and even on Machiavelli's building projects. Hardly a literary topic, but one of interest. His lectures were brilliant. Once or twice in the faculty lounge we had talked about Renaissance art and literature. At a faculty party I noticed him drinking "across a crowded floor." That last was a line from a 50s song. Dad used to sing it. But Ferrell was a mere acquaintance. What could he want with *me?*

At exactly 9:22 came a sharp rap on my closed door. I opened to find Rob Ferrell. How long legged he was. He could really cover the ground.

"Have a seat, please, Professor Ferrell. Take the armchair by the window; it's the most comfortable one." Bad move on my part. The sun coming in back lit his face, which went nearly black, while hitting me between the eyes. My battered old blinds needed replacing. Ferrell saw every square inch of me, and maybe through me, as well. But all I saw of him was a black outline illuminated by fine white teeth.

Because he was nearly six feet four, his feet touched my chair, the base of which was sun struck. This is why I had such a good view of his two-tone Italian shoes in tan with brown suede trim. They had side zippers and tassels. I was wearing scuffed loafers.

"I've come to proposition you," he said, tossing his large head of hair back as he did so, laughing. His auburn hair, thick and wavy, was shining gloriously around his head, halo like. Mine was brown, and didn't shine. This was because I cut it myself. I'd read that a good cut brought out the shine. Anyway, I couldn't afford a good haircut. Ferrell's remark about propositioning me amused him. My friend Molly, who teaches English here, and once dated Ferrell, said he was sexist. His statement and laughter proved it. He put one of his long fingered hands, and then his forearm on my desk. I hadn't said a word. I just watched the wall clock move toward twenty of. His jacket, green and gold tweed, part silk, part merino wool, was gorgeous.

"Your artistic sense is certainly reflected by that lovely jacket," I told him.

"Clothes, Candida, don't make the man, but thank you for the compliment." An awkward pause followed. I cleared my throat. He admired his Rolex watch, sparkling in the sun. Its beams interfered with my already compromised view of him.

"I'll make this quick," he said. "Garvey, (our new President, Roger Garvey) called this morning. He wants to make money for his new ice rink. He's heard that some new Silicon Valley investors may help us along. They're called venture capitalists. He thinks a huge new ice rink, with its money-making potential, may intrigue them; get them to underwrite the construction. He's very ambitious, you know." I didn't see where I fitted in. Prof. Ferrell explained.

"Roger, uh, Pres. Garvey, thinks we can raise some cash for the rink fund by offering a three week luxury art tour to Italy. He suggested you for the Italian cultural leader–or co–leader–and me for the art history leader. He's willing to pay us four thousand apiece for the job, and I thought that was pretty damn good for a three-week luxury tour. Are you agreeable?" Silicon. I had to think when I first heard that term? High school chemistry class? Was it in mainframe computers? I hadn't taken it in yet.

"I don't know." The money *was* tempting. "Would I have to recruit for this? I only have two small Italian classes, one small French one."

7

"Oh, it's not a trip for students. Garvey doesn't want the problems young people cause. We won't be *in loco parentis* or anything like that. No, this is aimed at their parents, grandparents, and any adults in the community able to afford such an expensive trip. This is Silicon Valley, you know." *Did* I know? I still thought of myself as inhabiting Santa Clara Valley. I remembered my childhood stints of picking plums, cherries and apricots in the orchards Dad's friends owned, those stretching between San Jose and Mountain View, not because we had to, but because it "was good exercise and educational," Dad said.

The more I thought about this trip to Italy, though, the better it sounded. In the first place, herding students in Italy would have been a big responsibility. In the second place, four thousand dollars would help me live on a salary of only $12,500 paid on a ten month basis. It was more than I'd have gotten in a state college. Altamonte was a very well financed private school, and California salaries—and houses—were higher than in most other states. The extra four thousand would get me nicely through summer's unpaid months; especially as the three weeks abroad would be for all practical purposes—almost free maintenance.

"Yes, that would suit me very well. I fell in love with Italy doing research on Boccaccio. My dissertation, you know." I pushed a copy of *Boccaccio's Bouquet*s his way. He thumbed through it, without much interest, snorting once at the cover art.

"Well, if that grabs you, the next thing is to find a wholesaler who knows his onions. I mean a travel broker who can get what Garvey wants built in—great class hotels in city centers; tickets to events, museums; most meals; a weekly banquet; a deluxe air–conditioned bus with driver and baggage handler—in short, the works—for $4,800 dollars apiece, single occupancy; seven double. This trip isn't Frommer's *Europe on Ten Dollars a Day*. Ten years ago, a deluxe three-week trip cost three thousand dollars. Now it's going to be hard to do it for near five. But we're aiming at the upper end traveler—not New Age hippies whistling "Bad Moon Rising" or Lead Zeppelin's rendition of "Stairway to Heaven." Rob sat back smiling indulgently at me.

"The trip will be the equivalent of traveling for gastronomy and Renaissance art, not music as the ultimate pitch." A pun. I didn't comment on it. I had been told that Ferrell had been a jazz musician as a young man growing up in Kansas City. And that he still kept up with modern music, plain jazz, hot jazz, cool jazz, or even heavy metal and pop jazz. He occasionally played in San Francisco's night spots, sometimes with the Hare Krishna crowd flitting about outside rock concerts. He played all kinds of jazz at clubs and private parties and was, Molly said, still giving cello and piano concerts of classical music in churches and private homes, beloved by older folks who valued his classical taste.

The Santa Clara Valley, scene of my childhood, had changed. Now, instead of the fame associated with fruit orchards and its canning industry, micro chips were displacing dried apricot chips. The smell of the old tomato canneries on highway 101 as you slipped into low-profiled San Jose with its blue, green, or yellow hills rising behind it, was less intense now. Even if I was hearing the term Silicon Valley often in 1973, a solitary journalist first used the term in 1971. I prefer the historic name I first learned to read on boxes of *Sun Maid* dried prunes my grandmother, Bubbie (Yid., grandma) Brondel bought.

I was involved in the retro activities of communicating by means of language, translated by dictionaries until students, hopefully, learned to think differently without the benefit of micro chips, which were, I learned, creeping into all kinds of machinery, changing the way everyone behaved.

Looking up at Professor Ferrell I asked, "Silicon? Isn't that an element in the earth's crust?" Ferrell gently chided me for my ignorance.

"Get with it, Candy. The term 'Silicon Valley' is a metonym for interactive digital media, made possible by kids with Stanford degrees working in garages, and venture capitalists on Sand Hill Road. Boccaccio's vocabulary is not the most recent one." I took his point, though I did not think I was given to much interaction myself. I did lean toward things digital, being a writer.

"Do you know any trip wholesalers, Candy?" he was asking now. "I don't, so I told Roger you had travel connections."

"You didn't," I said sharply. "I don't."

"Well, then, get some," Ferrell said rising. "Get some Candy, because I have two hundred students to your...what? forty? I don't have time for the small stuff. But we'll be meeting regularly, so you can tell me what you've found out by next week. Monday morning at nine? My office. Yours is so depressing."

And with that Prof. Robin ("Rob") Ferrell glided past my desk, shutting my door softly. I didn't have time to tell him that I am never now called Candy, and haven't been since my grandmother passed away when I was in middle school. He took a lot for granted. He seemed to me a self-promoter. I make a mental note to ask Molly. Her office is just across the hall from mine, but she was out today with a cold.

President Garvey, another self-promoter, is new here. He arrived at Altamonte in midyear. Without the undergraduate office assistant he got pregnant. Without his wife, who was divorcing him. Because of that scandal, he had lost his job of Provost at a private eastern university, and with it, the possibility of becoming its President. Then Altamonte's President, Hubert Reardon, suffered a stroke and tendered his resignation, which our Board accepted regretfully. Garvey heard about the vacancy and flew out to be interviewed. He had something on somebody in his former Administration, so they gave him a super recommendation. Six months later the story leaked out. Nice looking, tall, and still young at forty-three, Garvey earned a graduate degree from the Harvard School of Business. He is a former Olympic hockey champion, and two members of our Board had once played professional hockey. Some Arts faculty thought he just wanted a convenient place to skate.

The Department of Dance supported the rink. Ballerinas and modern dancers can do wonderful things on ice, developing new muscles. The student body will get regular rink hours. Literature majors didn't flex their muscles much. Performers are all about muscles. Tendons. Ferrell, too. One could not teach art history or paint the human body (he's an exhibiting artist) without such knowledge. Da Vinci, after all, dissected human corpses.

"When does this ice rink of Garvey's get built?" I asked at our next meeting in Ferrell's large, attractive office.

"Oh, our Board has lists of grateful potential donors. People who are thankful their kids can make it through a four year college. Roger schmoozes with the big donors. He wants a great architect for the rink, like Frank Gehrey or I.M. Pei who did the Kennedy Library. People pay handsomely to enter any great building, no matter what goes on inside." I nodded.

"Organized tours can be real money makers for colleges," Ferrell went on. "And for us as co–leaders."

"Co" meant together. From *cum* in Latin. What would Rob Ferrell be like as a co–leader? He oozed singularity. I'd spent one year alone in Italy, Rome and Florence, researching Boccaccio. As co–leader, I wouldn't have to traipse about in the hot sun carrying my suitcase from station to a humble *pensione* (bed and breakfast place). Four thousand smackers is three times more than I could make teaching summer school for six weeks.

Altamonte, a private liberal arts school for rich kids with poor SAT's, is very accepting. Our tuition is as high as Stanford's. Our brochure states that we welcome students who are "creative rather than merely studious." Rich peoples' children could not be shunted to community colleges when their friends' kids attend the Ivy Leagues. Besides, the millionaires in Santa Clara Valley would show their gratitude for a B.A. or M.F.A, and donate generously for new projects, new Chairs.

Altamonte does intramural sports only. We have our own teams for tennis, golf, swimming and gymnastics, yachting, weight training, and perhaps one day, ice skating. Students can major in these five unit courses, taught by retired pros. We give free room and board to dancers (ballet, modern), musicians and actors already gainfully employed in the arts of the City. We are big on Culture. We support talent. It in turn supports us.

Our Performing Arts Department got a great new theater with a glitzy metal façade. It seats 2,000 people, with reception rooms for social gatherings, complete with bars and serving tables that rose out of the floor, later retracting. These rooms doubled as ballrooms or green rooms. We hold fundraisers here. Our state of the art kitchen for Culinary Arts majors is in the basement. Behind the stage, we build sets. Our performers have space for storing everything from harps to dijeroos, hollow wooden tree trunks from northern Australia, carved not by tribesmen, but termites. Our administrators, like termites, bore from within, creating pipes out of which pour not just music, but a positive cash flow. The theater's twelve sewing machines employ women of color who sew costumes for all performances. Miss Iona Bergstrom, our Vice

President, a frumpy Home Economics major from Iowa State, wanted the college to offer "Clothing Construction" when the machines were idle. We did. Nobody enrolled. She wanted something that would give students a "hands on trade" despite the wealthy milieu from which they sprang. I suggested she rename the course "Fashion Design." Dozens of girls signed up, with a waiting list. Our Fashion grads find jobs with Dior in Paris, Versace in Milan, Balenciaga in Madrid, Ferragamo and Gucci everywhere.

As a Language Arts person, I was not surprised that "Fashion Design" caught on where "Clothing Construction" failed. A turn of phrase, a more appealing synonym, can dramatically influence behavior. I made the same point in my dissertation. Propagandists know it; terrorists, clergymen, politicians, radio talk show hosts, too. Shakespeare said "words, words, words" bored Hamlet, then a mere student, though a prince. A dramatist and poet, the Bard knew which words would earn his bread. Altamonte prepares beautiful youth to speak well, or if not well, better, hiding other deficiencies. Cicero orated about politics and friendship, not science and engineering.

Rob told me that a fledgling computer science program complete with a laboratory for students was set up two years ago at some college whose name I have forgotten. I doubt Altamonte will get into that stuff. The kids who enroll here couldn't decode English very well, let alone computer 'languages.' Computers might prove helpful to a few gifted scientists at colleges like Stanford, but language arts, as far as I could see, are what self–promoters and their kids need most. And self–promotion is what makes Altamonte such a great success. Rob is such a know-it-all, but he is dead wrong about the future of computers. I'm sure I'm right about this.

Our state of the art theater was a gift from a student's grandfather. While in tenth grade she had written "movie star" as her life's goal. Grandpa donated a state of the art theater *before* she matriculated. She left without graduating, but was making it in Hollywood, at least, before entering rehab centers in southern California. Here, she had tried to find herself. Weren't most people in the 60s doing the same? Drugs and partying did her in. Fortunately, her parents could afford to keep her in a luxurious rehab center.

We offer math and science at Altamonte, but most students flunk those in prep school. Here they take them again, plus business math. There are accountants for those mathematically challenged. Three-quarters of our students are remedial readers. This presents problems to humanities profs. A calculator can do math for you. Only your brain could form and express your thoughts effectively.

I try to make masterpieces of literature from Dante to Voltaire enjoyable for my students. Dad said we were direct descendants from Voltaire, *de Arouet*, having been Anglicized to give us the English sounding Darroway. My maternal relatives were Italian Jews from Lucca. After Mussolini's racial laws were passed, Grandma (Bubbie) Brondel and Grandpa *Massimo* Orefice got out. *Orefice* means goldsmith in Italian, so they were the Max Goldsmiths here. Mom kept her heritage alive in me to the extent that she was able. Dad resented her Jewishness–her plumpness. That's why he next married a skinny blonde Catholic–Chérie–after he divorced Mom. She, in turn, married Jim, a hefty blonde Protestant widower with three young children. If I seem older than my years, it's because I never had much time to be a child.

In the nineteenth century, the gardeners here were Italian immigrants. Altamonte means high mountain in Italian. Non-Italians undervalued hilly land, but Italians terraced it. They grew olives, grapes, tomatoes, fruit trees. Their flowers were fertilized by honey bees. The honey was sold in jars; the wine in bottles. Their flowers filled the stalls in San Francisco's Union Square. Vegetables were hauled down the mountain by horse carts to the City. The ladies of Nob Hill, the officers' wives at the Presidio, paid good prices. So did the Palace Hotel. The rest was peddled up Jones and Market and Geary. The Italians on Columbus bought the leftovers. Owners of rooming houses fed immigrant men from Apulia, Bari, Naples and Palermo leftovers. These skinny Italians ate little seafood (*frutti di mare*) in America, but lots of bread, pasta and minestrone made from bruised Altamonte tomatoes. The roomers' kitchen cooks added chick peas, lentils, pigs' ears and three day old pasta. For body. The men's; the soup's.

These immigrants became citizens. Neapolitans, the Di Fassulios, bought Altamonte's three hundred acres shortly after taking their oath of allegiance. This was about when Pres. McKinley was shot in 1901 by an anarchist *not* Italian, but a German Pole from Detroit. Being judged of sound mind, he was executed. Now they execute even those of unsound mind, too, providing they are poor.

The Di Fassulios had ten children. They lived on *pomidoro* (tomatoes) and fried bread, olives and olive oil. Slowly, they built a small agricultural empire. Several of their kids tired of farming and set up pizzerias in the City, where their *pizza alla Napoletana,* being cheap, made a big hit. Their children became produce wholesalers; theirs, developers. The developers produced bankers, and at least one Mafioso. The next generation produced doctors, politicians, a rocket scientist and an Alfa Romeo franchise dealer in Menlo Park. They all married and had lots of kids. No one knew how to speak Italian by the 1960s. Too bad (*peccato*).

Altamonte College occupies a mesa overlooking San Francisco Bay. The view is worth the tuition. Our white students come from wealthy homes from Hillsborough to Los Gatos. Few spent quality time with their fathers, who worked sixty hours per week and played golf on weekends. More spent time with their mothers, who stayed at home raising them. Betty Friedan found it a drag. The kids weren't so fond of their mothers. Overexposed, perhaps. Once in prep school, some moms found relief in afternoon love affairs, because they knew their husbands were doing it, too. Infidelity took off in the 1960s. *Open Marriage* sold well in bookstores. Since all the kids had swimming pools, tennis courts and jogged, they were the fittest kids in North America. Only the less fit poor people of color and poor whites served in Viet Nam, not having gotten college deferments, like our students.

Those, like the administrators, drive new cars. The faculty drive beat-up Ford Fairlanes, Chevy Impalas, Dodge Coronets, Pontiac Catalinas. My 1965 Volkswagen bug (orange) is barely hanging in there. I am in no position to buy a newer car, as I need to finish paying off a college tuition loan of five thousand dollars, which seems monstrous. Mom married a plumber who had three kids. She went to secretarial school in the City, but hadn't been a secretary for twenty years. She can't buy me a better car or help pay my student loan. Dad, a lawyer, could, but won't. On my visits to them, I feel more visitor than beloved daughter.

This four thousand dollar tour income will be a godsend. The bug needs new brake linings; the air conditioner has stopped working.

I leave Alviso after eight o'clock and get on route 237 to 101. I eat a piece of fruit en route or a packaged Danish, or even a "pandulce" from Alisio's Mexican Market. Bubbie Brondel called such stuff "nosherei" (snack food.) But all Italians love sweets. Next to opera and Salvation, sweets were an Italian's chief consolation. Dad kept them out of the house, helping me maintain my "Anglo" slenderness.

"Fortunately," Dad said, "your nose is straight, your skin isn't olive colored, you don't look Jewish, and you are slender." Both Mom and Dad were proud of my educational achievements, but I got stuck paying for a third their cost. I got big scholarships. A Woodrow Wilson. A Fulbright. The advantages of being a bookworm.

An impecunious academic, unmarried at thirty-two, with a lit degree, looking for true love. Perhaps on this tour. I am determined not to get fat touring. Overeating is an American plague. I know about plagues having written on Boccaccio's *Decameron,* about nobles escaping the Black Death.

Women's Lib, a term that dates only from 1968, might not approve my desire to find the right man. Many libbers didn't like men much. I have been on the Pill since I turned twenty-one. Still, at twelve, reading *Seventeen Magazine,* I figured out that girls who wore matching cashmere sweater sets attracted boys. I didn't happen to attract any—perhaps because my sweaters were mostly nylon.

By the time I was in college, I learned where I wanted to fit in. It wasn't with the sorority girls, but with those preparing for an independent career. I did not need to be called Ms. I did need to be independent. In fact, I thought Ms. or "Mizz" sounded terrible, the way chic ladies in big houses referred to their black maids in movies. "Miss Darroway" was fine by me. "Dr. Darroway" better. I had earned the doctorate. A professional job. Now for the rest.

I am not without marriage prospects. My main "squeeze" remains Tony Murphy. He didn't want to work in Puerto Rico, leaving Teresa alone on the ranch. He dated me because I was so fond of his *"nonna"* or grandmother, whom he loved dearly. She's going back to Florence this summer. I might meet her there. After Tony's teenaged mother got pregnant by an Irishman, Teresa raised him. Not knowing if your mother, your daughter, still lived was a deep-seated pain in their hearts that neither Tony nor Teresa talk about. Nor did I tell them how much I miss my own mother and father, because there didn't seem to be any remedy; besides, Tony never even knew *his* real parents.

Teresa, on her mother's side, is a Nepi of the Roman Renaissance Nepis. On her father's, a member of the royal dynasty of Sardinia-Piedmont and Savoy, a direct descendent of King Victor Emmanuel I. Her husband, a third cousin, and a Della Savoia, from the royal House of Savoy, dropped dead on a tennis court at thirty, of a heart attack, leaving Teresa six months pregnant with Tony's Mom. Teresa never remarried. She is in her mid-sixties and looks forty-five. After her husband's death, she lived with several men on a consecutive basis.

"Living in sin is not sinful," Teresa explained, "because Jesus loves us all, and the important thing is just to confess your sins before dying. Not necessarily to a priest."

"Extreme unction" she maintained, "was a later invention of the papacy; like purgatory." Teresa rejected hellfire and purgatory "because the popes made those things up when they needed more control over pagans, parishioners." Teresa is a garlic rancher, a countess, and knowledgeable about church history. She regards dogma skeptically. Teresa took up with a Sicilian-American who died in a car crash in Palermo. They lived in Sicily for five years, because her lover's parents were sickly. She speaks Sicilian when she cooks, Tuscan when she visits her mother in Florence, and Gilroy slang from a Gilroy rancher boy friend she lived with after her return to the States. He left her the garlic ranch, too, before dying of a brain tumor. Teresa's mother is still living at ninety-three in Florence, a princess (*principessa*) of Savoy. I hope I meet her and her other royal relatives on this tour. If it comes off.

Teresa loved the Sicilian recipes she cooked with her lover in Palermo. He was a professional chef. She does a tuna fried with lots of sliced onions (*tonno alla cipollata*) you could die for, and her sardine pie (*pasta con le sarde*) is the best in the world. Given her lovers (two more followed the garlic ranch owner), she strayed from Catholicism, but not religion. Everybody rebels in his or her own fashion, whether socially, sexually, or linguistically.

I have adopted the Italian accent of my Jewish mother, Lucia. Pretty standard Tuscan. I have not rejected my grandparents' Jewish-ness, though I was not taught *how* to be Jewish. A few years' attendance at an Episcopal church didn't take. Probably because Dad rarely went with me. Mom wouldn't go. Her family were anciently Judeo-Spanish, never *conversos*. (Span., never converted to Christianity). After 1492, they moved through Turkey to the Venetian ghetto, and perhaps other places, but to Lucca in the late nineteenth century.

For Teresa, one night last week, I made Florentine chicken (*pollo alla Fiorentina*) using a Tuscan Marsala that cost a fortune, and chopped fat pork from a Parma ham Teresa provided for the purpose. The wild mushrooms (*funghi prataioli*) Tony and I gather in Morgan Hill, using our guidebook to mushrooms. Tony was so entranced with my cooking, he nearly proposed. I am glad he didn't, but when I got back to Alviso, I cried. Too much garlic? Or too much friendship (*amicizia*), and not enough passion? For all my sedate ways and academic interests, I am passion's fool. There's a song that says "Everybody's somebody's darlin,' everybody's somebody's fool." Whose fool will I turn out to be, I wonder? More importantly, whose darling?

I do a book talk three times a year on a French or Italian novel for the Language Arts faculty. Besides me (teaching Italian and French language and literature), there is a part–time German teacher, a part–time Russian teacher, and a part–time Japanese teacher. Last year we added a handsome part–time classicist, a Jesuit priest, Father Sean O'Connor. He regaled students with Petronius and Ovid and really sexy Greco-Roman myths. His Superior thought these pagan porn. O'Connor disappeared after one semester. There went our Greek and Latin instructor. I wondered where he was now? Probably causing women to swoon wherever they've stowed him. Nothing attracts women as much as uniforms and cassocks. Or Irish eyes "when smiling." Jewish women were often attracted to their rabbis. My friend Molly Finkel is, though I am trying to get her to face reality. Her rabbi, Schlomo Schneider, will go back to his wife and kids.

I think Christopher Columbus and Samuel de Champlain failed us linguistically. We speak neither Spanish nor French in America. Columbus left Genoa a youth, never to return. He spoke only Spanish, his mother having been a Jewish convert (Span., *conversa)* from Spain. De Champlain would have spread French on the New England coast, but his successors were done in by Francophobia. The French mistreated the Iroquois and Onondaga, not to mention the British, who hated the French because they, like the Brits, wanted a sizable chunk of North America. Britain won over France, leaving us with the only foreign language no one really speaks anymore. English.

When I got back from my French class at five, I found a message from Ferrell. "Hi, Candy. Ferrell here. Must see you 5:15 in the faculty lounge. Urgent." Damn, I was going to go home and cut my hair. I can't afford professional cuts even in a humble place like Alviso! I hear they can cost fifty bucks in Palo Alto. Sixty in Atherton.

For some reason, I feel this trip to Italy will prove my own Renaissance. Everything that follows now will take place, not in the present, where I am stranded; but in the past tense–including the intimate past, from which I shall emerge triumphant. All that follows will fall–precipitously and not without trauma and tragedy–into place. It just has to.

CHAPTER II

ALTAMONTE TRIES IT ON

My father named me, Candida Abigail. Candida means white; pure. Abigail means "My father is joy." He isn't and never was, according to my mother. Abigail is just more baggage. Candida Darroway's enough. Dad hoped I would be every bit as distinguished (and grateful) as Candida Abigail suggested.

After my maternal grandparents died and my parents divorced, I was enrolled in a private boarding school. Being Candida was quite acceptable. They knew instinctively to accent the *first* syllable, not the second of my name. There I got my first blazer, worn with a blue pleated plaid skirt. Even in California, pants for girls were not allowed in boarding schools.

Sneakers were worn only in the gym, rubber thongs and shorts were banned. Our school blazer was navy with a school patch worn with a white Peter Pan collared blouse tucked into the skirt. Mom came to visit me every Saturday (she lived ten miles away), taking my blouses home to launder, returning them all starched late Sunday evening.

I associated school with blazers and pleated kilt skirts then. Now I reserve skirts for formal occasions, since they are regularly made of slinkier fabrics–jersey, velour, satin. In the early 1970s skirts were mini, midi, or maxi. The mini ones, in leather or satin were so slippery one could hardly control them when seated. They crept up. For informal parties I preferred a granny gown, in Indian cotton, all encompassing, unless one had a good reason to shuck out of it and into something much more encompassing–someone's arms, that is. But I only tried that once in college, and never again until I met Tony Murphy. Nor did I go bar hopping. I didn't talk to men not introduced by friends. I didn't go to church or to synagogue. What was left?

Tony Murphy, grandson of Teresa Della Savoia, who raised garlic in Gilroy, and whom I adored–Teresa, not Tony–within minutes of our meeting. We spoke Italian together immediately. Tony could speak it. He just didn't want to.

I must say I was feeling stressed. I conferred with Ferrell for the first time this morning. Had I failed the test? Had he decided I would not be a dynamic co–tour leader and told "Roger" that? Who called the President of the college "Roger"? They must be close friends.

I dashed into the ladies' after my French class and looked into the mirror. People have said I am pretty, but I never believed them. Well, sometimes I did. My hair was uneven. I was not often well turned out. I should aim for outfits. Matching ones. Supplement old clothes with odd treasures that languish at Goodwill. You'd be surprised what a wealthy community discards. Last week in Palo Alto's Goodwill I saw a violet suede jacket, Max Mara, like new, for ten dollars. I was tempted. But what would I wear it with? Dressing was like sex. One thing led to another. Before you knew it, you'd outgrown your own space. Closet-wise. Personality-wise.

I have been employed at this college for two years. The only close friend I have made on campus is Molly Finkel. She teaches English literature and has an office opposite mine in Buzby Hall. Buzby is the oldest building on campus. If you were ever on campus trying to locate it, you'd spot it quickly. It is our most neglected building. It hasn't rated renovation since it was built in the 30s.

Molly and I let our hair down (so to speak) when teaching got tough, or sex reared its head–or didn't. That doesn't mean we didn't have secrets, though we hadn't known each other that long. Molly's hair is a glorious red waterfall ending half way down her back. She is a secular Jew, but goes religiously to Friday night services at a *very* Reformed temple in Berkeley. Half the congregation has returned, she swears, to the Faith of their Fathers from Zen Buddhism. Hare Krishna. Jews for Jesus. Unitarianism. Wicca. Hard Liquor. Soft drugs. Excessive pre-occupation with feng shui. She has a crush on her rabbi. She knows it is hopeless. He is kind of separated from his wife and they date. I mean, he dates his *wife*! Molly, he lays. She is strictly on the side. This is a bad situation and I know she knows that. She is very intelligent. But since when was intelligence smart?

Before I saw Ferrell again, I resolved to get more information about him from Molly. Her office door was always open, so I knew she was there now. I knocked anyway. Molly, who has a tendency to overdo things, thought fruit was the way to stay healthy and had brought too many tangerines to school. She told me to help myself. I had eaten a skimpy breakfast—again—and forgot to pack a snack. The tangerines were delicious. I tossed my two peels into her wastebasket, after hers.

"Molly, I have been asked by Roger Harvey to co–lead a tour to Italy with Rob Ferrell. I have had one meeting with him. He gave nothing away. Kind of sexy, though, even if he is in his early fifties. I need to know more about him to protect myself, should the occasion arise."

"From yourself or from him?" Molly was now peeling a banana. She offered me half, which I accepted.

"From him, I suppose. I'm only after the four thousand dollars this co–leader thing pays. Not him. But I feel I should know who he is, exactly? I mean, married? divorced? gay? bi? Those Italian shoes! And is he kind? indifferent? capricious? ambitious? lecherous? cruel? Give me the skinny."

She peered at me over her diminishing banana and her eyes blinked above the peel, hanging around her hand. The peel reminded me of Jocko, the monkey in our third grade readers. "Jocko" took her time replying, flicking at the peel with her thumb and index finger.

"Well, he was married once, a long time ago. He is divorced, and he is not gay."

"How do you know all that?"

"How? Because we had an affair the year before you came here, one that lasted just over nine months."

"Hah," I said, laughing. "Long enough to make a baby."

"Yes." Molly tossed the banana peel into her waste basket. "And long enough to make one go away, too. I had an abortion at four months. He refused to marry me."

"Oh my gawd, Molly. I didn't know. I'm so sorry."

"You must not tell a living soul," said Molly. "His best friend is my Uncle Izzy, the cantor in Beth El Ner Tamid, the big synagogue with the dome in the City. Itzhak Finkel. Rob and Uncle Izzy play squash in the Jewish center every Sunday afternoon. Uncle Izzy usually wins.

But they are close friends. Uncle met Rob while playing squash. Rob has a membership there. I think there was some Jewish relative on his mother's side. And another thing, Candida. He likes young women; likes them slim and in a field where they cannot compete with him. Not art. Not music. You are young and slim. Do you play any instrument well? If so, keep it quiet. He plays four instruments well, and hates competition."

Molly had something else on her mind, because whenever she was most thoughtful, she twisted a lock of her red curls round and round her finger, and was doing it now.

"What else do you think is important for me to know about him? And hey, I'm not asking about his performance as a lover. What he did to you was rotten. Though he is exceptionally attractive, so I can see why you fell for him." She looked up under slant eyebrows.

"Was that a pun?"

"Molly! Of course not." If anything it was a cliché.

"Well, you're right, Candida. He is exceptionally attractive. Right up there with Paul Newman, Robert Redford, and Warren Beatty. You know! And he *is* exceptional. A real Renaissance man. They called him the "tripled tongued devil" in Kansas, where he grew up, because he played a trumpet like Miles Davis, "Bix" Beiderbecke, Winton Marsalis and Harry James." Molly loved big band music and listened to lots of it. When I visited her, we listened together. Those were mighty music men.

"There's a lot more to be said about Ferrell later. I have class, now." Molly packed her briefcase with stacks of corrected essays, her grade book, her literature anthology.

"But one thing is more important that all the rest."

"And that is?" I asked breathlessly.

"He just soaks up all the attention, all the admiration, and all the drama in any group. He's big, and people are in awe of him. Women especially. There isn't space enough in the universe for his ego. And the more devotion and attention he gets, the more that ego grows. He's kind of like a golem in Jewish literature, a monster like those they make in rubber and then blow up on the big screen to frighten adolescent boys at horror shows. He charms his audience while destroying them."

"Like one of those Indian snake charmers when the lid of the basket opens?" I asked.

"No. Indian snake charmers only charm the snakes. Rob even charms their baskets." Was Molly a bit bitter? Yes, about Ferrell, and now, about Rabbi Schlomo. To be traduced by two men in a row was hard. She deserved better. When she had left, and after I was back at my desk, I thought about the one ineluctable fact of tours. Flying.

On my first trip to Italy I crammed a pullover shawl into my carry on case so the air-conditioning wouldn't stiffen my neck. I packed Erica Jong's *Fear of Flying*, which I had never got around to reading when it came out. I packed a copy of the play *Mandragola*–Machiavelli's– on which I hope to write a long article, perhaps even a short book. I also carried a nail clipper, as my nails shred easily and biting them is undignified. The stewardess came around in half an hour with a cart full of soft drinks, wine or beer (three dollars) and peanuts. On that trip we had–in cargo class–three dinner choices: vegetarian lasagna, chicken or beef. Now they give you only two–vegetarian and chicken. This did not bode well for future airline travel, I mused. I suppose some day, they wouldn't give tourist class passengers any food at all. They'd just sell food. The next step would be forbidding you to carry your own sandwich on board unless you proved you had bought it in the airport mall.

I freshened up for my meeting with Ferrell. I had to be fresh. He was. If Ferrell were not so handsome, I probably wouldn't have gone to the trouble in the teacher's ladies' room to put on fresh lipstick, comb my hair and wash my face, using a paper towel and a tiny bar of hotel soap from my last tryst with Tony in Monterey. There, Tony and I had had pretty good sex at "The House of Seven Grables." The Grable family who owns it has four kids and a cat named Betty.

I found Ferrell in the Faculty Lounge, drinking Scotch and soda.

"Hello, Prof. Ferrell." He put his drink down on the coffee table and stood up when I entered, which I thought very gentlemanly. Most of Altamonte's male faculty had dispensed with the social graces; when, I couldn't say, but after most of them started wearing pullovers and blue jeans to class instead of shirts, jackets, ties and pants that go to the dry cleaners.

23

"Thanks for being so prompt, Candida. And please call me Rob."
Normally at this hour I'd be heading down highway 101 toward Alviso,
passing the houseboat dwellers as I went. Their lives, closed to me,
nevertheless represented freedom and gave me a sense of joy. Ferrell
had, according to Molly, a fabulous place in the City up the same
highway, Lombard to Telegraph, turn off at Pioneer, just under Coit
Tower, overlooking the Bay.

"What's the reason for our meeting, anyway?" I asked. He sat
down, leaning over the cocktail table between us. He smiled with just a
soupçon or hint of indulgence, the way you do with children who want to
know what's in the box you've brought them before you give it to them.
He took a long swig of Scotch, a good one by the smell. He never did
answer my question. I appreciated a good Scotch, beer, wine, but drank
very moderately. Discriminating between cheap and good booze was a
gift I acquired from my Dad, a connoisseur of good living.

"Something to drink, Candy? Thanks to Roger's secretary, Alice
Harvey, we should celebrate your getting a break on your first assignment:
finding a wholesaler for our itinerary. Harvey. Rhymes with Garvey.
Funny, don't you think?" I smiled, wanly. "Well, what'll you have?"

"Prof. Ferrell, I never drink before hitting highway 101, unless it's
mineral water (*aqua minerale).* He got up and brought me a bottle of San
Pellegrino. "Please don't keep me guessing. What's up?" He opened the
bottle, pouring half into my glass, setting the bottle ahead of the glass.
He also handed me a business card of someone named Charles Clark,
Esq. "Trip Wholesaler" with a San Francisco address.

"Peanuts?" He pushed a wooden bowl toward me, and, as my
stomach was rumbling, I took some. "I'm sorry to delay you at rush
hour," Rob said. "But this man will save needless hunting over your
weekend. That's the main point of this meeting, or one of them. I wanted
to ease your task, having dumped it on your shoulders. And do call me
Rob, not 'Prof. Ferrell.' You make me feel I'm still holding my pointer."
His pointer was the metal rod he used to indicate details of projected
images of paintings to students. Nothing physiological. Still, I couldn't
always repress thoughts of another word for his pointer–his "tool."

"While we are on the subject," I said, still munching peanuts,
"please call me Candida."

"Ah-h. I'm sorry. I assumed that you would prefer 'Candy' to Candida because it's so sweet. And informal."

Was this an implied compliment or implied insult? I wondered. Rob Ferrell was, as Molly said, a charmer. But I wasn't a snake, and I had no intention of swaying to his flute, which he probably played along with his trumpet, cello, piano, and saxophone. He nodded, as if he could read my mind. He was tapping his glass thoughtfully.

"Okay. Alice Harvey, Roger's Executive Assistant, was listening, as secretaries, now called Executive Assistants, will listen to the boss's conversations. She heard Roger and me discussing the tour." I was quiet. He continued.

"I guess you are too young to remember sanitation engineers were once called garbage men, and custodians, janitors?"

"No, I remember," I said, in a mature tone, which wasn't hard for me. "I think people deserve titles that reflect well on the honest professions they pursue." Did that sound stuffy? People said I talked like someone who had come of age in the 1950s, not the 1960s.

"I approve of your sensitivity to human dignity," Rob replied. He swizzled his ice around and gazed into his glass, and then down at me. Was he being ironic? Did he mean I was just sensitive in my rhetoric, but not really to janitors or garbage men? There was something compelling about Rob Ferrell, and something almost repellent. Although, that recent talk about him with Molly certainly made me prejudiced against him. Getting rid of dust and garbage was one thing. Getting rid of Molly's half formed fetus was another.

"Ah, yes. I appreciate the difference those upgrades make in terms of self–worth," Ferrell agreed. "I could hardly teach art history if I didn't appreciate the dignity of man's perception of other men, and of himself, now could I?" One of his elegant long fingered hands held his glass. The other was beautifully set out upon the arm of the overstuffed lounge chair. Like a doily in my grandmother's house, for display.

Human dignity. I thought of *The Renaissance Quarterly* article I had written on Pico, entitled "Pico as Democrat," in which I described his understanding of human dignity. Of course, I got some criticism from conservative colleagues who could not connect Pico's Neoplatonism with democratic ideals, not even that of human dignity. That was my first published paper, written before my dissertation was even begun. Still, even good democrats could turn against democratic positions. Pico wound up a follower of the authoritarian zealot, Savonarola!

"The Renaissance," I said tentatively, "touted the human capacity for doing good and doing well. Those were not necessarily the same, as you know." Ferrell nodded, stirring his ice cubes more slowly. Was he a Democrat? A Republican? Would it matter? His concept of dignity had not been too strong where Molly was concerned. Now, sitting across from me, he appeared the perfect gentleman. Dignified.

"Miss Harvey overheard plans for our tour," Rob repeated. "*Our* tour, Candida." I liked the way he acknowledged my name and the *we–ness* of this enterprise. He looked straight at me, I suppose to see if I did indeed like it; but I have a poker face. Nothing, I am sure, revealed my susceptibility to being manipulated. Ferrell kept on talking, but a hint of amusement played across his features, as if he had sized me up, and found me amusing, too.

"Alice reminded Roger (she was Ron Kearney's hire, you see) that her previous job was in European travel. In fact, ten years ago, she taught a course in Travel Studies at one of the nearby community colleges." I just stared, awaiting further enlightenment. Ferrell leaned back in his armchair–cracked green leather from President's Kearney's office–but good enough for faculty use now. He tossed his hair back, grinning as he had earlier in my office; the same movement. In this light I got a chance to appreciate again how good–looking he was and how much delight he got out of his vitality, satisfaction from playfulness.

Teresa once told me how most middle–aged men in the Beat generation thought they could rejuvenate themselves by hitting on young women who could have been their daughters. Teresa thought women needed younger men who could keep up with them–as long as they themselves could keep up–not older ones who clung to young women in order to relive their own lost youth.

Ferrell brought to mind the *Commedia dell'Arte*, comic theater begun in mid-sixteenth century Italy. Its characters were stock ones: lovers, parents, maids, counselors etc. Isabella, for example, was *always* Audrey Hepburn, wooed, as in *Roman Holiday* by the young Gregory Peck, or in *Charade*, by the older Cary Grant. Only lovers went unmasked, on the assumption, first questioned by feminist authors, that all lovers were similar. Perhaps the Renaissance directors felt with all that kissing, masks would have been a nuisance. Youth was beautiful. It made everyone happy to see. The other players wore masks and costumes revealing their character. "Pantalone," a Venetian grandee, gave advice, supervised others. Ferrell to a "P." There was a gullible and lecherous lawyer, who misspoke himself. Ferrell never did. He was too smooth. And not only very learned, like a Renaissance man, but a virtuoso in art, painting, sculpture, and music. Perhaps the outstanding figure in the *Commedia* was *Arlecchino* or Harlequin, a sad clown, painted by artists like Watteau, Manet, Picasso. Witty, nimble, and gay, Harlequin was a capricious and heartless lover. I couldn't see all the *Commedia* potential in Ferrell. Just some, derived from voracious reading, that told me life itself was a comedy, and also, a mystery.

Aside from Molly's testimony, I had learned a bit about Ferrell from students. For example, until two years ago, if they came late to his class, he used to pull out a track starter gun from his top drawer and shoot them. The blanks were loud. A young girl fainted. And she had arrived to class on time. After the blank went off, a yellow flag dropped on which was written, "You're late, you creep!" President Kearney had made Ferrell stop, lest someday he grab a gun some criminally insane person put there to fool him, and instead of blanks, a real pistol killed a latecomer. Not even a tardy student deserved that. Ferrell agreed, so that's history. Not art history; just history.

Molly told me he took instruction in carving wooden ducks, having spent time in Golden Gate Park watching ducks on the pond, a grown up Holden Caulfield. And there was something in Ferrell that reminded me of Holden, who wasn't so sure of himself. Of course Holden had been institutionalized. Ferrell merely taught at one. Big difference. Ferrell's ducks were not in Central Park, but in Golden Gate Park. His facsimiles were exact replicas; so exact, that when he placed a female on the pond's beach, the drakes went wild, quacking to get "her" attention. Ferrell took pity on the drakes and returned the "female" to his backpack. He sold his ducks to Gumps, a pricey jewelry shop in the City. Then he refused to sell them any more, though they begged him to, as they had sixty back orders. They paid him a thousand dollars a duck, Molly said, and charged customers $1,500. It was a profitable commerce, but he gave it up. Once he gave up on something, he never went back. Molly knew that.

Ariosto (d. 1533), whose novel *Orlando Furioso* regaled the d'Este court at Ferrara and influenced Shakespeare and Milton, was Italy's Jack Benny. My grandparents doted on Jack Benny. Where had all the great comedians gone? "Gone to flowers every one." Pete Seeger's voice was engraved on mind.

My Bubbie Brondel had more influence on my cultural and ethical expectations, even on my comedic and literary ones than my mom, who was trying hard to adjust to American norms, while Bubbie Brondel was grateful that her Italian Jewish ones still served her needs–on U.S. soil.

Niccolò Machiavelli (d.1527), seated in his study above Florence, in the old Etruscan town of Fiesole, wrote a play (1524) called *Mandragola* (*The Mandrake*), in which he wrestled with the cultural norms of his day. I might write a book on that subject. One book wasn't enough to catapult me into a university. Machiavelli wrote about politics, defense and governance. Ferrell, like old Niccolò, was similarly learned. Was he also Machiavellian?

I had heard how deep Ferrell's knowledge was of the slides he lectured on. He had another degree, but no one knew in what area. Some thought Ferrell had been a physician, or maybe a chemist. I wondered if, in true Renaissance fashion, he were also an alchemist; for he had the power to turn precious materials into dross, and common assumptions into grandiose, even grand, aspirations. That's what made him an artist. At any rate, he exhibited his paintings in our college library. He was a cellist of note, punning aside. He played a mean jazz piano when liquored up; classical music when sober, and his jazz rhythm was widely trumpeted, a pun that seemed appropriate for this Renaissance man. But exactly what character would he choose to play with me among those in the *Commedia dell'Arte* cast? Pantalone? Arlechino? Who could predict?

Dashing from the ladies' room to the faculty lounge, I was aware of my tatty gray slacks and treasured, but worn, maroon blazer, one of whose pockets had unraveled on top; one of whose three brass buttons

I'd lost. I got attached to buttons, and not being able to match them, never replaced any. I could not afford new shoes because cheap ones hurt my feet. I needed "comfort shoes" and they were expensive. I couldn't help thinking Ferrell might be pardoned for assuming I'd be a Candy rather than a Candida.

"About Alice Harvey's handing you just one name of a single trip wholesaler. This might be bothering you, Candida. Is it?"

"Well, I think if she were once in the travel business herself, she might have given us three or four names to explore," I confessed. Ferrell waved his hand somewhat deprecatingly, if gracefully.

"Look, Candida, she could have given you a list of ten. But would that have made you happy or burdened your heart? I assume she chose Clark because she trusts him most. If he doesn't come up with the right numbers, the best hotels in the most convenient places, the right meal deals, and a gala banquet each week–something really memorable at three of our more dramatic stops–I'm sure she has others who will. We'll give him our itinerary first. Next, we recruit our travelers. No travelers, no trip. I called you here to give you an idea of what must be accomplished. Get a notebook and start putting information into it in an orderly fashion. You've got a freshly minted doctorate. That shouldn't be challenging. Over the weekend, start thinking of the places you want to go to, and I'll do the same. We'll coordinate to get a reasonably practical schedule, one that will please us both. So how about meeting on Wednesday to confer? Let's make it a working lunch in my office. I'll bring deli sandwiches from the city. Tuna, corned beef or crab?"

"Crab would be nice."

"I have a coffeemaker, too. Do you take cream?" I nodded.

"I'll get some," he said. "We can work until your next class at…?"

"Three." On Wednesday, my lightest day, I did not teach until three.

"Good." He was enthused. "We'll aim for a finished plan by next weekend, Saturday, 20 October. We can get together at my place, working hard at coordination, and when we're all set, have a really great Italian dinner afterward in a little place I know near the Marina."

"Red sky in the morning, sailors too warning! Red sky at night, sailors' delight," I thought. Was Ferrell thinking of himself as a sailor?

And where did he see his port? The thought of staying overnight at his apartment made me extremely apprehensive, knowing what I knew about Molly. I was always a poor sailor. I didn't think sailing into any red sky would bring lasting delight. And Tony. No lasting delight there, I was fairly sure. But I didn't have to fear anything from Tony, whereas, I wasn't sure what I had to fear from Rob Ferrell.

"We'd best work it out here at the college," I said, with a quavering voice I blamed on allergies. "I live in Alviso, and it's a long way from there to the City. Alviso isn't so bad," I said, seeing his look of disdain. "It used to flood and still smells once in a while, despite the sewage treatment plant. But we have the largest bird habitat in the world. Anyway, I need to get back home early." Ferrell stroked his chin, and grinned.

"Don't worry. I have two bedrooms and two keys. You can go home Sunday after a breakfast of brioches and jam, and a great Denver omelet. Overlooking the Pacific. Place called Louis's, near the Cliff house. A girl from Alviso deserves a break from all that sewage. And Candida, we will just be working partners. Nothing more, nothing less. You can trust me implicitly."

So there was the pitch. A business card belonging to one Charles Clark of San Francisco; a plan to work on an itinerary; a tacit agreement to complete that itinerary in the apartment of a man old enough to be my father. I suddenly remembered I would have to tell Molly everything that had transpired. Would she think I was crazy? a wimp? Quite likely. She'd be right, too.

"Well, goodbye, until next Wednesday, Ferrell," I said, gathering up my purse and briefcase, in my best professional manner.

"Call me Rob, please Candida?" he said, jumping up suddenly and looking down at me from his full height. I, by the way, am five feet four inches tall. I was the right height for the Renaissance. I met all measurements. Men in the Renaissance were tall if they were over five feet seven. Ferrell would have to stoop to get through some Renaissance doorways. I wondered how low he would be willing to stoop?

"Goodbye, Rob," I said. It was only fair. He had called me Candida. I did not wait for him to make it around the table, but, being nearest the door, left alone. I took the path down the hill to the faculty parking lot. It was almost empty. No wonder. Six P.M.

It felt good to be back out on the highway heading home to the sleepy district of Alviso, where a person could hide. I had lots to keep me busy over the weekend. There was even a chance Tony might drive up for dinner at Vahl's Restaurant or a movie or something. The best part of my life was that the unexpected could usually be expected. And if not, it didn't matter much. Even as a child, my teachers said I was delightfully "inner–directed." Was I still? I was not entirely sure. It might be that as one ages, one sacrifices, of necessity, some of one's inner–directedness. Yes. When I thought about it, it seemed as we turned from childhood to adulthood that the world impinged increasingly upon us. Only some children lived truly private lives, protected by a charmed ignorance. The rest of us had not really been all that protected, nor kept in such ignorance.

CHAPTER III

THE "BOOT" FITS ALL

Outside the airplane window, only clouds. "British Airways will be landing in Heathrow in approximately seven minutes and thirty seconds," the stewardess announced. No sign of the approach; just gray clouds. I hoped the pilot knew where Heathrow was. A stream ran past it, the Thames. I preferred landing on the tarmac.

Heathrow sat close to its south bank, a meadow called Runnymede. "Bad" King John I, brother of King Richard I, "Lion Heart," signed Magna Carta (1215) there. American lawyers raised a monument to the Great Charter, putting John's image on it. John had reneged after signing. Pope Innocent III excused him saying the barons had forced him to sign. Innocent then acquired England as a papal fief. His feudal payoff? Dues paid Rome. Mine? helping tourists to a quality adventure.

Speaking of rivers, I have just begun to get my feet wet as co–tour leader. Ferrell and I would reach the promised land–Italy–safely, on dry land. In summer, Italy *is* dry.

"Getting your feet wet" meant beginning an enterprise (*The Book of Joshua* (3:9-30). Yahweh led the Israelites through the River Jordan on dry land, ordering twelve priests to step first into its waters. They carried His Ark. The Israelites stood well behind the priests, and only got the soles of *their* feet wet. Their followers came through on dry land, conquering Jericho without changing shoes. This was a variation of the Red Sea story in *Exodus*. Joshua "fit" the battle, "and the walls came 'tumblin' down." Before that, Joshua took Canaan. His principle was daring to get his feet wet.

Ferrell and I must get our feet wet; show courage. The *Ark of the Covenant was* the only media for Israelites. Errors were made. For example, Jericho was conquered in B.C. sixteenth century, not by Israelites, who may or may not have entered Canaan yet. Historians are not sure. Joshua's history was but a rewrite to build his image. It was written after B.C. 586, the year Nebuchadnezzar of Chaldea forced ten thousand Israelites to leave Jerusalem for Babylon. Joshua, successor of Moses, "captured" Jericho to encourage the Israelites in Babylon—three centuries later! Their captivity was among their darkest days. The *Hebrew Bible* was written to promote endurance for even darker ones ahead.

Some tours are best understood when they have ended. And of course, no event is the same for everyone. Each will have his or her own version. Many factors would affect their stories. These included the travelers' ability to take disappointment; their energy level; their sense of self. Some people could not take any reversal of dream reality if it clashed with real reality. Consider the effort. Travel meant work (*travaille*) in French. The Italian word is *viaggio*, from Latin for road, (*via*). When Italians speak of a road they use "via." When they want *you* to hit the road it was "Via!" (Ital., Scram!). The French saw travel as work, the Italians found a smooth road, *via*.

Who would prove the better tour leader? Me or Ferrell? He was a full professor, full of himself. I just made associate professor. Tall men become CEO's of large companies, commanding officers, judges. Short women usually wind up with such judgmental fellows. At least in novels. Ferrell was Moses the Lawgiver, getting Israelites through the Red Sea to Mt. Sinai. In the process, he slaughtered three thousand compatriots who disobeyed his orders. Or God's. God was Moses' stand in. Would Ferrell be God's? It wasn't likely to be a woman.

Who would conquer our travelers' hearts? Neither could conquer Italy. It had been conquered already, lastly by the U.S. Army in 1944. Just this January the draft was abolished. Fighting would now become as voluntary as signing up for a tour to Italy. Follow the flag! American troops left Viet Nam in March. But we had our own flag, the Altamonte College flag to follow. Tourists, like warriors, followed theirs. Therein lay safety, a successful tour. Our retractable flags bore the heraldic symbols of Florence the fleur-de-lis (*fiordaligi*) representing Florence, France, New Orleans, La., and Charlemagne, controller of large parts of Italy, (eighth–ninth centuries A.D.). Our golden lily was *so* right for Italy.

Heathrow was looming, but all we could see was fog. The English brag of fog as Benvenuto Cellini bragged of his exploits. A goldsmith, he wrote(1558-62) in his *Autobiography* things that concerned his many artistic and military exploits. No one bragged like he did.

The passengers were very restless now. Anita stopped reading her *Bible* and put it away. I was thinking of Michelangelo. When he saw Ghiberti's golden doors on Florence's Baptistery facing *Il Duomo* (the cathedral under Brunelleschi's dome), he called them "the gates of Paradise." Men have called their mistresses' legs the same. When a woman's swung open, they reaffirmed God's command: "Be fruitful and multiply." Michelangelo revered Ghiberti. I stretched my own legs, now, prickly and stiff from sitting too long.

Ferrell didn't think I knew anything about art. It would have really pissed him off if he knew how much art I have studied. He pissed off easily, but hid his irritation if necessary with a smile. He thought all I knew was language arts, the art of tongues. That's *so* Freudian. As with art, no woman could win a pissing contest with any man over sex, either. Men since Freud have labeled frigid the women who didn't care for them. Men who lived in prior generations were already acolytes of Freud's twisted interpretation. Medieval men thought women more libidinous not less so than men. Only women lived in real time, in real bodies, and were realists.

Ferrell believed a picture was worth a thousand words; literature fewer. I think the ancient Sumerians, who once used pictographs, switched to cuneiform writing because they had much more to say than artists. Nothing beats reading, writing, speaking. Not even the *Mona Lisa. La Gioconda*, (Joyous Lady). But if ever I saw a fellow woman hiding anxiety, it was she. Mona Lisa, like the song, was "laughing on the outside, crying on the inside."

Though lilies symbolized Florence, so did lions. Lions loved St. Mark. Did he love them back? Cats knew who did not like them and made straight for them. Poor St. Mark. He may have hated lions, but they represented him everywhere we'd go.

I was passing these last moments of a tiring journey pondering Italian history by way of distraction. Anita had closed her eyes. No one had talked to me but the stewardess–briefly. We should be landing at

Heathrow any minute. Lord, make it appear soon. Two days in London, and then, Rome. First a hot shower and sleep, then bring on the art.

I turned my thoughts to Venice mulling over St. Mark and lions. After Venice defeated Genoa in 1381, she devoured several neighbors and Mediterranean islands like the capitalistic lion she was. Gnawed their bones. The League of Cambrai stripped Venice of her land empire in 1508. Venice said goodbye (*arrivederci*) to Cyprus in 1571; Crete in 1669 and the Peloponnesus in 1715. See you again! But Venice never owned them again. Empires are about owning other peoples' stuff. Now Venice lived off tourists. A winged lion stood atop a pillar near the corner of the Ducal Palace (*Palazzo Ducale*). Another decorated the Cathedral of St. Mark's façade, with St. Mark looking uneasy beside him. A third lion graced a lunette of the cathedral on St. Mark's square (*piazza* San Marco), minus St. Mark. Saints could be spiritually present even when physically absent, like lovers.

Speaking of lovers, I wondered how Tony was doing without me? Getting more depressed, I'd bet. An engineer, he liked making calculations with no immediate human implications. Tony went to interview in some southern state for a job. Jobs had human implications. I doubted I would be among them.

St. Jerome had a lion, too. It guarded him in a cave in Syria. Albrecht Dürer, a Lutheran, drew Jerome in a proper book lined study. Protestant artists were not as free as Italian Catholics to paint nudes, and dancing nudes plagued Jerome's Hebrew studies. Ferrell would surely show us this work in the British Museum tomorrow.

Florence's lion, the *Marzocco,* was Donatello's. It's on our flag. Florence had a boar's statue in its market place. Ferrell put the *Porcellino* (Piglet) opposite the *Marzocco.* Probably lions ate pigs in real life, but on our flag all was peace. Altamonte spent three hundred bucks per flag, more chic then the umbrellas used by British tour guides. Reverence for art and respect for Italy, God's own culture garden, was what Altamonte's flag conveyed. Beneath its lily, Ferrell wrote "Altamonte College on the Peninsula." The girls in fashion design hemmed the silk banners. The shop guys worked miracles with collapsible rods. That's what real men do with their tools. Work miracles.

Our flag was our Ark of the Covenant to protect our travelers as chosen people. If we couldn't save them, money could. And they were paying for this luxury tour–$4,800 apiece. Even if I had had to pay I would have gladly, had I the cash. Italy had shaped me more than America. My education had led me back to my roots, which were Italian and French.

Bump, bump and bump! The landing gear made contact with Heathrow's tarmac. "Bravo's" filled the aisles. Everybody around us shifted in his or her seat.

"Ladies and gentlemen, we ask you to remain seated with your seat belt fastened while we taxi to Gate A 17. Remember. Things in the overhead compartments tend to shift during flight, so be careful when you open them. For now, please remain seated until the pilot turns off the seat belt sign and we arrive at the gate."

We were happy to touch earth again. S.F. to Heathrow in twelve hours. Sixteen from my house to deplaning.

I retrieved my overhead luggage. It had not shifted at all. One cannot believe everything one hears. We (Ferrell, W.L. Spotswood, Anita Marble and I) were so close to the front, we were soon on the ramp. Everyone was looking forward to luxurious service, deferential treatment. Who could have offered a better luxury tour deal than Altamonte College and its trip provider, Charles Clark? I knew the tourists would appreciate everything we had won for them.

During the flight I had envied Ferrell and Prof. W. L. Spotswood their camaraderie. Anita finally confided that she taught fifth grade English and art in a Catholic parochial school in San Jose. She told me her students were not often adept in English, but came from immigrant backgrounds where Spanish or Vietnamese was spoken; homes where people did not have books, and sometimes, little food or money. Her hands, when she touched mine were like ice. Perhaps she prayed so consistently from a fear of flying, like Erica Jong's heroine, Isadora Wing, in her brilliant new novel. Isadora also had cold hands. Did Anita suffer from fear of flying? Or did she pray from hope rather than fear? I wanted to ask but was afraid to interrupt such stalwart religiosity. Since I couldn't join her in prayer, I wished I could have joined in the hearty laughter and conversation that rang out from the professors across the aisle. Perhaps Ferrell was taking some sort of instruction from W.L. Spotswood, professor of Renaissance history from Madison. Or vice versa.

I learned how *not* to take instruction from Ferrell during the fall quarter. The college sent out three thousand brochures in early November, with our itinerary, including application forms. Ferrell designed the form and it was added to Altamonte's Winter Catalogue. Roger Garvey subsidized its late inclusion. Other applications were placed in hotels and fine restaurants. We handed out brochures and forms at several recruiting events in the City and two at the College, held in the theater downstairs, with Chardonnay, cheese, crackers. Several hundred well dressed and blue–jeaned sneaker wearers showed up. Rob held a twenty minute slide show on Italian art. I explained how I planned to make each "guest" conversant with important Italian phrases, and in which cities I would give mini bus lectures on books written by some famous author connected with our itinerary. The crowd seemed more interested in five star luxury hotels, plus banquets and cuisine. Only six lunches were not included. Free tickets to all major attractions were provided. Rob and I would lead them to far, far better places (museums) than they had ever known. *"Buon viaggio!"* (Have a good trip!) They could see by our happy demeanor how much fun we'd be! Most couldn't afford the tour. They came for the wine and cheese. And Rob's slide show.

We signed up several parents and grandparents of Altamonte students. Matilda Visconti, from South San Francisco, was a widow whose granddaughter, Elisabeth, was my least talented, but most beautiful, French student. Elisabeth persuaded her to take this trip to "stop living in the past amid Grandpa's dusty stuffed moose heads." Matilda joined, determined to find her family home. She didn't have an address, but knew it was dark red and in Milan. I doubted we could find it without an address.

"Our schedule will dictate," I told her. Elisabeth's own head lusted after her biology instructor, Jon Nicholson. I saw them on the parking lot one night, in his car, in, well, a state of spirited nudity. Nicholson was married. But with Matilda gone for three weeks they would have a large house to play in, instead of a cramped Toyota. Elisabeth was twenty-one.

There were also the Froehlings, Ellen and Bill, of Los Gatos, grandparents of one of our golf and yachting majors. Bill, a retired engineer, told us: "Ellen is always late. You'll wait for her a lot." Anne Gilmore of Menlo Park, in her mid fifties, wrote memoirs and novels she feared publishing. Two couples from Monte Sereno were in their seventies: One set, the Harkers, Betty and James, a retired geologist, were related to the founders of Harker Academy of Palo Alto, a military school now in Cupertino. The Harkers were age-mates with the Huntsmans of Saratoga and the Froehlings.

Ralph Huntsman was a retired Etruscanologist who had taught at the University of Pennsylvania before falling into a deep excavation in Volterra. At that time, still in his late forties, he had been watching a young grad student in shorts and halter on the other side of the same excavation, and nearly lost his leg because of it. He had fallen into the yawning gulf before him, and crushed his femur badly. Now, he walked with a cane. Jan grew roses and dragged Ralph to San Francisco's opera. Jan had inherited a major seed company fortune, and Ralph's small retirement was no obstacle to their cultured lifestyle.

Two married women in their mid–forties, Joan Lorimar from Pleasanton, and Andrea Smithwitch of Palo Alto, were lone travelers. Mr. Lorimar, one of those technical entrepreneurs, was starting up a new electronics business. He could not take off three weeks, as he was the only one of his three partners who could visualize the ultimate dream–"a tech" company that would supply a young electronics firm with the appropriate hardware to make its new software outperform three other new companies'–all competing with and stealing from each other. Andrea Smithwitch's husband, Dr. Arthur Smithwitch, Stanford's famous liver transplant surgeon, had a schedule not even God almighty would dare alter, and only the airlines or melted ice ever delayed. When anyone asked what he did he replied, "Liver's my game. The liver business." Andrea hated that.

Samantha Jones, a stunning divorcée in her late forties, lived in Atherton, where multimillionaires dwelt on so many acres apiece, they never saw their neighbors. Only the arrival of delivery and repair men, of maids and gardeners, caterers and lawn party organizers, tree trimmers and dog walkers, decorators and floral delivery trucks broke the semirural hush of their retreats–Tudor, Georgian or Renaissance. Samantha was traveling with Sam Perkins, a former stockbroker, then a failed realtor, whom she loved, but who was not a viable social replacement for her ex-husband. The latter had given her a generous settlement and the Atherton estate. Sam was pushing fifty and a recovering alcoholic. He was trying to dry out, and put his faith in Twelve Steps and Samantha, who made him sell his Condo in the East Bay and live in her rear cottage. There, like Lady Chatterley and her gardener, they had made passionate love, the passion of convenience.

Lynette Dryer, divorced, was a plain, boyish looking women approaching her forties. She liked to watch old movies at home alone. I often watched the golden oldies for the joy of seeing the great stars of the 40s and 50s–Katherine Hepburn and Spencer Tracy, Orson Wells, Janet Leigh, Bette Davis, Humphrey Bogart–more. They preceded America's change of taste from drama to the ecstatic, and soon, with Star Wars, to the galactic escape. This year's thriller, *The Exorcist*, was gory. I would not go see it when Tony, intrigued by the lines at the nearest theater, pleaded that we should.

Three more women had enrolled. One was twenty-eight, Anita Marble, who turned out to be my seat-mate on our flight, religious, repressed, and timid, though finely molded on a grand scale with a terrific cleavage. In high school she had studied singing and had a lovely voice. Her family, Italian businessmen, had their name changed from *Marmo* to Marble at Ellis Island. She was given this trip to their homeland in the hope she'd meet some nice Italian man and marry him. She had attached herself to me at our second meeting in the Altamonte theater, though on that occasion she seemed livelier than as my seatmate.

Two other women, mid-fortyish, Sandy Craigie and Belinda Smith, were lesbian lovers and business partners. They owned a costume jewelry store in Sunnyvale and planned to write this trip off as a business expense, shopping Florence and Venice intensively for beautifully designed, though poorly soldered necklaces, many of which broke within a month of purchase, but were worth having restrung. I was glad that Altamonte could stimulate the economies of Cupertino as well as Italy. Or was a tax write–off not an economic stimulus? I wasn't sure, not having paid much attention in econ class.

In mid-February a young guy Molly Finkel described as "a cool dude"–Matt Silverstein–like her, Jewish and red-haired, our age, attended one of the Altamonte tour parties. I made Molly attend, just to get her out of her apartment, the doldrums. Matt, like Tony, had just been laid off from a managerial position in a manufacturing company in San Jose. Everyone was jittery about the economy because of the oil shortage. Matt had majored in English at Reed College! Molly was enchanted. They could actually communicate about books, and not just in bed. Though both kinds of interchange were useful.

Matt felt that he needed an expensive Italian tour before he began to look for work, and his parents, well to do, were willing to pay for it. He took an immediate interest in Molly, who was very cute, and asked her to take the tour, too. She couldn't afford it. She had to teach summer school to make her rent. Matt was the first single Jewish guy she had met in months, if you discounted her Berkeley Synagogue acquaintances, "all more or less crazy," in her opinion. Anyway, she wanted to forget about Rabbi Schlomo Schneider whom she had been laying because he was still laying his wife, separated or not. She had hoped to meet the right man at that very Reformed Jewish temple, B'nai Israel, in Berkeley. But the number of young, single Jewish males there was not equal to the number of unmarried females, or married ones, for that matter. Even Jews had begun to swing in the seventies. Increasingly it seemed the bond of marriage was weakening. For men, it had never been that binding. And Molly was kind of hopeful that Schlomo would leave his wife. I wasn't. They had three small children. In most Jewish families, the parents stuck together for the good of the children even when they despised each other. The parents, I mean; not the children, who were innocent by-sufferers.

"Most Jewish men are "self centered duds, not dudes," Molly had lamented.

"So are most Protestant and Catholic men," I told her. "Agnostics and atheists, ditto." She and Matt exchanged phone numbers. He asked her out for the following Friday night. Her folks, who hadn't attended "Shul" (Yid., synagogue) since Molly's grandparents died, were happy that Matt was Jewish. Jewishness, I'd concluded, was (for secular Jews like me, those also atheists), a love of one's history, a loyalty to one's suffering ancestors. All mine were Jewish on Mom's side. I figured I qualified as Jewish without keeping the Sabbath holy. Molly was not an atheist. She was more a spiritualist with preponderant Jewish loyalties, but not wholly adverse to experimenting with other peoples' rituals, unless these were institutionalized. She was phoning Matt every couple of hours before out tour left, where formerly all she did was talk to me and correct essays. Their first date was a huge success. Huge. She promised to make him wear condoms. One abortion was enough.

All this recruitment stuff was running through my head—and more—as I tried to keep upright against a large metal pillar near our baggage rotunda. We waited and waited. My back hurt. My eyes were burning. I hadn't slept well before the trip. I could not sleep in planes. I nevertheless tried to encourage the tourists who came to me for reassurance.

"Of course, Belinda, of course you are going to get your luggage. They rarely lose anything on international flights." Did I know that? No.

"No, Ellen. I did not observe your suitcases being loading onto a flight to Barcelona. Be patient. We'll soon have our luggage, and then a wonderful room in a great hotel." I looked over to see Andrea Pellatierra, manager of Gumps jewelry shop in the City, holding hands with his wife, Maria, against a neighboring pillar. They had introduced Rob to the upper world of San Francisco's art colony. Indeed, to some who were just upper, not artists, but bought art. Bought Rob's ducks. Gumps was the most famous gift shop in the City. Andrea admired his carved ducks. Rob could not carve fast enough to fill the back orders. But he lost interest. Aside from ducks, he had carved a place for himself in San Francisco's *beau monde* (Fr.,high society). Occasionally, he hung an abstract painting in one of the trendier galleries. His works were always non–representational. I didn't ask why, not wanting to seem out of it.

Rob placed three dozen brochures in Grace Cathedral's porch on a table advertising religious events. Two Anglican nuns, an aunt and her niece, a beautiful twenty-three year old postulant, saw them and signed up. The aunt was Sister Agatha Rollins; her niece was Allison Rollins, sole heiress to the Rollins coffee and tea fortune. The aunt looked around forty-eight or nine, and Allison just looked beautiful, even in a wimple and light blue habit. Not all nuns were poor, vows of poverty notwithstanding. The Rollins' coffee and tea business began in the City in the mid-nineteenth century. A large billboard hung over the lip of highway 101 advertising it. A Turk drinking coffee; an Indian brewing tea.

Wait. Was that my suitcase coming down the conveyor belt? No. Damn. It looked like it, but no ribbon. I had tied a plaid ribbon to my handle. Anyway, the same Grace Cathedral gave us an assistant priest, a man in his thirties, with a Princeton Divinity degree and an M.F.A. in classics. Father Ian MacDonald. He lacked a permanent teaching or pastoral post, but his parents were deep in oil and urged him "do" Italy, as Reed's parents encouraged him. It had worked well for Henry James, William Dean Howells and E.M. Forster. Why wouldn't it help Ian find himself? It was a 1960s thing but with very remote precedents.

I sat down on the floor to ease my lower back. I spread a discarded newspaper, the *London Times* under me. Ferrell was watching. He looked as he did when rested, only for once, his tie was not tightly knotted. He had loosened it and it sort of dribbled over one of his lapels.

It had been Ferrell who dropped off brochures at the concierge desk of the St. Francis on Union Square, too, and at the Mark Hopkins on Nob Hill. It was at the Top of the Mark that Spotswood found a copy lying on the bar while ordering a Manhattan. At the St. Francis, a gentleman from Boston, a banker named Arnold Lodge, yes, one of *those* Lodges, had tossed our brochure into his briefcase along with his worn copy of *Tom Sawyer*, for he was an avid Mark Twain reader.

Someone (what was his name?) Del Vecchio, a young man, an Italian-American around thirty-three, did the same. Del Vecchio was a car salesman with an M.F.A. from Yale. Like most third generation Italians, he didn't speak Italian. His passions were the clarinet, which he carried everywhere; Italian cars, which he sold in Menlo Park; and marriage. *Italo-Americani* believed in starting families early to reap the blessings of many grandchildren in old age. That was one way they could achieve immortality, should the Church let them down any other way. Wait! I remembered his first name now. Clarinet. Reed. Reed Del Vecchio. Mnemonic aids, ever a blessing! Reed Del Vecchio lived in Palo Alto, on Waverly, with his parents, both physicians at Stanford Hospital.

Ferrell was now yelling, "Attention Altamonte Tour Group. Our luggage was placed in the rear of the plane because we were the first to board. So it won't be up for another fifteen minutes. Those people you see carting away theirs were on our plane, but boarded later. I'll stay right here at the belt. Prof. Spotswood will keep me company. As soon as our luggage starts coming up one of us will come and tell you. Meanwhile, there are benches opposite rotunda six." We were at ten. "Why don't you just go down there and rest until you hear from us?" Rob asked. "Standing up is a trial, I know, and the floor is pretty hard." The group started down the hall toward the benches. I went with them at Ferrell's suggestion. He and W.L. Spotswood remained behind.

Spotswood's application had puzzled me a bit. A noted professor of Renaissance history, with a long string of publications, I wondered why he had not simply applied for a grant? This was a pricey trip. I doubted he made a ton of money at Wisconsin, even with a chair. I had read several of his articles and his book on Renaissance education. I looked him up. Fourteen books on warfare and politics in Italy during the early Renaissance, one on education and three on Medici politics from Cosimo (d. 1464) through the return of Alessandro in 1532 as Grand Duke of Tuscany. He had graduated magna cum laude from the University of Missouri eighteen years ago. Ph.D. from the University of Chicago. Full professor at Columbia before taking the Eugene O'Reilly Chair of Renaissance Studies at Madison. A whiz in Latin and Greek, I wondered if he were fluent in Italian? With his credentials he could easily gain entrance to that ritzy resort place at Bellagio on Lake Como with all the other academic swells! I supposed they did more drinking than research there.

If I ever got such a grant, I might be tempted to play, too; down by the lake shore—Lake Como (*Lago di Como*)—so blue, with little villages creeping up from its shore into the mountains. Bellagio. Palm trees on the paths and hibiscus climbing up white walls. So arresting. Rose bedecked public gardens heady in the moonlight. Everything beckoned one outdoors, not into a library. Maybe W.L. Spotswood needed a change of pace in an atmosphere where not doing research, not even pretending to, absolved him of guilt. At fifty-three, he was Dad's age.

Ferrell, the same age, was squash partner and a friend of Izzy Finkel, who was not only the Cantor at the biggest Synagogue in the City, but Molly's uncle. Izzy creamed him at squash last month. For penance, Rob passed out two dozen brochures at the Synagogue. Four hit their mark: one was Jonah Schoenstein, sixty-three, President of the Altruistic Insurance Company that insured Altamonte College. Jonah's young second wife, Mindy, only twenty-five, told Molly she married Jonah on the understanding that they would have no children. Jonah had two boys who attended Altamonte. Mindy, a convert to Judaism —she was raised a Seventh Day Adventist—loved good clothes. She loved *good* clothes. She'd never gone to college. Mindy was just in front of me, walking with Barry's Schwartz's wife, Myrna. They were not much younger than I was. I was not going to be hippy, but Myrna might be as she aged. To be fair, she had had twins less than two years ago. That doesn't help trim one's hips. I knew the term "hippy" once meant large-hipped. Once it meant a "hipster" who knew the latest musical hits in the early 1940s. Now "hippies" since the mid-60s and into the present time, were young people who put a high value on non-violence, communal living and long hair, not to mention marijuana and other illegal drugs. Language was fascinating. So historical. I had chosen the right profession.

Mindy Schoenstein had been drawn since the age of fourteen to the doings of hippies in San Francisco and to radicals on the Cal Campus. After high school graduation, she headed West from Chicago to find a job in San Francisco. Jonah Schoenstein had just been divorced from his wife of many years, Leona. They agreed he should stay in their house in St. Francis Wood and their college aged sons could live with either of them, or at the college. Leona's classy new mansion in the Seacliff area had an elegant entrance hall, a divided marble staircase and a gorgeous view of the Golden Gate. Leona didn't even mind if Mindy made Jonah happy because she felt their marriage had outlived its usefulness. Leona now played as much bridge and mahjong as she wished without having to entertain her husband's business associates. For six hours a week she volunteered at the Palace of the Legion of Honor art museum as docent. Leona had been an art major at Brandeis. Mindy had found security; Leona, freedom; Jonah, love. *Divorce was as blessed as marriage*, I thought.

The synagogue also gave us Barry Schwartz, a banker, and Myrna his wife. Barry was in his late forties, and like Schoenstein, had two kids in college, but not at Altamonte. At San Jose State and at Chico State. Myrna, a brunette with black curly hair, was two years my junior. The Schwartzes had had twins–boys–after three years of marriage. Neither Mindy nor Myrna were your typical Hadassah ladies. They were hot chicks, though one was childless, the other a young mother. In my dreams, I was a young chick, too. Just not yet a mother.

The Schwartz toddlers were now being cared for by two adoring Bubbies, Jewish grandmas, plus a nanny from Peru named Maria Sanchez. Maria's lineage on both sides until the sixteenth century was Ashkenazi Jewish. One of her paternal ancestors, Hoseah, later called José, and soon a *converso*, (Span., Catholic convert) sailed with his parents and siblings, from Spain to the Crimea, after being forced into exile in 1492. His family, like mine, refused to convert to Catholicism. They spoke Ladino, part archaic Castilian, part Hebrew. Maria knew nothing of her remote ancestry.

José had made it his business to learn modern Spanish before leaving, buying old books from peddlers. He taught himself a fairly grammatical if quaint Castilian Spanish minus any Hebrew. Just nineteen, the youth was determined to make his fortune in the New World, and having left his family in the Crimea, went to Odessa, where he lived for a year as an apprentice trader, before making his way to a port in Greece. There he took ship for the New World. As chance would have it, he met up with an ex-swineherd of genteel Spanish background named Francisco Pizarro. José was with Pizarro when the latter conquered Peru, and smart enough to attend Mass with the other soldiers under Pizarro, before marrying a Peruvian Indian woman whom the Jesuits had converted to Rome in their mission church in the Andes. At José's wedding, his fellow soldiers got drunk on a local liquor of fermented gourds. José took the name of Sanchez after one of those men. He had by then almost forgotten Ladino.

Centuries passed, rumors of Jewish origins died. His descendant, Maria Sanchez, finding herself alone in the world at the age of twenty, managed to reach Los Angeles in 1968–best not to inquire how–and after several years as a housekeeper and occasional baby sitter in the Hollywood Hills, bought a bus ticket to San Francisco. There she found a job as nursemaid to the Schwartzes, partly because she looked like so much like Myrna's mom.

Maria Sanchez loved the twins, who, as they grew, seemed closer to her than to Myrna. So much so, that both Jewish grandmothers or *bubbies* joked about Maria being the twins' "real" mom! Of course it was just a joke. The nanny was Peruvian.

"If Myrna doesn't spend more time with those babies, though," Bubbie Blankenschiff, Myrna's mom, said, "the twins will speak better Spanish than English."

The Blankenschiffs, Myrna's maternal relatives, came from Odessa, where they had been in the shipping business. Before that they lived in the Crimea, alongside Hoseah's family. As they were all Jews and spoke Ladino, they naturally intermarried among their own kind. The term words for white ship, a description of the one they sailed on from Spain, got translated into German (*blankenschiff*) years later by clients from Munich who heard that these Jews left Spain on a white ship. The Blankenschiffs (as they allowed themselves to be called) prospered in their business. In Odessa their shipping company grew steadily. Just before the Great War, they shipped themselves to New York, and in the 1940s to Miami Beach where they helped develop inland areas and made a fortune in developing hotels for the "snowbirds" who came down from Canada and Chicago, Boston and New York, to warm their tootsies on hot sand. Grandma Blankenschiff was a widow and still lived in Florida. Her mother had sung her a few lullabies in Ladino, but Bubbie Blankenschiff had forgotten most of the words, if not the melodies.

Some of those words she mangled. But many were familiar to Maria from her childhood, even if she did not know their meaning, and the nanny took to singing them to encourage the twins to nap.

Grandma Schwartz's husband, Bernie, though seventy-seven, got the three weeks of Altamonte's tour to Italy off to fool around with his mistress, Betty, fifty-two, who did his wife's nails and Grandpa on the side. Grandpa was *very* rich, and needed catering to. Neither of the two *bubbies* catered much to anyone anymore but themselves and the twins. Myrna played bit parts at one or two amateur theater groups and shopped to get out of the house away from her twins, who were, after all, a constant headache. The terrible two's.

Altamonte's *Spring Catalogue* netted our last tourists. Meg Summers and Peg Springer, ex-nurses, twins. Both ex-wives of doctors, in their late forties. They lost their husbands to younger nurses, after having stolen them from older nurses. They got decent settlements and their children attended private schools. The ladies were still nice looking, despite some weight gain and a hint of future dew-laps. They were identical. Their habit of wearing matching clothes was less cute than when they were children, though.

Ferrell had rolled his eyes when I asked him if he could tell them apart, because I couldn't. He referred to them as "Megpeg." We turned in the list of thirty-one applications (plus us, making thirty-three) to Charles Clark, who was satisfied. Still, he raised the tour price by two hundred dollars to $4,800 and sent out contracts to be signed with hefty deposits in case someone changed his or her mind before 15 March. After that, each applicant would be liable for the whole cost of the tour.

I did not sleep with Rob Ferrell last autumn. In the first place, he treated Molly badly. In the second, maybe still the first, an affair with a colleague who collected precious objects like Molly, and then disposed of them didn't seem promising. I wasn't convinced Tony was the man of my dreams, but I did want to avoid nightmares about Ferrell's autumn invitation to spend the night after a day's planning session, even if he did know a great breakfast joint near the Cliff House. If he gave me a key to my own bedroom, I suspected he had a duplicate as well. So I arrived early–at 8:00 A.M.–at his house on Coit Tower hill. He was in his dressing gown and slippers.

"Hi, Rob," I said in a perky manner. "I thought I'd come early and we could coffee up." I held up two large cups of coffee that I had bought at the deli two blocks down the hill. "Lattes, for energy. The caffeine will help us pump out an itinerary in two hours." It took longer, but not longer than four.

He raised his two bushy eyebrows. "Where, Candida, is your suitcase?"

"Oh that," I had said blithely. "I figured we could finish the itinerary by two–then have lunch on me, overlooking Ghirardelli Square. I sleep better in my own bed. Insomnia."

"Perhaps, then," Ferrell said with some malice, "you'd better not go to Italy. You might miss some shut-eye." He left, returning minutes later in a black turtle neck, chinos, and sandals, bearing a tray of croissants, toasted bagels, jam and butter. "Here," he said gruffly, putting the tray down on his dining room table. "You want orange juice? I can squeeze some."

It wasn't necessary, but a nice offer. We got our itinerary done by two P.M. I took Rob out to Ghirardelli Square. He donned an exquisite silk sports jacket over the turtle neck, good slacks, Italian shoes. We ate *bouillabaisse* and sourdough bread dipped in olive oil and vinegar. *Crème caramel. Espresso.* He bought a fine bottle of *Pinot Grigio* and tipped the waiter handsomely. A delightful meal. When the sky began to turn orange and aqua over Alcatraz, we left. No, I did not re-enter his house, though I did need to use a bathroom. I stopped at a gas station in San Mateo instead. And yes, I made it back to Alviso just before its sky at last went black over Alviso's sloughs.

Morning, in London! Our hotel, the Savoy Regency, was in the City of Westminster, the ritziest real estate in London. The hotel was on a street where London's finest hotels stood proudly, within earshot of Big Ben. Ours was a four star hotel, not luxury, but almost, and so central. I found the purple, pink and aqua color combo of the lobby a decorative cliché. The breakfast room was delightful, though, in gold and white, with sheer drapes and tasteful Venetian blinds as well, in case the morning light proved jarring. Londoners saw so little sun, hardly anyone had the nerve to adjust the blinds, much less close them altogether. At 7:45 A.M. we gathered in the breakfast room as instructed. From our six tables (round, each seating six people), we looked out onto a small walled garden, filled with potted phlox and stock, heliotrope and larkspur. Ivy trailed the stone walls. A birdbath attracted four bathers, species unknown. Delightful. We all beamed at one another, though a few were too groggy to beam straight on. We were still strangers, except for the married couples. And even in their case, who could say?

Dudley, our local facilitator and baggage handler, handed out Altamonte College name tags, blank, with plastic covers and pins underneath and placed pens on each table. We wrote our names and titles to help us get acquainted. A plaque on each table said "Altamonte

College Tour." We took up six tables. Ferrell sat at mine with "Megpeg," in matching pink polyester pantsuits that would cut through any London fog, surely. Next to the twins was Prof. Spotswood and Bill Froehling. Ellen Froehling arrived late and the waiters fluttered about setting up another place for her. Our table was the most crowded after the seventh chair was added for Ellen. The women laughed at Ferrell's comments, and at the Professor's, just two inches shorter and slimmer than Rob, with a slightly ironic and sometimes corny sense of humor, but well mannered, and I would guess, kindly.

Our menu was a British breakfast of juice, tea, (coffee was available but had to be ordered, and we did not want to get off schedule) limply fried bacon with bits of bone in it, dry scrambled eggs and a limp fried tomato slice on the side. Apple or prune juice was placed beside a "porringer" of oatmeal. We finished our meal off with fresh fruit salad and headed through the lobby bus-wards, stopping only long enough to visit the "ladies" and the "gents," quaint British terms for the ladies' room and the men's. We boarded our bus, but had to wait for Ellen Froehling. Her husband said she'd forgotten her headscarf. Rob and I sat nearest the driver, and after Ellen arrived, panting, we headed out.

I lowered my window. Through it Big Ben tolled nine o'clock. Clarissa Dalloway was right, or rather, Virginia Woolf was in *Mrs. Dalloway*. There *was* a whirring sound that filled the air with tension before Ben's actual tolling from his tower attached to Parliament. "Ben" shared his space with other bells, as Ferrell and I shared ours with thirty-one strangers; not counting our driver and British facilitator. I wished Henry James, William Dean Howells, and E. M. Forster could have signed up. Hemingway, no. He would have had it out with Ferrell, both alpha males. Thomas Mann might have been interesting, but *Death in Venice* would have depressed him. It depressed me.

We'd be in the Savoy Plaza in Rome, on the *Corso*, a quiet enough thoroughfare. Our hotel in Venice would be on the Grand Canal (*Canale Grande*). It would be noisy at night in *La Serenissima*, the so-called 'quiet' city. But waking up on the Grand Canal with such a view would compensate for noisy revelers in gondolas.

I thought of my favorite Jewish authors, their ignoring of European culture except in its manifestations–denatured–in New York or New

Jersey. Many young women of my generation avoided reading Saul Bellow and Philip Roth. Bellow was softer in his rhetoric toward my sex, whatever the women's religious backgrounds, but as superior as Roth about their lack of culture. I forgave him because of his humor, pathos, and Jewish perspective on a world constantly betraying its own values by adopting those of the dominant Christian culture–which had ceased to practice them.

Besides, I could not accuse him of inaccuracy. Most men did treat women badly before I reached maturity. Regarding Philip Roth's *Good By, Columbus*, which made fun of bourgeois Jewish families (while Bellow merely escaped from them), I lamented the harsh treatment meted out to the young woman Roth's hero supposedly loved (Brenda Patemkin), making fun of the fact that she cared so much about getting her nose bobbed, having to wear eyeglasses. What drove her to "fix" everything about herself she found imperfect? And why did Roth ridicule her imperfections? Still, I admired his genius, misogynist though he was. I admired genius in all the great twentieth century novelists, even the overtly anti–Semitic ones, like F. Scott Fitzgerald, and Edith Wharton.

Oh, well. *We* are about life, not novels. Novels, love them as we do, are, at best, a last resort for living a full life after real life has been unkind or cruel, boring, or when we cannot afford a luxury trip to Italy. Thank goodness this tour would be a real life experience and not about some characters in a novel.

CHAPTER IV

I ARRIVE IN ITALY. ALONE.

So here I was, flying all alone on *Al Italia*, heading to Rome, plane half empty. I had had a wonderful time in London, and was shocked when, after we returned to our hotel for 'high tea' Ferrell said, "Pack up, Candida; Charles Clark just phoned. You leave immediately to check out our new, inferior accommodations outside Rome." My mouth dropped. *Bummer*, I thought.

"But we booked into the Savoy Plaza on the Corso," I said, suddenly recalling the hotel.

I once stayed at the Savoy Plaza, an older four star hotel, rather tatty in the 1960s, but charming. From my research months in Rome I knew it was close to one of my many *pensione* where I had showered in an old man's kitchen while he drank his coffee in his yellowed undershirt, and handed me a bath towel (*un accapatoio*) before I stepped into the low lipped shower stall.

One didn't forget having passed the Savoy Plaza, once having stepped between such an old man and his refrigerator into a mildewed shower with a cement floor and rusted drain. That shower was in his kitchen, even though my toilet was in my bedroom, where the closet once was. Before inhabiting that *pensione* for two nights, I passed the grand old Savoy Plaza at least twice a day, and had gone inside to look. Yes, its furniture needed reupholstering and the carpet was worn. But the ballroom had its own bar and was covered by Tiffany glass in multi-colored panes, the way Tiffany lamps used to glow in the rather dimly lit parlors of my Bubbie Brondel's old friends. It cost fourteen dollars a night at the Savoy, marble staircase, tubs on legs, overstuffed (if worn) bedroom furniture, and no old man in his yellow undershirt to hear you taking a shower behind his mildewed shower curtain. I paid seven bucks for the *pensione*.

So I had moved on the third day into the Savoy and enjoyed its decayed, but spotless splendors, its marble bathrooms, huge bedroom, and the chambermaids' laundry lines on the roof-top patio outside the French doors. The Corso began at People's Square (*Piazza del Popolo*) near the Pincio Hill where the Borghese Gallery sat. There reclined Canova's bewitching statue of Napoleon Bonaparte's sister, Marie Pauline, (*Paolina*) who married into the Borghese family. It was close to the *Piazza di Spagna* (Spanish steps), the Piazza Navona; and some of Rome's best boutiques. Last fall, I had checked out the Savoy Plaza, and finding it entirely re-decorated and ten times as expensive, made Charles book us into it. It was now a five star.

This morning, during my half day with no second night in London, our bus excursion took us past the Houses of Parliament. I heard Big Ben toll as we headed for the Victoria and Albert Museum on the Cromwell Road, South Kensington. The museum admission was free. This surprised all of us Americans who had started paying entrance fees for museums in the 1960s and who were quite amazed that the British were keeping free admission going. Some of our super advantaged tourists thought England would collapse and bring us all down unless it stopped providing cultural services paid for by the wealthy; "services the poor neither appreciated–nor deserved" according to someone in our tour group, though most approved of free school tours. As we entered, I saw the Directors had set out a plastic donation box, and on it placed a sign saying, "Anything you give will be appreciated." Jonah and W.L. dropped ten pounds into it on the way out. Arnold Lodge, the banker, dropped in twenty. Ferrell gave ten, and I gave five. Sam gave a pound. The rest of the group pretended it did not exist.

We spent two hours in Victoria and Albert's wondrous collection that held close to five million objects and had the largest collection of Renaissance art outside Italy. I cannot remember many of the marvels we saw. It was overwhelming. I recall Jacopo da Pontormo's portrait of Alessandro de' Medici, illegitimate son of Lorenzo de' Medici, cousin of Cardinal Ippolito de' Medici, also illegitimate. And Pope Clement VII, who relied on both to rule Florence in his absence. Ippolito's father was Giuliano de' Medici, Duke of Nemours. The bastard cousins, plus a distant relative named Lorenzino, a pal of Alessandro's, were put in charge of Florentine government. The Republic was dead after 1512. Machiavelli joined the unemployment lines for having served a republic. W.L. would know all about that.

Of his two illegitimate nephews, Pope Clement preferred Alessandro, made first Duke of Tuscany (1532), with the approval of Charles V, the Holy Roman Emperor (a Spaniard who owned much of two worlds, New and Old Spain and Germany), and who gave his illegitimate daughter, Margaret of Parma, to Alessandro to wed. Illegitimacy played a huge rule in the Renaissance. Does it in our age? There are so many more ways to practice it now.

In the Victoria and Albert Museum I stared up at Alessandro. I was reading diligently from a plastic coated description of the painting. His mother had been an African slave. Despite his subsequent good fortune, he shared none with her, and she lived in Rome with a passel of kids by her African husband, poor and unrecognized, but probably not unloved. Alessandro was quite dark, though dark skin is not unknown in a country so close to Africa. Nor is a dark heart. He finished his reign despite two cousins who tried to have him poisoned (1537), but not before he had become a real tyrant and libertine, a Medici tradition. Ippolito also tried to have him assassinated. Lorenzino, his best friend, helped. Sent on a mission to Charles V in Tunis to complain about Alessandro, Ippolito was himself poisoned on Alessandro's orders.

In his black suit and small white collar Alessandro looked sour. He could be a hell fire and damnation preacher in a nineteenth century black American Baptist church. Instead, he was Pope Clement's favorite nephew, Duke of Tuscany (1532). It must have shaken him to discover Lorenzino had betrayed him; consoled him to have had a pro-Republican but loyal historian, Francesco Guicciardini (d. 1540), offer him counsel and support him after 1534. We didn't always know our real friends. The fact that a first rate historian with anti-Machiavellian views tried to steer a cruel libertine like Alessandro straight put some shine on this most crooked of politicians. Even when good advice is not followed, and the counselor himself was sullied by the relationship. I thought Nixon; I thought Attorney General John N. Mitchell; I thought H.R. Haldeman. John Dean.

Turning, I found Prof. Spotswood smiling down at me in some amusement, at my absorption presumably just with the da Pontormo portrait.

"I would be happy to fill you in on Alessandro," said the Professor. I've written all about that era, you know, and lots about Alessandro." I didn't know, though I didn't say so.

"By the way," he continued, "I have wanted to tell you how much I admired your book on Boccaccio and the speeches you gave on Petrarch and Benvenuto Cellini's *Autobiography*. I sometimes infiltrate the Renaissance Lit conferences when they are in the same cities as my Renaissance history ones. Chicago, 1969? Philadelphia 1970? Atlanta 1972?" I stared at him wide–eyed. I had indeed read a paper in each of those cities in those years. His eyes were hazel like mine, only his eyelids were a bit slanted, giving him a hooded look of superior wisdom. He was, after all, twenty-one years my senior. But his penetrating look was full of good humor.

"I am sorry to say," I said in a rush, "that though I knew of your prolific scholarship, I haven't read much of it. I did use one of your books on education to explain something in Castiglione's *The Book of the Courtier*."

"Much obliged," said Prof. Spotswood, grinning down at me. While we stood looking at each other, the rest of our group had waltzed by, not stopping for Alessandro, nor us. Ferrell was hurrying them toward Raphael's ten "cartoons" on loan from the Vatican. He gave me a curious slanted look of his own. From Raphael's framed cartoons, sketches were made for the tapestries for the Sistine Chapel, woven in Brussels. The cartoons, in England for over three hundred years, featured one particularly distasteful anti–Semitic drawing. While Ferrell lectured the group on Raphael's cartoons, my thoughts drifted to the Italian side of my family, my Mother and Bubbie Brondel and Nonno Massimo (Grandpa Max), who died when I was only four, shortly after they arrived in New York via Canada.

My maternal relatives wandered back westward from their exile in the Crimea and Odessa. Some of them, after Italy had been gifted by Napoleon Bonaparte to his sister Elisa and his brother-in-law to rule in

1805, found their way to northern Italy, before settling in Lucca in the nineteenth century. My grandparents managed to escape (1939), with my mother, Lucia, born in 1923, in Lucca. The three entered Canada, (1940) and migrated after the war to upstate New York. While doing research on Boccaccio on my first trip to Italy, I had tried to locate the handful of relatives my mother remembered her parents having mentioned. I found references in 1930s newspapers to several, businessmen or artists, but after 1939, nothing. Italy had 70,000 Jews before Mussolini's formal alliance with Hitler that year. During World War II, she lost 7,500 of her own Jews, but sheltered 4,000 from occupied regions of Vichy France and Greece, setting up concentration camps for Jews, mostly in southern Italy. Others, as my old friend Luigi in Venice had done for his wife and children, found a refuge for them in the Italian Alps, where they were passed off as "nephews" or "nieces," sometimes accompanied by their mothers, always referred to as "distant relatives" or needy "friends of the family."

Mussolini let Jews stay with their family members in his concentration camps, where many, but not all, survived. There was no way to tell if any of my mother's family had, or if they were among the 7,500 "disappeared" Italian Jews, fate unknown. I found a Jewish cemetery in Lucca and put pebbles on all the grave stones I saw there, a practice something akin to leaving calling cards on the silver trays of Victorian gentry in New York, to demonstrate that someone cared enough to stop by; someone remembered.

Raphael's anti–Semitic cartoon, displayed before us here in London, was not his prettiest. It featured a Roman deputy whom St. Paul was trying to convert to Christ in the presence of a "false Jew." Practically all Jews in Renaissance literature were "false," like Shakespeare's Shylock. Bar–Jesus, the "false" Jew or more accurately, the one loyal to his own faith, was trying with all his might to dissuade the deputy from converting to Christianity. Paul, once a Jew named Saul, called on the Lord's power to blind Bar–Jesus with a sacred mist. I thought of mace and student protesters, but "sacred mist" sounded nicer. The deputy then converted to Christ, convinced of the power of the Christian's God. Enlightenment and salvation due to thick fog? Blindness as a conversion technique seemed odd, but didn't prevent some who saw through a mist blown about by others from seeing just as dimly. It happened often in politics.

With Ferrell guiding us, we compared the cartoons with four of the tapestries lent the museum by the Vatican. The tapestries had faded, while the painted cartoons had stayed fresh and bright. Prof. Spotswood or "W.L.," as he wished to be called, and I moved in closer to the group of tourists. Ferrell felt his presence, because W.L. was nearly Rob's height, though slimmer. And he was right behind Rob. If Ferrell tried to blow mist into our eyes, the broad back of W.L. would offer some protection. Cartoons were designs meant to suggest the completed work. But cartoons as we know them were usually funny, as Raphael's Bar-Jesus one was not. Cartoons could be cruel enough to kill–at least indirectly. W.L., sensing this, took my arm, and neither of us mentioned the harsher reality of Raphael's anti–Semitism or the papacy's–which was, after all, the root cause and also the occasion of the decoration of the papal apartments.

Then it was on to Trafalgar Square, at one end of which sat Britain's National Gallery. In its middle was a tall column, on top of which stood Viscount Horatio Nelson, in his tricornered hat, the Admiral who finally defeated the French fleet at Trafalgar, where he died in action (1805). His private life was interesting. While the French took possession of Naples, Nelson took possession of Lady Emma Hamilton, the English Ambassador's wife. For a year or more, the Hamiltons, Nelson, and the baby Emma produced, a girl christened Horatia, lived together happily in England. After Nelson's death, the grateful English erected this monument. Did little Horatia come here with her nanny to mourn the father she never knew? His last erection was now covered in pigeon dung. Still, it enhanced the square.

That day, too, we poured out of our bus into England's National Gallery. There our tour group regarded a painting by Bronzino of Venus and her son, Cupid. Ferrell loved myth, as I did. One might not be familiar with Bronzino, but most people knew something about Venus and Cupid, especially Cupid. He was on so many Valentine Day cards.

I once saw Bronzino's *Portrait of a Young Man* in the Metropolitan Museum of Art in New York. He wore a beret, a puckered padded jacket (in style again), and his collar, just a rim, white and ruffled. A finger of his left hand marked a place in a book nearly closed; his right hand (long tapered fingers) gracefully splayed at his waist. His look was very arrogant, and you knew he wasn't looking at you, though he might have if he thought it worth his while. I sometimes felt that way when Ferrell looked at me. He wasn't really looking at me but wanted me to look at him, a transactional analysis that eluded my grasp, even when I did in fact look at him. I guess things might have been different had I brought that suitcase up to Ferrell's place under Coit Tower? Coit. Coitus. Why on earth name a dignified tower Intercourse? Some people are very phallic.

Of course I, too, was oriented thus in that I was still young, still unwed, still looking, like many of my college friends were, for that great love of my life, a phallus toting man. I happened to have majored in Renaissance literature, but that didn't make me different from the Renaissance men and women who sought, and found, what they hoped would prove true love. It's just that I didn't make such a show of my search, or of myself. I was certainly not dead from the waist down, just because I taught Renaissance language and literature. I was also alive from the waist up, and that included heart and brain. Of course, my taste in clothing had been sedate, I had not been a hippy. And I preferred classical music to Motown–Stevie Wonder, Diana Ross, the Supremes–just names to me. So too with Rock, Hard and Pop, Heavy Metal, Country. Did that make me square? Unmarriageable? I hoped not.

Anyway, Bronzino's *Young Man* in the Met was flesh and blood. This Venus in London's National Gallery was fleshy, but bloodless. There was a difference. We didn't for a minute believe these figures lived. Not really. I wouldn't have meddled with the young man in the Met. But I might have pinched Cupid or caressed Venus's stomach, and I was neither a pederast nor a lesbian. Bronzino, a pupil of Pontormo, rendered *Venus, Cupid, Folly and Time*, (1550) as a mannerist allegory, learned, complicated, ambiguous. Cupid, Venus's son, was clearly making love to his mom. Having just kissed her lips, he fondled her left breast. Venus was not as overweight as a Rembrandt housewife, or a Franz Hals peasant. She was not as slim as a Botticelli, either. She was just *zaftig* (Yid., plump), a gorgeous handful of quivering possibility, with a practiced model's ability to pose. The kind of woman a man approached in a bar and bought a drink or two. Another youngster, Folly, prepared to throw rose petals at them, and three more figures hovered or crouched. Floating above, an old man, Father Time, sported amazing biceps and pectorals. He must have worked out for ages in Gold's gym. Apparently he wanted us to know that old age is no barrier to getting it on. A jealous older female who hated youth's much flaunted loveliness crouched, while two figures, perhaps inconstancy or falseness, did and didn't look on. I thought it quaint of Venus to have slipped on a snood or hair net, so she could be ready at moment's notice to send Cupid to his room and engage in a really adult fling without having her hair mussed.

The thought made me giggle, drawing curious looks from Ferrell's rapt audience, not only our tourists, but others who gathered around because Ferrell was very compelling. Ferrell himself took no notice whatsoever. W.L. eased me toward a water fountain some feet away, where we both imbibed. Two minutes later we were looking for rest rooms. Having emerged, we were surprised to find the group had vanished. We saw Ellen Froehling running frantically along the main corridor, so we ran after her, and the three of us found the bus waiting at the main entrance. Aboard the bus again, Rob grabbed the mike.

"Do you all have energy left for the Tower of London before returning to the hotel? No one did. He advised our driver to take us back to our hotel in time for 'high tea.'

"It would take a lot more than tea to get me high at this point," I whispered to W.L. Spotswood. "I fight jet lag for days."

Shortly after we returned to our hotel, Rob ran up to tell me the hotel plans for Rome had changed. Charles Clark had left him a telephone message at the desk saying that a new hotel, the *Albergo Buon Soggiorno* (Hotel Good Rest), twelve kilometers southeast of Rome on the Autostrada number seven, exit number five, Albano Lazio, had been substituted for the Savoy Plaza in the heart of Rome. The new hotel was on *Viccolo Chiuso* (*Blind Alley*), number six, the first turn to the right off Autostrada 7 (A 7), then the next left. I did not know if that *alley* were blind, but Ferrell was in a blind rage. I remembered the mist and blindness of Bar–Jesus in Raphael's cartoon. Was Charles

Clark underlining artistic prejudice or signaling mercenary prejudice? The latter, obviously.

"Candida," said Rob grimly, "You are going to be leaving here in exactly twenty minutes for Heathrow. Pack up right now. I'll have a taxi ready to run you to the airport when you descend. You will investigate this new hotel. If it is less than four or five stars, lacks good views, and is way outside central Rome, phone Charles Clark and insist on a change or we will sue him." To myself I thought, *Damn. What a drag. I'm going to miss the group's theater outing tonight. They are not only getting tea, but a great dinner in the theater district and Mrs. Warren's Profession, George Bernard Shaw's play.*

I knew what Mrs. Warren did for a living, though, and I was beginning to fear that we might have worked in related trades. What was the difference, after all, between a man ordering you to Italy, or into his bed and expecting you to perform? It wasn't money that made a woman a whore. It was obedience to the male will. Minutes later, having thrown most of my stuff into my suitcase and overnight bag, but still carrying a few cosmetics in my hands, I left the hotel lobby, where 'high tea' was being served on low coffee tables set up for that purpose in the lobby. A few of the tourists, told I was leaving, looked anxious. Anita came up and hugged me.

"Buon viaggio, Candida!" and handed me a plastic bag with three cookies and four tiny sandwiches. She had stuffed a napkin into the bag. Ian MacDonald, the assistant pastor from Grace Cathedral, offered to carry my bags down to the taxi, refusing to let our facilitator do it. He gave me a hug and kissed me on both cheeks.

"Whatever happens, Candida, know I will be praying Jesus for your triumph and safety. "I hugged Ian back, with tears in my eyes. I didn't even know the man. Jonah Schoenstein, our insurance man, joined Ferrell in warning me to stop Charles Clark from pulling "a fast one." W.L. approached, running down on my right, as Ian was running on my left. W.L. had a myriad of directions for me.

"Candida, do not enter any taxicab at Leonardo da Vinci (Fiumicino) airport not clearly identified as a *public* cab. Copy down any license number beforehand and get the name and service number of the driver, too. Find out *before* entering how much the trip to the hotel costs." To my astonishment, he slipped two hundred dollar U.S. bills into my jacket pocket. "Just in case."

I had no time to protest, and my hands were too full of my cosmetics to hand them back. I shot him a look of pure (at least I thought so) gratitude for his fatherly advice. And then I was in the taxi, heading for Heathrow. I felt like King John, going off to Runnymede– either to capitulate or do battle. I did not know which.

And so I winged my way across the Alps; Lombardy (*Lombardia*), once home to Germanic Lombards, and passing Milan (*Milano),* to *Friuli* (and Bologna); then across Tuscany, and Florence (*Firenze*). Over Umbria, and Perugia to *Lazio* (once Latium, and on to Roma (Rome), where we landed at Leonardo da Vinci airport. Smooth as silk. Would my luck run as smoothly?

Once in the airport it was down the escalator to the baggage conveyor belts, and there was no one around of whom to ask questions. I spotted my flight's baggage conveyor with four or five suitcases slowly making the rounds, and within ten minutes, mine, too, appeared, for which, praise God. I always praise Her in airports and hospitals, where one tends to need Her most. Still, I was an atheist. I didn't expect much. I grabbed the case before it could be eaten by those rubber fangs. No one bothered me as I went through customs, the young clerks behind the glass window just waved me through when they saw my American passport. I guessed they did not want to halt a conversation about Rome's soccer team, the *Lazio*, whether it did nor did not stand a chance to win their next hurtle.

I exited through the glass doors to the sidewalk. A sign there read Taxis (*Tassi*). There was nothing to be seen but a few family cars waiting at curbside to pick up lucky travelers, mostly men carrying briefcases with their suit jackets slung over them. No single women. No busses, either. No taxis. I decided to phone the new hotel. Perhaps they would send a car out for me. Any decent luxury hotel in the States would; even plain old convention hotels did. All I got from a sidewalk phone stand was a busy signal. After fifteen minutes of this strange sounding signal (different from that in the States), I decided the desk clerk had taken the phone off the hook, and was probably watching the "telly" as the Brits called it. I already missed England. I already missed...certain newly found friends. W.L. Spotswood, for example. Why had he given me two hundred dollars? The *telly?* I'd only been in London twenty hours and already substituted "telly" for TV? It was my fate. A linguist is condemned to go through life sounding phony as hell. Holden Caulfield would have agreed.

I was permanently tethered to my luggage and the sidewalk, just underneath the *Tassi* sign. It was now 12:40. A.M. No bus. No taxi. The last private car, a Fiat, picked up the last salesman, who was by now getting ready to fall into bed, I suppose. I cannot tell you how tempted I was to climb right in between him and his wife. I envied them a mattress. I went back into baggage, pulling my suitcase behind me, feeling as Franz Kafka felt approaching the castle, though he wasn't pulling a heavy suitcase. Suddenly, at the far end of the baggage room, I spotted a janitor (*un custode*), pushing a battered broom.

"Excuse, me, Sir. Where are the taxis, please?" (*Scusa, Signore. Dove les taxis, per favore?*).

His answer was "something" would come along soon, but no regular taxi. Too late. Rather a "*tassi independente*" which I translated as an enterprising private driver with a sign on top of his car saying "Taxi," the type W.L. had forbidden me to take. But what were my options? W.L. was sleeping in his comfortable bed near Big Ben.

Back on the sidewalk, at ten to one, a white mid-sized Fiat rolled up with a sign saying "*Tassi Independente*" on top. I failed to write down the license plate number.

"Good evening, Miss. Going to Rome?" (*Buona sera, Mees! Per Roma?*)

"No, no. To Albano Lazio." (*No, no. Per Albano Lazio.*) I got into the front seat and he hopped out, picked up my luggage and placed it in back of me. The doors clicked (ominously); and then we took off. I told the driver the hotel's name in Albano Lazio was the *Albergo Buon Soggiorno* "Do you know it?" (*Lo conosce?*) I asked. He didn't respond. A sign on his sun visor told me his name: Aldo della Grazia.

"Now that he knew I spoke Italian, the "Mees" disappeared. I could play on Aldo's turf. I snapped on the light over the mirror, took out my notebook and read the name of the hotel and its location.

"*Albergo Buon Soggiorno*," I repeated. "Take Autostrada 7 and the exit for Albano Lazio. Can you find it?" (*Autostrada numero siete, e l'uscita per Albano Lazio. Può trovarlo?*) Without the license number, how would W.L. know into which "taxi" I had stepped? Not that I had an envelope or a stamp. And by that time, they would have flown out of London, anyway. Perhaps someday we would have a device that could allow us to speak to a person wherever they were–without having to call into a building. Kind of like Dick Tracy's wrist radio. But now, not. Were those micro chips going to help? I doubted it, just like I doubted that silicon was going to erase Santa Clara. The Prince in Cinderella knew which pumpkin turned coach dropped her off at his castle, but neither W.L. nor Rob knew into which pumpkin I had stepped at Leonardo da Vinci airport, or which rat–no livery–was my coachman. Since Aldo was an independent, he wore no livery–no uniform–other than a military style hat with shiny brim. A soldier of fortune. Mine, no doubt.

Aldo was a fast driver, but regularly glanced sidewise at me, letting his eyes drift from the nearly empty highway to the end of my nose, and, I must admit, the ends of two other parts of me as well. Not that I am big busted, but I'm not flat chested, either. Men are men, wherever you find them. Some are just more covert than others. Aldo wasn't.

"Not your first trip to Italy, true, Miss?" (*Non è il vostro primo viaggio in Italia, vero signorina?*).

"Oh, I know Rome fairly well," (*Conosco bene Roma*) I answered. I really didn't.

Della Grazia. His last name meant graceful; also merciful. How could anything go wrong?

"But you don't know it well by night?" he pressed me–in Italian, naturally.

"No, not at night. Just in the daytime," I answered, speaking Italian with that weird exuberance it always gave me. For language freaks, a foreign tongue was like a martini. You felt ready for anything once you'd gotten it down, or spat it out, as in this case.

"Then what I can do for you–at no extra cost–is show you how beautiful she looks at night," he said. "Beautiful. Like you."

Oh, oh. I thought. Me, cities, females all. "She looks, she shines, she, she, she. The rural rube makes his way to the female city for only one reason, I told myself. Some kind of night life.

"I'll take you on a little excursion on the way to your hotel. It's not the same by daylight." I could only imagine what Ferrell or W.L. would say. Oddly, their imagined comments were identical... "Don't be a fool, Candida! Get him to take you to your hotel via the direct route! Pronto!" Funny word, that. In Spanish and Spanglish, it meant fast. In Italian, it meant "Ready" or "Hello?" You picked up the telephone and somebody on the other end says "*Pronto!*" which meant *ready* to speak, so start talking and don't waste my time! *Pronto contanti,* however, meant ready cash. Your money where your mouth was.

I felt into my jacket pocket. W. L.'s U.S. hundred dollar bills were still there. Ready cash. I wondered how much I might have left over if and when Aldo delivered me to the *Albergo Buon Soggiorno?* We viewed Rome from atop its hills (more than seven, if you count little sub-peaks): Capitolino (over the old Forum); Palatino (archeological dig); Vellian (a spur of the Palatino); Pincio (not officially one of the "seven"); Quirinale (contains Rome's city hall); Aventino (site of the Knights of Malta Square); Gianicolo (great residential area; spur of the Esquilinno); the Esquilinno; Viminale (other spur of the Esquilino*)*; Vaticanus (northwest of the Tiber). This last was once called Monte Malo, the Bad Hill, when a nobleman was murdered there in the tenth century. It is now called Monte Mario. People had forgotten the Malo bit. Or maybe that the guy was murdered. Was his real name perhaps Mario Malo? Who knew?

After we had run up one side and down the other of Rome with no hint of getting to my hotel, I became wroth. I was named Candida, so I could be candid (frank), though in fact the name once meant a bit simple in French. Simple? Of course I was, but I was far from being an airhead. I had credentials to prove I was not. Highways (*Autostrade*) did not run through the inhabited portions of Rome. They lay beyond it. I had forgotten that we had to get on one at Rome's southeast corners before we could exit at Albano Laziale. Simple was not the word. Stupid was. I turned to Aldo.

"Aldo. Hit the highway. Now." I added that if he didn't, I would consider him less than a gentleman. "Has anyone ever?" He shrugged.

A few moments later we turned onto the autostrada heading for the Alban Hills, twelve kilometers southeast of Rome! I was very quiet, the lights of the city dimmed, and within five minutes we were lit only occasionally by eerie neon strips on very high poles. Hardly any cars shone their lights into ours. We watched an overhead three car train crossing above the highway. Its engineer saluted us with a half-hearted toot and waved.

"What a coffee pot," (*Quel caffetiera*) said Aldo, grinning. I had never heard of a train and a coffee pot being compared to each other, and smiled in spite of myself. Finally, we took the next turn to the right off the autostrada and the first turn to the left a few yards later. We pulled into Viccolo Chiuso, no. #6, and its circular driveway in front of a small hotel. Across the street was a small brick building I thought was a garage.

"Here we are!" (*Eccoci!*) said Aldo. "That will be one hundred thousand fifty seven lire plus fifty-five *centèsimi* (cents) plus tip— fifteen percent is usual." I made a rapid calculation. Two hundred thirty-seven bucks plus fifteen percent tip for a taxi ride from the airport to the outskirts of Rome? Ridiculous. Larcenous. I immediately turned my hand to the window lock on the seat behind me, tugged it up, and jumped out.

"Leave everything in the car!" said Aldo. "You can get it later if you need to change a big bill!"

"I'll be back," I yelled, my heart pounding in my chest, carrying all my luggage and heavy purse, loaded with cosmetics I hadn't been able to pack properly. I staggered up three steps and through two glass doors. I dumped the luggage. I crossed the small foyer in two seconds, and stopped at the small reception desk. There sat a middle aged clerk in a suit and tie, neat as a pin. He looked up at me.

"Are you *Signorina* Candida Darroway?" I was in the right place. Or the wrong one.

"You are so far from Rome," I said, lamely, as if he could change that.

"Well, *the A* 7 starts in Rome's eastern suburbs. We are admittedly closer to *Albano, Signorina.*" *Albano.* The Alban Hills, I knew, were in the countryside southeast of Rome sixteen kilometers, several more than where this hotel stood. In those hills were five star hotels, golf courses, swim clubs, elegant shops. Watering holes for the rich. Think

Carmel. Palm Springs. Naples (Florida), not Italy. Maybe this would not be so bad in daylight, even if the lounge lacked everything but the look of a modest motel on some back road of Oregon. For now, all I could do, lacking Jonah Schoenstein's advice and Ferrell's, was to keep on truckin'–as they say.

"*Signorina*? Your taxi's still outside? You have a little problem, yes?" (*piccola problema, sì* ?)

"No," I shouted. "A big problem." (*Non. Una problema enorma.*) "I need your help. I got picked up by this driver in an independent taxi at Leonardo da Vinci, two hours ago." The clock over the clerk's head on the wall said 3:10. "And I got in, and he said he knew just where you were but for no extra cost asked would I like to see Rome by night? I said yes. Anyway, no other cab or bus was around. The airport was empty. Now, Aldo out there claims because he picked me up after midnight and I agreed to a sightseeing tour, though he did say before that there would be 'no extra cost'–I remember him saying that–I owe him...." Here I started to weep.

"A fortune," finished the clerk. But he didn't say that then, did he? No. You know what you really owe him? Much less." The clerk, whose name was Signor Salvatore Occhiuti (Ital.,*Savior Sharp Eye'd*) was not only Occhiuti, but acute. He handed me his handkerchief. He would save me from being cheated.

"Come with me, please, Signorina Darroway," said he, placing his hand under my elbow and leading me past my dropped luggage. At the curbside, Aldo was drifting off in his driver's seat. He had had a long day, too.

"You, there," said the desk clerk gruffly, from the driver's side of the car. Aldo's window was rolled down. The night was balmy. The slight breeze delicious. Aldo snapped awake. "You see that brick building across the street? It's a police station." I noticed a sign I had missed before. "Police. Quick Help." (*Polizia. Pronto soccorso.*) Signor Occhiuti continued, "The maximum fee you can charge this lady is forty-three dollars or twenty-four thousand, six hundred lire. She will pay you now. If you make the slightest objection, I will call for help. You'll be in that jail over there," jerking his thumb at the red brick building–"until bail is made. And if I were you, Aldo, I'd make it my business to stay away from this community. You give Albano Lazio and all Rome a bad name."

I started to hand Aldo one of W.L.'s two bills, but Signor Occhiuti snatched it away and gave it back to me. To Aldo he gave the sum in lire he just declared owed him and no tip. "I'll add his fee to your bill," he whispered to me. Otherwise, he'd drive off with the one hundred." I thought to myself how positively fab to have run into a man as helpful as Signor Occhiuti. Aldo took off rapidly with his much reduced fee. Mr. Occhiuti walked me back to the lobby. His son, a sleepy bellboy of fourteen, carried my luggage to my room. I opened the door. A large, plain, very clean room with a vase of real heliotrope greeted me. On the small coffee table was a bottle of San Pellegrino, a box of cold low fat milk, a large ham sandwich, four *biscotti* and a red apple. I turned to say thank you and tip him for his help, but the boy had already closed the door behind him.

I fell into bed almost at once, pausing only long enough to brush my teeth and splash cool water on my face. When I woke up, the sun was streaming through the curtains. I ate everything on my coffee table. I pulled the blinds behind the curtains. Five blonde cows with long horns mooed just over a wire fence that ran close to the window. Theirs was a spacious field, over-run with buttercups and Queen Anne's lace, "growing all over the place," like the old verse said. I remember Ferrell's admonition as to view. Would this view do?

CHAPTER V

ROME AT LAST

I found out that it would not do. The group arrived shortly after I descended for coffee. It was just noon, and I had just eaten last night's nocturnal snack. I hoped the milk might have come from the blonde cows next door. I had grown up in upstate New York with Holsteins and Guernseys, then moved to the Midwest where Jerseys and Brown Swiss predominated. But blonde cows? I never saw any as beautiful. Perhaps they knew that Italy was special and tried harder–art objects in their own right.

Our tourists came trooping into the *Albergo* tired and cranky. Barry Schwartz was reading the *New York Times*, muttering about the Watergate Committee's having learned that Nixon had recorded– actually recorded–incriminating conversations about the Watergate breakin. There was even talk of impeaching the President! Then Gerald Ford would be President, and Barry wondered how that bumbler could help the market?

The rest straggled into the dining room complaining about the long ride from Rome. Their "This is not what we came for's," "expected's" and "deserved's" unnerved me. But some people greeted me civilly, like Anita, who was glad to see me, as were Matt; Mindy, Jonah and a few others. The Huntsmans were pleasant, hoping I wouldn't worry myself to death when things went wrong.

"We've been on dozens of tours and something *always* does," said Ralph Huntsman, and Jan patted my hand maternally. Ralph, our Etruscanologist and his wife, Jan, were sitting with the Harkers. Betty Harker, was a bosomy grandmotherly type. Her husband, Jim, a genial retired geologist. Also at this "geriatric" table were the Froehlings. Bill Froehling, a former engineer, and his wife, Ellen, wanted very much to be part of something–the art world–most of all. They knew Ferrell from having taking art courses from him at a community center. They sat to my left, the three elderly couples of our troupe. Ellen looked sharply at me, before turning to her table mates. Bill, on the other hand, smiled, shrugging his shoulders as if to apologize for Ellen's curtness.

W.L. was the last person to join us at one end of this table. He drew up a chair across from mine. "Candida, Ferrell is mad as hell," he said quickly, quietly. "He expects that you will have given Charles Clark a piece of our collective mind and get us the hell out of Albano Lazio. Have you?"

"I have not even tried to contact Charles, having only recently awakened, myself. He is certainly asleep on Russian Hill in California where it's four A.M. There is a nine hour time difference, you know." I said this defensively. But I asked the clerk at the reception desk if I could use her phone to make an international call, and she ushered me into the hotel office. Calls to the United States were too special to be made in the reception area. The group appeared more bonded than in London. I had bonded only with cows.

I determined to use a firm tone when speaking with our trip provider. "Candida Darroway from near the Alban Hills, Charles!" I could tell from his first words he was trying to wake up, still in bed, no doubt. I determined to be his worst nightmare.

"We were supposed to be on the Corso in the heart of Rome, Charles. We're out near the Alban Hills instead. Ferrell is livid. He says we will sue if you do not do right by our contract, by us."

"I can't do magic tricks on 4,800 dollars apiece," said Charles, apparently gagging on phlegm. It was no doubt foggy in his neighborhood, and he seemed to suffer from sinus problems. "The Savoy Plaza said your numbers grew from thirty-three to thirty-six counting the driver and baggage guy. They claimed they could not manage rooms for so many for so little. Travel is all about profits, Candida. Hotels have bottom lines. Even our group rate must come closer to the one fifty U.S. they usually charge." A gagging sound and coughing followed. "Thirty-one plus two equals thirty-three," I told him coldly. "Not thirty-six."

Charles gurgled. "But our budget doesn't stretch to the Savoy Plaza, Candida. The *Albergo Buon Soggiorno* is a two star motel, yes, but near luxury facilities in lovely hill area just a few kilometers outside Rome."

"Sixteen, Charles, and we didn't contract for two stars. This is not even a hotel, and certainly not a luxury stop. It's flat as Nebraska out here. And the Alban hills are ten miles away."

"So what? Your bus could get you to Rome central in half an hour, forty-five minutes in heavy traffic. Your complaint is without merit." Before I could answer, he hung up. I dialed back. He picked up again.

"Yes?" he asked very slowly. I let him have it.

"Charles, a contract is a contract. You are playing fast and loose with ours and could be sued by Altamonte's insurance company. Altruistic!" He paused a second or two on his end.

"It's not my company they'll sue, it's your college. I doubt Altruistic Insurance will do much for your distressed tourists."

I thought as fast as a humanities major could when dealing with a dishonest businessman. "You don't get the picture, Charles. The President of our insurance company, Jonah Schoenstein, is on this tour. Our Board of Trustees is made up largely of *very* influential Silicon Valley venture capitalists resolved to make these trips profitable for reasons we won't go into." I thought of the profits to be made in professional ice hockey. "Venture capitalists won't take lightly lawsuits from deceived tourists. They know you are cheating, Charles. Their media resources are, as you know, unlimited. Their collective lawyers can beat yours. I'll give you one more chance. You make better arrangements for us in central Rome, luxury class, or the college will sue your company, *Travel Thrills*. Call me back in one hour with a four or five star, in central Rome. Otherwise, I will put into motion forces that will turn your *Thrills* into your *Chills*. And Ferrell says your Russian Hill condo is mortgaged to the hilt. If your company folds, your address will be Potrero Hill, (a slum), not Russian. Goodbye, Charles." I hung up and noted the time. Half past noon.

In the dining room, every table had already received baskets of bread, red and table red and white wine (*vino da tavola rosso e bianco*). Small plates of pasta and *pesto* were served by two teenagers in red vests, with black satin bow ties under chins just beginning to sprout a few hairs, still strangers to any razor. These waiters were local boys, being trained for their life's work.

The first course (*antipasto*) was a house specialty. *Pesto* (a sauce of ground basil, pine nuts garlic, olive oil)) was special to me, certainly. When I first discovered it, in Genoa (*Genova*), I swooned. Mom never made *pesto*–it wasn't native to Lucca. It now arrived on my corkscrew noodles (*fusili*), and the taste sent me through the ceiling. I'm not a big eater. I came to Italy that year *purely* for research and a few adventures, mostly literary or cultural. But not for calories. My father had not wanted a pudgy daughter like his first wife, and I listened carefully, having been trained to defer to men. I'm about language and literature, not cooking and eating.

A really genuine *pesto* had to have pine nuts, but virgin olive oil did it no favors. Too bland. The cheaper, stronger oils are best. A fine parmesan cheese (*Parmigiano*) from Parma was a *must*, though, as was lots of garlic. I used to put eight large mashed cloves into what I guessed was roughly a cup and a half of basil and chopped parsley leaves, and a bit more oil. The herbs were in roughly the same proportion. I skipped Italian parsley (too mild). I went for the familiar American kind. Basil (*basilico*) leaves have to be bright green, but if one must shop at Safeway, it could work out. Into the blender with all but the black and slimy ones. As they said in Florence, *Pazienza!* (*patience*). I never measure anything. Use your judgment. Anyone, having eaten a dish, as I ate *pesto* in Genoa, should be able to reproduce it adequately without a recipe. One didn't need a teacher for everything. Some people were born good cooks. And if not, with time came mastery. Didn't great Renaissance artists have to work hard as apprentices to their masters? Be your own master.

Unlike Teresa, Tony's grandmother, descendant of the royal family who once *owned* Genoa, ancestral home of *pesto*, makes it with pine nuts. I stopped using them. They made the sauce too slippery. I prefer a grainy finish. But the *pesto* of your heart may well require pine nuts! It's the heart, not the stomach most affected by cheese and oil, or salt and sugar. The salt is in the cheese. The pasta it went with turned to sugar in your gut. *Everything* was different from what it first appeared. Too bad we wouldn't be going to Genoa. I moved toward my table, now filled with Shoensteins, Schwartzes, W. L. Spotswood and Ferrell.

My research hadn't required research in Genoa, but I did take the train then from Florence to Genoa (*Genova*) anyway. I wanted to find Mazzini's tomb (1805-72), the great republican insurgent, inspiration for democracy during Italy's *Risorgimento* (revival). Mazzini probably read Machiavelli's *Discourses of Livy*. He preferred a free republic, not a dukedom, dictatorship, or an arranged "marriage," i.e., a Savoyard monarchy under Victor Emmanuel II, forced on Italy by a Sardinian finagler–Count Cavour–and a greedy French Emperor–Napoleon III. A fighter, but a journalist as well, Giuseppe Mazzini, who never lived to see a real democratic Italy, fought for and wrote about justice, liberty. His Doric style tomb is on the top of Genoa's hills. It was in Staglieno Cemetery, and I feared slipping on its steep gravel paths. Mazzini, father of modern Italy, was only now beginning to get his historical due. Sometimes great leaders of people wait a long time to be thanked. I should write some of these things down in a notebook, in case I ever write a novel. Most literature professors do.

Having tossing a red rose on Mazzini's funeral monument on that earlier visit, I had then wandered into a truly huge mausoleum, simply because the gate was open. It was filled with beautiful statues of rich Genovese families. Their marble sculptures–whole family groups–often included the Virgin and Jesus. Such displays of superfluous commercial wealth and ostentatious faith struck me as stuck–up. My reward for this critique was getting locked into the mausoleum for lingering. How was I to know that cemeteries and mausoleums kept hours? Death was for eternity, no? No.

An alarmed custodian heard my desperate cries from inside the darkening mausoleum and unlocked a door. I bestowed on this limping senior citizen a generous tip that cost me a complete dinner. That's how I wound up with "only" pasta and pesto and a double espresso. This *antipasto* or starter, as the English say, of pesto and pasta was very filling. Fulfilling, even. Sometimes, life hands us a prize when we expect a punishment. The reverse was also true.

Back at the table in the Albergo Buon Soggiorno, I noted Mindy Schoenstein was wearing a pink eyelet sundress that would cause problems if we did St. Peter's today. Shorts, tank tops, sundresses, mini skirts and sleeveless garments were all forbidden garb. Vatican guards in dark blue suits would be polite, but firm. They escorted you away from the entrance without hesitation, without remorse, one on each side if necessary. I purposely chose a grey knit pullover dress, high necked, with mid length sleeves, feeling storm clouds appear on the horizon.

W.L. was next to my empty chair. Rob, smiling, frowned ever so slightly as he greeted me, watching W.L. rise to hold my chair for me. The Schwartzes, Myrna and Barry, were to W.L.'s left, and the Schoensteins to my right. Myrna was wearing a low v-neck white linen dress. It was a beautifully detailed garment one couldn't find in Penny's, much less at Goodwill, my usual clothing sources. Myrna wore it with exquisite mid-heeled Stuart Weitzman sandals, brown networks of leather straps, gold eyelets and laces; themselves a work of art. Bloomingdales. Four hundred dollars with tax. I knew those sandals. I had stared at them wistfully at the Stanford shopping center before we left, frustrated that I could not afford them and still make my rent. The foxgloves, mounded in front of the store in giant earthenware bowls as high as my shoulder, had bowed their heads to me as I passed, sympathetic as only flowers can be to a human yearning for stylish shoes.

"Well, Candida?" Rob asked. "Have you talked with Charles Clark about this little Alban caprice?" Next to him at the table, Mindy, size six, who usually played with her food, upon tasting the pasta and pesto, opened her blue eyes wide and began to eat with real purpose.

"Clark will not change us. He claims the Savoy Plaza could not afford us rooms at the agreed upon price." Andrea Pellatierra, the manager of Gump's and his wife, Maria, exchanged knowing looks.

"We've met your Charles Clark before," Maria informed us. "He promised a sizable check to an art club for disadvantaged youths and never sent it."

"He didn't send a buck," Andrea intoned mournfully.

"And you let Clark bamboozle us, too?" Rob asked, lifting up his white wine glass, to inspect its color in the clear sunlight streaming onto the table from the window in back of us. Only when W. L. picked up his glass in the same fashion did Ferrell shoot him a dirty look and set his down sharply, spilling wine onto Mindy's pink sundress. Luckily, he was drinking white (*bianco*). Whereupon W. L. said "Cheers" and neatly drained his, red (*rosso*) smiling broadly at Rob. Mindy daubed at the wet spot with a napkin dampened in water, and went on eating. She was quite Stoical about it. Or maybe just hungry.

"I called him back and said Altamonte would sue if he didn't come through for us."

"Good girl, Miss Darroway," said the silver haired, handsome Mr. Schoenstein, whose long Ralph Lauren shirted arm was pasted around his wife Mindy's slim and now damp waist. "Did you give him a chance to redress his 'error'"?

"I did, Mr. Schoenstein. He's got until one o'clock to call me back and tell me we are scheduled for a five star in central Rome."

"Excellent. You are to be congratulated, Miss Darroway. And please call me Jonah."

"Candida, here," I replied.

"That's a funny name," Mindy said, swallowing her last piece of pasta. "Did your parents think you'd be a candid baby, one who told when she wet herself?" I smiled, but couldn't think of an answer that wasn't rude. Was she trying to be witty, or making light of her wine soaked dress? Jonah looked intently at me.

"You do know that I am the President of Altruistic Insurance, the company that insures Altamonte, don't you, Candida?" he asked. I did. I said I had informed Charles as well.

"Good," he said. "That will scare him a bit." He ignored Mindy's remark about candid babies. He had had enough babies, his two boys by his recently divorced wife were attending Altamonte College. Mindy was his reward for having engendered them.

"Here's what I suggest we do," said Jonah. "We let the hour run out while we dine on this surprisingly good pasta and await the entrée. I think it's veal." In Italy people ate veal as a matter of course, without worrying about how it had been produced; hopefully it wasn't raised in a dark box. Perhaps it had even had the run of the farm. The Italians and the French cannot live well without veal. Jonah continued speaking.

"After lunch, we will probably find your Charles hasn't called and never will. After which, I'll give Roger Garvey a head's up, and tell him to move us at once to a more suitable five star in Rome. Otherwise, the college is bound to be sued by some of our more disappointed fellow travelers, and having two kids at Altamonte, I do not want to see it weakened or embarrassed."

Neither of his sons took French or Italian, or hadn't so far. They were on the golf links often. One was a champion at the breaststroke. I wondered if he got tips on that from his father, whose hand had wandered slightly higher up from his wife's waistline. Bubbie Brondel would have been shocked. But open displays of affection are not in poor taste in the 1970s as they had been in the 1950s. Mindy did not seem embarrassed. The times that had been "A-changin'" in 1964 when Bob Dylan wrote that song, had certainly changed more, nearly a decade later.

W.L. tipped his head backward slightly and laughed. "You'd make a splendid Renaissance *condottiere* (leader of mercenaries), Jonah," he said.

"Schoenstein," said Jonah. "And you are... who, exactly?"

"Prof. W.L. Spotswood. My Chair is the Professor Eugene O'Reilly Chair of Renaissance History at the University of Wisconsin at Madison."

"Wisconsin?" asked Barry Schwartz, the banker, Myrna's spouse. "Isn't that where students picket the capitol building all the time to protest the wars in Southeast Asia? Bunch of radicals, like at Cal. They don't do that at Jose State or at Chico," he snorted. Those were his sons' schools. *No, they don't,* I thought. They don't know enough about capitalism, insurance, minimum wages, or real democracy to occupy anything but their mansions or frat houses. I said, "At Altamonte we try very hard, Rob and I, to occupy our students' thoughts." Barry looked placated. As for my own thoughts, I tried to keep them to myself.

Jonah had excused himself after the *antipasto*. It was 1 P.M. I went to the foyer to phone Roger Garvey. Jonah wasn't on the Board of Trustees, but he was paying two hefty tuitions for his boys, and he had it in mind, Ferrell said, that Altamonte deserved considerable support in his will. He wasn't so young anymore, though his wife was. He was, a very big potential Altamonte donor. What I appreciated about him was his take-charge instinct. Ferrell was no help at all.

Through the glass doors, I watched Jonah pace up and down punching the air occasionally with his left hand. Finally, he returned and took his seat. This time, his shirt sleeved shoulder brushed up firmly against my right shoulder and the uppermost portion of *my* right breast as he sat down again. Though he moved it immediately, he smiled at me doing so, instead of saying "I beg your pardon" or "Excuse me." They're putting softer cloth into the Ralph Lauren lines this season. My Dad wears them for his law practice. I know the lines. All of them.

Which reminds me my biological clock is ticking. Mom had found Dad at twenty. But she did not go to college and grad school.

74

And anyway, my parents proved (again) that rapture can dissolve in rupture. No "green magic" like *pesto* could heal the raw wounds of incompatibility, divorce.

What did Garvey have to say?" Ferrell asked. I told him Garvey said the big problem was that the Board did not meet in summer as the trustees were vacationing. "Garvey says he can probably help Charles get us into a fourth class hotel in the Trastevere district, since it is cheaper than central Rome; but he'd have to do it from his own rainy day funds, which are limited." While I filled them in, Schoenstein watched his wife Mindy play with her green salad (*insalata verde*). Ferrell was watching Schoenstein watching her. Middle–aged men were admired by other middle–aged men for snagging a young wife. And sometimes those marriages worked out. But not always. Still, I thought, there were plenty of age matched marriages that didn't work out, either. Marriage was a gamble, and those who thought they could draw the lucky card often erred.

Shoenstein had a loud bass voice, and our table was not far from the desk, that is, it was on edge of the lobby and within earshot of the day clerk, who at the moment happened to be an attractive woman in her thirties–Signorina Rivelli–her name in gold on a wooden pyramid. Miss Rivelli jerked her head toward Schoenstein and crossed over to our table.

Pardon, sir? (*Scusa, signore?*) I hear you must be in central Rome tonight, *Vero*?" (True?) Schoenstein looked up at her with interest.

"That's correct Miss, Miss…Rivelli." He read her name of the badge she wore. Ferrell, silent for some time, had waited for me to do all the repair work, but finally bestirred himself.

"*Senorita*, (the Spanish didn't surprise me) can you help us find a deluxe hotel in downtown Rome?"

"I believe so, Signore Ferrell. You lead this group, no?"

"No. He's a co–leader," I put in quickly. "We are *both* leaders of the tour."

"Well, Signore," she continued, directing herself exclusively to Ferrell (as women will to handsome men, especially European women), ignoring their fellow females completely. I hated that. It was a betrayal of what we women could do by ourselves. Signorina Rivelli, looked deeply into Ferrell's eyes. "My cousin Alessandra works at the five-star *Parco dei Principi* (Princes' Park) Hotel, on the edge of the Borghese Gardens in Rome. She just phoned. A luxurious dream, the *Principi.*" Signorina Rivelli batted her fake eyelashes at Rob. I could see how he charmed her. Sure of himself, his heavyset body, deep chest, auburn hair and white teeth perfectly set in his well shaped large head made him seem more self-assured, while his impeccable clothing (mostly Italian) could not help but win the hearts of those less well clad—especially Italians.

Ferrell leaned in. "And why are you telling about your cousin Alexandrina and this Hotel Principe?" he asked her, flashing a smile.

Signorina Rivelli lowered her voice. I had to strain to hear, as did W.L. beside me. "Her name is Alessandra, not Alexandrina. And it's the Hotel Principi, plural of the singular *principe* (*prince*). It's on the Via Veneto. Alessandra phones when business is slow, and it is suddenly."

"Why?" Rob asked. The Signorina gulped air. I think his leaning in toward her did took her breath away. I took this opportunity to look at W.L. His hair, unlike Ferrell's, was greying; and he was slim and athletic, rather than monumental. Where Ferrell's skin was deep reddish brown from the California sun, W.L.'s was white, like that of most Midwesterners, especially scholars who spend even summertime in libraries. Yes, he had freckles—on his forehead, the result of playing sandlot baseball as a boy. His eyebrows were not bushy, but sparse, and he never stared out at one from under them. When he had a question, his right brow rose questioningly, high above his fine featured face, its beautifully sculpted cheek bones, its kindly hazel eyes that changed color according to the daylight, now gray-brown, now golden green, but always with little brown spots. Like mine in fact. Well made, slim and aristocratic, he seemed ever in good humor, as if he and the world shared a secret joke, which he would, at any moment, divulge. The two men, of equal age and nearly equal height, both professors of distinction, could not have been more different. Ferrell could certainly be graceful and gracious on occasion; but W.L., one felt, was never anything less. I suddenly thought that had he not been a professor of history, he might very well have been a Lutheran theologian. Indeed, as an undergraduate, he had studied at a seminary. A scholar of religion as well of war and political mayhem, he was not now conventionally religious, just ethical and compassionate.

Signorina Rivelli explained. "Well, the *Principi* just had over one hundred cancellations for the next four nights! A group of Japanese businessmen, wives included, unusual for Japanese businessmen, came down with the flu. They're all in hospital in Iceland. They've cancelled their trip indefinitely." I thought, *over two hundred individuals, double rooms, many meals. That's a big loss to the Hotel Principi.* Opportunity appeared ready to knock.

Ferrell turned to face me. "Candida, you go phone this hotel and see if we can get a special rate. They are going to need a lot of drop-ins to fill that loss. My guess is they are now peculiarly open to bargaining with thirty-three customers for four nights. I bet we get a sizeable discount (*sconto*). I won't bother Charles Clark, and I'd rather not call Roger Garvey. If his board is out of town, his spine is, too."

I asked Signorina Rivelli to get me the number of the Principi's Director (*Direttore*) at once, and excused myself just as, (sigh) the caramel cream pudding (*crema caramele*)—my favorite Italian dessert—was being handed 'round. I left the dining room at the Signorina's heels.

"*Pronto?*" (Hello?) I heard as I finished punching in the number. "*Albergo Parco dei Principi. Che desidera, per cortesia?*" (Hotel Princes' Park. What would you like, please?) Then I explained I wanted the *Direttore*. When he picked up the phone, I expressed sympathy over his unexpected loss of clients, which a friend in the hotel business just spoke of to me.

"I'm sorry you have suffered this unexpected misfortune," (*Mi dispiace che Lei ha sofferto questa sfortuna inattesa.*") I added: "We laborers in the tourist business, (not mentioning that it wasn't my *real* business) "feel how threatening these cancellations are to a hotel's bottom line."

The *Direttore* thanked me. "So many people think running a luxury hotel has no unanticipated problems." (*Tanta gente imagino che la direzione di un albergo lusso non ha probleme inattese.*) "Instead," he told me dolefully, "it had many more (*molto di più*) than lesser establishments." I agreed. Then I got down to my real business.

"I find myself, dear Sir, (*caro Signore*) unexpectedly stranded with thirty-two other American tourists, an Italian driver and a trip facilitator, who share a room. They are uncle and nephew. We are desperate to get into a fine central hotel in Rome for four nights. *Signor Direttore*, can you possibly give us thirty rooms at a good price (à prezzo buono), we being a college sponsored art history tour."

A short pause, then: "How about each room at seventy-five dollars? including breakfast?" he asked. "That would be roughly a third of the normal cost if you walked in right off the Via Veneto." Delighted, I gave him my name and Altamonte's credit card number, assuring him we would arrive before the hour was out, traffic willing. When I went back to my seat, I told the group our good fortune. Ferrell immediately rang his teaspoon against his wine glass. He then rose to get our full attention.

"Ladies and gentlemen of the Altamonte tour group. I have just secured a five star luxury hotel on the edge of Rome's finest shopping street and of her most beautiful park, the Borghese Gardens." There was a great hand of applause, punctuated by "Bravo's" and Bill Froehling squeaking out, "Atta boy, Professor!" And that put the stamp on or rather off *my* getting us out of Albano Lazio and into one of Rome's outstanding luxury hotels. Professor Ferrell had corrected "my" unfortunate and clumsy "error," though I had often been told that my organizing skills were excellent. In fact, so were most of my other skills. All but my "heart" skills. Those had lagged. Gifted kids were often considered "out of it" and so left out on purpose, which didn't help them "get with it."

All this while Rob sat finishing his *crema caramele* dessert not having moved a muscle nor spoken a word to the *Direttore* of the Parco Principi. He even continued, unbeknownst to me, to repeat "his" triumph in my absence. He was a hero from that moment on, and from then on, I suspected difficulty achieving equal status with Rob among our group.

After a half hour of preparations, our blue and white tour bus, propelled by our Italian driver, Carlo Donizetti, drew up before the *Albergo Buon Soggiorno,* leaving with thirty-odd occupants. Just how odd, I would be left to ponder. This *albergo* had sold thirty-five meals, counting my overnight snack. Jonah told the desk clerk we would pay for half their loss of services for four nights, which was only fair, and they were delighted. I paid for my own night, a reasonable thirty-five thousand lire for which Jonah immediately reimbursed me in cash. I thanked Signorina Rivelli and left a note and a tip for Signore Occhiuti and his son, thanking the father for his kindness to me on my arrival. Then we piled into the bus, waiting only for Ellen Froehling, who couldn't find her reading glasses. The busboy found them beside her plate, and we took off, tearing out of the driveway and onto the New Appian Way (*Nuova Via Appia*) toward Rome (*Roma*) to which all roads lead.

I decided to introduce a few Italian expressions to our group, now that their stomachs were full and they were anticipating luxurious accommodations. Many would forget the Italian words and phrases I would model from their *Berlitz for Travelers*. Ditto for all Ferrell's efforts with Anunciations of Christ's conception (*Annunziazione*) and Depositions (*Deposizione*) from the Cross. But it would be more difficult for me than for him. Foreign language learning does not make as deep an impression as art on most people. It brought fewer familiar references, and no visual reinforcement. These factors created in most Americans a verbal frustration that soon gave way to those of inadequacy. Ferrell made pictures talk, so that the viewers needn't. Not even the best language teachers could so quickly make *talk* talk.

Even so, most tourists remembered less about the art they saw in museums than they did of the best meal eaten, the last caper, pine nut, and dessert (*dolce*). They could probably get just as much out of a trip if they didn't take one at all. They could buy an art book or two, or watch tours of Italy in their living room. It would save them time, money and anxiety. It would be more restful, and as instructive. Still, I was here to give language and cultural instruction a try.

"Attention, fellow travelers," I announced, using the microphone. "I thought you might learn a few Italian words and phrases on our way in. Get out your *Berlitz* so that you may follow along. Now, on page l: Ready? "No is....*Non*. Yes is .... *sì*." They were fair at repeating these monosyllables, though the Italian *No* has a has a softer, "o." No matter. "Good" (*Bene*). Next, "Please," (*Per favore*). They were following. "Very good!" (*Molto bene*!). And for manners' sake, "Thank you" is *Grazie– the z* has a *ts* sound, you see. Thanks very much" (*Grazie tanto*).

But after a few more expressions, their eyes glazed over, reminding of my Altamonte Italian 1 class. Foreign language profs are used to this. And now, here is Prof. Ferrell," (*Adesso, ecco il Professore Ferrell*"). Everyone clapped. I was the warm up act.

"*Amigos*," Rob said in Spanish, (*not Amici*). "We are on *Via Appia* heading for the Coliseum. They covered it with awnings when it rained, or when the sun was in their eyes. Then they could see which gladiator, Christian or African beast still had some life left in 'em. They differentiated among the wounded. A few gladiators got thumbs up, and lived to fight again. Beasts and Christians were dispatched. The Coliseum could be flooded for regattas, like the Piazza Navona where we'll lunch tomorrow. Then, keep your eyes pealed for the Arch of Titus. Pretty arch fellow he was, too, and no friend to Jews. Titus, Vespasian's son and co-ruler, destroyed Jerusalem during a Jewish revolt in seventy A.D. Beneath the arch you can see a menorah, and other Jewish property, spoils of the Roman victory. The arch was built (81 A.D.) by Titus's brother, Domitian. (d. 96 A.D.) Some of the 50,000 Jewish slaves brought back to Rome were forced to help build it."

The Schwartzes and Schoenfelds looked stricken at all this ancient anti–Semitism. I grew quiet thinking of my own Italian Jewish family disappeared from Lucca during the war. Rome was great, but essentially unkind to Jews. So, what else was new? Jewish historians have extra emotional burdens to bear, and many references in the greatest classical and Renaissance texts are there to denigrate Jews, a Western tradition. Not just Jews, of course, just *always* them, as well as other despised groups, which included women, of course.

W.L., seeing me so moved, grabbed my hand and squeezed it gently. I thought, Rob Ferrell wouldn't squeeze anyone gently. W. L. empathized with others.

"Titus," Rob explained, "had a Jewish mistress in Jerusalem whom his dad wouldn't let him marry." W.L. said quietly, "And Domitian wound up a poor military strategist and a madman, stabbed by his wife's slave at her insistence. They didn't lead such happy lives either, those brothers."

That cheered me. He was so learned. I thought of the nice priest, Father O'Connor, who had come and gone from Altamonte's part-time faculty, and whom I would never see again. He would have known about

Titus, too. I felt that he would not have approved how Titus treated Beatrice or her country. After all, Christ was once a Jew. Maybe always. Who really got to decide? Here was the Pantheon, where we made a quick stop. Ferrell herded us in.

"This is the largest domed structure of antiquity," he informed us. "Although parts of the original (built in 125 A.D.) are missing. A colonnaded court once adjoined the front façade. It is a concrete structure whose dome is one hundred forty-four feet in diameter, and has an open "eye" or hole at its top thirty feet wide. That's the only source of light, so we should return when the day is not so advanced. We'll see. You can also buy a postcard of the painting of its interior by Giovanni Pannini (his name means sandwiches in Italian!) in the National Gallery of Art in Washington, D.C. He painted it in 1750 and it is as much a masterpiece as the building itself." Some tittering. "We'll stop at the Trevi Fountain if the traffic in that square permits," he added.

"It won't," Carlo Donizetti, our driver, announced, his thin gold wire rimmed glasses glinting in the late sun, lending his greenish eyes an almost diabolical glint, though he was in fact a gentle soul and patient—until pressed too far.

"People off from work, tourists, school kids, they clog the narrow streets that surround it," Carlo explained to me in Italian. Our three coins might be tossed into the Trevi Fountain later. I then advised the group to toss their coins into the fountain tomorrow or the next day, earlier or later. Since I still held the microphone, I went on:

"We had hoped to visit the Villa Borghese today, group, but since our hotel sits next to it, we'll do it tomorrow morning. It will also be easy to stroll down from the park tomorrow to the Piazza *Santa Maria del Popolo* (the peoples' Saint Mary), and peek into its two churches.

Ferrell snatched the microphone from my hand.

"I want you to get a good rest in the later afternoon (our bus had already begun to climb up behind the Spanish Steps) (*Scala di Spagna*) and think of everything great that we'll do in Rome. Rest for three hours; or whatever else you prefer to do in bed; but assume the horizontal. Romans dine after nine P.M. So we'll gather in the hotel dining room at that hour. That may shock your American stomachs, but believe me, it's early for Rome." A general groan arose.

Carlo, five years older than Ferrell, turned to me after I had translated for him, saying: "Dinner at nine or ten is for grandees and rich tourists. We Italians eat at seven or eight. After all, tomorrow is a working day for most of us. We are no longer the grandees of Renaissance Rome!"

His was an inside story. We get so few of them. When one travels, there are various viewpoints that never get expressed. Carlo had taken me into his confidence as if to say, "Prof. Ferrell doesn't know everything, Signorina Dalloway."

"Call me Candida," I told him. "Carlo," he replied.

CHAPTER VI

BEST LAID PLANS

Ferrell came up at 7:45 P.M. to plan our second day in Rome. I had a whole suite; a blue and gold Empire bedroom with king sized bed, marble tub. Living room with a gold velvet *chaise longue*; a blue, white and gold Chinese carpet with peach blossoms on which bluebirds sat; a marble coffee table with an intricate scrollwork cornice. *Do* tables have cornices, like draperies, buildings? I didn't ask.

He intimidated me, so cold and impersonal yesterday. But when I opened the door–to my astonishment–he was carrying white lilies in a crystal vase which he placed on my coffee table. The scent was divine. I stammered, "Thanks."

"I bought them because they reminded me of something ineffably sweet. You, Candida." My jaw dropped.

He vaulted heavily onto the chaise, a pillow behind his head. "Have you given any thought to tomorrow's itinerary?" he asked.

"Only the Borghese Museum next door and the Piazza Navona for lunch," I responded.

"Logical and practical," Rob said.

"The last time I visited the gardens," I told him, "I fell in love with the sculpture of Paolina, Napoleon's sister, lying nude, only a drape over her hips. Funny, Rob, but your pose on this chaise reminds me of her. Though you are not half draped."

"Not on our first date," he answered. "Or is this our second? third? Anyway, I'm not holding an apple," he laughed. "Clever, Candida, to match us by pose. Canova made her Venus, you see, the apple being one of her sacred symbols. Just remember. She's marble now, but conceived of sea foam. I'm neither that hard, or that soft."

If this were verbal foreplay, I ignored it. He could be my father. That's what my peers would say! But not Molly. She had had an affair with him. Still, how could a woman my age fall in love with a man Ferrell's?

"At least *we* are neither hard nor insubstantial," I said, returning his serve. "The Napoleonic era was about war, but also, art and love. Paolina was ready to award the apple to a lover, or eat it if he stood her up. We have just an hour to plan our tomorrow's sights before our dinner. Paolina married a *Borghese*, a name that means middle class in Italian. War, religion and social class were disciplines whose codes they honored, though onerous."

Rob put one hand to his brow, as if peering out over a plain. "I see you as Portia in Shakespeare's play," Ferrell said, his glance penetrating. Consider this, Counselor: Paolina's hair-do wasn't mussed; so we don't know if she put duty before lovemaking. Or, just sat, beautifully coiffed, eating her apple all alone."

We laughed. This man, so self assured, Dad's age, was so amusing. I thought of Tony, back home, who wasn't. And of Molly, my gentle, impetuous friend, wading out beyond her depth with Ferrell. She had loved him. Naturally, she had not confided in her Uncle Izzy, nor to her parents in New York. Matt Silverstein, unlike Ferrell, was her age, her religion, her hair color, and a lit major.

Ferrell was surprised that I knew about Paolina (née *Maria Paola Buonaparte, (1780-1825)*). She, unlike Nefertiti or Mona Lisa, was a *whole* woman, not another bust. That whole being was large, sensual. Even half nude she remained dignified. A class act, neither bourgeois nor merely royal. Divine.

I wondered what Ferrell's commentary on Canova's Paolina would be. The Villa Borghese was early seventeenth century. Italy offered a steam table (*tavola calda*) of artistic treats. Paolina's creater was Neo-Classical, not Renaissance.

"After the Villa," Ferrell said, running his fingers through his hair, "we descend to the Peoples' Square (*Piazza del Popolo*) and the Church of Santa Maria del Popolo. We'll see the whole square from the Pincio. There's an alley leading from it down to the Piazza." Rob could not, once started, stop lecturing. Even if just to me.

"The Piazza del Popolo, Giuseppe Valadier's nineteeth century square has two semicircles. Sety I's obelisk, erected by Ramses II, is central. Ramses II was big on erections. Augustus brought the obelisk over from Heliopolis (B.C.10). We'll see the two lion fountains beneath.

But the Church of St. Mary will be our focal point. Pope Sixtus IV, a *della Rovere*, commissioned it. After his death (1484), Pinturicchio and others frescoed two chapels. (1484). Hard men, the della Rovere's, perhaps because their name meant oak!"

At last, he stopped for breath. He didn't need to translate for me! If I thought Rob might pause long enough to let me say something, I was mistaken.

"Sixtus IV, a Franciscan scholar," he continued, was also a briber of his enemies. He elevated his nephews to the purple. One abetted Giuliano de Medici's murder over a question of Neapolitan rule. Pope Sixtus IV helped his nephew because Giuliano's brother, Lorenzo, supported the French candidate, Sixtus's enemy. Renaissance popes rarely shepherded their flocks, but fleeced them or drove them over the cliff. The family's 'warrior pope,' Julius II (1503–1513), beautified Rome, even while fighting off foreigners." He paused. Then, "The *Della Roverese* had acorns on their shield; you know, nuts. What was the significance of nuts to fighters, Candida?"

"Same as Medici balls?" I asked.

Rob roared. "You show promise, Candida." I didn't remind him that I sometimes broke one, like last October when I refused an overnight at his apartment.

"The chapels in the church of Santa Maria del Popolo were frescoed by Pinturicchio and his pupils," Ferrell pronounced. "We'll skip the twin Baroque churches on the other side of the square. Bernini helped with one. But we've his improvements to St. Mary's façade, and his fountains in Piazza Navona."

"Just one fountain, no?" I asked.

"Two" he said; "That of the Four Rivers" (*Fontana dei Quatro Fiume*) and "The Moor" (*Fontana del Moro*)."

"Oh," I said lamely, "I forgot the 'Moor.'"

"Doesn't matter. The original was replaced by a copy. I don't mean to patronize you. You're young, and your strong points are literature and language, not art." Handsome of him.

"Then what?" I asked.

"A walk to Navona down Via Repetto," Ferrell mused, "then out to the Tiber under the sycamores. Or plane trees? Shady, anyway. Dodging dog poop, we get monumental views of the Palace of Justice; Castel Santangelo; Hadrian's tomb. With the Vatican City in the distance. Hills galore. We'll see the outside of Hadrian'stomb today, but do the Sistine Chapel tomorrow. We'll walk past Augustus's tomb and the Palazzo Borghese where Paolina once lived. The Borghese still occupy a part of it, called the "Harpsichord" (*Il Cembulo*), for its irregular shape."

"We won't walk to the Vatican surely?" I asked. Rob looked startled.

"Too far. Carlo picks us after our lunch in Piazza Navona and drives us there."

"The devout Christians will be very moved by St. Peter's," he mused. He furrowed his bushy eyebrows. "And classicists and history buffs, also art lovers. Evangelical Protestants, our Jewish contingent, Unitarians, agnostics and atheists will have to make do with art and architecture. But St. Peter's splendor appeals to all."

"I agree, Ferrell. I was very impressed when I first visited the basilica. And I'm Jewish on my mother's side, though I'm Gallo-Roman Catholic since the fifth century on Dad's, with a detour through Anglicanism. Jewish by Hebrew law, though. Not anything religious. My mother wasn't keen on raising a Christian kid after Mussolini's racial laws ruined her heritage, her family in Lucca. Dad was a country club Anglophile."

Rob looked up. "I'm a Baptist, myself, dunked in a river. Now, an atheist like you. And Candida, you don't look Jewish."

"Oh? How do Jews look?" I asked.

"More beautiful than Catholics from St. Peter on. Beautiful on all sides."

"My sides, like my heart, are my own affair," I said, primly, blushing.

"Ah, Candida. You're thrice blessed. Unburdened by myth, authority, conscience."

"But conscientious," I insisted.

"Even conscience may be a mask," Rob rejoined. "Remember Carnival?" (*Carnivale*). He was smiling, sitting opposite his lilies, the bedroom twenty feet beyond, doors wide open. Why did he play these games? And were they games?

Silence. He looked at his fingernails. I looked at the lilies. He looked at the lilies, his fingernails and me. We could have been museum pieces, but for the tension. But he was suddenly all business again.

"Lemme see. Carlo takes us from St. Peter's to the top of the Capitoline hill (*Campidoglio*, where we view the Roman Forum (*Il Foro Romano*). I'll point out the main ruins from the hilltop. Too hot to be out there in July. As for the museum there, except for the equestrian statue of Marcus Aurelius, of which a copy stands outside, only Bernini's *Head of the Medusa* and *The Dying Gaul* are tip top, but they're in all the textbooks."

"By then we'll be tired," I interjected.

"We'll pass by that gawdawful birthday cake of Victor Emmanuel II's. Then hit the Trevi Fountain. This time we stop. Everybody tosses his coin in and makes a wish. We'll dally by the Spanish Steps. Carlo risks a ticket at the Trevi, the Steps, but who cares? Altamonte will pay. Above the Piazza di Spagna, we'll see the Keats-Shelley House; just the exterior. We'll dip below Bernini's Barcaccia Fountain (*Fontana dell Barcaccia*); and stroll two blocks down Via Condotti, drooling at leather goods; high, unaffordable fashion. Then it's back up the Steps to the Trinity Church of the Mountains (*Trinità dei Monti*). From there, excellent views of Rome to snap before sunset," he announced triumphantly. I nodded, he was winding up. "Carlo whisks us to our hotel. Rest. Then, dinner in Trastevere." There. Rob, had planned our whole first day in Rome. It was 8:30. "Oh, Ferrell, get out of here! We dine downstairs at nine. I must shower and change," I cried. With that, he fled, pausing only to get a long whiff of lily scent.

I let the steam from my open shower de-wrinkle my blue gauze, low-necked dress, hung just outside in the steam's path. Blue beads from an old friend. White ballerinas. On the living room chaise, Rob's Mont Blanc pen. I tossed it into my purse.

The dining room of the *Principi* was formal, with amber pillars; candelabra holding electric "candles;" gold draperies; oyster white velvet chairs and vases of roses everywhere. The ceiling had clustered chandeliers. Round tables for four were draped in gold satin, a synthetic fabric that released stains. Even the rich may be sloppy eaters; the best waiters spill soup. I stopped briefly at every table containing our tourists, before finding my own table. I knew some tourists still blamed me for the Alban Hills fiasco.

I asked the elderly Harkers, Betty and James, "Did you enjoy our view of the Eternal City today? Do you like this hotel?" Betty and James were voluble.

"We cannot *tell* you how beautiful our room is overlooking the pool," Betty cooed. We're grateful to Rob for getting us out of Albano Lazio."

"Well, really, I did," I said.

"No, you stuck us there. You chose a crooked wholesaler!"

"No, I did not," I said, evenly. "I was given his name by Ferrell who got it from President Harvey's Secretary, a former travel agent."

The Huntsmans were taken aback. "Well, I'm sure you'll be careful now, dear." Jan's answer showed she did not understand what I had told her. As Americans we tend often to be judgmental without all the facts, and reject them when we hear them. I hoped the fact that *I* had not chosen Charles Clark, would sink in. Ferrell was spreading this rumor. Even when he was charming, as he was when flirting with me in my suite just now, he was, like Alpine weather, variable (*variabile*).

To the Etruscanologist, Ralph Huntsman, I said, "You *must* help Prof. Ferrell at the Villa Giulia. Etruscans are not his specialty, but yours. Your granddaughter Cynthia wrote an essay on Etruria in Italian for me!" Ralph said he had had to help her. I had suspected as much.

"We *all* need help, Ralph; Rob will appreciate yours. Cindy will be a good Italian student if she sticks with it." She wouldn't. I had given her a gentleman's C *only* because Altamonte College doesn't approve of D's. It discourages our students.

Although most of the tables were set for four, at one with six places sat Joan Lorimar, whose husband was starting an electronics business in Pleasanton. Ferrell had confided to me that he and Joan had been lovers twenty years earlier, when she had been his student at Altamonte. Their affair lasted three years. Since her marriage, she had had nothing to do with him, though her son was currently studying art history with Rob. Now, they were seated side by side.

"You will be able to tell your son about everything you see tomorrow," I told her. "He'll think his mother studied art history with Prof. Ferrell!" She looked up at me startled.

"I did once, when I was his age," she said, blushing. "Ferrell–Rob and I– are old friends."

Their table mates included the Froehlings. Ellen, jealous of Ferrell, whom she was proud to call a friend, shrank on hearing Joan's confession. Beside Ellen sat Matilda Visconti, determined to find her family's home in Milan, though her only clue was her ruby ring and the color– red. Her granddaughter Elisabeth was no better a French student than Cindy Huntsman was an Italian student, and her mind was not on French this summer, but on "making out," as the younger students say.

"Matilda, I hope we find your family's home in Milan, but I wish you had an address. Meanwhile, enjoy Rome." Bill Froehling winked at me. He was as ingratiating as Ellen was baleful.

Next to Matilda sat Andrea Smithwitch. In her later forties, she was very attractive, though a bit overblown. I had been reading about women between forty or fifty being considered more desirable to older men, who did not feel as responsible for any emotional damage they might cause. Andrea, married to a famous liver transplant surgeon at Stanford, lived in Palo Alto. She was still beautiful, so I guessed I had a few more years left of appealing to men. A woman's beauty had more elasticity these days than when Mom was my age. She remarried, of course, but the thing was, she married the first man who asked her. Jim, a widower, and nice enough, had three kids under six to raise. Now women could wait longer, until they found just the right man. And they didn't necessarily have to marry, either.

"Andrea," I smiled, determined to establish personal relationships with as many tourists as possible, "Your application said you majored in English at San Jose State University. We must have a chat about that. Some of my friends teach in the department there." She looked dismayed.

"Renaissance Literature, most particularly. My professor thought highly of me." Here she simpered at W.L., seated a table away, but watching both of us. Sam Perkins sat between Andrea on his left, and on his right, his lover Samantha Jones, she whose rear cottage had no weeds growing between the stones of the path that led to the mansion. Sam was reading the wine list. I said I hoped he would like the wines Altamonte had included *gratis*. Sam had little income, being a kept man. He smiled up at me. His teeth needed capping.

"After the fourth glass, they all taste the same," he laughed. Samantha, his lover and patroness, did not. Blonde, blue-eyed slim-hipped, she kept Sam in her cottage out back. She was perhaps fifteen years his junior, and very possessive of him. It's just that while he was good in bed, he was not socially acceptable as a husband.

Matt Silverstein sat with others at a table behind a pillar, dreamy-eyed. When I got closer I noticed a sweetish smell that could only have been marijuana. I knew Mollie smoked pot. One more reason why they'd be a good match. Now he was sitting next to Anita Marble and the lesbians, Sandy Craigie and Belinda Smith, were opposite him. These jewelry partners (and lovers) were having a quiet tiff, more apparent by their expressions than their words. Anita looked uncomfortable. Matt, I noticed, had grasped Anita's hand under the tablecloth and she was unable to disengage it.

"Does the *Principi* suit you?" I asked, to deflect their attention from flesh and feud. Anita nodded solemnly. Belinda and Sandy said respectively, "Yeah," and "Sure." Anita "never dreamed of such splendor." She had purchased this tour with part of a small inheritance from an aunt, who left most of her money to *The Nation* magazine. Her aunt disapproved of Republicans and Catholicism.

"Matt, have you heard from Molly?" I asked. He dropped Anita's hand at once, and she could now put both elbows on the table, which was proper when dining in Italy.

"Sure, we dig. Great chick. Molly said she'd ring you up. So far, we've had four phone conversations from Europe, two from England. Is England Europe?"

"Only culturally," I told him. "The English Channel separates it from the continent." I resolved to phone Molly myself and see what Matt was saying about the trip so far. I needed feed-back.

"My phone bill will be on the moon," Matt said. "Maybe Molly can split it with me. She's teaching two summer school composition courses at a college called 'Canada,' like the country."

Cañada College was a community college on the Peninsula. It was *not* pronounced like our neighbor to the north. Either Molly had a wry sense of humor, or Matt had not caught the tilde on the "ñ." "*Two* composition courses in summer is punishing!" I gasped. "She'll exhaust herself with all those compositions." But Molly had a tuition loan to pay off, too, and did not have mush cash in the bank. Matt's parents were rich. Maybe they'd pay for his calls.

"I'm glad you're in touch, Matt. Give her my love."

I passed the twins' table, Meg and Peg,–Meg Summers and Pat Springer. Divorced nurses; nice ladies; mothers of nearly grown children, abandoned in middle age by their ex-husbands, both doctors. They were wearing lavender pant suits and pink quartz jewelry.

"Thank you for correcting your mistake," they chorused. I was taken aback. "Yesterday's hotel *fiasco*," Peg stage-whispered.

I told them, too, the fault was not mine; that I alone corrected its consequences. There was much to be nipped in the bud, and the bud was now in full flower. The twins sat across from Sister Agatha and Allison Rollins, aunt and niece, who looked up as I passed. Nuns rarely have judgmental views, until they are in a classroom. This tour *was* kind of a class, for we were learning much about art, Italy and ourselves. Also, about Charles Clark.

"I know you will have much to marvel at in St. Peter's, Sisters Agatha and Allison."

"Oh, yes," said Aunt Agatha. "We are braced for it. Knowledge of medieval history and the Reformation will fortify us against its excess." Her niece smiled, fingered her silver cross and looked dreamily at Ian MacDonald's profile. Ian sat beside her. I hadn't noticed how dashing this Anglican priest in his mid-thirties was until now. He probably found Allison adorable in her blueberry habit and creamy wimple. So young, so pure. He taught church history at Grace Cathedral's High School to kids not much younger than she. Spiritual and sexual purity were two of his best units.

"We have a connection," he said as I paused briefly beside Rev. Ian MacDonald.

"Who's that?" I asked. He flicked a bread crumb from off the table cloth. The crumb landed on Allison's plate. She picked it up and ate it, slowly, smiling at Ian. I thought it was the most intimately consumed crumb ever.

"I was at Princeton studying classics with Sean O'Connor," said Ian, while watching Allison eat his crumb. "He became a Catholic and then a Jesuit priest, up from Anglicanism–or down–depending on your point of view."

"I haven't one," I said. Ian was unruffled.

"Sean was a part-timer at Altamonte, no?" he asked.

I nodded by way of confirmation. "But he disappeared before I got to know him. We only said 'hi' a couple of times on campus or in the hall. Different schedules. Where is he now?" Ian looked blank.

"I don't know. Our Princeton friends don't either. We'd like to, but Jesuits play their cards close to their chests." Did O'Connor have any to play? I wondered.

"Well, if you hear of him, Ian, give him my best," I said, passing on to the center most table in of the room, where there was one empty chair and three men–W.L. Spotswood, Ferrell, and Arnold Lodge. I joined them, scraping my thigh against Mindy Schoenstein's metal studded Versace handbag. She had slung it hip high over her own chair at the table behind this one. I knew instantly a jagged metal stud had torn the skin of my upper thigh. Served me right for wearing a miniskirt, though they were all the rage in Italy. I pulled the brief material back and rubbed my thigh with ice from my water glass. I dipped my napkin repeatedly in my glass of ice water and held it to the wound. We all watched as the napkin dyed the water red and redder. W.L. handed me his napkin, and Ferrell his ice-water. Arnold went to the desk for Band-Aids.

Before I sat down these three had been discussing *The Last Tango in Paris*–with an aging Marlon Brando and a much younger woman. They hadn't seen the film, but it was said to be a porno "flic." My accident had interrupted their guilty pleasures. At first they smiled at my awkward entrance, for Mindy's bag reverberated noisily against her chair, as I brushed against it. Mindy didn't notice, but each man here smiled differently, like the three headed Cerberus, guardian of Hades. This mythical Greek dog ate live meat. When I was applying ice to raw wounds, they knew I'd been butchered. Three heads aroused. When Arnold returned, they watched him paste four large Band-Aids over the still bleeding parts of my thigh. Mindy remained oblivious to the event, due to a sheltering potted palm.

As for meat, was I to be fed to Cerberus? I'd only had one real boy friend–Tony Murphy. My sophomore year of college I lost my virginity to a boy in my French linguistics class–another virgin. The blood reminded me of him. We could hardly look at each other after that and sat in chairs so far apart diagonally, we didn't have to. Look at each other, I mean. Two of my Cal professors offered to take me to bed. One to a motel. Another to Mexico. No and no. A third, Prof. Moravia, Italian linguistics, asked for a date, but he was almost three times my age. I refused, tactfully. My French literature professor was half in love with me, but the other half of him was in love with men. I did not lead a great date-life in college. I did get my M.A. in one year and my Ph.D. two years after that. You might say I avoided complications stemming from drugs and sex. Unfortunately, I *am* accident-prone. I am trying to find sexual meaning in my life without getting slutty about it. The three men staring at my grazed leg were solicitous. If they had not yet managed to see *The Last Tango*, they had managed to see a great deal of me.

Dinner began with the broth of Pavia (*zuppa Pavese)* chicken soup with a raw egg tossed in to produce strands of cooked egg white. Romans use Parmesan (*parmigiano)* cheese from Parma to make their "Roman" version. Next, skewered baby lobsters, followed by *Rissoles* Roman Style (*coppiette alla Romano*). These were fried patties of beef, ham, *parmigiano*, white raisins and pine nuts, breaded, deep fried, then smothered in gravy. This Roman specialty is as garlicky as anyone from Gilroy could wish, and "home cookin." Even though I'm not southern, Rome is. This dish was accompanied by creamed artichokes, and many glasses of *Est!Est!Est!*–a highly rated white wine from Montefiascone. The Frascati, naturally, was from Frascati, just south of Rome. I thought it was a bit too sweet, what Italians call *cannelino.* Our dessert (*dolce)* was black cherry jam tarts with vanilla ice cream (*gelato alla vaniglia*). I divided my tart between the men. I ate only the ice-cream. Had I been one of the dishes served, each would have ladled me up. To satisfy what appetite? Then I remembered I had a weapon. Opening my purse, I aimed Ferrell's Mont Blanc pen at his heart.

"Rob, you left this on my *chaise longue* when you brought me the lilies." Now Arnold and W.L. had to recognize that I had just one, not three, heads. A girl must assert her individuality at *any* cost, though it may be her own. The pen put a period to their fawning over me. Equals again, I stood up to announce a brief meeting in the hotel lounge to discuss tomorrow's schedule.

We assembled in the lounge; its armchairs in jewel colors, striped and solid, around cocktail tables, intimate islands on a Persian carpet sea. At one end of the lounge was a stupendous red marble fireplace, flanked by slack jawed lascivious woodland deities (*Sileni*). They looked down as if to say: "Who gives *you* the right to intrude? Your group are not Sicilian prophets (*Galeolae*); female deities (*Nymphae*); Greek academics (*Graeciae*); Persians sages (*Magi*); or women inspired by heaven (*Sibylla*). You are uncivilized wanderers (*Nomades.*) Tourists!

Had I drunk too much wine at dinner? It helped kill the pain. I was glad the *Sileni* were attached to the fireplace and could cause us no harm. Having lowered myself–carefully–into a striped love seat, I was immediately joined by Prof. Spotswood, who offered me a glass of cold lemonade with two straws.

"Relax," he whispered, his hip pressing on my thigh, still tingling from its scrape. "Ferrell is going to run this show." W.L. was right. Dressed in a plaid madras sports jacket, he looked attractive, and I could see that Andrea Smithwitch was smitten. But the professor was no flirt. He merely nodded to her. W.L. seemed in need of real affection, unlike Ferrell who struck me as a cowboy, despite his accomplishments, a man who just wanted another notch on his belt.

The love seat was narrow, so I bore with the light pressure on my hip and thigh caused by W.L's. He was big, if slim. I smiled at the folks on the other side of the table. They included Andrea Smithwitch, Anne Gilmore, Arnold Lodge, Samantha Jones, Sam, and Lynette Dryer.

Ferrell was poised to speak with one elbow atop the fireplace mantel and one foot on a short step stool. Andrea kept trying to catch W.L.'s eye, but he gazed steadily at Ferrell. To my astonishment, and probably to Andrea's chagrin, he carelessly picked up my right hand, intertwining his long slim fingers with mine. Hesitating to pull it away, I nudged my evening purse over both our hands, carefully. I was still holding the lemonade in my right one.

Andrea, whose B.A. was in Renaissance literature, was stunningly dressed in a low necked orange chiffon cocktail dress. She kept crossing and uncrossing her pretty legs, sighing loudly enough for W.L. and me to hear, as her armchair was directly opposite us. She was a woman who craved attention, perhaps because her husband gave all his to livers. Her green velvet armchair looked striking against her orange dress. She leaned forward toward our love seat.

94

"You know, W.L.," she said loudly, "I wrote my senior thesis on *The Faerie Queene*. By Edmund Spencer. You should read it." W.L., smiled saying, "Must have been difficult."

"I'd be glad to send you a copy if you give me your address in Madison. It's not published, but nobody has equaled it or given a sharper interpretation of how manners changed Tudor politics." She dipped into her evening bag handed W.L. her card.

"Thank you so much, Miss Smithwick. Very kind." Fishing into his wallet, W.L. came up empty. "I'm sorry," he said, turning toward her. I don't seem to have any of my own cards with me."

"Smith*witch*, she replied, sweetly, but with a slight hiss to compensate for background noise. "Mrs., not Miss. And *witch*, not wick. Now don't lose my card!" I thought *I should order cards, too.* I exchanged papers with colleagues after conventions. It always seemed pretentious before, but now cards seemed useful.

Across the table sat Anne Gilmore, still handsome in *her* 50's, her hair still black, except for a white streak in her bangs. Unlike Andrea, she was a widow. Her application said she was a novelist, unpublished, hoping to find material on our trip for a novel about an Italian tour. Italian novels, she had been told, sold like hotcakes; everyone was mad for Italy. I thought of Henry James, William Dean Howells, E.M. Forster, Ernest Hemingway, Thomas Mann. I leaned across the narrow coffee table toward Anne.

"I hear you are thinking of writing a novel about a tour to Italy," I said sweetly. Will any of us play a role in it?"

"Oh, I don't know if I have enough fortitude to do it," she said. "I don't know much about art, and the number of characters presents problems. I may lack the imagination to create real characters of thirty-some tourists–and the courage to ask personal questions. I probably won't have the nerve, though somebody else here might."

Travel novels. They *might* be interesting reading if done right. The challenge was not just to describe where people went and what they saw, but how it changed their behavior, their conceptions of self, other peoples' lives. I thought of Luther (a religious reformer), walking from Wittenberg to Rome; Calvin, another such, walking to Ferrara, and Montaigne, a philosopher of ideas, an observer of himself and all mankind, walking to Rome from France via Innsbruck. Each of these men of genius wrote at the peril of their own lives. They weren't novelists, of course. Novelists imperil their characters' lives. God (and Gutenberg) gave Luther a wide readership; the people gave him credit. Calvin's reviews were less favorable, but the Geneva Consistory was an awesome publicity agent. Each writer used his journeys for his own purposes. That's what writers do. Later, Grand Tours of Italy were thought to "finish" young men. The women, naturally, were finished before they started out. Few did by themselves. The best poets of the nineteenth century did; the best novelists followed them.

But suburban Californians from the Santa Clara Valley? Could an F. Scot Fitzgerald, a William Faulkner, or a John Updike have made much of such flaccid personalities as some among our group? Fitzgerald would have made them spoiled heirs and heiresses; Faulkner, incestuous southerners; Updike, lechers. Better to leave them in some small Midwestern town where they could lead normal lives. Cook. Run the fire department. Keep a shop. Pull teeth. No, I didn't think a nice woman like Anne would be up for a novel about Silicon Valley folks turned loose in Italy. And I never intended to write one, either.

Arnold Lodge sat on a red plush chair perfectly framing his snow white hair. On his lap lay *Tom Sawyer*, in the middle of which he had stuck a purple bookmark. Now he was looking intently at Anne. I thought it would be nice if two people in later middle age, widowers both, could find in one another real attraction. Probably no sex, though companionship relieves loneliness. I listened to Ferrell with half an ear. I was thinking about Tony in Gilroy, and about W.L.'s long hip to knee ratio. His leg began to feel really good against mine. I had to check myself remembering that he was Dad's age. Like Ferrell. I think if Dad had been there for me after my parents divorced, I wouldn't constantly be so attracted to older men. He had jinxed me by starting a new family. And with a young woman Chérie–I thought a phony. The Holden Caulfield thing again.

Perhaps one day I *would* write a novel, and make all my characters happy, complete people, as few in this life (and lounge) seemed to be; novels in which everybody finds true love, at least a good job, either because of a pair of eyeglasses found on a library shelf; a pen on a *chaise longue*; a lost ring recovered; a talent playing western soul music.

I had read the applications of the tourists and reviewed them mentally, as Ferrell droned on. I recalled that sandy haired Samantha Jones once sold real estate in Atherton. Her ex, the tycoon she worked for, left her the mansion, and a handsome alimony after five years of marriage. She had traveled here with Sam Perkins, whom she hoped would prove to her the depth (if any) of their affection. Our Lady Chatterley was also an A.A. member. The fact was, real estate sales and her ex-husband had driven her to like drinking, too, though not as much as Sam. Her gardener noticed how well beaten was the path from her rear door to Sam's front one. He didn't need to use weed killer around the flagstones any more. The weeds stopped growing. He thought of their own accord.

I looked at Lynette Dryer. Her "ex," president of an insurance company, gave her a large settlement and married an older woman, his private secretary.

"No children. Thank God," she said when I asked. Lynette had sat next to me on the bus back from the (almost) Alban Hills.

"It would be impossible for me to re-marry," she said, but not why. A petite woman, she wore fake jewelry, and patronized the shop that Belinda and Sandy ran in Cupertino.

"I left the real stuff back home in the bank vault," Lynette confided when, worried, I told her about our tour's insurance policy." Tonight she was wearing some of the "fake" stuff, sitting with her suppliers, Sandy Craigie and Belinda Smith–lesbians, lovers, businesswomen. Anita Marble was part, but not actively part, of their group. She had a place beside them, but looked displaced. Lynette chatted with Sandy, the "male" of the Lesbian pair, a Tennessee hillbilly who made her own unisex metal jewelry. Sandy sold this line in the Haight, and moved to the "burbs" when she and Belinda discovered each other. They imported their stuff from all over, but Venice and Florence were their main sources. When I asked how Sandy got into the jewelry business, she grimaced.

"I took to wearing my own creations in junior high," Sandy answered, "leather and metal with an occasional pink or yellow daisy, to keep people off my back, and me off mine! My evangelical, homophobic parents never caught on. As soon as I left home, I came out. I thought my mother might keep some of the pieces I left behind. But she tossed them into the dumpster. She wears pearls to church. My father picked two of my necklaces out of the dumpster and soldered some of their 'ballsier' parts onto a belt from which he hung fishing tackle. When Mom asked him about it, he said 'It's a good way to keep fishing lures organized.' He didn't wear it when he went fishing with the deacons from church, though," Sandy grinned. "They would have thought it too feminine."

To these women's left, five feet removed, sat Matilda Visconti, a "duchess" in a gold armchair, talking to young Reed Del Vecchio. Reed loved classical music, jazz, and Alpha Romeo cars, which he sold in Menlo Park. They were not speaking Italian, but using Italian gestures. Their hands spoke Italian for them, as once their ancestors had. Dad had not approved of my using Italian hand gestures. I thought W.L. Spotswood might speak Italian, too, as the scholar of Renaissance history that he was, but so far he had not. He had moved closer to Ferrell, who, I realized, amused him, and whom he may have secretly felt bore watching. And though W.L's eyes wandered around the room searching (for me, I guessed), I was now far to his back with Reed Del Vecchio, and Matilda, effectively hidden behind some Chinese screens.

I noticed Reed stared often at Anita, who was unaware of it. Sometimes, I feel people are like Edgar Allen Poe's "The Purloined Letter," a detective story in which a "lost" letter is in plain sight, ever so near, but invisible to all but Poe. So, I concluded, many of us were "lost letters," waiting to be discovered where we were "hiding"–in plain sight–opened, and read.

The Gumps jewelry store manager, Andrea Pellatierra and his artist wife, Maria, who made pots, were listening intently to their friend Ferrell's description of our next day's activities. So were the Froehlings. W.L., far up front, was now pressing Sister Agatha's thigh, for he had sat down next to her on a love seat like the one we shared before. He pressed in on Agatha, quite unintentionally. Those seats were not broad enough to be discreet. She seemed acutely aware of this. For relief, she crossed her legs, and kept leaning over to a strait backed chair where sat her niece, Allison, lost in thought, twisting her cross. Ian McDonald sent little signs to Allison, which she ignored. Ian had left off his priest's collar. He was wearing a pale yellow Arrow shirt with a blue tie. He stared at the young novice from his church with an intensity that made me wonder if it was her soul that worried him, her wistfulness, or just her inattention to his staring? his tie?

Arnold was chatting with the Huntsmans and Harkers, while Anne came around and straddled the arm of Jan Huntsman's chair, who took her hand in her own and patted it. Anne and Arnold looked at each other as if they were surprised to have recognized an old friend, though they had to my knowledge, not met before.

At one end of the great fireplace the Schwartzes and Schoensteins sat in separate armchairs, oblivious to Ferrell. Mindy was eating chocolates bought on the Via Veneto, offering them graciously to all but Jonah, who waved them away, with long, slim fingers, perhaps because at sixty-three he worked hard to maintain his shape for a wife twenty-five. She could have passed for his granddaughter. They were way across the lounge, and though I usually keep myself from temptation, I suddenly craved those candies. When Matt Silverstein seated himself with them, I slid 'round the outer edges of the lounge, until I was abreast of them. Jonah, seeing my approach, moved over to make room for me, patting the sofa beside him with those long, bony fingers. He had several times given me advice about not letting men taking advantage of me—drawn from his own experience, perhaps? Nonetheless. Jonah, who eschewed sugar to keep fit and trim, took great pleasure watching the people around him enjoy his superb (kosher) chocolates. I had always admired people who could enjoy life vicariously. The box was passed my way, and I sank my teeth into a dark chocolate covered cherry filled with kirsch *liqueur*. Heavenly.

Why should I feel left out of my mother's culture, Jewish, even if I were an atheist, not even agnostic? I needed a roost like any other bird, though I'd be lost at a Friday night service. No Hebrew. No practice. I knew more about Catholicism, Anglicanism, than Judaism. Matt took another candy and pushed the box toward me. I chose a milk chocolate filled with raspberry flavored cream. I was suddenly filled with pleasure. No wonder candy makers generally succeed. God must have invented raspberries and chocolate, even if not the universe.

I was reminded of what the Greek philosopher, Epicurus (not an epicurean in common parlance), thought good eating was in his day a piece of aged cheese on holidays. To be a real epicurean one should be a philosopher. But we have perverted the word to mean gourmet. How philosophy, cooking, gods and language spoil with the passage of time!

Matt mentioned that "Molly was weary of teaching, only a third of the way through summer school." He had two Jewish cliques to fit into. One was the Conservative temple in San Francisco, well-to-do, Byzantine in appearance. Beth El Ner Tamid. The other, Molly's, B'nai Israel, an ultra Reformed temple in Berkeley and very laid-back. Matt, at thirty-one, was fascinated by the hippy culture that had been apparent even at Reed College, and was much more so in the Bay Area. He got a kick out of saying "Our Crowd" to describe his conservative temple, but he preferred Molly's. Only I seemed not to belong to any crowd. Did I lack an emotional as well as a spiritual gene for cohesion? Where did I belong? I was neither Christmas nor Hanukkah.

Finally, Ferrell finished. "Comments?" he asked. Ellen Froehling wondered if we would see "the David" tomorrow?

"No, Ellen," Rob said gently, "but you'll see him in the Accademia museum in Florence, and Donatello's younger version in the Bargello there, too." She smiled up at him as if to say, "I know you wouldn't try to trick me like Candida would." Of course she did not say that. My imagination was working overtime.

I stood up to remind everyone to dress soberly for St. Peter's tomorrow. "No shorts, halters, sundresses, bare midriffs, backless dresses or miniskirts. No beachwear or suggestive slogans on T-shirts. On the outside of the Church, if lost, look for our Altamonte College flags with the pig, bear and lilies. Inside, keep together as a group. The basilica has innumerable side chapels, stairways, exits and a crypt down below the Bernini baldachin before the altar. Don't wander off. Stick together. Pay for any candles you light. Prayers are free."

As we were leaving, Jonah Schoenstein put a sack of sugared almonds into my hand and, smiling slightly, kissed my forehead, before catching up with his child wife. Now what was that all about?

CHAPTER VII

HIGH SPIRITS, HOLY SPACES

We breakfasted in the dining room, emperors' busts looking down from a shelf above. Had I dreamed last night Joan Lorimar said, "No, I think not!" to Ferrell's "Are we still kids?" Voices drifted through opened windows. Did Sandy offer Anita a "nightcap" as Belinda was "blotto"? Did Belinda say thickly, "Try Lynette." Did one of them borrow a nightgown?" "*Forse che sì, forse che no.*" (Maybe yes, maybe no).

That slogan decorated the Gonzaga palace in Mantua (*Mantova*) on my last research trip. I wrote post cards sitting on the town square in a light rain, calling the palace "Gone soggy." Bad puns lift one's spirits.

Last night in Rome I took a Sominex. Too groggy to eat the chocolate on my pillow, it melted under my cheek. The group straggled into the Principi's breakfast room under imperial inspection. Anita joined W.L.; Ian MacDonald joined me, wearing his clerical collar again. Belinda joined the twins, Meg and Peg. Sam and Samantha sat together, not speaking. Joan sat with Matt and the Schoensteins; Lynette and Sandy seemed glued to one seat and looked radiant. Bill Froehling sat alone. Ellen slept through breakfast. Bill had a tray sent up.

Ferrell, Arnold Lodge and Reed Del Vecchio kept Anne company. The emperors look dour. We were watched by a government long fallen, its heads of state stone deaf to our pleas. Their lack of insight into our problems had become traditional for all subsequent heads of state.

On the terrace, sheiks' head gear in red lozenges on white flowed alongside black beards, rested on white robes. Their wives wore black burkas. Oil sheiks didn't drink with their wives, except orange juice on terraces. At casinos, they drank cognac with other men's. They would meet in Rome to preserve liquidity for gas guzzlers, for themselves.

Our breakfast was American—scrambled eggs, toast, fried potatoes and bacon, stewed prunes. The Harkers, Huntsmans, and Froehlings took generous helpings of prunes. When I breakfasted in Italy's bars, there was no orange juice or fruit, just small boxes of stale cornflakes and warm milk. Cream filled *dolci*, (sweet buns) and *caffelatte*. Hard-boiled eggs of unspecified antiquity in large jars. I bought *Motta* ice cream on sticks if I were still hungry. The cashier gave me my change in hard candies (*caramele)*, lire being in short supply.

The *Direttore* entered, bowed at my table and asked, "Everything all right, Miss Darroway?" (*Tutto bene, Signorina Darroway?*)

"Yes, Sir, everything is fine." (*Sì Signore, tutto bene.*) I did not need a *Motta*.

This morning, the Villa Borghese Museum (*Galleria Borghese).* Our trip facilitator, Gianfranco, Carlo's nephew, handed us tickets. Built for Cardinal Scipio (*Scipione)* Borghese (1615), the museum held alabaster, porphyry and marble gods and goddesses. The trip took five minutes. The collection was Camillo Borghese's, Paolina's second husband's. Inside, Paolina, bare breasted, hips draped, sacred apple in hand, left little to the imagination. Her marble "flesh" compelled attention.

Venus Triumphant! (Lat., *Venus Victrix*). Ferrell walked deliberately around her, pausing before her belly. Turning to an enlarged group–he attracted other tourists–he began:

"Canova, the great Romantic sculptor, gave us this neoclassicist Venus. An approachable goddess, she aroused other divinities' jealousy. We worship at her feet." Anita, who *was* at her feet, blushed. Paolina's real marriages couldn't compete with mythical romance. Whose could?

"The problem was," Rob remarked, "that Canova failed to keep his distance from Paolina's flesh. *Marble* flesh, I mean." While speaking, Ferrell bent closer over Venus's navel, not keeping his own distance. His auburn hair brushed her full breasts. Straightening, he asked, "Can anyone explain?"

Then W. L. hazarded, "You meant Canova lost his artistic authority by making Venus a real woman about to jump into bed with her first caller? Not a goddess, but a tart?" Professor Spotswood's hazel eyes twinkled.

Ferrell gazed intently at W.L. (what *did* W.L. stand for?) He stood beside me and Paolina's left shoulder. Both men were nearly the same height as they leaned toward each other nose to nose; Ferrell, massive, W.L. athletic, trim. Ariel vs. Caliban.

"*Very* good, Spotswood," Rob told him. "You see," Rob told us, "Paolina lost her first husband, a general, to yellow fever. She married Camillo Borghese, next, of the family that gave Rome Pope Paul V (1605-1623). Camillo 'collected' Paolina, a rare piece of work, Napoleon's sister. She 'collected' him because he was enormously wealthy. Both were 'collectibles.'" We enjoyed Ferrell's breezy explanations. "Paul V," he continued, "completed St. Peter's façade and canonized many saints, including Ignatius of Loyola. Paolina, no saint, tired of Camillo. She returned to Paris where her tarty behavior upset Empress Marie-Louise, who banished her from court (1810). For Camillo, art was more precious than his wayward love. He displayed his wife's charms publicly."

Arnold Lodge interjected. "When a lady asked Paulina how she could have posed nude, she replied, 'The studio was heated.' Perhaps that story was apocryphal. If not, Paulina, like Freud much later, thought sexuality self-evident." Arnold was quiet for a moment, then added, "Obviously her morals differed from those of Becky Thatcher in *Tom Sawyer*." None of us could imagine what possible connection there might be between Paolina and the little girl in pantalets who so attracted Tom Sawyer.

"Oh, Arnold, Anne said, "give us the punch line."

"Only," Arnold replied, his eyes twinkling, "that Becky heard Tom confess he had once been attracted to their classmate, Amy Lawrence. Becky broke off their engagement. A good thing, too, as they were still in elementary school." Laughter. Arnold laughed at his own absurd comparison of an historical *grande dame* posing nude with a come-thither smile, and Becky Thatcher who held her own dignity at a higher value than Paolina Borghese did.

Anita was a large-breasted, attractive brunette. Had she really borrowed a lesbian's nightgown last night? I couldn't imagine her posing as Venus, though her name *was* Marble, changed at Ellis Island from *Marmo*, i.e., marble in Italian. My right hand, caught in W.L.'s comforting grasp, had grown stiff. W.L. looked at me raising an eyelid ever so slightly. Hazel eyes were so expressive. I lowered my own. Abruptly, W.L. dropped my hand, now tingling, just as Ferrell turned his gaze from Paolina's raised shoulder to her lowered leg. Had Ferrell seen us holding hands?

Next, Bernini's *Apollo and Daphne*. All eyes were on Ferrell, but
I began this lecture. Father, like Apollo, was once a god to me. He
had given me Nathaniel Hawthorne's *Tanglewood Tales* when I was
seven, insisting I report to him on my reading every day. I knew he
was trying to make me smart. Those were the days, unclear to me then,
when Dad was cheating on Mom with first one secretary, then another.
I confused Dad with Apollo, both handsome, compelling. That's what
the secretaries had thought, I realized now.

"Here is Apollo," I told the group, "also called Phoebus, son of Jupiter
by a Titan's daughter, Latona. She antagonized Jupiter's wife, Juno, who
persecuted her. Persecution by the gods was common, especially where
a woman was a married god's mistress and her persecutor his wife!"

The group murmured their comprehension. Apollo drove the sun's
chariot, but preferred art to cars. He invented music, poetry, eloquence,
medicine. Like Jupiter, he made love to many women, including his
half sister, Calliope, muse of music. Apollo hated a spurned advance.
Daphne tried escaping. The pitying gods turned her into a laurel tree.
Apollo pursued her. He placed a circlet of laurel leaves on what once
was her hair. Laurels were sacred to him. He won many.

I added, "His rival for Daphne was Leucippus, who posed as a
huntress. Like Apollo and Leucippus, men pose. Women must guess
at their imposture. Daphne's heart remained wooden. Soon she was
all wooden. Apollo had 'tree'd' her." I bowed, raising my hands with a
forward flourish, just as Daphne had done. Leaves had emerged from
Daphne's. Ferrell played Apollo. Would I play Daphne? Not a chance.

Rob's follow-up was fine. "Bernini trained in these gardens," he said
to us, with a broad sweep of his arm. "His versatile sculpture included
many materials; wood, cloth, bark, leaves; female and male flesh–done
by gods at work, Bernini's. Apollo's. Divine *fiat*. This was godhead
acting on human and plant growth through marble and time; the one
thing we have little of. Bernini made the sweep of Apollo's hand time
itself. Daphne's limbs testified to his force, swinging forward wildly,
tree limbs in a storm. Her left leg had become a tree trunk. Thus man's
dependence–women's still more so–on divine will, battling lust, losing
love, life." I identified with alliteration, and also with lust love and life.
I was, after all, thirty-two.

W.L. whispered, "You've won."

"Won what?" I asked breathlessly as we dashed on to Bernini's *David*. "One off Ferrell," W.L. replied. "Your explanation was more dramatic. The group was riveted. Men, are competitive. Sports and testosterone make them so."

I knew women played for keeps with no real advantage. W.L. knew the rules. Few other men would have stated them so clearly. He, like Ferrell, had a powerful intellect, but W.L. was more sensitive to feminine emotions.

Once we had arrived before Bernini's *David* Ellen shrieked. "Look, Ferrell! David *is* here!"

"Ellen loves proving people wrong," Bill explained. "She values Ferrell as mentor and dinner guest, but has turned her guru into her alter ego. *She* is now the art critic. She shreds all our magazines to make collages. Calls them 'post modern art.'"

"Rob, dear," Ellen chortled, "You erred last night. David *is* in Rome, not Florence! Shame, shame!" This dowdy woman of seventy-two made the schoolgirl's gesture for shame. Rob bit his lip to keep from laughing.

"Now Ellen, I am sorry if I misled you. There are several sculptures of David, the young Jewish hero who defeated a Philistine giant, Goliath. You forgot that in Florence we'll find not only Michelangelo's lordly *David*, but Donatello's young adolescent one, and also Verrocchio's apprentice in a leather apron, having just severed Goliath's head."

"Was David the one who started beheading people in the Middle East?" asked Mindy. Myrna grimaced. "Don't you know the story of Judith and Holofernes? Didn't the Seventh Day Adventists teach you *anything* in Sunday School?" Mindy was undaunted.

"We colored all the *Bible* stories you colored, and more! Judith and Holofernes were for Halloween." Barry and Jonah winced at this second reference to beheading in the *Hebrew Bible*.

I continued my historical discourse with the confidence my once trusted father early instilled in me.

"This David is not a calm young patriot like Verrocchio's, Donatello's or Michelangelo's, all motivated by justice. Look at this face. This is a young hood, a murderer who betrayed King Saul; enjoyed killing and was Saul's lecherous successor. David, unmindful *pater familias*, seduced Bathsheba, killed her husband Uriah by sending him into battle unprotected. The list of his sins was long. You would avoid him on a dark street corner! Bernini's message was, again, time. David begins his lethal pivot, that calculated movement that releases the slingshot's stone."

"I never knew David had committed so many sinful acts," Mindy said thoughtfully.

I continued my recitation. "Jews and Adventists, all biblical literalists, took these stories as gospel. David only had a slingshot. But God was on his side! *I Samuel.*"

W.L. whispered into my ear. "The *Bible* is about stories, who tells them and why. Beware the media!"

Ellen remonstrated. "I bet *you* didn't know there were three Davids in Florence, Candida." I just smiled at her.

We passed an intriguing Titian, but Ferrell ignored it. This painting, *Sacred and Profane Love,* featured a woodland setting where a sumptuously clothed woman, left, was seated on a casket. To her right, a female nude held aloft a flaming lamp. A cupid-like figure in the center peered into a slightly opened casket. In the background lay a town. Titian raised the classic ideal of sacred nudity and the vanity of rich garb. The lamp was divine knowledge or philosophy. Learned Greeks didn't distinguish. Now, Italy was a fashion hub. If we went naked, the fashion business would suffer. Italy would fall. Renaissance artists tried to reform prejudices against nudity. Reforming fixed notions was a tough job. I knew from teaching.

Sam Perkins fell into step with me. W.L. went to the men's room. The others headed to the exit. Together, Sam and I scrutinized a painting called *The Sick Bacchus (Bacco Malato),* by Caravaggio (1573-1610). Bacchus, the god of wine and orgies, was crowned with grape leaves, face sickly yellow and lavender. Death neared. A sunbeam radiated off his right shoulder. His right hand held a bunch of Thompson seedless, greenish-yellow, like his skin. Black grapes rested on a slate table. Two hard green peaches would never ripen in time for him to eat. His sparse drapery was tied with a brown bow that flopped onto the table. His mouth bore a humorless smile. His tragic eyes stared Death in the face.

"This is what sexual excess and alcohol did to him," Sam was crying.

"Sam! Can I help?" I queried.

"Hold my hand," he said, so I did.

"I am that fellow, Baccio," he burbled.

"No, Sam, *baccio* means kiss in Italian. You are Bacchus, in Italian, *Bacco*. Rhymes with taco." Sam grabbed me and kissed me full on the lips. Perhaps he was hungry for tacos; more likely for a drink. Maybe just grateful for my holding his hand.

"You are so sure of things, Candida. So smart and sober." Sam didn't know it, but I had lots of doubts about myself. True, I was not a recovering alcoholic or a failed stockbroker or realtor. That could lead one to drink. He confessed that Samantha had saved his life.

"But for Samantha and the AA. I wouldn't be around."

"She loves you, Sam?"

"Yes," he sniffled. "We make lots of love. She comes with me to Alcoholics Anonymous, too. She drives."

"Oh?" I asked.

"Well, we have a drink before we leave, to buck us up. Then we chew mints or sen-sen. Twelve Steps. Tough love." I knew about the steps from her mansion to the cottage, the trampled weeds. Sam recognized himself in Bacchus. Perhaps it would help him. I wondered if I would find myself represented in any art and be helped by it? I might say that like Athena, I had sprung fully armed (intellectually) from my dad's head. For without his training of me from an early age, would I have acquired so much wisdom? Pursued two advanced degrees? Lots of girls I knew at Smith just married millionaires' sons, and then went to New York's upper west side or to Westchester county, where their suburban routine gave them little scope except opportunities to join book clubs, become den mothers, or have affairs with sons of other millionaires–or their fathers. Mature lotharios, like Dad, controlled their daughters' fate not merely through positive childrearing techniques, but by failing to provide the proper role models of what a real man should do with his family–protect it–not run away when the going got rough. Fatherhood was not only a intellectual and spiritual thread that ran through all religions, but should have been a paean to motherhood, to nurturing.

W.L. emerged from the gents' and we three made a run for the group waiting for us outside. Ellen, also late, scurried to catch up, purse and sun hat churning, one sandal flapping. I knelt and strapped it for her. She couldn't see the holes. She thanked me.

Rob was swinging his pocket watch, on the rim of the Pincio hill. He did not like to be kept waiting. Samantha, keeping close tabs on Sam, ran over. Lucky for Sam I hadn't left any lipstick traces.

A view over the hill's rim; a plunge down the narrow alley, W.L.'s hand steadying me over broken pavement. Maybe he steadied himself. Suddenly, I needed steadying. Men Dad's age were not sexy, I told myself. Not.

Inside Santa Maria del Popolo, piety, bewilderment, belief, disbelief. I was transfixed, not by the Holy Spirit, like Bernini's St. Theresa pierced by God, but by art. It was fairyland; the view from a giant Ferris wheel into a theme park of holy images.

I recalled Petrarch's climbing Mt. Ventoux and his view of Vaucluse—God and nature fused. My early morning ski lift atop Mont Blanc when Apollo slalomed over the glacier. Hilton's *Shangri-La*, where reality was imaginary and imagination real. Hudson's *Green Mansions*, in which tribal ways were sacred and true forever, and nature and man one. Tolkien's *Lord of the Rings* taught that Power corrupted all who sought it; love and charity healed—mystically. The church merged mystical whimsy with natural grandeur.

Petrarch or Francesco Petrarca, "Father of the Renaissance" (1304-74), was Boccaccio's friend, a cleric, diplomat, courtier, lover. He poured out his love of Laura in his Sonnets (*Canzoniere*); not to the mistress who bore his daughter and son. He was crowned (1341) first Poet Laureate since antiquity. Reading St. Augustine on Mt. Ventoux turned his thoughts from scenery to soul. He inhabited courts, archives; palaces. He determined man's place beside God and woman's. Now, under the dome of the Chigi Chapel, we were surrounded by art, created by man to glorify himself, God. We might each try to find our place in such a universe, or not. Jews, Protestants, Christians, agnostics and atheists were so many Sauls on their way to or from—Damascus.

"This church," Ferrell was explaining, "is one of Rome's richest collections. Raphael drew cartoons for the dome of Creation, finished by Luigi da Pace et. al." Looking up, I wondered if any of us believed in creationism. But surrounded by such art, who could *not* believe in divine creation? Where could you find a tiler who worked as fast? Teresa's new kitchen took two weeks and didn't make any of the guide books to Gilroy. Atheists had two handicaps, of course. Science. Logic.

"The Chigi," said Ferrell, "has an octagonal plan based on the Creation of the World, sun, and six planets, each moved by one angel."

"Which angel put up the cash?" asked Ralph Huntsman, whose every Etruscan dig had been sponsored by *National Geographic.*

"Raphael's patron, the Sienna banker, Augusto Chigi. He moved to Rome and built not just a house, but a reception palace (the Villa Farnese) for entertaining cardinals, popes, and their mistresses; now an art museum. See that pyramidal wall tomb with Latin inscriptions? Chigi's. Next to it, Bernini's *Habakkuk and the Angel.*"

"Habakkuk?" interjected Matt. "A Hebrew prophet! Maybe Chigi was a Jewish banker in Catholic drag. Perhaps he wouldn't have a memorial if Raphael hadn't been his friend. Raphael's Hebrew name means 'God has healed.'" Ferrell stared. Matt, who had been bar-mitzvahed, knew his Hebrew. He seemed exhilarated by this hypothesis. Barry Schwartz, who had struggled with Hebrew, shrugged.

Matt was turned on by Habakkuk. "Habakkuk rejoices that the Lord used Chaldeans as instruments for Jewish redemption; bad tasting medicine heals. Catch my drift?" If we didn't, he explained. "Nebuchadnezzar, a Chaldean, dragged some Jews to Babylon (B.C.586). Divine punishment administered by the Chaldeans, bad medicine." But who were the Chaldeans in Bernini's day? I asked myself. The Bourbon kings of France.

Ferrell, annoyed, said, "Chigi wasn't Jewish, Barry. God worked in wondrous ways to save the righteous, is all. Here, God works in a catholic manner." Had Rob meant catholic with a small 'c' or Catholic with a large 'C'? It was too much for Barry. The church that excited Matt, made Barry nervous.

"Bernini finished this chapel in the next century." Mindy contributed. She ticked Bernini's feats off on her fingers. He finished this church's façade; this chapel; the façade across the piazza (of Santa Maria Montesanto); Habakkuk; the colonnade of St. Peter's for Pope Alexander VII (1655-67), other stuff."

W.L. finished up for her. "Stuff like the Constantine statue at St. Peter's; the portraits of several ecstatic female saints, including Saint Teresa of Avila and blessed Ludovica Albertoni. St. Francis once lived in a hospice connected with her." Stonily, Ferrell eyed W.L., who took no notice. Jonah was astonished that his young wife knew so much about art.

"Ludovica Alberoni," Ferrell said, turning toward W.L., "was a nun who died in the 500's. Her descendant, Cardinal Alberoni (originally, Albertoni), had Bernini (1671-74) sculpt her on her death bed in ecstasy, with *putti. She's* in Trastevere, in a church once associated with St. Francis's stay in Rome. To be honest, it's a toss up as to whether she is having a religious experience or an orgasm."

W.L. looked especially jolly at that. "Passion is passion," he observed. "Putti or no."

Sister Agatha piped up, "Any passion makes us putty in the hands of man or God." A nun's pun on *putti*?

Sandy Craigie muttered, "Or putty in the hands of women." Allison moved closer to Ian. He started to put his arm around her shoulder, then stopped, batting away an imaginary fly.

"Glad you mentioned that Chigi's family produced Alexander VII. A number of papal families besides the Medici rose from banking to the Holy Office," W.L interjected, adding: "Or should I say from the unholy office of banker to the Holy one of banking on God?"

"What banking?" Ellen queried blankly.

"Oh, banking on the sacrifice of his Son. Salvation through the Son. A big investment, no?" W.L. smiled beatifically at Ellen, who finally took his meaning.

"You're a free thinker, Professor," she sputtered. "We sent our grandson to Altamonte to escape liberals." She was wrong. Most professors were not liberal; and both Ferrell and I, who were, taught at Altamonte! As for W.L.'s views, I did not know his well. I wished I did.

"You know," Matt said, "Chigi *might* have been Jewish, even if Habukkuk was a minor prophet."

"So was Jesus once," said W.L. "And many regarded him as a Jewish nuisance."

"Even the Son of God had to find his comfort zone," grinned Ralph.

Ferrell ignored Spotswood, Spotswood, Ellen, and Ellen the rest. To Mindy, Ferrell said, "About Bernini finishing stuff. Some people start things, others finish them. The process of art is like life. Your parents started you and you'll have to finish the job, especially since Jonah is so much your senior." A long silence. Then Jonah turned toward Ferrell.

"And possibly, Professor, someone will finish you off one day." I was aware that at Altamonte College, the two had had a long history. About what I didn't know.

"Roundheaded arches," Ferrell intoned, "on four walls; entrance arch open, the others 'blind.' Here, the *other* Jonah, the one in the whale, 'prefigured' the Resurrection." Jonah Schoenstein went to look, but decided his second marriage was *his* resurrection. He believed in satisfied shareholders, a youthful figure, a satisfied wife. He believed in Israel. He believed in Gold's Gym. He did not believe in the story of Jonah nor that being vomited out by a whale was consistent with resurrection, whatever the *Hebrew Bible* had to say about it. Whales, vomit, God's forgiveness, maybe. But resurrection? That was too Christian a concept for Jonah to swallow.

The Baroque Cerasi Chapel was an opened jewel box, revealing two Caravaggios. In the *Crucifixion of St. Peter*, left, Peter had requested he be nailed upside down, so as not to compete with Christ. He had had a sense of humor. A heavy fellow; the workmen struggled to position Peter. Why not have spared themselves the trouble? The workmen lacked Jewish humor. *Perhaps having denied Christ three times, Peter wanted a still more horrible death to make up for those denials,* I thought.

In the *Conversion of St. Paul*, to our right, Saul was depicted after Christ's death en route to Damascus to persecute Christians. He lies on his back, arms extended, fallen from his horse, which lifted a hoof to avoid crushing him. An old man looked on unemotionally. No sign of God, Christ, or the Holy Spirit.

"Hard to tell from this painting," Ferrell grumbled, "if Paul is being rewarded for his conversion or punished for his persecutory designs. Caravaggio was a brawler, but a believer. Paul lost a battle, but won a huge victory. All light came from the future saint. Caravaggio knew Paul was blessed for eternity, if not helped up after his fall." Ferrell stepped back sharply, so he could look at both paintings at the same time.

Ferrell had recently read a new biography of Caravaggio. "His art is difficult," he told us, "like Caravaggio; a slum dweller and a killer. The more realistic his sacred images, the more effective in saving souls. Away with platonic idealism! Caravaggio made holy people street people. Eventually, the clergy accepted his realism. He got away–literally–with stoning Roman Guards, beating up a fellow artist; hitting a waiter in the face with a plate of Rome's famous creamed artichokes. The man he killed had apparently beat him at tennis! Having painted so many Adorations; Resurrections, Martyrdoms and Virgins, he won over Cardinals and Popes. Paul V was willing to exonerate him for murder, but Caravaggio died before, barely thirty-seven, convinced that mystical experiences occur within the context of physical sensuality and sex."

In this address on Caravaggio, a painter unknown to our group–Ferrell had performed the professorial sage, indeed, king. And from his throne he was both wise and regal. It was when he got you alone that his regal nature dissolved; whereas, there was something about W.L. Spotswood which suggested natural, not regal, authority. I was beginning to differentiate between authorities.

The group sighed, nodded, or looked puzzled. Their ideas of mysticism and artistic sensuality were as yet unformed.

I thought of St.Teresa of Avila and St. John the Divine; of Hildegard of Bingen and the nun she loved who was sent off to head her own convent. I thought of Abelard and Heloise, of Santa Clara and St. Francis. Sensual dimensions to all these clerical loves abounded. Had it escaped their mystical *o altitudinos* (highs)? Hardly. Caravaggio knew what made mystics lovers and lovers mystics. I hoped to learn.

Till now my own altitudinous experiences were on Mont Blanc's ski lift and an elevator to the top of the Empire Sate Building as in *An Affair to Remember*, Tony's favorite oldie. In my case, heights did not entail the sensual passion I wished for, but the phobia I suffered from. Vertigo.

Ferrell concluded, "God had converted him, but Paul didn't have a clue."

Then W.L. said, "Paul's experience made as much sense as ours do. We haven't a clue about our future, nor understanding ourselves. I tell students: study *your* history, or you will have to *invent* it, which is much harder."

Rob had tons of facts, but less philosophy than W.L. Philosophy grounded me. Facts suffocated me. What would pick me up off my ass if I, like St. Paul, were to fall off my horse into a slough of invented facts? Philosophy might.

"Can we trust arbiters of artistic style more than arbiters of biblical truth?" asked Andrea Smithwitch. Excellent question. Andrea had learned something in college. W.L. looked at her, so fetching in green gauze. Before she could draw him out—or in—Sister Agatha recited:

"'God moves in a mysterious way / His wonders to perform,' William Cowper. *Olney Hymns,* (no. 1, 1779)." Once an English teacher, Agatha quoted an enlightened poet, not the *Gospel,* which I thought telling, though I was not sure what it told. Cowper suspected God worked by letting people pick themselves up from the dust and only later giving them a brush up, or off. Did Andrea feel she'd been given the brushoff? Her husband had received a Nobel prize for transplanting livers; all she got was a B.A. in English literature and his exhausted body at the end of days spent transplanting livers.

"Caravaggio died at Naples," Ferrell continued. "He was arrested after a fight and jailed. Released, he watched the boat on which he had packed all his possessions set sail for Rome. Already feverish on the beach, he died before his thirty-seventh birthday."

I was thirty-two! Biological clocks didn't tick for men. For kings like Henry VIII, yes. Would I wind up on some beach without issue? And would it take some guy I couldn't count on—or care much for—to change all that? Heaven forfend."

First to exit Santa Maria, I saw a terribly lame gypsy boy, hobbling on one crutch, holding a tin cup. He was begging as he crossed the piazza. Seeing us emerge, he dodged noontime traffic, and ran to a safety island near our curb. When traffic slowed, he hobbled over, dodging a taxi. Mindy's eyes popped, but Jonah gave the boy ten thousand lire, and W.L. the same.

"A performance like that," said Jonah, "merits a reward." Ferrell and the others, just through the doors, had not seen the boy run, but watched him plead for lire.

Ellen lectured on the evils of begging, and criticized W.L. and Jonah for helping the boy. "Cripples should learn to be useful."

Bill went around her back and dropped another ten thousand into the child's cup saying, "He needs new shoes."

Maria Pellatierra said, "Bet his take will go to his father or uncle, not the shoe store."

Arnold related how when Samuel Clemens was in Rome (*Innocents Abroad*), "the author, whom we call Mark Twain, seeing Rome's poverty so widespread, suggested that the poor steal from the Church."

Agatha said she couldn't approve of that, even if the Catholic Church had acquired its wealth by war and chicanery. An Anglican, she didn't mention Thomas Cromwell's acquisition of England's monasteries, acquired by war and chicanery.

Like gypsies, governments and religious institutions cheated, stole. I resolved to read *Innocents Abroad*. After all, weren't we all less innocent having witnessed corruption at home as well as in Italy, and done little to stop it? Arnold, Bill, W.L. and I were trying to educate our tourists, but even we scholars were "innocents abroad." When our group left the curb, the boy ran back to the island, before hobbling–or running– depending on traffic, to his place across the square. There, a burly man emptied the "crippled" boy's cup into a shoulder bag. He boxed him on both ears and fled down an ally. The boy waited for other tourists to emerge from other churches. He would have to redeem himself.

We followed Via Repetto to the Tiber under plane trees. No breeze. We saw the Palace of Justice, and Hadrian's tomb, which morphed into the Castel Sant'Angelo by the sixth century. It became a fortress for popes under attack. They had enemies, but also friends. I needed more friends, and I was unsure who my enemies were. I told the group about a man whose friends included kings and popes.

"He supposedly killed their enemies, when not making luxury goods for their personal use," I told the group. Benvenuto Cellini (1500-1571) had been a master goldsmith, brawler, and gilder of truth.

"Look, everybody! (*Guardate, ognuno!*) Castel Sant'Angelo. Cellini (1500-1571) fought the troops of Emperor Charles V there, and his *Autobiography* claimed he shot the Constable of Bourbon, too, who commanded Emperor Charles V's army; wounding Philibert, Prince of Orange–both enemies of the French king, Francis I. '*Forse che sì, forse che non.*' The facts were not certainly known. Cellini's clients included

Augusto Chigi's sister-in-law, for whom he reset the diamonds of a 'gilded lily.'" Were Ferrell's lilies "gilded?"

Dad had warned me against "gilding the lily." In Cellini's case, it paid off. Asking no payment but his client's pleasure, he was rewarded when her servant tossed him a sack of gold. Lesser remuneration came his way playing in Pope Clement VII's band, though his heart wasn't in it.

"What instrument did Cellini play?" I asked Rob.

"Cornet," he said, having played that and trumpet, too, in his Kansas high school, earning the nickname "Triple-Tongued Devil." Among his later instruments was Molly, whom he played false.

"I just remembered," I said brightly. "Cellini cast a huge vase for the Bishop of Salamanca, who delayed paying him." Ferrell gave me a look. I stopped. Rob finished up on Cellini.

"Francis I of France commissioned Cellini's Nymph of Fontainbleau (in the Louvre) for his garden, and a unique salt cellar with two golden gods, now in Vienna. In Florence, we'll see his *Perseus* holding up Medusa's head in the Loggia of the Lanzi, in Piazza Signoria." Rob smiled beatifically right at me. "Cellini's most obvious trait, aside from talent, was his personality. As Candida told you, like Caravaggio he was a brawler, forgiven for murder by Pope Paul III, who could not pardon him when Benvenuto wounded a papal notary."

"I guess popes had to draw the line somewhere," Anne, a widow, observed. She toyed with writing her travel novel about a tour through Italy, suspecting the job would be too hard for her. I hoped to get to know her better, though Arnold was taking up her time now so my chances for a chat with her alone were reduced. As they walked along, he put a protective arm around her shoulder, so intimate a gesture; so public a sidewalk.

"They overlooked a lot of sin for art's sake," Arnold said. His family had collected many degrees, many public offices. Lodges had edited many journals, published works of history. Held seats in the Senate. One was a governor of Massachusetts. Lodges were emissaries to foreign countries, even the Vatican. A cousin had been nominated to run as Nixon's V.P. in 1960. They collected many honors. Would Arnold "collect" Anne?

We shuffled through dry leaves beside the sluggish Tiber (*Tevere*). "Some people," W. L. maintained, "brag about what they do, and others, what they don't do. Cellini lied about both." W.L. seemed to have drawn Ferrell's own portrait in just thirteen words.

Anita, walking beside Reed Del Vecchio, was talking, not about Cellini, but cars, for Reed sold Alpha Romeos. They didn't hear Ferrell's command to cross the street. I ran ahead to herd them, a poor shepherdess. I recalled paintings of Marie Antoinette at the Petit Trianon. Never got her satin gown dirty; never chased a wayward lamb. That shepherdess was herself led to the slaughter (1792).

We straggled toward the *Campo Martio* (Field of Mars). There, a year before grasping power (B.C. 28) Octavian, later Augustus, built his tomb, now decayed. We peered into it, briefly through tall weeds and a rusty grill. "To each his own," observed W.L. (*Lat., Suum cuique*). "Cicero." Did he mean to each man his own grave? W.L. had a classical education and often expressed his own thoughts through the lips of some Greek or Latin sage.

Sam said, "Augustus should have provided for the grave's eternal maintenance."

"It wasn't always so," mused Rob. "It was a gardened jewel when Augustus built it." The modern *Ara Pacis* (Altar of Peace–B.C.11) stood nearby, housed in a modern steel and glass structure. We glanced at its altar to Augustus and his dysfunctional family including a toddler grandson who was clinging to his mother's skirts.

"Babies, thank goodness, don't change," said Jan Huntsman, a grandmotherly soul.

"Nor do dictators, however much they may smile," Andrea said, pressing against W.L., smiling.

"*Hamlet, Prince of Denmark*," W.L. said, regarding her carefully. "Like Augustus, Hamlet's uncle smiled a lot for... 'one may smile, and smile, and be a villain.'" (Shakespeare, *Hamlet, I, v.,106*). W.L. was adept at quoting Renaissance authors as well as classical ones. Andrea looked happy, vindicated by her own vagueness. I wondered what gave her, a married woman, the audacity to try out her limited learning on an erudite scholar? W.L. knew why the comparison between Augustus and the King of Denmark was appropriate. He knew I knew. Suddenly,

I wanted to talk about Augustus and Hamlet's uncle with W.L. Lie. I just wanted to talk with W.L.

Sister Agatha remarked, "Augustus was famed for morality." Ferrell quibbled. "Famed for fooling a bunch of Senators into passivity; starving his daughter, Julia, slaughtering his enemies, and murdering his granddaughter's husband," Rob rehearsed, dryly. I wished he hadn't pricked the Sister's bubble. We all imagined some heads of state to be moral and competent. Few were.

We passed the Palazzo Borghese, once Paolina's home. We didn't pause, as we were anxious for lunch. The rectangular Piazza Navona, built on Domitian's stadium (first century A.D.) had two Bernini fountains and the Church of St. Agnes (*Sant'Agnese*), a virgin martyred for refusing to marry a pagan. Couldn't love have converted him? It did her.

"Ah-h!" chorused the group, once we drew near to the Piazza. Sam said, "Smell that food!" Aromas of fried shrimp (*scampi fritti*), stuffed Italian pancakes (*cannelloni*), noodles with ox duodenum and tails (*rigatoni alla vaccinara*), and frying pork fat (*strutto*), matured a year. The smell of garlic, rosemary and anchovy paste drove the group wild. Unfortunately, I lost my appetite. I often feel hungry; smell food, and lose my appetite before I use it. Kind of like relationships. I'd never had a really good one that satisfied my appetite—or nourished my soul.

Ferrell said, confident and in charge, "Our reservations are for *Da Peppo*, just behind Bernini's Four Rivers Fountain, an informal restaurant (*trattoria*)."

Its Italian name meant simply, "At Beppo's."

"This is one of our prepaid lunches," Ferrell announced. Happily we approached *Da Beppo*, shaded by awnings. Who said there was no free lunch?

They seated us at two long tables near the fountain. Green tablecloths, small bouquets, signs saying, "Welcome, Altamonte College" lent a festive air. Cypress trees (*cipresse*) in tubs gave privacy to what was in fact the public square, chief entertainment besides ourselves.

We had a choice of four appetizers: mixed cold cuts (*salumeria miste*); artichokes (*carciòfi*); mixed seafood (*frutti di mare misti*); or raw vegetables in a hot sauce of anchovies, garlic, and truffles (*bagna cauda*). The second course was pizza; *margherita* (tomato, cheese and basil); *napoletana* (anchovies, ham, capers, tomatoes, cheese and oregano; or *siciliana* (black olives, capers and cheese). Each table had big bowels of mixed green salad (*insalata mista*). Desserts included three flavors of ice cream (*gelati tre sapori),* or sponge cake (*cassata siciliana)* garnished with sweet cream cheese, chocolate and candied fruit. We ordered individually, four waiters (*camerieri*) to a table. Beer (*birra*) and wine (*vino*) flowed.

Sam and Samantha drained two glasses of each. I drank sparkling mineral water (*acqua minerale, "gassata"*). With W.L to my right, and Ferrell to my left, I needed a clear head. Across from us, the Huntsmans and Harkers chatted happily. They discussed Etruscan art, the geology of various Etruscan areas, Jim Harker having been a geologist. Rob was charming, almost the perfect host. He offered toasts (*brindisi*) to us all, the college, to me (!) and the owner of Da Beppo.

That was Signor Beppo, a man in his late seventies, who watched over us, anxious that we enjoy his hospitality. He watched Rob and W.L. closely. I watched him watching them. I ate very little, a phenomenon Mom called "Candida's cancellation"–present at table, but appetite cancelled (*cancellato*). I nibbled at my salad; played with my pizza, and ate every crumb of my *cassata siciliana*.

W. L. was not only attentive to me, but to Rob, who acted as if he couldn't trust himself to trust W. L., nor not to. The same way Rob seemed to feel about me. He did and did not care about me, but intensely; in perfect equilibrium. Why both men were flanking me now was a puzzle. *Rob should have seated himself at the second table*, I thought, to qualify as a really perfect host. Perhaps he liked the view of the fountain up closer, with its four river gods symbolizing papal significance on four continents. Neither man trusted the other in my company. Perhaps because only when we were all three together, they did? *"Forse che sì, forse....."*

Finally, Rob rose and signed the bill Signor Beppo had already prepared for the head waiter, who gave it to a cashier inside. Most people went inside to use the facilities. I waited outside, alone. Signor Beppo approached me.

"Signorina Dalloway," he said. He knew my name! "I wish to warn you–for the love of *Dio* (God). Be alert. You are running a particular risk." (*un rischio particolare*.) With that, he disappeared into a rear entrance. My stomach tightened, and for a long moment, I really felt something akin to fear. I broke into a cold sweat—on a hot day. What did Signor Beppo mean by the phrase "*rischio particolare*"? He knew *nothing* about me but my name.

Then, on to St. Peter's! Carlo swore when two bikers (*motociclisti*) swerved in front of him near Angel Bridge (*Ponte Angelo*), thereby risking becoming "angels" themselves. The bus emptied. Ellen emerged last. The doors caught her purse strings. Bill yanked them loose, tearing one, but knotting both around her neck. Ferrell and I unfurled our flags, as the square, Bernini's design, was crowded.

The first St. Peter's, Constantine's, was built over the assumed spot of Peter's martyrdom (68 A.D.). It was replaced at the beginning of the fifteenth century; completed in the eighteenth. We entered, watched by Vatican guards as we passed through bronze doors of the former basilica, "with reliefs by Filarete," Ferrell intoned (mid fifteenth century). St. Peter's was supposed to provide relief. We stood in a basilica six hundred fifteen feet long, under Michelangelo's dome—unfinished in his lifetime—four hundred forty-eight feet tall. The basilica's size militated against comfort.

A few prayed, perhaps for relief from our fellow tourists, who swelled down the right hand aisle by the hundreds, pausing before Michelangelo's statue of Mary and the dead Christ, the *Pietà*, a statuary pair damaged last year by a hammer wielding madman who broke Mary's arm at the elbow, damaged her eyelid, chipped her nose. Mary got a nose job, orthopedic surgery and a blepharoplasty.

After the thirteenth century statue of St. Peter, Arnolfo Cambio's work, Peter's foot had thinned from too many kisses. I wondered how much bronze one pair of lips absorbed kissing that toe? Was bronze carcinogenic? Lipstick was.

We progressed to the baldachin, Bernini's (1624). Four columns twisted up toward Michelangelo's dome, demarcating the presumed spot of St. Peter's tomb below the altar. The site of Peter's martyrdom and burial was not scientifically settled. Constantine's guess (fourth century)—the Vatican hill site—had a definitive influence on the Church, based on an ancient marker; second century). Excavations (1939) produced no proof that Peter's remains had been located. Faith, as usual, trumped fact. With so much to see, there was little interest in climbing five hundred thirty-seven steps to the summit of the dome and more to the cupola. I'd leave that for another trip to Rome.

We filed up the left hand aisle, glancing casually at stations of the cross; side chapels, stained glass. Ferrell turned taciturn. Perhaps as an ex-Baptist he was revolted by such obvious religious authority, even if he were himself an authority on so much that was religious, namely, religious art? Ambiguity here. There was so much in life. Anita and Reed walked ahead, two 'Italians' amid the barbarians. Sister Agatha said "hello" (*Salve*), to some Poor Clares in Latin. Perhaps they thought she was Catholic, not Anglican. W.L kissed Peter's foot!

"Why?" I asked, noting his hazel eyes (grayish-brown) sparkling with humor. "Oh, Peter suffers pangs of conscience, and is emotionally needy. He denied Christ three times. That would have bothered his conscience."

"And you don't think having this church and holding the keys cheers him up?" I asked.

"A Jewish fisherman? Nah! How would *you* feel if *your* toe was sucked?" W.L. could be acerbic and off-color, too. Was his observation a joke, an act of mockery, or a veiled invitation? Were the keys to be mine? Was I a rock on which to build, or just dense, like a statue?

Sister Agnes announced that she would "be dining with the Clares this evening," and would ride with them to their convent and take a taxi back to our hotel.

"Tell Allison not to wait up!" she directed, and trooped off with the Franciscan Clares, a blue-bird among brown sparrows. Ferrell was exiting the Filarete doors. We hurried after him.

Reassembled outside, the group marched down the left colonnade to view Charlemagne, victim of a mediocre eighteenth century sculptor. His horse looked more lively than Charles (d. 814). The reverse march gave us Bernini's Constantine, eyes on the sky, reading, "*In hoc signo vinces.*" (By this sign, you will conquer). It was on Pall Mall cigarettes, my first Latin lesson. Dad was still smoking then. Constantine's horse was faster than Secretariat, who won the Triple Crown last May. Constantine had won out over three Roman rulers. Historians point out that he kept all their power and the title Chief Priest, *Pontifex Maximus*; like later, the popes did. He never outlawed paganism, only converting to Christ on his deathbed (337 A.D.) Prudent. He built churches to show his good faith. What would ours be, I wondered?

My faith had been in my father. Dad had taught me to stand alone, given me a superior education when still a young child. But standing alone and being quite alone are two different things. Which would prove my fate? Only time would tell.

CHAPTER VIII

HIGHER SPIRITS IN COMMON PLACES

Our bus waited. Carlo was reading *L'Osservatore Romano*, a Catholic paper. Carlo, a believer, was not a churchgoer (*Credente, ma non praticante*). In Italy, women went to church more than men, who frequented bars, cafés, and *bocce* ball games–and women.

We were off to Trastevere for dinner! Ellen waved Carlo back after the bus emptied. She had left her shawl in the bus. While she retrieved it, the cars behind the bus honked mercilessly. Shawl in hand, she waved coquettishly at their drivers.

Trastevere was medieval in appearance, peopled by international riffraff, some very rich; restaurant goers, revelers. It was less crowded than central Rome. Tourists enjoyed the district's reasonable prices before returning to their lodgings. Romans conquered the Etruscans here. They named it Trastevere (across the Tiber), but avoided taking up residence here for several centuries. Jews and Syrians arrived in the first century A.D.

In the third century, Catholics moved in. They may have convinced Pope Calixtus to found Rome's oldest church there. Some say their motive was a cheaper building site; others, that oil gushed up here on Christ's birthday, sign of the site's holiness. There was a problem with Christ's birthday. Mithras, an old Persian god, shared it. Considered a savior by Rome's legions, Mithras was the name in which Rome's legionaries had been baptized. Later, they shared a sacred meal in his honor. Any special rewards (booty) for good behavior, i.e., victory in battle, were provided by the god as well.

"Did Mithras have sacred oil?" I asked Rob. He thought a moment. His answer was generic.

"In antiquity, as you probably know," he said thoughtfully, "oil was a sign of salvation and was used in lamps for lighting, cooking, and as a soap substitute."

I still wondered why it was a sign of salvation? W.L. stroked his chin. His eyebrow went up; he was thinking.

"Oil was early regarded as a purifier. A kind of soft soap. Romans used it in their baths." W.L. smiled before continuing. "In *Psalm 22* the Lord anointed a believer's head with oil just before his 'cup runneth over,' and Jesus reproached a Pharisee who invited him to dinner, for *not* having anointed his head with oil (*Luke 7:46*). It may have had a significance of welcoming, caring. An unknown woman there won Jesus's approval because she bathed his feet in her own tears, and dried them with her own hair, before rubbing costly myrrh on them. She was Mary Magdalene and carries an ointment jar in Renaissance paintings of her, there being oil in myrrh. Her act was devotional, but also sacrificial. It may be, Candida, that oil was precious because the Middle East was so dry. Everyone needed moisturizers."

Jonah Schoenstein, whose insurance business was international, and who, as an ardent Zionist, was particularly interested in things that affected Israel, said, "The West still thirsts for Middle Eastern oil." Ralph Huntsman looked thoughtful.

"Neither of you really know," Ralph told them, "if oil were sacred to Mithras. But you may be on the right track. Oil was prized in ancient times as a panacea for many ills, including mortality. They anointed the head of the dying with oil, and still do in Roman Catholicism. We prize it now for running all our fancy machinery. The olive tree was sacred to Athena and the Minoans on Crete long before Christianity. Latins planted olives because they learned of the utility of olives from the Greeks in *Magna Graecia*, (Greater Greece, i.e., southern Italy)," Ralph paused, before adding: "The ancients cooked with olive oil, traded with it or for it; took it as a laxative. They rubbed it on athletes' bodies to make them harder for opponents to tackle. Oil lamps lit rooms and terraces for parties!"

I thought about all these uses of oil before adding my two cents' worth. "But today oil threatens the environment and makes us dependent on foreign fuel which will eventually impact productivity. The need for oil is politically dangerous. Look at how the Saudis held us hostage over oil this year. And Germany's Black Forest has been turning brown from all the gas emissions." I looked at Ralph for confirmation.

"Did you know," Ralph responded, "that the first person to calculate the rate and danger of carbon build up from burning fuels was a Frenchman named Joseph Fournier in 1824?" I didn't. I did know the word *four* meant oven in French. One of those linguistic coincidences I so enjoyed.

"Stop!" Matilda cried. We should be thinking of how lucky we are to be among Trastevere's merry makers. *I* say, let's explore this old cobble stoned quarter, so medieval, and forget about oil. Enjoy the oil already wasted flying here in the first place. Otherwise, I'll feel guilty for being rich enough to have made the trip!"

There was a nobility about Matilda. She knew we were wastrels. She just didn't want us to suffer on vacation. Sin first, do penance later. So aristocratic (*signorile*).

Whispering to W.L., I asked, "Have you noticed gas stations in Italy called 'Agipgas?'"

"Oil companies are gypping everyone," W.L. answered, "because of our dependence on oil." Here, his voice got suddenly quite loud. "Nobody seems overly concerned except a few environmentalists. Look at the fuss raised by Rachel Carson's *Silent Spring* (1962). Her protest against DDT was actually the first bell to ring out for the environment."

"Well, fine," Rob asserted gruffly, "but DDT is *not* made from oil."

"As for Agipgas," W.L. said ignoring what DDT was or wasn't made of, "it is certainly an ironic name for an oil company. English speakers can see the humor in it. In Italian a "gyp" is what? Another word, no?" It was my turn to nod.

"A gyp in Italian is either *inganno, truffa or furberia*," I said.

W.L. replied, "Ah, the whole world does not speak the same language."

"Let's think of oil in its third century context," I pleaded. Matilda rolled her eyes." Here at Santa Maria in Trastevere," I explained, sitting on the steps of the fountain before Mary's church, "legend says we are perched over a sea of holy oil." In fact, we were sitting there to rest, oblivious to what the ancients knew of Trastevere's geology. Who cared?

Jim Harker, a geologist, did. "Volcanoes and precious metals and marble were really the main geological interests of the ancients." No mention of oil.

I went on. "The *purported* reason why this church was built here in the first place was the holy oil under this square. The *real* reason was cheaper building sites than in downtown Rome. Now, people in Trastevere's restaurants dip their country style bread (*pane di compagna*) into olive oil, oblivious of geology or the environment. They are mere revelers."

"When they drive their cars down here," W.L. said evenly, "they consume fossil fuel, and help ruin the olive crop. Automobiles are choking our tourist centers, too, and our lungs–with exhaust." Reed Del Vecchio, whose livelihood was selling cars, looked sober. He and Anita had been sitting on the other side of the steps listening to our seemingly endless comments on oil.

"I'd like to be more helpful about tailpipe emissions," Reed said, "but the industry isn't ready to produce non gas burning engines. Sorry."

W.L., to pour oil (of a sort) on troubled waters, quoted Cicero: "Oh, what times! Oh, what moral standards!" (Lat., *O tempora! O mores!*), a lament for corrupt times. I thought this a perfectly cogent way to wind up a convoluted conversation about oil, religion, salvation, agriculture, entertainment and modern transportation.

This square was the heart of Trasteverian nightlife. On these steps rested Rome's joy seekers, and those who had found it. We wanted to find it and were privileged to sit here looking for it.

Ferrell announced, "We must look into the Church of Santa Maria before strolling to Saint Cecilia's, close by. Cecilia has been called the patron saint of romantic love and music. If anyone still believes in love," he added, with a quick snort. "We'll look at her house afterwards. We'll admire her neighbors' medieval homes, too, still on cobbled streets, with wash hanging over ivied balconies. It wouldn't do to think only of night life in Trastevere."

Next to me on the steps sat Anne and Arnold. Anne thought people resembling Allison and Ian had just ducked into a nearby tavern. I mentioned it to Rob.

"How annoying," he said. "If we don't wait for them, they may get into trouble." We were all glad to rest a few more minutes, though. Our day had been quite athletic.

"Anne," I said, while we waited for our two clergy persons to leave the bar, "I want to talk about your novel of a group touring Italy. It's about us, isn't it?" She laughed, clasping her knees, letting Arnold rub the tired places between her shoulders blades. Years as an accountant had left her back muscles and shoulder nerves compromised.

"No, not exactly. Yes, maybe. But I'm just taking notes now." She drew a spiral notebook from her bag. "I haven't put much into this yet."

"Do we merit a novel?" I dropped my voice, "We're not so interesting a group."

"You think not?" she asked. "I find us fascinating. Too bad we don't get to talk much, Candida, since Ferrell" (she dropped hers, too) "keeps us on the go. When he talks of art, it seems more significant than *us*. But when Arnold talks about the two of us, it seems more significant than art."

I wondered which *was* more significant? Renaissance art or the private lives of our contemporaries? The question was worth asking. After all, our lives were very short–great art would last so much longer, or as the Romans had it from Hippocrates, (Lat.) *Ars lunga, vita brevis* (Art lasts long, life is short). I was curious if Anne had something on me in her notes, but was afraid to ask. I did not wish to compromise her project or crowd her artistically. I was pretty sure, though, that she would never finish that novel. So many people start them; then, finding it difficult, abandon them. Novelists and novels are "stuff such as dreams are made on," (Shakespeare. *The Tempest* I, v., 103).

In high school, I played Miranda. A story's characters take over while authors sleep. Not that I took over Miranda. Rather, Miranda took me over. I was looking for my Prince Ferdinand even then. In a similar vein, hadn't a number of our tourists switched roles–partners–last night in the hotel, when people were pairing off, petitioning each other for tenderness and nightgowns; wishing to revive youthful memories; share sexual thrills? If this happened in real life, why not in novels? I had, so far, been a purely academic writer. I'd never seriously considered writing fiction. One might lose control of one's characters. Of one's self. The creation of dream worlds might prove "a particular risk," to quote Signor Beppo.

126

Before entering Santa Maria in Trastevere, two attractive strangers joined us. A woman in a pink minidress, wearing high-heeled fuchsia slides and carrying a large fuchsia bag stood arm in arm with a fellow wearing Gucci sunglasses and white flannel pants, topped by a neat striped sports jacket and a foulard. They looked like socialites (*il bel mondo*), but on closer inspection proved to be Allison Rollins and Ian MacDonald. Seeing them, Ferrell whistled. The sound alone hinted at cynicism. His charm drew crowds; it did not encourage relationships. Whereas W.L. shared his immense knowledge to guide lost individuals, Rob used his to herd them. Or so it seemed to me.

"Do we owe all this to Aunt Agatha dining with the Poor Clares?" Rob asked.

Allison, laughing, replied, "All this is owed to Versace's summer sales, Prof. Ferrell." Ian looked happy, but said nothing. Allison was an heiress, and could afford high fashion with her credit card. Maybe Ian's family could, too. He had gone to Princeton. Neither were earning real money.

Our peep into Santa Maria was brief. Inside was a glorious Byzantine dome. Christ and Mary were seated. The Virgin wore a gold crown, flanked by male saints, looking like waiters. Christ waited on them all. Below, a semicircle of twelve sheep. Do suburbanites know how smelly sheep are, how stupid? I had herded them on a friend's farm once, with a smart dog. Did Christ own a dog? Why did Christians call people sheep? Why did Christ carry a shepherd's crook? The implications were obvious. I thought of William J. Lederer's book *A Nation of Sheep* (1961). Followers could get into plenty of trouble.

Then off to Saint Cecilia's church. I would have loved to explore one of those medieval apartment houses we passed. They looked humble, but some were renovated. Rich foreigners bought them. As we picked our way along narrow cobbled streets, Rob retold a fifth century legend in which Saint Cecilia, a noble Roman girl, was early betrothed to a pagan named Valerian. After the engagement she told him she had vowed her virginity to God at five.

"Do five year olds know about virginity?" Myrna asked.

"This one was precocious," Barry muttered.

"Probably she waited a while to tell him," Sam responded.

"Why did she wait so long?" asked Belinda.

Allison, thoughtful, replied, "Perhaps she knew about virginity at five, but not how it might work in a relationship. More likely, she did not get to see him for ten years or so."

"Anyway," Rob continued, "an angel told her she had made the right choice. Valerian wasn't sure, but said he'd honor her vow if he could talk to the angel first. 'Impossible,' Cecilia replied. 'You were never baptized.' On his way home Valerian got baptized. He returned to see his fiancée talking to the angel. Although his brother had also converted, they never spoke to Cecilia's angel. They were martyred before they made their approach." Ferrell's voice was so inexpressive it was easy to see that he lent this story no credibility. Perhaps an idle monk had made the whole thing up? They were the media moguls then. I knew. I had written a term paper once about Pope Joan, traceable to a salacious, perhaps disappointed and irreverent monk.

We trooped into St. Cecilia's, just as the priest was saying, "Go. Mass is over."(*Lat., Ita, missa est*). The communicants, left. Marble columns from the Baths of Caracalla, and a Byzantine dome were lovely; but the exquisite altar under which Cecilia lay outdid them. She, too, had been martyred after giving her possessions to the poor. She had angered Almachius, a Roman prefect, whose Latin name meant blemish (*macula*). This detail was itself suspicious. Anyway, Almachius, who may have lusted after her, ordered Cecilia steamed to death. She lived three more days, and would not die without the last sacrament. Then she was beheaded.

But here she was whole, holy and beautiful in sleep. Her marble head was wrapped in 'cloth,' face down on a marble mattress. Her skin looked creamy, sculpted of pure white marble. Perhaps it was due to the result of all that steam. She lay in a red marble niche with blue lapis trim, surrounded by two nude male angels atop her effigy, and three cherubs (*putti*) below. Red and white marble panels screened her niche. She was not in ecstasy, just sleeping on her side, wearing a nightgown identical to my favorite Eileen West one. If I wear any at all, it has to be an Eileen West. Cecilia had impeccable taste.

When this saint's remains were exposed in 1599 by Cardinal Sfondati, he found them uncorrupted. She had led a pure life. Guido

Reni painted her as a violinist, though the common instrument of her day was not the violin, a late Renaissance instrument, but the organ, invented in the third century. The way she slept, her nightgown, her lack of orgasms touched me. At last, art I could identify with. Like Sam had with Bacchus. Of course, I gave my old clothes to Good Will and not, like Cecilia, directly to the poor. Some of the stuff I gave away wasn't in the greatest shape, and giving it directly to the poor would have been embarrassing.

I uttered a prayer of gratitude for Cecilia, Muse of Music. Our first names both began with "C." Cecilia, Candida. *Piacere,* (pleasure to meet you), my dear sister, (*mia cara sorella*).

Back toward Santa Maria's, we found a tavern (*osteria*) near the square. Out in front were tables, but the garden and a small band of musicians (St. Cecilia would have liked their music) were in the garden out back. They were tuning up in the tool shed. Ferrell, W.L., Anne, Arnold, Allison and Ian, Anita and Reed, Joan, Samantha and Sam, all followed me through the dining room out into the garden. The sky was exceptionally clear, with stars hanging low over red hibiscus that hid the building next door from view. When we had drunk several glasses of wine, those stars seemed to hang even lower.

The men ordered the wine. *Lazio* or Roman vintages were not prized. W.L. ordered a red Falernian from Campania, "Highly praised by Horace," he averred. Rob chose a white Trebbiano, fruity but not sweet; and Arnold supported Latium (Lazio) by ordering a Castelli Romano red he had tried out (with Anne) privately. We were munching bread sticks dipped in olive oil. Our waiter brought a revolving lazy Susan of marinated vegetables and sauces for dipping.

Lazy Susans. The return of the 1950s. My parents were still married then, but fought at the dinner table while I spun the Lazy Susan around for something to do.

We were all giddy by now, and the menu was long. Four of us couldn't read in the dark or had not brought reading glasses. To speed things up, Rob said, "I'll order for us all." Our waiter approached. Rob ordered veal scallops in Marsala wine with ham and sage *(Saltimbocca*

129

alla romana;) eggplant (*melanzana*) as a side. Mom used to call eggplant the poor man's veal. I would have preferred greenbeans (*fagiolini verdi*). Italians eat veal without making as much of a fuss about it as some Americans. Veal is a necessity, not a controversy. Germans stick to pork, which was, biblically speaking, controversial, too. But people had to get protein somewhere. Even the author of *Genesis* admitted that. Who was the biggest hero there? Abel who raised sheep, or Cain, who raised vegetables? Abel, that's who. All I could do was hope Europe's farmers would continue to avoid the "factory farming" that was replacing family owned farms in the U.S. Matt confided that he wouldn't eat veal, but he ate pork and shellfish, which weren't kosher. It was hard to make sense of other peoples' dietary prejudices and best, I thought, not to try.

After the main course, a salad with artichokes, mushrooms, onions (*insalata con carciofi, funghi et cipolle).* Arnold ordered two more bottles on his credit card, and W.L. one on his. Ferrell bought a white from the Castelli Romani, another test for old Latium (*Lazio).* I thought, if the dinner hadn't been good, nobody would have remembered.

Then the band struck up. Arnold asked Anne to dance. W.L. led me out past the dropped purses and chairs to the center of the dance floor. Rob grabbed Joan He didn't even ask her. He grabbed her arm and pulled up. Anita and Reed, hardly moved on the dance floor, just rocked slowly in place, while Allison and Ian spun round the outer margins of the floor behind the orchestra and into the toolshed. They disappeared for what might have been ten minutes. When they whirled out again, Allison's dress was partly unzipped in the back, revealing...no bra. How comfortable. Maybe Versace didn't sell underwear?

Sam proclaimed his inability to dance, so Samantha danced with one of the busboys, and then by herself. She had downed a lot of Felernian red. Horace (inhabitant of that region) was vindicated. Matilda, however, went up to Sam and, putting her veined hands on his sloping shoulders, they danced together slowly, behind the bandstand. Sort of like *Harold and Maud*, the film so popular the year before last.

Dancing with W.L. was not like dancing with Tony. W.L., a lithe dancer, held an affirmative hand on my lower back, guiding me through steps I usually fluffed; around chairs I usually bumped into. The twirling movement—and my whirling head—the stars and the red hibiscus blooms, made me recall the dance scene from the movie *Anna and the King of Siam,* and I said so.

"Ever been to Siam?" W.L. leaned down to ask the question. "Ever made love to Yul Brynner?" His eyes were laughing down at me. Yul Brynner? That sexy, bald-headed movie star who played the King in *The King and I?* Dad took me, aged ten, to see that production on Broadway. I remembered how grown up I felt to be alone with Dad at the theater. I don't remember where Mom was—perhaps they had quarreled before the show started. W.L. had lots of hair, just like Dad did, with a trace of gray at the temples. His hair was a shade lighter brown than mine, and a little more curly. He was not bald like Yul Brynner! Only later did I grasp his meaning. And much more.

Shortly afterward, Rob cut in. Dancing slowly, he informed me, "Candida, I phoned Carlo. It's after eleven, and our coach will soon turn into a pumpkin." Surely he got it wrong. Shouldn't it be a giant zucchini? (*zucca*). This was Italy after all! Suddenly the thought of walking back three blocks to Carlo's bus stand seemed challenging. But W.L., who found and carried my purse, took one of my arms, and Rob the other, the first time I recalled him ever touching me. The management let us go with a profusion of "Good night, folks. Have a great vacation." (*Buona sera, signori. Buone vacanze!*).

At the Albergo Parco dei Principi, still holding onto W.L.'s arm, I took my bag back, and waited for the elevator to descend. "Thank you," I said, for his steadying arm, for carrying my purse, for dancing so well, and now, for accompanying me in the elevator and helping with my door key card. I had had a little more wine than usual.

"Oh, it's too early for thanks," he replied, and as the door swung open with a light downturn of its brass handle, we entered my suite. The gold *chaise longue,* the coffee table—Rob's lilies, all opened now—filled the living area with their too heavy scent. "Oh-h-h! I said, as W.L. bent down and, with two fingers under my chin, tilted my face upward toward his. Opened, the lilies looked slightly obscene, but before I could ask W.L. if he thought so as well, he asked me something.

"Do you think you could spare any further comments until after I've kissed you?" he asked. Before I could think about that, his lips were on mine, gently, having fitted them onto my slightly parted ones like a master craftsmen, perhaps a locksmith, whose success or failure depended upon precise measurements.

"How did that feel?" he asked, stepping an inch or two backward as if, whatever my answer proved to be, he was measuring my reaction with oh, so intelligent hazel eyes, one eyebrow slightly arched.

"Like beginning a Bach organ fugue," I murmured, thinking of the Fugue in E Minor whose first three measures are in middle C, the melody tentative; but by the fourth measure the left hand had introduced two notes in the lower octave suggesting this was going to lead, if not to a great climacteric, at least away from lonesomeness into a duet, interweaving two themes, two with repetitive elements, counterpoint, and permutations of what at first was neither intuited nor continuously developed, but finally coalesced, carrying the listener to a new reality.

W.L. considered my response. "Good, you are musically sensitive. Are you in other ways as well?"

"Oh St. Cecilia," I thought. *"Strike a happy chord for us on the organ or the violin, however anachronistic!"* The very word "organ" gave me a thrill while W.L. unbuttoned the row of crystal buttons that started at my back neckline and ended at the point of the great divide, where a woman's hips are pushed out by her buttocks to sculpt that roundness missing in men. The buttons were the mainstay of this flimsy dress, as the two contrapuntal themes were the mainstay of Bach's fugue. The garment fell to the floor, a soft rayon jersey heap of pink and white flowers–a wilted bouquet.

I bent to pick it up. W.L. took it from my hands and hung it by a shoulder loop on a hook in the armoire. I felt a sudden cool airiness envelope me, as having gently pushed me onto the bed, he pulled my half slip and panties off my feet, gaily hurling them underhanded up into the armoire. But now, as he began pulling off his own blazer and unbuttoned his shirt, watching me watch him all the while, I turned down the bedspread myself, and disappeared into the bathroom, taking care to lock the door behind me.

There are some things one doesn't want to share with even a familiar lover, and certainly not with a new one. When I reemerged, W.L. reached for my breasts, kissing each nipple, before he, too, disappeared into the bathroom, where I heard the shower running. Men do not close bathroom doors. One is lucky if they close the toilet seat.

Teresa once said, when I was complaining about Tony's personal hygiene, that "If a man showers three times weekly, he's a treasure worth keeping." And she was an Italian aristocrat! Tony showered four or five times a week, but he always came to me damp and clammy. He just didn't towel himself dry, so the bed was damp as soon as he climbed in.

W. L. showered and toweled dry, emerging with a wonderful scent that I first thought might be shampoo or cologne. But it was more certainly just his skin, for he did not wash his hair that first night, nor even shave until morning. He was simply the nicest smelling person I had ever met, due to some genetic anomaly. Being near him clothed, as I had been when we trooped through museums or sat at tables together, I thought it must be aftershave; but being near him naked, I suspected there was more to it. Or rather, less. Deeply, I breathed in his lovely scent.

"I shower thoroughly because I do not wish to offend if I work up a sweat," he said. "Do I smell clean?"

"Better than clean," I said. "Just one more thing," I pleaded. "What is your name? I cannot call you W.L. and make love to you!"

As he lowered himself on top of me, one hand between my thighs, gently pushing them outward, he smiled and, pausing first to put his tongue deep inside my mouth, withdrew it long enough to say "Westcott, my mother's maiden name. Westcott Lawrence Spotswood. Call me Wes." I called him many things after that, but I don't think Wes was one of them until morning. Someone knocked on the wall behind our headboard a couple of times. Our headboard knocked more than a couple. I heard people laughing and talking in the night, filing down the hall. Doors opened, doors closed. Mostly, though, I heard music, first, Bach fugues, which I had practiced every at home; then, as our lovemaking grew more lively, his *toccatas* (from *toccare,* to touch). In a fugue state now myself, I heard snatches of the *A Major* and *A Minor*; and the *Theme from Albinoni*, which I adored and worked ever so hard on last year. Before we fell asleep around two, exhausted by the day and amatory excess, I heard Bach's mighty *Concerto* and *Fugue in C minor*, with its thunderous finale.

At last we slept, my head on Wes's chest, and once, uncomfortably heavy, his on my belly. I had to get up and use the bathroom due to the pressure. Somewhere around five, barely awake, his arms enfolded me, and soon, we were way out, far beyond the tides, far beyond Bach or Palestrina, floating back, drifting forward, now wet, now dry, now at the very height of a passion I had never experienced before. Palestrina (1525-1594), I had learned last night, was the music master of Santa Maria Maggiore, and later of several popes, before returning to Santa Maria Maggiore. I distinctly heard, not his Masses, but his motet, "*Song of Solomon*," whose opening words were: "I will sing the song of all songs to Solomon/that he may smother me with kisses."

I was indeed being smothered with them, and Wes wasn't particular where they fell, just as Palestrina wasn't where his madrigals, complex polyphonic vocalisms, fell amongst secular text, including Petrarch's. Was I the secular text? I was pretty vocal throughout our lovemaking, though I don't recall what I was saying, even singing. I was certainly not unaccompanied.

Finally, the sun woke us up definitively. Wes was lying on one elbow, looking intently at me as my eyes fluttered open, stroking my left breast to wake me. He was a great lover. Yet, despite his prowess, I detected a note of insecurity. Why? He was so much older; he knew so much more than I. His working equipment was well oiled. Perhaps it was not insecurity, but, instead, concern for me. He wanted me to feel secure. The mantel clock said seven A.M., so I discouraged his overtures.

Breakfast was at eight. "So, what do you think, Candida?" my lover asked, swinging his long legs over the edge of the bed, as I eluded his grasp and headed for the bathroom. "How did it work for you?"

"I had lots of help. You were wonderful," I said. "So were Saint Cecilia, Johann Sebastian Bach, and Palestrina. I can tell you last night was for me a sonata; a nocturne; a symphony, a concerto of sensual satisfaction. Of love and trust. Everything music gives, you gave me."

"None of the other senses? Just the auditory?" Wes asked, grinning. "Far be it from me to boast, but I thought we hit each and every sense in the lot."

I threw a pillow that hit him on the shoulder. He was dressing fast, and as I approached the armoire to choose my outfit for today, he caught me in his arms and gave me one very hard (and stubbly) kiss, before buttoning his blazer and disappearing out the door. "See you at breakfast," he said. How, I asked myself, does one eat breakfast while treading on clouds?

Then my eye spotted something lacy on the armchair. It was brand new, and I hadn't seen it before. An Eileen West nightgown! Snow white with six tiers of tucks on each sleeve, six pearl buttons on each arm, and a dozen more from low neckline to below the waist making it easy to get into. And out of. I counted fourteen tiny rows of tucks for the hem.

"Cecilia, dear, Patron saint of lovers," I said aloud, "The music was sufficient. The gown is magnificent, but you shouldn't have." Whatever Ferrell might have thought about romantic love being extinct, I now knew it was entirely alive. And blessed. And I wasn't even Catholic.

CHAPTER IX

PASTIMES AND PAST TIMES

To save time I brushed my teeth while showering. Rob "knocked me up," a Briticism he thought amusing, to set the day's itinerary. Charles housed and fed us. But what we did daily was not set in concrete.

Etruscans first. Then, the Sistine Chapel. Last time I stood in line for tickets to the Vatican Museum, my rear end was pinched three times. I put a guidebook into my underpants. Tonight, our first banquet. I hoped it would be somewhere pretty.

I chose cotton underwear, an unwired bra. Cool comfort. I threw over them an Indian print, with billowing skirt. Elegant hippy. My wet hair stuck out in points. I'd admired this dress in Bloomingdale's, so upscale. One hundred twenty-five dollars. Tony couldn't afford it, but Teresa helped him buy it for me last Easter. He's Catholic. It would have hurt his feelings had I refused. I'm not Easter. I'm Spring! I miss him as a person with whom one shares the burden of not having found the right person.

Three raps. The mirror told me I was *not* the fairest of them all.

"Come in, Rob." I opened the door for him, voice strained with the cries of love past. Last night, Princess of Love; this morning, of Frogs.

"Morning, Candida. You look frightful!" Rob dropped heavily on the chaise, overflowing its delicate frame. Glancing into the bedroom he saw the shipwrecked bed tossed by the stormy seas of lovemaking, roiling sheets, pillow crests and troughs; the tides of passion all run out.

"Need more sleep?" Rob asked, solicitous of a sudden. I could take the group out–Ralph as co–leader. We'd scarcely miss you." I didn't deign reply.

"O.K. We'd miss you, but we could *spare* you." He gave me that diagonal smile one could interpret as mirth, sympathy, or disdain. I *was* sleep shy. With a comb I created not a hairdo, but a hair don't before the hall mirror. I didn't want it drying in peaks and troughs, like my bed. "Bed head" we called bad hair at Camp Winnipesauke. I was an Indian

Princess aged twelve. My parents dropped me off, relieved to have two weeks to fight in peace and calm.

"It's Villa Giulia and Etruscans this morning, right?" I queried.

Rob grunted. "Yes, but for only an hour. Etruscans are not Renaissance. Many tourists will remember them as Italy's Apaches. There was truth in his statement about the Apaches. Italy was the wild West then, not the cultivated East." A rap on the door.

"The maid," I said. "She thinks I'm at breakfast." Opening it, I found … Wes.

"Wes," I said, hissing. "What *are* you doing *here*?" He strolled in.

"Oh, hello, Ferrell," he said, seeing Rob on the chaise. "I dropped by to ask Candida if she'd found…"

"Something you left behind last night?" Ferrell asked, smirking.

"A pen I lent her in the *restaurant*," Wes replied. "So she could jot down a new book on Machiavelli. After which my Mont Blanc pen disappeared."

"I haven't seen it, Wes. I'm sure I gave it back. I think you put it into your inner jacket pocket. Check last night's jacket."

"Right," he said, He smiled ingenuously and left. I shouldn't have called him "Wes." However, Ferrell hadn't noticed. I confirmed his itinerary suggestions: the Sistine Chapel; then lunch in a nearby joint, close to where Carlo parked? Or near the Roman Forum? Nero's house? Actually, those places were hot. How about some fresh air?

"Fresh air?" Rob repeated. "Good idea, Candida. I *would* miss you if you weren't here! By the way, why did you call him 'Wes?'"

"He asked me to. It's his name." This was not a half truth, perhaps a quarter truth. Rob let it go at that, but tapped his pen on his notebook and forgot where he was in our itinerary.

"Aha!" Rob's face lit up. "Air. Yes. How about the Tivoli Gardens? It's just an hour bus ride northeast of Rome, twenty-two miles. And breezier there. Cardinal Ippolito d'Este's most pious act was building a sixteenth century retreat for jaded clerics fearful of Rome's malarial marshes. Pastimes for priests! He built pools at Tivoli and waterfalls; trucked in carved nymphs; a few were human. For entertainment. The hierarchy knew how to have fun! Water games. (*Giochi d'acqua*) with hydraulic grotesques. They dampened guests who walked by, but not their enthusiasm."

Four miles south of Tivoli was Hadrian's Villa, (*Villa Adria*), an emperor's re-creation of a Hellenistic town, with copies of the Emperor's favorite imperial buildings. Rob's enthusiasm was itself a waterfall, until you dampened his spirits.

"Hadrian," (117-135) I recalled, "was big on travel, architecture, no? And still bigger on Antinous, his young Bithynian catamite, who disappeared floating down the Nile on Hadrian's barge."

"Suicide or murder?" Rob asked.

"Agatha Christie might have written it up as suicide, like *Death on the Nile*." My joke (*Gioco; pl., giochi*). Rob joked a lot, but now I was joking with him. Between us it seemed we toyed with each other in a humorous manner–when we weren't at odds. The games Ferrell played; those Candida did, (*Giochi di Ferrell. Giochi di Candida*).

"Our first banquet is tonight," I said. "Let's invite Carlo, Gianfranco, his nephew, and Maria, his wife."

"Great idea, Candida," Rob said.

"Where *are* we dining?" I asked. Rob consulted his notebook. "Charles booked us into '*Lo Scarpone*,' (The Rustic Boot). Highly recommended; a vine covered outdoor terrace seating 200 on the Janiculum hill, (*Monte Gianicolo*). Fish, a specialty. Views of all Rome."

"Sounds wonderful," I said, mechanically. I remembered Signor Beppo's phrase: 'particular risk.' Ferrell was ambivalent, but vaguely possessive. Wes *had* possessed me, and not vaguely. Two men Dad's age; each tall, dark and handsome; each attracted to me; though one, (Ferrell) was jealous and even at times, snide; but occasionally, courtly. Good cop, bad cop. *Good dad, bad dad*, I thought. Ferrell never laid a hand on me, except to help me out of the tavern in Trastevere. Never patted my hand or head, whereas Wes was very demonstrative, even, to my dismay, in front of Ferrell. Was Ferrell irritated because I had not stayed overnight last Fall, but took him to lunch instead? *Was* sex more addictive than caffeine? marijuana?

"Breakfast time, Candida. Fix your hair."

"Of course," I said.

I was suddenly back at Lake Winnipesauke, a skinny twelve year old, where a male counselor bossed me around. He was a college kid on whom I had a crush. I doubt he noticed me. Just made sure I was presentable at mealtimes.

Not a skinny kid now. Did Ferrell notice? Wes did.

"By the way, why did W.L. ask you to call him 'Wes?'" Rob asked. "Short for Wesley?" He closed the door before I could answer.

"Westcott," I muttered after he had gone, "not Wesley." Who is *anyone*, really? Why "Rob" with connotations of thievery? Or Candida, of naiveté? Who are any of us, really, and how can others know? Snow White asked her mirror. Mine was draped with dark cloth, like mirrors in Orthodox Jewish homes after someone had died. One day, though, those cloths would come off, and I would see who I really was. In the breakfast room, the *Direttore* came up and asked if all were well? I nodded.

"Everything is fine," (*Tutto bene*). He bowed, and returned to his post.

I sat with the Shoensteins, Mindy and Jonah, and Matilda Visconti, wearing the ruby ring. It had been in her family six hundred years! I urged her to use the hotel safe at night. Jonah, our insurance agent, echoed my admonition. The stone, a round *"cabuchon"* or cabbage-shaped ruby, was an inch across, set in beaded gold with leaves and half moons; I'd never seen any jewel as beautifully set.

Matilda explained. "My family thought it valuable." Flashing in the sunny room, it left a pool of blood on the ceiling. In relief (*intaglio*) with "Gian Galeazzo" carved on it, probably during the 1380's.

"It's a man's ring," Mindy observed.

Matilda told her, "My great-great-grandmother had a Milanese jeweler reduce the circlet so that she could wear it, since she had no male heirs. All the Visconti descendants were poor when the family arrived in Queens in 1890. They debated whether to sell it, or keep it as a verification of a noble past. They had nothing save this ring to authenticate royal lineage."

"And your mother's family?" asked Anita, also of Italian extraction, but working class.

"Hers," Matilda said, sighing, "were starving near the shore of Lake Como (*Lago di Como*) before arriving in New York. Some moved up the Hudson to Amsterdam, where they worked in the Mohawk carpet mills. Others stayed in the city. Four of the five girls in my mother's family—my aunts—got jobs in the Triangle Shirtwaist Factory (1911) and three burned to death because the employer locked the doors to prevent 'lollygagging'. A fourth girl—only fourteen—jumped off the roof and was run over by four horses pulling a beer wagon. Two uncles sold newspapers before they became bellhops in the old Waldorf Astoria. They supplied bootleg liquor and prostitutes to traveling salesmen. My grandfather, father and uncles, moved to upstate New York to cut gloves in Gloversville, or stayed in the city to become furriers or tailors. One male relative made out pretty well as a junk dealer in Amsterdam."

"What a strain on the women in those families," said Maria Pellatierra, also an Italian-American. Matilda agreed, adding:

"My paternal great-grandmother had just two kids in order to keep the ring in the family's possession. That meant no sex at all! Not that the Church cared. They only worried if you *had* sex and prevented conception in any way but the rhythm system. 'Rhythm and blues' meant babies and hopelessness. No sex meant your husband 'worked late' and got his 'consolation' elsewhere, arriving home happy and drunk."

Everyone laughed but me. I had forgotten how Petrarch and Galeazzo II, Gian Galeazzo's forbear, were related, and was annoyed by this memory lapse. Did too much sex dull the brain? Had one night of love with Wes "blown my mind"?

Mindy said, "I'd make a pendant of it, Matilda, because your finger is too small; the stone too big." Matilda shrugged. "Most people think it glass. I should get it appraised, but if it's valuable, I'd worry about wearing it. It matches my bathrobe, anything red or pink and this dress. The ring might be fake after all." Jonah shifted uneasily, but he was an insurance guy, not a jeweler.

"I advise you to get it appraised while we're here in Italy," Jonah told her.

Having breakfasted royally, we assembled in the lounge where Ralph told us of Italy's Etruscan sites—Volterra, Orvieto, Gubbio, Fiesole, Bologna. He was an expert on Etruscans, but that fall in his forties put an end to his digging. Ferrell instructed Carlo to drive us to the Villa Giulia in order to spare older tourists extra walking. We piled into the bus. Andrea Pellatierra sat beside Matilda, and stared at her ring. Maria was across the aisle. Andrea was a gemologist. Moments later, we arrived at the Villa Giulia. Gianfranco handed out tickets.

Andrea asked Candida, "Do you think Matilda would let me examine her ring with my jeweler's loupe? I brought it along." I said he should ask her himself. Maria grimaced. "He'd sooner leave me behind than that loupe. Not that I'm out of the loop, but it's amazing what gets into his. If Queen Elizabeth II were our guest for dinner, he'd wangle a look-see of the royal tiara. And because Andrea is so genteel, she'd hand it over." We all laughed.

"Tools of the trade," Andrea said lamely. I knew how he felt. The tools of my trade were language and literature. I'd feel lost without them.

A wall map showed the spread of Etruscan culture (B.C. 900 to 200). From Etruria, now Tuscany (*Toscana*), north to Piacenza and Mantua (*Mantova*); east to Rimini; down the Tiber to Orvieto, tomorrow's stopover. The Etruscans had absorbed Rome (B.C. 600); taken Greek Cumae ("home" of the learned, if imaginary, sibyls in southern Italy (*Magna Graecia*); spreading to Naples and Pompeii. They went as far east as Elba and Corsica.

Ralph said, "Etruscans are controversial. Theories abound. They came from Asia Minor *pace* Herodotus. The Chaldeans taught them to prognosticate using raw liver. The Minoans called them *'Trrhenoi'* and taught them all they knew. Or vice versa. Neither spoke an Indo-European language, so how they learned was a mystery."

Learning always was, I thought, and as a teacher, I knew.

"They were *'Tursha'* or 'sea peoples' in Egypt; *'Tusci'* in Italy." Ralph paused.

Barry hooted, saying, *"Tushy"* means rear end in Yiddish. *'Tusch'* is singular and means half-assed!" Barry's joke unconsciously revealed that he was learning Italian grammar, but he was unaware of it.

"Singular indeed," said Ralph, but he meant Barry, as exotic to him as the Etruscans.

"Etruscans called themselves *Rasenna*," Ralph explained, "and archaeologists think earlier arrivals, Villanovans from Central Europe, mingled with Etruscan newcomers, and other Orientals—Greeks, plus

Semites. Through trade, the Etruscans began (after B.C. 900) to borrow from their neighbors, making products superior to those borrowed; e.g., intricate jewelry." Here, Ralph indicated a gold earring, Persian-like, but fancier.

Myrna, formerly a successful model for *Vogue* and *Elle,* asked, "I wonder how the lady lost her other one? Maybe left it in her lover's bedroom?"

Mindy, brighter than Myrna, but not the "bunny" Myrna had been answered, "Maybe he ordered another to match the lost one and gave the pair to yet another mistress."

Ralph couldn't cope with pseudo history, ceding the floor to Ferrell. Rob pointed to a stunning ornament in a tall thin case.

"Look at this oval onyx pendant—brown and gray-blue, set in gold leaves; beading on the inner edge; neckband, heavy, ridged; with two gold pendants, one male, one female. So original, don't you find?" He directed this last remark to Andrea Pellatierra, who nodded. He had never sold anything like that at Gumps.

"We haven't mentioned the Etruscans and death, Rob," Ralph reminded him. "They made death cheerful; built condominium-like tombs into hillsides. Each family's necropolis was decorated—with flute players, scenes of marital bliss, eggs, intercourse. Now, eggs and fertility have become our Easter decorations (like rabbits), not Christian symbols. Italians still give candy eggs at Easter! Again, not a Christian symbol. Their Etruscan predecessors associated life with the ovum, so they felt close to the female principle. Indeed, they loved women, dined and went to concerts with them, like today's Italians, not ancient Romans." I thought the Etruscans learned to respect women from goddesses who "ruled" in Asia and Asia Minor, possibly their first homeland.

Rob thanked Ralph and moved on. He couldn't avoid the subject of Etruscan death, for right before us stood the famous terra–cotta sarcophagus on which a loving husband and wife sat in semirecumbent postures, adopted by Romans for dining, not death. "This terra-cotta piece from Cerveteri (sixth century B.C.) was a burial casque. Villanovan forebears used little hut-shaped pots or urns for cremated remains," he informed us.

"Was burial the Etruscans' big thing?" asked Belinda.

"No," said Ralph. "Enjoyment was. They felt they earned it."

"Did any of their sarcophagi have two women on their lids?" Belinda asked. Ralph said he "was afraid not."

"Then," Belinda said, "they were not as advanced as you think." Ralph raised both arms. He could not rewrite the sexual mores of Etruscans.

Rob wanted our attention. "Look how tenderly this couple sit here on their tomb lid together. The man has so enveloped his wife's shoulders, she feels secure. One wants to celebrate their nuptials, their lives together, their deaths. The simple pleasures of sensitivity and sensuality."

Wes smiled, asking, "Under which categories, sensitivity or sensuality, did death fit?" Rob frowned, but did not reply.

Ralph informed us that "heterosexual love displeased Greeks and scandalized Romans, but death didn't bother them much. Sex with mistresses was okay, and love of boys. For Romans, loving your wife was a sign of weakness or mental aberration, same as for Greeks. Etruscans were unapologetic about heterosexuality; they loved their wives." Sandy grimaced as did Belinda. At least our lesbians could identify with Greek culture, homo-erotic as it had been in the best social strata.

"Oh," Anita said, sighting a Medusa's face with snaky locks, grinning monster's head, dangling tongue and flashing eyes.

"That's called a 'grotesque,'" Ralph said. "Etruscans found Medusas amusing, like Halloween masks."

Rob said a different treatment was given the same theme in Bernini's head of a beautiful Medusa. "This Etruscan Medusa *is* funny. But Bernini's makes one weep from the horror of a beautiful woman's fate, and we share the horror as she turns into a snaky monster."

I couldn't handle horror. I could scarcely cope with the horrible collectibles some people used in home decoration. "The horror tales of the brothers Grimm," I observed, "were not funny. They were intended to be moral lessons written to scare children into being good. Modern horror films were intended to frighten every age group. Goodness has been downgraded."

"Etruscans didn't moralize," said Ralph. "They played with dice; loved sports, music, painting, company, sex. The grotesque was not intended to disparage the beautiful, but to remind us to appreciate it. Losing ground to Greco-Roman culture, they began illustrating death as crossing the River Styx, like Greeks. Winged devils replaced wild orgies and eggs on tombs. Hope abolished, in came the dour, dire, dismal."

"Too bad! (*Peccato*)," Maria murmured. Ferrell, however, heard Michelangelo's call. At the Vatican Museum the limelight would be on him and Michelangelo. Summoning Carlo, we left the Villa via the Tiber to the Sistine Chapel.

Artistic fashion was inexplicable; some fashions the Church deemed unacceptable. Belinda, Lynette, Sandy and Myrna Schwartz wore skirts too short for admittance, despite my warnings. Reed Del Vecchio and Barry Schwartz wore Bermuda shorts.

The Schwartzes mumbled, "Catholic hypocrisy," but Reed *was* Catholic, and said nothing. The Sistine ceiling images were mostly nude, not just bare-kneed.

Sandy yelled when the guards escorted her out of the line, "*And God created knees!*" To no effect. Anita, modestly dressed, wanted Reed to accompany her. He insisted she go on in, and the "refuseniks" agreed to meet us at Rinaldo's *Rosticceria*, (grill), visible from the corner where Carlo picked us up yesterday.

The Sistine Chapel was part of the apostolic palace of St. Peter's. It had 1,400 rooms, chapels, galleries. Popes called it "home." They didn't queue up to see the Sistine Chapel. We needn't have, either, but Charles Clark "forgot" to make group reservations for us. After waiting in line in the hot sun for forty-five minutes we envied the "*refuseniki,*" who by now were drinking cold beer in Rinaldo's. Only when Sister Agatha threw her arms out, sighed loudly, and gracefully fainted onto the pavement, did a museum guard return with water for the fallen nun–not knowing she was Episcopalian–announcing:

"Your group may proceed to the head of the line, for the love of God. *Per l'amor di Dio,*" he added. Allison, fanning her aunt's face with cardboard found on the sidewalk, looked up at us.

"She's okay. She minored in theater," Aunt Agatha opened one eye and shut it quickly. She was acting in our interest. Her "Where am I?" was very convincing.

Pope Julius II had asked Michelangelo to cover a crack in the barrel vault with a fresco one hundred thirty-one feet long, and forty-three wide. Thousands of tourists fought their way down long corridors leading to the chapel, and like salmon in a congested stream, flowed past Roman statuary, the Raphael Rooms. Dipping to the stream's bottom, they reached Michelangelo's ceiling, and the *Last Judgment* in the Sistine Chapel. The experience spawned satisfaction for art lovers and the pious, while some, exasperated by the crowds, vowed to buy the best art books on the Chapel and look at Buonarotti's work in their own living rooms, sparing necks, toes.

With modern mass tourism had come sweaty crowds; dour Vatican guards, zealous tourists of the law and order types. One yelled at me for taking no-flash photos! (*senza flash*). Yes, certain behaviors were reported, and you could be ejected, deposited in front of the Vatican Museum store, encouraged to buy postcards, rosaries, and books illustrating what you had just paid thousands of dollars to try to see, but due to the crowds saw only with difficulty, unable to hear your guide's comments.

Ferrell was probably brilliant in describing such miracles of art, but few of us heard even him due to noise. I remembered what Duane Becker, a Renaissance lit scholar, once told me at a convention: that in 1963, when he'd been a grad student of twenty-two, and before international tourism was so prevalent, he came here to a chapel practically empty. He lay on his back on the floor for fifteen minutes of uninterrupted observation. Prone, he viewed the paintings of a man who didn't even know how to draw when he began, a sculptor by trade. Now, Duane would be trampled if he tried such a pose.

What was more ludicrous? Christ condemning lost souls to burn in hellfire, or God giving Adam the Finger? Ferrell kept lecturing, eyes raised, red lips moving, white teeth gleaming, while I tried to answer my irreverent question. Great art, like religion, may suspend reverence, or instill it.

Leaving, we passed the gift shop. No one stopped. Ferrell and I left last, like good shepherds should. Everyone else was already on the sidewalk when I saw him lift from a hallway display rack of Vatican T-shirts a large navy blue one, slipping it deftly into the bag that held his gear. It was all done fast. I wasn't sure he knew I knew.

At Rinaldo's *Rosticceria,* our *"refusenicki"* had their own notions of everything they did not see, and even quarreled with each other as to what was and was not in the Vatican collections. Rinaldo's collection of hearty food was not debatable. He had it all. *Buon appetito*! (Good appetite!) The beer was cold, the mineral water warm, and carafes of *vino da tavola,* (table wine) were less astringent than the vinegar. We ate, drank, and, paid up without complaining, though Ellen balked at tipping. "Tip who?" she asked; "For what?"

"The busboys, the kitchen staff," I said, pointing to a jar with lire near the cash register. Italians do not usually tip in such establishments. The tip is supposed to be included in your bill. Most Americans tip anyway.

Upon entering the bus, I invited Carlo's family to join us for the banquet tonight. *(Carlo, voremmo invitarvi, Lei at sua moglie, et suo nipote, al banquetto nostro stasera).* He accepted with pleasure

Ellen and Bill entered last, she having met up with a post card vendor, strings of cards over his body clipped to chains about his chest.

Ellen brandished several vertical folders of scenes of the Sistine Chapel. "Half what they charged at the Vatican shop," she announced gaily. She did not realize the cards were old, made shortly after the restoration of the Chapel done in the 1930s. Indeed, there was a plan afoot—but it wouldn't happen for several years—to restore the ceiling again. Its restoration jobs dated from the seventeenth century.

Ferrell grabbed the bus microphone. Wes drifted to a seat in the rear. Matt had the one beside me.

"Molly has sprained an ankle and is on crutches. She sends you her love—if you still need any," he said, eyes twinkling. What? Had Molly learned about me and Wes already? It was just last night we made love for the first time.

"You deserve *everything* good," Matt said earnestly. "Molly supports everything you do." It couldn't have been Matt, who was no tattletale.

Ferrell would hardly have told Molly. After her abortion, they never spoke again. It had to have been Ferrell, nonetheless. He must have phoned Uncle Izzy after he had left my bedroom this morning, preceded by Wes, whom he suspected of having 'lost' something–or found it– in my room. Wes had found...me and lost his heart! Yes. His Mont Blanc pen was a red herring. Wes had tried to put Rob off track. However, Ferrell was *on* track, like a bloodhound. And now, so too was Uncle Izzy, who phoned Molly to discuss her friend Candida's relationship with an older professor from Madison. I could imagine their conversation:

Uncle Izzy: "*Nu, Miriam,* (Yid., So, Molly) that's some friend you have. A fast worker, I hear."

Molly: "*Nu*, Uncle Izzy, that's some friend of *yours*: A real scoundrel, (Yid., *schmoynitse).* So much she would say. But no more. Nothing about her affair with Ferrell.

Matt moved to the back of the bus. Wes came to sit by me. Andrea Pellatierra, clutching his loupe, crossed the aisle to sit beside Matilda. Ferrell, to my right, was giving Carlo orders, which I had to interpret. Andrea got another good look at Matilda's ring, but without daring to ask if he could use his loupe on it. Maria, I noticed, looked liked a wife who knew her husband was drawn by a professional interest in rare gems he could not ignore. She folded her hands and sat alone. After thirty-seven years of marriage, Andrea still thought his wife the most exotic jewel of them all. And Maria was a jewel. Once a P.E. teacher in a high school, she was now involved in the art scene of San Francisco, and had done some extraordinary ceramics in her garage studio. Andrea put several of her pots in Gumps where they sold at impressive prices.

We were going to skip the Forum. Carlo announced it was one hundred degrees F. outside at one o'clock, and clearly, our group was not up to a forced march through the Forum's unshaded ruins. Carlo parked in the shade up the street, and we walked back, Wes's hand under my elbow; Rob, at the foot of the steps, watching everyone leave the bus. If only I had worn a sleeveless T-shirt and shorts. Only, I wouldn't have been able to see all I *didn't* see due to the crowds in the Sistine Chapel. I would have had to join the "refuseniks."

Carlo drove down boulevards named Lungo Tevere *(*Along the Tiber*)*;*Vaticano;* *(*Vatican Drive); Anguillara; (Serpentine Way)

Janicolo; (Gianiculum Road); Farnesina; (Farnese Palace Way); Sanzio; (Approval Way); Ponte Palatino; (Palatine Bridge)– following the Via del Circo Massimo; (Circus Maximus Road), Rome's oldest racetrack, between the Palatine and Aventine hills. The track had been an oval course, 660 yards long; the Circus had held over 200,000 spectators who watched one hundred chariot races a day!

We passed the Arch of Constantine. By now we felt him an old friend, and viewed him from our bus. His was the best preserved of Rome's triumphal arches, commemorating his victory over his co-emperor Maxentius (d.312), the last of the four rulers making up Diocletian's tetrarchy. Maxentius's death left Constantine (d.337) sole ruler. He wasn't Christian yet, saving baptism for his deathbed, when he would be incapable of committing any more sins. I wondered if he went to Heaven for prudence or piety?

The Coliseum had held a mere fifty thousand spectators. Romans had sat under awnings protected from sun and rain while animals, humans, and gladiators were slaughtered. The victims were long thought to have included Christians. Now, some scholars weren't so sure that Christians met there deaths there, showing us how little we know of what we were "certain." Gladiators, not considered human, could be freed to fight again by a thumb's up gesture from the spectators. If freed forever, it was to honor their skill in killing, Rome's highest virtue.

We entered when the stadium was free; though at night, with lights and performers, one had to pay.

"Oh, it's cool in here," Anita said, as she and Reed fell into step beside Ferrell and me, with Wes just ahead, flanked by Andrea Smithwitch on his left and the twins on his right. Meg and Peg were wearing coral pantsuits with aqua blouses.

"The corridors were wide so crowds could exit rapidly," Ferrell explained. Some of us went to photograph the arena floor to which wild animals had ascended on lifts. Others wanted to climb the steep stairs for panoramic views of the Palatine Hill, Arch of Constantine, and the Corinthian, Ionic, and Doric columns upholding the structure. Some columns had been used by architects willing to destroy antiquities for their own new Renaissance buildings. Some of those columns were now in St. Peter's; others in private villas.

Climbers included me, Anita, Ian, Allison in pedal pushers and T-shirt; Reed, Matt, Myrna, Mindy, Barry and Wes. Ferrell stayed below, saying, "I'll sit this one out."

I was worried about Wes, our oldest climber, my newest lover. One climbs in brilliant sunshine, and the stairs were very steep. "Are you sure your knees are up to this?" I asked. He gave me a reproving look, a crooked grin.

"If my staying power is in question, Candida, then you should have asked last night." Fortunately, nobody heard him, as our little troupe mounted like goats. Wes and I joined them, last, breathless and sweating, on the fourth level.

"An impressive view," Barry admitted, mopping his brow with a bandana. Mt. Kilimanjaro without snow."

"Do they still have snow on that peak?" Matt asked. "I heard it was retreating."

I said, "We ought to retreat ourselves, as we have more to view and it is already after two."

We clambered down, finding the descent more of a strain on our knees than the climb up. Wes, the last down, was limping. I looked at him searchingly, but all he said was "An old baseball injury. Knees aren't quite as good for all things. But more than adequate for others!" I didn't say a word. I heard Bach's fugues and toccatas again. Love! I was in love with Wes.

Last night I was only in love with what Wes was doing to me, for me. No longer merely the loved object, I had become the objective of a hunter of men, Diana, goddess of the hunt. I, Candida Darroway, had brought down my sacred prey; not Boccaccio, Petrarch, Machiavelli etc., but a professor of Italian Renaissance history, holder of his own chair! Was I now Chairwoman? Or was Wes just enthroned in my heart? I thought "*far out*," borrowing Matt's hippie phrase. I was indeed far out, and farther in. I floated in happiness.

There was a refreshment stand across the street beside our bus, and Ferrell said drinks were on him! Most of us were very thirsty, so we bought orangeade, lemonade and iced coffee with crushed ice (*arranciate e granite di caffe*). How marvelous (*Che maraviglioso*) when you thirst for something, and find it.

Tivoli's famous gardens were part of the Villa d'Este, an estate built in the mannerist style for the governor, Cardinal Ippolito II d'Este, a relative of Pope Alexander VI. Cardinal Ippolito (1509-72) patronized the poet Ariosto, whose *Orlando Furioso* I had taught my advanced Italian class. He showed how man could assert himself against nature–and win. His architect, Pierro Ligorio, created a mythical garden (1550) on the former site of a Franciscan monastery, diverting the Aniene River one mile to the site to create hundreds of fountains, all diverse, in descending terraces. Some fountains chirped like birds. Others shot skyward or thundered over rocks into placid pools of lily pads, wild iris, bamboo, water hyacinth. Some clerics may have divested themselves of clerical habits–literally–and taken girls–or boys–to swim in vine draped pools.

Cardinal Ippolito, determined to outdo Hadrian's Villa Adria. Renaissance men sought not to imitate, but exceed, antiquity. Much of Tivoli's marble was stolen by Ligorio to construct the Villa d'Este. Renaissance architects despoiled pagan art to make art for the Church and for churchmen.

We traversed Tivoli's upper terrace; photographed the plain below; and spread out toward the Fountain of the Great Cup, perhaps Bernini's, where water poured from a natural looking unnatural rock into a shell-like cup that had never graced any beach.

Matilda, Maria and Andrea sat beside Ligorio's Oval Fountain, cascading from an egg-shaped basin into a pool with marble nymphs. I watched with Wes as Andrea Pellatierra took his jeweler's loupe and, in the beam of light from the sun through the trees overhead, examined Matilda's ring, first bending down over her hand, and then, peering up, holding it aloft.

"Suppose it falls into the pool?" I asked Wes nervously.

"It will get cleaner," he said, smiling. Ferrell came over, chuckling softly.

"Andrea is one of the world's authorities on gemstones, my co–leader chided. "He won't let one fall into a pool, nor come up with a theory that won't wash. Matilda will be better off for letting her ring pass under his loupe. She doesn't know about jewels. What one doesn't know can be dangerous." I filed Rob's cliché away for future reference.

Neptune's fountain had two large water jets and six smaller ones, plus seven waterfalls on different levels. Above it was the Water Organ, topped by the d'Este falcon crest. Falcons were birds of prey. D'Este daughters intermarried with Milan's Sforza. Marriageable noblemen and women were prey for each other. Illegitimate d'Este sons became dukes of Modena, Reggio. Later in the sixteenth century, a d'Este married Renée, daughter of King Louis XII of France. Ferrara, home of the d'Este dynasty, was full of art, letters and intrigue. The family needed a retreat position. Ippolito gave them one. The hydraulic organ played tunes every two hours.

I dipped my hand into its basin. I doubted if anything could beat a Bach fugue heard lying on one's back while looking up at your lover dipping into your private basin. The Rometta Fountain was on the next level. Some of our group walked that far. Others, just to the Oval Fountain.

When I was six, my parents took me to Niagara Falls. The tourists looked like yellow ducks in their yellow rubber rain coats and broad brimmed rain hats and boots before stepping behind Niagara's thundering cascade. Twenty-six years later I gave up on the fact that I would always be safe if Daddy kept me from falling.

The Hundred Fountains fill a trough, and one can walk on a broad path as far as the Oval Fountain without danger. I liked these fountains the best. Carlo would soon pick us up and whisk us to Hadrian's Villa. Most of our elderly contingent were milling about, waiting to be collected and guided back to the bus. Walking now up the last flight of steps toward the villa's façade, Ellen complained of aching feet. I had a clean bandanna in my purse. I dipped it into the cold little stream that flowed beside the rock steps we had nearly finished climbing. In the bus, I wrapped first one of her unshod feet and then the other in the wet bandanna, knowing that cold water reduces swelling.

"Why, Candida, how thoughtful of you!" Ellen said. One of the twins, seated across the aisle, then ripped off her Indian scarf and poured some water from a water bottle over it, handing it to me. "Here," Peg said," have another foot cooler. Ellen will get relief twice as fast."

Ellen smiled beatifically at us both, and was comfortable during our brief ride to Hadrian's Villa.

I noticed Andrea Pellatierra's face was very red. Over exertion? I asked if he felt well.

"Oh, I'm very excited," he said. "I found something quite amazing with my loupe, and it has may have raised my blood pressure a bit." Maria handed him a small bottle of water and a white pill.

"I told you, Andrea," Maria said, "a gem is just a stone. Don't get too enthused over these things." But her tone was wifely, concerned, and she was, I noticed, taking his pulse as she spoke. Meg and Peg asked Maria what his pressure was and advised her to keep him calm. Strokes were always possible.

Matt caught took my arm as we walked to Hadrian's model town, with lagoons encircling the ruined buildings, and a feeling of fairyland wafting about, except inside the small reception area, with its reconstructed plaster model of the town Hadrian died before finishing.

"So, Matt? Did you like the Villa d'Este?" I asked.

Matt nodded. "Terrific. I'm sorry Molly couldn't be here, too. Romantics, scholars, artists and poets all found inspiration there. Without them, would there even have been a Villa?"

I smiled at his enthusiasm. "But Matt," I said, "without the poor they taxed and exploited, would there have been any romantics? any elites? any art? The poor paid for it, and the elites preened themselves on it. Matt, who came from a proper upper class family of a businessmen and lawyers, was socially liberal, but economically conservative. I then switched topics from art and economics to sex, though they are sometimes quite similar in execution and no sex is wholly satisfying if not done with an art and economy apropos to it alone.

"Matt, I've figured out what you said earlier about my 'deserving love.' If you don't mind, I'll phone Molly as soon as we reach our hotel. I fear Ferrell has been indiscreet, and worse, that Uncle Izzy will weasel out of Molly things he ought not to know—about all of us. Please give me first shot at Molly before you phone." Matt agreed. Since it was after five, we left the Villa Adria. Hadrian's major edifices were the Pantheon in downtown Rome and his tomb, now the Çastel Sant' Angelo.

Fortunately, we were in Rome before six, when traffic gets very thick. Though Wes followed me up to my door, I smiled, shook my head, and closed it. I needed to talk with Molly privately. Sometimes men just get in the way.

"It's me," I said, when she answered. "I just learned from Matt that Ferrell has spilled the beans—my beans, not yours—to your Uncle Izzy." I said.

"Oh, yes, Candida. I'm mortified. Uncle Izzy is a perfect sieve, and Ferrell told him about your affair with one W.L."

"Wescott Lawrence Spotswood," I said. He holds the Chair in Renaissance history at Wisconsin. Our, um, relationship began last night. Why in God's name did Ferrell tell Izzy?"

"Oh, old men get their jollies that way, didn't you know?" she asked. Vicarious living. Or loving."

"Does that mean he also told Izzy about your abortion as well?"

"God, no!" said Molly." Rob likes his membership in the Jewish Community Center; squash games with Izzy."

"If I tell Rob to cool it, never discuss my relationship with Wes again, could I mention *your* affair, your abortion, his desertion of you? Could that be a stick to beat Rob with? If I were to tell him that I would rat him out with Uncle Izzy, wouldn't he be more discreet? Would you mind?"

"Go for it, Candida. Rob is having at you, dearie, diddling you through a lover of *your* choice. Graphic language. "Just remember," she said, "you're at risk if Rob gets jealous about the sex. Be careful." Then we were cut off.

Molly was the second person to use the word "risk" in connection with me because of Ferrell and Wes. Signor Beppo was the first. Whatever the risk, I was certain I could minimize if not avoid it. Despite the times that had been "A-changin'," I did not intend to "let it all hang out," or "go with the flow." The 60s bard, Bob Dylan, had sung "If you got nothin' you got nothin' to lose."

Well, I had a lot to lose, and I had no intention of losing them: my reputation as an up-and-coming literary scholar, a job at Altamonte College—until I found a better one. I wasn't sure about keeping Wes, given the distance between us, but I longed to make him my future. Even if Rob were jealous of what I did have and what I could do and was, he would not get the best of me. I had every intention of defending my territory, interests, accomplishments. I had plenty of them to defend, and thus, plenty to lose.

CHAPTER X

DONE IN IN ORVIETO

This morning I woke to find myself in a strange room, Wes's, smaller than my suite in the Principi. My head felt heavy. I had dreamed I was in Cincinnati, giving a paper on something by Machiavelli–but couldn't recall what it was I wanted to say. I had left the paper in a restaurant just beyond the city center. I called, but the cook said he had just wrapped chicken entrails in its pages and had incinerated it. I was sad that Wes had not shown up to hear my paper. The dream bothered me, even with Wes softly breathing beside me. It took some time before I fell asleep. It seemed only minutes later (it was two hours) that Wes was pulling my too large T-shirt up and fondling parts of me that *really* needed to visit the bathroom. "Oh Wes!" I moaned, "I need to pee!"

I rolled away from him, pushing Cincinnati from my thoughts. On his bathroom floor lay my used underwear, and last night's dinner dress hanging by a sleeve from the dripping shower head. I needed to brush my teeth, but his was the only toothbrush available! I picked it up, tentatively, squeezing some of his toothpaste, not without guilt. Still, when I made love to him, even sucked him off, I hadn't felt the least guilt, just joyous abandon.

So why worry about a toothbrush? I was using his equipment; he had used mine. Was *he* out there feeling guilty? Women had to learn to live like men, at least until men learned to live like women.

My Latin teacher, Miss Grundling, quoted Publius Syrus, a liberated slave and licentious playwright (second century A.D.) about this: "Other people's things are more pleasing to us, and ours to other people," (Lat. *Aliena a nobis, nostra plus aliis placent*). I had no siblings. Other peoples' things were heavily charged for me, while other people, it seemed, just charged heavily when one used theirs. Wes wouldn't.

155

I tossed his T–shirt onto a chair, slipping into my still warm slot. He laughed with delight and began licking my nipples. He was into me before I had had time to confess about the toothbrush. I had never felt so clean.

"You taste delicious," he enthused finally. Cunnilingus.

"Oh, Wes, its *you* you're tasting. How egotistical." Then I told him, "I borrowed your toothbrush." No answer. He was busy. Soon, I was dreaming again, far from Rome and the Principi. I was traveling in interplanetary space. It was balmy, rainbow colored. Far below I saw Wes and Ferrell, waving up at me. Or Wes was. Ferrell may have been giving me the finger. It was hard to tell in such thick rainbow dust.

I woke again at 7:05! I couldn't tell Wes to get out of my room, because I was in his. I kissed his forehead. "Wake up! We have to get packed and eat breakfast! Gianfranco will be taking our luggage from the hall soon. Tonight, Orvieto. "I know the hotel. You'll love it!"

While Wes recovered from post coital languor, I dressed. My shoes were in his bedroom, with my panty hose. I dressed there so he could use the bathroom. I slipped out when decent, hoping no one would see me in the same dress I wore to last night's banquet at *Lo Scarpone*. I was a bit overdressed for 7:20 A.M., and one sleeve was wet. It had hung over a dripping shower head. My outfit fairly shouted, "This woman slept in somebody else's room last night!"

Fortunately, the hall was empty except for a room maid who paid me no attention. I took the elevator down. Inside, a well dressed Italian businessman with glossy briefcase. He merely smiled and said *"Buon giorno, Signorina"* (Good morning, Miss), for which I blessed him. He might have made some awful remark about my partying so late, or living immorally, or pinched my bottom. But, no. He was a perfect gentleman. Or gay.

There wasn't anyone on my floor, either. Fortunately, my room was close to the elevator. I slipped inside, tore off my dress, kicked off my heels (I had already kicked them up!) and in no time donned a khaki outfit, with flapped pockets, bone buttons, and woven army style belt. Tan sandals, and a camouflage scarf completed the outback look; a perfect leading-a-tour-through-Italy costume. I used to wear clothes. Lately, I preferred costumes. Something had happened.

Teresa happened. She took me shopping at the Stanford shopping center. She bought me six outfits, and new accessories for all, including three pairs of new shoes. Garlic paid well this year in Gilroy. Whenever we spoke of fashion, Teresa's accent became almost French. I had not noticed this before. Perhaps because she was part Savoyard, and fashion runs deeply in both Italian and French bloodlines? In Gilroy, when we cooked Sicilian, she sounded Sicilian, having lived in Sicily five years with her Sicilian lover, his parents. She was planning a visit to Florence this summer. Her royal and noble relatives were aging, though not her older sister, who refused to. Perhaps while I was in Florence with the group, I could drop by for cocktails and meet her relatives, also, Tony's? We had three nights scheduled in Florence.

It would be wonderful to hang out with Teresa. And yet, having reveled with Wes of late, how could I really get back to the place where Teresa and I had been so close? We shared Tony, among other things. I could see now that Tony had been too immature, though sweet. He had depended on me to make all decisions, when what I longed for was a man who would help me make my own. With Tony it had been, "Where shall we dine tonight?" "What movie would you like to see?" "What outfit should I wear?" I had been his big sister. With Wes, I knew I had someone who could give *me* sound advice, as Dad had not been willing to do after he remarried.

Too late I remembered I hadn't showered. I did yesterday, after a quickie with Wes! Well. So what? A shower a day was my rule. Only if one considered sex dirty had I sinned against hygiene. It's not sex that I had a problem with, apparently, but mental sludge. How to rid one's mind of it? Cleanliness was next to godliness, they said. And though I didn't believe in Her, I did believe in good physical and mental hygiene.

I sprayed my favorite perfume, *Cabochard* by Grès, behind each ear. My hair looked curlier than usual from Wes's body heat; perfect for travel. Curly hair rarely looked messy. It was the straight kind that cried, "Comb me!" even after a night of celibate rest; especially if there was a breeze. I packed quickly.

Molly and I went to an MLA meeting once in Los Angeles, sharing a room to economize. Her packing was painful. She went ballistic. "Don't ball everything up, Molly," I had told her.

"It won't all go in again," she yelled, stuffing the overflow into her bulging briefcase—and mine. The secret, I told her, was to keep small articles flat in drawers, big ones on hangers, not removing them when packing. Just fold.

Barely 7:30, now. I lay on the chaise reliving last night's banquet. Carlo's wife, Madalena, had sat by me, Carlo by her. Carlo said I was a good person. I returned the compliment. Madalena had invited me to visit them at their lakeside apartment near Rome.

"That's so nice of you," I told her. To my right, Anita; to hers, Reed. Arnold sat with his arm around Anne.

"I love sitting near you, Anne. You make the meal for me."

Reed said to Anita, "I love sitting near you, Anita. I could make a meal off you!" Such was the difference between the older generation and the younger. The first was romantic, the last, appetitive. Anita wasn't even blushing.

I had asked Anne, "How's the novel going—in your head, I mean?" She answered slowly.

"I begin to see how the pieces might fit together." This was so tantalizing I wanted more. But the waiter had brought the *antipasti* and started taking orders for our second course (*secondo piatto*). Across from us, Wes. On his left, Andrea Smithwitch, his married, middle-aged but still gorgeous, shadow.

"Andrea," I asked sweetly, "How do you find living in Palo Alto among the Stanford medical faculty? You must go to exciting parties, since, unlike humanists, doctors can afford to entertain grandly. What's it like being a medical faculty wife?" Too late I remembered Meg and Peg, each having been divorced by doctor husbands, seated behind us. They turned around in their chairs to listen.

"My husband," Andrea had answered, "talks only of donors and blood types, matches and flight times for livers, operating teams and operating rooms." Then, "And frankly, my dear, I don't give a damn for medical parties. Surgeons are all assholes. And their wives reminisce about Smith, Mt. Holyoke, Wellesley. *I* got my degrees from San Jose State. Their kids attend private schools so they can go to Ivy League colleges. I don't have kids. I am bored out of my gourd at such parties. The doctors talk surgery. If you dress up, their wives think you're after their husbands. I studied the English Renaissance, not livers, not child rearing. And I *like* dressing up."

I might have commiserated, but she turned back to Wes, ignoring me completely. Wes raised one eyelid and put his foot over mine under the table. His foot said, "Candida, your time will come." But not yet.

Andrea was telling him she had written a paper in her senior year at State on Sir Francis Knollys, jailor of Mary Queen of Scots. Wes knew nothing of Knollys, but listened patiently. By that time I was conversing with Madalena, again, otherwise linguistically stranded. She could speak with her husband; but at a dinner party, what wife wanted to? Carlo, fortunately, was not too talkative. Madalena, a secretary in a used car business, told me Carlo thought our group bewitched by Ferrell, whom Carlo didn't trust, and many of our tourists thought me too "detached," begging my pardon (*Perdoni!*)

I said, "Don't worry about it, dear," ("*Non vi preoccupa, cara*"). I didn't want to interfere with the group's experience, only enable them to have a fuller one. How was that "detached?" Matilda, seated at the table's corner, seemed wholly into the next table's conversation. But she leaned briefly toward me.

"Don't pay attention to that, Candida. You are doing just fine," before returning to her chat with the Pellatierras, Samantha Jones, and Sam Perkins, who were discussing her wine red ruby ring over ruby red wine.

Our mixed hors'oeuvres (*antipasti misti*) arrived on balsa wood trays that gave everyone easy access. The variety was delightful: bone marrow on toast (*crostini col "Merollo"*); anchovies cheese-stuffed; (*acciughe ripiene di formaggio*); truffles of Piedmont (*tartuffi alla Piemontese*); various sea creatures that had crawled, crept, or hidden in sand. My favorites were crab salad in the shell (*granseola*) and breaded scallops (*cape sante*). I nibbled at giant sauteed snails (*Bovoloni*), which were not, admittedly, seafood. They must have been too big to work their way out to the beach, so ate everything in gardens instead. Their smaller cousins in California ate my garden. Eating their big Italian cousins was my revenge. Snails versus gardeners: gastropodic cannibalism.

I had studied Montaigne's essay on cannibals. It wasn't about snails, but tribal customs in the New World, and what one could expect from "savages." About as much as one could expect from Frenchmen or American tourists, actually. Art and literature, culture, knowledge, and animosity, are related. Bovoloni taste better than one's enemies (whom cannibals ate) because of the garlic, olive oil, parsley (*persilio*), fennel (*finnochio*) and a splash of sherry (*Vernacchia*). Bovoloni took *their* revenge by killing my appetite (*appetito cancellato*). When hunters and gatherers we had gorged on what we had walked days to find; now, riding mostly in a bus, we ate much more. No wonder some of us were gaining weight.

There was dancing after dessert, a *cassata* (brick of mixed ice cream) with espresso. The Viennese orchestra played Viennese waltzes. Their "revenge" for having lost Italy? Strauss waltzes. I loved Strauss, sweeter than dessert. I danced three waltzes with Wes, rescuing him from *La Smithwitch*, who only "frugged" and "twisted." I danced one with Matt, for Molly. I danced three with Jonah (Mindy didn't dance because the Adventists had not approved, though she *had* learned the *hora*, and danced it at weddings and bar-mitzvahs. The Viennese didn't play horas. Jonah was a superb dancer, the kind you watched on television, in movies. He realized I wasn't that good, but didn't seem to mind.

Smiling down, he whispered, "Candida, if I were you, I would advise Prof. Spotswood not to be so attentive to you in public. Try to keep your relationship under wraps, so to speak. His attentions make your co–leader edgy; and, having worked with Rob Ferrell in various capacities at the college, I assure you that when edgy, he plays rough. He's a jealous fellow, despite his charm, talent, and good looks."

My throat was too dry to reply.

"And, Candida, my friend, because I hope to be your friend, he's at that dangerous age in life, which I passed ten years ago. Fifty-three."

"Oh?" I said, thinking of Wes, Dad. "Yes," Jonah said solemnly, "an age when men go berserk. Male menopause. They want that last dollop of sexuality, that last drop of youth's sweet elixir." Jonah of course, had married a twenty-three year old two years ago. And still wanted it. But he meant well.

"W.L. is a gentleman," I said.

"Candida, Candida," Jonah sighed paternally, smiling down at me. "W.L. is your lover. Ferrell feels insecure outside every spotlight. From a man's perspective, my dear, Ferrell may feel you put him in the shade, though, as far as I know, he has not asked you for any 'light?'" He stopped talking, looking at me inquisitively. I didn't feel the dance floor a good place to explain about last autumn's overnight that never happened.

"Call me if you get into trouble with Ferrell—any time, day or night." The waltz ended and Jonah, bowing, went back to Mindy.

When I got back to my table, Wes was in the men's room and Andrea by herself. I asked her, "Just out of curiosity, Andrea, how old is your husband?"

She looked startled. "Not that it's any of your business, Candida, but he's fifty-three."

"Oh," I said, sweetly. "Did you know that Wes and Ferrell are the same age?" A funny look passed over her face and tears appeared in her eyes. "Here," I said, "have a Kleenex. The whole world gets to be fifty-three if they don't die first."

I thought of 'Nam.' I wondered if she got my meaning? Her battles were strictly domestic. Having smudged her eye shadow, Andrea went to the ladies' room.

On my way there a few minutes later, I passed Arnold coming out of the men's room. He drew me aside and asked if I had heard the sad news.

"What sad news?" I asked, apprehensively.

"I just saw on television—he gestured toward the T.V. over the bar— that a Delta Air Lines flight landed short of Boston's Logan Airport." Lodge lived in Boston. "There was poor visibility. The plane stopped short of the runway. I hope I don't know any of the casualties. Eighty-nine people were killed immediately; only one survivor. I had to tell somebody."

I gave him a hug and some advice. "Don't tell Anne. Phone one of your children. The names of the dead might be in the *Globe* by now." Arnold nodded, soberly. Though air travel was safer than automobile travel, all of us knew our adventures were not without risk. Life wasn't. So much for Signor Beppo.

The next morning we said *"Arrivederci Roma!"* as Carlo by-passed the A1 toll highway to follow Route 53, which passed between two lakes through hilly scenery. On the left, Lago di Bracciano, a crater lake formed hundreds of thousands of years ago, once home to Neolithic villagers who'd arrived without depending on hunting or gathering. They built homes on the lake shore, domesticated animals, grew fruit and vegetables and ate bread of whole grains stored in pots. They sailed in from who knew where, settled on the lake, grilled trout of an evening and ate it with bread and vegetables. The lake level rose gradually. Their village sank. It was now 400 feet off shore, if you wanted to dive for it.

Would our lakeside cities disappear? Everybody talked about Venice sinking under the sea one day. The lost Atlantis, if it ever existed, had so submerged. I wondered if it could ever happen back home? Would seas one day swallow America's coastal cities? Lago di Vico, ten miles from our first stop, Viterbo, was a popular camping site. I would have loved a stay by the lake, but Wes wasn't a camper. Besides, I was earning four thousand bucks as co–leader, a godsend to me.

Viterbo, sixty-four miles northwest of Rome, was a walled thirteenth century city; an Umbrian hill town. Its medieval district, San Pellegrino, was near the Springs (*Terme*) of San Pellegrino, its water now sells at Safeway. It was called the Pope's springs (*Terme dei Papi),* famous for medicinal benefits. Its mud beautified skin. Etruscans had their own spa. The springs held 21,000 square feet of water, one hundred thirty-eight degrees Fahrenheit.

When my parents took me, aged four, to Saratoga Springs, New York, I refused to drink the "stinky water;" sulfurous. Mom thought it might cure me of bed-wetting and a higher opinion of books than parental guidance. They gave me little of that, anyway. It did cure me of bed wetting, I guess, since I don't do that anymore; but not of reading.

In one quarter sat the Romanesque Cathedral of San Lorenzo (*Il Duomo*); the domed cathedral built on top of a Roman temple of Hercules. Ferrell alluded to its recent history.

"The church was bombed by our guys in World War II. There's a Crucifixion attributed to Michelangelo here, but we'll skip it. We're not doing art here, just coffee and a short walk." The group murmured its approval. They'd already seen a dozen crucifixions. I speculated on why Christians often built churches over pagan temples?

"Here in Viterbo, Christians built a cathedral over the temple of Hercules, a Greek demigod," Robb said, as we gathered on the piazza having all clambered out of the bus.

"Why build on pagan foundations?" asked Anita, who thought it sacrilegious. Sister Agatha explained, "Christians were showing pagans that God was stronger than Hercules, a pagan." Anita accepted Agatha's explanation.

Wes remarked, "Jesus, being a woman's son by God the Father, was, from a pagan's viewpoint, just another demigod, surplus stock in antiquity."

"Not after the Council of Nicaea (325 A.D.) he wasn't!" retorted Sister Agatha, unsympathetic to pagan or to Orthodox Christian theology. "Orthodoxy did not believe Christ coeternal with God or of the same substance, because Mary was human," said Sister Agatha, stiffly. "Jesus, however, remained untainted by her humanity, and was no pagan demigod." I thought, "*No, indeed. He was a Jew.*"

Allison had come to believe that the cosmos was created by a female force–the mother of everything.

"I like to think all good comes from the female. I think all these old Hebraic-Christian traditions sadly patriarchal." Her aunt looked aghast. Perhaps Agatha had forgotten that Anglicans wouldn't have existed had it not been for Henry VIII's need for a male heir and Anne Boleyn's eyes. Such corruption, the papacy had objected. Such practicality, Thomas Cromwell, Henry's adviser, had enthused, eyeing Catholic church property. Protestantism, like Roman Catholicism, had debatable foundations.

Ian, trying to smooth over what could not be smoothed, observed that "Christians recycled resources to save souls, to equip armies of soldiers and clerics and win pagans to Christ before resentment boiled over."

"Whose resentment?" Allison asked, the pagans' or the Christians'"? This novice was rapidly becoming a Sophist, a logician. Ian, no. They were sitting together near me, so I heard their conversation that followed. It was a real argument, using the politest of expressions. Before we arrived in Viterbo, she slipped her cross into her fuchsia pocketbook.

Wes, seated across the aisle, said, "Everyone is tribal, Allison. And tribal custom had a solid foundation for those who built on top! We are still building on primitive foundations." Wes took a broad view. Ian, like Agatha and Anita, thought building over pagan temple foundations rightly humiliated former devotees of Satan and helped "bring them to Christ, the only *enduring* foundation." Their view, unlike Wes's, was purely confessional.

"Only this Cathedral didn't endure," Ferrell informed us. "It was bombed by us in World War II. Italians rebuilt it. Their penance for being on the losing side."

"It's solid enough now," Ian retorted, with some complacency.

"Perhaps," Ferrell replied. "But have you been inside an Italian church on Sundays? Attendance at Mass has fallen sharply." Even solidity was not all it appeared.

I decided to talk of volcanoes, now an impersonal, once a religious topic. "This is one of the more seismically active regions in Italy. Vulcan, Roman god of volcanoes, hid out here anciently, his hideaway after the Etruscans arrived. In the thirteenth century, the papacy hid out in Viterbo, too, to escape their enemies and Rome's heat."

I recalled Petrarch's reproofs of the popes during the "Babylonian Captivity" (fourteenth-fifteenth centuries) when they were living large in Avignon. The papacy was still avoiding Rome for tactical reasons then. I thought of how the Prophet Elijah kept disappearing in the *Hebrew Bible*, also for tactical reasons. I was rather sympathetic to disappearing when things got tough. I could disappear into my own thoughts; go for a walk; slide underwater in my bathtub. I might, under duress, hop a train and explore a place where no one knew I'd taken refuge. Dreams were convenient escape mechanisms. Of course, duty always called me back. No place was forever duty free.

"Viterbo's Gothic papal palace dates from the thirteenth century," I said, "and was for many years a papal residence. Here, for a brief time (1267-1268) Thomas Aquinas, serving the Curia, counseled Clement IV (1265-68). Then Clement died. Fortunately, Thomas regained Paris."

"Why fortunately?" Sam asked.

I explained that for three years after Clement's death, Viterbo's residents revolted. That was because they were obligated by law to feed the cardinals and their entourages until a papal successor was chosen. The cardinals put off choosing, perhaps because they enjoyed living off the locals. Thomas would not have appreciated having his studies interrupted by agitated townsfolk who latter removed the palace roof to speed the election and rid themselves of unwanted "guests."

"Sometimes it's not the foundations of faith that are the problem, but the height to which the faithful will go to save themselves from their leaders," Wes remarked. "In this case, the palace roof." A few people clapped. Others chatted or gazed at the scenery. Professors were often ignored.

Viterbo had a wonderful main square. We inspected the narrow streets, the decentralized little piazzas, flower draped balconies, hanging flower gardens, Etruscan vaults and arches, buildings draped with local underwear hung to dry. Tiny squares boasted grand fountains. Larger squares, smaller ones. This old quarter bloomed with potted flowers on every stairway. Did inhabitants remember their rural past? think certain flowers warded off evil spirits and aging? Aging probably wouldn't be so bad if one could do it with the right person. I pitied young people who didn't have the right partner with whom to share youth. I also pitied the lonely elderly.

On the main square we ordered drinks at a sidewalk café. I chose iced coffee, a superior version (all *granite* differ); sweet with bitter undertones; no whipped cream, but frozen vanilla ice beads, making the bitterness delectable. It came with a rolled wafer that I wolfed down. How like life, I thought. Sweetness, bitterness, then dregs and crumbs.

Orvieto, thirty-two miles north, beckoned. Upon a mesa five hundred fifty feet over the plain of the river Paglia, it was a spectacle from afar. Etruscans built no fortifications. Christian counts built many against Lombards, Tuscans, and the Empire's regent, Manfredo, Frederick II's bastard. Germans rulers lusted after Umbria. Today, Orvieto had a military base that trained Umbrian youth so they could keep the Soviets at bay, with a high "wall" called NATO that included Germans, the very ones Italy fought against in The Great War, and with in World War II.

"Germans and Italians were blood brothers, even if each was sometimes out for the other's blood, I told the group.

"Speaking of blood," Rob remarked, "Orvieto profited by a 'miracle'(1263) in nearby Bolsena. An Irish priest doubted communion wafers, once blessed, were really the body and blood of Christ. Then he saw one dripping blood. Pope Urban I ordered the construction of Orvieto's cathedral to honor this Miracle of Bolsena. This cathedral, built on the foundations of an Etruscan temple and two earlier Christian churches, commemorated this miracle, similar to others throughout the twelfth century. But the Cathedral turned out to be the real miracle; an architectural miracle of great beauty."

Wes told us that Pope Urban asked Aquinas to write the doctrine of Transubstantiation because Urban believed in this miracle and that Thomas believed in what Urban did. The result was the Feast of Corpus Christi, largely ignored until the Council of Vienna (1311). It was only in the mid-fourteenth century when the papacy, 'captive' in Avignon, needed more pizzazz, that the Feast went onto the church calendar." Rob listened rather impatiently to Wes's explanation of Orvieto's miracle, Transubstantiation, the "captivity" of the church that recalled the Babylonian captivity of the ancient Hebrews.

The Duomo's Gothic façade was a many colored triptych, with biblical scenes. Twenty-four sculptures decorate the porch (*loggia*) that divides the triptych, halfway up the façade. Illiterates could "see" the Creation from *Genesis*; redemption; the Resurrection, the Last Judgment, Heaven, Hell. It was a billboard for faith. The nineteenth century Swiss historian, Jacob Burckhardt, lauded it. Pope Leo XIII, later in that century, called it "The golden Lily of Italian Cathedrals." Lilies were a key to biblical history and to many a woman's heart. Only not to mine.

We entered the cathedral. Lynette, glancing at the painted altar pieces, said "I prefer this to St. Peter's because one can see it all at once, and forget it at leisure." Rob forgot nothing. He had all this stuff in his head. What he had in his heart was anyone's guess. I doubted it was me.

"This reliquary," Rob began, "of silver-gilt by the Sienese goldsmith, Ugolino di Vieri, was commissioned by Orvieto's Bishop in 1337. Its shape duplicates the cathedral's façade. Inside, lies the chalice-cloth of Bolsena. If any blood dripped onto the cloth, we cannot verify whose. The priest was mythical. The stories varied. We moderns have equipment for coping with fables. We have carbon dating."

That was true; yet we still had to apply under the Freedom of Information Act for "sensitive" facts. The Warren Commission will release those of John F. Kennedy's assassination only in 2050. Sometimes, even the government leaks secrets, but *we're* the government. Those are *our* secrets. In the Middle Ages, one applied to the Church. All *theirs* were kept from the public, too, but skeptics and doubters were called "heretics." Applying for verification of any doctrine was dangerous. Sensitive facts were almost never divulged willingly by power. Not much has changed in that respect since medieval times.

"Now to the 'New Chapel' (of *San Brizio*), where precious frescoes by Luca Signorelli, reminiscent of Michelangelo's, exist. The reason they are reminiscent," Rob explained, "is that Signorelli started the technique of foreshortening, giving a sense of realism and immediacy to drawing. Luca asked to be paid partly in the white wine of Orvieto. Michelangelo, who used foreshortening in the Sistine Chapel, was paid in cash."

"Creativity grew on thirst," Wes told me, drawing alongside. He had opened a small notebook and began taking notes on a Latin tomb inscription. "It says the departed died of thirst," he announced, straightening up. "It's not Signorelli's tomb," obviously. He had the wine of Orvieto." Ferrell, overhearing Wes's joke, scowled. I had noticed that Rob grew touchy when Wes and I encroached on topics he considered his own.

Lynette Dryer, reflecting on cultural borrowing, e.g., Michelangelo's from Signorelli said, "I once borrowed another kid's idea for some project on light refraction. I illustrated it much better. But my sixth grade teacher gave me a D."

"She was jealous of you," said Belinda. "Or the other kid was her pet," Sandy opined.

"You think?" asked Lynette. "Could I look her up and tell her about Michelangelo copying Signorelli?"

"I wouldn't." Belinda advised. "She might give you an F. Most teachers are vindictive." *But not more so than lawyers, cops, bankers, generals, politicians, clerics, and the CEO's of health insurance and energy companies*, I thought. I should have said it out loud.

The Signorellis *were* amazing. "This one," Ferrell told us, "shows two angels, one red winged, one green, blowing ten foot trumpets, while below, cupids (*putti*) swim in a rocky pool. Lower, figures once dead, are putting on flesh; some completely fleshed out, climb out of white sand, others still have bare skulls. A group of a skeletons wait to receive their flesh."

Barry shrugged. "A flesh futures market..." Being a stockbroker, he knew. "That's what 'flesh-pots' must mean. An entrepôt for new flesh stocks. An intermediary market. I guess the angels bought flesh short and sold long. That's why the trumpets are blaring. They had no ticker tape machines in those days."

We couldn't help but laugh at this attempt by Barry to put what he knew to use to explain what he didn't. Flesh pots? Barry knew about withholding stocks and stock futures. He did not know that fleshpots meant brothels, another deal entirely. How wonderful language was. How it could enlighten our understanding while lightening the heavy load of human suffering; help us better to understand religious art, and sometimes, throw us off track. Allison doubled up at Barry's use of "fleshpots," but her aunt and Ian reproved her mirth. This was a church, after all. The "flesh" Allison was putting on was that of a humanist skeptic, a postulant nun. What else was possible? Pregnancy, I supposed.

"Signorelli painted Antichrist," Ferrell pointed to the real Antichrist being thrown out of heaven about to crash into crowds listening to his false words. "He is disguised as Jesus. Now, if you come with me closer to the front and look up over the altar," Rob added, "You'll see Fra Angelico's *The Judging of Christ and the Prophets*. Signorelli added the Madonna, Apostles, patriarchs, doctors of the church, martyrs, virgins."

Ferrell gave me one of his famous smirks. "Mary is dutifully and *humbly* leading this group to Christ." He put an added emphasis on "humbly." I had been quite dutiful and humble on this trip. At last, a woman–a Virgin, no less–was leading travelers to their destination. Ours would reach a destination, too–San Francisco. It made me happy that Mary, a humble Jewish woman, had led appreciative travelers to safety.

It was too late for a lunch, but not for a snack at a cafeteria (*tavola calda*). We headed down a hilly street. At the bottom we found one with a few tables out front. Self-service. We chose food from steel containers holding beans, pasta, sausage, and meat balls, fried fish, and rice mixed with beans (*risi bisi*). An upper shelf held salads. I selected a noodle salad with chicken and artichoke hearts for an entrée, and a small glass of the Orvieto's cold white wine. I sat at a shady table, and immediately, Ferrell joined me. So did the Pellatierras, Andrea and Maria. Wes, late in getting through the line, sat with Arnold, Anne, Matt, and Jonah and Allison. Another table, the loudest and longest was all women but for Sam, who looked happy.

Arnold Lodge was retelling the tragic airplane disaster at Logan. "I felt immense pain for my city, but such relief that I knew none among the many killed." His tablemates listened wide-eyed. Jonah caught my eye in approval. He probably thought I had sat at a table other than Wes's for prudence's sake as he had advised. Was sitting with Ferrell really safer? Jonah, after all, did not trust Ferrell, and he had no reason not to trust Wes. All social realtionships were fraugt with ambiguity. One couldn't avoid all risks, not from airplane crashes, not from sexual rivalry, not from the misapprehensions of others.

Ian looked hungrily at Allison, dining with Sister Agatha and the twins. Allison avoided his gaze. Agatha did not! She and Ian were getting to be good friends. With me at Ferrell's table were Maria, Meg and Peg.

Meg said, "I was so sorry for Andrea last night. It's clear to me she is stuck in a marital rut with her liver surgeon."

I said, "If she feels that way, I too, am sorry." The twins were happy that I agreed with them.

Andrea Pellatierra talked about Matilda's ring. This practiced jeweler, manager of Gumps in San Francisco, decided it was a Byzantine jewel of great antiquity, maybe sixth century, reset in the late eleventh or early twelfth century and engraved in the middle of the fourteenth by the Duke of Milan, Gian Galeazzo.

"If this is true," he said, "the ring is not only much older than I at first thought but of incalculable value."

Ferrell, enjoying beef meatballs (*polpetti*), asked "How much, Andrea?" Andrea paused. Matilda was chatting in the rear of the patio with Belinda and Sandy out of earshot.

"Well, don't quote me. I need information in Florence from the dean of Italian gemologists, Prof. Luigi Balestreri. My guess? One hundred million dollars." At this point, I tipped my wine glass over, and most of it ran over Ferrell's tan chinos. Thank goodness it was Orvieto's white.

"Candida!" he said, irritably, "Why must you be so clumsy?" I remembered in Albano Lazio, when he poured white wine over Mindy's dress, he didn't apologize.

"Sorry, Rob," I said, using my napkin to soak up the excess on the paper place mat. This was not a fancy place. I did not mop up his pants, the wine having fallen into his lap.

After lunch, Carlo drove us to our hotel, the Palace of the Peoples' Defenders (*Palazzo dei Capitani del Popolo*) on the central market square. The Palazzo was one of the most impressive buildings in Orvieto. Begun in the late eleventh century, modified in 1280, it was crenellated for defense purposes. Now banners hung from the crenellations. On the second floor, trifurcated inset windows, arched and decorated with carvings. It lacked only a moat and a princess with golden braids, waiting for her lover to climb them and rescue her.

Carlo and Gianfranco took our bags in through the central door. A small elevator held four people. Ferrell and Wes were large, so I was the only other rider up to the second floor, where I knew the desk clerk was stationed. The group stayed below, looking up at a remarkably wide, white marble staircase leading past statues in niches to a landing on the noble second floor, a landing topped by a stained glass windows, whereon stood a unicorn, a falcon, a stork (an Etruscan motif), shields and crests, with a crown on top underscored by Seneca's motto: *Fallaces sunt rerum species*. (The appearances of things are deceptive). Seneca, a wise teacher had a brutal pupil, the Emperor Nero.

On the second floor was a desk in one corner of the dismal breakfast room. A small, nervous man in a maroon vest with a white shirt and black trousers rose from behind his desk, and came to meet us. It was the same Signor Pignarello who had been here when I first stayed at this hotel four years ago.

"Do you have time to sign in the Altamonte tour group?" Ferrell asked facetiously, since the place was empty. Signor Pignarello consulted his book, and then, into two canvas sacks, placed thirty four keys (one key for Carlo and Gianfranco, who, since they were family, and Carlo spoke almost no English, preferred always to share a large room).

"It's easy, Signorina Candida," said Signor Pignarello, who remembered me well. "All the keys beginning with number two are on the second floor, in this brown sack. Those beginning with three are on the third floor, in this white sack. People may ride up to floor two, but those on floor three must walk up one more flight and carry their own luggage by hand. So give the two hundred something keys to elderly tourists, please. Your rooms are all ready, with towels, and soap, shampoo and hairdryers." He was very proud of this newest addition—hairdryers. On my research trip I carried a small hairdryer with an adaptable plug for European current. He handed Ferrell a restaurant menu, a place called "La Lanterna" (the lantern) with an address.

"I recommend it highly; the chef has won several culinary awards. It's just two blocks away, below the square, beneath a sign with a brass lamp on it. The food is superb and reasonable. The service, excellent. Would you like me to make a reservation for you?" he asked.

"Oh, yes," I answered. "That would be kind." The convenience of a short walk to a neighborhood restaurant where we could dine as early as eight o'clock was wonderful. This fussy little man wished to please, but irritated Ferrell. Homosexual men made Rob irritable. I wondered why? Perhaps at some point in our culture, homophilia would become acceptable, but not yet. What was needed, I supposed, was a civil rights movement.

Wes and I went back to the group. Ferrell was directing Gianfranco and Carlo to stack our luggage at the top of the landing the second floor.

"Here are your keys," I said, explaining the desirability for the less hearty to stay on the second floor. Some of the second floor folk lined up for the elevator, riding up four at a time. It was a very long staircase. The rest followed me up the marble steps. They were a masterpiece of architecture, slightly curved, broad, with statues on the left side. I knew the rooms to be beautifully furnished, spacious, with floor to ceiling windows; canopied beds with brocade spreads; oriental scatter rugs on parquet wooden or tile floors; each uniquely furnished with antiques in distinctive color schemes. The bathrooms had been re-done ten years ago, but some older nineteenth century marble tubs remained, and deserved to for their beauty, re-fitted with new faucets and drains.

I drew no. #311 and Wes, #318 across the hall. I turned my heavy key in my key hole. Enormous room, gold and green, with a huge bed, canopied, and a matching spread. The armoire would have held all my clothes, including those in Alviso. The room faced onto the market square below. The bathroom tub and sink were green marble; shiny brass faucets gleamed. White towels lay neatly piled above the sink on glass shelves. Two huge bath-towels hung behind the door. There was a bidet and a long mirror on a mahogany stand.

I washed my face, and went to see if the elderly were happy on second floor. I knocked on the first door. Matilda opened. Her room was gold and white, with antique French furniture and views of the rose garden. She was delighted, and hugged me. Next door, the Huntsmans were housed in royal blue and white, but Ralph found the mattress too hard. I said I'd inquire about a change of rooms. Leaving, I met Ellen and Bill in the corridor outside. Ellen was upset.

"Is anything wrong with your room?" I asked. Their mattress was too soft. I knew they could swap rooms with the Huntsmans and told her so. "Anything else?" I asked.

"I'll tell you what else," Ellen burbled. "I just found a dead rat behind the bidet. Imagine. This is not the five star you promised! Your job was to get us our just desserts. If you weren't so involved with W.L., you'd have told Charles Clark that Altamonte was suing him." She had been talking to Ferrell.

CHAPTER XI

RAPT IN ASSISI

A rat had crept into the Froehling's room. It had died there, but not of hunger. The *Capitani del Popolo* sat in a market square, where farmers, bakers, and produce vendors sold their wares six days out of seven. Some debris filled drains, some gutters. It wouldn't be hard for rats to proliferate.

The Huntsmans took the Froehlings' room. They preferred a hard mattress, and theirs was right for Ellen and Bill. A maid disinfected the area where the rat had breathed its last behind the bidet. Signor Pignarello arrived with a bottle of Orvieto's best wine, glasses, and "calming" biscuits for both couples. Ellen relaxed at once, he reported, leaving me to wonder what Italians put into "calming biscuits?" In Berkeley people put marijuana into brownies.

I took a deep bubble bath. My hair fell naturally into its best pattern–wavy over the forehead, but not sticking up where I had a cowlick. I hung up the white dress I planned to wear to *La Lanterne*, with gold sandals, Teresa's gold evening purse, and turquoise beads for color. Everything matched! I had never had stuff that matched before. So little else in life did.

An hour later, Wes arrived in tennis shorts and T–shirt. "For relaxing in," he said. "Though there are better ways." His nose was sunburned. "There's time" I said, glancing at my travel clock. "It's only seven."

"Darn right," Wes chortled, and in seconds had stripped off his clothes and leaped into my bed. He pulled my nightgown off over my head and hung it inside out over the bedside lampshade. Tidy soul. After that, I had no time to think of how to categorize Wes, because his lovemaking, at first tentative, rapidly turned innovative, strong, fast and self-assured. Suddenly, I was waltzing with Fred Astaire–always three steps behind–until I, Ginger Rogers, once Candida Darroway, was wafting in high heels down a winding golden staircase that never, ever, reached bottom until–out of breath–it was hard to breathe with what was suddenly thrust into my mouth—I let out a loud cry of pleasure that might have disturbed people next door if the Duke's architect hadn't built his walls a foot thick. The staircase departed without us, through shuttered windows, while we both lay, utterly spent, sweaty, arms flung out to dry.

I felt drugged. I saw us from a ceiling much higher than ours, in microscopic detail, to the last hair, freckle, feather. We were like two seagulls on a white beach having landed from the Pacific Coast. Unfortunately, no ocean here. An oversight on the Goddess's part?

I knew little about Wes. How to mine the post-coital phase when there were so many years to catch up on?

"Wes," I asked, "I know your wife died of cancer, but how long ago? Do you ever miss her?" Pause.

"Five years ago. And no. I missed her years *before* our divorce. Not after. She was a divorce lawyer, a partner in her firm."

"Oh," I said. "You weren't happy together?"

"Are most divorced couples?" he asked. "Or rather, we were happy when our kids were young. Then not so much. Followed by not at all."

"What happened? Had you found a lover?"

"No. She did; her firm's president. She sued me. They had the advantage. I had the savings of an Associate Professor, plus four thousand dollars yearly in textbook sales. Out financed, outsmarted, outnumbered, I was out in the cold. And Madison is very cold. She took the children. I got the books. Fortunately, she did not need alimony and waived child support. I contributed to my kids' education, anyway; the pride of poverty. She paid the lion's share. My son is interning in plastic surgery. My daughter attends Smith, and is betrothed to a dental student." They'll be able to take the old man in if my retirement goes south." I couldn't think of anything to say, so he continued.

"I didn't date after the divorce. I needed a woman to love. Wanted one desperately. But I was so busy writing to get a promotion, and teaching four courses a year, I found I had no time to look for a wife. I told myself it didn't matter." A long pause. Wes turned his face away from me toward the window. Then he turned back, and raised my chin up a trifle with his long slim fingers, so that our eyes were on the same level.

"Look, Candida. I've fallen in love with you. And you know that. I have to think you are beginning to love me, too." I nodded, and kissed his shoulder.

"Oh, yes. Yes."

"Well, you must be very careful from this moment forward. Consider the difficulties. I am, regrettably, twenty-one years your senior. That is not usually a recipe for happiness, though it could work. You yearn for and deserve a normal marriage. I'd marry you tomorrow, if I thought it was the right thing for you. But there are problems. Take children. I've had two, grown up now. If we married today, and you got pregnant tonight (I shivered, entertaining the possibility)–what next? Your life is on the West Coast, and your job prospects. Altamonte College is superior to a Wisconsin high school, and to a distant state college outside Madison. Do you even know how to drive on ice and snow? Would I want you to? I'm on the campus, holding a Chair that lets me live well in Madison. I don't have youth. I don't have a job at Berkley, Stanford. And the Bay Area's housing prices suck. He smiled and sucked my left nipple for emphasis. You'd be wiser to call this off. I *should*."

My shoulders heaved and I hid my face in the pillow. Wes sighing, went on.

"My dad lived to be nearly one hundred and four, but I'm not Dad. I might have twenty more years. You probably have sixty. I might be dead before our children left for college. Could you educate them on your salary, Candida? If our kids were brilliant and won scholarships, yes. If you became a full professor at Stanford, they'd get reciprocity in another private college." I sniffed. I held our whole future in the palm of my own hand. What he had in the palm of his was my left breast. I kissed him, saying, "I do love you. I cannot give you up." That afternoon we spoke no more of parting.

From the *Capitani* to *La Lanterne (The Lantern)* was two blocks. The chef had chosen our meal. Two long tables in pink linen. A cozy gas log cast light and shadows on place settings. The chef's stocky mother greeted us, holding a photograph of her son receiving a gold cup, first prize in Umbria's culinary competition. Two of his other dishes took second and third.

"My Arnoldo is up there with Umbria's finest chefs," she assured us. The photo beamed back. Arnoldo himself came out from the kitchen to greet us.

"Tonight (*stasera*) you will dine on stuffed geese (*oca arrosta ripiena*), after a first course of pasta with anchovies, a regional specialty, and one of my first prize dishes." Then he bustled back to his kitchen, his pony tail tucked under his tall chef's hat, with only a rubberband showing just at the nape. Were outstanding chefs in Italy also hippies? At home chefs were royalty. No ponytails.

"First, second, or third prize?" Anita asked the waiter who served our first course. He shrugged. "Who knows? I'm an employee, not a biographer." (*E chi lo so? Sono impiegato, non biògrafo.*)

Arnold Lodge took one taste and paused. "Of course, one must like anchovies." Anne said, "And pasta starters."

Fortunately, the Italians don't kill an appetite with an *hors d'ouevre*; they awakened it, like the kiss Prince Charming planted on Sleeping Beauty. Not like those Wes had planted on me recently. The main course was so dramatically presented, we yelled, "Bravo!" as Arnoldo led three waiters out, each bearing a goose on a platter, the birds stuffed with baked mussels, a local specialty. Arnoldo himself carried the fourth goose, stuffed with bread dressing, decorated with preserved and fresh fruit. He had been told that our Jewish guests could not eat shellfish, so he made a kosher goose for them, which he sat down before Jonah Schoenstein and Mindy, Barry Schwartz and Myrna; Matt.

The nearest large lake was Trasimeno, one hundred kilometers north of Orvieto. But fresh or frozen, the mussels were delicious, baked in grappa and bread crumbs, stuffed in a well-browned goose, bordered by homemade sausages and black truffles *(tartufi neri)*.

"The waiters marching with the geese remind me of a picture in a nursery book," said Joan Lorimar, to my right. Then, turning toward me, added softly, "I must talk with you. Walk back to the hotel with me?" I said "Of course," recognizing urgency in her voice.

The vegetable, broad beans (*fava*), with sautéed onions mixed with herbs and a olive oil was seductive. After a heavy meal, dessert was light, pine nuts *fondant*, (*pinoccate di Perugia*), an Umbrian treat. The nuts, candied with orange peel and sugar, arrived with coffee. Ancient

Romans finished their meals with nuts, too. We were reenacting a classical tradition.

Arnoldo's mother asked us to praise her son's art. Arnoldo stood at the door as we left. We praised his cuisine because it was praiseworthy. He beamed and bowed. The waiters bowed. Arnold Lodge and Ferrell bowed back.

"Thank you, ladies and gentlemen. Come back soon," (*Grazie, Signori, Tornate fra poco*). We'd been his only customers.

Joan Lorimar fell into step with me. I saw Wes approaching, but held him back with short chopping gestures.

"Candida, I have to tell you something unnerving," Joan whispered. The street lights, so bright near *La Lanterne*, suddenly went out, a power failure that plunged us into darkness. We held hands to steady ourselves. Knowledge is empowerment, and I needed power just like this quarter of Orvieto did.

"Last night, on top of the landing, I heard Ferrell tell Ellen that you were sleeping with W.L. I was right behind him, and he's awfully big. Ellen didn't notice me, nor Rob. I froze, because, well, he shouldn't have told your private business to her. Ellen is a vindictive type." She paused. I took a deep breath. Most older people remained prudish about sexual matters despite the Beat promiscuity of the 50s and 60s. Hippies experimented with idealism in the 70s as with pot and sex.

Joan continued. "Ferrell lured me into his room at the *Principi* in Rome, to 'reminisce about old times' at Altamonte, when I was his student, his lover. We still know people in common and we keep in touch. I took him at his word. Well, he dragged me onto his bed, and I wasn't prepared. I said 'No' but...he is very strong. I wound up doing something I'm very sorry for. and I...I have reason...to fear him. My husband is not the forgiving type, but a hard nosed technical engineer. One day he'll have a very lucrative electronics firm. We have two children, one nearly grown up. I intend to preserve my marriage, even if it is imperfect. I just want you to know that Ferrell may tell others about your affair, as he might about ours. He is capricious and inflicts pain if foiled. You should have some way to...to..control him. I don't. He responds to controls, though, the kind he recognizes as having adverse consequences for him."

I thought at once of Molly's dark secret; the "stick" she had offered me if it were necessary to use one."Did he say anything else about me?" I asked.

Joan hesitated, "He said you were a 'loose' woman; 'slut' was the actual word, and 'in cahoots' with Charles somebody." I thanked her for her courage; hugged her for her pain. We walked slowly on dark, uneven sidewalks. The hotel *Capitani* was black. Our hearts sank because a darkened medieval castle is creepy.

"Anybody got a flashlight or cigarette lighter?" Ferrell asked. Sam had a lighter; Sandy Craigie and Matilda feeble key-chain lights, which illuminated only their pocketbook contents.

"I have matches," said Jan Harker. "I collect them for my grandson." She lit a match. We entered the main door of the hotel by its light. The clerk had gone to bed. By virtue of matches, we made it up the stairs. The elevator was not working, naturally.

I remembered candle sticks on a serving stand near the kitchen. I groped my way, aided by a sudden moonbeam, and found the stand. Squatting down I located four candlesticks, each with a candle. "Eureka!" I shouted.

Jan lit the candles. Four flames burnt a hole through the second floor darkness. Folks with rooms on second floor were escorted by Wes and Rob, each with a candlestick. Those on the third floor followed Wes, Rob and me up the long curved staircase, our shadows goblins dancing on the walls and ceilings. Wes and Rob had left two candlesticks on second floor. The Harkers had matches to share. Two candlesticks ascended to the third floor, with one departing amongst those whose rooms were at the far end. That left Wes, Rob, and me near the head of the staircase, with one between us. Rob or Wes would ultimately have to do the best they could by moonlight and memory to navigate their darkened rooms.

Once on third, I said, "Wes, please go on to your room. I must speak with Rob alone."

"No way," he said. Ferrell said *he* didn't care to be part of a threesome; but when he opened his door a crack, Wes suddenly placed his hand on his back and shoved him inside, drawing me in with him.

Wes sat on the bed, I found the desk chair. Even one candlestick wasn't much light in a large room. Rob fell heavily into the one armchair.

"Well, Candida," Rob said, are you going to announce your engagement to W.L., here?"

"No. I just want to warn you, before a witness, that if you tell anyone else besides Izzy and Ellen about my private life, or suggest I am in cahoots with Charles Clark, I have Molly's permission to tell about your affair with her; and how you forced her to abort. I will phone Uncle Izzy first."

"And you think that will do it?" Ferrell asked.

"Maybe not," I conceded. "We'll see. But you will tell Ellen tomorrow morning you were mistaken in your facts, and that she must spread no rumors or else must leave the group; Orvieto to Rome, Rome to San Francisco. And if she rejects the arrangement, I'll phone Roger Garvey and tell him you are a rake who injured Molly Finkel and have been taking our undergraduate females to bed for years. Also, that you swiped a navy T–shirt from the Vatican gift shop." Wes laughed. Ferrell whistled softly.

Of course, President Garvey, except for not stealing a T–shirt, had acted similarly, but probably learned that careers can be terminated for such antics. Wes and I left Ferrell, taking the remaining candlestick. Wes's lips found mine as the flame guttered in the corridor, and after kissing me, said softly, "Candida, dear, go to bed. I'll help you with your key. See you at breakfast." He managed to turn my key in #311 and I sailed in, pausing only to don my Eileen West nightgown, the new one given me in Trastesvere by Saint Cecilia or whomever. In my sleep I was arguing with the saint that martyrdom was her thing, not mine.

I awoke at 5:30 A.M. A racket floated up from the market with wagons rumbling, truck doors slamming, dogs barking, geese honking, roosters crowing, hens cackling, and hoofed creatures neighing and braying. I put my head under my pillow. Useless. Even closing the windows and shutters had no effect. The farmers had arrived with cheese and fruit and bread; biscuits and olives; all kinds of produce and animals. No knock on my door. I supposed Wes was as tired as I from our late night exploits. I realized that when Ferrell irked me, I called him by his last name. When he behaved well, and he could, he was "Rob."

Hardly anything is all one way or the other. He could be pleasant when it served his purpose. Was I a psychologist? No, but I was growing wiser.

Despite doors slamming, I recognized some voices. The traffic was from my side of the hall to Wes's, where rooms faced onto the garden, protected from the market noises.

Lynette said to Sandy and Belinda, who shared a room, "It's noisy, can I come in?" A door opened and shut.

Ian begged Allison, "Open up, sweetie."

She replied, "Go away, Ian." I opened my door a crack.

Aunt Agatha was saying softly, "Join me, Ian!" I could not have heard anything had I not opened my door a crack. The hall's acoustics were superb.

Peering and hearing added to my knowledge of who was doing what with whom. If Ellen or Ferrell told tales about me and Charles or Wes, I could turn the tables on them! Knowledge was power. The soul of discretion, I had been the goat for other peoples' discontents. I'd done no harm. "Do no harm" is the doctor's motto. I am, after all, a doctor. Of French and Italian literature, granted, but a doctor. I shut the door again, but not before Reed called to Anita. They had become a couple, like Wes and me. Still no one knocked on my door. I lolled in bed free for an hour or so before rising. Solitude had a sensuousness all its own. At seven I showered, toweled my hair semidry, ruffled it with my fingers. The hair dryer Signor Pignorello boasted of didn't work.

I put on my blue denim traveling dress with its long skirt and matching unlined jacket, long sleeved, which I would carry. Today was a cover–up day. Assisi! I dressed for the basilica. I wore tan sandals. Platforms. Nice. From Teresa. Brown olive wood beads completed my "costume." Didn't they hint at a rosary? All I needed was a cross. What a good Catholic I could have made!

Wes was half way down the staircase when I caught up with him. The Froehlings had just admitted Ferrell, whose back quickly vanished into their room. We looked at each other. Wes raised one eyebrow, saying, "It doesn't hurt to take the offensive."

"Against the offensive?" I asked.

"Against offenders," Wes replied.

A group of American teenagers were leaving the breakfast room, looking glum. They had arrived last night after we left for the restaurant. I saw two ladies with them. They looked like teachers. Teachers stick out like sore thumbs.

What kind of class are you?" I asked.

A teenaged boy answered, "Third year Italian from Hoboken." I asked them, How was breakfast here today? (*Com'era la piccola collazione oggi?*)" "A fiasco," (*Un fiasco),* replied the same youth, minus the New "Joisy" accent he revealed speaking English. "My advice? Eat elsewhere." Their teachers shook hands. We chatted a bit in Italian. Theirs was excellent. The boy was their best student. When he spoke Italian, it was goodbye Bayonne, hello Tuscany! His grandparents were proud of him. However, they spoke Sicilian and found his Tuscan almost incomprehensible.

Inside, tables were decorated with paper placemats and cocktail napkins, folded into slim triangles. Our group, totally silent, seated themselves. Two waiters brought coffee and baskets of yesterday's rolls, as their small dimples and wrinkles proclaimed to me, who had eaten yesterday's bread when a student. The bread was already on the tables, as were pitchers of evaporated milk for coffee. No cream or butter here. No fresh fruit. No flaky croissants, either. Plastic plates, cups, saucers, and knives. Spoons, no forks. The whole breakfast consisted of coffee, stale dinner rolls, jam or honey, and, if you were thirsty, garish liquids of yellow, orange, red, and purple in large plastic containers against the wall.

"Juice," said the waiter, pointing. "Help yourselves."

I was thirsty, and so was Wes, who brought me a cup of orange liquid. It was *not* juice. Jonah and Mindy followed him. Jonah eyed the liquid he carried (bright purple) suspiciously as he poured his coffee.

"Candida," said Jonah. The meal last night was delicious. The rooms here are splendid. A power failure is not the hotel's fault. This hasn't been a catastrophe. Personally, I think this old castle a treasure. But it should not be confused with the luxury hotel the group contracted for. I wouldn't want anyone to sue. So....here's what you must do. Phone Clark after breakfast and demand the hotel in Assisi tonight be a five star. Else we might have rough sailing–you, me, and Altamonte College."

His tone was a combination of avuncular and conspiratorial. Jonah was a businessman with sensitivity, not a usual type. He implied that we two were equally in this thing together. I couldn't help but be flattered. I saw why Mindy could not resist his marriage proposal. He was her husband and my friend.

Our group looked glum, and as I finished my meager breakfast first, I was the first out. I had to phone Clark privately, so I ran up the flight of marble steps to my room. Breathlessly, I dialed the number, breaking my last best fingernail. He was not wholly awake.

"Hello Charles, Candida Darroway in Orvieto. The consensus is that the rooms here in Orvieto are lovely, but the amenities not. Our breakfast was wretched. Also, the rooms facing the market square were noisy after 5:30 A.M. A rat got into one of the rooms, and mosquitoes (*zanzare*) for lack of screens. I would guess this is a three star hotel. Correct?"

"No," Charles said. "Two. But while not luxurious, it is central and its rooms are splendid."

"Yes, Charles, but our contract is also splendid, and it states *luxury* hotels, centrally located, *not* two stars. The group is upset, and I get the flack. I need to tell them that our next stops will *all* be five or at least four star lodgings. What's for Assisi tonight?"

Charles was fooling with notes. "Ummm...uh, lucky you. Country inn, classy, very expensive, one kilometer from the Basilica of St. Francis. Large swimming pool. Floral gardens. Panoramic views of Assisi, good dining."

"All right, you'll hear from me if there are complaints. Please review the remaining hotels to make sure they meet our contractual standard. Is that clear?" Charles yawned and hung up.

Returning, the group looked at me warily. "Good morning, Candida!" said Ferrell, in a voice of false friendliness. "I thought I'd take our guests on a quick walk to St. Patrick's well. I don't suppose you're interested?"

"Of course I am," I replied, indignantly. I realized that the alternative was to go back to bed with Wes. I'd be written off as a guilty co–leader, a betrayer of the contract, possibly in cahoots with Charles Clark. We set out for St. Patrick's well after our terrible repast. St. Patrick was supposedly born in Britain to Roman citizens, then enslaved by Irish pagans. It was touching that this well was named for a saint far from "home"–which for Patrick was Britain, Ireland, France, then Ireland again. Never Orvieto.

This well was begun by Pope Clement VII (1527) to provide Orvieto with water during a siege. I confided to Wes that I hated holes, including St. Patrick's well–two hundred forty-eight steps deep, a double helix arrangement. It gave me vertigo just to look into it. The shaft was a straight two hundred and three foot drop!

"What are other holes you hate?" Wes asked.

"Well, black holes in space. Moth holes in cashmere sweaters. Gopher holes in my garden; pot holes on highway 101; and holes left in my heart made by people I loved who disappointed me." After all, I really did not know this man with whom I had fallen in love. A psychologist would have a field day considering my current entanglement with two men, both about Dad's age, one of whom kept cutting me off at the pass, the other of whom had not only made a pass at me, but had become my lover, *my passport to happiness*, I thought.

"I'll remember that," Wes said, squeezing my hand. The well was impressive. The idea of water and life through its presence, seemed a prayer in stone, built by the Florentine architect Antonio Sangallo. I thought of the courage of the laborers who risked their lives to build it.

Ferrell came up to us. "I talked to Charles," I told him. "He guaranteed deluxe accommodations in Assisi, a kilometer from the basilica." Ferrell grunted and walked on ahead. Ellen scurried to catch up with him. On our way back to the Capitani, people bought pastry to make up for the skimpy breakfast. I ate an almond tart that Wes handed me, after he downed something fearfully chocolate. Ferrell bought bags of cherries for us to eat on the bus, which was parked, packed and ready to leave for Assisi via Todi.

Todi, our one stop before Assisi, was twelve miles further on Route 79. Rob passed the fruit around, and we spat cherry pits out the windows, planting trees for posterity. Todi is a dramatic hill town. We parked below its walls and climbed up to its hilltop rim. Legend said the Etruscan town plan was for the Tiber plain. But an eagle grasped the plan in its talons, and placed it on the hill's top, hence the view. Romans called Todi *Tutere*, and it was famed for defending itself. Frederick II, Holy Roman Emperor, ruler of Sicily, couldn't get his arms around it.

Nearing the top, we saw a statue of Jacopone da Todi. Sister Agatha insisted on stopping. "I wrote my Master's thesis on him at Cambridge," she announced. Who knew she had attended Cambridge?

"Who was he?" Myrna inquired.

"An aristocrat and lawyer. His wife expired during a party. He quit law and became a lay brother of the 'Spiritual Franciscans.' A newly minted poet and mystic, in accord with St. Francis, he believed clerics should live like Jesus and the disciples, not like grandees. For his audacity, Boniface VIII had him imprisoned for life in 1298."

Mindy said, "I thought all monks were spiritual."

Agatha sighed. "Unfortunately, spirituality wasn't typical of all clergymen, then or now."

Allison, in white slacks and a tank top, said, "It all had to do with poverty, because St. Francis favored it," she explained. "The Spirituals were Francis's truest followers. The majority took their cue from the popes, though, who feared poverty as dangerous for papal prestige. Poverty meant homelessness, wandering. Wanderers empathized with the laity, whom they never met in convents. Innocent III made sure Francis would obey him. Then he let him fraternize with the poor, a Christlike endeavor. Subsequent popes rejected that idea. They did, though, let them keep their *vows* of poverty." *Double think*, I thought. *There was so much of it in the world.*

Ferrell added, "This whole poverty thing will reappear when we get to Assisi and see what most Franciscans did after Francis's death (1226). No homelessness for them; no camping out, begging for food; no preaching at crossroads, in towns, none of that."

Agatha walked around Todi talking of Jacopone. "He wrote over a hundred vernacular poems, including the *Stabat mater dolorosa*, about Mary in tears after the crucifixion. It was set to music by Palestrina, Pergolesi, and Anton Dvorák."

On to Todi's piazza. Wes said, "Aunt Agatha left out the part where the poet, critical of Pope Boniface VIII, was excommunicated; then imprisoned for life. King Philip the Fair (Philip IV) of France sent some thugs to frighten Boniface, due to disagreements about clerical treason and a crusaders' tax. Boniface, roughed up, died (1303) soon after the encounter. A new pope, Benedict XI, freed Jacopone after Boniface died (1303). Jacopone then entered a monastery." Wes knew a great deal about the fourteenth century. Ferrell, ignoring Wes, pointed to a church we were passing.

"That's where they entombed Jacopone, in San Fortunato." We didn't enter, having already paid our respects. The *Piazza del Popolo* was enclosed on three sides by a cathedral and three palaces. There was much to see here, if one had the time. One of the palaces held an Etruscan museum. Nearby was an Etruscan necropolis. Ralph's eyes gleamed, but we had to get to Assisi.

We climbed the steps of the cathedral, built over a temple of Apollo.

Ferrell said, "The choir is the only thing worth seeing in this thirteenth century church." He condemned a huge rear wall copy of Michelangelo's *Last Judgment*, as "Not a great job." I kept mum. What you didn't say couldn't be held against you.

Leaving Todi, I reflected that Jacopone had anticipated Petrarch. Both were Renaissance men, forward looking for their times. Both took clerical vows, wrote poems in Italian, defied a pope, studied law, marriage, piety. But now, we were heading to Assisi, back to the Middle Ages, to Francis (*Francesco*) Bernardone, "the Little Flower," who spoke to birds, Innocent III, Saint Clare (*Santa Clara*); and at last, to the whole world. Still, he, too, was a vernacular poet.

Francis began as a knight who fought against Perugia. His side lost. He spent a year in prison. Released, he heard God command him to rebuild his Church, and thought He meant a little ruined chapel near Assisi. He stole some of his father's fabric to buy supplies. Signor Bernardone, a wealthy cloth merchant, was wroth. He locked Francis in his room. Perhaps Francis reviewed the Latin and French he had forgotten, but had been educated in; for he was groomed to be a gentleman. I took the microphone from Rob's hand, as he had nodded off, his heavy eyelids drooping on his flushed, full face.

"Having crossed the Tiber and arrived at Mt. Subasio behind Assisi," I told the group, "you are now in a position to look northward to the Tescio valley, and turning, to view Umbria's plains to the south." That's how my guidebook read, as we entered the city of Assisi, jammed with cars and pilgrims.

Carlo parked opposite the twin Gothic doors of the "lower church" begun in 1228. Above, the basilica, with its giant, lacy rose window beneath arched trefoil Gothic doors. In the center, a Romanesque bell tower. At one end of the front façade, a shorter, domed tower's *loggia* overlooked a deep stairway tucked between high walls. A long colonnade ran down one side of the lower courtyard. We exited the bus. Allison had donned a full sleeved blouse and shed her flip–flops for shoes and socks. Only her face and hands were bare. Anita wore a long skirt and linen tunic, with a lacy buttoned front. A heavy silver cross dangled between two firm breasts.

Reed helped her down the steps, though she didn't need help. She was a strong, attractive young woman, the picture of self–sufficiency and health, glowing with new found love. Finally, Ellen disembarked, last as usual.

Ferrell spoke of the rose window: "The work of one *Pietrasanta*," done in the late fifteenth century."

I laughed, explaining, "The name Pietrasanta means 'holy stone' in Italian." Jonah laughed too, and several others. Pietrasanta's fate was in his name. He carved stones for holy places. Something meant to be. So much wasn't. The basilica, for example. Francis's opposition to a permanent building. Ignored. Leaders often are, as I knew now from my experience with the group.

There was an upper and lower church. Four stories high, the cloister could be seen for miles when you left Assisi for the plains below. From aerial photos, it appeared a giant honey comb, with a huge ladle sticking up out of its pot–the basilica's tower.

Entering the lower church, our attention was drawn to St. Francis's brown robe displayed in a case, with his rope belt, and nearby, slippers that Saint Clare had made for him, embroidered with pansies. For remembrance.

"Clare never forgot him," did she?" asked Matilda.

"No," replied Sandy, a recovering Catholic. "As a young woman, she kept slipping out of her fortified family home to hear him preach."

"Slipping out of a fortress?" snorted Belinda. "Clare pushed open a thick oak door, reinforced with metal, a door normally requiring two strong men to open."

"Be poor like Jesus." That was Francis's message. Both he and Clare came from wealthy homes, but acted like hippies. I thought of the flower bedecked kids in San Francisco's Haight Ashbury. The city was named for Francis. Unlike most of his now cloistered Franciscans, hippies slept in city parks in and begged for food, for money. I was struck by the similarity of the hippies' protest against parental and societal expectations and those of Francis and Clare, the saint for whom the Santa Clara Valley was named. There *was* no St. Silica.

And now that I thought about it, other lost souls besides hippies were pretending to be leaders; far out ones, like Jim Jones; Indian gurus in Oregon's ashrams. At Esalen, south of Carmel, folks sat naked in hot tubs soaking up seminars on spirituality. Marsha Hunter Mossman was a prophetess in San Jose. L.Ron Hubbard wrote *Dianetics* for 'clearing' the spirit in his "church" called Scientology. Did *any* church clear the mind? Didn't all religions aim at clearing bad spirits out only to fill them up again with different values?

After Francis cut off her blonde hair, he set Clare up in an existing convent, and later, in her own, as Abelard had earlier helped Heloise become abbess of his abandoned one. When Clare fasted too strenuously, Francis made her eat bread and drink water. Had she helped inspire his *Canticle to the Sun*? (*Cantico del Sole*). Clare was anorexic, and spent years in bed, too undernourished to do anything but give orders to her sister nuns. No matter how weak she was from fasting, Clare certainly managed to open up opportunities for female religious, and to win from the Pope a promise that her Order of Poor Clares could stay poor. Lady Poverty smiled on Clare as she had on Francis, but *not* on this basilica.

Its central Romanesque nave rested on low pillars. "Here," Ferrell said in the nave, "is Saint Martin's chapel. Very medieval in theme. St. Martin of Tours, son of a soldier, (d.397) renounced a military career before being named Bishop of Tours. Reminiscent of Francis's renunciation of *his* father's trade and *his* assumption of the religious life." We were overwhelmed. The grandeur of the art in Assisi was more moving than the classicism of St. Peter's, perhaps because it was so personal and thus, more believable. How many teenagers still rebelled against their parents? I had done so myself though I took care to hide it more.

The lower chapel contained St. Francis's crypt. Ferrell did not even bother to lecture. Agatha, Anita, Sandy, Reed, the Pellatierras–in fact, all our Catholic and pious Anglicans knelt and prayed. Wes and I, the Schwartzes and Schoensteins, Matt and a few others, including Ellen and Bill, the Betty and James Harker, Ralph and Jan Huntsman, remained standing. Ferrell and Wes kind of twiddled their thumbs, until Ferrell, caught sight of Wes watching him. Both twiddlers stopped immediately. Wes was quite capable of these harmless charades. He'd started twiddling as soon Rob began. Wes had an elfin sense of humor. He made my heart laugh.

Also down here was a portrait of Francis preaching to the birds, aligned on a tree branch and on the ground. "This fresco," Ferrell said, "artist unknown, has very modern coloring." But the idea of someone preaching to birds wasn't modern. Not all my students paid me as much attention as these birds paid Francis.

There were portraits of Francis and Clare that looked like illustrations from *Vogue* circa 1935, only with golden halos (by Simone Martini). The right transept held Cimabue's *Madonna* enthroned with the *Babe* and angels.

"Francis," Rob pointed out, "stands to one side, as if he could not believe the august company he kept. This is the best portrait of Francis I know of," he added. "He wears a halo in the Italian Byzantine tradition."

Mindy piped up, "His big ears stick out like one of Disney's seven dwarves." Unflappable, Rob continued, "His eyes may seem perplexed, but are marvelously questioning." Mindy wasn't through.

"It's as if he were asking, 'What am I doing here? I should be out preaching to the poor, not standing beside a fresco of the Holy Family in a fancy church wearing a golden halo. I should have it melted down and give the gold to the needy.'"

"Mindy!" Jonah said, at times taken aback by his young wife's directness. Rob unperturbed, took over. "His right hand bears a nail's puncture wound; his torn robe reveals a deep gash in his side. The stigmata, you know, and the soldier's stab wound, given Christ."

Ralph Harker thought somebody must have broken Francis's nose, because it wasn't straight. "Perhaps in prison?" Ralph asked, "or while fighting against Perugia?"

"Maybe his father broke it for him, after his fabric went missing," Lynette murmured. "My dad punched my brother out for pawning his gold watch."

"Francis's biographer, Tommaso Celano," Wes said, "was a brother Franciscan and personal friend. He wrote in his *Life* (1228-30) that Francis's lips were thin (they weren't in this fresco;) shoulders straight (they sloped here); and beard black and shaven." Here his beard was reddish brown and an inch long! A biographer who knew Francis personally was more trustworthy than an artist like Cimabue (1251-1302) who may never have held the *Life* in his hands, and could not have met Francis, who died (1226) a generation before Cimabue's birth. For that matter, why did Jesus so often look Nordic? It was fascinating to me how artists had made representations of historical persons recognizable without access to authenticated source material. Still, who *really* saw a saint, even while he lived? Many thought they saw a madman in St. Francis, and the same was true of many who saw Christ.

The Upper Church was *too* splendid, mocking Francis and his "Lady Poverty." It was also noisy, with too many guides explaining in their own languages details of the collection, including Giotto's cycle of thirty-three scenes (1297-1300) from Francis's life, plus five by another artist. Most striking were the saint giving his cloak (originally lent by the bishop and never returned) to a poor man; a chair reserved for him in Heaven; another poor man of Assisi spreading his cloak before Francis; and Francis renouncing worldly goods, wearing only that cloak his bishop handed him when Francis stripped down to his underwear before Assisi's townsfolk. Pope Innocent III was shown approving Francis's *Rule*. Thirty-eight pictures in all.

Ferrell could not explain each one, thank goodness. After he had done what he could, I realized Anita was missing.

"Wes," I asked, "have you seen Anita?" He could see out over the crowds. Well, Reed's over there all alone," he offered. I went over to him.

Reed said, "I had to go to the men's room downstairs, and Anita said she'd wait for me. Not seeing her when I emerged, I thought she'd grown bored and had gone up to join the group!"

I told Ferrell the group should get some fresh air on the balcony and hastened downstairs to look for Anita. Wes and Reed followed. The stairs were crowded and we had to fight our way down.

Anita was nowhere in sight. I sent each man to one of the chapels, while I checked the ladies' room, calling her name. No answer. I then walked the long corridor to where St. Francis's robe was displayed. I recalled wooden doors off that corridor. Anita, who disliked crowds, might have opened one, seeking a little peace while Reed was in the men's room.

Suddenly, I heard faint crying. But where? The hall was empty. I knocked on one of the closed doors, but, turning the handle, found it locked. I tried the next one; also locked. I crossed the hall, and opened what was a library, seemingly empty.

Then I saw her on the floor in a corner. Anita had pillowed her head on her arm, her skirt halfway down her hips; her left leg bleeding; her white blouse badly ripped away, at the front.

"Anita, Anita!" I cried, "What has happened?" Slowly, blinking, she told me the appalling story of attempted rape.

"I wandered down the hall to wait for Reed to finish in the men's room. There was a line outside it. A Franciscan monk, not young, middle aged, heavy set with powerful shoulders, almost as wide as Ferrell's, emerged before Reed ever got to the door." By now I had helped her to a sitting position, cradling her upper body against my chest, my shoulder. The front of her skirt was ripped to her knee. There were bloody scratches on her right leg and left arm where sharp fingernails had torn her skin, leaving four parallel stripes of raw flesh. The worst bruises were on her left forehead and cheek. They would need stitches. Blood splattered the floor, the podium, a fallen breviary.

"He...he...said he had something of Francis's that ordinary tourists weren't permitted to see, ... in this room.." The room was a library, with locked bookcases. "I thought I'd...just take a quick look, and then go back and Reed would...would be out of the restroom waiting..." After a moment she went on. "Oh, Candida. I thought he was trying to find keys to some locked case, but he was…trying to remove an under garment instead. He lunged at me, tore my blouse. Pushed his hands down into my bra. He pushed me up against that lectern, all the while lifting up his robes, trying to remove his undergarments. I fell. My forehead hit the podium's corner. I tasted blood on my lips. I can't button my blouse. It doesn't seem to be on me in front." Pieces of her tunic–the lace parts on which the buttons and button holes were sewn–lay on the floor. Most buttons were missing.

"My legs hurt," she moaned. "He pushed me down. Pulled my skirt up. I screamed and kicked his belly. Hard." Her walking shoes had short but heavy heels. Anita was five feet eight or nine, with strong arms, and muscular legs. She was large bosomed. Definitely not a size six.

"He fell on top of me. I screamed and another monk came to the door. He didn't come in, but saw us, then ran away calling for help. But nobody came!"

"Did he take your pants down?" I hated to ask her that.

"He tried to, but stopped when the monk ran off shouting. He left then. I wasn't raped, just mauled."

I took off my jacket and very gently introduced Anita's arms into it, though it was not a good fit. I couldn't get the three top buttons to button, only the last two. But Anita had tied a long scarf tied to her purse handle. I untied it, and arranged it over the gap where my jacket didn't close. It covered her bra top and cleavage. I found three safety pins in my purse to pin her ripped skirt from the underside; so that, if you didn't look too closely, Anita looked clothed.

There was no way of hiding the black and blue swollen mark on her right cheek, her bleeding forehead. I found three small Band-Aids in my purse and applied them to her forehead over the deepest wounds. Spotting a holy water font, I went to it and dipped her handkerchief into the full basin. Then I proceeded to wash much of the curdling blood off Anita's torn face and bloody lips, the latter, fortunately, not cut. Together we walked slowly, hand in hand, back to the Upper Church and out onto the balcony.

"Oh, what happened?" chorused several ladies, while the color drained from Wes's face, and Reed staggered, clutching Rob's arm to keep from falling.

"Oh, nothing," Anita, said softly. I slipped on some wet tiles in the ladies' room and hurt my leg and my face. I'll heal." Meg and Peg, both registered nurses, were examining her leg wounds, facial ones. Meg had her Bactine spray in her bag, and used it on the opened wounds, even the ones I had covered, telling Anita to close her eyes.

"Your face won't heal without stitches," said Meg. Peg ordered Ferrell to tell Carlo to bring the bus to the lower church's rear. *Would Anita's wounds heal? Some would,* I thought to myself, *and some surely would not.*

CHAPTER XII

COURTING FAITH IN ASSISI; FREEDOM IN GUBBIO; PERFECTION IN URBINO

Assisi's *Terraza Rosa* (Rose Terrace) was three stars, the town's *finest* hotel. There *were* no better hotels here. Assisi, was small, buses packed; kids wanting icecream, parents a parking place, grandparents, a bathroom.

Anita went at once to her room in the *Terraza Rosa*, where Meg and Peg, the two R.N.'s, attended to her legs, arms and right side. Her deepest cuts were on her forehead and right cheek. Her right arm, now bandaged, was mostly black underneath. The hotel manager phoned an all night surgery. Anita was taken there by ambulance for facial stitches. Meg and Reed, worried sick, sat in the recovery room with her until certain she would not wake up until morning. The surgeon told them her release would occur after breakfast. Anita would be in pain and require medication for several days, but would be alert and mobile. In California, plastic surgery would hide any scars stitches left.

Jonah later assured her that, "the trip insurance would pay for all of it."

"Poor kid," Meg said, when she and Reed arrived back late that night. "Nothing can repay her for this trauma." At eleven A.M. we were to meet with Inspector Francesco Bianco. Would he side with the Order, or with order in Assisi? The town existed mainly on its tourist trade, and good relations between the Basilica of St. Francis and the police.

I told the group tomorrow's departure would be delayed, and recommended their visiting St. Clare's church, while Rob and I accompanied Anita to the police station. Our tour had been blighted. The excellent cuisine served that sad evening did not make us jovial, but I did manage to eat, if not dinner, a large serving of dessert–Umbrian *pestringolo* (fruit cake with figs, walnuts, pine nuts and honey). Few danced, though I went through the motions because Wes wanted to ask about Anita's prospects in a more private setting, out near the pool, while a small orchestra played and no one could overhear.

Assisi's stars shone brightly over the roses. We felt the pain that Anita was even then experiencing, having facial wounds sewn, bandaged. Attempted rape, like rape itself, was a violation of human dignity. We feared for Anita's emotional recovery. Walking her out to our bus, in the late afternoon, everyone had speculated on the cause of her injuries. Carlo had asked point blank: "Did someone rape her?" Wes had asked, "You'll tell me what *really* happened, Candida?" Rob wasn't speaking. He seemed about to once or twice, but then, retreated into stony silence. He had said in Trastevere he didn't believe in romantic love. Perhaps not in rape, either. Or perhaps he was just not able to talk about such things unless they appeared on canvas or marble.

It occurred to me that Rob had only once or twice touched me– when we lunched in San Francisco's Ghirardelli Square. In fact, apart from my walk from the bus to the Hotel Principi after Trastevere, he had, to my recollection, only taken my arm to steady me, with Wes on my other side. I inferred that he did not relate normally to women. Not to Molly, anyway. On and off he seemed attracted to me. Even Joan had not portrayed him as tender, though they had a long history. I thought making love to Rob would be like making it with a statue by Michelangelo. Not the David. One less animated. Maybe Moses; just as self-righteous, but more inner directed.

Seated on the hotel's terrace restaurant, each registered apprehension over Anita's assault in a private way. Myrna Schwartz remembered her twins, Michael and Murray, nearly two, in San Francisco with Grandmas Schwartz and Blankenschiff and Maria Sanchez, the Peruvian nanny. Both bubbies moved into the Schwartz manse during our tour. The house, in St. Francis Wood, a ritzy neighborhood in San Francisco, had a walled garden, eight bedrooms and four floors, counting a finished basement and remodeled attic where Maria lived. Jonah had described their house. The new staircase led from Maria's quarters down a wall into the back garden.

Myrna and Barry went inside to phone home. She hadn't talked about her twins much, and I wondered if she missed them? Before her marriage, Myrna was a fashion model. Barry, a banker, had taken this marriage on with abandon, Jonah told me, and parenthood again with trepidation. Barry was sure *his* mother, Ethel, took good care of the twins, along with Maria, whom Jonah told me, over drinks on the patio, was also his mistress.

Mrs. Schwartz had left Palm Springs and Barry's dad, Bernie, seventy-seven, to amuse himself with *his* mistress, Ethel's hairdresser. Those two gambled, drank, and Ethel said, did "abnormal things" in bed. Well, you couldn't do "normal" stuff with a man his age on meds for high blood pressure. Ethel didn't care. Barry had a retro impression of his parents, as middle-aged children often do. He thought she still cared what Bernie was up to.

"Mom hates leaving Dad, but loves the twins so much," he said when the couple returned to our table, along with their friends the Schoensteins, Wes and me. Last night I dreamed about these people–Myrna's mother, Rose Blankenschiff, fifty, recently widowed, and her boyfriend, Mel; and someone named Hosea. All this modern and ancient data was interwoven with my mother's fifteenth century relatives who, on a white ship, along with Hoseah's family, relatives, and Myrna's ancestors, had fled Spain (1492) because they refused to convert to Rome. They sailed east to the Crimea; later, to Odessa. Hoseah, later José, sailed still later to Greece, and took ship to Peru with Pizarro's conquistadors.

Mom's ancestors left the Crimea for Odessa; then, being traders, sailed west again, arriving centuries later in the Venetian ghetto, where they stayed for many generations before heading for Lucca in the early nineteenth century. There they were befriended by the Orefices, a Blankenschiff girl marrying an Orefice boy in the 1830s, and another at least once again in the later century. Their descendants, my grandparents, lived in Lucca until Mussolini's racial laws made it imperative to leave, which they did (1939), landing in Canada and after 1945, in New York.

I began having vivid dreams about the late medieval past in fifth grade. They persisted intermittently, but intensified during grad school, when I dreamed exclusively about the Italian Renaissance–in Italian. I've never shared these dreams, though most were innocuous. Some might think me unstable if I revealed how much I *could* learn of the past through dreams, though not of periods earlier than the later Middle Ages or Renaissance. From dreams of later eras, I simply receive facts. If I have a direct connection with the fourteenth through the sixteenth centuries, it reflects my graduate studies at Cal. Dreams gave me topics for articles, sometimes, but most importantly, deeper knowledge about people and events I could never otherwise have researched. About the Schwartz family for example, and Maria, and my mother's forebears. I regard my dreams a special gift. They make me tolerant of people like Signor Beppo, and closer to other prophets who once dwelled among us, but who are often maligned for misleading people. No information exists not flawed in some way. The sibyls knew this. Plato, too. Even J. Edgar Hoover and Nixon in their saner moments knew this. Trust me.

Mel Feingold, and Rose Blankenschiff met in the Peace Corps. They got into my dream last night! There Rose admitted attending a "fat farm" near Tempe, Mel's home, useful for one so "zaftig" (Yid., plump). She and Mel renewed acquaintance. He sold "used" car parts to "chop shops," warning Rose always to lock her car doors. They enjoyed a rambunctious sex life in Tempe six times a year. No strings. For the first time since her husband's death, Rose felt young; desirable. There was magic in Mel's hands, tongue. The rest was touch—and go. When she went, that was okay. When she came, bliss.

When Myrna's grandmother died, the family's tenuous grasp on their European past faded. Myrna would have been shocked to learn about her mother's present— her affair with Mel.

Nor did Barry suspect that Ethel and Bernie were happier away from each other than together. As for his older sons, Mark and Alan, he knew they lusted after Maria. Normal boys. He didn't know they gambled with Grandpa Bernie in Palm Springs. Bernie taught them Life Lessons. They learned poker in college. Barry's twins, Michael and Murray, were just babies. Ciphers. Mark and Alan revered Grandpa Bernie as a role model. He was into Smirnoff's, Benny Goodman, women much his junior, once show-girls in Vegas, now Ethel's hairdresser. Not girls. Women. The two were distinct species. Bernie taught his grandsons about that, the racing sheets, but also how to get a virgin into bed. He taught them what every college boy should know: that life is a gamble and winner takes all. Bernie graduated from the School of Not So Hard Knocks. He'd made it. Now he had it made.

Maria Sanchez was twenty-three. She looked like a younger Rose, ivory skin, auburn hair. Rose, at the first sign of gray, went auburn. This increased the strong resemblance between Rose and Maria, often mistaken for mother and daughter, to Myrna's annoyance. Even Grandpa Bernie said that Barry's nanny looked like Rose, with whom he had flirted at Barry's wedding. But he was too old for her, recently widowed then and not interested in the geriatric set.

Maria never heard of a maternal ancestor named José, of his borrowing the name Sanchez from one of Pizarro's officers. At nineteen José was in Peru with Pizarro, subsidized by Emperor Charles V. Together, though not acquainted, they ascended the Andes, where Pizarro befriended the Peruvian ruler, Atahualpa, and then executed him. By this time Pizarro had noticed that this José kid was intrepid, fearless. He saw to it the boy was promoted and given the best fighters to lead on raids.

A *converso* (Catholic convert), José married a Peruvian Indian girl in a mission church after capturing her village. He forgot his old religion when he left Odessa, but sang songs from ancient Castile, till he died (1582) in a rancho in Cuzco, near the site of the native palace where Maria's forbears had labored. The songs José sung, his descendants hummed, whistle or strummed on guitars. For centuries, they recalled a few words. The tunes remained after some words were lost, which was good since many of the words were Ladino, though how censorious poor Peruvians living high in the Andes were about Hebrew inflections is problematic.

Maria had an aquiline nose. A model's nose, like Myrna's. She rarely went to confession and grew up in poverty. Her father made his way to Mexico and then, reportedly, the States. He never returned, not phone calls, not cash.

"Maria found her way to the States," Barry told us, but provided no details about how she became his twins' nanny. Barry's rewards for her services made her mother's life in Peru comfortable. He did not pay into Social Security for her, however. Her future was her affair. Her present, his.

"Maria never questions our authority," Barry bragged. She avoided Mark and Alan when they visited from college. They found her irresistibly attractive. They told her she looked liked family. Maria said, "Lots of people look alike," and resisted attempts to get more friendly. Barry was enough.

When Maria, Rose, or, less often–Myrna– put the babies down for naps, they sang or hummed the same quaint tunes once heard in Castile, in Peru, and now in San Francisco's classy St. Francis Wood neighborhood. Myrna at last accepted Maria as a sister. It helped that Myrna took chloral hydrate to sleep after making love with Barry, who snored loudly. She never heard anything until daylight. Never heard him make his way from her bed to Maria's upstairs via the outdoor stairway.

"The bubbies adore the twins," Barry told our table after the couple had phoned. "My older boys are counselors at Tahoe this summer."

"Yeh," Myrna said dryly, "the bubbies are glad. The twins say 'fuck' and 'shit' because of them. They repeat naughty words because people laugh." Turning to Barry she added, "*My* mother doesn't laugh. Yours thinks it's cute. She's just happy Bernie's in Palm Springs, where he and her hairdresser, gamble, drink and fuck."

So now our table knew a bit about the private lives of the Schwartzes and Blankenschiffs. Their more remote history remained remote. It was open to me because of my gift. Dreaming. These people were my distant relations, though we'd just met. Yesterday's tragedy in St. Francis's basilica probably sent my subconscious into Renaissance overdrive. History was not only around us, but in us. And we were in it. It was knotted, like the Gordian knot. We don't see the knot or have a blade sharp enough to cut it. Alexander the Great had the edge on us.

After dinner, Wes knocked, but fell asleep in two minutes. I disengaged from his embrace in order to think about the Schwartzes; bubbies; babies; Barry; Bernie, and the ignorance of families about their nearest and dearest, let alone forebears. I fell asleep and dreamed again.

I was with Isabelle and Ferdinand in late fifteenth century Spain; with Pizzarro and José, another distant relative, in Peru. When I awoke, I knew that I had not just dreamed of unknown relatives, but was with them. It was not the first time. But the most intense. I had never made the acquaintance of Maria but knew intimate details of the Schwartz and

Blankenschiff families, and how their histories once intersected with that of the Orefices, and my mother's folks, also Blankenschiffs, who had left Spain with their nephew, Hoseah, and sailed with his relatives on a white ship to the Crimea.

More urgent today was Anita, who would soon be back in the hotel. I prepared myself to accompany her to the police. When I awoke at 6:00 A.M. Wes had gone, but the note on my pillow said, "You will need strength for the interview with the Inspector. Wish I could come, too. I love you, Candida. Wes." I wondered how many lovers would be so thoughtful?

I packed and re-read the introduction to *The Book of the Courtier (Il Cortegiano)*, Castiglione's portrait of court behavior at Urbino, tonight's stop. The author had explained how the work had, through mischance and his own rush to get it written before a thorough correction, somehow escaped its author entirely. It was "corrected" by unknowns, and "mutilated." I thought, *if I ever wrote a novel, I would let no unknown editor mutilate it. I would do it myself.*

Soon we would be meeting with the Inspector, an Italian cop who knew nothing of Anita. Would he focus on her rashness, wandering off into a locked room with a monk who "promised to show her something of interest?" Her story wasn't published, like Castiglione's; but like his, was filled with ambiguities. How would they be corrected?

Sure, this was 1973, not 1528, when Castiglione's book was finally published, after almost all the people in it had died. In Anita's story there were only three characters; Anita, her attacker, and an unidentified monk. History was always incomplete. Only the telling of it gave it an appearance of completion.

At 8:30 A.M. Anita and Reed entered the breakfast room. Anita's left forehead was bandaged, and her left eye was black. A large square Band-Aid hid her stitched cheek. Had it not been for her ordeal, none of us would have wanted to leave this hotel. Even the checkout time was 3:00 P.M., a message to guests that they deserved to stay longer. As it was, the group was glad to be leaving the scene of the crime, for Urbino, via Gubbio.

We left for the police station first. Wes wished us well. I wished I could have thought of an excuse for him to come, but couldn't.

The police station was medieval, but modernized, a glass and chrome entryway, palm-filled, having been added. A pretty, feline looking secretary sat opposite the entrance. She said *"Buon giorno."* I *"Buon giorno"* 'd her back.

"Inspector Bianco is expecting us at eleven. I'm Candida Darroway, professor and co–leader of an American college tour. This is Professor Robert Ferrell, our fine arts leader. And Miss Anita Marble, who was assaulted in the basilica yesterday."

The secretary frowned, not understanding English. I repeated it in Italian. (*Facciamo parte di un gruppo collegiale di turisti americani ed abbiamo un appuntamento col Ispettore Bianco alle undici. Mi chiamo Candida Darroway, professoressa–guida del gruppo. Il Professore Robert Ferrell, la nostra guida delle belle arte. E la Signorina Anita Marble, membro del group, vittima di un assalto nella basilica ieri.*) She beckoned us inside.

"Inside" was a hall with coffered ceilings, oriental rugs and short, arched oak doors. She knocked once at the second door. A muffled Italian voice called *"Entrate,"* (Come in). The secretary bowed, and withdrew cat–like to her glass cage.

Francesco Bianco was handsome, in his late forties, but with a still boyish face and gray eyes that missed nothing. We introduced ourselves. He invited us in perfect Southern American English to sit before his desk, on which were a vase of daisies and bachelor buttons and a pad of yellow note paper. His pen was tucked behind one ear.

"I did not have the grades to attend the University here," he said. "But an Aunt and Uncle in Nashville got me into Vanderbilt. They built the university a new chemistry lab, and suddenly, I was in. I stayed long enough to earn a doctorate in American Literature and acquire a Tennessee accent." Rob whistled. Anita said, "I have a cousin who went to Vanderbilt.

"Small world!" the Inspector remarked. We stared at each other. In other climes, at other times, we might have been friends. Inspector Bianco broke the silence. "Then we are three American doctors of fine arts and letters? And you, Miss? What did you study?"

"Oh," Anita answered, "I went to the College of Notre Dame in Belmont, California. I have only a Master's in education. I teach art and English in a Catholic middle school in San Jose."

The Inspector asked her to tell him exactly what happened from the moment she separated from Reed in the lower church, to when rescued by...?

"By me," I said. "Only not rescued. Just found."

Anita recited the sordid details–the monk's offer to show her Francis's personal things; his ripping her blouse half off, then pushing her up against the podium, where she cut her forehead, her cheek. She showed him the deep scratches where his nails dug into her legs trying to get her skirt off; the ones on her arms made before she kicked his stomach. She rehearsed her fall to the floor and how he sat on her pelvis, ripping her blouse to away in front, plunging into her bra, pausing only to finger her large silver cross. At this point Anita said she had yanked out a number of his beard hairs and he had bellowed in pain. She placed those hairs to one side. A monk unlocked the door and entered, but ran away calling for help. That's when her assailant ran off without raping her, but showing his contempt by spitting at her neck, a detail she had not told me before. Anita, looking straight at Bianco, drew from out her purse a ziplock bag containing the scarf she'd worn yesterday.

"First, I wiped his sputum off my neck with this scarf, and then wrapped my cross in it. I gathered up the beard hairs as best I could before Candida came. I put those in a cellophane gum wrapper. I thought if you sent them to a police lab, you might be able to identify him by the hair, or else, by a fingerprint, which I'm sure he left on the cross."

The Inspector carefully placed her cross in one specimen bag and the hairs, still in her cellophane wrapper, into another. He wrote on them both. It seemed a long while before he finished labeling the specimens.

"These might help identify the attacker," said Bianco, in his southern drawl. "Not many women would have thought to save such evidence. Anything else?"

Anita showed how observant an art teacher could be. "He had a small, round white scar between bushy black eyebrows. His beard was gray streaked," she said. "His lips extremely red. His upper left eyetooth was broken. He was about three inches taller than me. I'm almost five feet nine. I'd guess he was nearly six feet tall. He had powerful shoulders, like a weight lifter and a convex front. He was around fifty." She sat thinking. The Inspector took notes. Then she added:

"Oh, yes. He had a tan birthmark between the right toe of his left foot and the adjoining toe up to its first joint. He wore sandals, so I saw it. He spoke no English except–'Good day,' 'Yes,' and in the library, 'Beautiful woman,' which he repeated twice. I don't speak Italian," Anita explained, "but my folks did. I understand much. I understood when he asked if I wanted to see Francis's intimate possessions, locked away in a library." We all looked at her in silence, contemplating the picture she had painted in words.

"I was stupid," she continued. "I accepted because St. Francis is my patron saint. My middle name is Francesca. He understood the word 'no.' It's a similar sound in Italian, and my repeating it enraged him."

Inspector Bianco dropped his pen and leaned back in his chair. "Your position would not be very good in a criminal case, since rape did not occur. If you stayed in Assisi and state officials, including a psychiatrist, a woman's right's committee, a government appointed defender–lazy fellow–interviewed you, you'd need to hire private counsel. Then there's the Order's legal staff. They'd review your case with several inquiries including a committee of Poor Clares. The sisters are tough as nails, not feminists. Finally, a verdict rendered by a council of the Orders and our Office. A decision on guilt would take up to eight months, if all went well. It seldom does. With luck, the attacker might be banned from the basilica during tourist hours. You might receive a letter of apology, from the Abbot's chief secretary. I don't suppose you'd care to stick around for such torture, Miss Marble?"

Anita said only, "No, I must work. Teachers' meetings start September first."

"It seems unfair," said Rob, "letting this skunk off so easily." Why did I suddenly think of Molly?

"Yes, I know," said the Inspector. "I have a daughter almost her age. Also pious. I will inform the Abbot. If the lab work on the hair and cross proves effective, any brother we question will have fingerprints and a hair analysis taken. If they match, the attacker *might* be dismissed from the Order. That doesn't do Anita much good..."

Anita interrupted. "Oh, it does. I'll know that no other woman will be at his mercy in the future. I am not guilty of more than foolishness. Other women might be as foolish, and come to worse harm."

We rose. Inspector Bianco shook hands. He gave us his card. "By November, I should have something to report. Let's hope. (*Speriamo*). We were back in the hotel lounge again. It was only noon. We could have visited the Church of St. Clare, too, but decided not to. Back at our inn, the pool beckoned, and the desk clerk brought us lunch, courtesy of the inn, served us at poolside in a small cabaña.

We met in the lobby, bathing suits in hand, and changed in the pool's rest rooms. Meg said Anita was not to get her wounds wet, for fear of infection. So, she sat on the rim of the pool and cooled only her feet off in the water.

Rob swam laps for twenty minutes or so, splashing water onto the concrete, but not in Anita's direction. I did my sidestroke keeping an eye on her as much as possible. Then, we both climbed out, delighted when a waiter appeared bearing crab salad, assorted sandwiches, black olives and potato crisps, plus bottles of *Orangina* and cookies. Our swim had given us big appetites, though Anita only drank fruit juice and nibbled on carrots and a cookie. The group arrived, having enjoyed the Basilica of St. Clare (*Santa Chiara*), its wide piazza with red and white striped façade framing a panorama of Umbria's plains. Clare's basilica held her remains, plus a cross that once spoke to St. Francis, who spoke to crucifixes and animals normally speechless. A heavily veiled nun stood watch over this crucifix.

"How creepy," I remarked. Sam arrived with Samantha, just then. "Real creepy, Candida. Why would she guard a crucifix?"

"Francis thought of the cross as heavenly security," Samantha offered, she who often restrained Sam's ebullience.

"Oh, well," he rejoined, "When in Assisi do as the assassins do." Everyone looked at me to correct his mistake, but I did not know the Italian word for "Assisi's inhabitants." So Sam's "assassins" became our word for Assisi's inhabitants.

At three o'clock we made our getaway. The two most medieval hill towns in Umbria, Assisi and Gubbio, are thirty miles apart. Gubbio lies due north of Assisi. Hardly had we seen the basilica disappear behind us than we began to anticipate Gubbio, downing (*biscotti*) and figs (*fichi*) that Matilda bought to remind us of Assisi's sweetness, however bitter for Anita.

When asked about Anita's interview with the Inspector, I said, "She was treated with utmost courtesy. The police will continue investigating, and send a definitive report. Her attacker will be caught and punished." To hint at justice soothes those not injured.

Ferrell suggested I talk about Gubbio's literature. Gubbio had none that I knew of, only a tale of St. Francis and a wolf. "My comments will be brief. A bit of religious 'history.' I began. Briefness always went over well where history was concerned.

"What's with this wolf?" Matt asked. "Oh, a bad wolf (*lupo*) was eating the Iguvians. St. Francis entered the forest and made a deal with him. "If I get the locals to feed you, will you cease devouring them? They are very dear to God, as are you." The wolf licked Francis's cheek and growled, "O.K." (*Va bene*).

"That's it?" Matt asked.

"Well, what more did you want? Wolves aren't big on conversation." Laughter.

Since Italian lessons were not popular, most of the group remained at the *Buon giorno; grazie; prègo; Buona sera;* (Good morning; thanks; Don't mention it; good evening; excuse me and goodbye) level.

"Gubbio," I said "home to Paleolithic cave dwellers, lies at the base of Mt. *Calvo*, meaning 'bald' in Italian." I slipped this in unobtrusively.

A few *were* listening. Wes grinned as if to say, "You can't lose for winning." I pressed on.

"Gubbio's original inhabitants lived on the plains. Then, Gauls, Etruscans, Umbrians, Eruli, Goths and Romans, whole armies forced them up the hill to found Scheggia, the first Etruscan town. They were attacked by Totila (d.552), last Ostrogothic king, and again by Emperor Justinian's General Narses (sixth century.) The eighth century abounded with Germanic Lombards. Kings Liutprand (d.744) and Astolfo (defeated by Byzantines,756) and Desiderio (d.774), finally caved. Charlemagne proclaimed himself King of the Lombards as well as of Franks. By the late eleventh century, the Iguvians freed themselves, defeated Perugia, and stayed independent for several centuries."

Rob looked up, but I had studied the medieval centuries in a guide book forgotten by one of the Principi's tourists and had taken notes.

Barry asked, "Did they tax businessmen for defense?"

"Oh, yes. Don't strong governments always?"

"Did taxes cripple business?"

"Barry, taxes protected Iguvians until 1387. Then Perugia attacked again. The Holy Roman Empire expanded into southern Italy, lured by the sweet smell of Perugia's success."

"You mean taxes were a means to higher ends?" Barry asked.

"Yes! Sometimes taxes were the *only* way to ensure the survival of rulers and ruled, even when they no longer spoke the same language." Barry looked thoughtful. But I was no apologist for imperialism, whether territorial or economic.

"In 1183 the Iguvians began losing to Perugia, a dissident city state. Early in the thirteenth century, Emperor Otto IV confirmed Gubbio's former liberties! Otto had other fish to fry. The popes demanded Gubbio's loyalty, but the city was taken over by anti–papal Montefeltros, dukes of Urbino. Gubbio became Urbino's protectorate, and pro-imperial (1387 to 1508)."

"Anyway, in Urbino tonight we'll 'fraternize' with Castiglione's courtiers," I announced gaily. Wes grinned, knowing I was glad to leave medieval history behind and get on to something Renaissance and literary. I continued. "Castiglione's *Book of the Courtier*, as I tell my students, is a how-to manual: how to succeed by impressing your boss and his supporters." Rob smirked. Most of the tourists found little humor in literary references to books they had never read. Many preferred private conversations or staring out the bus window, or contemplating dinner. Why not? What else are vacations for?

"Didn't the commune of Gubbio protest being taken over?" asked Reed, for whom 1960s protest movements were still definitive solutions. His Democratic grandparents had defended unions and the common (white) man. He held Anita's hand, determined to protect her from further predators, as Roosevelt protected defenseless workers from predatory employers.

"Ah," I said. "They couldn't rebel. Urbino was incorporated into the papal states when Montefeltros married della Roveres. The della Rovere Pope, Sixtus IV, made Federigo Montefeltro, his favorite nephew, Duke of Urbino (1444). Federigo married a Gonzaga of Mantua (*Mantova)* whose only son, Guidabaldo, died childless. Urbino went to a cousin,

205

Francesco Maria della Rovere, nephew of the della Rovere Pope Julius II. Julius laid St. Peter's cornerstone in Rome and fought French invaders. The della Roveres then ruled Urbino, Gubbio, and other towns until 1644. Finally, the Papal States took possession of them all."

"You mean Gubbio became a papal pawn?" Mindy asked. Wes took over, and took the mike from my hands.

"Yes," he said clearing his throat. "But in the Napoleonic era," he told her, "its independent spirit was rekindled by Murat, Napoleon's Grand-marshal and briefly, King of Naples. Murat married Napoleon's sister Caroline. Murat *claimed* to be a revolutionary, but caved to Austria to save his throne. Austria executed him for his loyalty. The French were major players in the control of Italy, but Italy proved uncontrollable. And still is." Laughter. Wes smiled broadly. He loved his own humor.

Ellen interrupted. "History is boring, you two. We're here for art."

"Thank you, Ellen," Wes told her. "Yours is a common opinion." Ellen didn't get the double-entendre. I noticed Ralph Harker laughing silently on my left. I was glad for Wes. "My jocks feel just as you do, Ellen. They hate history," Wes added.

"The more history you know, the better you appreciate art," objected Mindy. "Those people who fought for life and liberty got to create the beauty we're here to see." Jonah, who once thought Mindy intellectually challenged, now saw that she was actually smart. He told me he thinking of sending her to Altamonte college or, if she qualified, to Cal.

Carlo let us out on the brick Piazza Grande with the Mayor's palace (*Palazzo de Podestà*) at its southeast end. He gave us two hours to stroll about Gubbio. This first palace was plain, so we headed into the grand *Palazzo dei Consoli*, across the square, a huge crenellated building with a bell tower dominating Gubbio, where the "Tables of Gubbio" rested.

Ralph Huntsman lit up. The Tables were bronze plates on which Umbrians wrote Etruscan words in Latin letters, lacking their own alphabet. He read some of the passages to us about religious rites performed at gates and passageways, like birth and death. Iguvium (Gubbio) was already a sophisticated society—religious, philosophical, and like our own U.S. in 1973, semi-literate.

We strolled the *Via dei Consoli*, admiring the famous majolica. Rob described a festival for Saint Ubaldo (d.1160), a meek Bishop of Gubbio who prevented Frederick Barbarossa (Emperor Frederick I (d.1190) from sacking Gubbio as he did Spoleto (1155). "Not bad for a meek cleric," Bill said. Marriage to Ellen had schooled him in weakness.

Rob took the microphone. "A word about the 'candles' (*ceri*). Every 15 May, Gubbians (Iguvians) place images of Ubaldo and two other saints on wooden holders or 'candlesticks' and carry them up Mount Ingino, where Ubaldo is buried. Each weighs four hundred pounds, but Ubaldo is so honored for winning eleven victories over Gubbio's enemies."

Ian was walking with Agatha. Allison with Belinda, Sandy and Lynette. The younger women admired the majolica ware next to a leather goods shop. Ferrell dashed into the latter, returning moments later wearing a wide brimmed leather hat that gave him the appearance of Charles Bronson in *The Magnificent Seven*. He pulled the brim down sharply on one side and posed for shots. Several tourists (not ours) snapped his picture, and two Danes asked for his autograph. They thought Rob a movie star. Rob wrote "From Charles Bronson, Hollywood, 1972." Then back to the Piazza where Carlo waited in a hot bus with Gianfranco, eating ice cream cones.

From Gubbio to Urbino is twenty-five miles. In a swank hotel a mile outside Gubbio a wedding party coagulated on a lawn, bridesmaids in lavender flanked the bride in white. Would I ever wear white? I thought my chances slim. There was not much to see for a while. Woods and fields. Like our Midwest. Rob told Gianfranco to buy sandwiches (*panini imbottiti*) and soda pop at a stand, for we had not stopped to eat since leaving Assisi.

Like children on a long automobile trip Sam and several other tourists asked repeatedly, called out "Are we almost there?" Andrea and Wes sat in the back of the bus. Wes kept nodding; Andrea talking. Good luck, Wes, I thought. Agatha and Ian were having fun with their sandwiches, taking turns holding pieces of their own up for the other to bite.

Urbino sat inland near the Marches (*Marche*), east of the Apennines, fifteen miles west of the Adriatic. Its towns were hard to reach by public transportation. To the near northwest lay San Leo, original home of the Montefeltros, dynasts of Urbino. Ralph, also a geographer, told us the

Marches were mountainous in the north, part of the Apennines, but level to the southeast and to the sea. To Urbino's west, *Monti Sibilini*. I loved it being named for the sibyls, wise women of early Rome who wrote, but said nothing. At least, nothing understandable. If I could only hold my own tongue (hard for an academic) I would be wiser too, and get more writing done. But the sibyls were prophetesses, and they learned things by dreaming. I felt close to those dreamers, writers. I, too, wrote books and had prophetic dreams. I just didn't tell anyone about them.

Rob, reaching for the "mike," observed, "Urbino peaked under Federico da Montefeltro, whose court was a cultural center of Europe. It had Italy's most beautiful Renaissance palace, and the largest library in the *quatrocento* (fifteenth century.)" Our hotel, between the ducal palace and university, was once a convent. Its lunette was a Luca della Robbia. The *Albergo San Domenico* (or Hotel Saint Dominic), had four stars, gardens, cloisters lined with comfortable chairs and great art. But only thirty-one rooms.

We were thirty-five people but could adjust downwards. Sam and Samantha took one room; Anita and Reed, also; Arnold and Anne, Gianfranco and Carlo. Wes and I got the last double. Rob, hearing this, leaned toward us and said loudly, "What a relief. I thought I might have to let Candida sleep on my chaise." Signor Bertelli dispensed keys. I had saved Rob from having me as a roommate. Perhaps Joan? No, she took a separate key.

Light refreshments in the cloisters before a brief visit to the Ducal palace across the street. There Montefeltro Dukes held sway until fertility failed in the early sixteenth century. Federigo's courtiers valued "platonic love." Cardinal Bembo lectured on it, but his works were sometimes sensual discussions, not so platonic. Plato set the ideal for platonic love that was the work's theme, but little love was platonic during the Renaissance. Otherwise, the della Roveres wouldn't have controlled Urbino for 136 years after the Montefeltros ruled for 121.

There was a difference of fifteen years in the reigns of Montefeltros and Della Roveres. Yet, as little of Urbino as we had seen, I would not have wished to lose even fifteen minutes, let alone fifteen years, of its rule.

Throughout history, sex was contentious, fertility capricious; neither less than true love. I'd choose the latter any time. How *does* one make two souls one? Agatha Rollins and Ian fed each other bits of their sandwiches (*panini imbottiti*). I was hoping to feed my soul mate different tidbits, more intellectual, and be nourished all my days.

Cardinal Pietro Bembo (d. 1547) wrote passionate poems, *Gli Asolani (1530)*, from his villa at Asolo. The Church hadn't changed much. He gave it a small push. I suspect platonic love, which Bembo praised publicly, never worked in any age, nor in his. No one tells all. If they did, would there have been any Renaissance? Any *us*?

Ferrell directed us to visit the ducal palace now, because we would not have much time to spend there tomorrow. We crossed the street. *Tavole calde* (cafeterias) were wafting dinner smells toward us from the square.

Crossing the Court of Honor, we paused to admire Luciano Laurana's (1420-79) architecture. "Laurana also worked in Mantua on designs by Mantegna, arriving in Urbino in 1466," Rob said. "He worked here until 1472, then alternated between the two cities. He knew the great Florentine architect, Leon Battista Alberti."

"Look at the inscription over the second *loggia*," said Agatha. Translating from Latin, she read: "Federico, Duke of Urbino, Count of Montefeltro and Casteldurante, Standard-Bearer, (*Gonfaloniere)* of Holy Church; captain-general of the Italian League, raised this palace from its foundations for his glory and that of his descendants." There was more about his victories, justice, mercy, faith, etc. What do we carve over our houses? Our street number.

"Ah, the Renaissance!" I raved alliteratively. "Fight, fuck (Had *I* said that?), faith, friends, family, fame, fabrication." Ferrell countered, "Art, architecture, antagonisms, adultery, adventure, amenities." Wes added, "Murder, Macchiavelli, misogyny, machinations, misalliance, mayhem." We threw our heads back and laughed. Professors are ham actors.

The group stared, then passed inside and entered the Room of the Angels (*Sala degli Angeli)*, a spacious ante-chamber to the ducal apartment, named for the baby angels (*putti)* on its fireplace. "Here," said Ferrell, "we're in the company of gods, as Renaissance artists, poets, philosophers, scholars, fighters, and church hierarchy frequented this hall. We're back with Castiglione's courtiers and rules for conversing, courting, courtesy and courtesans." *Especially the latter*, I thought.

"What did they talk about?" Mindy asked. "Bravery in war, or manners at court?"

"Both," said Wes, "but especially of the proper relationships between the sexes. You know, we don't use the word 'court' today just when we sue people, but also when we go a 'courting.'"

"Like Froggy in the old nursery song," Joan added. Ferrell stared at her wistfully.

I remembered the greatest defense of women's talent was made by Giuliano de' Medici, youngest son of Lorenzo "the Magnificent," who hid in Urbino during the French invasion of Florence." Wes, expert on the *cinquecento* (sixteenth century), looked up.

"Oh, yes," he recalled, "Giuliano ('Il Magnifico') was mostly contradicted by Castiglione's cousin, Cesare Gonzaga, soldier-diplomat; a man who gave women credit only for chastity." I thought of Anita in Assisi, now Reed's lover. No longer "chaste," was she less lovely?

"Well, respected women were surely those who had the least sex," Joan said, as if reading my mind. Ferrell blushed. Her comment reminded me of courtiers who preached female chastity after having destroyed it in upstairs boudoirs.

Back at the hotel, in the lobby, Ferrell announced restaurant reservations at the *Hotel Bonconte* in Wall Street–a short walk past Raphael's house, yards from our hotel.

I wanted to wash my hair and rest until dinner. Then I remembered that I was sharing a room with Wes, so no rest. I washed my hair anyway, but got the pillow case wet because he wouldn't wait for the hairdryer. But in Italy, things dried fast. When we left, I didn't have a hair out of place. I pinned the damp pillow case to a chair on the balcony to dry in the breeze.

The *Bonconte* hotel restaurant had a wall painting of Renaissance fighters attacking the Montefeltro palace. It was Piccaso-like, only more garish, less gifted. Ferrell insisted on seating himself directly opposite it and to my annoyance, I was obliged to take the seat beneath the painting. Ferrell stared at me, as did everyone else looking at that painting. Joan Lorimar sat to Ferrell's left. I wondered about that, considering what she had confided to me in Orvieto, that she wanted to avoid Rob. Here she was, beside him, though she had taken a separate room. Rob was fiercely attractive, if on occasion, threatening. I could not afford to alienate him, being his co–leader. Joan could do as she pleased. A case of gnarly attraction, no doubt.

This foursome was held together by professional discourse; male chauvinism; sexual desire and Renaissance courtesy. Courtesy not in the sense of manners, but *of men*; authority; justice; right order. Courts. Patriarchy, status, a burning desire for female love, lust, which we women returned, but discreetly. Even the menu was fixed (*prezzo fisso*). Wine excepted.

The Marches (*le Marche*), site of Urbino, featured largely Umbrian cuisine. Dinner began with a soup, (*minestra di passatelli d'Urbino*), spinach in a beef base, and dumplings made of ground beef, smoothed to a paste, mixed with the spinach. To this paste were added butter and grated Parmesan, five beaten eggs, soft bread crumbs, nutmeg. One of the best soups I ever ate. Good food was an experience, not just a meal.

The entrée was *pollo alla maceratese*, chicken casserole, baked in meat stock. When soft, it was cut into serving pieces, reassembled as a whole chicken, and covered with a sauce of beaten eggs, lemon and pan juices. Superb. Joan said she would add cognac, not lemon juice. The men got every drop of lemon sauce on their plates by using their bread to soak it up. Very Italian. Very male.

The chicken was followed by trout from the Nera (*Black*) River. The owner liked to fish, and put trout on the menu. Wes bought a Verdicchio esteemed in the Marches; Rob a Sangiovese, red. We polished them off. Then came Umbrian cochineal cake flavored with a liquor (*Alkermes*) made with cinnamon, nutmeg, cloves and other spices. The cake was doughnut shaped, with a cross piece over the hole, and little balls of cake batter over all that, covered with meringue browned in the oven. It would be called coffee cake or *Kafee Kuchen* (Ger., coffee cake) in Milwaukee or Munich; in Urbino, *ciaramicola*.

Wes and Rob drained Arnold's bottle of dessert wine, orange in color, but it gave me a headache. Wes spoke mostly to Joan; Rob mostly to me. Only occasionally all spoke together. Jonah watched from across the dining room.

"Why did you talk so much to Joan?" I asked Wes back in our room again.

"So she wouldn't feel left out of intellectual discussions. Now, something less intellectual." Wes carried me to the bed, removing my dinner outfit.

"Wait," I giggled, "what would Cardinal Bembo say?"

"I'm no Bembo scholar," Wes replied "But I know what Giuliano de' Medici said in *The Courtier.*"

"What?" I asked.

"Who does not realize that without women we can get no pleasure or satisfaction out of life?"

CHAPTER XIII

AND THEN, TUSCANY!

After breakfast we revisited Federigo's palace. There wasn't much great art left now. Bound for San Gimignano and Siena tonight, that was just as well.

Wes volunteered, "Federigo invited artists from all over Europe to Urbino to paint religious art, portraits of the poets, clergymen, dukes, duchesses and their relatives who dropped by."

Sandy nodded. "Belinda and me appreciate artistic presentation. We make our jewelry displays look like Renaissance artists might want to paint, or one of those duchesses wear."

The couple would write this trip off as a business expense. Their jewelry was displayed in Cupertino on silk scarves, art deco ware, appearing to a lower middle class clientele as real art objects, so different from what Gumps' patrons bought–real gems mounted in gold and platinum, fashioned by top designers, and often, quite tasteless. Italian glass, agate and alabaster, simple stones gracefully designed, were "genuine" works of art for Cupertino's "duchesses"– schoolteachers, clerks, housewives.

"Federigo ordered quality art from the best artists," Ferrell said. "He valued artists while popes demeaned them as mere artisans and made them work faster."

"Like Michelangelo under Julius II?" asked Ellen.

Rob struck a thoughtful pose. "At the time, Michelangelo was on scaffolding under the Sistine Chapel roof and vulnerable. Julius threatened to have him thrown down if he didn't work faster. Julius also contracted with Michelangelo to do his funerary monument of forty huge sculptures. Never completed, Michelangelo satisfied his heirs with only three statues: *Moses*, and two *Slaves*."

"Michelangelo probably identified with the slaves," Andrea Pellatierra noted wryly.

We entered Federigo's *studiolo*, a cubicle once hung with paintings, *trompe l'oil* (Fr., eye-fooling) intarsia and objects so three dimensional you thought them real, not painted! It was as small as many cubicles where modern workers labor. A few such studies, Francis I's, (a de'Medici), in the *Palazzo Vecchio* in Florence, were large. Modern cubicles are made of particle board, decorated with stuffed toys, coffee cups, fake flowers, and photos that 'personalize' work space. Output, not art, is prime.

"Oh, look!" Mindy viewing Federigo's *studiolo*, cried. "It's empty."

"Its treasures were shipped to Florence by the last duchess before Vatican armies attacked," Rob said. "Most went to the Uffizi. She married the Medici Duke to keep her Urbino 'dowry.'"

A portrait of the Duke and his little son, Guidobaldo, now hangs in room 25. Federigo wears a red velvet robe, ermine tipped, over steel armor, as comfortable as we are in pajamas. He was reading, while Guidobaldo, a child of three, stood beside him in a long gown, holding a candle. Guidobaldo would lose this palace to a della Rovere cousin for failing to produce an heir.

"He looks like the kewpie dolls I got at carnivals," Matilda recalled. Guidobaldo did look singularly porcelain. His yellow hair came to a pointy curl over his white forehead.

"Let's go see Raphael's "*La Muta*" (Mute Woman) now," urged Rob. "She *may* have been Maddalena Doni, a plain Florentine noblewoman."

"She might be almost pretty if less sad," Arnold Lodge said gallantly.

Rob mused. "Some critics thought the letter she held was a nobleman's marriage proposal."

"Perhaps he liked quiet women," Lynette suggested, also plain and quiet. "Though Candida said *the Book of the Courtier* favored women speaking wittily on many topics," Lynette recalled, sighing.

"But women kept quiet on political power." Allison grimaced. "Forget political power! Women rarely got to choose their own husband."

"Their marriages were *part* of political power," Belinda reminded Allison.

"Maybe," Sam hazarded, "the guy who proposed to *La Muta* wasn't talkative. Maybe Lynette nailed it. They got on well, but silently."

Ferrell laughed, saying, "*La Muta* might even be Raphael's self-portrait!" We move closer to "her." It occurred to me that in Renaissance portraiture, there was about as much fidelity to facts as in modern media."

Wes quoted Seneca: "*Fallaces sunt rerum species.*" (Not everything is as it appears to be.)

"Woo-hoo!" Matt sang out. "I hung with some transvestites from the Castro district in S.F. and upset Dad because they weren't what they appeared."

Allison stared at "La Muta." "I think she has lots to say! She speaks volumes to me."

We moved to Piero della Francesca's *The Flagellation of Christ* (1454), a study in perspective. A Roman soldier was whipping Christ, tied to a Corinthian pillar and nearly nude. A seated man (Pontius Pilate?) and a turbaned figure stood watching, backs to us, the latter figure possibly Mehmed II, Ottoman conqueror of the Byzantine Empire (1453). This was an allegory. Mehmed II was not Christ's contemporary. In the right foreground, three males turned their backs on Christ. To illustrate spiritual detachment?

"The raised whip appears suspended in time," Rob commented. "One feels it is suspended for *all* time, like Salvador Dali's folded pocket watch." Surrealism was not my favorite genre. I liked paintings to speak directly to the problem, the viewer.

"Allegories," Maria asserted, "were common in Renaissance painting. " The group grew glassy-eyed.

Ferrell replied, "Maria, the artist may have wanted to say that the present was related to a similar, not an identical past. We aren't sure who six of these eight figures are," Rob explained. "The man with forked beard might have been Federigo's father; a cardinal, or the former duke's adviser. The barefoot teenager in red was once thought Federigo's half brother, Duke Oddantonio, made Duke of Urbino at sixteen for defeating the Sforzas, papal enemies. Now, some critics say an angel, because of his bare feet and vacant look."

"Nonsense," said Agatha. "God could afford sandals for angels; and lots of privileged leaders look vacant." Rob turned to the painting.

"The balding man in blue looks only at the bearded guy. The seated figure *might* have been the Byzantine ruler John Paleologus, whom Mehmed II defeated, not Pilate. But della Francesca researched Pilate's house in Jerusalem, so some critics reject the Mehmed identity."

"Why would Paleologus turn up in Jerusalem with his conqueror to watch Christ's flagellation?" asked Wes. "Seems implausible."

"Wait, there's more. The older men in the foreground may be clerics. The heavy guy, Mantua's ruler, Lodovico Gonzaga. Oddantonio lived a wild, expensive life, and may have been murdered along with two advisors. Perhaps Federigo was involved. Oddantonio's grave is unmarked. And Federigo pardoned everyone connected to his death."

"Wow," said Matt. "A Renaissance cold case!"

We cope with inadequate information. I derived most of mine from reading, but the records were incomplete. The *Flagellation* revealed parts of stories not comprehended then or now. It reflected Piero's perspective, but depended on ours. Wasn't good art always a conversation between painter and viewers; good literature between author and readers?

Time to leave for Tuscany (*Toscana*) lands once Etruscan. To speak the best Italian, one must speak the best Tuscan. Siena, Lucca, Pisa and Florence contend for the honor.

Our southwesterly descent, Urbino to Siena, was forty-two miles, and included two stops. First, San Sepolcro (Holy Sepulcher), in the commune of Arezzo, birthplace of Piero della Francesco (c.1420), a pilgrimage point for his admirers.

"Park here!" Ferrell ordered Carlo.

"*Ecco, il Museo Civico,*" I said on the speaker. I was *supposed* to be teaching them a modicum of Italian. "That means, 'Here's the City Museum.'"

Room three held Piero's *Lady of Mercy (Madonna della Misericordia)*. Huge, blonde, Mary wore a green cloak over a red gown. It sheltered eight patrons, four men under one arm, four women under the other. She protected Piero's patrons. Mary was the largest part of a polyptych (1445-1462), i.e., folding panels that took Piero over seventeen years to finish. It depicted seven saints, an angel, and the Crucifixion. Stunning. Its patrons got their money's worth.

Another work, a *Resurrection* did not lack humor. A bloodless Christ, pink robe dropped to reveal his bare chest with the lance mark on his right side, held a white banner with a red cross. He was emerging from a marble sarcophagus, his right foot balanced on its rim. Below him, four men were sound asleep. One was Piero! I wondered why the artist painted himself asleep? Self–deprecation? A statement of human frailty? The woodland background was half wintry and bare, half summery and green. I compared how I felt last fall and now. In fall, bare of hope; now my heart was a summer garden. The resurrection of Candida, the result of Wes's love! But wasn't the other *Resurrection,* too? Wasn't love what saved?

Mindy, once Christian, now Jewish, said, "It's nice to see Mary in Christmas colors," and Agatha said Christmas cards with this painting were for sale here if Mindy wanted to send some out. Mindy sighed. She didn't send Christmas cards any more.

I taught Dante's *Inferno,* skipping *Purgatory* and *Paradise,* less dynamic. No really bad sinners. *Most people saved themselves,* I thought. Some think God will. Or not. Libraries have been written for and against. No one really knows.

Wes was a Dante buff. "Neither Dante nor anybody else could write about man's soul without reference to St. Augustine's views on predestination. God predestined men for Grace, as well as hell. The key? Faith. If he predestined you to believe (unmerited faith) you were saved. (Lat., *Sola fides)."*

Wes was a *pro forma* Lutheran. Did he feel himself saved? When I questioned him, he waffled. He didn't *really* know. He'd gone to seminary. The catch was, without God's Grace, you could not even *believe* and could not therefore *be* saved. It was perplexing. Thank goodness Anglicanism hadn't taken with me. All I wanted was to save myself by finding a mate, rearing two children and publishing good books on Renaissance lit so I could get promoted, and they could attend a good college. They would, of course, be exceptionally bright.

Two faded frescoes, Piero's work. Rob passed them by. The warm museum and Rob's spiels put us in trance mode. Soon we'd be in San Gimignano, where fine views, fine art, and good food abounded. We left the museum and boarded our bus. Some Americans called our first stop 'Saint Jim'–easier to pronounce than San Gimignano, where we would lunch in the Hotel Bel Sogiorno, (Fine Stay). The finest art cannot feed the body. Only the soul. If I spoke often of souls, it was because English had absorbed Christian theology. We atheists need another word, but "spirit" was also Christianized. "Sensitivity" or the older word, "sensibility" might be a useful substitute.

The road out of San Sepolcro twisted. Piero's pilgrims caused heavy traffic. Maseratis, Fiats and motorized bikes *(motociclette)* shot along on the center line, one the commune let fade, endangering all.

Rob kept watching his Rolex. I wore a Timex, though Tony, unemployed, had wanted to buy me something more chic. Ah, Tony! I think of you. Sometimes. I hadn't thrown him over, nor he me. We just went our separate ways…me to Italy, Tony, to look for a job in Texas, in Louisiana. Would that he could find whatever he needed to make him whole. Me too.

Rob said to tell Carlo to take the short cut to "Saint Jim," through Castelina, turning just before Poggi Bonsi (Good Wells.) "Carlo must turn south at Poggi. It's quicker. Fewer trucks, busses. Tell him, Candida."

"Carlo, please turn south as soon as you get to Poggi Bonsi. It's faster." (*Carlo, per favore….Ferrell dice di girare al sud appena arrivato a Poggi Bonsi. E più presto.*)

"I don't think so," (*Non mi pare*) Carlo said, peering ahead through wire rimmed glasses. Suddenly, a red Lamborghini whizzed by with a half inch to spare. Reed cheered. "Those 'Lambos.' Great maneuverability!" We had come close to extinction, but Reed lauded Italian engineering.

"Lamborghinis were not as well balanced as Alpha Romeos," Reed admitted. But was Reed perfectly well balanced? Was anybody?

In ten minutes, our bus headed down toward the Al highway (autostrada) from Florence to Rome. We passed Montevarchio on our right, and soon after, would pass Castelina, Poggi Bonsi.

"Okay," said Ferrell. "Tell Carlo to turn south just *before* we hit Poggi." A strange glint appeared in Carlo's eyes. Eight miles later Ferrell said, "Tell Carlo to turn *right* now for Castelina."

"Yes," Rob smiled, turning on his not negligible charm. "This will take us straight into San Gimignano." After a few minutes on this road, which paralleled the Al, a sign said "Tavernella di Pesa." Carlo shrugged. The Al super highway was now very close, and the traffic's roar ominous.

"A mistake!" Ferrell shouted. "I wasn't this close to the A1. Carlo should have turned left, not right." I translated. Carlo kept driving.

"Did you tell him?"

"Of course."

"Well, at any moment," Ferrell reasoned, "we'll see the fourteen towers of San Gimignano." Actually, thirteen. At least seventy plus in the medieval era. Many–most–had fallen. Earthquakes? Poor architects? Invaders? Early medieval history wasn't my bag. Guidebooks called this village "the Manhattan of the Middle Ages."

Ferrell again: "Look to your left, and back, Candida. What do you see?"

"A couple of churches on two hills. Oh, and a ruined castle."

"The towers should be coming up any second," Rob said, sweating profusely. I recalled a story Dad read to me–*Are We Lost Daddy?* In it, the daddy kept looking for a white barn for his turn-off, but it had been painted yellow. They missed their turn; we our towers.

Ferrell barked: "Tell Carlo to turn left." We turned. "Now, when we round this curve up ahead, towers!" he predicted. None. We were descending a hill, leaving the superhighway behind.

My co–leader: "I'm sure Carlo took a wrong turn. Tell him to go back to where we made our first right." I told him. In a rutty farmhouse drive Carlo negotiated a turn back onto the same road down which we had come, heading south. He was mumbling in Roman dialect now. Fifteen minutes later, we reached Colle Val d'Elsa, a city in the Elsa River valley.

"Tell Carlo to park. There," Ferrell said curtly, "where the sign says 'Autobus.'" I looked. There was a red X through "Autobus." Carlo leaned his head out the window. A policewoman was approaching.

"Is this San Gimignano?" he asked.

"No," she answered. "This is Colle Val d'Elsa." We were twelve miles *south* of San Gimignano. We had wasted an hour with Rob's 'shortcut.' Rob was deflated. He scarcely took his eyes off his lap. Carlo, following the policewoman's directions, swung our bus around toward Poggi Bonsi again.

From there, it was a little over seven miles, through olive groves and vineyards, patched with large golden squares of wheat or plowed land only a bit more intensely gold than wheat, stitched together by narrow lanes leading to farm houses, and to country inns once farmhouses. These were hidden from view by the inevitable cypress (*cipresse*) that lined Tuscan driveways under skies so blue, so full of nimbus clouds, one wanted only to be let off to spend the rest of one's life face up in a Tuscan field.

Suddenly, around a bend, stood San Gimignano on its hill, with several of her remaining thirteen towers. Then, the wall surrounding the most visited hill town in Italy appeared, with thousands of cars attached to it, like pendants strung along a collar to fit a giantess. Busses parked elsewhere. Carlo dropped us on a gentle incline leading to the Porta San Giovanni leading uphill to a small park at the end of the town's main street, *Via San Giovanni*.

Our elderly members needed to rest. Ferrell, Wes, Gianfranco and I walked a short distance to drink stand, returning with plastic trays of lemonade glasses. Extras were not wasted. We started walking through a town once an Etruscan village (third century); become a town (tenth century) named from a Bishop of Modena, later canonized as St. Gimignano. He defeated German barbarians. Nothing could save the town from them now, as Germans filled nearby hotels with swimming pools, from which they launched repeated attacks. Still, the current conquest of "Saint Jim" is not from Germany alone, but the world.

Strolling the main street, we reached the Plaza of the Well (*Piazza della Cisterna*), and sat on its steps to eat ice cream on sticks, purchased from a Motta stand. Beyond the short wall protecting this square, fields and farmhouses shimmered in heat under a Tuscan sky, now cloudless. We would have this view down the street at lunch in the *Bel Soggiorno*.

Beyond the *Cisterna*, the *Collegiata*, a church turned art museum. Its walls were frescoed by Lippo Memmi, who did *New Testament* scenes, and Bartolo di Fredi, *Old Testament* ones that Rob faulted, calling Fredi "that crude Sienese populist painter." A ghoulish *Last Judgment* by Taddeo di Barolo (1410), at the entrance. Ferrell was no longer depressed. Art criticism was his profession, his hobby. He would indulge.

Gozzoli (1497), a Florentine, produced a prickly view of St. Sebastian in underpants bristling with arrows, holding one in his right hand, a pen in his left.

"Silly pose," Ferrell remarked, "unworthy a man so talented." *La Smithwitch* asked if St. Sebastian were shot by critics of something he wrote.

"Authors suffer the slings and arrows of rotten reviews," she said. I had to admit that when she wasn't chasing Wes, Andrea had a sense of humor. Or had it when she *was* chasing him; but then, I didn't. Piero della Francesca was right. Life is about perspective. *Things are not what they seem.*

Ferrell said, "If you want more Gozzoli, wait until Florence. "Gozzoli's clients included the wealthiest merchants, and his *Journey of the Magi to Bethlehem* would reveal The 'Magi' as Medici 'princes' *before* they *were* princes!" (1512).

Wes added, "The Medici always acted as if they *were* legitimate royalty. The *Journey of the Magi, etc.* is pretty art. Nice costumes, fine chargers, family 'shots' of dictators!" Gozzoli's painting awaited us in the Medici Chapel at Florence.

Royal (unchallenged) power is a question we Americans might well ponder, since President Nixon's collusion in spying on the National Democratic Headquarters in the Watergate building. That was two years ago. Now, in mid 1973, we had read on Italian newsstands that Nixon secretly taped conversations in the Oval Office, tapes to be subpoenaed by the courts to determine any cover-up. Where would it end? Machiavellian politics were still alive. Would Nixon give up the presidency? He couldn't turn the U.S.A. into a dukedom—could he? Or stage a come-back if he left office like the de' Medici had done when the French were driven out? It couldn't depend on his own perspective, could it?

In the Civic Museum, di *Bartolo's Virgin and Child*, which Dante visited (1300) representing Florence's Guelph faction. Upstairs paintings by Gozzoli, di Freddi. A wedding night scene showed a couple getting into bed; risqué for the fourteenth century, or any since. Their queen sized bed was covered with a checkered spread, with a hard pillow roll trapped in the top and bottom sheets so you couldn't toss it. Cheap French hotels use them to break American necks. Here, it was softened by smaller pillows, on one of which the nude bride (bare boobs showing over the coverlet) rested, awaiting defloration by a hesitant groom standing on the other side of the bed. Wes, started to say something, but I shushed him. I don't trust lovers in public when the topic is sex.

Ferrell was already commenting on the scene with a remark critical and profound: "What you don't see is usually far more erotic than what you do." I considered that what you *didn't* see may not be erotic, either, but I was thinking of Tony. Sometimes, eroticism fails because we expect too much. The result might be embarrassment first, resentment later. Could confusion over what love and eroticism were—and were not—have caused Dad's endless affairs and immediate remarriage?

There was more in "Saint Jim," but it was 1:00 P.M., and we had lunch reservations at the Bel Soggiorno for 1:15; rather late for Italians.

"I'm beginning to dig art," Sam admitted, walking beside me on our way out of the museum. "I wish I had a year in Italy to look at it all." Samantha reminded him that he would miss his normal routine, and their AA meetings.

"That'd be one of the best features!" Sam exclaimed. "I don't think as much about alcohol in Italy. Why do you suppose?"

I supposed that in Atherton people were less sociable, substituting material comforts for time spent with close friends. In Italy there was much diversion, less boredom. Here, the spirit (or sensibility?) could drink in art, history, and savor life. The Italians did not make a fetish of food or drink. They simply enjoyed eating with friends, as they had for thousands of years. The cure was good company.

Would this "cure" work on complaints besides alcoholism? "Directions. Dine with folks you care for at home or in your favorite *trattoria*, sharing *one* bottle of a good Chianti. Invite a stranger to join you. Stir in any art that stirs *you*; savor with smiles and laughter. Stress, infidelity, and snubbing the poor should soon disappear." Would Medicare cover this treatment?

The Hotel *Bel Soggiorno*, run by one family for five generations, dated from the thirteenth century, though only a beamed ceiling was original. Plate glass windows divided by thin vertical strips of wood revealed breathtaking hillside views. Three long tables longitudinally placed, seated most of us, and as the windows took up three sides of the dining room, everyone got the view. We might have been in Carmel Valley; in Livermore (away from the atomic labs); or looking out over

Napa's vineyards. No wonder Italians felt at home in California. Only antiquity, the Middle Ages, and the Renaissance were missing.

Rob presided over the left table; Jonah the center one and Matilda was "Mamma" for the third; which included Belinda and Sandy, Betty and James Harker, Ellen and Bill. Those who stopped to use the bathrooms, five of us, wound up at a table for six at the very front of the central window with steep valley views.

Our thoughtful waiter removed the extra chair. "So the Devil doesn't occupy it," he said, smiling. Carlo, Gianfranco, Wes, me and Andrea Smithwitch made an unusual combination. Only three of us understood Italian. Wes read it. Andrea thought she read Wes. Naturally, it fell to me to play translator, hostess, "Mamma." Who would have thought that I, Candida Darroway, who drudged away alone in Alviso grading papers in a shabby shack, could have carried off all three roles with aplomb? Alviso was full of boat dwelling "hippie" clones who lived on old houseboats. I would prefer a large Edwardian in Berkeley. I did not feel laid-back. Until bedtime.

The waiter informed us that, by accident, the meal prepared for our tour, squab, was not available. A new waiter had served several groups of tourists the roasted pigeon breasts on skewers baked with alternate bits of lean ham, bay leaf, stale bread chunks and mushrooms intended for us. He presented us the regular lunch menu with a flourish, and told us to chose anything that would not exceed the price of the squab.

Pigeon. I did not trust pigeons all that much. Whenever I ate "chicken" in Venice, the pieces were so tiny I *knew* some independent vendor had bagged them on Piazza San Marco at three A.M. Our table decided we would all have roast veal, (*vitello arrosto*), baby green beans (*fagiolini verdi*), and roasted potatoes (*patate arroste*) with a local rosé (*rosato*) and the good white wine (*Vernaccia bianco*) of the region. I was very happy to "make do" with this substitute.

Carlo said the *rosato* was on him, and Wes paid for a bottle of *Vernaccia*. Was it too much for lunch? Of course. But when it reached our table, it was after 2:00 o'clock, and we had not eaten since breakfast in Urbino! We did justice to lunch.

Wes was sorry we didn't have time to visit *San Agostino* (St. Augustine), whose choir was covered with Gozzoli's frescoed cycle of the saint's life. He was fond of Augustine, often referring to his raffish, persecutory, *at times* holy life, and his frightening theology of predestination. Wes was a cool Lutheran. Luther, still an Augustinian friar, hit upon St. Paul's remark concerning the just, who live by faith, being saved from predestination by the Grace that made faith possible. *(Romans* 1:17). I was glad I wasn't involved in either of those scientifically–or religiously?–unprovable propositions. The latter involved circular thinking; the former, unvarnished sadism. Thank God I hadn't majored in Reformation Studies.

"Wes," I told him, "Several of us are going to go shopping after lunch. Arnold wants to buy *Vernaccia.* I have my eye on a ceramic planter my African violets can't live without. Perhaps you'll find a book on Gozzoli's frescoes of St. Augustine."

Andrea assured us that she "coveted some silk scarves" next to the book store, "so we could go together." Franco and his nephew spoke softly in their Roman dialect. I felt it unnecessary to interrupt, except to remind Carlo in Tuscan that he had to drive afterwards, and to go easy on the wine. Italian men don't believe wine and driving are incompatible. Men everywhere don't. Wine makes half of all men defensive highwaymen, and the other half, aggressive ones; the soldiers of fortune or *condottiere* of the twentieth century

When our food arrived, my spirits lifted. But just as I began to cut my first piece of meat, lunch was interrupted by a blood curdling scream! Waiters came running, and even the chef deserted his ovens with his hat askew to see if someone was injured. Ellen Froehling's pale blue dress had a dark purple patch spreading over her heart! Andrea, faint, or feigning faintness, buried her face in Wes's neck, after screaming, "Ellen's been shot in the heart!" But there *was* no shot. I did think it possible that Ellen had no heart, but didn't say so. Anyway, this was Tuscany, not East San Jose! I went to Ellen, now hysterical.

"Ellen," I said firmly, putting my hand on her shoulder, "Chill. Let it go." But Ellen was too old to know "chill" meant calm down. "Ellen," I repeated, "calm down, no one has injured you." Ellen was impassioned.

"You clumsy dyke!" she shouted at Sandy, "You stupid, ugly, dyke. You've ruined my new Bloomingdale's dress." Belinda, seated at the next table rose to go support her partner who, in passing Ellen on her way to the rest room, had accidentally jostled her arm, just as Ellen was lifting a full glass of red wine. It had poured all down the front of her dress, then onto the white table cloth, now red, dripping onto the floor. Spying Belinda, Ellen began again. "Dykes!" She screamed. "No decency. Scumbags of the earth!" Then Bill stood up and commanded Ellen to go to the restroom, where she might try washing the front of her dress. A housekeeper in the hotel appeared to help her, and Ellen, still spitting epithets, was led out.

Sandy, shaken, sat next to Belinda, whose arm encircled her waist. Drawing a deep breath Belinda said firmly, "The term 'dyke' is demeaning, its origin unknown. Sandy and I are lesbians, like Sappho, poetess, educator. We are members of the Daughters of Bilitis, an organization formed in San Francisco (1955). Some think Bilitis an island near Lesbos; others, Sappho's friend. If people regard it an organization akin to the Daughters of the American Revolution, as some do, it lends respectability to a maligned sisterhood." At this point Belinda, a quirky humorist added, "You might call us a service organization."

Her irony made Wes and Jonah smile, Rob clasp his forehead. True, the dictionary says "dyke entered American speech in 1942." It's a perfect rhyme for "kike," which "entered our American speech in 1904." Both were used to stigmatize minority groups. How easily such words soiled those who used them.

After lunch, Ellen was given a robe to wear. The stain was treated with a special solvent, and her dress emerged like new, washed and dried in the hotel's laundry room, ironed by a housemaid. Bill chatted with the owner's son, waiting for Ellen to emerge, as tidy as she had begun the day in Urbino. Then they entered the main street where shortly, Ellen froze. Sandy and Belinda were buying dishes at an outdoor stall. Much to their surprise, Ellen went over to the couple and apologized for her outburst.

"I hope you can find it in your hearts to forgive me. I think I drank too much wine. Lucky I didn't have that final glass. I am very sorry for the embarrassment I caused."

Sandy answered her with admirable control. "I forgive you, Ellen," she said. But Belinda gave Ellen a quick hug, saying, "Everyone has

done things in life that are regrettable. We respect you for your apology."
And with that, the two couples went their separate ways.

I forgot in which store I had seen that planter. Andrea entered the
silk scarf shop, and Wes and I the book store, where we found excellent
Gozzoli reproductions of the St. Augustine cycle in a paperback.
Leaving the shop with Wes's new book, we caught up with Anne and
Arnold, who announced that he had just bought *two* cases of Vernaccia,
and had had them delivered to our bus. "Whatever happens in Siena and
Florence," he said, eyes twinkling, "we won't go thirsty."

With Arnold and Anne, and the rest of the group straggling up the
crowded street, we walked back to the Porta San Giovani. Carlo brought
the bus up and everyone boarded, stowing purchases in the overhead
nets. I was sorry to leave San Gimignano. A quarter mile down the
road, people splashed in a *de luxe* hotel pool, and as it was hot, I envied
them their luxury.

Carlo turned up the air conditioner. At Poggi Bonsi, we turned south
until we hit Route 2, which took us through several towns before Siena.
Our hotel there, the *Villa Scaccia-Pensiere* (Dispel Worries), sat on a
ridge just outside the city's old wall, with a heart–stopping view of Siena
from its terrace. A nineteenth century building, it had four stars, rose
gardens and a swimming pool.

We would be dining late, lunch having ended after three! Our dinner
reservations were for ten P.M. at the Old Tavern at Divo's. (*Osteria Antica
da Divo*). Now all I cared to do was to head for the pool, where Ferrell,
Joan, Anita, Reed, Wes, and most everyone but the elderly folk were
congregating. Bill, who liked to see women in bikinis, came without
Ellen, and sprawled in a deck chair, eyeballing the younger set who
wore them–Allison, Mindy, Myrna, and even, Andrea Smithwitch, who
probably should not have, but wore the briefest of all– a yellow polka-
dotted one, no less. I wore my old navy one piece that Esther Williams
would have chosen. With age it had lost its elasticity, its color. I needed
a new suit. Not many people were swimming. I ached for exercise,
and executed fourteen laps all side-stroke. Wes, who wasn't a great
swimmer, managed five or six lazy laps and went out to dry off, leaving
Mindy, Jonah, Matt, Rob and I to share invisible lap lanes, avoiding the
shallow end where older tourists were just chatting, cooling off.

The sun had not yet set and it was still hot. I gathered up my large towel, wrapped it around me, and retreated quickly, feeling a bit like an ugly duckling in my old suit whose seat was, I realized after it was wet, sagging.

Wes had already left. Ferrell was still toweling off, and called to me to walk with him back to the hotel. We had something more in common than our employer, for his shabby swim trunks, like my own baggy suit, should have been tossed. We both wore rubber pool shoes, and when we entered the hotel from a side door, they squeaked comically on the tile. The *Scaccia-Pensiere* had three floors, and our rooms were on the third. I didn't have a clue where Wes's was. Arriving by stairwell at the third, I discovered to my chagrin that Ferrell's room was next door to mine. I supposed the management, honoring us as co–leaders of our group, had given us superior rooms side by side. My room was elegant and large, with a *loggia* overlooking all Siena.

As we stood wrapped in our towels, fidgeting with keys, Rob said, "Candida, I've got a bottle of *Americano* in my room. I'd like to share with you on our private *loggia*." So. He knew the *loggia* linked our two rooms. I didn't.

Stalling, I asked "What is *Americano?*"

"A popular Italian aperitif, vermouth with bitters, brandy and lemon peel."

"I was thinking of a brief snooze," I said weakly. Rob's eyes gleamed.

"Rest afterward. It's only 5:45. We're not dining until ten o'clock, and won't leave the hotel until half past nine. I'd like to talk over how we'll spend our one day in Siena."

I thought fast. Wes hadn't said a word to me about the late afternoon, so maybe a half hour with Rob on our *loggia* would work out. I did not want to alienate him. That would be unwise.

"Okay," I agreed. "Let me shower and change." We closed our doors, and I sped into the bath, whose tiny floor tiles in red, black and white fitted together in such a way that one could be drawn into the pattern by staring at it too long. Handsome. Hypnotic. Like some men in their 50s.

I donned a summer skirt in black with pink roses, and topped it with a pink cotton tank top. My pink bra straps showed, but I have never felt decent bra-less, like the hippy crowd at Cal and in the Haight. No bra burner I! An unlocking sound next door. Rob, with his back toward me, appeared on the *loggia*, taking in the view. I went out barefoot, the tiles still warm. I was properly dressed for an ad hoc patio party.

"Hi," he said, boyishly.

"Hi," I said girlishly. We sounded like characters in John Updike's novel, *Marry Me*, where the reader was never certain who would stay married to whom.

"I brought refreshments," he indicated with a jerk of his head a table on which were two small glasses, a tall bottle, some crackers, Italian salami, a runny triangle of gorgonzola cheese, and wizened black olives that, despite appearances, were quite delicious.

Removing the red, white and blue label pasted over the bottle cap, Rob smiled. "A compatriot." Having poured us each some liqueur in the funny little water glasses Italians use for wine. He clinked our glasses.

"Well, Candida, old girl, here's to Columbia!" The label had one of those Columbia images on it, where a radiant woman in a white dress held up a sparkling torch of freedom and looked solemn, like a child holding her first sparkler on the Fourth of July.

I murmured, "*I'm* not old. *You* are." I instantly wished I could have taken it back. I was not unaware how potentially menacing this tall, handsome colleague could be. His expression did not change.

Actually, it was "Columbia" not Rob, who hit back first. The heated tiles under my bare feet, the sun shining directly into my face, followed by the 47-proof brandy–made me hot all over, and, as the Brits, say "tiddly." I had drunk too fast because of the heat and my nervousness drinking alone with Rob.

"What did you say the alcohol content of this "compatriot" was?" I asked, pitching myself into his left side as I lost my footing.

"I didn't." He laughed, steadying me. "Never ask a friend how much money he's worth, how much alcohol is in his drink, or how old he is. It's crude."

I blushed. "Crude like Ellen calling Sandy a 'dyke'?"

"Gawd. That *was* a scene. I'd no idea Ellen was a homophobe."

"Oh, Rob. She's known you for years, and often invites you to dine."

He shifted his gaze toward Siena. "I have accepted two of her dinner invitations, yes. The Froehlings took two of my lecture courses at a senior center. But know them well? No. That's Ellen social climbing. As if knowing *me* provided social status." Somewhat bitterly, he added, "It doesn't."

Turning back to me he said, "Don't drink the rest of that, Candy. We are going to have cocktails on the Piazza del Campo before dinner. Pace yourself."

That was kind, though I had stopped drinking anyway.

"Tonight's Osteria Antica da Divo, where we're dining, translates as Divo's Old Tavern, as you know," Rob explained. It's a short walk from the Campo, where our cocktail bar is located." He cleared his throat. I merely nodded. Then he launched into tomorrow's itinerary.

"The Duomo is a must," he said. "It has too many marvels to count, and will take all morning. After lunch, the Palazzo Publico, the crenellated town hall is not only the best gothic palace in Siena, but has a Civic Museum (*Museo Civico*) which boasts fine paintings by Simone Martini, Ambrogio Lorenzetti. Funny about Martini–the artist, not the vermouth–his best work, the *Maestà* (majesty; a word describing the Virgin enthroned as Queen of heaven, surrounded by saints and angels), was also his first."

I said, "It would be nice to walk in a few medieval streets, to get the flavor of the Middle Ages. The plague (1348), killed three quarters of the city, filled those streets with corpses, collected each morning for mass burials." This thrilled my students. Why are the young such necrophiliacs? Because they think they'll never die.

My phone rang next door. Wes, no doubt. I told Rob that I was grateful for the snacks and the *Americano*. In fact, the last had gone to my head. He knew it would. Preparing my exit, Ferrell came up from behind, put his arms around my shoulders and lightly kissed the nape of my neck. He had never touched me that way before. His arms dropped suddenly, when I turned quickly, eyes questioning.

"Surprise you?" he asked.

"No," I lied.

"Then this won't, either," he said, wrapping his arms around me, kissing me hard on the lips, forcing his tongue far back on mine. He stepped back to judge the effect. Risk. What Beppo and Molly had warned me of. I felt myself start to shake, and moved backward unsteadily, my right arm behind me, reaching for the handle to my door. Finding it, I stumbled over its threshold into my room, pressing what I thought was the button that locked the door to the *loggia*. On the patio, laughter, and a clinking of glass.

The alcohol produced a feeling of dizziness and, yes, elation, balanced by self-loathing, sexual desire—my underwear was sticky—and guilt. What had I done? I climbed onto the bed and found myself crying softly, eyes wide open, gazing at the beamed ceiling, painted with pastel flowers and vines. Yes, the *Americano* had rattled my brain, but I did not recall giving Ferrell any come hither signals. Was it my bare feet? Perhaps he was a foot fetishist? No. A man. He sent me a message. Not a love letter, but not hate mail, either. I was recalled to the present by a ringing telephone.

"Candida Darroway here," I said groggily.

"I know *who* you are, I want to know *where* you are!" Wes.

"Room 312 on the third floor."

"Comb your hair. I'm coming up."

A minute or two later, I saw a paper being pushed under my door; a breakfast menu. I opened the door then for some reason, and noticed the number on it was 311, not 312! That was Rob's number! I shut the door, brain muddled. I waited, heart drumming, legs trembling. a minute later, a muffled knock. Then, Wes's voice: "What the hell do you mean, 'partied out?'"

Ferrell: "Sorry, W.L. A *private* party. We didn't send out invitations." Inaudible exchange, then, "Bullshit."

"Ass-hole." A door slammed. I opened mine and peeked out. There was Wes, leaning against the opposite wall between Rob's door and mine, a study in indecision. He was trembling.

"Wes," I whispered, "I made a mistake. About the room number."

"The question is, Candida, how many, and what kind?" Then, he crossed into my room.

"I don't think I made any other," I responded gamely. "Just the half glass of *Americano*. It's very popular in Italy."

"I bet it is," said Wes. He came closer. "I think that particular 'American' is still on your breath. Is the other one?" And with that, Wes strode over to the blinds, closed them tight and began removing

230

my clothes. In zipping off my underwear, we heard a loud rip. My underwear.

"I owe you," he said. Then, removing his shorts and T-shirt and kicking off his sandals he said, "On second thought, you owe me!"

Whatever it was he thought I owed him, I paid. By 8:30 whatever was outside was as sore as what was inside: my heart, conscience and another part. Never let it be said that a man of fifty-three cannot combine inventive sex with a dash of ferocity, a cupful of tenderness, a few touches of perversity, ending in a French kiss and a sharp slap on the behind.

"That was certainly uncalled for," I said, rubbing my backside.

"I hope so, darling. I hope so," Wes replied, and with that, dressed and slipped out the door of my room, saying, "See you at nine-fifteen."

CHAPTER XIV

SOULS IN SIENA

I was asleep in Siena. I was fighting consciousness. I dreamed of last night's dinner near the Campo, in my white wraparound dress, the one that dipped in the back to the belt, and sitting, revealing a knee, a thigh. I was sipping an *Aperol* (non-alcoholic bitters) at an outdoor café above the piazza (Campo)–until the waiter told me my drink was made of insects! Insects bite. And something *was* biting my shoulder! Wes." I lay yawning as the day was dawning.

"Who asked you here?" I mumbled.

"You did, don't you remember? After we got back from dinner at one A.M. You should remember. You begged so piteously for me to come in. I demurred at first, naturally, but then went to my lowly room (he was on the second floor) for a tooth brush. I know you're picky about lending yours."

I was awake now. "No, I'm picky about borrowing *yours*. That's diff." Wes had both arms around me and was nuzzling my neck, breast, belly, my... I never got to finish the last word, which isn't polite anyway, and all I think needful for anyone to know is that we needed a shower afterward. We showered together. Italian hotels give you huge, thick bath towels. Rarely washcloths, but plenty of bidet towels, larger than wash cloths, but workable. Wes toweled off my back, and as he did, I hesitantly broached the subject of my tipsy chat with Rob yesterday, and Rob's not so innocent boasting–when Wes knocked on his door–that he and I were having a "love fest" with the *Americano*. Rob was occasionally unbearable, but not always. He had been almost charming on the balcony. It was something I couldn't discuss yesterday, and because I couldn't, Wes was considerably more assertive, even aggressive, this morning, though deliciously so. We women had seen too many movies about wounded male lovers to overlook how infectious those wounds, neglected, grew. But, despite love making with Wes this morning, I still needed to know what he thought had happened on the *loggia* yesterday. My parents' history proved misapprehensions fester with time.

"About yesterday on the *loggia*," I began.

"What about it?" Wes asked.

"I swallowed that liqueur fast because I was nervous and it was hot out there with Rob."

"Hot and nervous. With Rob. Why nervous with Rob?"

"Because I was waiting for your call."

"And I did call. Then what?"

"I couldn't get there in time."

"There" meaning to your room?"

"Yes," I said meekly. "That's where you phoned, no?"

"It's about ten feet from the balcony. Why couldn't you get there?"

I thought a minute. Why not, indeed? Because I didn't want to leave the balcony? Because I was curious to know how far Rob would go? Of course, I knew he wouldn't do anything. Lie. I thought he might. All I said to Wes was that there was a table out there that blocked my way past it to my door.

"Ah," said Wes. "So why didn't you ask him to move it and excuse yourself?" I thought another moment.

"Because I am co–leader, after all. I did want to know our itinerary for Siena." Also, I *did* want to see what Rob might try. But I couldn't say that to Wes. Some women, like some men, are sexual egomaniacs. Sometimes, so am I. Though it is embarrassing to have two men evaluating your every move, it's fun to evaluate theirs.

"Actually, the phone stopped ringing when I started to leave," I told Wes. Disingenuous. I suspected I could have had both of them for lovers–but only when Rob was nice. And only if I had not been seriously searching for the one I loved, and not just for fleeting conquest. Besides, knowing Molly's tale of woe, I knew Rob would not provide the forever kind of love for which I was searching.

"One man is all you need care about, it seems to me," said Wes, as if he were reading my mind. He was conventionally right, and I was quiet for a few minutes.

"Anyway, I turned my back on him, and he came from behind and kissed my neck."

"And….?"

"And I turned around." Wes jumped in here.

"Saying what? Doing what?"

"Nothing much," I answered. "He asked if I were surprised by the kiss?" I said 'no.'" This time I was not lying. I wasn't at all surprised. But I shouldn't have told Wes that.

"Candida, that denial was his ticket to come on to you again! You should have said 'Yes, and don't ever do that again.' Then what happened?"

"He kissed me on the lips and put his arms around my back." I neglected the French kiss part.

"After which, you….?"

"… ran back to my room and cried."

Wes looked thoughtful. We were both nude, but he was concentrating on my face. I might have been wearing a raccoon coat. "Candida, you are well named! You are naïve," he finished.

"Naïve? I think I'm a cool customer," I said, my voice wavering. "I've been on my own since prep school. I'm not naïve. What makes you think that?"

"Because you do not realize how alluring you are to clever men twice your age. I know because I am. Almost. After hearing your speech on Boccaccio in Chicago, I felt incredibly drawn to you. I didn't introduce myself because I was afraid I might frighten you. An older scholar in the audience; next thing you know, you'd think: 'He'll ask me out for a drink; then to his room.' Naturally I'm a middle aged sex fiend, as you've since discovered. But I flatter myself that I don't normally frighten young female professors. I love your *whole* self–face, body, mind. But most of all, your spirit, your talent for writing, speaking, your knowledge and sense of humor. And I can't resist your nose. I love your nose." I was speechless. "How can you love my nose?"

My rather "Semitic nose" had been the bane of my prep-school life, and appeared to be on the grow after thirteen. Mom offered me a nose-job as a prep school graduation 'gift.' I told the surgeon I wanted a straight nose with no bump; a classic nose, like those on Greek urns. Unfortunately, an Irish nursing nun with an up-turned nose worked in the operating room with the surgeon. She urged him to give me a nose like her own, up-turned, Irish. I was shocked when the swelling went down—as far as it could, and my nose stayed up-turned.

"Your nose wrinkles when you're unsure of yourself," Wes told me. "It just knocks me out." I, too, was "knocked out." How many men love a wrinkled nose?

"But, Candida, you've got to let Rob know that his little assaults are not appreciated. Otherwise, he will hit harder. He won't back off. I don't believe you know how to tell him to."

"Of course I do," I said hotly.

"No, I think you are flattered by his attentions. Even though you do understand that while Rob wants women sexually, he wants what he doesn't like. And to be honest, Candida, I don't think he *likes* you. He just *wants* you. I know why he wants you. But not why he doesn't. Every heart has its reasons. And there are lots of perverted hearts out there. He is like the character in the *Commedia dell'arte*, Arlecchino. Harlequin. An unreliable lover."

I was jolted to hear him articulate what I had thought months ago, upon learning of Rob's treatment of Molly—Arlequino, the deceptive lover. I hadn't had the courage to admit that I, too, found him attractive. On the other hand, he frightened me. For example, last night at the *Taverna da Giulio*, he never alluded to the episode on the *loggia*. Now that I think of it, he didn't say much to me at all, but was very deferential to Wes, whom he had just hours before taunted.

I nodded at him, saying, "You are right, Wes. I didn't really get it before, but now I do. I played into his hands, unwittingly. I'll be careful in the future." Wes kissed my unwrinkled nose. I dressed for the day in Siena. Wes put on last night's wrinkled clothes and went to his room to change and shave. He had already showered.

Our breakfast on the terrace gave us the protein to spend a whole day in an art-filled Tuscan hill town; not easy work. Ferrell had, however, set us a leisurely pace, since one day scarcely justified our climbing medieval streets a few feet wide that ran from Siena's three high ridges and sloped precipitously down to the Piazza del Campo, either fan shaped, shell shaped, or bow shaped, depending on which novelist or art critic you were reading.

235

There, late in June, Siena had held its horse race, the *Palio*, (banner) awarded to whichever *contrada* (district) won. The horse assigned to each *contrada* was blessed in each parish church. It was considered good luck if the horse relieved himself while the priest was blessing him, though not, I suppose, by the church's janitor. The town's districts had banners with distinctive insignia–a wave, a tower, a goose, a giraffe, a wolf, and so on. Rob Ferrell should have come earlier for the race, waving the wolf banner. I was obviously the goose. And Wes? The tower of strength. I wasn't big on horses or screaming fans, corralled by policemen and barriers, while horses ran free, sometimes killing themselves, their jockeys, and occasionally, an onlooker on a turn. We had missed the *Palio*'s banners, costumes, jockeys (mostly Sicilians) and horses.

Carlo had dropped us close to the Duomo, our morning's stop. We got the full impact of the cathedral's external beauty. Dedicated to the Holy Virgin Mary of the Assumption, it was indispensable to a tourist's Sienese experience, full of art that demanded attention. It sat atop the town's first church, begun in the tenth or eleventh century, depending on your guide book. This one was begun in 1215 (the year Magna Carta was signed) and completed in 1263. The campanile and some higher structures were halted by the plague of 1313 and never completed. It was remarkable for its marble stripes of black, green and white, and much else. I addressed the group first.

"Notice how the five rows of the *campanile* (bell tower) have but one aperture on the first level, two on the second; three on the third and so on until the uppermost level has five."

Anita asked why that was true, and Rob answered: "architect's preference."

Anita said, "*I* think it may represent the stages of man. When we were small, as this campanile was when started, there was but one idea to cling to: the nurture our elders provided. As adolescents, we were filled with the light of education, or apprenticeship in a trade. We were growing up. In the third stage of life, we expanded our interest to physical desire and reproducing our kind. In early middle age, the fourth stage, we acquired the control of adulthood and contributed more to our community than just children. But in the last stage of life, when we are closest to God, as the campanile also grew ever closer to Him, we achieve spiritual understanding, and these five windows light up the last landing on the tower of our life, just before our spirit flies up over the belfry to heaven." Who could have guessed that Anita was, besides being an art teacher, and religious, a poet?

Reed kissed her non-wounded cheek. "You are my inspiration, Anita, and if that wasn't what the campanile's architect had in mind, he should have had." Rob, too, complimented her on her poetic explanation.

"I'm going to incorporate your allegory in my next lecture on the Duomo of Siena," he announced, as graciously as anyone could have responded. "I'll even give you credit for it, Anita, dammed if I don't."

Still outside, we admired the three arched doorways, the giant rose window, the corner towers of clumped pillars, each topped by a turret, and the striped side of the building with four gothic windows above the first pillared line of wall; the blue dome against the campanile. We were too busy snapping pictures to do more than nod and grunt at Ferrell's comments.

"The lower facade," he explained, "was once decorated with statues by Giovanni Pisano, now in the civic museum. The upper half, added in the fourteenth century, is decorated with nineteenth century Venetian mosaics." Seneca had nailed it. Appearances *weren't* everything.

Siena and Florence were once equals, but at odds for four hundred years, until pro-imperial (Ghibelline) Siena reached its height, under a Council of Nine (1278-1355). After that, her fortunes varied. Vanquished (by Charles IV of Anjou), she was victorious in defeating Florence (1526); then was incorporated into Grand Ducal Tuscany after a terrible siege (1555) against Phillip II of Spain. Her population plummeted from twenty to eight thousand starving souls. The "saved remnant" preserved and rebuilt Siena's medieval heritage. Lucky for us tourists who could ponder that other Middle Ages, not the sickly, superstitious one, but the creative and aesthetic one to which we moderns seem so often inhospitable.

"If you thought the Middle Ages were mostly dismal, I think you'll find this Duomo dedicated to Mary's Assumption will change your mind," Rob hazarded. "The master architect until 1265 was Nicola Pisano. His son, Giovanni, designed the lower half of the façade, begun in 1285."

Sam countered, "That's ridiculous. Wouldn't you have to have the lower finished before the higher could be?" Rob explained that the façade is different from the structure itself– "the face is not the skull" he tossed off. His witty metaphor reminded me of all the things about him that mesmerized students and tourists alike.

Rob again. "When we get to Florence, we'll view at least two medieval churches whose façades date from the nineteenth century."

"Every old girl needs a face lift once in her life," said Matilda, sagely. Meg and Peg nodded knowingly, as each had had one.

"Buildings are not women," Ralph protested.

"True," his wife said, "but women can use all the upkeep they can get! Why not churches?" Everybody laughed. We entered the Duomo's center door.

"How to describe a gasp by thirty-three tourists at once?" I asked Wes.

"As a late January wind rushing over Wisconsin's prairies toward me walking to my office on Bascom Hill," he replied. Because this interior overwhelmed, I whispered, "More like a hurricane than a wind, Wes. Too much, too much!" Art causes a tempest in the brain of those whom it touches deeply. It is mind–blowing.

Now Rob was directing us: "Look how Romanesque pillars leave an imposing central space. And catch that cornice frieze with the papal busts over main arches," he insisted.

My own preoccupation was the floor, tiled with images in red, white, and black. I was afraid to walk on them, but who can hover above a cathedral floor? These inlaid mosaics covered the whole of it! It took forty artists two hundred years to complete. At one point you can see the She–Wolf of Siena, the one the ancient Romans believed suckled Romulus and Remus, because Siena, once a Roman town called Sana Julia, believed itself founded by Remus' son, after Romulus and Remus quarreled over Rome's boundaries. The fact that there was no Romulus or Remus or suckling wolf was beside the point. In Siena and Rome, this legend was fact.

Rob pointed over his head. "See that hexagonal dome? Bernini's. The coffers are *trompe l'oeil* meaning 'fool the eye.' They're only painted. Neat trick, no?"

I was getting allergic to things that only appeared to be what they really were, but I loved finding Socrates, whom Christians forgave for his pre–Christian birth. I loved finding Dante and the sibyls in the south transept facing the Chapel of the Virgin of Siena. St. Jerome and Mary Magdalene were in marble. Bernini. I climbed the pulpit by Nicola Pisano et al. I fantasized that teaching French and Italian grammar from this pulpit would make it sink in quicker.

Before we left, we viewed Donatello's *Feast of Herod*; his tomb monument of a bishop; his *St. John the Baptist* in bronze overlooking the font, surrounded by eight Pinturrichio frescoes (1504-05), plus four early Michelangelo sculptures of Peter, Paul, Gregory (with help from others) and Pius II, Siena's native son, near the entrance to the Piccolomini Library.

Rob insisted, "We must look at the library ceiling." He strode into a hall housing Pius II's books. "Enea (Aeneas) Silvio Piccolomini's nephew, the future Pius III, commissioned this library to house his uncle's collection. Aeneas Sylvius Piccolomini (1458-1464) was a humanist scholar before he was Pius II. The Pinturicchio ceiling (1502-1503) portrays mythological subjects."

Looking up, Wes remarked, "These would have pleased Aeneas, scholar of German culture, and a poet at the court of Emperor Frederick III as well as secretary to the chancery in Vienna."

As Wes spoke, a cloud Ferrell's face clouded over. Wes was looking up at the paintings and didn't notice. Gazing upward, my lover said, "After Aeneas gave up his scholarly role, he lost his sense of humor, becoming a serious churchman, then pope. Old Pius. He is famous for his statement, 'I see no good on the horizon,' made when he was trying to unite Christianity in a crusade against the Turks, around 1460. When Christians proved unenthusiastic, he wrote Mehmed II a letter urging him to convert from Islam to Rome and become the Patriarch of Eastern Christianity. Humanists were capable of liberalism and insensitivity in equal measure. While a liberal humanist, Aeneas Sylvius favored church councils, which meant less power for popes and more for the hierarchy. Once he was Pius II, he shut down the last council. Scholars turned administrators make arbitrary moves."

Rob moved toward the door, and we left in single file, ducks in a row. Everyone took a last look around. I hated to leave the Duomo, passing under the Last Supper rose window, one of Italy's first stained glass masterpieces. If only we could remember all we have loved; but art, like joy, leaves us long before pain and humiliation does.

It was almost lunch time. Sister Agatha, in "civies" wanted to see the home of St. Catherine of Siena, the woman who persuaded Pope Gregory XI to return to Rome after the Church had spent much of the fourteenth century in Avignon, a papal possession then. Gregory finally went to Rome, but died of kidney stones, slightly more than a year later (1376).

Italy insisted on an Italian pope, Urban VI (1378-89) and cardinalate. The French cardinals returned to Avignon, having elected a Frenchman (Robert of Geneva), cousin of the French King, their own pope. Clement VII. Pronounced a heretic by Rome, Clement was regarded as an antipope in Rome. Giulio de' Medici freely took the same name and number in the sixteenth century (1523-34).

St. Catherine of Siena (as she became) tried to end the Schism, as the split between the Roman and Avignonese churches (and after 1309 those and the Pisan church, too). Who knew what she could have accomplished had she not died (1380) aged thirty-three, a Sienese mystic of immense will, but little education; a Dominican sister who never hesitated to tell male superiors what to do to satisfy her–and God! At least she had tried to put an Italian church back together again, and for all Italians, trying counted.

Allison, ex-postulant and budding feminist, agreed with her aunt that a visit to Catherine's house was essential. Ian, friends with Allison since becoming Agatha's lover, despite their age difference, now treated Allison as a niece. All three held hands on the back seat of the bus ride to Via San Galliuzo, near the Via di Santa Caterina, in the contrada of the Goose (*Oca*) where Caterina had lived, with her huge family. Her mother gave birth to twenty-five children.

Allison, reading from a handout, told us, "Her original house stood near Siena's most famous fountain, but the building called *Casa di Caterina* encompasses it now, an imposing structure with enormous double *loggias* and a tower around it, which would have made a great study had it been there in Catherine's day. Her twin died at birth."

Could the world have taken two of her sort? Suppose one had sided with the French? "At seven," Allison intoned, "she dedicated her virginity to Christ. She dropped out of family life while demanding one of the two rooms of her family's dwelling for her own use, in order to engage undisturbed in the reception of 'mystical visions.'" *Most children would have been disciplined and lectured on selfishness*, I thought.

"Mystics lack discipline," said Jonah, startling me by seeming to guess my thoughts.

Allison continued. "She then took instruction from a Dominican priest."

"We'd call it tutoring now," Jan Huntsman said.

"Why would she need more instruction when she was already getting visions from God?" asked Mindy.

Allison couldn't stop reading. "Her house contains many of her dictations and other items of historical interest. The '*Casa di Caterina*' stands behind an iron grill."

"I suppose the neighbors, like her own family, living in squalor, criticized Catherine for not helping out more around the house," Peg said.

"It goes to show how little one's neighbors understand our lives," said Bill. Ellen frowned. She did not speak to hers.

Wes told us that, "A number of her siblings died in the plague of 1348. Three quarters of all Sienese did! Let's say her family, too, was reduced by three-fourths. Then there may have been only twenty left; still a crowd. But if *they* didn't all survive, Catherine thrived, though she died at thirty-three. She left behind three hundred eighty dictated letters (she couldn't write) to leaders of *trècento* (thirteenth century) society; kings, popes and cardinals."

Allison, reading further, added, "And twenty-six prayers, plus a *Dialogue* (*Dialogo*), records of her ecstasies, from that 'inner cell' where she communed with God."

Anita, educated in parochial schools, thought that "the oddest thing was that when she died in Rome, they cut off her head and encased it in a bronze reliquary, which can be viewed in the Church of San Domenico (St. Dominic) nearby; also one finger. Her torso stayed mostly in Rome. A few body pieces were given other European churches as relics." Catherine, obviously, was made of stern stuff, even sterner than bronze, which is less stern than the ability to dictate to a large family. Rob listened quietly to Wes, Anita, Allison. Female saints were not really his bag unless until some great Renaissance artist painted their portraits.

Matilda picked up Allison's folder. "Catherine must have derived some of her determination from her mother, Lapa. It says here Lapa lived to be eighty-nine years old and walked behind the procession carrying her daughter's head and finger into the church of Saint Dominic." Allison thought about that for a moment.

"Perhaps that was Catherine's way of giving her mother the finger!" she said reflectively.

Agatha, hearing her niece speak flippantly about a saint, frowned. "Catherine should inspire us all to press on, at whatever cost, to obtain exactly what it is God is aiming for." *Why couldn't he do it without help?* I wondered.

Jonah said, "There's an old Pete Seeger folk song that says the one can only achieve by doing things for yourself," but only a few of our older tourists revered Pete, though he was still performing. Jonah remembered a few words: 'Ain't nobody here can do it for you, you gotta do it for yourselves...' And for others, too," Jonah mused. Jonah occasionally gave voice to my very thoughts.

"Of course, Catherine did not undo the Schism by herself," Wes said. "She was just one forceful voice. It took many clerics, kings, and several church councils to accomplish that." Ferrell was busily inspecting a cornice while Wes was talking, and made no comment. His lips were firmly set, but Wes went on.

"In fact, it got *more* complicated after Gregory's trip to Rome. At one time, there were three popes, and France stopped obeying any at all at one point after the Pisans split from Avignon as well as Rome. Not until the Council of Constance (1414–1418) met in the next century was the Schism ended." Religious history had overtaken art history, and we were feeling fatigued. History tires most people out.

Upon leaving Saint Catherine's, we returned to the Piazza del Corso for lunch. A number of *trattorias* (informal restaurants) had set up tables on the sidewalk, and we chose one close to the top of the *Campo* with an unobstructed view of Siena's most central monuments, the *Palazzo Publico* (town hall;1297-1342) and its imposing *Torre del Mangia* (Tower of Eating). It was Italy's second tallest tower. Its bell rang out over the countryside in times of danger. Eating and living were synonymous. Was that the point? Bubbie Brondel used to say, "Mangia mangia" at every family dinner, though I remained a rather skinny child.

When we were all seated, Rob, as if in his lecture hall said, "The tower's flat-topped solid parts between the upper crenellations of its battlements were designed in the imperial Ghibelline fashion. Its base was protected by macchicolated galleries built on corbels around the top of the structure."

Sam asked, "What's macchicolated? What's a corbel?"

"Macchicolated," Rob explained, "means an opening in a floor so defenders of a tower can throw down projectiles, or missiles from a platform on the tower. A corbel is the platform that leans away from the tower, supporting weight, enabling defensive maneuvers. The Sienese were nearly as proud of their tower as of their Duomo—both designed for salvation," Rob added.

Precise terms explained, we now grasped the nature of medieval towers. It paid, I told myself, to learn how to defend oneself, and part of self-defense is precise vocabulary. Rob was teaching me unaware of such instruction how to protect myself. Words were my weapons of choice.

Lunch was not pre-paid, so we all ordered individually. I chose anchovy pizza and beer, and Wes ordered a fish salad (*insalata di frutti di mare misti*.) Matt said it was clearly an ice cream and coffee lunch day, and his "Magnifico" consisted of twelve dips of *gelati diversi* (different ice creams) topped with nuts, cream, chocolate sauce, caramel sauce, maraschino cherries and two banana slices, floating atop a coffee flavored liquor. Only a man of thirty-two could afford to lunch on so much ice cream, goo and caffeine.

Rob chose *canneloni* (rolled pan cakes of thin lasagna stuffed with beef); Arnold and Anne, *lasagna verde* (green tinted spinach pasta stuffed with spicy beef), and small salads. The twins, Meg and Peg, and the Harkers went the spaghetti route, though the pasta, a generous serving, made the small dollop of sauce in the middle look pathetic.

I recalled Mom's *Bolognese* (meat sauce for spaghetti) and how it covered the whole pasta, with lots left over when the plate was tipped. Anita and Reed, Sam, and Samantha ordered a splendid Leghorn (Livorno) Fish Stew (*accacciucco alla Livornese,*) a Tuscan one–dish dinner, with eel, squid, a crustacean called *calla squilla mantis,* whiting, hake, octopus, cuttle fish and crayfish.

Sam yelled "Boy! A seafood tsunami!" and the Froehlings, Huntsmans, Matilda and the Pellatierras cheered. "Chalk up another for Poseidon," Ralph, a classically trained scholar, exclaimed. "Poseidon was the Greek god of the sea, the Roman Neptune," he explained.

"The next time I see that on any menu," I said to Wes, "I'll have it." "And the next time Poseidon sees you on the menu, he'll have *you.*" I looked up questioningly. "What was that supposed to mean?"

Wes, munching thoughtfully, replied. "Only that Poseidon seduced every beautiful woman he could find, and had dozens of children by the most beautiful maidens from Libya to Asia Minor. He was just the crafty kind of 'waiter' who, after bringing a lady her menu, fed upon her."

"Oh," I said. "Well at least, he didn't show the hesitation that typified a man like Ferrell." Wes stopped munching. I wished I had not said that.

"Poseidon, who invented the horse by pounding the sea floor with his triton, was king of all the oceans. Ferrell, who is often a horse's ass, is only king of that small pond called Altamonte's Department of Fine Arts." Our waiter approached, and Wes paid for both our lunches.

"Why, Wes," I said, breathlessly, "I do believe you are jealous of our leader."

"Not at all," said my lover, taking me by my arm and steering me toward the group, now departing for the Civic Museum, "I am jealous of no man, unless he possesses you."

"Then," I said, "I erred. You are not a jealous man."

"Only of my happiness. And you are my happiness."

We swept down the Piazza toward the Civic Museum and the tower of medieval defensive precautions. Precautions! Good Lord. Had I taken all my pills? I hoped so. I hear they are planning even better ones for the near future. In the meantime I remembered an old German saying, "Every woman has her day; but men are always dangerous." Fertility was gender sensitive.

We entered the Town Hall (*Palazzo Publico*) with its city museum. The city fathers gave Siena's artists display space. To us these artists were largely unknown. The council chamber stood open.

"Let's look in here first," said Rob. "Here's a map of the world as they knew it in the fourteenth century. Ambrogio Lorenzetti's."

"Parts are missing," Sam observed. "Did Lorenzetti realize that?"

"Nobody did," said Rob, grinning. Remember 1492 when 'Columbus sailed the ocean blue.'? Well, he hadn't sailed yet. That's why, Sam."

Ferrell was endearing again. Opposite, another *Maestà*, Simone Martini's. Samantha mulled over the painter's last name.

"I'd hate to go through life bearing the name of a cocktail," she said. I pointed out gently that "Martini" was just the Italian way of saying Martin, a name common in English.

"Oh, of course. What a dumbbell I am!" Samantha sighed. I assured her that where foreign sounds are concerned we all made mistakes–until we learned the word, and then, it seemed normal. Samantha shot me a smile that made me think language teachers really could make the world a happier place, and the pittance we earned was supplemented by immense satisfaction.

Joan Lorimar, who rarely asked Ferrell anything, though she had been his student as well as his lover–maybe that was why– now asked one.

"Did the councilmen pray for divine guidance in this chapel next to their chambers before passing new laws and taxes?"

Rob arched his eyebrows, but before he could respond, Arnold, who had been a member of Boston's city council for several years, answered it for him.

"Wouldn't most councilmen seek divine guidance before they raised taxes? Wrong decisions in the Middle Ages might have proved dangerous to the councilors. They have in Boston." Ferrell laughed.

"Excellent, Arnold. And in fact, there were cases, and not just in Siena, when unpopular councilors were murdered by their critics. Of course today, we just petition for their recall, or watch political action committees unseat them, photograph them with their mistresses, or quote something they thought they said off the record. Then the columnists ridicule them, and they lose to a worse candidate at the next election."

Anita thought it lovely that "the councilmen looked to God for guidance."

But Ian mused aloud that, "It's easy enough for clergymen to 'know' the mind of God, but they may learn that what they think God wants might not be the case."

"Render unto Caesar what is Caesar's, but just make sure you don't render what is mine!" Barry, a stanch Republican, warned.

"Let's get out of here and see what else there is of note." Ferrell hadn't expected so much philosophy and civics to surface, but we were, after all, not an under-educated group; though appearances could be deceiving.

"Not only for defense, but town councilors also provided for garbage disposal," Ferrell said, as we crossed the hall. I wasn't sure how much prayer that might involve. But globally, I thought, people better pray that their councilors were inspired, because we had a lot more "garbage" now than in the Middle Ages.

The only other thing we looked at in this museum was the Hall of Peace (*Sala della Pace*). Jonah remarked that its very name indicated that it must contain the most precious thing in any age, for we knew how violent the medieval and early Renaissance periods were from paintings. If there was anything our forbears had learned regarding peace, we needed to pay attention.

This Hall, decorated by Ambrogio Lorenzetti (d.1348), had frescoed cycles of Good Government and Bad Government (1338-9). Lorenzetti, an allegorist, was influenced by Byzantine styles, but also by the naturalism of the Florentine Giotto, hence he was a transitional figure between medieval and naturalistic art.

"The famous *Allegory of Good Government,* farthest from the windows, is a painting in three layers, like a pudding-filled cake," Ferrell observed. "The lowest layer shows a procession of good councilors, contemporary Sienese. Above them (middle layer) is a stage on which sits a lady in white, Justice. She points to scales of justice. Virtue, at her feet, is also female."

"So justice and virtue are associated with feminism?" Allison asked. "You wouldn't think so from what we know to have been the dominant attitude of men toward women in this period." Rob smiled patronizingly at Allison, but did not take time to answer her observation. He went on with his lecture.

"You see the scales of justice are held by Wisdom, floating above Justice's throne. Justice was divine, thus male. To the left, a criminal is beheaded. To the right, good citizens receive their just rewards. The top layer of this "cake" held Mary, Queen of Heaven, patron saint of justice. Other figures included a male judge, and next to him, a blonde lady in white, representing Peace."

If anyone other than Allison and I noticed the inconsistency of a male judge, but a female patron saint of justice, no one said anything. Art history can be rewarding, but Rob could induce a hypnotic state that discouraged analysis.

"In the Middle Ages," Matilda told us, "Italian women, not often blondes, lightened their hair by soaking it in urine before lying in the sun. It might have been a worthwhile, though smelly, process if a dye job brought peace. Peace here *is* a blonde, one who saved sons and husbands from slaughter in war."

Ferrell looked nonplussed, but it all made good sense to us women, some of whom had lost their sons or fiancés in Korea and Vietnam, and before that in world War II.

"The *Effects of Good Government* and *Bad Government*," Rob continued, "were works that depicted familiar Sienese history and the nearby countryside. In *Good Government*, prosperous city folk were dancing or trading. In *Bad Government*, Siena endured crime. The sick roamed about a city whose infrastructure was crumbling."

Myrna, who did not often comment on artworks, noted that *Bad Government* looked "a lot like some of the poorer sections of San Francisco and Oakland." The artist, we learned, died in the plague (1348). To make matters worse, in *Bad Government*, the countryside was suffering from drought. In California, we knew about drought.

Meg and Peg, who were Girl Scout counselors, as well as nurses, took girl scout troops camping in forests. They were moved. "Colorado, where we were raised," Peg informed us, "and where we still own a cabin behind Denver, has had a bad drought this year. Forest fires have destroyed thousands of acres, hundreds of homes, and our favorite scouting campsites. Is bad government at fault?"

It struck me as an interesting question. If governments didn't cause drought in the fourteenth century, were they less innocent in our own era? Or had the scales of justice just moved from heaven to energy companies who fed our love affair for automobiles, a mode of transportation that some scientists were thought might raise temperatures around the world, endangering more than just the forests and camp grounds of Colorado?

We were impressed by Laurenzetti, but no one seemed enthused when Ferrell suggested we might catch the original sculptures of the Gaia Fountain (*Fontana Gaia*) by della Quercia, a replica of which stood on the Piazza del Campo.

"The original sculptures are lodged in what for over a thousand years was the hospital of Siena," Rob told us, "and there's a chapel in that same building where St. Catherine used to go and pray at night." Silence. We were tired.

"Or," Rob said, "We could just sweep quickly into the National Art Museum (*Pinocoteca Nazionale*) and view Lorenzetti's landscapes. They were probably the first truly secular paintings of Western Art." We had, it seemed, had enough art of all kinds for the moment, though we admired Lorenzetti's allegories.

"We should," Rob was wheedling us now, "*really* see the last Byzantine master, Giotto's mentor, who tried to breathe new life into Byzantine art forms. His name was Duccio (d. 1339), and he was Cimabue's student. We saw his Madonna in the Duomo this morning, but I forgot to draw your attention to it."

"Part of the altar?" asked Mindy. "I saw it." Good for her. I didn't. But despite Rob's entreaties, we had had it. Many were thinking of a cold drink on our terrace, a swim, a nap, making love.

Sometimes even Rob knew when he was beaten, so we summoned Carlo. Back to the *Scaccia-Pensieri* we drove, an ideal place in which to forget one's cares, which was what the hotel's name meant, of course.

Nearly half of us had drinks out on the patio, including Agatha and Ian, Allison, Matilda and the Pellatierras, the Schoensteins, Matt, Anita and Reed, Wes, me, Arnold and Anne and of course, Rob. The rest went inside to nap or shower, write post cards, or phone home. We ordered drinks. I ordered my annual Scotch and soda, usually reserved for literature conventions; Wes, a Manhattan, Rob, a gin fizz, Matt, a Heinekens, and the rest Cynar (made from artichokes), Cinzano; Campari and Coca-Cola, the last considered fashionable in Italy.

"Where are we dining tonight?" Arnold asked. Rob told them. "At the Old Tavern of Divo's (*Osteria Antica da Divo*), near the Duomo, carved out of tufa rock by Etruscans. Ralph will love it! The food is outstanding; the atmosphere romantic. All you lovers should be happy," he added, eyeballing Wes.

"We shall be!" Wes responded. We watched Siena's sun drop lower into a sky orange above, but topping the hills with aqua and blue. A beautiful palette for an art-filled city. Around 7:15, we broke up. "Dinner at 9:45. Be down in the lounge by 9:00," Rob warned.

I walked Matilda back to the side entrance; Wes, Arnold and Anne walked to the front one. In my room, I ran an opaque bubble bath, slid under the water, slowly exhaling. When I re-surfaced, Ferrell was sitting on the end of my tub, watching me, a slanting smile on his florid face. Had I summoned him with errant thoughts, or yesterday's kiss on the *loggia*? I hadn't wanted to. Had I?

CHAPTER XV

FLORENCE: MANY ROOMS, MANY VIEWS

Don't ask me what my plan was. I had none. Too proud to scream, I slid back down under the bubbles. If by chance Ferrell had murder in mind, all he had to do was hold my head under water. Alfred Hitchcock's leading man might do it. At least I wouldn't have to explain to Wes how Ferrell got into my bathroom. I didn't know! When I thought I might die of burst lungs, I eased back up.

Ferrell was gone. I would never tell Wes about this. Never! I toweled off and went to bed to rest up from the shock, wrapped in the hotel's terry robe. Wes knocked on my door. Wordlessly, I admitted him. Wordlessly he untied my robe, tore off his shirt and tennis shorts and inserted himself. Without more than a deep gasp or two, I came. So did he, and rolled back off me. We were on automatic pilot. I knew why *I* was, and Wes, doubtless, had his own reasons. I would never ask a lover what those were unless they affected me adversely.

"Wes," I said. "Something strange happened a little while ago. Ferrell got into my room from the *loggia* and entered the bathroom when I was underwater, wetting my hair. He sat on the corner of the tub, watching me. Before I rose up, he was gone. He never said a word."

"What?" Wes asked, propping himself up on one elbow, gazing into my eyes. "Candida, I told you, without reproving him, he will keep pushing." Wes got up and went to the patio door. It was closed and locked. He came back. "I see you locked it after he left," he said.

"No, I hadn't pushed the button all the way in; or else, I pushed some other metal protuberance. I found it locked later. *He* pushed the inside button," I told him. I began to see that Wes was right, though. Ferrell was a man who pushed. I would have to push *back*. Now that I had told Wes–though I had vowed not to just a half hour ago–I felt safer.

We had just enough time to return to our starting posts to dress for dinner. Everyone was in the lounge at 9:00 sharp, as directed. Usually,

250

I followed directions. I had an aunt who had told me, "Promptness was the courtesy of kings." I thought since queens were women, *they* could dally. Dad disabused me of that. He was a stickler for promptness, so I was always on time–when not early–from a young age. Doctors, dentists, teachers had all remarked on my promptness. I was outrageously early with Wes a little while ago, but then, so was he. Sometimes, it worked out best that way. Speeding toward Florence in our bus this morning on the A1, I had leisure to relive last night's dinner.

Inside *Divo's Osteria* tufa rock stuck out in irregular bumps, and though the restaurant had few decorations it did have a smashing modern painting of unisex figures in citrus colors, a painting that covered the rear wall and drew all eyes. The floor tiles were standard deep red, the tables for four wooden, and the menu, superb. It was a five star restaurant–not as Americans know them–but an informal restaurant. Very romantic. We started with mixed appetizers: thin slices of garlic bread (*bruschetta*); rolled eggplant, cheese-stuffed; crispy quail with a reduction of vinegar and leeks, and vinegar-soaked thinly sliced potatoes; smoked salmon (*carpaccio*) with avocado; watercress and oats soaked overnight–the German *muesli* in a salad.

I thought the quail wonderful, but how many appetizers could one sample and save room for the main course? After pasta and clams, the second course was meat. I nibbled at the first, and waited for the second. I had ordered a half portion of roast rack of lamb baked in the *Vernaccia* wine of San Gimignano as a base for its sauce. It was served with fennel cake. There was also duck breast with braised vegetables, and rabbit thigh stuffed with spinach, mushrooms, and Pecorino cheese. The potatoes were *au gratin*. Wes ordered the rabbit, but as rabbits had destroyed my vegetable garden in Alviso, I avoided revenge. "Vengeance is mine; I will repay, saith the Lord." (*Romans* 12:19). I'm not Him, or Her, but last night's bath made me wary of the idea of revenge. I was not cut out for it. Anyway, the Italian pudding, *tirra missù* (pull me up) plus cappuccino for dessert made me less vengeful and pulled me up from the depths.

That would have been sweet, except that just as the last morsel disappeared, Ian, dressed in pastoral garb again, stood up and asked us for a special blessing. Blessing? Weren't we blessed enough to be going to Florence tomorrow?

"I would like a silent blessing from you all when I sit down, having first announced, that the day after tomorrow, Agatha and I will be wed in the U.S. Consulate in Florence–a civil ceremony at 11:00 A.M. Agatha joins me in this invitation, as she will in our life together. After the brief ceremony, in a place yet to be decided, we invite you all to join us for *antipasti* and *spumante*, Italian 'champagne;' somewhere we can dance and make merry."

Agatha, wearing the same skirt and blouse she had worn all day, said nothing. She stood up quickly, smiled at everyone, and sat down again. I thought how fortunate for her that she would be able to spend her declining years with a man twelve years her junior, so that he would most likely be taking care of her in old age, rather than vice versa. Allison looked generically happy, also embarrassed. Perhaps she thought aunts approaching fifty not cut out for making merry. In Trastevere she had made merry with Ian herself. She was sweet and very pretty. A rose waiting to be plucked. Of course, you could pluck a chicken, too. Was I a rose, or a chicken?

Our hotel in Florence turned out to be a bona fide five star, a short walk from the Duomo, the Hotel Helvetia and Bristol. Once a private palace, its luxurious rooms were so beautiful that when the bellhop opened my door on the fourth floor, I just blinked. My room was a deluxe double, in wine and gold, with two queen size beds, two easy chairs, a dining table, cocktail table, fireplace, and before it, a love seat. A huge mustard yellow marble bathroom sported gold taps. My view was of Giotto's tower and Brunelleschi's masterpiece, the dome of the *Duomo*, properly, the Cathedral of Saint Mary of the Flower (*Santa Maria del Fiore*), the essential landmark of Florence. I thought of E. M. Forster's novel, *A Room With a View*. Wouldn't Forster's Lucy, a romantic girl, have preferred the Bristol to a rooming house on the Arno?

On the coffee table sat a huge bouquet of white lilies, still closed, in a crystal vase. The card read, "For someone ineffably sweet." Unsigned. I remembered the identical bouquet with similar sentiments Ferrell had handed to me in Rome. These were from him. But the fact that he had not dared sign his name was most disturbing because of his behavior in Siena. Not collegial. Flirtatious. Presumptuous. And, if Wes were right, taunting. But now, again, I wasn't sure. The bath scene in Siena was macabre, even threatening, and ambiguous. I thought of Signor Beppo's warning on the Piazza Navona. Was I running a personal risk? He thought so. And Molly, and Jonah and Wes. But lilies?

The second thing that struck me, after placing my suitcase on the luggage rack, was the phone flashing. Three calls. First, Molly's voice: "Hi, Candida. I miss you *so* much. I can't wait to talk about your trip. Or finish summer school. Just remember: be wary of *you know Who*! I had a bad dream about you and him. Bye for now." Dreams were my thing. Molly never dreamed. She warned.

The second voice was Theresa's! "Candida, honey, phone me at 0064-83-43-71 as soon as you get in." Theresa had made the trip to Florence as planned. Great. Dialing her number I heard the usual "Pronto!" (Here), an old fashioned response, also used to indicate readiness, that told me the call was being received by a butler. "Pronto," I responded. "This is Miss Candida Darroway. I'd like to speak with Signora Teresa Della Savoia."

"One Moment, please." (*Momento, per piacere*).

Then Teresa's familiar voice. "Candida! At last! (*finalmente)*. I thought you'd never get here. I lost your itinerary."

"Oh, Teresa, great to hear your voice. How did you know the right hotel?"

Teresa laughed before answering: "That, I remembered."

"Unfortunately, Teresa, we only have two and a half days in the city, and tomorrow, would you believe? our two clergy persons are getting married in the American Consulate at 11:00 A.M. I can't come out today, and tomorrow, I could only make it over for dinner. Our third night is a banquet at the Ristorante Michelangelo—on the *Piazzale* (a large elevated square) at 9:00 P.M. I have to attend. What's best for you?" I could hear Teresa thinking.

"Two possibilities, Candida. Dinner with us tomorrow night, say eight o'clock? We are getting older, so we dine earlier. Or, my first choice would be *before* your dinner at Ristorante Michelangelo. We live near there. Hercole, our chauffeur, could pick you up at your hotel at 5:30 and, after our visit, drop you at the Piazzale Michelangelo at nine. That would give us three hours to chat, meet my relatives, have drinks, nibbles here in our little villa. I will invite twenty people and twelve of the mobile ones will show. What do you think?"

"*Lovely*," I thought. But what I said was, "Listen, Teresa, I'm in love! With an older man, a Professor of Renaissance History. Can I bring him with me?"

"Naturally, *cara mia* (my sweet one), if you are formally engaged, with a ring and all, I mean." I was caught off guard.

"Teresa, I'm not *formally* engaged, I'm just in love. What difference does a ring make?"

"No difference at all–in Gilroy. Every difference in the world in Firenze. You see, my family is very Catholic, very proper, very old fashioned. At least the women are. They would be shocked if you came with your lover to see me, especially since you used to be Tony's girlfriend."

I had to admit she had a point. "Oh, I forgot about that; I mean, about Tony. Can I bring a snapshot of Wes at least? Can I show it to you when nobody's looking?"

Teresa sounded conspiratorial: "I want to see *several*, Candida. We'll hide in my bedroom and you can show me then. Ercole will pick you up at your hotel at 5:30 P.M. Friday. *Ciao, bella*!"(Goodbye, beautiful).

I was so excited. I would always love Teresa, always think of Tony as a ...brother? Cousin. That was it. A cousin. Now, for the third call. Room 302. I dialed.

"Hello, it's Candida, Wes."

"What's your room number?"

"405," I said.

"Be up in fifteen minutes. Prepare yourself!" Suddenly, I felt a strong pulling sensation in my nether region. The approach of ecstasy, or just a full bowel? I ran into the bathroom and did everything needful. Then a knock on the door.

I ran to it, with a smile on my face and threw the door open so hard it made a black mark on the paint.

"Rob!" I said, speechless. He smiled, strolling in uninvited, as if it were his room, not mine.

"How *do* you do it, Candida?" he murmured. "I have only one queen sized bed," he confided. "And no foreplay....Gawd! I meant to say no *fireplace*! I don't have a fireplace like yours. My room doesn't have a separate sitting room, either." Then, "I see you got my flowers."

Okay. It's wishy-washy, but most women who have just received a *second* bouquet of lilies in a crystal vase with a poetic (if unsigned) card would find it difficult to throw the flowers or their giver out. Only *not* if their actual lover were on his way up! Still, most women weren't co-leading tours with the "Prince of Lilies." I remembered the fresco from Crete of that name, only their prince was a lot slimmer than Ferrell, whose powerful six-four frame, beginning to flesh up around the middle, still rippled with muscles across the back, shoulders and long forearms. Was Rob prince or potentate? His little acts of thoughtfulness—if they *were* such—complicated things.

"I guess," I stammered, "you came to discuss our itinerary?"

"No, to apologize," he said, looking everywhere but at me.

"Please, Rob, look at me. What are you apologizing for?" I did not add "this time."

"For entering your bathroom in Siena. Really, Candida, that was uncalled for. I frightened you, and acted the total cad." I noticed he used the past tense, as if, now, at this moment, the present, I couldn't possibly think him one.

"I *was* surprised," I said politely. *Having a uterus caused politeness,* I thought. Many contemporary feminists would have criticized my thinking that; would have been incensed that I could fall for the old "biology is destiny" line.

Turning to Rob, now Nancy Drew not Wonder Woman, I asked, "How did you even get into my room back in Siena?"

"You didn't fully close your door off the *loggia* is how," Rob answered. "I was going to close it. I did afterwards. But then, I thought it would be better to apologize for kissing you without a proper lead-up. You know, it was half in fun!"

"Which half? The apology? Or the kiss?" I asked, smiling, despite my fear that Wes would soon pop in on us.

"Umm, how about the apology one hundred per cent, and the kiss fifty? Or maybe, the apology fifty, and the kiss, one hundred?"

"But why sit on my bath-tub?" I asked. "To have more to apologize for?"

"Confound it, I don't know! Soft in the head? Appreciation of the female form? A poorly conceived death-wish? Whatever you like."

"Well, Rob, don't do it again. Ever. I accept your *loggia apologia* (Lat., balcony apology). It was hot. We'd both been drinking. But I cannot accept the bathroom invasion. As for our itinerary, we'll talk after lunch. It's already 10:30. We can eat lunch behind the Duomo, a student *mensa* (Lat., table). In Italy student dining commons are often open to the public. The service is cafeteria style; the food is good, tasty and cheap. I suppose the Duomo *is* our first stop?"

"Yes. Then Orsanmichele, Palazzio Vecchio, maybe the Bargello. Pass by, but not enter, the Uffizi and on down to the Lungarno (sidewalk and drive along the Arno River). Then, cross the Ponte Vecchio (Old Bridge); up Borgo San Jacopo; on to Via Santo Spirito, gaze at that church from the outside, and so back to the Hotel Bristol. If that's too much walking, we'll call Carlo to drive us back from the Ponte Vecchio. He'll take the Lungarno and I'll point out whatever."

"So, there is this afternoon's itinerary–should we survive it." He smelled a lily, and looked obliquely up at me afterward.

"Thanks for those," I said. "But you really shouldn't have."

"I really did," he said, and left abruptly. I immediately shut the lilies into the armoire, the best arrangement I could think of. Just in time. Wes rang my door buzzer not a minute later. No use upsetting him with another bouquet. I kicked Rob's card under the skirted armchair.

"Now," I said brightly, having opened door to my lover, "What would you like to do before lunch?"

Wes didn't hesitate to answer. "You know damn well," he said, and shucked out of shorts and T–shirt. Unassuming in public spaces, he was full of fire and vitality in private ones.

"One bed or two?" I asked, as if serving lumps of sugar at tea. Wes snickered, climbing into the only bed I had turned down. *I* was the sugar, but we both drank from only one cup; passion. And drained it.

"Happy?" he asked me, leaning later on his elbow, peering deep into my eyes.

"I've never felt so happy; so complete. Completely fulfilled."

"And completely filled," he replied, kissing my nose. After which, he ran back to his own room to dress for our awesome itinerary. But why take a Renaissance art and language tour if you cannot put up with so much passionate expression, culture?

Lunch was convenient. It was the only place near the Duomo, and though heavy on pasta and soup, good and inexpensive. Back in the Piazza del Duomo or Cathedral square, we heard Rob orate on the octagonal baptistery of St. John (*San Giovanni*), where Dante was baptized. It faces the cathedral and is Florence's oldest building. Made of variegated marble, its doors were the most famous in the world. The oldest, the North, by "Il Pisano" (1330-36), had twenty-eight sections on the life of St. John the Baptist, plus allegories of the cardinal–and theological–virtues.

"Since the Renaissance cardinals were not too virtuous," Rob said, "I call this the door of wishful thinking." His joke made my thoughts wander. "Wishful thinking?" What did Rob wish for, really, where I was concerned? Unlike Wes, who was consistently ardent and caring, Rob blew temperate, warm, icy. One never knew in advance. Yes, he had seemed disappointed in his apartment under Coit Tower when I had evaded his sleepover invitation. Yes, he had taken pains to let me know he was the President's friend or confidante. But if he were confident that he could get me fired from Altamonte for not sleeping with him, he was much mistaken. I had not compiled a C.V. with as many publications as I had to make that probable, let alone possible–which it was *not*. Altamonte was lucky to have me. Rob would have been even luckier if he could have had me, which he wasn't.

The South Door was Lorenzo Ghiberti's (1403-24). "He had helpers," Rob said, "Donatello, Uccello, et al. He, too, made twenty-eight panels, from the *Hebrew Bible* and the *New Testament*, very naturalistic. But only Ghiberti's East Door, facing the Cathedral, won Michelangelo's highest praise: 'The door of Paradise.' Ghiberti labored twenty-seven years (1425-52) to complete it."

Barry winced. "Parents probably hesitated to have kids baptized in winter. The unfinished door must have let in lots of cold air–rough on babies." Barry, with small twins, naturally thought of their comfort, and of the little Florentines of long ago. Our Jewish members were especially taken with this door, its stories from the *Hebrew Bible.*

Ian, an Episcopal priest, also enthused over it. "Here Adam, Eve, Cain and Abel, Noah, Abraham and Sarah, Isaac, Jacob and Esau, Joseph, Moses, Joshua, Saul, David, Solomon and the Queen of Sheba live and breathe on this door, gilded, as if the God of Israel had just breathed life into them. Amen!"

I was surprised to see Sheba on the door. After all, she was not Jewish, but a *shiksa* (Yid., gentile woman) from Punt. Still, it was moving to see Ian so moved. Art and religion function in much the same way, offering the beauty of hope for securing eternal life. I supposed the Queen of Sheba made it into heaven, too, if Solomon did. She was his trading partner and greatest admirer. Maybe another paramour.

The Duomo. Its steps reeked of urine, for the homeless sought relief there. Once inside, we admired the three naves. Rob said, "Their pilasters support the ogival vaults." *Ogival* was a new word for me.

"An ogive," Rob explained, "is a ribbed or diagonal arch across a Gothic vault. The interior was begun around 1296, by Arnolfo di Cambio," he intoned. "This was built on the site of an older church."

Cambio meant change in Italian. "The architect changed with Arnolfo's death in 1301," Rob observed, "death being the biggest of all changes. Giotto was already working on the campanile next door. He took over the direction of the church, too. Then, Francesco Talenti completed all but the cupola in 1369." I repeated the name Talenti to myself. Who couldn't guess the name meant talents? Talenti had many!

"Talenti didn't have enough talent to do the cupola," Rob declared. "That was an object of a competition Filippo Brunelleschi won instead (1420), finishing the work fourteen years later." So. People can be loaded with talents, but someone else turns up with the very one they lack. Things were not so different in the Renaissance than in more prosaic ages, I told myself. We just have to work hard not to be jealous of others' triumphs. Was I guilty of jealousy? Wes knew more about the politics of the Renaissance than I ever would, and Rob, about its art. I was pretty sure I wasn't jealous of Wes. Why then jealous of Rob? I would not have been if we were not in a competitive relationship as co–leaders. If we were not in some vague sexual competition as well? I would not go down that path.

Before leaving, we gazed at Michelangelo's other *Pietà*, a work he intended for his own tomb, but left unfinished. Here, instead of Mary holding the crucified Christ, Nicodemus (with the face of Michelangelo) did.

"After working for years on it," Rob noted, "Michelangelo discovered a flaw in the stone, and smashed it (1555). His servant Antonio, who needed money, sold it. Another sculptor finished the female to the left, and the work wound up in the Duomo's museum."

Maria Pellatierra, a potter in her spare time, said it was always a mistake to smash an imperfect work that still spoke to many, if not to the craftsman. "Beauty is in the eye of the beholder. It depends on one's view. Even the artist may have a mistaken view," she said, gently admonishing Rob. He smiled at Maria. But I thought he really went with Michelangelo's view. A great master must please himself. A mere craftsman may please everyone or anyone else. Rob stopped carving wooden ducks after proving he could do magnificent ducks. He did not deign to be a mere craftsman of many similar objects, but an artist of original works. That's why Gumps could not fill all its duck orders. Andrea Pellatierra took the loss philosophically. Through Andrea, Rob penetrated San Francisco's most prestigious art circles.

Before leaving, we looked up at the church from the square. Anita said, "I cannot believe this façade is as old as the dome."

"Correct, Anita," Ferrell told her. "The façade was not completed until 1887, by De Fabris." Only in 1887? We were surprised. It matched Giotto's campanile completed twenty-two years after Giotto's death (1337). De Fabris. His name came from the Latin verb *fabricare*, to make.

"De Fabris certainly made a name for himself," Lynette said.

"Yes, but his is not a household name," objected Reed. "Who ever heard of him before?"

He had a point, I thought. All things, including art, are shaped by circumstance. Even that of ignorance. Especially ignorance. Before one knew what De Fabris had accomplished, he was a nobody. Now we knew, his accomplishments meant a bit more, at least until we forgot him. The history of the Duomo will always include his role, giving the first face lift to a medieval church. I knew from my last stay in Florence that Santa Croce had received a face-life in the nineteenth century, too. Tomorrow we would see San Lorenzo, a church still waiting for its face lift. And needing one badly.

As we passed Giotto's campanile, Agatha and Ian were walking hand in hand together heading toward Orsanmichele. Sandy and Belinda, also held hands, as did Anne and Arnold, Anita and Reed, Wes and I; but none of the elderly married couples, save Andrea and Maria. There was probably a warning there. I could have been wrong. My view was that of young (Wes being young at heart) lovers. Or youngish lovers. Agatha, after all was no longer young, nor Anne Gilmore, nor Arnold, nor Joan, nor Rob, nor Wes; yet obviously they were leading active sex lives still. Especially Wes. I could vouch for that.

"Just think," I murmured to him. "Most of these lovers never even *dreamed* of finding romance on this tour or knew about each other, before this trip started."

Wes muttered, "They dreamed of it, but dismissed it as unlikely."

"And Matt!" I went on, "Matt speaks to Molly every day. How enchanting to see Eros (Cupid,) still putting two and two together."

Unfortunately, I didn't know that Ferrell was just behind us, all alone. What was he feeling while I effervesced loudly on love? He didn't have Joan, except on loan, so to speak. That was a problem for him. Was I another? I did not know. Yes, he could be a bully. But not always. His personality was conflicted. I felt Rob could not, putting it simply, decide whether to be good or bad, and that the conflict was not only tearing him up, but those around him. *Conflicted personalities cause others pain, but to themselves most of all,* I thought.

The Church of Orsanmichele, a square Gothic building with a low crenellated tower was built as a granary with arcades for merchants, designed by di Cambio (c.1290). The structure replaced an ancient church of Saint Michael with its own orchard. The "or" in Orsanmichaele reminds us this was once one. This church is not di Cambio's work, but was rebuilt (fourteenth century) by Simone Martini, who closed off the old arcades, filling them with beautiful portals and three lacy windows. Between the pilasters he placed statues–patron saints of craft guilds who commissioned Ghiberti, Andrea del Verrocchio, Donatello, Talenti and finally, Giambologna (b. Spanish Netherlands; d. Florence,1608).

Sam asked, "So this church is dedicated to manual workers?"

Rob, beamed at Sam. "Yes, it is a monument to those who were manual laborers, plus a few bankers and merchants. In the Middle Ages, manual labor was considered honorable employment. Today hand labor is scorned."

Sam looked thoughtful. When he had worked, he sold stocks, houses. Did that count as working with one's hands? No. He thought it would be nice to paint a picture and hang it in Samantha's cottage.

We left Orsanmichele for the nearby Piazza della Signoria (Government Square), where we could walk at leisure not menaced by cars. We viewed wonderful statuary and fountains; the old city hall (*Palazzo Vecchio*) and Orcagna's Porch of the Lancers (*Loggia dei Lanzi*,1382). After we saw all we could, we would relax at a café. Was there a better living room (*salotto*) for the world's lovers and art lovers? I doubted it.

But first we climbed to the top of the *loggia*, "To get our bearings," Ferrell pronounced. It sat, we observed, at one corner of the piazza, past the Uffizi, back to its right and beyond, the Arno River. It was roughly opposite the Palazzo Vecchio, the old palace that still served as Florence's town hall. Between them, they formed a doorway into the square. Under the *loggia*'s roof, Cosimo the Elder, first Medici ruler of Florence, (d.1464) had housed his lancers in barracks.

In the distance a graceful, pointed tower of the Abbey Church (*La Badia*), and a shorter, crenellated building, rectangular in shape, (*Il Bargello*). The last word once meant police chief, but now it was the museum where Donatello's young David stood, as demure as a young girl, having just slain a giant, Goliath. There, too, was Donatello's original *Marzocco* lion, one paw resting on the Florentine shield. This lion was on our flag.

Down on the piazza, the bulky five story town hall, a fortress outside, a palace inside. To its left, a tower by di Cambio. It was clocked, corbelled, crenellated and accommodated bells. Way up flew the flag of Tuscany, crest barely visible from below. Looking at the Palazzo's exterior, Neptune's fountain to the left, with horses and a raised platform in front of the town hall itself, the *arringhiera*, from which we get our word "harangue;" a soap box where officials expressed official views.

To the right of the palazzo, a replica of Michelangelo's David. The real one was in the Accademia Gallery (*Galleria dell'Accademia*). On the left, Bandinelli's Hercules triumphing over Cacus, three headed son of Medusa, and a robber (1534). *If Cacus had hired a good defense attorney, he might have gotten off with community service*, I thought. After all, he'd been out here for centuries entertaining tourists.

Once down from atop the *loggia*, Ferrell led us past its inner statues. On the steps, two Medici lions; a restored Roman copy of the Greek work–*Menelaus supporting Patroclus*; on the far left, Benvenuto Cellini's *Perseus with the Head of Medusa* (1545-54). On the far right, the tortuous *Rape of the Sabine Women*, a spiral of marble by Giambologna (1583).

Samantha remarked, "It looks like he had snakes in mind when he did that."

Rob explained that the figure was "in the style called mannerism, where everything strains for effect, movement, the unexpected. This twisting figure (*figura serpentina),* is the first statuary group without a dominant viewpoint."

"Oh, what fun!" Ellen exclaimed. "No dominant viewpoint."

"No dominant viewpoint!" Allison sneered. "It's pretty simple to see that the viewpoint is statutory rape! What's more dominant?" She made a sour face at Ellen and we passed on to *The Rape of Polyxena*, a diagonal sculpture by Pio Fedi (1865). Two rapes and a beheading in less than three minutes.

"Aren't there more still more rape sculptures on the rear wall?" asked Sandy. There were. Three.

"What would you expect at a military headquarters?" asked Belinda.

Rob cleared his throat. "The three ladies on the back wall also represent the *Rape of the Sabine Women.*" Rome's early settlers needed wives and offspring.

"Plus," Ralph added, "there's a barbarian prisoner named Thusnelda from Trajan's or Hadrian's era" (late first to second centuries A.D.), discovered in the sixteenth century. That's really when archaeology began to get a grip on the Western mind."

Wes, scholar of Renaissance warfare, not archaeology, remarked casually, to calm the feminists (of which I was a proud, if wimpy member), "The whole point of war is to take what your enemies value most–first their women as sex slaves, then other citizens for other kinds of slavery. Equal opportunity for the defeated to suffer injustice."

"It hasn't changed all that much," Belinda asserted. "A good reason for doing away with war."

Agatha remarked, "What would Jesus say?" No one replied. Everybody knew.

"The Renaissance didn't value pacifism, did it?" asked Matilda.

Wes turned to her. "Oh, there were pacifist writings and even long intervals of peace–between wars," Wes explained. "It would bore you to name all those who took part on each side, and the peace treaties, some of which lasted a long while before war broke out again. The views of humanist writers and state officials, kings and popes, varied according to time and circumstance–and views of what would benefit whom most. But a whole literature on peace, starting with Erasmus's *Quarrel of Peace* (Lat., *Querela Pacis,* 1517) reproved Machiavelli's defense of strong military defenders in *The Prince,* (drafted, 1513), followed by his *Art of War* (1521). Those works rehearsed a humanist debate that went on into the seventeenth century. Shakespeare, who wrote several plays about the glory of war, finished his career with *Troilus and Cressida,* in dispraise of militarism. Candida surely knows all about this." Wes looked at me, with a half smile thrown out like a small bouquet.

Rob, with his slanty smile, asked, "Did generals also speak in dispraise of militarism?"

"No, I think just poets and scholars. Generals rarely wish to fade away." Wes's broad smile indicated how much he enjoyed the art of conversation. Military history was his specialty.

"Gen. MacArthur was no exception," Sam volunteered, and he recited that World War II general's statement: "'Old soldiers never die; they just fade away.'"

"He didn't wish to. That's true. Truman wasn't up for an attack on China," Wes reminded us.

"We aren't ever going to finish the argument on peace vs. war, are we?" asked, Anita, despondently. "Diplomats will go on engineering impracticable peace treaties that cause more wars and desperate men will look on war as the surest way to enrich themselves or the state! The state will then do them favors and desperate men will have to return them."

"Anita, dear," Wes replied, "desperate men have to fight. They are not the ones who enrich themselves. Those are the guys who design the wars that desperate men die fighting in."

Ferrell sniffed, saying, "W.L., *never* end a sentence with a preposition." He then walked us over to a figure to our left, where he stopped before a large equestrian statue of Cosimo I, the sixteenth century Grand Duke of Tuscany, his horse with curly mane and tail, his master balding, probably a curly beard worn to distract from his shiny pate.

"Giambologna," Ferrell informed us, "made both rider and mount look as pleased as punch with themselves," he said. "Here you have a man who enjoyed a good fight." Rob admired this work. "Cosimo's son, Cosimo II, paid the sculptor in cash for this monument. His father was worth every penny of it. His descendants ruled Florence until their line ran out in 1737, when the title Duke of Tuscany passed to the husband of Maria Theresa of Austria. In council rooms, banks, on horses and on beds, (the ultimate battleground), the family of de'Medici had a very long run." Ferrell's eyes shone as he finished.

Wes nodded. "Counting the years from the Republican rule of Cosimo the Elder in the 1430's to 1737, roughly three hundred years of de' Medici governance, with just a few interruptions." Did successful fighting make absolutism respectable? I wondered.

"Enough political history," Jan Huntsman moaned. Her left shoe had begun to rub a blister on her heel. "My foot is killing me. Let's sit down at that café and have something cold to drink."

Betty Harker said, "Hear, hear." She, too, looked worn out, and her husband, Jim, a retired geologist, looked almost as beat, even if the rocks in the piazza, which ordinarily engaged his attention, were excellent specimens, now incorporated into such impressive statues, such magnificent buildings. These older folks, Betty and Jim, Jan and

Ralph, chose the first shaded table they found on the piazza, town square of Florence.

"Iced-lemonade for me" (*granita di limone*), said Ralph. "With a gooey pastry," he added. Jim and Betty ordered frozen coffee drinks with whipped cream toppings (*granite di caffé*).

"For me, cold coffee (*caffé fredda*) will do fine," Matilda said, sitting wearily beside them at the nearby table, where she was joined by the Froehlings, who wanted cake with cappuccinos (*dolci con cappucinni*).

Meg and Peg, in banana yellow pant suits-with walking shorts and looking very much like banana splits, ordered lemon cake (*torta di limone*) that matched their outfits.

Not much in life did match, I thought. Did Wes and I? We had not thoroughly discussed that. Perhaps his view of matching would differ from mine? A good match means well-suited. A couple whose interests dovetail. Were we one of those? The taste of warm red wine, cold beer, good sex, a love of Italy and its history and literature might not be enough! I didn't want to think about it now. But one day we must. I wanted children. That would take negotiation, a lifetime commitment.

"Whew" Jonah exhaled, as he and Mindy, Barry, and Myrna, joined Wes and me. At the next tables, Rob sat with Joan, Sam, Samantha, Lynette, Sandy, Belinda. Rob was so close to me I almost touched him with my right elbow. In fact, once or twice his left elbow bumped my right one; intentionally, I thought. Surely there was something of the "love-hate relationship" in Rob's attitude toward me, an expression that had recently taken root, along with "transactional analysis" in psychology, whatever that was. It occurred to me that Rob had sought to remind me that he was not out of the picture, and that it would cost me to get him out. I had no idea what price he'd exact. I preferred to sit beside Wes, but Rob was still there as a kind of lightening-rod to counter atmospheric conditions.

Did he think I owed him something? I didn't. Roger Garvey chose me to be the co–leader–not Rob. And if I needed anyone to testify to my good behavior, my determination to serve the needs of our tourists, I had a powerful witness in Jonah Schoenstein, who knew the politics of our school inside and out. He was, I felt, another lightening rod to counter Ferrell's "electrical impulses" from shocking me. That, and my growing scholarly reputation, would protect me. Wouldn't they?

All of us ordered spring water (*aqua minerale*). All took great pleasure in the moment, seated in shade in the heart of Florence without Ferrell lecturing on art!

Around five o'clock, we headed for the Arno River and its wonderful old bridge, the *Ponte Vecchio*. Carlo was waiting to pick us up, because our older folks were not up to walking the six or seven long blocks back to the hotel. We were just passing the rather ominous, if cheerfully yellow, Uffizi Museum (*uffizi*; offices), former Medici offices in the sixteenth century. The structure led to the Ponte Vecchio. Suddenly, Wes whispered, "I want to go shopping with you on the Ponte Vecchio tomorrow."

I shook my head no. "Wes, that bridge sells very expensive jewelry."

"Nevertheless, I want to buy you something expensive."

What was he thinking? I recalled Teresa on engagement rings. We had talked but once of marriage, and briefly, of its insuperable difficulties.

"I still owe you two hundred dollars, you know, and I haven't repaid you yet. The jewelry on that bridge will be far more expensive," I reminded him; warned him.

"When would I have given you two hundred dollars?" he said, raising his eyebrows, feigning memory loss.

"In London, as I was rushing towards a cab. You remember, Wes! I owe you."

"Nonsense, you don't owe me a farthing," he said. "I'm the one in your debt, Candida! After I first heard you speak in Chicago, I was your secret slave. Very secret, I admit. But look how much you have given me."

"Not so loud," I said. "You admit you gave me those two hundred dollar bills in England, don't you?"

"If you keep mentioning them, I'll give you three hundred more. Then you'll owe me five. You'll never get out of debt with your tuition bills besides. Anyway, you've already repaid me."

"How?" I asked.

"Ask me again back in the hotel," Wes replied, his eyes twinkling. "But the Ponte Vecchio tomorrow. I insist."

"Do you always get your way?" I asked, indignantly.

"No. Only where you are concerned," he said, laughing out loud. I was glad Ferrell was on the opposite corner. We were about to cross the Lungarno (boulevard that runs along the Arno) to join him, for Ferrell had unfurled his tour leader flag on the other corner and was waving it. Carlo could more safely pick us up from that side.

In the clear yellow light of late afternoon the Ponte Vecchio looked golden. Beneath the roof was a passageway connecting the Pitti Palace across the river to the Uffizi, Vasari's innovation. We crossed over to our bus, which had forced other passers-by to duck into shop entrances. This city was designed for horses or horse drawn buggies, not tour buses. We climbed into ours, gratefully.

"Where's Ellen?" Bill asked. She had been walking with the Harkers and Matilda, who informed him that "Ellen got interested in some Gucci sunglasses displayed in a little window around the corner. She said she'd catch up." Looking directly at me, Ferrell said, "Go get her."

I found her around the corner, raptly gazing at the Gucci display.

"Ellen, please, the bus is waiting around the corner." I took her hand, and we made our way there. She got in safely, but Carlo wasn't aware that I had not entered, too. Perhaps Ellen's wide straw hat blocked his view of me. I heard a hydraulic hissing sound, and the rubber edged door of our bus smacked me on one side of my face and head. I staggered back down the two steps of the bus and fell on the street, my head landing on a heap of packaging material that had just missed a garbage can (*rifiuti*) on its pedestal near the street corner. It was lucky for me it had, or I might have had a cracked skull, a concussion. I couldn't get up.

The bus doors hissed, and out ran Meg, and Peg, both nurses. Wes and Ferrell were just behind.

Meg asked, "Can you stand, Candida?" I couldn't.

Peg yelled "Ice!" and dashed into a bar near the corner, re-emerging with a huge plastic bag (*sacco in plastico*) of crushed ice. This she held to my face and head, placing a scarf over my face, so it would not burn my bruised skin.

267

Next, Ferrell and Wes carried me into the bus, laying me on the back seat. This would be the closest I'd get to a *ménage a trois*! The thought would have made me giggle except I hurt too much, even with Meg holding the ice on my right leg. Peg took my pulse. Meg kept Bactine in her purse, and sprayed it on my bruised leg, pushing up my skirt to see if the bruises went higher. As the skirt had lifted in the fall, they did. Meg removed the ice from my calf, which was cut and bleeding, past my knee to my thigh. Maria Pellatierra, once a gym teacher, untied a draped scarf from her waist and bandaged my lower leg, making a tourniquet from what had once been a lovely Indian print, pure cotton. It was the lower leg that was bleeding profusely. I could feel warm blood trickling into my sandal.

I was trying not to cry. Then I was drifting along a crystal path, lined with lilies, until I felt Wes and Ferrell carrying me down the bus steps. The nurses followed. I hurt all over. My face was wet with sweat, tears, blood. The doorman ran for a wheelchair. I was wheeled into the elevator; whisked to my room. Ferrell had picked up my room key. Meg put two bath towels on the mattress to protect it, before Wes lifted me on top of them. The desk clerk arrived almost immediately, carrying two champagne buckets of chipped ice.

Mindy and Meg took turns applying cold compresses to my entire right leg, and the lower left leg. They applied compresses to my arms, using icewater to get face towels cold enough to reduce the swelling. Peg called the hotel desk for a doctor. Within fifteen minutes one arrived.

"Fractures are possible, but I feel nothing broken," the young doctor said. He bandaged my right leg and put some large plasters over my right cheek. Then he gave me an injection and I left Florence.

I left through the window with Brunelleschi's dome before me, making straight for it, arms widespread as I wafted up and over it heading for Alviso. While occupied in steering with outspread arms, I glanced back. Wes and Rob in armchairs by the cocktail table were chatting. Rob got up and opened the armoire, lifting out the vase of wilted lilies. He set it on the table between them. He patted Wes, now asleep, on the shoulder, and left, pausing to sniff a wilted lily. A blue puddle beneath me (the Atlantic Ocean) was soon crossed.

I was over San Francisco, where I avoided impaling myself on the pointy Transamerica Building, before rising over the Embarcadero and out to Highway 101. I thought about checking my mail at Altamonte; but, failing to make the turn toward the hills, I continued above the freeway until the Alviso turn-off.

Once inside my wire gate–I lived in the poor Hispanic section–I saw, to my dismay, that my flower garden had been leveled by rabbits; that I had forgotten to cancel the *San Francisco Chronicle* and *San Jose Mercury*. Inside, the electricity was off. I groped my way to bed, fell asleep on sheets used by unknown lovers who had broken in and made love on them, leaving several condoms down by my toes. But the flight, without benefit of airplane, was wearing. I slept for a whole week on the soiled sheets of unknown lovers.

CHAPTER XVI

MORE VIEWS THAN ROOM

The power came back on. I had enjoyed a week in my own bed! But now, the dome below told me I had returned to Florence. Yes, back in the Bristol. I hurt when I moved, but needed to use the bathroom. Wes, fully dressed, was asleep on the *chaise longue*. "Wes," I called, "I need you!" He began to stir, as if being whipped in a mixing bowl, arms flailing. Suddenly he awoke.

"It's okay, Candida. Don't do it yourself!" He reached my bed in a flash. I was trying to get one leg over the mattress edge, but my body wouldn't follow.

"Here, grab my forearms," he said. "Move slowly. Now, slide your other leg. Good. I'm going to be holding you; push your butt off the bed. Got it? You're going to plant both feet on the carpet at the same time." Then I was standing, unsteady, clutching Wes's arms.

"Bathroom?" I nodded. Nodding hurt. Slowly, holding Wes holding me, we reached the bathroom. Could I sit on the toilet without toppling? Wes grabbed me under both armpits, and sat me gently down.

"Good girl, darling. Do your thing."

"Turn around, please?" I asked. He did, but every muscle, I knew, was taut, waiting for a cry of distress. When I finished, he flushed, lifted me back up and walked me over to the yellow marble sink.

"Here's your toothbrush and paste." Wes loaded my brush and filled my glass. "Brush. I've got my arms around your waist." My right side was aching. A knock on the door.

"It's Meg," a voice called. I have some pain pills for Candida."

Wes yelled, "Wait a minute, Meg." He then pulled up the bath chair with his toe and seated me on it. "Don't move," he directed me. He ran to the hall door and let Meg in. She entered the bathroom, brandishing a pill bottle.

"'Morning, Candida. The doctor called these in last night. Pain pills, one ever three hours. There's codeine in them. Let's see your bruises." She pulled up my night gown. My leg looked like hamburger meat.

"Hmmm," Meg hummed. "Could be worse. The swelling is down a bit. You'll be bandaged for several days to keep infection at bay, yourself from bumping into things, which could start the bleeding. You'll feel better in half an hour," she said, holding out a pill and refilling my glass. Next, she whipped out a thermometer. "Just 99.3" She took my pulse. "A bit high, but that's to be expected. I wouldn't overdo today. No walking, no stairs. Rest this afternoon."

The phone rang. Meg answered. It was Ferrell. "Who is this?" he asked loudly enough for me to hear from the bathroom.

"It's Meg, Rob. I just gave Candida a pain pill."

"Good," I heard him say. "I know she isn't up for the Bargello, the Pitti or Uffizi museums. But I'm guessing she will not want to stay in her room. Can I talk to her?"

Meg said, "She's in the bathroom, Rob. Why not tell me?"

"Okay. The desk clerk says there are horse carriages that would allow her to see things from the outside. A few places she could even enter if Wes carried her up one or two steps. I could, but there's the group to guide. The list of places to see and a cane—the hotel's—will be at the desk. I'll have the desk clerk call the buggy for ten."

"How thoughtful of you, Rob. I'll go along with them to help her out. I'm an R.N., you know."

"Kind of you, Meg. I'm on my way to breakfast. Have a good day, all three of you!" Meg thanked Ferrell. Such kindness resembled that of a happy marriage. Molly said Rob had married young, but she knew little more than that he had been divorced at twenty-five. Perhaps, though, tenderness, like a vestigial organ, remained long after anyone ceased caring.

We ordered breakfast for three for my room. Meg wanted to see how I felt after the pain pill kicked in before we left. I felt very cared for, if groggy. I started to tear up.

Wes said, "There, there, my dear, don't cry. You have your own private nurse. Your own private Wes. In a few days you'll be your old private self."

I couldn't be my old private self when I was sharing my most private self with Wes, I thought. And that was all to the good.

Breakfast arrived, and the fried ham and eggs tasted good. Better was the pitcher of orange juice. I drank more than my fair share. Meg said that was all to the good, given my slight fever.

Meg dressed me, choosing a skirt with a rubber waist band, not pants.

"Your bandages will show, but this will be easier to manage in restrooms," she said. Nurses are so practical. She found my widest loafers, rubber soled. "Your feet are swollen," she informed me, "and you need traction."

Wes had gone back to his room to shave and shower, but he came back to walk me, cane in hand, to the elevator, and into the lobby. We all met at the front desk around ten. As we did so the horse and buggy arrived. The driver's name was Guido; the horse's, Alfonso. Meg stepped up into the carriage first.

Wes carefully hoisted me up the step, helped by the doorman. Meg's arms wrapped around my waist and hauled me the rest of the way in. Wes sat outside with Guido. This carriage was meant for lovers. But Meg could hardly have been expected to ride with Guido, and Wes found it entertaining on the buckboard. He even managed to get out some Italian, while Guido prompted him in not too wretched English. Men need to bond with other men. Wes had been cleaving to me, and Andrea, despite her marriage to the liver surgeon, to Wes. Wes enjoyed Arnold's company, but Arnold had found Anne, as Wes me. Wes wasn't interested in Andrea. He felt sorry for her. Mixed company–a tour group *is* a cocktail–conducive to chatter, but less consoling than straight Scotch. Wes might have bonded with Ferrell in other circumstances. They were both scholarly, big, handsome men, deeply into Italian history and culture. But I was the bitters in their drink–neither could stand the taste of me in the other's mouth.

"Our first stop, San Lorenzo," said Guido. The Church of San Lorenzo, redesigned in the first half of the fifteenth century by Brunelleschi, was not finished until a generation after his death (1446). It was still minus a proper façade. Its rough hewn stone was dreary, a distasteful gray-brown, though yellowish in the sun. It had only a couple of horizontal set-backs, a filled in indentation above where a window should have been but wasn't, and under its arched roof, a small grilled hole suitable for a pigeon roost. Three main doors, the central one taller, sat above a narrow concrete skirt, and seven shallow steps led up from the street. Consecrated by Saint Ambrose, Bishop of Milan (c. 397), Ambrose had also baptized the adult (and adulterous) St. Augustine; but in Milan, not here. Rebuilt in Romanesque style (1000) and again by Brunelleschi (1421-46), the Medici completed San Lorenzo (1460).

I knew its three naves and Corinthian columns; coffered ceiling and works by Donatello (d. 1466); but I couldn't get to what I would have liked to see again, the Laurentian Library, where I had researched Boccaccio. Too many stairs. Cosimo the Elder (*Il Vecchio*) had done well by humanists, providing they could climb stairs.

We drove around to the red-domed Chapel of the Princes on the back side of this church. The Medici Chapels were accessible without stair climbing. Handed down by Meg, Wes and Guido, all taking a part of me and placing a cane in my left hand, we entered. Slowly. This structure, begun in 1604, followed Giovanni de' Medici's own design. It was an octagonal chapel with a cupola, and its walls were covered with finely worked marble and bronzes. Walking slowly, with Wes's arm about my waist, I took in the sixteen coats of de' Medici arms. But the grand sight here were six porphyry sarcophagi, with statues of the grand dukes from Cosimo I to III. In the New Sacristy by Michelangelo (1520) were the three most famous tombs, two finished. Near the left entrance was that of Lorenzo, duke of Urbino, with the two figures that rested on it, Dawn and Dusk. Opposite, the tomb of Giuliano de' Medici, duke of Nemours, and at either end, the figures of Day and Night. Lorenzo "Il Magnifico" and his brother were buried near the right wall. Their monument, though incomplete, bore the Madonna and child.

Half of those statues seemed lost in thought, a hand to their chins, or heads, eyes downcast. If they looked straight out it was in search of solutions. Those they found served them well enough. Less well their subjects. The Statue of the Night was a bosomy female with right forearm supporting her head. She reminded me of a woman traveling in tourist class, trying to sleep in a cramped aisle seat. The Statue of Dawn, also female, looked as if she were overwhelmed by tasks assigned her. I had often felt I looked like that before hitting the highway to Altamonte College. The statue of "Dusk" to her left, was an old man with an unfinished face. But in the dusk, he hid his disintegration. I couldn't describe the Statue of the Day because it was of a muscled middle aged man who looked like he might kick your teeth in if you described him.

Wes bent down to look at me. "Enough, Candida," he said, and picking me up in his arms, carried me out to Alfonso, who whinnied. Guido hopped down and helped Wes place me in the back seat. Meg followed, holding my cane. She was a solid women, who intimidated several Malaysian tourists she saw touching the statues. She did have a stick, my cane, and looked authoritative. To me she was an angel for having left the group to supervise my recovery.

Wes said, "Guido, the Piazza San Marco. Then on to the Accademia. Perhaps she can see the David. My lady Candida would enjoy that." I loved the way Wes referred to me as "My lady." It made me feel like Isabel Archer in Henry James's *Portrait of a Lady*. Not only did Isabel live in Florence (with an American cad, a collector of precious items); but she had the grace to see it through, no matter how wounded, which was more wounded psychologically than I was physically.

"Then," Wes was reading, "past the foundling hospital (*Spedale degli Innocenti*) to the church of Santa Croce, and the synagogue (*sinagoga*). Ferrell's list. He remembered my Italian Jewish origins. *How nice of Rob*, I thought.

"After that," Wes intoned, "we continue down to the Arno and on to the Ponte Vecchio, where I'd like to stop for twenty minutes to buy a present for this lady. Lastly, return to the hotel. What do you think, Guido?"

Guido's job was not thinking, but managing Alfonso in heavy traffic. But he did nod, replying, "Expensive, but possible." (*Costa piutosta caro, ma possibile.*)

The market (*mercato*) on the Piazza San Lorenzo was full of scarves, glass, beads, alabaster, shoes, leather jackets, handbags. Meg was alive with interest. "Oh, Candida! See that red leather purse? Isn't it stunning?" I gently turned my head to the right, and saw the lovely red bag.

"It is, Meg. I bet it costs a fortune!"

Wes told Guido to stop beside the stall. Leaning over, he pointed to the red purse and asked, "How much?" (*Quanto costa?*) The stall owner raised it on a hooked pole for our inspection. It was soft and creamy. "One-fifty" (*Cento cinquanta*) he told us. Realizing we were Americans, he quoted the price in dollars.

"Too much," (*Troppo*) Wes said.

"One twenty," (*Cento venti*), the vendor countered. Final price," (*Ultimo prezzo*).

"Other colors?" Wes inquired. (*Altre colore?*) I was surprised he was doing so well in Italian!

"*Caramèlla, verde, nero*," (Carmel; green, black), the man answered.

"Candida," Wes asked me, "which color do you prefer?"

"Oh, if I were buying, carmel," I replied.

"Two then," Wes said. (*Due, allora, "Rosso. Caramèlla*). The vendor's face lit up.

"*Allora, sconto*" he smiled broadly. "*Cento dieci ciascuna.*" (Then a discount. One ten apiece). Wes handed the man two hundred twenty dollars in lire (the amount in *lire* a seemingly enormous sum), and the bags, each in a snazzy plastic sack (*un plastico*), were handed up.

"Oh," said Meg. "I'll write a check, Wes."

"Nope. Present," Wes said. "Look at all you've done for Candida, and before for Anita. Look at all you're missing – the Pitti Palace, the Uffizi, Bargello, the Davanzati. Present from me to you!"

Meg was flustered, but Wes would not listen to protests or offers to repay him. Then he got out of the front seat, and went around to the back of the carriage, pulling out the "Altamonte College on the Peninsula" flag (which he had lifted from my room), extended it, and stuck it in a small brass pendant holder he had spotted.

"Now, we are safer from being run over by cars, and your Altamonte College gets free publicity," Wes said. So Donatello's *Marzocco* lion and the *Porcellino*, or boar, flew above us within a border of red Florentine "lilies," really irises, native to Persia, and prominently advertised our school on silk fabric—woven in Florence! The Florentines identified our red "lily" as a symbol of their own. I did not know who first introduced that "lily" symbol to Florence. But, as St. Matthew said of real lilies, they were "of the field." *(Matt. 6:28)*. Florence was surrounded by Tuscan fields.

Meg had a thermos and paper cups. From her bag she pulled them out. "Time for another pill," she said. "You're stiffening up, Candida." I took one, and sipped. "Drink up!" she said, so I drained the cup. "Water anyone?" she asked, taking a gulp herself. Guido said *"per favore"* (please), but Wes waved it away.

"You three are the lushes here," he teased. We were on our way to the Church of San Marco and its little piazza. Guido took Via Martelli to Cavour, and soon we were at Piazza San Marco, with its thirteenth century church, several times restored (by Michelozzo, Gimbologna and Pier Francesco Silvani (1678). Although I had been here before, I knew I couldn't go inside. I remembered Michelozzo's paintings, and under the altar of the Chapel of Saint Antonino, an Archbishop of Florence, his remains, entombed by Giambologna.

Ferrell thought all this art unknown to me, but I had really been moved by San Marco, the convent, its art, its sacred objects. One didn't have to be Catholic to find Catholic art touching. Yet the Dominicans, as an Order, were cruel inquisitors into conscience. Torturers, as well as educators. There was a difference even then.

This convent, San Marco, was commissioned by the first Cosimo de' Medici (d.1464) for the use of Dominican friars of Fiesole. One was the famous Fra'Angelico (angelic brother) who painted such sweet angels and left so deep an impression. His second floor frescoes, one for each cell on both sides of a corridor, were superb. I recalled a fresco based on *John 20:17*, (Lat. *Noli mi Tangere)*, where Christ said, "Don't Touch Me" as per *the Vulgate*. In my *English New Testament* this was translated, "Do not cling to me." The disparity went to show what power there was, and what variation, in translation. But Christ's own Translation, i.e., his Ascension, had not yet occurred, and that seemed to be his reason for standoffishness. He explained something of that to Mary Magdalen, his friend, telling her he had not yet ascended to the Father. I didn't understand *why* Christ said it. Mary must have suffered a feeling of loss when he withdrew. Many women experience a sense of loss after withdrawal.

Girolamo Savonarola, prior, had lived here after 1491. The Dominican from Ferrara, spurned by a woman whom he had loved, ruled Florence harshly (1494 to 1498), admired by a few, but unable to effect moral reform. It was hard being moral when it meant no art, no luxuries and frequent confession of sins. They hanged him in the Piazza della Signoria on 8 April, 1498, after torturing him. He died reconciled with the Church and his arch enemy, Pope Alexander VI. Savonarola was critical of Alexander Borgia's immorality–five illegitimate children by unknown women, and three more by Vanozza dei Catanei (including Caesar (*Cesare*), *plus a* brother whom Cesare *may* have murdered; and Cesare's sister, Lucretia (*Lucrezia*), whose first (of three) husbands he had murdered. Lucrezia's marriages served the family's fortune. Not hers for love.

Savonarola respected the pope's right to have him tortured and burned at the stake! Of late, the Church had been talking about getting him started on the road to sainthood, a case of love thine enemies, not an unknown principle to me. San Marco was full of art and history, but I could not have climbed to the second floor to see Fra Angelico's frescoes. So we clopped down the Via Guelpha to the Accademia and David, Michelangelo's masterpiece.

I loved Wes; I loved David. I called out to Guido, "Stop, Guido." (*Si ferma qui Guido*) And to Wes. "You've got to get me in to see David or I'll die."

"Here," Meg said, "take another pain pill." Although Wes thought the exercise might be too much for me, I would brook no opposition. Guido said the steps were few and shallow. When people waiting in line saw me being carried, they let us by. They probably thought I was dying of some wasting disease (I had lost three pounds), and I *was* pale. Wes carried me halfway up the corridor in his arms to Michelangelo's masterpiece, then gently stood me on my feet. Meg took one arm, Wes the other, and we finished the brief trip right up to the roped off pedestal. I couldn't help it, but tears were falling down my face.

Having looked again at Michelangelo's David, the most famous king in the world, I could not but be moved. Finished by the twenty-five year old sculptor (1504), David is every young man's inner self. Confident, handsome, strong, beautifully proportioned, straight of nose, pious. And a born killer.

In bed with Bathsheba, or on the battle fighting his father-in-law, King Saul, David represented virility, success, everything men wanted and claimed women did. And he knew it, flaunted it. David was the Judeo-Christian stand-in for the Greek demigod Hercules. Or the Jewish stand in for those Christian brawlers, Saints Michael and George. Being Jewish, David was sentimental, and sentimentalism was dangerous in a ruler. I wished I had known him. In Ferrell, I sometimes thought I had.

"Well, Candida, now that you've seen your ideal man, and before you faint, I'm getting you out of here," Wes muttered. Jealousy? He threw me over his shoulder this time, like a sack of polenta, and marched off, leaving Meg to thread her way through he crowds, carrying my cane and the thermos.

"It's easier to carry you like this," Wes said, "The other way hurt my back." And so, having looked upon the face of David, the body of a Greek-like demigod, I was obliged to look at the backside of my American lover, without the superb *gluteus maximus (Lat., buttock muscles)* with which Michelangelo endowed David.

Of course I said nothing of that to Wes, who placed me in the back seat of the hackney cab, just as a policeman *(poliziotto)* approached to ticket Guido. When he saw that I was disabled, he crumpled the ticket and waved us on. One cannot help loving Florentine policemen, the demigods of modern Italy.

Meg poured me another cup of water and handed me another pain pill. I thought I could do without it, but she insisted. "You take them before you're in pain. Not after. And you are due for one now." I obeyed. Nurses and schoolteachers have an authority not easily resisted.

We were passing the Hospital of the Innocents (*Ospedale degli Innocenti*). It sat on the Square of the Holy Annunciation (*Piazza Santissima Annunziata*), where everything was in proportion with everything else. The *Spedale,* as modern Italians called it, was completed by Brunelleschi (1434). Between its arcades were medallions with chubby boy angels (*putti),* fashioned by Andrea della Robbia of glazed terra–cotta; winged cherubs in white, swimming on blue sky. Opposite, a convent by Antonio da Sangallo and Baccio d'Agnolo (1525), whose real name was Bartolomeo Baglioni. *D'Agnolo* was a corruption of *Angelo*, his father's first name. The names of Renaissance artists were as varied as their works. Many had nicknames, like kids at prep schools in England and New England. How sad that we Americans have to stick with our given names, or use generic nicknames like Butch, Bob, Babs ....Candy.

Renaissance artists were freer in their identities than we are. Whatever name we went by, our government knew who we *truly* were, and woe to us if we should use a nickname on an official document, or misspell our mother's maiden name. We could be kept off a flight list; not get a job; a passport; unemployment benefits–perhaps even a death certificate–although, it wouldn't matter much to *us*. Just to our family.

Guido drove around the square. We admired the Church of the Holy Annunciation, (thirteenth century). It was continually reconstructed up through the eighteenth. Its portico, begun by Sangallo, was finished by Giovanni Caccini (1621). Inside was the tomb Giambologna designed for himself and other "Flemish artists who died in Florence." Curious, but even the dead preferred to be with their own kind.

Wes asked if I were tired. "I'd be more tired if I were in bed all day," I replied.

"Stop at the synagogue, Guido," I yelled out. It was only a few blocks down the Via degli Alfani, and I had been there before.

"I want to go *inside*, Wes. I have a special prayer to say for my Italian family members." Guido, who understood more English than I had realized, turned around. "You're Italian, Miss? I wouldn't have thought so." (*Lei e Italiana, Signorina? Non l'avevo mai pensato*). I wasn't going to go into my mixed heritage. Nor pray for any Christian relatives here. They raised unholy hell when Dad married my Jewish mother.

This synagogue dated from the 1870s, though the city's Jewish population was over a thousand people after the fourteenth century. It was a beauty, Moorish-Byzantine of style, church-like in appearance, with a dome, apse, pulpit and pipe organ. I sat on one of the back prayer benches, not oblivious of the fact that there was separate seating for women–upstairs. I hoped I didn't spoil the prayers of the next man who sat here, but I couldn't climb stairs. I just lowered my head and made up a prayer for my mother, still living, in which I wished her luck in raising her husband's children, grandkids. His kids were her family now. I was an addendum.

I prayed that she would not realize the pain caused by marginalizing me at fourteen, when she'd first met him. His kids were cute then, and I was a floundering fourteen year old with issues. I didn't understand then. I prayed longer for my Bubbie Brondel, because she had given me unconditional love from my birth to her death, dying just a year before my parents' divorce. What would she think—or did she know?—that I was in an orthodox synagogue, praying for her, wherever her ions might be; for she had been cremated (not orthodox) and had Mom toss her ashes off Moss Landing in California. Even if she had wound up in Japan, I knew she was watching over me while her spirit was eating sushi. My Bubbie loved fish.

I looked up at Wes, and he got me back to the coach. There's a term "hackney coach." It suggested something often used and common, i.e., hackneyed. I didn't ever want to feel that way myself. We Renaissance scholars were an elite group. We might be underpaid, but we were not common.

Santa Croce was easily reached from the synagogue. Guido took the Via dei Pepi to the Piazza Santa Croce, a Franciscan church designed to hold huge audiences in which the enthusiastic piety of its preachers would transform an errant Florence. It never happened.

Now Santa Croce was a cenotaph for famous Florentine souls, not a house of spiritual change. The church, with three Gothic naves houses the tomb of Michelangelo by Vasari; Dante's cenotaph (by Ricci, 1829) is also there, though Dante's remains are in Ravenna. Once banished, always banished, except in the case of the Medici, of course. Machiavelli had his monument there by Spinazzi, (1787). Leonardo Bruni, a great humanist, had his tomb by B. Rossellio, (fifteenth century), as did the composer Rossini (d. 1868). Not even the Barber of Seville could have gotten him out of his present fix. Memorial stones of the Ghibertis, Lorenzo and Vittoria, were here. And the tomb of Galileo Galilei (d.1642). So many great Florentines were buried in Santa Croce. Besides Giotto, the artists who decorated their last resting places—as today interior decorators decorate the homes of the wealthy—were impressive:

Michelozzo, Giovani del Biondo, Donatello, Andrea della Robbia, Lorenzo Batolini, Agnolo Gaddi, Libero Andreotti, Bernardo Daddi, Maso di Banco, called "Giottino" (little Giotto), Volterrano, Cimabue, more. Even Ferrell couldn't have done them all justice. Overwhelming how many talented souls were born or worked in Florence, buried in Santa Croce.

All the more perplexing, having loved E.M. Forster's *Room With a View*. In that novel the scene in Santa Croce concerned a missing guidebook, as if any guide, printed or living, could do more than just locate this city's parts. Forster's tourists, like ours, were not art *afficionados* or even seekers after themselves. Their seeking out Florentine beauty was just doing what one's class dictated must be done to belong. An Italian tour. You simply *found* the parts, not bothering to make them your own. Reading Forster, one learned almost nothing about Santa Croce–like the English tourists whom he "led" there. The heroine, Lucy, met the hero, George Emerson, inside Santa Croce. He and his father, neither of her social class, served as her guides that day. George turned out at novel's end not merely to have been her Florentine "guide," but her life's. They married, though her friends thought him an inappropriate match. Would my friends find Wes inappropriate due to the difference–not in our social class, which was equal–but in our ages, which differed so? Was it any of their business? Wouldn't they say the same about Agatha's marriage to the younger Ian?

Wes told Guido to head for the Ponte Vecchio, and Alfonso took off at a gallop straight down Borgo Santo Croce, into the Via dei Vagelli (dyers' vats) and on until the Ponte Vecchio appeared. We descended. Meg and Wes helped lift me out of the carriage like a precious jewel that might otherwise have rolled into the Arno.

Guido said, "Take your time. Alfonso and I will find you again on the same corner of the Lungarno." They disappeared in heavy traffic.

"Wes," I said, "I don't want to seem ungrateful, but going into any shop on this bridge is foolhardy. One or the other of us might regret such a purchase some day."

Meg excused herself saying, "I'm off to see what those Africans on the sidewalk are selling. Maybe I'll get the perfect stocking fillers for my nieces and nephews. I'll wrap up Christmas while you two wrap up your future."

I turned to Wes. "Look, we haven't even discussed our future. We aren't a couple. Just a couple of lovers! You just bought me a lovely purse. No expensive jewelry, please."

"Oh, indeed we have a future together," Wes replied. "We've just delayed entering it, because we both know that it has as many disadvantages as advantages. We are eminently reasonable, you and I, Candida, as well as besotted with love for one another. Here's what we haven't faced up to. On your side, the disadvantages of marrying me are greatest." He began enumerating. "First, I am as old as your father. Second, I do not want more children. I've had two, that is adequate. I'm glad they're grown and beginning to paddle their own canoes." I looked way up toward the hills above the river. "Third, if I married you," he continued, "and I would *love* to marry you, Candida–you know that–you would lose your job at Altamonte, which, while not a great one, earns you more money than you could make in Wisconsin, in or near Madison. I have to earn money there, where my Chair is. It would be different if I had one near you." He was explaining the situation while tourists drifted all around us, making selections when we couldn't even make a choice.

"I'm not too old to be hired in California, Candida, being, well-established in Renaissance studies." I loved his humility. He was a world class scholar in the field. "But so far, no senior Renaissance positions have turned up in California. And you know how expensive houses are there."

I didn't say anything, just held onto his arm for balance and directed my view to the other side of the Arno somewhere halfway between Via Tornabuoni and the Piazzale Michelangelo.

Wes, getting no response, added, "I've a perfectly nice four bedroom, two bath home on a tree-lined street in Madison, within walking distance of my office on Bascom Hill. Our weather is rotten, cold and icy in winter hot and humid in summer. But I'm a Midwesterner. I can take it. You, on the other hand, are a California blossom–with a touch of chronic bronchitis. And you would be lucky to find a job in a high school, let alone the University. Faculty wives without your credentials get jobs in our nearby high schools. Those places wouldn't touch a scholar like you. You are overqualified. A state college job would be a long commute. Really untenable, as Milwaukee would be–too far for a married couple who need to be together every day, not just weekends. And, you want kids." His reasoning was relentless. "So, if I bought you an engagement ring, it would remind you not of possible advances in academe and the nursery, but of a life closing down, no research, no teaching, no dates, and unbearable loneliness. You might not love me as much then. I have considered all this ever since we met, and cannot foresee a happy solution."

I knew he was right. "So why buy me any jewelry, Wes? It's a waste of your hard earned savings, and for me, a token of inevitable parting."

"We might meet during vacations, Candida. And at your literary conventions, when they coincide with mine. There's Christmas. Easter. Summers. Letters. Phone calls. And when you do marry, well, I'll know that you will have children, and pray that every one of them–especially the girls–look just like you, laugh like you, and eventually, make love like you. I'd have something to rejoice about, knowing that I had once had such love myself." Wes teared up. But he was not to be swayed about the jewelry.

"Now, we are going to buy you a lovely present in one of these shops of gold." He paused to blow his nose. "Here, I like the name of this one. *The Golden River.* And it's right near the pickup point. No walking. Let's see what it has to offer two problematic lovers," Wes said.

There was only one other customer inside, an elderly man, looking at cuff links, and several clerks standing idly by, bored.

"How may I help you?" asked one, a tall woman, whom the French would call "*une belle laide*" (an attractive ugly woman). She was wearing a chartreuse silk shirt and black tapered pants. About her long neck hung five or six golden chains, very fine and in good taste.

"Perhaps an engagement ring? A diamond? A sapphire? Sapphires would go with the lady's eyes." Mine weren't blue. Was she near sighted?

"Not today," Wes said diplomatically. "No, today I'd like to see a gold necklace."

"Something like one I'm wearing?" she asked.

"No, heavier," Wes replied, opening his thumb and forefinger to show a half-inch gap. He saw a case that glittered in afternoon sunlight lighting up it display. The clerk followed.

"How do like this one with the broad etched links?" she asked me. I shook my head no. "Perhaps this, with the flat broad links? Or–but this is a masterpiece–the one of plaited hearts and keys? So romantic." She saw my look of disapproval in the mirror. Undaunted, she asked, "Possibly a twisted rope design?" Wes just looked the case over at his ease, giving the clerk no clues as to his own preference.

"Candida, come look at these." He had forgotten to keep hold of me, and turning, I nearly fell, cane in hand. The clerk looked concerned, and ran out from behind the counter to steady me. Hang on to the counter, she urged.

"Oh, darling," I'm so sorry," Wes said. "I forgot your condition."

"Condition?" Perhaps the clerk thought I was pregnant? I blushed. Then she did. But it wasn't any of her business, and she was all business, because Wes was now excited about some necklaces he had glimpsed–not the least expensive items in the case, either.

"How do you like this one?" he asked, his arm around my waist, pointing to an exquisite, broad, intricate gold collar.

The clerk brought it out and laid it on a dark blue velvet display pedestal.

"It's too dressy for my lifestyle," I said, hesitantly. *I love it,* I thought.

"Well, what about the twisted rope piece?" Wes asked.

I said, "It's nice, but too old for someone my age."

The clerk agreed. "I know just what this young lady might like." She went into the back of the shop, opened a safe and returned with three necklaces so gorgeous they took my breath away. She placed each one on a velvet stand before us.

Three Byzantine ropes of twisted gold wires curling endlessly on and into each other, in three lengths. The gold cores were heavy, their surfaces held tiny multi-colored medallions, and the clasp of the twenty-four inch necklace was a lion's claw covered by a golden rose that swung shut, clasping the claw, creating a stunning nape interest. It could be turned forward to form a pendant, as versatile as it was beautiful. The clerk clasped it around my neck, as she stepped back, Wes kept his arm around my waist, as we looked into the mirror.

Except for my bruised right cheek, I looked liked one of those advertisements in *Vogue* or *Elle*. The twenty-four inch necklace, in 18 karat gold, was perfect on me. Not like my old hippie Indian or African beads, in random sizes and colors, some chipped or missing. Even Audrey Hepburn, Hollywood's "hippie," was transformed by Hollywood into the more appealing "Holly Golightly" shopping for jewelry at Tiffany's. Holly expected older men to reward her with gifts for her company. Had I become like her? A throwback to pre-war geishas of Japan? I knew women in the Renaissance were "bought" by rich men dangling gold and titles before them? Wes was very noble, but a duke or count he was not. He asked the clerk, "How much is this necklace?" It was "only" three thousand, nine hundred and fifty dollars," she said.

"No, Wes," I said aghast, "that's foolish," I protested, kicking my "inner geisha" to the curb.

"I think it suits you to a 'C,' Wes said, 'C' for Candida."

"I could offer a small discount of fifteen percent?" the woman said to Wes, while looking at me.

"A bargain," Wes said, smiling at her. Before I knew it we were moving out of the shop, a small bag with an empty satin box; the chain on my chest. It caused a sensation on the street, as we emerged, and when Meg spotted us, she was enthralled.

"Please don't wear it when you're alone. It must have cost a fortune," she added.

"It did Meg," but Wes insisted." I felt like a princess in a story book. I gave Wes such a kiss I nearly toppled over. Several nearby street vendors clapped. Fortunately, Meg was holding my arm or I might have fallen on *them*. Just then, Guido and Alfonso appeared. We headed back to the hotel, clopping over ancient cobble stones. I could not take my eyes off my chest.

When we got back to the hotel at 4:30, I was so tired I wanted only to sleep. Meg came into my room with me, and found a night gown in the armoire. She slipped it over my head and turned down the covers. She was strong enough to get me under the covers without hurting me– much–but made me take another codeine pill with a glass of water. On her way out, Wes came in.

"Now, Wes," Meg said reprovingly. "Don't do anything rash. I recommend complete rest!" I was still wearing the necklace. When he saw it, he kissed that, too. "Sleep as long as you wish, darling. The group are going to dine out near Santa Croce. But not you. And not me. I'll hang out around here. When you wake, give me a call. The Helvetia and Bristol has one of the grandest dining rooms in the city. Sleep well, princess!"

I slept for four hours. When I awoke, it was nearly nine. And I was hungry. I dialed Wes's room. "Hello, there, Sleeping Beauty," he said. "How are you feeling?"

I laughed. "Hungry as a tiger. I feel like going down, not eating up here."

"In that case, I'll dress for dinner, but I'll be up in fifteen minutes to help *you* out of bed and dress. I'll reserve for 9:30." Then he was here. He eased my dress over my head and got my right arm through with minimal discomfort. He found my codeine pills, and handed me one with water before we set off.

"Look at you in the mirror," he said, before we left the room. My dress was a violet colored silk, and low necked. The necklace gleamed against throat, just clearing my cleavage. I looked up at Wes questioningly.

"Will I do?"

Kissing me lightly on the mouth, he answered, "You will be the most lovely woman in that dining room. Because you are."

The dining room was an Edwardian masterpiece. Its ceiling curved at all four sides, until it met with a clear glass skylight, from which dangled two dramatic iron chandeliers. The end of the room was mirrored, giving the impression of endless depth, *a good impression for scholars*, I thought. The chairs, in gold and white velvet, were mostly tables for four, with flowers on each lacy cloth. Small oriental rugs in matching tones punctuated the shining parquet floor. One felt as if one had stepped into the pre-World War I era where the sight through the skylight's glass was still optimistic, and everything, even Italy, seemed about to improve tenfold–for Westerners in Florence. I then spotted Arnold and Anne, almost hidden by a potted palm tree, their backs familiar in the glass behind. Our waiter asked if we would like our friends to be seated at our table. Very shortly they were, and we could speak quietly with them.

"Oh,Candida!" Anne exclaimed when seated. I was wondering if you were all right? Rob told us you and Wes and Meg drove about seeing the sights today. How did that go? And are you in much pain? Could you walk into any building, or did you have to stay in the jitney?"

"I was pretty good on codeine," I told her. I entered San Lorenzo, and the Medici Chapels. I saw the outside of San Marco. Wes carried me into the Accademia to see the David. Skipped Santa Croce. Entered the synagogue. Meg and Wes were selfless."

"And you walked into a jewelry shop on the Ponte Vecchio, if I mistake not!" said Arnold, winking at Wes."

"Oh, yes. My new necklace. It is a present from Wes."

"And I thought it was a high school graduation gift from your Dad," said Arnold, his blue eyes twinkling under his lovely white hair. From my father? Of course, Arnold was joking. Anne leaned over for a closer view.

"And *I* think it's an engagement gift from Wes," she said." Are congratulations in order?" I looked at Wes who smiled at Arnold and Anne.

"It's a kind of pre–engagement gift because we haven't the opportunity now to marry. Hopefully, in the near future." That made them happy, as they, too, planned to marry, only in the very near future, when we got back to the states.

Anne said, "When you two do tie the knot, we hope we'll be on your guest list, as you will be on ours." She squeezed my right hand.

"Ouch!" I said, and we all laughed. Was there a single part of me that did not hurt from that fall from the bus step onto the pavement? We decided to dine on the same items, as it was late, and the restaurant wanted to close before midnight. So, for our appetizer, we hit upon chicken livers on toast (*crostini di fegatini di pollo*) which certainly reminded me of my half Jewish, half Italian childhood, when my Bubbie Brondel gave me chicken liver from the roasting pan where sat, in all its glory, a fat stuffed chicken she often made for Friday night dinner. But these livers were made with ham fat, sage, lemon juice and grated Parmesan cheese, plus sage and onion. I hated to admit it, but they were better than Bubbie's. I was glad I wasn't obliged to tell her, dear departed soul. Her livers (and chicken) were made only with love, not ham.

For our main course, we chose young grilled ox (*bistecca alla fiorentina with beans* cooked in a bottle, *(fagioli nel fiasco)*. The steak was a slice of a young ox, grilled with olive oil over the right kind of wood. You couldn't possibly cook this on the Peninsula. How would you ever determine "the right temperature?" Or find a cut of "young ox?" The beans, white ones, were cooked in a wine flask over a charcoal brazier. The trick was to use fresh haricot beans cooked in water, olive oil, two cloves of garlic, sage and no salt! Straw stuffed into the neck's bottle allowed steam to escape, but not flavor. Both dishes were accompanied by mushrooms, cooked like tripe (*funghi tripati*), which turned out to be cooked in olive oil, crushed garlic, tomato paste and oregano.

Anybody who wants to eat like a Florentine must put olive oil on and into everything. Garlic helped, too. The result was distinctively Tuscan. The truffled mushrooms were a great compliment to the tender, smoky beans. A custard tart for dessert, with, Wes insisted, vanilla ice cream to top it off. The waiter disapproved, but Anne and Arnold dumped theirs into their espressos, while I humored Wes by eating my ice cream off my tart. Delicious. This marvelous meal was washed down by Chianti and a Moscadello from Siena.

Anne and Arnold had dined in our hotel, rather than at Santa Croce with the group, because, Arnold said, "though pleasant the group was sometimes too predictable," and Rob "could get on one's nerves." Still, Rob had been "a stalwart leader" today, showing them the Davanzati Museum's Renaissance furnishings; the Bargello with Donatello's David; the Uffizi and then, the Pitti Palace. For those still able to walk, the Boboli gardens behind it were a treat.

"The gardens were gorgeous," said Anne, "but some of the older tourists just sat in the shade, too weary to walk through them. I kind of wanted to join them," she confessed wryly. Arnold said he would do his best tomorrow to fill us in on their favorite paintings, but they were now more interested in what we had seen. I told them about our day. Finally, we bid each other farewell in the lounge. Wes and I went straight to my room. He helped me in the bathroom and he helped me undress. Then he undressed to his shorts.

"Oh, Wes, I can't. I hurt too much," I protested.

"You won't hurt, I promise," he said, lifting my night gown up and carefully drawing my bandaged, bruised legs apart. His fingers caressed my private parts, his kisses poured onto my belly, my *mons venere*, and then where his fingers had been. He lingered, licking me eagerly, and I couldn't help but think of my cat at home. She, too, could make do on very little. I giggled despite myself.

"Just lie still and enjoy it," Wes said caressing my forehead. "No self-consciousness now. We'll forget about me tonight. Go with the flow, Candida." And I went. And I came. And Wes left, happy at having pleasured me.

CHAPTER XVII

RINGS, ROYALS, RISTORANTI

My leg itched. I couldn't scratch. Someone knocking–at 6:45 A.M.? "Yes?" I called out groggily. "It's Meg, Candida. May I come in?"

I could not move my right leg. It was too stiff. My bruises itched. Meg had suspected that. She had my room key, and entered, carrying a white tray of nursing stuff. Scissors, three styles; a file; disinfectant, spray and cream; band aids; tape; anti-itch cream and more pain pills.

"These pills won't make you sleepy," she said. "The doctor said to remove the cumbersome wraps; replace them with lighter ones. We'll get rid of the ace bandages and packing. Itching today?"

I nodded. Once I got my right leg over the edge of the bed, I could navigate. For short distances. Barely. I used the facilities, brushed my hair, my teeth.

"My hair needs washing," I said sadly. "Today is Agatha's and Ian's wedding, and later, I visit Teresa. At nine P.M., our banquet at the *Piazzale Michelangelo*! The views will be great. My hair won't." How self-centered. Most of us are when we hurt.

"I'll help," Meg assured me. "Sit in the shower on stool. Watch it! There's a step up. Now, let it rain! I'll pour shampoo into your hand. Do your hair. I'll soap your back. We're not saving bandages."

After, she toweled me off, she helped me to a window seat.

"Sit there, Candida. It's the best place to cut off those bandages." Nurses are so efficient. Their tasks are self–evident. Harder to discriminate in literature, though the possibility of causing pain was less. Literature could heal, but it couldn't bandage.

As Meg worked away on my ankle, I got a muted view of what others had seen in Technicolor. Now, my right leg was greenish black, with crusted blood, maroon in color. The flesh on the left leg, not torn, was yellow, blue and aqua.

"Not too bad," Meg said snipping away at the right leg's wrapping. "The ankle and lower calf are the worst. Less drama past the knee."

There had been less abrasion higher up, but more muscle trauma, which was why I was so stiff and shaky.

As the bandages fell, the packing came off with just the color of iodine: dark yellow brown. I ached from torn muscles, courteous enough not to bleed, discourteous enough to make me stiff. Meg offered me a pain pill as one offers a guest a chocolate. I swallowed it and drank water.

"Now this will sting, so hold on." She sprayed the disinfectant on my legs. I gasped. Wasps had attacked.

"You do know how to make a girl cry," I moaned. Meg spread moisturizing cream over my leg, which helped ease the sting.

"Gosh, you're lucky," she remarked. I *was*?

"These upper lacerations just missed by a hair's breadth being candidates for stitches. As it is, you'll heal in several months. By Halloween you'll be your old self, skinwise. Lucky your leg hair is blonde. Shaving might open the wounds. Don't. Let them heal. No nylon hose for a month or so. They'll make itching worse and tear the new skin."

Meg understood torn flesh. I wondered if she understood broken hearts? Not that mine was broken. Yet. But after leaving Florence for Venice tomorrow, after Padua (Padova) Vicenza, Verona, Milan, would I ever see Wes again? Broken skin was nothing compared to a broken heart.

I dressed for the wedding. With lighter bandages, I could wear pants, and chose light blue *crêpe de chine* with a matching satin blouse and my necklace. Indeed, I hadn't taken it off since the clerk had fastened it. I wondered if it would grow on me, literally? Would I wear it with shorts, my baggy swimsuit?

Meg forbade high heels. Flat sandals offered stability. My bag held little to destabilize me. Sunglasses. Comb. Lipstick. Pain pills. Kleenex, passport. Some paper *lire*. Enough. Wes phoned to see if I could make it down to breakfast on my own. I told him Meg was here, to help me walk down. We walked, me using the cane, arm in arm, hip on hip, down the hall. A well dressed lady gave us a dirty look as we passed.

Meg said, "Rest today when you can. Rest beats codeine." *But nothing*, I thought, *beats love*. That was all I wanted. I made a mental note. "Memo: all Candida wants is love."

The group had gathered in the breakfast room. Agatha wore a white crepe dress, with a high neck, but intricate lacing from the back neckband to the low-backed waist. Agatha had one. A waist, I meant. Who knew? Belinda and Sandy had found a silver necklace in Florence perfect for Agatha's dress. Their wedding gift. Ian had bought her a very small engagement ring, a diamond, in Siena, probably, with matching gold band. Allison found the white dress on Via Tornabuoni near the Pitti. She asked me if I liked it.

"It takes ten years off her age," I told her.

"That and her new hairdo," Allison agreed. "The hairdo cost half as much as the dress! You'd never guess she was wearing a habit three days ago." *Or that you were, too, just last week*, I thought.

I inspected Ian, just to see if together, they matched. He had been cultivating a small mustache since Assisi, which put a few years on him. He wore a seersucker suit, tan and white striped, with a white vest, tan shirt, white tie.

"Ian looks smart, if somewhat older than his mid-thirties." Allison, blonde hair cascading down her back, replied, "It's his new mustache, the vest."

Rob guided me to the center table where Matilda, Bill (Ellen was late) and he were sitting. Matilda said she and Andrea Pellatierra had a nine o'clock appointment with *Professore* Emiliano Balestreri of the University of Florence, but would make the wedding at the American Consulate, no. #46 Lungarno Amerigo Vespucci.

Long tables bordered the breakfast room. All I wanted was a roll and coffee, fruit and yogurt. Rob brought me cantaloupe, muscatel grapes, a peach, and vanilla yogurt. A waiter made a stop at our table with orange juice. Ellen came in blinking, lost. Bill led her to a table unoccupied by anyone else, and sat down there with her, having brought along his coffee cup and a croissant. I thought how tactful he was. He didn't want Ellen to accuse me of accusing her of causing my fall. I wouldn't have. Still, had she not been window shopping, I would have remained in the bus unharmed.

Wes entered, handsome in a navy blue suit and white shirt, red tie and white carnation. Wes was Ian's best man! I guess those two Protestants had talked about theology in private, but Wes had not mentioned it before. He looked more like the groom rather than best man. Allison, maid of honor, wore a pink dress with ruffled skirts. A large pink rose was pinned to the top of her head. She looked a prom queen. I sighed, listening to the quiet ticking of my biological clock. Of course I could put off childbearing for a while yet, but I couldn't ignore the opportunities that were cycling past each month.

Andrea Smithwitch waved at Wes, but he had spotted Rob, Matilda and me and joined us. Andrea went to sit with the twins.

Rob: "Wes, I never realized until now that you are a handsome fellow."

Wes: "Thank you Rob. Same to you." Rob, in a pale blue chambray suit, white shirt and navy tie looked like a boy off to Sunday school. Both men radiated male magnetism. It had drawn Andrea's attention. And mine.

Something about a wedding–even a civil ceremony–made people euphoric. As for Agatha and Ian, they seemed nervous. Nuns didn't usually marry, except Jesus. Katie Von Bora had married Martin Luther, an ex-friar when Lutherans were called Evangelicals. There was no "Church of England" then. Henry VIII was still Defender of the Roman one. Katie, a noblewoman, and Martin, a peasant's son, had no doubt been nervous before theirs. Anne Boleyn should have been. Lust and holy words can "unite" flesh, but only true love souls.

After breakfast, Ian told us that a luncheon in the heart of Fiesole would follow their wedding. There would be *spumante*, wedding cake, and everything in between. Agatha was rich.

After breakfast Jonah said to a few of us, "The champagne is my gift, but we'll need a tangible object for the couple, and of course, flowers for their table." Myrna volunteered to look after the flowers. As for tangible gifts, I recalled matching silver wristwatches for men and women in "The Golden River." I told Jonah that if he bought them, we would all contribute to their cost. I remembered a sign on the counter saying "rapid engraving," (*Intaglio rapido*). Jonah called from the front desk. The store promised to have those watches at our hotel before 10:30 A.M., fully engraved on the rear of each case. I went with him and carefully spelled the names of the bridal pair–in Italian–so there would be no errors in spelling. How fast Italian service was at this jewelry store. They'd been master merchandisers for over five centuries. At home, engraving would take a week.

At half past ten the parcel arrived. The reverse side of both watches had the bride's and groom's name, today's date, the place (Firenze) and a tiny lily beneath. Jonah paid for the watches, the flowers and wedding cake as well as the *spumante*! He absolutely forbade me to ask for contributions from the group. Jonah was a generous man.

Mindy was curious about my royal cocktail party. I told her the *Sardi-Piedmontese-Nizzardi-Genovese* (men of Sardinia-Piedmont-Nice and Genoa) were once Dukes of Savoy, which after a war, became part of France (1860). One member of Theresa's family, Victor Emmanuel II, became King of Italy (1861). During his rule Italy lost Tuscany, the Romagna, Parma and Modena. Savoy, Piedmont and Nice went to France. The acquisition of Naples, Sicily, Umbria and the Marches made their cession less painful, and the dynasty continued their reign until shortly after World War II.

Though deprived of Savoy, the family had chosen as a last name Della Savoia, a name that signified owning something that legitimizes—even if they owned it no more. Royalty suffered from nostalgia. No matter how much they kept, they treasured most what was lost. Still, a dynasty by any name smelled sweet—if it were yours.

When Mindy asked how I had met these "royals," I said that my ex-boy friend's grandmother was a countess, also a garlic rancher in Gilroy.

"Gilroy, garlic capital of California?" she asked. "They make garlic flavored ice-cream there!" I assured her I hadn't tried it.

"What do you plan to wear this evening?" she demanded.

"What I have on. I have bandages to hide." She looked me up and down." Candida you're a perfect size six. So am I. I've got the right outfit for you. Come to our room—Jonah, dear, get lost for an hour? Thanks, sweetie." And to me again: "I'll lend you an outfit for queens." We linked arms because my leg throbbed. On the way out, the same elderly lady who had made a face at me and Meg, saw us thus entwined and muttered again under her breath.

We took the elevator to third floor. From her armoire Mindy pulled out a pair of black silk *charmeuse* pants; bell-bottoms, belted low with a gold buckle. They flared into cascades of gold striped ruffles, three layers at the ankle. These pants one didn't buy at J.C. Penny's. My love of pretty clothes extended back to a girlhood watching 1950s movie stars wearing high fashion–when I had not yet shed my penny loafers and felt poodle circle skirts.

"Wait until you see the blouse," she said. Out came a white silk, notched collar blouse with sizable black diamond lozenges and tiny gold lines connecting them. The buttons were hidden under a flap, the French double cuffs had gold cuff links. Its neckline, low, required a halter bra which Mindy also provided. I didn't own one. Now, the necklace was all that stood between me and my cleavage.

"Wear it with gold heels," Mindy advised.

"I can't. Meg's orders. All I have are flat Carters sandals." Mindy wrinkled her nose. "Here, she said, opening a cloth bag she called her "embellishments" bag, from which emerged two giant gold pom–poms on stretchable bands.

"Cover the tops of your Carters with these, and you'll have evening sandals! Take this wrap in case it gets breezy up on the Piazzale." Mindy handed me a white satin cape lined with gold cashmere knit.

"My goodness, you are a one woman fashion boutique." She laughed.

"Jonah insisted that we get out in the City. So we do opera, theater, concerts, parties. His first wife read mystery novels in the evening and wore long black coats."

I tried everything on. The effect? Stunning. I did not feel like Candida Darroway. A 1950s movie star, yes. A diva, certainly. Too bad I couldn't sing.

Mindy said, "I've been watching you. You're made for high fashion but are disguised as a drab professor. I was once disguised as a Seventh Day Adventist! Sorry your leg's injured, your cheek's bruised. I have some makeup that will hide that. After leaving the Adventists, I went to modeling school for a while, but the owners were sharks. Bastards, really. I found work as a fileclerk later, and the boss–Jonah– proposed."

I put all my "loot" in a bag for this evening, and gave Mindy a hug.

"Wait till they see you at their castle," she enthused.

At nine P.M. Wes knocked. I let him in. "You look stunning," Candida. Blue suits you."

"So do blue suits, you," I replied.

"You don't suppose we have time for a little romp, do you?" he asked. "I would have to borrow a couple of hangers."

"How alarming," I said. We both laughed.

"No, Candida, I'm not into S & M." We looked at each other, then hugged.

"Yes, a little romp sounds right," I said. This man was so deep into me, why not as deep as possible? He was already unbuttoning his shirt, and his jacket was on the back of my desk chair, not on a hanger. Suddenly my blouse was off my head and Wes's fingers under my waistband.

"I'll do the rest" I volunteered. "It's not fair that you do all the work."

Two minutes later we were happily exchanging kisses; tender, tender caresses. Two minutes after that...well! I didn't know what heaven might be like. I didn't believe in it, either. But loving Wes was heaven to me. Though he was very careful about distributing his weight, our lovemaking did hurt my wounded legs. But it hurt so good.

10:45. Carlo waited at the front of the hotel Bristol. The Consulate was a few blocks away down the *Lungarno*. Arrived, Wes took one of my arms and Meg the other. Behind a polished door with "American Consul in Italy" engraved on a brass plate, were three carpeted but shallow steps down into a foyer. Wes, whom Ian had asked to be his Best Man, helped me navigate them, then went straight to the Duty Officer to identify our party.

A second officer led us through a wide door into something more like a ballroom than a judge's chambers. A mahogany table sat in the middle. Behind it sat a white haired gentleman in a navy suit. He rose to greet us after the Officer announced us as "the MacDonald-Rollins wedding party from California." Rob took Wes's place at my side. Since the accident, he seemed subdued, more caring. As for the other injuries— those of the Siena loggia and his bathtub caper—we never spoke of them. Nor of lilies or spilt wine.

Agatha in a fingertip veil and Ian approached the table, where the white-haired civil servant, the Hon. Archibald E. Griffin, shook their hands, Ian's, Agatha's, Allison's, Wes's.

"Would everyone else please step back fifteen feet?" Mr. Griffin asked. "It's a safety precaution." *A useless one*, I thought. Most guns shoot farther than fifteen feet, and a sneeze spreads germs farther still. It was impossible to protect oneself from life's risks.

"I, Archibald E. Griffin, American Consul in Florence acting in accord with regulations appertaining to matrimony granted me by the United States Department of State, do hereby, solemnly pronounce you, Agatha Rollins, and you, Ian MacDonald, man and wife. You may kiss the bride." Then, "Please sign here, here, and here." A pause while they signed. The couple then turned to face us. We applauded them, congratulated them. I felt something else should have happened, but nothing did. We left.

The trip to Fiesole was five miles from Florence. Here, in the early sixteenth century, Niccolò Machiavelli penned his apothegm to Caesar (*Cesare*) Borgia and to authoritarian government, *The Prince*, because he deemed undemocratic tactics necessary to preserve the state. *The Prince* did not win him steady employment. An authoritarian book may provoke more than flatter an authoritarian employer.

The Piazza Mino was the heart of Fiesole and overlooked Florence. *Da Mino's Ristorante* provided blue umbrellas for shade. The bridal table was bedecked with three floral arrangements, white gladiolas and blue iris. Broad steps led up to a porch, beyond which was Da Mino's interior dining room.

"Congratulations Agatha and Ian; Long Life" read a sign like a Jewish toast. Matt had made it, using crayons. He had taped it to the bridal table's front edge. Soon Wes and I, Rob, Allison, Jonah, Mindy, Belinda and Sandy were seated there. Rob sat on one side of me, Wes on the other. Anita came up briefly and whispered something into Rob's ear. The waiters came with sweating bottles wrapped in napkins, and filled our *spumante* glasses.

"To the bride and groom!" we stood and toasted the happy couple.

"Speech, speech!" Matt yelled.

Ian rose saying, "We are so pleased to celebrate our nuptials with you in Fiesole. I think you are probably more amiable wedding guests than I would have had at home, so thank you for being here. Agatha, dearest?"

Agatha's "speech" was about behavior, spiritual and not. "I would like you to join me in a short prayer. 'Dear God, we have tried, Ian and

I to follow in your footsteps. We have not always done so. But by your Grace and with Your love, we intend to resume our service to you, Lord, to Jesus, and to the Holy Spirit. Amen." Then, as an afterthought, she added, "I do have other family here today; my niece Allison, maid of honor, and now my wonderful husband, Ian." We all echoed "Amen."

Certainly, all couples needed protection because, as my parents demonstrated, wedded bliss is not for everyone, nor achieved by all who wed, nor once achieved, easily sustained. I looked at Wes, "and his eyes blew a kiss when they met mine," words from an old song.

The wedding lunch began with an antipasto (starter) of eggplant and gorgonzola cheese. The main course was petrale sole *"fiorentina,"* stuffed with spinach, and garlic bread crumbs, rolled up and baked in a sauce with cream, sherry, *peccorino* (sheep's milk cheese) and butter. The salad, Ligurian style, had chopped anchovies, cucumbers, sweet peppers, black pitted olives, hard-boiled eggs, tuna, and pearl onions, thinly sliced in olive oil vinaigrette; a meal by itself. The wedding cake? A masterpiece (*capolavoro*). Six layers of chocolate almond cake with white frosting made of powdered hazelnuts, hazelnut liqueur, egg whites, and honey. The bride fed her groom a thin slice first, and he fed her one, after. A silly, but symbolic, tradition. Each must sustain the other.

Photos were taken, and then, as the cake was served, Reed, carrying his clarinet case, Anita, and Rob headed for the interior of Da Mino's. Just inside was a piano—a well–tuned upright. The owner placed a microphone and speakers just over the door step, with both doors opened. Reed, clarinet raised to his lips, waited. Alerted, everyone turned toward the front porch. From the piano, Rob's long unseen fingers sent out a brilliant, improvised, much arpeggio'd introduction to "O Promise Me," Reginald De Koven's wedding classic. It had brought tears to eyes at countless weddings. Reed raised his instrument and joined in a piano-clarinet restatement of themes struck by De Koven and Rob. Reed did a solo variation, dropping to a sweet *pianissimo* reprise of the melody, with Rob joining in.

Anita, in a clear, mezzo–soprano, looking innocent, but voluptuous, in a lownecked pink dress began to sing: "O Promise me that some day you and I will take our love together to some sky, Where we can be alone and faith renew, and find the hollows where the flowers grew...." She looked at Reed, as she sang. They made a handsome pair.

Those maudlin words without the music would not work, I thought. But with a good pianist, which Rob was; Anita's strong mezzo–soprano, and Reed's haunting clarinet, they did. When the last stanza ended with references to "God's message," "souls," "organ rolls," and "O promise me, o promise me!" many wiped tears away with the backs of their hands, their napkins. An elderly gentleman, seated alone, used the end of his necktie.

Rob rejoined us, I said, "Rob, you were wonderful!" I meant his piano playing. "Yes, I am wonderful," he said. Throwing back his head, he laughed so happily, that the elderly man, seeing him, stopped crying. A smile broke out over the man's withered face. Probably he, too, had laughed loudly at a wedding, and took a bride to wife.

Back in my room, I kicked off my shoes and somehow, climbed onto the bed. The next thing I knew, the phone was ringing. Wes was asking, "Are you awake yet? You're being picked up at 5:30, you know."

"Thanks for the wake-up call, darling," I said groggily. "Sorry you weren't invited to Teresa's party. Only your pictures will be admitted."

"Okay," Wes said. "But when I get to be King of Italy, their dynasty goes into exile. To Newark, N.J. Let them try to find anyone who speaks Tuscan Italian there." I thought of the kids we'd met in Orvieto. There were a few!

"Oh, and another thing. I cannot wait to see you at nine sharp at the Piazzale! Have fun, sweet girl. Until nine." Wes rang off.

Ambiguity haunted speech. Have fun "until nine" and then stop? Of course Wes didn't mean that. Have fun because you're a "sweet girl" but sweet only "until nine"? Nor that either. And how about, "I cannot wait to see you at nine sharp?" Did that mean if I arrived later, he wouldn't have waited?–or that he wouldn't have been glad to see me? Or that he himself would be not be there until nine on the dot, and before then he wouldn't care? Or, did he mean I must look "great" at "nine sharp," but after that, it wouldn't matter how I looked? Wes didn't mean all the ways one could wait, be, look, or act "sharp." As for the word sharp, he did not define it. It had over a dozen meanings. Just imagine if one didn't know the speaker well, or at all, and had only the text. What could be learned from it? Very little.

I thought of the philosopher Jacques Derrida, that pesky Frenchman with his theory of Deconstruction, in which literature professors had been indoctrinating their grad students, telling them that only words have meaning; forget context, whether historical, cultural or psychological. Words had nothing to do with their authors!

Derrida's 1971 book on the "marginality" of linguistics, literature and philosophy was bunk. If he and his ilk were hung up on the spoken text only, they were enemies of western civilization. Deconstruction of civilization had been tried in many ways before Derrida. Glad he wasn't on our tour. Rob and Wes would make mincemeat of him. My disapproval of Derrida was a function of my inability to "go with the flow"–to take every new fad as a God given addition to the sacred vessel of our cultural heritage. That heritage needed protection. And how.

I ran a shower, washed my hair again, tousled it for that new feathery look, letting it dry however it would. I put on Mindy's halter bra which made me feel all cleavage. I eased into the ruffled bell-bottomed pants, nearly losing my balance.

"Calm. Be calm," I said to myself. At least I didn't have to cope with a garter belt because Meg forbade stockings. I put on the print satin blouse, and fastened the pants' buckle over my navel. Why did they make these designer pants so low slung?

I stepped back, carefully, to check myself out in the armoire mirror and apply the eyeliner and the pancake makeup in just my shade. It did hide the bruises on my face. The woman in the mirror did not appear to be me. I hid my old sandals under gold pompons. *Ecco*! (There!) Fashionable feet. I passed on toe nail polish, though. Too slutty. My black evening bag, tiny, fit the few essentials I could carry without losing my balance. One *gettone* (token for a telephone call). *Basta*! (Enough!). The bag, from Lerner's, was a knock-off; but of a designer original. Mindy's satin, cashmere lined cape completed the outfit. I could see myself as the fashion model Mindy meant me to be. My inner model and my academic self joined hands. I locked my room door and limped out with the cane to the elevators.

Two young men, sporting longer haircuts, stopped when the door opened and tensed when I got in. They both followed me into the lounge. There sat Rob and Wes, one on each side of a small table, facing the lounge entrance. Not there by accident, they were waiting for me. The young men stood back, watched me greet them, then turned and left.

"A good afternoon to you both, Wes, Rob. I'm waiting for my ride to Teresa's. How do I look?"

"You well know you are…breathtaking," Rob replied, lowering both eyebrows, a trick of his when he had private thoughts.

Wes answered, "Candida, what are you doing talking to two old professors? You should be chatting up royalty, nobility, moguls, movie stars."

I grinned. "Teresa doesn't invite movie stars." Too bad. I was just right for Harrison Ford, Richard Gere.

Just then the desk clerk called my name. I had to leave. "See you both at the banquet," I said, waving at them. Wes got up and came out to the limo with me to help me in. Rob rose and bowed, rather subdued, though determinedly elegant in his formal farewell. They were dear, each in his own way, of course.

The chauffeur, Ercole, was waiting right by the door to his limousine, under the hotel's canopy, "*Signorina Darroway, per caso?*" (possibly?).

"Yes, here I am," (*Sì, eccomi qui*), He held open the rear door. But I told him I preferred to ride up front. Wes lifted me up onto the front running board of Ercole's old fashioned limo and I settled myself in, taking care to fasten the seat belt. "I never get much chance to speak Italian in Italy," I told Wes. He understood. He gave me a peck on my cheek and closed the door.

It felt good to chat in Italian with Ercole. He lived on the estate with his wife, and both were old employees of Teresa's family. He had played with her as a child, he told me, though he was the gardener's son. His wife, Paola, took care of the linens, as had her mother and grandmother! I wished someone would take care of mine. Of course, I only had one set of sheets; two small tablecloths; four real Irish linen dinner napkins. They required ironing. Starch. So I didn't use them. Ercole pointed out the landmarks.

"There, *Signorina* Darroway. We just passed the Lungarno Serristori (road along the Arno), and are heading to the St. Nicholas Gate. (*Porta San Niccolo*). "So, a right turn at the Great Square of Michelangelo

(*Piazzale Michelangelo*); then the Galileo Road." (*Poi, Viale Galileo Galilei*).

"*Grazie*, Ercole," I responded. He was trying to help a stranger get her bearings.

Still climbing, we passed San Miniato a Montici, an eleventh century church set upon its punitively steep stairway. We turned off the Viale onto a winding lane passing two villas, cypress trees guarding their entrances, until we turned down a gated drive, marked "Private Drive"(*Via Privata*), rolling through olive orchards. Suddenly we were in front of Teresa's villa–a rococo, colonnaded affair with three marble verandas down three sides of the building. Ten Doric columns ran across the front porch.

The gardener had placed flower urns between each column, and green and white settees, wicker easy chairs, cocktail tables, a hammock, and porch swing at one end. The veranda reminded me of an asylum for people suffering from personality disorders, or old age, the staff determined to get them into the fresh air for several hours every day.

The driveway circled a pool whose rim held statues of mythological grotesques–mermaids, satyrs, centaurs, nymphs. Two dolphins on their tails' ends spouted columns of pool water at pool's center. The grotesques got bathed daily.

I mounted to the porch and Ercole held open the door. Down one of two curved marble flights came Teresa, her arms outstretched. Paola, Ercole's wife, followed her. Paola curtsied to me.

"Candida!" Teresa laughed, you put us all to shame in your gorgeous outfit. You have become the Princess, and I, Cinderella (*Cenerentola*)."

Teresa wore a long grey jersey skirt and black silk shirt, with only modest coral beads for color. I wondered if I had overdone it with Mindy's swag?

"Oh, Candida," asked Teresa, wide-eyed, touching my necklace. "From Wes?"

"Yes," I said. "But no ring."

"Well, I wished things could have turned out for you and Tony, but it was always a long shot. I hope Wes is the one. He could have bought several rings for what he laid out for this! Never leave it in your hotel room! Now, come and show it off to our 'gallery of ghouls.'" She spoke *sotto voce*, of course.

Teresa led me through a wide hallway into "the family room" (*salotto famigliare*). This was forty feet square, with windows along one side of the left veranda. The brocade drapes were pulled back to let the late afternoon sun enter between the columns. The room was a delight. Cut blue and yellow velvet brocade on the chairs and sofas; oriental rugs with navy backgrounds on the blue and white tiled floor. No child had ever smeared gelato on this furniture, crayoned on this yellow satin "wallpaper."

Teresa put Mindy's cape over two side chairs, where we could chat if other conversation failed, or my legs did. For now, she walked me slowly around a semicircle of settees, a few outliers with their backs turned so their view was toward the colonnade. All her family were soberly attired in black or grey. At least I had on black pants, though ruffled, and gold trimmed. I had a cane, too, I hoped they noticed.

A dozen people were present. Those past seventy-five were withdrawn. The rest were either talking among themselves or staring– at me–not with approval. Five of the old gentlemen, did, however, nod. One licked his lips. The ladies, in their late seventies or eighties, put their glasses, on chain necklaces, on their noses to peer at me, before lowering them back to flat or concave chests.

I smiled and expressed my pleasure at being here. "Good evening. Pleasure to make your acquaintance." (*Buona sera. Piacere di fare la vostra conoscenza*). Then they, too nodded and repeated "*Piacere, Signorina*."

The "young" men were, if in their forties, Teresa's nephews. She had a sister, Silvia, and two brothers, Arturo and Salvatore, the younger set's parents. Salvatore, a brother two years Teresa's senior, was sixty-nine. Arturo, the baby, was fifty-three, but could have passed for forty-five. Teresa said Arturo was "a terrible snob." In a corner speaking with the old Duke, Arturo turned to look at me. Appreciatively. Teresa guided me around the room keeping an eye on this well preserved 'baby' brother. Perhaps he was not as snobbish as she thought? Salvatore bowed deeply when I was introduced, and kissed my hand. Silvia, Teresa's older sister, was still upstairs, perfecting her "toilette."

"Silvia always makes an entrance," Teresa explained. Arturo wore a black tuxedo (he was going to a wedding later), and was introduced as "the noted industrialist" of Alto Adige. The family owned timber near Vipiteno, south of Innsbruck. Arturo was Chairman of the Board. In fact, he was too bored to chair anything but a ski lift, and spent his winters at nearby Innsbruck. Other pleasures, at Monte Carlo, were farther off. There he not only tried his luck at the casinos but at chasing– and catching–young women. But he soon let them go again, like fish, underaged. His title was Count of Bolzano. The old Duke of Bolzano, his uncle, titular head of the dynasty, looked at me out of narrow, slant eyes. He only nodded to my "Piacere, Signore." Should I have curtsied?

Bolzano had belonged to the Habsburgs after 1513, then Bözen; but in 1919 it became part of Italy, renamed. The Duke's title was a thumb in the eye to Austria, owner of Austrian Tyrol before 1918. Arturo regarded the German speaking Italians in *Il Tirolo* as "the foreign" element, and the Austrians as "the enemy." Some thought he was referring to the Soviet Union.

Two of Teresa's nephews in their early thirties seemed quite nice. Enea, (Aeneas), Salvatore's son, and Ubaldo, Arturo's. Enea was the shy heir to the Duke's title, Enea IV of Sardinia–Tyrhennea. I thought the heir looked sensitive and would make a gentle Duke Enea V, though there were no more public duties for him left to perform under Italy's current constitution. Teresa said if we were lucky, he might play his violin for us.

"He's gay," she whispered to me as we moved on, "That's why he is so sensitive. The dukedom is not what it used to be, but he wouldn't have to play the fiddle for a living. His father, Enea IV, is hanging on to life and his title at 89." Ubaldo, Arturo's son, stood up to give me a quick kiss on both cheeks. He was Teresa's favorite nephew: "Count of Savoia-Liguria," she said introducing him. "He is engaged to be married to a wealthy duchess in Brussels." The engagement was in its fifth year. His fiancée was torn between marriage to him or to Christ. Ubaldo went there twice a year to pledge his undying passion.

Suddenly, a loud, rather grating, laugh was heard from above. "Silvia's entrance is imminent," Teresa intoned. Sylvia swept down the staircase in a loud print gown of lavender, green and orange, scarves flowing off narrow shoulder straps, beads of all lengths and colors hanging between pendulous breasts. Indian bangles lined both arms. When she raised those well muscled, if wrinkled arms, to give me a hug, it occurred to me that Sylvia was lesbian. She wore false eyelashes, a "rug" a shade darker than her own thinning hair and feminine fashions, but worked out with heavy weights. Her hug caused me considerable pain.

"And you must be the lovely Candida," she said, adding, "I always knew Tony was a fool." I was not sure in what sense she had meant that. She had obviously had a drink or two before the party. Older than Teresa, her face was heavily lined. Her mouth was a little bow, shaped by bright red lipstick that did not reach its corners.

"Dear Candida, I am Teresa's sister, Silvia." Teresa gave her formal title. "*La Contessa Della Savoia e di San Remo*, my older sister, Silvia." At this Silvia wagged a finger at Teresa saying "Ah, but not by much, *cara*." In fact, by seven years.

I was overwhelmed. Teresa might have prepared me. Silvia spoke rapid Italian with a Savoyard or Piedmontese accent. I had to listen carefully. Actually, she had little to say, but it took longer. Then she went over to one of the distant chairs, turned it, and returned with this upholstered wheelchair, wheels hidden by its fabric skirt. A push bar that ran along the back near the top was all that differentiated this chair from others in the room. Silvia delivered its ancient occupant, the Princess (*Principessa*), Arturo's, Salavatore's, Teresa's and Silvia's mother; Enea and Ubaldo's grandmother, and Tony's great-grandmother.

Silvia gave her mother's title: "The Princess of Sardinia-Savoy and also, rightly speaking, Piedmont." (*La Principessa Della Sardinia-Savoia et anche, giustamente, Piemonte*).

Teresa whispered, "Really, only of Sardinia, but we kept the name Savoy, though the territory itself went to France. Piedmont went too, but we humor her. She is almost ninety-four." Then, with a slight bow toward the old woman she said, "Mama, I would like to present to you *Professoressa* Candida Darroway."

I felt I was being introduced to a gorgonzola cheese gone dry in the refrigerator. This ancient woman, wearing a tiara of diamonds and rubies, was the great great granddaughter of Victor Emmanuel II, King of Italy (1861) (d. 1878). Her connection to Italy's last king, Humbert II, who abdicated in 1946, escaped me, but I did not escape her. She turned her gray eyes on me like a ray gun.

"So. You're Candida, Theresa's *protégée*. (*Allora, Lei e Candida, protégée di mia figlia Theresa*).You might have married my great-grandson, Tony Murphy." She looked through a lorgnette, adding, "But you didn't, (*Ma non ha fato*). I'm glad. You need a man with virility (*molto virilità*); so Tony was not for you. Have you considered Silvia's sons, or Arthur, my son, as a mate? You just met, of course. I understand your Italian is flawless, your French, too. You're pretty, intelligent, talented. Our family is getting short on brains. You could help us regenerate. If we hadn't blown Savoy, you could live there and speak French. Never cared for your paternal ancestor, Voltaire. You are named after his novel, *Candide, vero?* (right?) Were your parents free-thinkers? Voltaire despised Catholics, though he took care—wily fellow—to die in the Church. I regret he damaged it before his death-bed conversion. And after."

I tried to mollify her. "I was named Candida because *Candide* was unprejudiced, unlike Voltaire, who was not fond of Jews. Who was? Candide desired a well-ordered society." The *Principessa* failed to hear correctly. "You are right my dear to uphold prejudice as the value most favorable to keeping society in order. And Voltaire was anti–Semitic, I'm happy to say. Mussolini understood the value of such order and prejudice as well." She was "glad I thought so highly of him."

Teresa signalled me to hide my shock, and because of her age, I kept smiling. Silvia made a wry face. The *Principessa*, unaware that she had misunderstood me, not to mention insulted my ancestors, wasn't finished. "Since you take advice," the old princess cackled. "Pursue one of our family as your husband, and you, too, will wear precious stones." She tapped her tiara. "Maybe this. Of course, you'll need baptism, religious instruction and confirmation, being half Jewish. But Holy Church does things fast for people like us, so you might pick out one of the boys now. All it would take is his approval and Rome's would follow. Or, you could marry a professor, eat aged cheese and moldy bread."

I recalled Epicurus had once suggested that his friends bring him an aged cheese on holidays. Voltaire advised cultivating one's own garden, but it was very hard on the fingernails.

Then the Principesssa: "Just remember: clever people don't do the planting, but the eating. Good luck in the garden of your choice," (*Buona fortuna, cara, nel giardino della scelta vostra*).

With that, she motioned to Silvia to wheel her out into the hall, where an elevator whisked her to her room, for she dined alone, retiring early.

Finally, Teresa and I had a chat about Wes in her bedroom. I told her all I thought might interest her about him. Being Teresa, she asked, "How is he in the sack?" I praised his performance. She enthused over his photographs and thought him handsome. He was.

"Perhaps he'd be better for me than for you," she said. We laughed. We returned to eat a few hors d'oeuvres (*antipasti*) and a white wine of an unknown provenance. Enea was just ending a violin piece as we entered. He bowed deeply.

I had to leave; it was past 8:30. Teresa called for Ercole. The nephews accompanied me to the door. In the hall, Arturo, Teresa's brother, whispered that he had a chateau in the Italian Alps, and looked forward to receiving me there. I could tell Teresa whenever I wished to come. An unfortunate choice of a word, "come."

The nephews, Ubaldo and Enca, invited me to their villas, too. Enea, whom Teresa thought gay, whispered into my ear that he was not; it was a pose that kept the family from marrying him off.

"I don't intend to marry," he said, simply. "But I do screw women." How better to prove himself straight than by being straightforward? I kissed Teresa goodbye. I'd see her in Gilroy. She said Tony sent his best wishes, and was dating a woman from Louisiana. She thought it might be serious. I was happy for him.

The Ristorante Michelangelo had a spectacular view. From its piazza, one saw Florence halved by the Arno, and below the dining area, Michelangelo's statues–five replicas of his works, all weathered green. David and his companions, copies of the four Medici tomb sculptures, had been afflicted with gangrene. The Green Giant and his oxidized friends forever awaited an invitation to dine. Perhaps the staff had reservations about seating statues. From here the Duomo still loomed large, the Ponte Vecchio seemed a toy bridge. The golden, red tiled palaces and museums were framed by broad green tree tops and tall cypress trees (*cipresse*).

The group was on the upper terrace, under the portico. Rob was in the middle of the first table, facing the view, Agatha and Ian to his left, Wes sat on his right. Jonah was opposite Rob; Mindy sat beside Jonah, and Agatha opposite Ian. My chair faced away from the city view, but my eyes were on Wes anyway. He was view enough. When he raised one eyebrow I knew he was asking, "Have you been royally entertained, Candida?" And, "How royally?"

Our meal was served. It crossed my mind that in the Renaissance, poisoned dishes were common. Poisoned relationships even more common. Our antipasto? Truffles, Piedmont style. The Della Savoia dynasty had lost Piedmont. Our first course (*il primo*) was Sardinian *Culingiones*, ravioli Sardinian style with spinach and cheese stuffing. Teresa's family still owned Sardinia.

Our second course (*il secondo*) was entrecôte of beef, *Niçoise*, (style of Nice) with *pesto*, typical of Genoa, also ceded, though not to France, but Italy. Still, a double blow to the family was a double loss! When the dessert came, it was a cake called *gâteau de Savoie* in French, *panettone* in Italian. When Louis XIV of France ate some he said it tasted like one baked in Milan. No wonder! The dukedom of Savoy stretched halfway from Neûfchatel, Switzerland, to the Mediterranean, including the Alpine passes between France and Italy; north nearly to Lyon and south from Turin (*Torino*) to Milan (*Milano*), also once the Della Savoia's land.

Why wouldn't Teresa's relatives be risk takers all? Everyone ran risks to "correct" down-turns in the economy. Everyone gambled—on land, stocks, horses, love.

Our food was enhanced by a white wine, Bogheri Bianco, for the first course; Tuscan Brunello di Montalcino, a classic Chianti, for the second. There was a story about that rooster on the Chianti bottle, and it was not to Florence's credit, because she once starved a rooster to win a horse race against Siena.

Tomorrow, the Vèneto, Padua (*Padova*), and Vicenza to the west— would prove our mettle. Was our departure for Venice something to crow about? We would in due course find out.

CHAPTER XVIII

VENICE VIA PISA, WITH LOVE?

All the bags were in the halls for Gianfranco to pick up by seven A.M. We breakfasted early, and were in the bus by 7:45. Lunch in Pisa, due west on the A11. Some grumbled about an early departure. We'd been out late last night. We'd never left so early. My leg was stiffer today. Agatha and Ian seemed dazed, married for ever and ever, unable to get away for a while. They already were away—and could not retreat to their own room for privacy—sharing one. Before we left Florence, we stopped at a church!

"What the fuck?" Sam, who had been preparing to sleep until Pisa, proclaimed irritably.

Samantha put her hand over his mouth. "That's not nice talk," she said.

Rob, said, "Okay. Everybody out for a quick look at Santa Maria del Carmine (thirteenth century). If Mass is in progress, be quiet. You shouldn't miss seeing the Masaccio frescoes here."

The original church had burned (1771), but the frescoes in the Brancacci Chapel were saved. Some were by Filippo Lippi; others, Masolino. Our sleepyheads wanted only to reach Pisa to see how far the Leaning Tower really leaned, and be photographed leaning with it, so friends at home could laugh at their originality.

Original sin was what we were here for; Masaccio's representation of the expulsion from Eden. Though misogyny made Eve responsible for all sin, at least *Roe Versus Wade* (1973) would make it possible for women to make love without the burden of unwanted pregnancies. Choice. No one could chip away at it or try to take it from us ever again.

Mass started. Latecomers dipped their fingers into the holy water fonts and bowed before the altar, taking aisle seats so as not to disturb more punctual worshippers. We made our way to the Brancacci Chapel. The priest before the altar knew we were here to worship Masaccio, not Christ. The *Tribute Money* fresco, painted shortly before his death at age of twenty-seven (1498), was a testimony to the artist's progression from old style figures to more realistic Renaissance ones, achieved through careful use of the light source, making flesh look solid under clothing.

Masaccio saw every muscle. His models for Adam, Eve, Peter and Christ were tangible, with heft and depth. His illumination depended not just on light, but on shadows that reminded us that what was obliterated and narrow on a wall might be greater than what seemed so clear in real life. Reality may be just that small sliver we saw so briefly; "through a glass darkly," as St. Paul said (I *Corinthians*,13:9-13).

I wondered if Rob would explain how our sense of reality was so dependent on shadows, without details, but he didn't. Instead, scarcely mentioning Masaccio's artistic technique, he just pointed out that St. Peter was looking for money in a fish's mouth, told by Christ that he would find enough there to pay the tax man.

Anita remarked, "This is Jesus's critique of government, isn't it? I mean, the value of the state and its money is reduced if even a fish carries it in his mouth? That belittles governments, doesn't it?"

Anita had again, as in Siena, surprised Rob with her acute observation, even if she were only a middle school, not a college, art teacher.

"My very thought!" he said, in response, and his jaw dropped to reveal two gold crowns. But they, I knew, were a tribute to his dentist's art not a government mint. Here Christ was scarcely more dominant than his disciples. All looked equally anxious to get rid of this intruder, the tax man. We never have appreciated governments who taxed us, but gave us only war and want in return.

The greatest work was the smallest: a slim panel depicting the expulsion of Adam and Eve from Eden for original sin. We all joked about the lack of original sin's originality, but our whole civilization had been shaped by this couple's disobedience and guilt, at least for believers. The fear of the Lord. Was that the story's purpose? Wouldn't men be fearful enough in a world of scarce resources? For what was more punishing than life in barren regions as opposed to a garden tended by God? Did mankind need to be punished forever? No couple, Masaccio may have felt, could have repented more. Was not repentance valid? How long did mankind have to repent eating an apple?

The artist made Adam's regret and Eve's anguish poignant. They were misery personified, as an armed angel in a fiery red robe drove them out the garden gate. Only Eve had bothered to cover her sexual parts. Adam was oblivious of his. How like a man.

Back in the bus, Rob told us that Pisa was once a thriving Atlantic port. "It silted up, and is now six miles from the sea," he explained. Like Florence, who conquered it (1406), Pisa spanned the Arno. The Florentines had a saying: "Better a corpse in the house than a Pisan at the door." The Genoese had defeated Pisa earlier, (thirteenth century), so Pisa was a two-time loser. Everyone hated losers.

"The Medici tried to breathe new life into Pisa by re-establishing the university (1574)," Wes observed, "but the town itself never recovered. It was bombed by the Allies in 1944."

"That made it a three-time loser," Reed figured. Without exploring its majestic villas, we made for the green field called Field of Miracles (*Campo dei Miracoli*). "Oh, what a magnificent cathedral" Matilda exclaimed.

"It was built in 1064, and faced in bands of marble." Rob further proclaimed it "one of the finest Romanesque buildings in Tuscany." Its colonnades, apse, dome and bronze doors were by Bonanno Pisano (1180), first architect of the Leaning Tower or campanile. This free standing campanile became a symbol for all Italy. After Bonanno had begun it, its tilt became steadily more apparent. That flaw delighted travelers for eight hundred years, not because it was off-center—so were many travelers—but because it was exquisite.

"That proves that one can err and still be redeemed," Barry Schwartz mused. "If Adam and Eve had been told that, they might have persuaded the angel to give them a second chance." It was the cleverest observation Barry had ever made, and it came from the head of the dysfunctional Schwartz family.

The circular Baptistery stood alone. It took over a hundred years to complete. Pisa went broke. Finished in 1246, it was the tower from which Galileo proved by his famous experiments with falling objects that gravity matters. The Romans, with their emphasis on "*gravitas*" (Lat. seriousness) always knew that. With gravity everything—whole empires—fell into place. Without it, they just fell.

Allison, who had studied theology, recalled that "Galileo's own life, like the Leaning Tower, was off kilter, considering he was denied his liberty for claiming that the earth moved around the sun. To be imprisoned meant that someone believed you had not gone straight. Yet Galileo went straight—straight to the truth of scientific evidence."

"The Pope should apologize to Galileo soon," said Anita, a new silver cross gleaming between her large breasts, replacing the one left behind in Pisa with Inspector Bianco.

Jonah, whose business was insurance, looked at the tower with the others, ruminating. "Two things about this Leaning Tower. First, had my company been asked to insure it, we would have been fools to do it. It's had a history of instability." Bill Froehling, a retired engineer, not half as good looking as Jonah, wearing wire-rimmed glasses and with his bald spot shining out of his wispy salt and pepper hair, wore a smile as he drew near Jonah. It was as if he had hurried up to hear Jonah's punch line.

Bill, turning to him, said, "Yeh. Your company wouldn't have insured. So what was number two?"

Jonah glanced down at Bill's balding head ruefully. "Two is that we would have been damn fools not to have. Look how long this tower's been standing. Look how much business it has brought this town! Sometimes, what seems to be risky is a good long term investment, with unexpected returns. *I thought of my love for Wes, its unexpected returns.* Jonah went on. "Take beauty," You can't insure beauty for its full worth. And beauty attracts—nothing attracts like beauty." He knew. He had married Mindy.

Ralph, however, was less concerned with the tower than with Galileo's experiments. Moving his cane deeper into the soft grass, as if to get a firmer grip on his thoughts, Ralph said, "I've always thought how wonderful that the learned world took Galileo's rationality more seriously than the Church did, which took its own mistaken ideology of the universe for a fact. And as you say, Jonah, the tower proved that a mistake may be forgiven if the whole work is exceptional otherwise."

"Are you comparing the flawed campanile there to original sin, Jonah?" Mindy had just caught up with her husband. As a former Seventh Day Adventist, she had been taught carefully about sin.

"I think rightly so," Ralph mused. "Builders and scientists may err, but we are human, like Adam and Eve. Pisano and the popes, too, along with us, and even Galileo. 'To err is human.'" A good line for one of Ian's sermons, perhaps, but the pastor was now strolling with his arm around Agatha's waist and not thinking of sermons.

I, Candida Darroway, could not help but think that there was a good deal to be said for forgiveness. I had forgiven Rob his bathroom invasion. Wes had forgiven me for forgiving Rob. As for Dad's desertion of our family, well, I knew I would master it one day. Forgiveness is highly underestimated. I could not imagine Italy without Pisano's *tour de force*. Art. Religion. Science. Superstition. Error. Desertion. Each exerted its own kind of force. Our tour group exerted its own.

We had no lunch reservations in Pisa, and as we left the Field of Miracles we kept our eyes peeled for a restaurant (*trattoria*). It wasn't long before we smelled pizza, and saw overhead a sign: *Pizzeria Rinaldo*. Was this the miracle the Campo provided us? No, another, more important miracle. I spied someone familiar, leading a group of college students toward us. It was my old professor, Dr. Antonio Moravia, still recognizable by the grizzled crew cut he had always worn, and always a bit too high. He was frailer than when I'd last seen him, nearly six years ago. Drawing closer, he exclaimed, "Candida!" and once abreast of our group, kissed me on each cheek.

"Dr. Moravia! How nice to see you again."

"Candida," he repeated. "Are you on tour? You should be in an archive researching another book."

I confessed that I was co–leading a group for Altamonte, and that I *was* writing another book, just not at the moment.

"And are you perfectly happy?" he asked, with the same piercing look Signor Beppo had bestowed on me, and the *Principessa* had given me last night.

"I'd love to talk, Professor, but my group is entering this pizzeria for lunch …."

"Have lunch with us instead, just around the corner. My treat. I have something important to tell you," he added. I accepted, first telling Wes where I'd be, and to summon me when our group finished lunch. Wes said he'd come around the corner when Carlo was ready to leave for Venice. He was pleased my former professor wanted to tell me something important.

"Go, Candida." Wes wasn't crazy about pizza, but he gave me a big slice of space when I needed it. He was very intuitive. Wes, however, walked me back to Moravia's restaurant, as my gait was still not quite steady since falling from the bus in Florence.

Back at the *trattoria*, Prof. Moravia, the famed novelist's second cousin, began enthralling his students with one of his bawdy tales of famous authors he had known personally, not excluding Alberto Moravia. On this occasion, he was winding up a story about Umberto Eco, a close friend.

"*Cara* Candida," he exclaimed, finishing his story, as I seated myself next to him. When I was his student, he had tried to date me. I was forty years his junior! I had refused, but tactfully, explaining that it would be risky for him to date his seminar student. Which it would have been. Risky for me to refuse, too. I had a friend at Cal who dated her Spanish Prof. When she refused his advances, he gave her a B in the course, a bad grade for grad students. That spring he was fired. True, he hadn't published, but one of the reasons alleged for firing him, was that he had brought Cindy to a faculty soiree whose guest of honor had fought in the resistance against Franco. Shortly after that, the guest was exposed as a Basque revolutionary, a commander of ETA. The consulate issued an arrest warrant for him. He escaped. To Cuba. My friend's professor, to a junior college.

I respected Antonio because I got an A in his course, even though I refused his advances. If he wasn't a man of total reserve in his sixties, he must be so in his seventies.

"Candida, your name is on a list of possible candidates for a tenure track job in Romance Literature" he said, as I was passing the olives.

"You're not serious?" I asked, Suddenly, my hands were shaking like aspen leaves in Tahoe, or tule grass in Alviso.

"*Cara mia* (my dear), I do not joke about anything but the authors I have known and their silly novels. But I assure you that you are on the list. Not a short one. I think there are four other names. But Prof. Murtree, our new Chairman, was saying recently that they were following your career closely. Your articles on Renaissance linguistic ambiguities have impressed the senior faculty."

After such earth shaking news, I had to calm myself to make conversation with his students, curious about this "older woman" in whom their professor took such an interest.

"By the way, Candida, when does your tour end?" Antonio asked.

"In less than a week," I answered. He tapped his index finger on his forehead, a familiar gesture from seminar days.

"From which airport?" he asked.

I swallowed before answering. "Malpensa" (Milan's airport).

"How about flying to Palermo instead of the States? I'll buy your ticket from Milan, and pay the difference between your old and new flights to San Francisco. I have a lovely villa on the ocean and no one with whom to converse. You'd have a whole floor all to yourself. My sister, *povera matta*, (poor crazy woman) had to be sent to an institution. My wife died five years ago."

After ruminating on whether I *would* "have the whole floor to myself," I replied, "Oh, your invitation is so tempting, Antonio. *Had he developed total reserve?* I wondered. But I *must* go home. My sister's wedding, you see. I'm Maid of Honor." I wondered. Not if it were honorable to lie, but if I ever had told him I was an only child? "Thanks, anyway."

"Pity," he said. "Marriage," he added.

The dessert was arriving when Wes came in and, after being introduced to the professor, told me that our group was now boarding the bus to Venice. Antonio arose, creakily, to kiss both my cheeks again.

"It was a pleasure to see you Candida. Come visit me on campus." I promised. Wes and I crossed the street. Rob had spoken with the Gritti Palace from the pizzeria and had bad news.

"Candida," Rob said, his face clouded over. "Charles left a message for us at the Gritti, which I just phoned. It seems we have been poured into the canal, so to speak. I called Clark myself to say that our lawyer would chew his ass, but he hung up. How could you have chosen to do business with Clark? You obviously did not make clear to him in our Albano caper outside Rome that his word must be his bond."

I was shaken by Ferrell's hostility. "Rob, I was the one who got us into the *Albergo Principi* in Rome. You took the credit, but I did the work. And where there were no in-town five stars, as in Assisi, we got a marvelous three-star, the best in town, and luxurious!"

I knew I would never have had the experience of such high living had the college not paid this trip, even if a few hotels were not class as luxury ones. Many people my age would have envied such privileges as we had, and I was cool with that, too. I supposed my preference for elegance rather than crash pads might have been in part innate, and not inherited from Dad. Good taste made it easier to associate with a mature crowd, with the older men I seemed attracted to. But this was my assignment, not a matter of choice. I wasn't totally spoiled, though, so I said, "The Orvieto hotel was only a two star, but the rooms were splendid, and it was one of my favorites."

"Except for the stairs we had to climb and the dead rat in my room" Ellen hissed, indignantly.

"Yes, and the bad breakfast and hard mattresses," Jan said.

"Not to mention the noise from the marketplace, Betty Harker, added.

The rest of the group stopped chatting and strained to catch every word of this altercation.

"Where in Venice does Charles intend to lodge us?" I asked.

"On the Lido," Rob answered, not even in Venice. That's a sand spit, five miles from St. Mark's square (*Piazza San Marco*.)

"It's over seven miles long," I told him, "an outer island between Venice and the Adriatic," I explained. "It has every kind of hotel from five star to *pensione*. Beach goers love its miles of golden sand, and you can drive cars there unlike Venice. Venice had a plethora of footbridges over waterways (*rios*) so one could walk free of cars, but one walked too much. The Lido had peace, excellent shopping, and in autumn, much of the Venice Film Festival," I explained.

In prior centuries, the island was the only place Venetian Jews could be buried, though they lived in a Ghetto across the Ponte Guglie in central Venice. Useful to Venice as money lenders, once Jews died, their remains were deemed intolerable. The Lido cemetery received its first Jewish corpse in 1389. Now, Venetian Jews had as much right to be buried in town as anyone else.

"Did you know," Wes asked, "that on Lido beach in 1204 crusaders gathered to be rowed in Venetian ships to Jerusalem? Instead, the Venetians made them loot their Christian competitors at Zara, and conquer Christian Constantinople. Pope Innocent III was embarrassed, but could not get the Westerners to move on to Jerusalem."

Rob to Wes: "At least the crusaders found quarters in Constantinople. *We* are still homeless." Then, turning to me, he said: "Use the pizzeria's phone and tell Charles to find us a suitable five star on the Grand Canal or we'll kick his ass."

Did I mention that Venetian canals smelled in summer; that ocean water on Lido's beaches was clean; that drunken singers in gondolas were noisy outside the Gritti? Did I mention the howling feral cats in Venice? Feral sounded too much like Ferrell. Both howled periodically.

I phoned Charles, the group all ears. I resolved to be calm. One must look at the humor in life, not dwell on misery; especially one's own. I'd look back at this incident as one of the most embarrassing conversations I ever had; like taking a bath in public, with people counting your moles and pubic hairs. But the only phone was on the cashier's stand.

Charles picked up. His sinuses sounded bad. The City is foggy in summer. Good, I thought, let him suffer. He claimed he had not at first been give the true price of rooms at the Gritti. He said I'd been told months ago rooms facing the Grand Canal would run three hundred dollars for a single, four for a double. He said the Manager told him just three days ago that their rates for scenic rooms had increased by fifty percent. Our agreement had a proviso—I didn't know this—Charles did—for our displacement if the price rose; or if a larger tour group booked within one month of our arrival. They claimed they had alerted him at the time. Charles claimed he told me. He hadn't. Our canal views had been absorbed by fifty-five Japanese. Charles said we might yet have gotten rear rooms if I had confirmed from Florence that we were on our way in and would arrive within a few hours. Some Scots had taken them. He gave me ten hotel names and numbers to call.

I hung up and started phoning. I didn't yell at Charles. I did not, as Rob had, threaten to have anyone kick his nethermost region. I'd been taught before Dad left us to know that when one kicks others around, one loses dignity and control. I needed both now.

I called the Pesarro Palace, a four star; booked through the end of August. I called the San Clemente Palace, five stars; ten rooms left. I called the five star Bauer near San Marco, but their first multiple vacancies were after 15 September. I called the *Hotel Corte Canale Grande* (a four star). Their accommodations had been courted–by Ethiopians. I tried my dear old Fenice Hotel (*Albergo Fenice)*, but they only had two vacant singles. There was a summer opera season, and they were just around the corner from the *Teatro Fenice*, (Fenice theater). Paolo, the desk clerk, single, hoped I'd drop by for a drink. He was off duty at five P.M. tomorrow. Nice guy, Paolo.

I tried more numbers in Wes's *Frommers.* Six in Anita's *Fodor's* and four from my own tour guide. No dice. My eyes were bleary. I was hoarse. Finally, Charles rang back. Luck! He had found us a four-star on the Lido. It was only a quarter mile walk to the ferry stop, with a garden, 32 available double rooms, and a Turkish bath. New mattresses and newly re-decorated.

"What's it called?" I asked Charles, shouting.

"Hotel Four Fountains." (*Albergo Quattro Fontane,)* he answered. "It has a country inn appeal, but no fountains." Charles said, though his voice was cracking up, "something something .... Tudor ...elegant rooms....red gold .....fireplace...something....rooms.....attractive..wire..... something....new......plus....air-conditioning.....terrace.....breakfast ..... beach half mile." Then, perfectly audible, "Besides, it brings your tour back nearly on budget, which is just under five thousand dollars, Candida, *not* just under seven thousand." And with that, he hung up.

I looked up the *Albergo Quattro Fontane* in two guide books. It existed. To San Marco by water taxi, which had group rates, was only twelve minutes; fifty-five on the slower ferry vaporetto, line 2. There was a schedule. We would have to consult it. The guide books listed the price of the *Quattro Fontane's* rooms. Under one hundred U.S. dollars for a double. That beat the Gritti Palace by nearly two hundred dollars. But, as I said, though the Gritti was on the Grand Canal, and in the heart of Venice, the noise and the smells of Venice could cost you, too. Sleep.

I was beat. I thought I would be an ambassadress of literary culture, and instead, had become a *condottiere*, a mercenary leader of troops who appeared (falsely) to have betrayed my side. *One day I must write an article on force in the Renaissance*, I thought, even if that were more Wes's strength than mine. Still, *Force and Femininity* would be a winning title for one of the new feminist journals. Travel magazines might use it for protection of lone female travelers. No, on second thought, it would scare off lone female travelers.

We stopped at a gas station–Agip. (*Agip stazione di rifornimento*) over the A1, a vast tourist center for refueling people and vehicles. The "gip" part evoked Egypt, shipper of oil from the Gulf, not a gyp in price. But that, too. All the money we paid for fuel would jip us eventually of our pulmonary function; our ability to grow food. Oh, well. Tourism contributed to that nightmare. Nobody's hands were clean. If I worried about such things, I couldn't restore my tour group's confidence in me. They hadn't lost it in Rob. He let trouble run off his back like water off a duck's back.

These rest stops were convenient. We have them in Illinois and Wisconsin. I remember stopping at one between a convention in Milwaukee and a flight from Chicago's O'Hare. In Italy, they actually served good food.

Wes helped me down at the "Bologna" stop. The city was not visible, but Carlo said it was close by. The smog was thick in Emilia-Romagna. As he passed me, Carlo said in Italian what we said when the turkeys were getting us down: "If I were you, Candida, I'd ignore all these complaints."

And Wes: "Candida, dear. You are under great pressure now. From Rob. Charles. Some of the more spoiled group members. But Jonah and I want you to keep a smile on your face, even a phony one, for your welfare; not anyone else's. When peoples' expectations are not met, they can turn on whomever they think responsible. Not on Rob. He's too slick. It will be you who gets pushed and shoved. So, be friendly to all. Jonah and I are supporting you, and ultimately, Rob will have to as well. Maybe later rather than sooner. I can't tell. There's something missing in his make-up. Love." After a moment Wes added, "You can always say what is perfectly true: this tour wholesaler was suggested by the President's secretary, Miss...?"

"Harvey," I said.

Wes nodded. "Harvey. Right. And that way even if the Lido is a disaster, you will suffer less. Not not at all. Just less. Jonah told me to tell them that our next hotel–Verona was it?– will be better."

"I know, Wes. But Verona is just one night. Venice–pardon–the Lido, is three."

"Can't be helped," Wes said, patting my shoulder. "You have friends here to protect you. Just remember that, darling." Wes called me "darling." That buoyed me. He would keep his cool whether the ferry to the Lido took twelve minutes or forty-five.

"What I could use now, is a drink." Wes said that was "reasonable." So, in the Bologna stop, after ordering hamburgers, we wandered to the bar. I ordered a Scotch and soda, Wes, a Manhattan.

Sam and Samantha were already at the bar, Sam licking the salty rim of a Margherita and Samantha sipping a whiskey sour, looking dreamily at the lemon disk placed on her glass rim. Our hamburgers–Italian style–with *pesto*, ketchup capers and olives–went very well with the Scotch and soda. I could not help but think of a few of the grad students I'd known at Cal who would have shunned alcoholic beverages for vegetable juices–celery, carrot, and loathsome cabbage juice. They'd have passed up beef burgers for tofu Sloppy Joe's (on whole wheat buns). Not me. I ate one hamburger a year, and wasn't having any Tofu. Slimy, colorless, disgusting stuff.

Samantha, without looking up, was watching me in the glass behind the barman. "My ex-husband," she announced, "would have sued the Gritti Palace for what they've done to us. I think you should have held your ground, Candida. Travel agents are famous for fucking clients over."

Was this the same Samantha who had recently reproved Sam for using the F-word when we had not yet left Florence but stopped to see the Masaccios?

She turned her back on me then, but Sam, who loved alcoholic moments, moved closer to me, leaning out toward me from his barstool.

"Hey! I want you to know, Canada," (sic) "I don't give a fig about the Gran' Canal." Then, turning to Samantha: "D'ja hear me say 'fig'? You're the one who just said fuck." Samantha sniffed.

Had they had two rounds already at this bar? Samantha's remark, and obvious hostility to me, would prepare me for more grumbling, more complaining from some of the other tourists who shared her disappointment.

I, too, had been looking forward to the Gritti Palace, Ernest Hemingway's favorite Venetian hotel. But unlike them, I had no one nearby to blame. Charles was in San Francisco. He had dumped the problem into my lap and then found us a place on the Lido. Ferrell encouraged complaints by implying that Charles and I were mutually responsible for these glitches.

Leaving the restaurant for the bus to Venice, seated in my usual place across from Carlo, the rest of the group filed in, most staring straight ahead, instead of making the occasional comments to me on a recent adventure, though admittedly, a lunch stop was not thrilling. Both Jonah and Mindy smiled at me as they passed, his white hair above her blonde head, forming a kind of platinum aureole as he leaned down over her to catch her words. Matt smiled too, but it was a pitying little smile, as was Matilda's, Anita's, Sam's, Joan's and even Anne's.

Arnold said, "Don't let the turkeys get you down, kid," which I appreciated. My dissertation adviser had given me a coffee cup with that slogan and silly turkeys on it. I kept pens in it.

We arrived at the railway station at 7 P.M. I inquired about the next "rapido" (fast ferry boat; *vaporetto*) to the Lido. It had already left. We could take a slow vaporetto that left in five minutes, but would not get us to San Marco before nine. We would not arrive at the Albergo on the Lido before ten and would dine as soon as we got in. Carlo, a Roman, had no idea of how to get around in Venice. He looked at his written directions, though, and parked the bus near the railroad station in a guarded lot. He and Gianfranco caught up with us crossing the *Ponte degli Scalzi* (Bridge of Discalced Friars). Some few of our group decided to take just one piece of luggage with them for convenience and to avoid paying more for their ticket, as our prepaid *vaporetto* tickets included just one suitcase apiece. A second bag would be at the tourist's own expense. But two would have been cumbersome without a porter *(facchino)* since everywhere in Venice there were bridges to climb, and we had to climb our first one before boarding the *vaporetto* (ferry boat) up the Grand Canal (*Canale Grande*).

I was glad I had but one piece of luggage. Wes insisted on carrying it as well as his own to the boarding point, up over the bridge from the station.The bridge was really all I could manage without carrying a valise, too. I still had pain in my legs, shoulders, hands. Gianfranco produced discounted *vaporetto* tickets. Charles had taken the trouble to reserve in advance. The ticket agent waved us through. We took line no. #2 which would take us more rapidly up the Grand Canal with a transfer to the Lido. If we were lucky, we might find a water taxi at San Marco, which would be much faster.

There were many "Oh's" and "Ah's" on the part of even our most disgruntled tourists. "Oh," Belinda leaving the pier. "I feel as if I'm in a movie. Look up the canal. It's full of mansions."

"It's better than the Hamptons, the Hudson, Miami Beach!" Sandy affirmed. "We've got to do serious shopping for our store here. Not just waste all our time in art museums."

I thought about how materialistic these businesswomen sounded and knew the Venetians would have approved. Their main business was business. Art came later.

The no #1 would have taken us more slowly up the Grand Canal, stopping at every landing, but we didn't board. We had had a long trip from Florence to Venice via Pisa. We were not in the happiest of moods. Those who passed us by in motorboats, gondolas and water taxis seemed to be. Many waved at us.

"I have a motorboat like that one," said Barry, and a sailboat docked at Sausalito." Lucky Barry. Just thinking of his equipment made him happy. Was he also thinking of Maria? She was part of his equipment, too.

We had entered a new world. Most of us did not own boats. And there was something disconcerting about a city of lagoons and no freeways, no ranch houses, no Edwardian homes in Old Palo Alto, or four acre estates in Hillsboro or Atherton. I thought of Rob's chic apartment beneath Coit Tower, where I had refused to sleep over, refused him. Dark waters, like dark cities at night were, however romantic, threatening to people not well adapted to darkness. I, at least, was used to the nearby sloughs in Alviso. The sloughs of male emotions were less familiar territory.

Once aboard the no.more rapid #2 we passed *San Marcuola* on our left, the Palazzo Vendramin Calergi, "one of the finest early Renaissance palaces in Venice," Rob told us. Matilda, said, "I know something about that house. Richard Wagner lived and died there in the last century (c. 1883). My great grandfather and great grandmother were guests in that house just before he moved in. They attended a ball there, and she wore this ruby ring there."

I had forgotten to ask her or Andrea what Prof. Balistreri thought that ring was worth, or where it had come from originally. I had been too handicapped in Florence, too rattled. It was probably the most interesting story any of our group had to share. Those near her could not but wonder at her excitement. Imagine knowing where one's great grandparents had gone dancing! All I knew about my own parents' dancing was that they did the fox-trot and two-step once when Benny Goodman played the Waldorf Astoria in New York. I knew nothing whatsoever about my Jewish-Italian great-grandparents. Had they ever gone to a ball? I doubted it. Rob told us the next great palace was the Golden House (*Ca' Doro*), built (1430) by a father and son, the Bons, who designed the Doge's palace, too.

Ellen, in her usual abrupt manner, said, "Doge is spelled like 'dog' only with an 'e' on the end." Wes covered his mouth with the back of his hand. Bill, embarrassed by Ellen's childlike statement, asked, "When will we get to see that palace?" He tried to divert attention from Ellen's inanity, and now, his eyes glinted behind his wire frames as if the effort drove him a bit mad.

Rob said "In about seven minutes at the rate we're going." Bill wanted to know if we could see the inside of the Doge's palace. Rob told him, "Tomorrow." Bill seemed satisfied, and now at least everyone knew how to spell it- with an 'e' at the end.

I turned to get a last glimpse of the miracle of Gothic lace and variegated colored marble, on the *Ca'd'Oro*, the Contarini palace whose façade contained gold leaf, vermilion and ultramarine. Their most beloved family member was a fourteenth century Doge. He won Venetians over by melting down his gold and silver plate to crush Genoa in a war. The family produced seven other Doges, and a Cardinal. They had earned their stay on the Grand Canal. We hadn't.

We passed under the Rialto Bridge (1591). "That's a great place for you to shop for jewelry," I told Sandy and Belinda. "Prices are low, and their beads are all from the shops of Murano or Burano."

"We'll go out to those islands the day after tomorrow," Rob said.

"But," I insisted, "if you shop on those islands, you'll pay three times or more for what you find on the Rialto Bridge and Market." Belinda and Sandy, looked at me with owlish stares, but made no comment. Well, at least I'd told them how to save money.

Then we sailed under the bridge, the only way to cross the Grand Canal until an iron Accademia bridge was built (1854) by the Austrian military. In 1933 it was so rusty the Venetians replaced it with a wooden bridge, which looked pretty rickety now. We passed *Ca' Foscari, Ca' Rezzonico*, an art museum, another art museum, and the eighteenth century *Palazzo Grassi* across the canal, now used for art exhibitions.

Suddenly, the Accademia museum appeared on our left, right after *Ca'Rezzonico*. Left, the *Palazzo Corner-Contarini* (papal families needed more than one mansion). This mammoth, three storied white structure with two *loggias* above and three grand doors below occupied a "corner" of the canal. But corner in Italian was *angolo*, not c-o-r-n-e-r. The name was a mere coincidence. So much in life was.

Next to great white palace, a tiny *palazzo*, the *Barbarrigo-Minotto*, whose ninth century owners defeated barbaric Lombards. Their name memorialized their barbaric (German) foes.

It took a big person to memorialize his enemies, or else, a proud one full of self-importance. One had to choose, because everyone had enemies. I shivered, not because the evening air was chilly, but because some of the tourists were chilly toward me. This *Barbarrigo- Minotto* palace wasn't as interesting as the family, which produced two doges, a saint, and a ballroom totally frescoed by Tiepolo (d. 1770). Personally, I would have preferred their ballroom to their doge or saint. Doges were just politicians. Saints were often a pain in the neck to live with. But the art of Tiepolo was divine. They should canonize great artists.

I knew we were lucky to be gazing at so much architectural beauty, at the sun setting in the west, lighting up windows that reflected back, but did not reveal their secrets. Those, I suspected, were either so magnificent or so dark that to know them would numb us. The *vaporetto* was a humble conveyance, and the faces of passengers expressionless from daily cares. The laborers of Venice had made this trip up their sparkling canal for over a thousand years, faces blank.

"Oh, look," Lynette shouted shortly before we began to slow down for the *Piazetta* San Marco and the pier beyond in order to dock. "There's the *Palazzo Gritti*, our would-be hotel but for Charles Somebody and the Japanese." I didn't tell them "Papa" said the Gritti was "The best hotel in a city of great hotels." That was after he wrote *A Farewell to Arms*, surely? By then he could have afforded staying there.

One could not penetrate the depth or contents of this water given the angle of light that cosmeticized it, deserving of our admiration. Upset when we started, approaching San Marco's *molo* (pier), I couldn't help but say, "Wes, Thank God for Venice. Thank God for *"La Serenissima"* (Venice's nickname; the Very Serene One). Turning back and to our right just before reaching the pier, the church of *San Giorgio Maggiore* (Saint George the Greater) was so illuminated by the sun's last rays it seemed to be ascending into the misty atmosphere; while to the left, *Santa Maria della Salute* (Saint Mary of Health), built (1630) out of gratitude for Venice's having survived an epidemic, was a Baroque thank-you card, already turning pale blue, retreating back up its many steps like the "great lady standing on the threshold of her salon," as Henry James had described it.

Now we were, if not keepers of salons, at least, stand-in ambassadors, as Strether's Massachusetts connections were in James's *The Ambassadors*. We were not ambassadors to Paris, though, but to the Lido. Our embassy there would be the *Albergo Quattro Fontane*.

Tomorrow would dawn again. The sun would strike these inland waters, the lagoon and the *Canale Grande*. And we, now chasing the last light of this day westward in a *vapporeto*, toward the Adriatic, would chase the sunlight back again to make an official visit to San Marco on the morn.

CHAPTER XIX

PIAZZE, PALAZZI, CAPOLAVORI

We arrived in the dark, water splashing the vaporetto's prow. Anita whispered, "*I* don't mind the Lido. It's part of the adventure." Once on land, the Four Fountains Hotel (*Albergo Quattro Fontane)*, would be our "home" for three nights.

"At the Gritti," Ellen complained loudly, "we wouldn't be walking a mile to our hotel."

"Less than a quarter," I objected, quoting a guide book.

Sandy asserted, "We'll see." Just how far from dock to hotel, we never knew. Once we reached the *Albergo* and ascended its veranda, the distance from the pier shrank retroactively. Mr. Bartoli, the night clerk, welcomed us.

"I am honored to have such distinguished guests," he said. Ellen visibly softened. The foyer was lovely. In the living room to the right, roses stood on each table. Oriental carpets on polished floors seemed grand yet homey. The lighting, from peach colored lamp shades, was inviting.

The reception area, tucked under an imposing oak staircase, was decorated with antiques; the library, well furnished with books, easy chairs and ottomans. It looked like a prosperous home, like coastal Maine. Ah, Maine. Bar Harbor, Camden—my parents had taken me there several summers.

This hotel had three floors. Wes, Rob and I were on third, with a door (locked) between each. Rob's was a corner room at hall's end. My room, in green and yellow, had antique nineteenth century furnishings. There was no time for anything more than the quickest wash up and comb out. The kitchen staff had held dinner hot for us. It was 10:20 P.M. We left our rooms simultaneously. Wes and Rob each held one of my hands for the long descent. I was still not as steady as I had been before the fall. This help from Rob astonished me, after his coldness to me all day. An odd threesome, we walked slowly down the staircase, and turned left. In the living room a few travelers were chatting softly. The elegant dining room beyond was red with gold accents. Very 1920s. F. Scott Fitzgerald and Zelda would have felt at home here.

At one end of the hall, a fireplace, two tables for four drawn up in front of it. A large buffet stood beneath windows overlooking a veranda. Wes and I joined Anne and Arnold and the Pellatierras at a table in the middle of the room. To our right, Joan and Rob, opposite Anita and Reed. To our left, the newlyweds, Ian and Agatha, red-haired Matt and blonde Allison. I could see Joan's eyes gleaming as Rob leaned toward her, filling her wine glass.

I was no prude, but I felt uneasy on Molly's behalf when I noted that under the table, Matt had grabbed Allison's leg and was stroking her calf! I would not tell Molly. Matt was making a big mistake about Allison. I couldn't explain why, but I knew he was. Her expression, as unmoved as her leg, didn't help. Joan certainly knew what she and Rob had in common–a collegiate romance–and what they did not. Her husband in Pleasanton. The Huntsman's, seeing the Harkers were seated with the Froehlings, sat down alone, and I was glad to see them joined by the Schwartzes; for the Shoensteins, had already joined Meg and Peg. So, new dining combinations formed tonight. Carlo and Gianfranco sat together, as usual, at a table for two, though Gianfranco had spoken some English with Matt out by the desk. Lynette, Belinda, Sandy and Matilda sat across the room, where, occasionally, the ruby ring cast red shadows on champagne colored walls.

Dinner arrived promptly. The first course: rice with peas (*risi e bisi*) was followed by thin slices of liver fried with sliced onions (*fegato alla veneziana*). Andrea Smithwich asked if she could have chicken instead of liver and got it. Our pasta substitute was maize (*polenta*), which Venetians formerly thought a product of Turkey, and still called *granoturko* (Turkish corn). Our *secondo* was seafood; a whole sun-dried salt cod (*baccalà alla visentina,*) surrounded by lobsters (*gamberi di mare*), shell on for color, cracked for easy serving. Around the edges of each platter, bream, mullet, sole, eels, sea bass. These platters were masterpieces (*capolavori*); followed by lemon ice to clear our palates. Next, A salad of chicory (*radicchio*) and pitted muscatel grapes in a vinaigrette of lemon juice, olive oil, parsley and Parmesan cheese

(*Parmigiano*). Dessert? Rum cake topped by whipped rum and shaved chocolate. We finished with espresso or cappucino.

As for wines, oenophiles rejoiced. Valpolicella from Verona; Bardolino from Garda; Soave, from Verona. Now I guessed what *Two Gentlemen from Verona* must have done with their afternoons! Merlot, Riesling and Cabernet, Santa Giustina, Daldaro (dry white) from ...I forget. There were Trentino wines, too, Tiroldego and Marzemino. Our table consumed four bottles. Andrea and Arnold were connoisseurs. I had two glasses and sleepily refused another sip.

Besides food and the day's disappointments, we spoke of Prof. Balestreri's view of Matilda's ring. The cabuchon style was late fifth century Byzantine. Its setting was seventh century, but altered in the late fourteenth by Lombardy's Visconti ruler, Galeazzo II, inscribing his name, enlarging the gold circlet. It matched the description of a ring Empress Irene sent Charlemagne, (late eighth century) when she proposed their marrying.

Charlemagne had had enough women. He, like Irene, favored icons in the Church; but thought a woman who made war against her son and blinded him to preserve her throne, *too* iconic. And, having robbed the Avars, who earlier had robbed Irene's churches and monasteries, Charlemagne already owned many of her Byzantine artifacts. So he gave her the go-by, (but kept the ring, her stolen valuables), furnishing his cathedral at Aachen and his palace with her stuff. Einhart, royal biographer, did not mention that besides adultery, larceny was one of Charles's bad habits. A monk, and fond of his master, Einhart kept some of Charles's sins to himself.

From Charlemagne the ring passed to his grandson, Lothar, who wooed a Lombard princess named Desideria. She received his ring but dumped Lothar. The ring went to the Lombard treasury. As Lombard power waned, their neighbors,' Florence and Milan, waxed. Pavia paid protection money to Milanese viscounts (royal administrators) in trinkets, including the ruby ring. They had no more land or cash.

The Visconti, a name derived from the job of viscount, mastered their Lombard masters holed up in Pavia. They won archbishoprics in Milan. Giovanni Visconti, Archbishop of Milan (1349,) now Duke of Milan, too, won Bologna, Genoa. After his death, two nephews,

Galeazzo II and his brother, Bernabò, divided the Milanese estate. Bernabò went east; Galeazzo II (d. 1378) west. Galeazzo wore Irene's ruby.

Galeazzo's II's son, Gian Galeazzo, imprisoned Uncle Bernabò, (1402) where he was poisoned. Gian Galeazzo donned the ruby and became the strongest Duke of Milan and Count of Pavia ever. He married his daughter, Valentina, to his ally, Prince Louis of Anjou's son. Two months later, the late Bernabò's daughter married the French king's brother, Charles VI, becoming Queen of France.

A feud between the descendants of uncle and nephew ensued. Gian Galeazzo's son, Gian Maria, lost Lombard cities and was assassinated (1412). His brother, Fillipo Maria (d.1447) took the ring. He rebuilt Visconti territory, reorganized Milan's silk industry and married his only daughter to a *condottiere* (soldier of fortune) named Francesco Sforza.

Francesco wanted his father-in-law's fortune. King Ferdinand V of Aragon was Fillipo's heir, but Francesco took the dukedom of Milan, anyway, and the ruby ring. Visconti blood passed not just to *condottiere*, but to European royalty. Visconti girls married Valois kings. Bernabò's great-granddaughter, Catherine of Valois, wed King Henry V of England. Widowed, she married Owen Tudor. Their son, Edmund, sired Henry Tudor, who claimed the English throne by descent from King Edward III, becoming King Henry VII of England.

Other Visconti girls married Habsburg Emperors and Bavarian princes. They did better through marriage than their male relatives through war. As it turned out, sexual unions seemed cheaper than warfare, but in turned caused other wars. *I must ask for Wes's opinion on this conclusion,* I thought.

Lodovico "The Moor" was Francesco's Sforza's younger son. Wes and I had looked at his portrait in London, discussed his ethnicity in London. Invested with Milan by Emperor Maximilian, Lodovico patronized Leonardo da Vinci, Bramante, and other talented artists at his court, a red fortress. But Lodovico died a prisoner of King Louis XII of France. Louis's dynastic claim to Milan was through Valentina Visconti's union with Louis, Duke of Orleans, Louis XII's father. Thus ended Sforza rule. Matilda's ancestors had evened the score with the Sforzas, who displaced the Viscontis by marital means.

Matilda was clueless about dynastic history. I doubted she would have retained it if she heard it. Only an historian of Renaissance history could keep everything straight. Even Wes had no knowledge of the ring. He explained the history of the era to Andrea, who had to consult Prof. Emiliano Balestreri, the Florentine gemologist, about the jewel. Wes took notes in a small notebook on what Balestreri told Andrea.

Pope Julius II's Holy League attacked Louis's Italian territory (1511). Louis made a truce with all his enemies except Austria, and went home to rule France. The ruby stayed in Milan's treasury until the Habsburgs invaded Italy (1527). Then, imperial commanders restored the ring to the Emperor, who gave it to an aunt, who was an Austrian Duchess, *born a Visconti*. If chickens could come home to roost, so could ruby rings.

Andrea Pelatierra paused in his conversation with Wes to sample the Tiroldego making its way around our table. After a hearty draught, he said, "Prof. Balestreri lost track of the ring's whereabouts, guessing that before the Habsburg defeat (1918), it was on the finger of that last Duchess's descendant, Matilda's great-grandmother who danced at the Palazzo Vendramin-Calergi on the Grand Canal before Richard Wagner (d.1883) rented it."

Due to a family falling out (the Emperor Franz Joseph was by then very old and temperamental) Matilda's parents left the Austro-Hungarian court in 1890. Because of the quarrel, they left without much money. Still, her mother, the duchess, whose grandmother had danced wearing the ruby on the Grand Canal of Venice, thought to sew that ring into the hem of her winter coat before she and her consort, with two young boys, set sail for a new and democratic life in New York City. Matilda was born in 1900. Since she was the girl, she received far less education than her brothers, though her parents did teach her the rudiments of French and Italian at home, in case it became possible to go back to Vienna someday. They spoke French, German, Italian and now, English, thought they couldn't say a word in Hungarian! Matilda grewup quadrilingual. Her parents never sold the ruby ring, though they were sometimes pinched for lack of money. Matilda felt it best to marry young, and at seventeen fell in love with a young Italian from Naples named Fernando d'Aragona. His family migrated to Queens from Naples about the same time her own family arrived from Austria.

Like Matilda, he knew nothing of his royal descent from the House of Aragon, which had once controlled Navarre, Saragossa, Catalonia, Majorca, Valencia, Sardinia, Sicily, Naples and several medieval French fiefs: Provence, Rousillon and Montpellier. Neither knew they were distant cousins, either, but it didn't matter. Most of Europe's royalty related one way or another.

A mobster from Naples, Bonafacio Batello, had settled in the lower east side a few years earlier. He had once fought Fernando's father back in Naples over a piece of property, a fishing dock beside the old Castel dell'Ovo (1154) the Egg Castle, 1154)–and lost. The property had vast marketing potential. So Fernando took his bride's last name, Visconti, to hide from a defeated and potentially dangerous Batello. Fernando and his bride had met over fish! Fernando liked the symbolism, since it hearkened back to Naples and his father's dock victory. Still, the royal couple, who knew almost nothing of their exalted status, lived in dire poverty in a two room apartment on the fifth floor of a cold water tenement that had no elevator.

Matilda, born nine months after their wedding (1898), was told throughout childhood that the ring was all that remained, except for a red house in Milan, of family wealth. The ruby was willed her by her mother, for Matilda was the only surviving child of this royal couple. Her two brothers, seventeen and eighteen, were both killed in World War I, one on the Piave front, the other at the Battle of the Somme.

Matilda went to the city college of New York. Her mother gave French and Italian lessons. Her father had received an education in Naples. He taught European history in night school. Fernando sometimes wondered if his family name, d'Aragona, might have had any connection to the House of Aragon, but concluded his relatives had taken the name of their Neapolitan employers for whom they gardened, landscaped, and did odd jobs. Some very odd.

Having discussed so much of Matilda's history on several bottles of wine, our table threw in the towel after one A.M. I was curled up on my mattress when I heard the intervening door between Wes's room and mine open. He had picked the lock with a corkscrew lying on a refrigerator in his room. How we found the energy after such a long day and evening to make memorable love, I cannot say. All I recall is that it was fulfilling, more so than dinner. But then, dinner feeds only the body; a joining of bodies, the soul.

When Wes rolled away, I said, conscious stricken, "Oh, Wes. I forgot to take my pill this morning." I wondered, sleepily, if one could start a dynasty without a ruby ring?

The next morning, breakfasting outdoors, sunlight on the Venetian lagoon shrank the distance from San Marco to our Albergo.

Belinda said, "I guess it's not a mile to the dock."

Ellen guessed, "At least a half."

Rob shrugged. "Less than a quarter." Soon we were boarding a water taxi for San Marco after a six minute walk to the pier. We'd be at San Marco in twelve minutes.

The vessel cut the waters, dividing them for us alone. We passed the arsenal where Renaissance galleys took a day to build, an assembly line system that overwhelmed the Turkish fleet at Lepanto (1571). We passed San Zacharias's church (ninth century) housing Giovanni Bellini's sumptuous *Madonna and Child with Saints* (1505.) It was close to the Doge's Palace on the *Rio Palazzo*, over which hung the Bridge of Sighs *(Ponte dei Sospiri)*. Prisoners sighed on their way to trial, death, prison. A pineapple shaped knob faces it.

Prisoners got no pineapple. The Portuguese conquered the Azores, pineapple plantations, the western slave trade (fifteenth century), the spice trade to the East Indies, and a sizable chunk, not of pineapple, but of the New World. After that, Venice became a tourist trap, a place where novelists, poets, movie directors, and academics went to paint, write, drink, make love, and die.

Lynette cried out, "Look! The Doge's palace!" It looked like a pink cake with candy canes of white marble and crosses. People walked in arcades below, oblivious to the beauty on top. Lynette, usually quiet, quivered with excitement at having recognized a major site.

"You cannot concentrate on beauty as a tourist," Sam mused. "You'd never get from pillar to post." Pillars and posts were all over this palace, as were grilled windows. But then, it was not just the Doge's home, but an official building, too. Security was always an issue.

Andrea Smithwitch wondered about the attic. "They probably stored incriminating documents there. Drier than their cellars. Exculpating evidence, too. Corpses in Greek Vases..."

Matt interrupted wickedly with, "Preserved in olive oil. In case the oligarchy killed the wrong man."

Sandy wondered if Casanova's carnival masks were up there in a box. "He wore a different one for every woman seduced." *Seduction was always a matter of masks*, I thought. Fidelity alone goes bare faced. I thought of my parents' crumbling marriage; of Mom's fidelity and where it had gotten her when Dad's "attic" held so many masks.

"Casanova ended badly," Jan Huntsman warned Matt in grandmotherly fashion. "Young men hide their identity without masks. It's your behavior that does you in, not your attic." I remembered Matt holding Allison's calf at dinner last night.

As our vessel sped toward the dock (*molo*), we couldn't see all of Piazza San Marco, just the *Piazetta* with St. Theodore, first patron Saint of Venice, atop one column; St. Mark's winged lion on another. The landing stage for gondolas, beside the little square. A clock tower (*Torre dell' Orologio*) at the rear of the St. Mark's square read 9 A.M. when tourists think only of breakfast. That tower on the north side of the Piazza (fifteenth century) was gilt with blue enamel, phases of the moon and signs of the zodiac. It was built for sailors, just as the Campanile was to serve as their lighthouse. I wondered what shoals I might be sailing into unlit, and if I'd get to a well lighted shore? I couldn't drown. Could I?

We disembarked. Ferrell raised Altamonte's flag. Its lion symbolized St. Mark. We walked to the palace's "Document Door," passing "the Moors," sculptures of four men Venetians believed Muslims plotting to steal the Basilica's treasures. Instead, they were Roman tetrarchs from Diocletian's day (third century). How quick Christianity had been to blame Muslims–and Jews–for Christians' fears, crimes.

Once in the Doge's palace, we passed over the Lagoon courtyard with busts of Venetian Doges, each with a distinctive hat. We passed the Compass Room (*Sala della Bussola*) and the Lion's Mouth (*Bocca di Leon*), a mailbox for denouncing one's neighbors. Doges encouraged spying, like Nixon in Watergate. This January five of seven in the

Watergate break-in pleaded guilty. Venice's Council of Ten was more open. The sign under the Lion's Mouth box read: "Secret denunciations against whoever gathers favors and offices or plots to hide the truth." Leakers and spies were rewarded! Modern democracies tried and imprisoned them.

Sam wanted to see what Casanova saw crossing the Bridge of Sighs, before escaping by a hole in the roof. Sam admired him. His own life had offered few successful outs other than alcoholism. Lacking a hole through a roof, Sam escaped through a hole in reality. By drinking.

We passed Sansovino's Mars and Neptune (1554), climbing the Staircase of the Giants (*Scala dei Giganti*.) "The Doges were installed into office here and given a unique cap," Rob explained. Betty Harker wondered about measuring the doges' heads? She once sewed hats for Schiaparelli.

"Thankfully the doges spent liberally," Rob said. Sansovino's Golden Stairway (*Scala d'Oro*), with stuccos by Alessandro Vittoria (1558) lowered unemployment, like the WPA projects in the 1930s. The stairs led to the Doge's apartments and offices.

Rob intoned, "This Republic, like most Renaissance ones, was an authoritarian government run by the elite for the elite." The group looked startled when Wes added, "Just like ours." Jonah whispered to Barry off to one side. *Their* crowd was elite, as was Arnold Lodge's and Samantha Jones's. Who else could afford a luxury tour? Even Wes was a member of the academic elite, like me. The part without money or power.

Wes looked at coffered gold ceiling philosophers, law-givers, holders of the scales of justice, too elevated to identify. Maybe they had no identities, but illustrated virtues rarely practiced? In the Great Council Chamber, ten men had made decisions, most questionable, but not to *be* questioned. Here hung the Tintoretto brothers' *Paradiso*, among the world's largest paintings. The masses looked up to Mary, the Holy Spirit, Jesus. Baby angels cavorted. Some saints looked up enraptured. Others paid no attention. Meanwhile, the piazza was filling with tourists. It was enough for them to say, "So this is Venice, Italy."

"Rob," I whispered, "let's get to the Basilica before it's too jammed to see anything."

He nodded. On the way down, a rising human tide sloshed up Sansovino's staircase.

Outside again, we admired San Marco's splendors, pigeons swooping everywhere. Over the basilica's façade, five entrances, numerous pilasters; and above, bronze horses, replicas of replicas–brought from Constantinople (1204). They were copies of Roman or Hellenistic originals that once decorated Constantinople's race-track. Their sculptors were unknown.

Napoleon stole them (1797). Returned after the Treaty of Vienna (1815), Austria claimed the horses *and* Venice. People loved horse flesh and have rustled them–and people–down through the ages, whether marble, bronze, or flesh. Venice, once the Wild West of the Byzantine Empire, had become a merry-go-round by the sea, complete with horses and gondolas.

Thirteen inverted cones decorated the basilica's roof. They topped gothic arches with mosaics. "Fortunately," Barry observed, "they are too lofty for Ferrell to lecture on." Above, five huge Byzantine domes, with smaller domes on top and crosses above.

Anita said, "No wonder the four 'Moors' hugged. "The upkeep on all this must have been worrisome."

"Venetians believed," said Ferrell, "that Muslims (Moors) smuggled St. Mark's relic to Venice under a load of salt pork."

Wes said, "Like the horses, Mark never really belonged in Venice."

"Nor the Madonna of Nicopeaia," Rob continued, "an icon stolen during the Fourth Crusade (1204). When Venice surpassed the Byzantine world in trade, she stole valuable art objects from Byzantine lands. Injustice plus creativity equalled mass tourism, trade." My co–leader hurried us into St. Mark's.

Inside he pointed to the "*Pala d'Oro*," or altarpiece, (tenth century) work of medieval goldsmiths, with 1,927 precious gems. Two hundred fifty panels included eighty-three examples of *cloisonné*, variegated enamel bound by thin strips of gold bent to any required design. A few were dated and signed. Here were the jewels of St. Ambrose of Milan worked up by Wolvinus Magister Phaber (835). An Anglo-Saxon gem was called "the Alfred Jewel" (849-899). King Alfred would have been proud.

Andrea Pellatierra, who knew his jewels, whistled. "Suppose the Church sold pieces of this *Pala d'Oro* to multi-millionaires in San Francisco? Those guys would imbed fragments into their Jacuzzis; decorate Ferrari dashboards; have inlays made for basement bars; jazz up soap dishes for bathtubs. If we could get this *Pala d'Oro* out the door, we'd have money for art supplies and art teachers from East Oakland to East San Jose," California's poorer school districts. Maria, herself an artist, wished we could do it.

Rob took up the theme. "We could rehire art and shop teachers, fired years ago. Shop classes could make *Pala d'Oro's* for churches, shopping malls." He explained how *Pala d'Oro's* could stimulate American manufacturing, train poor kids for careers in building and the arts.

Wes looked up. "Rob, you're right. We could introduce *Pala d'Oro's* to Protestant churches, Lutheran, Presbyterian, even Unitarian ones. Leave out the Virgin; put in Luther, the Saxon Princes; quotes from John Calvin's *Institutes*; engrave Unitarian ones with their non-creed: "We respect everybody and try to promote the search for what is provable and psychologically healthy by discussing social problems and world events in a comfortable setting over a good red wine."

I could see Rob directing *Pala d'Oro* designs at art camps for the non-college bound. He liked kids. He was good with his hands, as his production of carved ducks for Gumps had proved. He was good at so much, he should have been the happiest of individuals. How little we know about the human heart.

Jonah listened attentively. He'd been thinking. "Why not *Pala d'Oro's* for synagogues? Put Abraham and Isaac on them; Moses with the Ten Commandments that nobody obeys, but all admire? And Islamic *Pala d'Oro's* could feature scenes of Hagar and Ishmael, related to Abraham, though unacknowledged by most Jews and Christians as family. Perhaps we could reduce hostilities in the Middle East. Jonah was probably thinking of the disastrous Arab-Israeli war of June, 1967. A whole new *Pala d'Oro* industry for an interfaith world community to discourage old animosities. Stimulate economies. Employ welfare recipients. Personally, I didn't think this would fly, but even without *Pala d'Oro's*, encouraging American manufactures might create an American Renaissance, restoring the can-do attitude that made us great in the earlier twentieth century. "The mosaic of *Christ in Glory* under the central dome (thirteenth century), is Byzantine, as are the other domes," Ferrell told us. "Look at that *Dome of Apostles* (twelfth century) touched by tongues of flame."

"You're like one of those Apostles, Rob," Joan said shyly, "I mean, you're an apostle of art; your lectures flame up, like sermons spreading light..." *Whew,* I thought. *What was going on with Joan? Psychological transference?*

"Art theft," Rob told us, taking no notice of Joan, once attained sanctity if you believed God wanted your church or city to have it instead of a culture that had already stolen it. Anyway, Pope Innocent III, embarrassed when his Fourth Crusade took a whole city with its hinterland, didn't bother to return the Madonna of Nicopaeia, so dear to Venetians here, or the horses on Saint Mark's. He didn't return many other icons. Why bother when the crusaders kept all Constantinople for over sixty years?"

Andrea Smithwitch, seeking male attention, sidled up to Wes, asking if would he like to see the *Loggia dei Cavalli* where the *real* fake horses were?

"I'll ask Rob," Wes said gallantly. Ferrell graciously assented. So we all went to look at the horses in the basilica's museum. They were stolen from Constantinople by crusaders (1204). Andrea grew up on a horse farm outside Lexington, Ky. She loved horses like Andrea Pellatierra, jewels. *Silly filly,* I thought. She hung on to Wes's arm while we walked, forgetting her husband and his livers as we passed another great organ, one I would have loved to hear. The real fakes hadn't looked any different from the fake fakes on the roof.

I wouldn't go out on the balcony overlooking the piazza, since I did once and had a bad siege of vertigo. The protective rail was just three feet high. The effect for the vertiginously challenged was... vertiginous and challenging.

The *Genesis Cupola* in the atrium displayed the *Creation of the World* in concentric circles. The artists never heard of the theory of mass. Yet they speculated how it came together. They thought God did it, but the *Bible* underwent hundreds of translations. Some of His or Her activities were lost. Some, poorly translated. Every edition aimed at reality. But who in ancient times grasped it? Who, for that matter, did now? We must prove our own truths.

Emerging, the younger members of our group, *without inviting me*, left to take the elevator up the campanile. First started in the ninth century, the campanile was rebuilt over the years. Its present form dates from 1514. All three hundred twenty-three feet of it fell down in 1902. The rebuilt structure (1912) was dedicated to St. Mark on his one thousandth birthday. It had a *loggia* and belfry with five bells. Each bell had one function: announcing executions, or telling workers when to start their workday, etc. Above the belfry, the Lion of St. Mark and a lady representing Venice stood watch. She was Justice (*la Giustizia*). Ladies always represented justice without ever being consulted about making laws fair to females.

We wandered over to Florian's coffee shop. The orchestra played. We didn't realize there was a music tax of 5,000 lire.

"Oh, well," said Lynette, when somebody grumbled over the music tax, "If we aren't willing to pay the piper, no tunes." She liked her joke, not realizing that it was a cliché. Most of the world's jokes were, but it was the first time I had heard her laugh. No laugh is ever a cliché. People should take laughter–like tears–as unique expressions of human feeling.

Florian's was tucked under the homes of city officials (*Procurati*), Sansovino's fifteenth century structure on the north side of the Piazza. Entering Florian's one enters a time warp. It first served patrons in 1720, when Floriano Francesconi was owner. The paneled interior was cozy, but dark. I preferred the brightness of the *piazza*.

Now, at half past eleven, it was filling fast. Harassed parents chased adorable children *(bambini) who* shooed off pigeons, or tried to catch them. Half the world's pigeons live here. Pigeon feed, sold in bags, gave feeders a chance to be photographed with pigeons on their hands, heads. From afar pigeons were okay. But not on one's head, or on one's plate where their tiny body parts posed as chicken.

The waiter placed Rob's and Ellen's espressos before them. Then he turned to serve Wes and me our *granite*. Ellen rose to avoid a pigeon dive-bombing over her. Rising, she jostled our waiter's arm. Half of Wes's *granite* spilled onto her blouse. She couldn't call the waiter a pervert, as she had Sandy and Belinda in San Gimignano. Not until later did she learn that a pigeon had splattered her hair as the coffee doused her shirt. Ellen's hair was itself dung colored, so at first no one noticed. But when she patted her hair, she became hysterical. Her fingers emerged covered with smelly guano. Matilda took Ellen into Florians' ladies' room and cleaned her up. They emerged just as our youngsters returned from the campanile.

"We got a view of everything but the Grand Canal!" a fact clearly stated in my guide book. It couldn't be seen from the campanile. They should have invited me to go along. I'd have told them.

We took a vaporetto to the Accademia museum where art students with sketch books were eating their bagged lunch before returning to class in a building that housed the world's greatest collection of Venetian paintings. Giorgio Massari's Accademia (eighteenth century) was a white, well-balanced museum. Classical.

"Napoleon Bonaparte, created the collection," explained Rob. "Bony moved some of the greatest works from palaces and churches to the Accademia in 1807."

In the first hall, Paolo Veneziano's polyptych (1325), the *Coronation of the Virgin* led Anita to remark: "It contains a few anachronisms. St. Francis was not the Virgin's contemporary." I supposed heaven was filled with anachronisms, a by–product of going to heaven with spirits arrived over the centuries. But I said nothing.

Betty said, "The frame is garish–too many flowery curlicues." In her garden these plants they would have gotten a good staking. It was hard to locate the Virgin, surrounded by so many male saints. I knew nothing of Veneziano, but wished he had given Mary more prominence in her own coronation. I'd always admired the sibyls and the female oracle at Delphi. Male seers and advisers hadn't been as farsighted as one might have wished. Mary might have preferred the company of female saints, like Theresa, Catherine, Hildegarde of Bingen, or St. Clare. On the other hand, Mary was Jewish, and Hildegarde, not yet a saint outside of Germany, where she bore that honorific, was a fierce Jew-baiter in the eleventh century Rhineland. Better that Veneziano left Hildy out, however musically and pharmacologically talented. Her cures did not extend to Christ's fellow Jews. She thought it better to burn them locked into their synagogues. As St. Bernard made clear in his letters to her, the Jews were not the enemy. It was the Muslims!

Rob led us to Carpaccio's works (d. 1525/6) on St. Ursula. "Sometimes said to have been born in Britain (more likely Rome)," he said, "she sailed to Jerusalem with either eleven or 11,000 virgins, fleeing rape by the Huns. Returning, they ran into Huns. All except Ursula were raped. She got engaged to Ereus, Prince of Cologne. Ereus was a classical name, not a German one. Ursula was either a fourth or a ninth century saint, (accounts vary). She may have married *before* her martyrdom. The Huns invaded Germany during the fifth century, and ought not be blamed for rapes that might have befallen ninth century virgins, when Huns were scarcely a memory.

The card under the picture explained that her "life" was a composite of old Scandinavian tales; massacres in Roman Cologne; mayhem in fifth century Chalon. Had a monk mistaken Chalon for Cologne? "Facts" need checking, along with spelling. The Church canonized her after a lifetime devoted to educating virgins. If we wanted an accurate obituary, we'd best write our own. Before dying, of course.

Carpaccio's scenes from her "life" began with the *Meeting of Prince Ereus* (1495). They sailed to Cologne. *The Departure of the Betrothed* shows her on board a ship. In the *"Dream of Ursula"* (c.1500) she lies in a canopied bed, tightly blanketed in red, with white sheets folded over them. There is no other pillow! A blonde angel with a sword guards the foot of her bed.

"Ursula is dreaming" said Sandy. "My guess," Allison hazarded, "is that she dreams of seducing the angel."

"Shhh," Agatha hissed, no longer a virgin, and probably not a candidate for martyrdom, unless Ian was impotent, which I doubted. "A betrothal is not a marriage. The angel is guarding her virginity," sniffed Agatha.

"Carpaccio," Rob said, "painted like Shakespeare wrote, revealing in different scenes great theatrical elements before theater was well developed. Carpaccio was the Cecil B. De Mille of the early sixteenth century."

We moved on to Gentile Bellini (d. 1516) and his *Miracle of the Reliquary of the Cross.* The Doge sent Bellini, a leader of Venetian painting, to Constantinople in 1479 as painter to Sultan Mohammad II. Bellini's *Recovery of the Holy Cross*, (1500) a large painting, shows that he remained solidly Christian despite his sojourn at a Muslim court. His painting shows buildings on both sides of the Accademia bridge, crowds of people, gondolas. Several clerics swim about in clerical robes. The relic of the Cross crosses the bridge above the swimmers.

Agatha was distressed. "I don't understand why priests are in the canal swimming. It's undignified. There's one in a boat. He could have picked up the others."

Rob shrugged. "Perhaps the mood was like that at Mardi Gras. The joy of proximity to the real Cross, though a mere splinter, made some onlookers toss decorum to the winds, bodies into the canal." Agatha looked dubious.

Belinda told her, "People aren't all happy at Mardi Gras. Or any other holiday. Suicides soar at Christmas." A light dawned in Agatha's eyes. Sometimes the enlightened are taught by the ignorant.

"Different strokes for different folks," Sam intoned, an unconscious pun on swimming clerics.

Rob looked at his fingernails. "Possibly these canal leapers performed a sacrifice, since few in prior ages could swim." I noted that Bellini chose stiff, rigid figures to balance the ecstatics. It's the Cross of Christ arriving, not rice and peas, served to Doges on St. Mark's feast. *Get with it, Venetians*, I thought. *Engage your souls.* Had commercial success deadened them to spirituality?

Pordenone's (d.1539) *Blessed Lorenzo Giustiniani* Altarpiece (1532) engaged us next. Jonah said, "What biceps. The guy on the right there."

Rob said, "The "guy" was Lorenzo Giustiniani, a Venetian nobleman, who appeared in a skimpy fur with superb musculature, displaying gorgeous biceps, abs."

"His left foot rests on a book," Wes said, disapprovingly. Wes respected books more than muscles.

"Probably a training manual for wrestlers," said Barry.

Rob explained. "Lorenzo was the heir of a great Venetian family, the Giustinianis. He had decided to reform the clergy and laity like St. Francis and beg his living. He caused a scandal. He left his widowed mother and five younger siblings unprovided for. He wrote tracts for holy living, and writers usually starved. Eventually, Pope Nicholas V consecrated him Archbishop of Venice. The Doge said Lorenzo was the only man with whom he could communicate the thoughts of his soul." *Do souls think?* I wondered.

Wes knew that Lorenzo was charitable. "When the Turks captured Constantinople (1453), his frank speech on poverty alienated some Senators," Wes told us.

"The rest of Venice called him a saint," said Rob, itching his chin. It was then I noticed that a mosquito had raised a bump there. I fished around in my purse, found a tube of anti-itch cream, and handed it to him. He opened it, dabbed at his chin, and kept on talking. "Lorenzo had Alexander VIII canonized in 1690, perhaps because Alexander was a Venetian. The sainthood was announced belatedly (1727) by Benedict XIII." Passing close to me, he said, "Thanks, Candida. That hit the spot." He kept the tube.

Bellini's earlier portrait of Lorenzo (1464) was made when Lorenzo was merely "blessed." It shows an elderly figure with a tight cap drawn about his ears, blessing others with two fingers pointing up, like a pope. His face was withered. One realized how much a harsh lifestyle cost a once strapping aristocrat; here, he is a codger near death (1455).

Ian sighed, saying, "To think of all life's pleasures he set out to miss. A saint indeed." Ian had grabbed what pleasures he could when, losing Allison, he took Agatha as lover and wife. But he didn't envy saints. Ian was an Episcopalian pragmatist, not a Catholic idealist. Henry VIII and Thomas Cromwell put the Church of England on a more pragmatic track.

We paused before Bellini's *Madonna and Child between St. John the Baptist and a female saint* (c. 1504). We admired the broad landscape, new for Bellini. We saw Giorgione's *The Tempest* (c.1507) where a woman, not too young, suckles her child while a storm approaches. A young shepherd wearing shorts looks on from a distance. Her husband? a voyeur? She seemed unprotected.

Agatha, now protected by Ian, averred, "He *may* be her husband. Some women marry younger men." That seemed an autobiographical remark. Perhaps experience is the key to understanding art. Paintings speak to us directly then. We saw Veronese's *Feast in the House of Levi* (1573), "commissioned as a *Last Supper,* but changed," Rob explained, "with Veronese's self-portrait among German soldiers mingling in the entourage of Jesus. Called before the Inquisition for taking liberties, Veronese replied, 'Artists, like poets and madmen, can and must take liberties.' Don't clerics?" Rob smiled at Ian.

Veronese's canvas was an architectural study of three marble arches, a palace *loggia*, many diners beneath it, and a radiant sky outside.

Myrna, not religious, but involved in Jewish life, commented, "If the *House of Levi* were in Venice, the rich Levis would have had to take their dead to the Lido, just like poor Jews. Death is no respecter of wealth."

Rob, concentrating on the painting, said, "Veronese was a classicist but less classical that the more rationalistic Roman classicists. Veronese held to perspective, color and design, but drew more on Venetian architecture and illusionist perspective." Illusion versus classicism? I found illusion disillusioning. Classical truths seemed more enduring.

Napoleon brought Veronese's *San Zaccharia Altarpiece* here from the church of that name. Rob hurried past it. Gentile Bellini's masterpiece, the *Procession in Piazza San Marco* (1496), drew his attention. Of all the masterpieces we had seen, this was the one that impressed our group most, too. On a huge canvas, the entire façade of San Marco was revealed in minute detail. The whole piazza was filled with a procession of clergymen in white, holding relics, scrolls, candles and other holy objects, while to the left, milling about, noblemen chatted. Others lined up to peer into ancillary buildings. In the left background, two nuns discreetly placed among hundreds of male figures, stood alone. The predominate colors were gold, black, red, pink, white, and gray.

Oddly, something was missing in Bellini's photographic approach. Pigeons. None in sight. Perhaps the breed had not yet been introduced? Or everybody kept theirs in cages to eat. This canvas was medieval looking, stiff. It took Bellini longer than other late fifteenth century painters to give up a medieval rigidity that made life appear arrested, static. A procession isn't static, but this one wasn't moving. Yet it *was* well worth seeing. Rob said Bellini painted it for one of the artisan guilds (*scuole*), which paid handsomely for large works.

We looked at Lorenzo Lotto's *Young Man in His Study.* In black against an almost black background, he had white hands and wore a white shirt whose sleeve ends tied with silver string, silver beads. Dainty. A diary, or bound handwritten volume, lay on a desk, as did a folded letter. Around the letter, a gold chain and gold ring amid a handful of dried, pink rose petals. The book rested on a blue silk scarf with many folds. The young man looked at the viewer as if to say, "What would you advise me to do with these? Insist that she keep them for old times's sake? Or give them to another woman as soon as I find one?" He didn't want to reread her so definitively folded letter. How young men in the Renaissance suffered!

I looked up at Wes, no longer a young man. He was not suffering. I did not know if he felt this was his Renaissance, too, but I felt it was my very own.

Rob led us to another Veronese. Veronese was the subject of his doctoral thesis. This painting blew my mind. The *Mystic Marriage of St. Catherine*. St. Catherine, dressed in a gown of blue and gold brocade, on a step before the Virgin, in a red, gold and navy cloak. The nude Infant lay on her lap and raises his right arm. To give Catherine a blessing, or just wave at her? She pokes two fingers into his tummy. The baby keeps smiling while Catherine holds her right hand over her heart. Overhead, a host of cherubs flit about, witnessing this "marriage." A female saint throws her arms up in wonder. As well she might. On the steps up to the Virgin and child, four musicians, perhaps two of whom were angels, read a large book, possibly of music. A stringed viol or cello rests against the steps. Two lute players jam on their instruments. Catherine's face is somber. But if you were marrying an infant, you wouldn't laugh, either.

Ferrell found this "less illusionist and more realistic than some of Veronese's others," but I thought it *delusionary. A grown woman marrying a baby!* I kept my mouth shut. I was already in trouble for the Lido thing, and Rob had not been so nice to me since we arrived on the Lido. I had no illusions. I was not popular with half the group, and I felt it keenly.

We left the Accademia uplifted but exhausted. Some insisted on drinking in a nearby bar. I told Wes, "I'm off for the Rialto Bridge to buy glass beads."

"May I join you, Candida?" Wes asked.

"Okay, they have men's stuff, too, and you could use some unspotted neckties. Also, there's a book store where I buy paper backs (*tascabile*)– all novels. Wes shortened his steps to match mine.

"Good stop. I need reference books; they could order them for me and ship them. I won't ship the ties; I'll spot them up here," Wes said, laughing. We waved to the group. Fast trip by water taxi. We were on the Rialto Bridge in four minutes.

Today's art was lovely, but the group wearing. I had been toying with an escape plan, like Casanova, but no roof. I said nothing to Wes. Tomorrow the group was off to Murano, Burano, Torcello. Murano was known for its glass blowing; Burano for its lace making and lace making museum (*Museo del Merletto*); and the last a peaceful island, where fifteen hundred years ago, the first Venetians found refuge from rough Germans invaders, before Venice was founded. It had an ancient cathedral (ninth through eleventh centuries). Until its canals silted up and malaria settled in, Torcello was a city of ten thousand, gradually abandoned after the twelfth century and now romantically empty. Except for tourists.

After choosing six glass necklaces in lovely colors, and having nearly paid for them (Wes got his credit card out before I did mine), we made our way back to the Piazza San Marco over many bridges. We stopped at the book store I had frequented several years ago. I bought six novels. Wes ordered two reference books on the Veneto and had them sent to Madison. With my novels, I would have company everywhere I went–the joy of novels. You enter into lives of people who take you over, satisfy your longing for love without compromise, adventure or risk.

At seven we were back at the Albergo. Wes followed me into my room, and wordlessly, undressed me. My skin felt both hot and cold, my stomach pulled by invisible wires. Wes kissed my neck, my breast, and, leading me to the bed stroked my legs with his long fingers, separating them with gentle, but definite motions. His fingers entered me first. Sweet torture. When he gave himself to me, I shuddered with pleasure.

Ours was not a mystical marriage like St. Catherine's, but a melding of adult bodies and minds. When we rolled apart, I had a smile on my face, whereas Catherine had looked sad. That was one difference between mystical marriage and earthly romance. There were others.

345

CHAPTER XX

TRY ME IN TRIESTE

I had no connection with Trieste. A student named Fausto, a native of that city, had been a grad student at Cal when I was finishing my Master's. I had coffee with him several times in the Golden Bear coffee shop, only because most of the graduate students didn't dare speak Italian with a native. He hardly spoke English, which was why he majored in Italian. His real interest was soccer, and he had a soccer scholarship. He reassured me that I had a good accent, which I derived from Bubbie Brondel and Mom, though after my grandmother died, and Mom had no one with whom to converse in Italian, we both spoke more and more English. At boarding school I studied French.

Four Italian courses at Cal seemed to have revived my childhood fluency, and added a literary vocabulary that had naturally been missing. Fausto was a jock, and aside from a few coffee "dates" at the Golden Bear, we had little to do with one another. He disliked Italian novels, and I had no interest in soccer.

I had never been to Trieste. So, why did I go there? Maybe because William Dean Howells (*Italian Journeys*, 1867) had something to say about it. That was one of the books I bought yesterday. Then, I was feeling rather blue after dinner, when only Wes, Jonah and Mindy seemed friendly. Perhaps I chose Trieste because if you leave out the first "e" you get the French word *triste*, sad. I suddenly felt sad, with half the group cool towards me, the others, frosty. They had wanted to stay at the Gritti Palace. Trieste wasn't far from Venice, but far enough to give me a feeling of distancing myself from the group. From Ferrell. I would take the first morning train. Alone. A Casanova cast off and out, undetected. An avenger of wounds. A rebel in revolt.

I took with me besides, *Italian Journies*, a sweater, my purse, sunglasses, sun-screen and my swimsuit, in case Trieste had a beach. Also toothpaste, floss, toothbrush and my bronchial spray. I found a train schedule at the desk, and decided on the 6:45 A.M. from the railway station (*ferrovia*). I hired a motor-launch to get me there without the need for rising at 4:00 A.M. I wrote a note and stuffed it under Wes's door. "Don't worry about me. Have fun at the islands (Murano, Burano, Torcello). I'll be back by train around eight. I need time to think. Love, Candida."

I took an orange lying on the Albergo's sideboard, and put it in my bag with two paper napkins. It was still dark when I left. I surprised the guy with the motor boat, who was eating his breakfast, but put it aside and extended a hand as I climbed aboard. "Good morning, Miss. Where to?" (*Buon giorno, Signorina. Dove?*) "To" is implied in "Dove." So many things are. Implied in each other, I mean.

I felt talkative. The railway station, please. I'm going on a little excursion to Trieste, you know." (*La ferrovia, per favore. Sto per prendere una scampagnata a Trieste, sai.*) Of course he didn't know. Who did? Not that it was any of his business, anyway.

So I was a little startled when he asked, "Are you staying several days?"(*Rimane qualche giorni?*)

"No, no. Only today. Do you know Trieste?" (*Conosce Trieste?*)

"Not at all," he said, (*Affatto*). The rest of the trip was completely silent, until, at the dock nearest the railroad station, he asked, "Can I take you home this evening, and if that's possible, at what time?" (*Posso riaccompagnarla stasera, e si e possibile, a che ora?*).

I told him about eight, but that I wasn't certain, and it wasn't necessary to meet me. *I might be back earlier,* I thought.

"No, Sir. It isn't worth the trouble. Another time." (*No, Signore, non vale la pena. Sara per un'altra volta*). Then I thought, *what other time could there possibly be?* It was me, Candida, through and through. Not willing to hurt anybody's feelings by flat-out rejection. I had been rejected too many times and knew how it hurt. And then, having paid my fare, told him goodbye, (*arrivederci*). I walked quickly away, stopping only when I reached the station's ticket-window (*lo sportello*).

"Trieste, first class, round trip ticket." (*Trieste, prima classe, andata e ritorno*) I told the man. He gave me the ticket. I gave him lire, the exact change.

What track? I asked. *(Che binario?)*

"Three," he answered, (*Tre*). I went out into the arrival and departure hall, and walked to track three. I pitied those with heavy suitcases. It was still early, but to my dismay, there were trains labeled *Trieste* on tracks three and four. Damn! I couldn't determine which to take, so I showed my ticket to a porter (*facchino*) in the usual bright blue smock and black visored cap.

"Excuse me, Sir, but which train do I take to Trieste at 6:30?" (*Scusi, Signore, qual è il treno per Trieste, partenza alle sei a mezza?*) He told me to follow him, and I did, down track four, three cars from the area where they sell soda, candy, sandwiches, comic books, magazines and other junk.

He pointed to a car with an open door and told me to make myself comfortable, next to the window. It was one of those older luxury trains that one hardly sees any more in Italy; but Trieste, I suspected, was not a popular destination, even from Venice; and not at this early hour. Still, I was pleased the train was so old, and so empty, and that I might even have a car to myself. At least for now I did. I had grown so used to being surrounded by the group in the bus, and in all the other places we went, en masse. Being alone was such a luxury. For short spells.

The pale blue faded velvet interior with dark wooden and brass trim seemed delightful, homey. The porter handed me in, and told me, twice, to keep watching out the right hand window. I thought he seemed a bit off, excited, but dismissed it. After all, railways don't hire Renaissance men as porters.

He left. There really was nothing else to look at but the next train, also empty on track three. The schedule said the trip took two hours from Venice, ninety miles from Trieste. A relatively short trip. I hoped that I could get some coffee and rolls on board. And pretty scenery to look at. Scenery soothes the heart rejected from some other setting. Scenery is tolerant by its very impersonality. I busied myself with my orange, getting it half peeled, before glancing out the window.

Oh Lord! There was the *facchino,* standing in the opposite window, not more than six, seven feet away, with his fly open, his organ in both hands. He was shaking it at me. The grin on his face was diabolical, imbecilic, lewd. His member was long and thin, like a white worm, except for its bright red tip. I drew the blind hastily, and found myself crying but giggling at the same time, as the wheels below me began slowly to roll, leaving Venice and the *facchino* behind. It occurred to me he undoubtedly felt rejected, too. Having only the lowliest of jobs, and no recourse to travel, he hit upon foreign women. I finished my orange, and pulled out *Italian Journeys* for company in the empty car.

Howells seemed more most interested in peasant girls bearing loads on their heads, and the superior looks of Trieste's women to Venice's. He did have nice things to say about the Austrians' re-building of Trieste, entranced by the number of public stairways one could climb to the hills above the port, to parks and castles. I was reading a dated travel memoir to what used to be part of the Austro-Hungarian Empire, now an Italian port city. I felt closer to Howells than to anyone but Wes, remarkable as Howells died in 1920. Some day I shall read his other books on Italy, *Venetian Life* (1867), and his novel, *Indian Summer,* (1886). Howells was fifty when he wrote the latter, nearly Wes's age and in love. I'm having a love affair in Italy with somebody who is in his own Indian Summer. I needed that book.

No one will remember my love affair with Wes over a hundred years from now or would know how I felt unless I wrote a novel about it. I might, when I'm old and gray, like Howells, and can scarcely remember the details; how Wes felt when his tongue was in my mouth; his penis thrusting deep into my vagina and his weight crushing my rib cage on a hot night when the air conditioner was turned off and Italy's mosquitoes (*zanzare*) were competing with my lover to see who could thrust their respective probodes deeper. When all was still again, which noise—my lover's or the mosquito's—would be more disturbing? Wes's slight snore, or the sharp whinge of a mosquito that, unlike my lover, was still engorged as it winged its way about our hotel room? Which, indeed, left me with the most enduring lump—that in my heart, or a bump on my leg or arm? Only a lover could leave an itch no hand or thought could alleviate, scratch as I might, mull as I must. *Be careful, Candida,* I thought. Either way, you'll run the risk of scarring. And broken skin heals faster than a broken heart.

Someone had to write stuff down or there would be no memory, no history, no us. Julius Caesar wrote about Trieste in his *Gallic*

Commentaries, (B.C.52-53). The place wasn't under Rome's control until 177 B.C. Caesar made it a colony though, and renamed it Tergeste. Venice captured it from the Lombards in 1202, and Trieste sought protection from the Habsburgs in 1382, growing into a prosperous port under the nineteenth century Austro-Hungarian monarchy.

Still, two-thirds of its inhabitants were Italian speaking by 1910. Since Italy had entered World War I as part of the Triple Entente, her reward, delayed until 1947, was that small sliver of land, Trieste, and a smaller splinter of Istria, guarded for nine years by the British and American armies. After a treaty was signed in London (1954), Italy finally (*finalmente),* took charge of what she had wanted so long.

The trip took three hours. The sad *facchino* with the sadder organ had put me on the milk run rather than on the fast train to Trieste. Had he done it deliberately, I wondered? We made several stops, each too brief for me to get out and buy breakfast. At Portogruaro, a young couple with plastic breakfast boxes, carrying covered coffee cups, came rushing down the aisle leaving only a hint of flavorful steam to penetrate the closed glass, wood, and velvet box in which I was imprisoned, a lonely queen, and a hungry one, in the glass cage reserved for me by the Italian National Railways Company (*Ferrovie dello Stato*).

Arrived in Trieste, I made my way to the huge Square of Italian Unity, (*Piazza dell'Unità d'Italia*), an imposing space surrounded by great façades of the late nineteeth and early twentieth centuries, when Austria was the cultural and artistic arbiter of everything. The rather stuffy name of this piazza dates only from 1955. Although I was not yet ready for tourism, hungry as I was, I couldn't help but notice the City Hall, 1875, (Palazzo Comunale) where Mussolini proclaimed his infamous racial laws, where my mother's family lost most of their rights, and some, as a result of those, their lives. All of Europe had some bad memories recalling a gruesome past. One cannot escape these, which follow the tourist, too, just as his most basic physical needs follow him through the continent's finest cities.

I needed a café, and chose one close to the docks. Hunger could push every thought other than your stomach into a cupboard. I had just seated myself under a yellow and white-umbrella when, unbelievably, I heard my name called.

"Candida, Candida from Cal, isn't it?" in English, but with a heavy Italian accent. Turning, I saw a man close to forty staring at me through very large, lightly rose-tinted wrap around sun glasses. I didn't know him! I did not have a clue.

"Excuse me?" (*Scusa*) I said, haltingly.

The man persisted. Don't you remember me, dear girl? I'm Fausto Cardinello! Soccer player, and, an all-but (i.e., no dissertation) in Italian from the University of California. Berkeley."

"Oh, my God, Fausto!" Of course he hadn't written a dissertation. He had never seriously thought of getting a doctorate. He went to Cal to play soccer. I would never have recognized this stocky, balding man in rose-tinted metal rimmed sunglasses, blue jeans and an old sweater for the plain, slim, but tidy looking young graduate student I knew back in my Cal Italian classes, and the Golden Bear coffee shop, hard by the campanile, a copy of Venice's own. This man was barely a copy of himself.

"Come for a walk with me and we'll talk," he said, lifting my left arm to aid in the process. I did not want to leave this dock-side café where I had hoped to eat, if not breakfast, then lunch.

"But, Fausto, I'm very hungry," I protested.

"I understand, and you'll eat. Believe me."

I told him that I had not even breakfasted; had taken a very slow train to Trieste, and that I needed to eat *now*. He assured me that his car was parked behind the Piazza, and that he "would feed me at once," then show me "the sights" of Trieste. Like Howells, he warned me there were not that many. That was okay, given the number of monuments and museums I'd already covered with the group. We were soon zooming around a curved street at the base of a high hill, the Via Capitolina. Screech! Fausto stopped the car, a beat up Volvo, which he said he "got for a song." I believed him. We parked at a curb and got out in front of a tiny shop whose window read, "Superlative Ice cream by Rizzo."

"Here we are; my favorite ice cream parlor in the world," Fausto proclaimed. I was astonished and, I had to admit, offended. I thought I had made it plain I was not looking for dessert, but a meal. Even pizza would do. Pizza and beer. I was not wedded to gourmet lunching. But sugar before protein? I didn't think so. I said as much to him.

"Bear with me, *cara*. I have a plan. You eat ice cream now; later, you dine with me and a couple of married friends like an Empress of the Sea! As it happens, the three of us are going for dinner at a world class seafood place just the other side of Venice. You come with us, and we'll spare you the horrors of that train ride back. The place where we'll dine is world class. This ice cream is just to sharpen your appetite for tonight." That in itself could sound threatening. But I trusted Fausto–I had no choice–and I disliked the idea of taking the train back. It might be fun to dine with him and his friends in a "world class" seafood restaurant.

"But I'm wearing only a cotton sundress," I objected. "How will that look in an elegant restaurant? And my shoes! Straw wedgies."

"You can buy yourself a dress here if you like," he said. There's a boutique just below my friends' apartment. Emilia, my friend's wife, is now watching it for Louisa, the owner. Alessandra, my wife, gets a discount because Louisa is her oldest friend. Alessandra is visiting her parents this week in Naples. But rest easy. Emilia will give you a discount, too, Candida," he pronounced, before adding, "Candida? You never were so tight up–is that how you say it?–in California."

I did not regard myself as uptight either at Cal or now in Italy. I overlooked Fausto's misapprehension. But I had to correct his pronunciation.

"The word is uptight, Fausto. Not tight-up."

Our order, or rather his for both of us, arrived. Towering globules of multicolored ice cream, diverse flavors, topped by three different syrups, nuts, marshmallow, maraschino cherries and real banana slices. I started with the banana. I knew I needed the phosphorous and potassium. I could not remember which one bananas had. I progressed to the cherries and ice cream, though I could not finish. The two-thirds I did eat took the edge off my appetite. And off much of my enthusiasm for Trieste. But, when Fausto asked, "What have you seen so far in the city?" I had to tell him.

"Almost nothing, just the square where we met."

"That won't do at all, Candida. Trieste is a lovely city. I'll run you up to the top of the hill for a look at the fortress and basilica. The first is from the fifteenth century; the second much older."

The "Castello" (fortress) stood high on the Capitoline hill overlooking the sea, the city, and a huge park below, not to mention the Basilica di San Giusto, (St. Justus) where the ancient city used to be on the fifth century site of a former Roman temple. The church, as we discovered, had Roman columns on the lowest story of its campanile. Inside (we merely peeked into it), wonderful mosaics (twelfth century) of Christ, St. Justus and St. Servulus, whoever the last two were. To my surprise, Fausto crossed himself, and knelt before the altar. Theoretically, most Italians are Catholics. But the younger ones, the ones with college degrees, usually aren't practicing. When I remarked on this to Fausto, he laughed.

"I have to practice. It takes forever to get the hang of it."

The north apse showed the Virgin in Majesty between the Archangels Michael and Gabriel, and below, the Apostles. All except Michael looked Jewish. I recalled both Dad and Rob having said something about my "not looking Jewish," and feeling irritated they had. I felt irritated now for having thought that all but Michael "looked Jewish." I knew people couldn't look like a religion, for goodness sake. Our language has been corrupted. Yet here, Michael was the very epitome of the Germanic blonde crusader. And I recalled that in boarding school days a Jewish preppie with these same blonde looks had asked me to go to a movie. I refused him, thinking he was German, probaby Lutheran. Only later did I learn he was Jewish, not German. And now I was in love with a Lutheran, though not a German. History had corrupted us all. Westerners *had* tried to capture Israel. Here, the archangel fought *for* the crusaders, with whom he may have identified—the big blonde Germanic thug. Only, on what grounds did anyone believe in Saint Michael, or in saints, period? Belief was not fact. What I did know was that it was nearly impossible to escape one's prejudices.

"I'm glad we skipped the inside of the castle," Fausto said. "We got the best it had to offer in views of the town and the sea from the parapet." After that, we wandered through the park back to the old Volvo.

"I'm going to drive you around Miramare Castle, high above the sea. My friends live on the other side."

Howells described the peninsula where sat the castle as a place where "Art has charmed rock and wave ..." It was built for the Archduke

Maximilian of Austria, the one shot in Mexico (1867), having been placed on Mexico's throne by Napoleon III of France, and unwanted by the Mexicans. His wife, Charlotte ("Carlota"), lived at Miramare after Max's execution. But she moved, dying in her native Belgium in 1927.

"She was mad as a marched hare," Fausto informed me.

"A March hare," I replied.

"*Grazie tante*, Candida," he replied. "I begin to lose my English in a cooked hat," he lamented.

"A cocked hat," I said patiently, though one should be very careful with verbiage relating to the male organ, even if Flaubert denied there was such a thing as a synonym. When writing *Madame Bovary*, he proclaimed there wasn't, and insisted an author choose the precise word, not one with nearly the same meaning. Still, even if Fausto's English had deteriorated, I hesitated to use the word "cocked," preferring to spare myself from a bawdy joke or become the target of bawdy behavior. Fausto, though, was a perfect gentleman, and probably unaware of the word's diverse meanings in English.

We drove northwest four miles around a lovely promontory with the Miramonte castle commanding a wonderful watery view. After another mile, we arrived at some condos, where Fausto's friends, Emelia et Rodrigo Giacometti lived. On the first floor of theirs was Louisa's dress shop. Alessandra and Fausto lived on the other side of this highway, away from the sea. But Emilia's and Roderigo's location was more desirable. It was also more expensive, which is why Emilia gave up her living room on the first floor so that Louisa, who owed Fausto money, could run a dress shop here, helping Louisa repay Fausto's loan and Emilia and Roderigo enjoy a sea view.

After introducing me to these friends, Fausto mentioned my need for a dress and Emelia took me down to Louisa's shop. Louisa, a petite blonde, promised to "treat me like she would her own friend."

Emilia said, "Thanks, Louisa. Give her the special discount." She went back upstairs to dress for our dinner out. Louisa was *simpatica*. But she certainly wanted to sell me something. Anything. There wasn't much foot traffic here.

Upstairs, Fausto intended to borrow one of Roderigo's shirts and a jacket, no tie, for our night out together at this elegant restaurant. The men were the same size, and it would save Fausto the trouble of traveling to his own apartment to tidy up.

Emelia came down while the men were thus engaged, wearing a simple skirt and blouse. She chatted with me and Louisa, while I flicked through the dresses in my size. I really loved an attractive lavender rayon number with a bit of Spandex in it to keep it from wrinkling. It had a low neck, capped sleeves, and an appliquéd bodice with a bias cut skirt and a cascade of ruffles that extended from the waistline on the right side to the hem on the left, swirling across the dress front. Very chic. It was on sale for a mere 65,000 lire. Although Louisa couldn't discount something already on sale, the dress was a mere twenty dollars. It even matched the sweater I had brought to ward off the mists of evening. I put my sundress into a bag. I bought a pair of ballerinas, real violet leather, with glass beads from Murano, discounted to 30,000. I could always use them as bedroom slippers at home. I put the wedgies into the bag.

Suddenly, I couldn't wait to start for Venice, missing Wes in a rush that almost knocked me down, wishing he could see me in my new clothes. I shook Louisa's hand and wished her good luck with her business venture, which was relatively new.

Upstairs in what was left of Emelia and Roderigo's apartment, I asked, "What do you do, Emilia?" I noticed that Fausto looked more presentable, though none of them were dressed for an elegant restaurant but me.

"I teach sixth grade," Emilia told me. "Fausto is the athletic director in our middle school." *That's what happens if you didn't finish your dissertation*, I thought. You spent the rest of your life playing games. Well, Fausto never did like Italian literature. He was smart, but not literary. Soccer was his game.

"Fausto's marriage has not worked out so good," Emelia whispered, when we were in her bedroom. Alessandra is a feminist. Fausto loves kids, but she wants to keep her job at the university library; so no kids. I think she loves her job more than Fausto. His students adore him. Roderigo wants to fix him up with dates, even though he's still married." I felt that Fausto and I had something in common. We were both looking for the right mate. Though Fausto had one already, and I did not, neither of us were certain about getting or keeping love. Life was so problematic.

We started for the Veneto in thick traffic. Roderigo sat up front next to Fausto. Emelia and I piled into the back seat. The seat was uncomfortably hard. We "felt" every line painted on the road. That had not been true when I sat up front. The springs were gone. Worse, Emelia lit a cigarette as soon as she climbed in, and Roderigo did the same. Only Fausto and I were smoke free, but "free" for only a minute. The smoke grew thick fast. Fausto rolled down his window immediately and I mine, but the air had begun to cool and the draft was annoying. I reached for my sweater. I had my bronchial spray with me and used it several times. It was empty by the time we reached the Venetian lagoons, and I was still coughing frequently. My eyes were watering, sinuses filling. I thought how red eyes would clash with a lavender dress. As a child I had had asthma, nearly outgrown. I have graduated to something called "chronic bronchitis."

"Does this smoke bother you?" asked Roderigo from the front of the Volvo. "You should have said something." He put his cigarette out. Emelia threw hers out the window.

"You really should have," she said, with an odd look. But I'd had so many odd looks in the last few days I was immune. Anyway, talking made me want to cough more. In my mind I thought of a smart aleck-y reply: *"Only a drug abuser would have ignored the connection between smoke and a coughing companion."*

I thought of Wes. It helped some. I loved Wes. I missed Wes. Milan loomed ever closer, and we would soon be separated by two thirds of the United States. Perhaps, forever.

I didn't feel elated when Fausto yelled, "Here we are; we've arrived" (*Eccoci arrivati!*). I felt apprehensive. It was after nine o'clock. There were no clues to our geographical location, save water and a wooden restaurant building, for all the world like one of those clam shacks we used to eat in on the Maine coast, when Mom and Dad were still married, and we were still a family.

"Where are we, exactly?" I asked Fausto, looking in vain for San Giorgio, the Campanile, Santa Maria della Salute—any recognizable sign of being in or near Venice.

"We're twenty miles south-west of Venice," said Fausto, whose heretofore inert face, was now full of joy and anticipation. "We are at the ultimate fish eaters place on the Venetian coast. You will see, Candida, something you have never before dreamed of."

And he was right. For when we entered the swinging door I saw one of the barest, least decorated dining rooms ever. Perhaps four or five of the thirty or so mismatched tables and chairs were occupied. No tablecloths, no elegance. A large blackboard near the entrance read "Catch of the Day" (*Pesci di Giorno*). There must have been at least thirty scribbled on the board in yellow chalk.

Finally, a slovenly looking man in a soiled white apron arrived. Seeing Fausto, he lit up, slapping Fausto on the back.

"Good evening, Fausto, you old devil. Why haven't I seen you this summer?" (*Buona sera, Fausto, vecchio disgraziato! Perchè non ti vedo quest'estate?*).

"Busy, too busy," replied Fausto, shrugging his big shoulders. (*Occupato, troppo occupato*). Then he asked for "the regular," (*Il Normale*). We sat down on hard wooden chairs with no cushions. Salt, pepper and paper napkins in a holder and basta! (That was all).

"Fausto," I asked, watching both Emelia and Roderigo light up cigarettes again. "What is *"Il Normale"*?

"The works," he answered. He, Emelia and Roderigo looked happy as...clams.

The prompt return of the waiter brought us–without our asking–a clear fish soup with chunks of stale Italian bread floating on top. Soup of the essence of shrimp. It did taste like shrimp, though none were visible. That was followed by a thick chowder of oysters and chopped cod, in something like a cream sauce, but with an unidentifiable goat-like smell. I felt my nose wrinkling. Bread arrived. I took a chunk. There was olive oil for dipping; no butter. The bread, a bit hard at the end of the long day, grounded me. Indeed, it nearly filled me up. I felt it soaking up the last of ice cream eaten hours ago in Trieste.

Next came scallops in parsley, giant sea scallops, each looking like Sugar Loaf mountain in the Carrabasset Valley of Maine.

This valley marked the end of the Appalachian Trail. Dad took me on it. Mom feared heights; like me now–and stayed in the hotel. Dad was busy teaching me about mythology, Greek and Roman, mostly, but about American Indians at trail's end. There was a plaque that told about the Indians. I hated to think how much I missed him when he walked away from Mom, me, and our home a few years later. There were no plaques to mark the event. Every trail ends, but the sea makes that still plainer, especially if you've no boat. The sea for non-sailors is the end of the trail. I had no boat.

Our waiter, smiling, came back with a plate of broiled eels. He asked why I hadn't finished (or started) my sea scallops. Don't you like them, Miss? *"Non le piace, Signorina?"* He was very solicitous.

Everyone looked at me.

"Oh, yes. Very much," I lied. "Can you show me where your rest room is?" He made a grand gesture and told me to follow him. The ladies' room was outside, down the pier on which the restaurant sat, and inside a plain door with peeling green paint marked in French: *Toilette Unisexe.* (Unisex Toilet). I tried not to look at the raised yellowish urinal in the corner. I gave my all directly into the hole in the floor over which was a brownish grate, that once had been white porcelain. A *trou* (Fr., hole). I hadn't even seen one in years. Some bar in Bari had had one, but that was years back. Paris was replacing theirs. There was a faucet, but no soap. I cupped my hands and drank. I vomited again. I rinsed my mouth out. I rinsed my hands and wiped them on toilet paper, hard and grey like that on Italian trains.

Arriving back at the table, Fausto assured me I had missed one of the best dishes, squid boiled in its own ink. I asked how many more dishes would be sailing into this "regata"?

Fausto missed my irony, and asked, "Do you mean meal? The word is *'pranzo,'* Candida. Your Italian is rusting. You said, *'regatta.'"*

The dinner sailed on without me. I did not talk much. Emelia started smoking. The three of them ate voraciously, talking of things that came and went–mostly of the successive dishes. There were fifty fish courses and dessert was–icecream. Watching them eat with such gusto made me queasy again. I got up to walk about on the front pier. I saw them through the window, oblivious of my non-presence, which to be sure, wasn't there when I was with them anyway.

Around 11:30, they finished dessert, and I came back in time to thank the waiter for his lovely service, fine cuisine, "elegant" surroundings. I was babbling, not being fresh. I was spent with fatigue, fear. Fear that I might never rejoin the group I had been so determined to separate myself from. Fear that Wes would be upset with me and worried sick because it was so late, and I was still far from the Lido.

Fausto paid for my meal, but I left a hefty tip for the waiter. He had worked hard on our behalf, after all. There were no other patrons in his restaurant, now. The meal was expensive, too. I left twenty dollars and hoped for forgiveness if that were not enough. Forgiveness from the waiter, my companions, the fish I had parted company with in the latrine.

We climbed back into the Volvo and within a mere twenty minutes or so our approach to Venice from Mestre, her industrial subuerb had begun. Mestre, where Hemingway's Frederick in *A Farewell to Arms* had been heading in a train filled with cannon, the train he jumped off short of the station to avoid arrest.

Fausto deposited me at the train station, the *ferrovia*. I walked over the bridge of the Discalced Friars to catch a vessel to the Lido. Should I take the slow *vaporetto* or a faster water taxi? Or blow my remaining cash on a motor launch? The latter. I discovered it was operated by the same man who had taken me this morning to the same landing. He recognized me, too, though I was more elegantly dressed now. What did he think about that, I wondered?

"*Buona sera, Signorina*. Nearly home again," he said in Italian "Your friend left an hour ago, having waited for you to show up from seven o'clock on."

My heart raced. "My friend?" I asked.

"Yes, a *professore* from Weesconsin. He met all the trains from Trieste, and in between, before coming to this pier to see if he somehow missed you." He left by water taxi an hour ago." We made a quick trip to the Lido, dodging gondoliers who cursed us as we passed because of our wake. Wake. A terrible word, really. Once into the Albergo, I tiptoed up the stairs to the third floor, so that the elevator would not give me away.

No one was in the halls. Not even the desk clerk was at his post. I helped myself to an an apple this time. Quietly, I turned the key in my lock, and undressed in the dark. But as I was undressing, Wes, seated in my armchair, with a double Manhattan, put it down and grabbed my hips, pulling me into his lap. His lips smelled of a quality bourbon. His finger opened my lips and he stuck a maraschino cherry into my mouth. Then he kissed me hard on each breast.

"I have been waiting for you," he said.

"But only an hour," I replied.

"More like seven," he said. "I got there early." After that, I must plead the right to keep my mouth closed. Other parts, no.

CHAPTER XXI

PADOVA, PALLADIO, VICENZA, VERONA

"Good morning, Rob," I said. The hall was empty but for us.

"Where have you been, dear co–leader?" Rob said, mixing disdain and caution.

"Sleeping," I said sweetly. Nothing of Trieste. If he reported me AWOL, let Roger dock my pay.

"Candida, you have damaged yourself by disappearing. Do you realize the worry you caused me? Jonah? Wes? Have you any idea *at all*?"

I hadn't given it much thought. I *had* acted carelessly. I supposed Wes had shown my note to Rob. That probably made it worse–jealousy plus wounded authority.

"I apologize, Rob. I was thoughtless."

He sat me down in an antique hall chair. "You caused me not just worry, but real pain. You acted like the personification of the Beach Boys' 'California Girl'–out for fun, heedless of others' feelings. You must think very little of me to skip out without a word, treat me so casually when I ...thought, when several times I tried ...." Here Rob's demeanor changed, as if "Off" had been pushed, and he couldn't find "On." Wordlessly, he retreated to his room. A crash. Should I get help? Could he...? From the third floor? No. His ego exceeded his stature. He had thrown something at a wall, not himself out the window.

I pressed my ear to his door. Wes, leaving his room, saw me leaning up against Rob's door. "Spying on Rob?" he asked.

"Of course not, Wes. He confronted me in the hall, annoyed about yesterday. Then a crash in there. That's all."

"Well, isn't that enough?" asked Wes, his gaze on mine.

"Let's eat," I said. "I was on a starvation diet yesterday. I went to Trieste–for a little peace," I added, "as I indicated in my note." *I hadn't given my destination in that note*, I thought.

"Well, your peace disturbed us. I only found out *where* you went from the boat guy. Making love to you last night helped."

"Love, being disturbed or the boat guy?" I inquired.

"Don't be cute," he responded. We did not speak after that. I got a few nods and even a smile or two from our crowd on the terrace. Anita and Meg asked if I had had any untoward experience yesterday. They were so kind, one a teacher, the other, the nurse who had been so attentive to me in Florence.

"Not at all," I said. I didn't mention the *facchino*. Icecream. Fish. Smoke. "I just needed solitude." Anita said, "Like St. Catherine. She prayed when she needed it."

Meg, having worked in E.R., nodded."We can't be on call all the time," patting my shoulder, before rejoining Peg, again in a different outfit from Meg's. Now they looked like individuals, not clones. Joan looked away when I caught her eye, but I suspected my Trieste caper was not the cause. Rob's dissatisfaction might be. Or hers with him. Or his with her. The possibilities were, if not endless, various.

Jonah said, "My dear, you gave us a scare. I'm glad you're unscathed." He bent to kiss me on the cheek. Mindy waved and continued loading her croissant with jam.

Leaving the Lido by the *rapido*, we arrived at the train station, where Carlo had parked our bus. Our bags, sent ahead, were already stowed. Padua (Padova) was thirty miles from Venice on the A 4. Rob left the microphone untouched. I didn't.

"Good morning, Group. It's going to be a great morning in Padua." (*Buon giorno al Gruppo. Sara una buona mattina a Padova*). I hope you all enjoyed the outer islands yesterday."

Sam asked about Shakespeare's play, "Two Gentlemen from Padua."

Andrea Pellatierra corrected him, "Sam, that was *Two Gentlemen from Verona.*"

"You sure?" Sam asked.

"Yep," said Andrea. "His first play, probably. About the foolish behavior of people in love." *Obviously a must read*, I thought. Yesterday, I was foolish.

Wes, next to Andrea Smithwitch, said, "Andrea, *not* being in love is what makes people foolish." She nodded. Ellen frowned. Rob sat across the aisle from Wes. After looking at Wes keenly, he, too, nodded. The two men began to talk quietly to each other, as they had on the airplane coming over. In other circumstances, they'd have been friends. I couldn't hear what they said. Freaked me out. There. A good counter culture description. They wouldn't be talking about me, would they?

Padua (Padova). We would see a Renaissance university; a nineteenth century coffee house and Giotto's frescoes, before leaving for Vicenza. We had a lot to do. Our final destination, Verona, would put Venice some one hundred fifteen miles behind us. Tonight, Verona; then Milan for three final nights in Italy.

In Vicenza, we would marvel at Andrea Palladio's (1508-1580) structures–a theater (*Teatro Olimpico* (c. 1585); an official court building; and just on the periphery, the *Villa Rotunda* (mansion with rotunda, (1550-52). We hadn't visited his Venice church, San Giorgio Maggiore, though we'd seen its lovely exterior across the Piazetta San Marco. The group would be very surprised by a cocktail party in Vicenza. I had accepted an invitation from a friend, Enrico Della Pace. His villa had a great lower Alpine view. *"On a clear day you can see forever..."* I remember his singing to me in English while we looked out over the mountains from his back balcony one evening. My research year abroad.

I called Enrico a friend. Just one I didn't know well, having met him that once. Some people were born friends, some lovers, some enemies. However, if a woman called a man a friend, everyone wondered how friendly. Intimate? O.K. We weren't lovers. We dodged temptation. Our noses didn't fit when we kissed. And Enrico was unhappily married. For the second time. That's a lot for Italy.

The party was for four o'clock. To be late would be thoughtless. Yesterday I was. But thirty-three thoughtless unknowns (*sconosciuti*) would be Overwhelming Thoughtlessness for a volunteer host. And did he volunteer? Yes, to see me again. I had sent a Christmas card saying I'd be co–leading a tour to Italy this summer. His invitation arrived a week later, so touching since we'd met only once. Well, two evenings in a row. And one afternoon. Was that three times or one?

It was a great opportunity for the group to visit an Italian home. Enrico wasn't just anybody. His cousin had been premier of Italy!

Enrico represented a large French office supply firm, and was sales manager for all northern Italy.

His (second) wife was away. I'd never met her. She was studying psychology in Florence. No children. In the U.S., Enrico would be better off divorced. But to divorce twice in *Italy* was to become an untouchable. It would have embarrassed his already embarrassed family. Catholics had recently won the right to divorce in Italy. But not in the Church. Or public opinion.

Padua, population two hundred twenty thousand, was a Renaissance medical center. Its Piazza of Fruit (*Piazza delle Frutta*) was the site of its court building. Its Nobleman's Square *(Piazza dei Signori)* was bordered by arcades filled with boutiques, wine bars and cafés. The Council of Nobles (*Loggia della Gran Guardia,*1523), was now a convention center. At one end of the square was a military headquarters (*Palazzo del Capitanio, 1599-1696*), with an astronomical clock (1344).

"Clocks give so much trouble" Lynette complained. A divorcee, fussy in taste, she was neither especially feminine nor "butch." *Asexual,* I thought. She loved jewelry, and that drew her to Sandy and Belinda's shop in Cupertino. Or it may have been their "Beat" attitudes and off-beat lifestyle that fascinated her. Lynette had received a large settlement from her ex, president of an insurance company. Nevertheless, she dressed in denims and plaid shirts. A closemouthed woman, she may not have been a lesbian, but she and Allison had found companionship with Sandy and Belinda. *Not all friendships were based on sexuality*, I thought. *Sympathy was very important.*

Lynette had a thing about time. "Everyone feels terrible when they don't know the time, are late to work, or forget the day of the week." Matilda agreed that life must have been freer before clocks.

Sam, in a boozy baritone, yelled, "Right on." Had he been drinking? Samantha liked a drink or two as well. She attended his AA meetings as well as garden parties, and made sure they got to all appointments on time.

"Even the rabbit in *Alice in Wonderland*," Sandy recalled, "repeated, 'How late it's getting.' The thing to do is enjoy the moments, not keep track of them."

"Oh," Reed said, "timing gear in a car is very important, ladies."

"And in sex, crucial," grinned Matt.

Molly worried about Matt's lack of a job, because, well, she didn't earn enough to make setting up house possible, and Matt couldn't find a teaching job at this time on the Peninsula. Understandably so, even if he had a Master's in English. Teaching jobs were scarce. The times were out of joint. As for time, I'd feel lost without my Timex, which, it occurred to me, rhymed with sex, where every moment mattered. I understood where Matt was coming from.

Every town in Italy adhered by coffee. Italians drank so much, they left no room for breakfast other than a sweet roll. They ate a big lunch; a late dinner. But they had a steady diet of beauty, antiquity, art, fashion, soft leather and Catholicism. In Italy people feel wholly at ease. In their own city. But *only* there.

For example, Enrico lived thirty miles from Verona, but didn't trust the Veronese. He said southern Italy (*Il Mezzo Giorno*), famous for volcanoes, oranges, poverty and the Mafia, started in Verona. It didn't. He said Italy could do without Sicily, Calabria, Naples. He would have annexed Locarno, Mont Blanc and Innsbruck in a heartbeat, if Switzerland, France and Austria wouldn't object. He was provincial *and* sophisticated, an uncommon binary. For added privacy, Italians spoke local dialects. Unless they lived in Tuscany. Tuscans didn't need privacy. They spoke Tuscan. To the rest of Italy, they sounded affected, if intelligible at all. There were radio programs devoted to teaching Italians Tuscan, since so many spoke mostly dialect, especially old people and the very young.

"Our first stop in Padua," Rob announced, "will be the *Caffè Pedrochi*, a coffee house disguised as a classical temple, a meeting-place, (*ritrovo*) for intellectuals since 1831."

"Cool!" Matt said, though coffee was generally hot. Gianfranco, who never said anything much to anyone but Carlo, was just nineteen, and not a whiz in his English class. Now he asked if he could speak about Pedrochi's. Coffee houses were his term paper subject last year at the Gymnasium (high school). His English, if not literary, was adequate. Gianfranco cleared his throat.

"The Caffè Pedrocchi she sits ona the corner of Via Oberdan, where it goes cross-criss with Via VIII of February. Pedrocchi, Antonio, *architecto classico* and a some other guy from Venezia, his name I am forgetting. It has three halls, each one a color of Italy's flag. The one white has white chairs and floors(*suole*); the one red, chairs and *soule* to match, and the one green, well, you know. The *Piano Nobile* (first floor above the street), is Renaissance. The building hasa the art museum. The besta thing? Great coffee."

At this point Matt yelled, "Got it man; we're for it!" Gianfranco muttered something. Having regained our attention, he continued: "Caffè Pedrocchi's flavor of mint espresso with frothy cream, wona the first prize in last year's competing. Caffè Marocchino has three layers: espresso; hot chocolate and creamy foam. My favorites, *Frangelico*, with hazelnut *liquor (liqueur)* and caffè Stendhal with chocolate and cream whipped are *so* good." Here Gianfranco rolled his eyes and patted his stomach. "There's Amaretto with cream whipped, and caffè Veneziana with brandy. They make Irish coffee and Turkish coffee so-o-o good." With that, Gianfranco bowed and sat down. Everyone clapped. Who'd known he spoke that much English? Carlo looked proud of his nephew's speech, though he could not understand it.

Once inside, Wes ordered two banana rum espressos, with "cream whipped," one for me. It came with cinnamon sticks. The stick was like a magic wand and sent Wes into a deep reverie as he waved it back and forth. Rob tried Moroccan delight mixed with hashish. He was more mellow afterward. Later, he might be less. I had no idea how a bit of hashish affected a man his size. If I ordered it, I'd fall asleep, hallucinate. I'm guessing. I don't do drugs. Dad's smoking caused my asthma. I had no interest in pot like many Cal students had. Molly and Matt smoked it. Not me.

The Italian "drug" of choice is coffee. They had a different take on it. With us, it was a drink. With them, an art form.

"Next stop, the Scrovegni Chapel," Rob announced. After Carlo found a parking place, we walked two blocks to view this chapel (*Capella degli Scrovegni*), built by Enrico Scrovegni (1303). It would, his son, Enrico, thought, spare his dead father the pains of hell, where Dante "put" him for usury. *The Inferno* scared Enrico Sr.'s son, Enrico Jr., for a rich man's son usually had some sin to expiate (e.g. St. Francis stole his father's cloth); so Enrico had himself painted on his knees before the Virgin, begging forgiveness, (*Last Judgment*). The chapel frescoes spoke to man's hopes and fears.

Petrarch, Giotto's friend, owned one of Giotto's Madonnas. He was convinced that the ignorant did not understand Giotto's greatness, because his art was not just pretty. But I thought it both pretty and great. I had described Petrarch's writing as "grand *without* vulgar prettiness." Well, art, writing, love and life intermingled in such a way that no one could perfectly analyze what made each great, or for whom. *Art was personal*, I thought.

Here, surrounded by frescoes (1303-05), we considered how incapable we were of judging their grandeur. Beauty, perhaps. Grandeur, no.

Looking at the *Expulsion of the Merchants*, (money changers is the English term) Christ driving them from the temple, gave Barry pause. A banker, he looked uneasy. He was a major synagogue donor. Last year he had recarpeted–at his own expense–his whole temple in a blue Karastan with gold leaves and dots. It was *his* temple, and no one was going to drive *him* out. Still, he was a money changer.

We looked at a nativity, where baby Jesus and his family were leaving their town–to pay their taxes to Tiberius Caesar. It made Myrna think of her twins, scarcely two, and of Maria, their nanny, so like her mother. The twins resembled Maria, too. *Life was full of coincidences*, Myrna thought. Neither Myrna, who looked like her father, nor Barry, nor Maria suspected any family relationship. The similarity of Maria's appearance with Myrna's mom and the babies was a coincidence, Myrna thought. But Maria *was* family. And Myrna's was part of my own, though I couldn't prove that, and she didn't know a thing about it. I had learned it while dreaming. I should have been named Sybil, since I knew much about a past I had not personally witnessed, not even read about, but dreamed of. I never even knew a woman named Sybil.

Mary's Presentation at the Temple. Raised to the right rear wall, it was a rhythmic study of grief, the *Deposition from the Cross* (*Deposizione*), the tragedy conveyed in the curvature of mourners, wild gestures, hovering angels. One had to elbow one's way about, for many were crammed into a tiny space. A chapel was not a basilica. Even the shortest person could appreciate the fresco of *Injustice* on the lower right wall, where mayhem reigned.

I had read that Giotto was regarded as the Father of the Renaissance, though Petrarch was more often so called. Both put a high premium on nature, naturalism and narrative drama. They left Byzantine traditions behind. Could a great movement of intellect and art *not* have two fathers? The laws of art did not apply to children. A child could have only one biological father, true. But he could have a non-biological parent who adopted him and became his father. Joseph as opposed to God, for example. *Art did not mimic nature; nature mimicked art*, I thought. The thought of children set my biological clock to ticking. Ticktock, ticktock.

"Giotto, one Father of the Renaissance," Rob explained, "was a man who used his time (1266-1337) well before his clock ran down." The trouble with a woman's was that it unwound faster than a man's, though most men lose half their sperm by fifty, and by seventy, most lose it all. Oh, Charlie Chaplin had his last child at age 73; Cary Grant his first at 60, and Saul Bellow his last at 85, but most mens' clocks don't go ticktock. Their hearing fails first, anyway, so they aren't bothered.

"And the Mothers of the Renaissance?" Allison asked. "Were their contributions painted over?"

Rob waved his hand dismissively. "Oh, they were artists' models, mothers, mistresses. Noblewomen bought art from male artists. Ladies hadn't given birth to creativity yet.

He ignored known female medieval artists. Nuns were painting as early as the tenth century. Ende of Spain did. In the early eleventh, there was a woman named Frögard of Osbey, Sweden, its sole rune master, or rune mistress. Later in the next century, Hildegard of Bingen was dictating her dreams to a female artist who was an excellent illustrator. In the twelfth century, Gruda of Germany illustrated her own works. The Bayeux tapestries had shown what eleventh century Norman women could do with just needle, thread, and linen—illustrate the Norman Conquest of England, (1056).

In the mid-sixteenth century, one family produced two female artists: Sofonisba and Lucia Anguissola, portraitists. Female painters proliferated as the Renaissance drew to a close.

"Women were only procreative," Rob said, more interested in explaining the Scrovegni Chapel then discussing female artists. I should have challenged him, but it would do no good. I felt myself as creative as (potentially) procreative, though I had given birth to just one book and a few articles.

We visited the *Teatro Anatomico* (anatomical theater) in the University of Padua (sixteenth century). Five tiers high, it had a raised table in the center. "Cadaver table" sounded grim, but "examining table" sounded too modern. And everyone examined was already dead. Students must have strained to see from the higher tiers on dark days. Galileo taught physics here from 1592 to 1610. Among other famous professors was Gabriele Fallopio, for whom Fallopian tubes are named. The very thought of Fallopian tubes recalled my hopeless, hapless eggs, sliding into oblivion. One egg might have become, if fertilized, a great female artist.

Arnold said, "I'm glad I didn't go to medical school as my mother wished."

"Banking was a cleaner profession," Anne said, with twinkling eyes. Anne could be very ironic. I hoped she got her novel of this tour published. It might not sell well, though. Irony escapes many readers.

Agatha looked stricken. She was unlikely to have progeny, having waited until forty-eight to marry. I still had a chance, though not as good a one as if I were twenty. Fertility declined throughout one's twenties and thirties. Much faster in one's forties. Some people fulfilled their biological mission at later dates. Many didn't. Of course, with the world so populous now, that was just as well.

We experienced a terrible gas shortage, with long lines at the pumps because of the Yom Kippur War and OPEC's decision to punish us by decreasing the world's supply. Our world did not need more people. That's what the Erlichs' book declared five years ago. Population was a "bomb" waiting to detonate. Birth control? Yes. I could control my fertility, but not the energy supply. Roe v. Wade, recognized my right to determine my biological destiny; it said nothing about driving a car. On to Vicenza. Once there, Rob recovered his old jauntiness, and I handed him the mike.

"The city of Vicenza was a late Renaissance bloomer," Rob told us. First Roman, then Lombard, it later fell to Emperor Frederick II, before the Scalageri rulers of Verona ruled it until 1387. That was when

Vicenza fell to Milan's Visconti. Matilda sat up straight hearing her name. She had been dozing. Indirectly vindicated in Vicenza, she knew nothing of her family's conquests cruelty. This eventually included the Habsburgs' crimes, too, for Visconti girls married into a dynasty no less unprincipled than their own.

In the latter sixteenth century, Vicenza came under the sway of Venice, but by then, Venetian Spain and Portugal had surpassed Venetian prosperity, leaving Vicenza scrambling for Renaissance grandeur, without a rich patron's help.

Vicenza was greatly aided by a talented former Paduan stone carver named Andrea Gondola. His Vicenzan patron, Count Tressino, renamed him Palladio, after Pallas Athena, Greek goddess of wisdom. The Count admired classicism. That change plus intense study of classical art, enabled Gondola (now Palladio) to sail into neoclassical history, studying Vitruvius, a Roman architect (first century A.D.), who wrote a great architectural treatise.

"Palladio died before his Olympic Theater (*Teatro Olimpico*) was completed (1585)," Rob informed our group. "It was based on models of ancient Roman ones. It was a perfect example of perspective achieved through permanent stage 'streets' appearing in greater depth than a tape measure testified, achieved by raising the street level so viewers in semicircular seating saw the set as part of a large city, though the 'streets' were only fifteen feet long. Above the stage façade, carved figures wearing togas lent dignity to the plays, depicting the donors' faces. Famous for its acoustics, the *Olimpico* had an inner room for musical recitals, a lobby where patrons displayed fine clothes, discussed the acting, purchased a glass of wine. No sign of a men's or a ladies' room, though.

"Palladio's career extended to Venice, too, where, besides San Giorgio, he built at least one other church. He changed the landscape of downtown Vicenza and its environs forever, the only things worth seeing in this burg," Rob declared. "We'll drive past Palladio's other buildings next," he told us, "leaving the city center briefly to visit Villa Capra Valmarana, also called *Villa Rotunda*. Its design is a dome over a cube; contrasting terracotta roof tiles; four marble columned entrances;

and over the triangular pediments of each, statues. It's his only villa with four entrances, and the most beautiful."

Sam asked why anybody needed four entranceways with grand sets of steps?"

"To elude your family?" asked Jim Harker. Jan looked nonplussed. Jim seldom made jokes about family. I recalled a jingle about Venetians being all great men, "gransignori" and Vicenzans cat eaters! (*magna-gatti*).

"Do you know that jingle," I asked Rob, "about gentleman of Venice (*gransignori*) and the doctors *(grandottori)* of Padua?" He didn't. Wes remembered something about Vincenzans being cat eaters (*magna-gatti*) and thought it dated from the plague era (c.1689) when mice and rats were over-running cities like Vicenza, and food was scarce. Venice sent them their feline surplus.

"But," Wes chortled, "the city's cooks roasted the cats, plump from their diet of rodents." A collective groan went up from our cat fanciers, our squeamish. I, Candida Darroway, thought those categories covered the whole world.

"Like Hoover hogs," said Andrea Pellatierra. "In the Great Depression. That's what folks in Texas did with armadillos: cooked 'em." I knew that historically, man ate what was available. Everyone in California knew what happened to the Donner party.

"Palladio's first work," Rob said, "was a building downtown (1549). He was rebuilding Vicenza until death took him. He made nineteen villas for *gransignori,* and many public buildings. The *Teatro* was finished by Vincenzo Scamozzi."

As we passed through the town center, Rob pointed out half a dozen other Palladian buildings, including the Palace of Justice, (*Palazzo della Ragione).* Whenever I heard the word "*ragione*," I felt uneasy. In English it mean reason, but in Italian it implied authority and power. That's what made the Renaissance as scary as it was inspiring. Governments commanded the obedience of the masses, who feared cruel punishments with little hope of justice.

A child of democracy, I rejoiced that our government wasn't authoritarian, and never tortured suspects or spied on its citizens or claimed as "evidence" what was suppositious. We preserved our

Constitution, our Bill of Rights. Democracy. We neglected the arts as a matter of course.

This palace of justice had rounded arches, triple columns. Its balustrade bristled with gods. The militia headquarters (*Loggia dei Capitani, 1557*) was the city council chamber now. Palladio's Chiericati (1550), was a museum.

"I like museums," Sam said. "I never used to, but I do now. I think the Borghese on the Pincio hill blew my mind. Yeh. That museum blew my mind *back* to me. I saw things I never saw even during my better hangovers." The power of art ought never be underestimated.

Rob said, "Palladio's neoclassical effects were of inferior materials, for lack of the wealth Venetians no longer had. Brick and mortar, not marble, lie behind these stucco façades. Many of these buildings are empty."

Samantha asked if Vicenza was been kind of like "a Hollywood set," a "back lot" like F. Scott Fitzgerald described in *The Last Tycoon*, "all false fronts?"

"Exactly," Rob agreed. Samantha had attended Wellesley. In her junior year, she was expelled for being drunk in chapel. She "finished up" at San Jose State, and was painfully aware of how much social prestige she had "blown."

"It's an impressive square," Samantha remarked. "But interior emptiness may have made Vicenza's citizens (*Vicentini*) 'hollow men' in T. S. Eliot's sense." No one picked up on Eliot. I only had one course on twentieth century poetry, and now felt that I should read poets like Eliot, Cummings, Yeats. These poets had had their own twentieth century renaissance. No one's rebirth should go unnoticed. Minutes later, the *Villa Rotunda (1550-52.)*

"Oh," Sandy said, "It looks like the White House."

"No," Anita disagreed. "The façade of San Giorgio Maggiore in Venice." Classicism embraced each of Palladio's buildings.

"The rotunda is in the middle of the central cube," Andrea Pellatierra offered. "And there are *four* colonnaded entrances with projecting porches under the belvedere.

Rob explained, "Some thought his style 'dry' compared to mannerism, the preferred mode of the late sixteenth century." I thought the Villa stunning enough to prove the critics erred.

Suddenly, it was 3:40. We retreated to central Vicenza. I directed Carlo to take the road out of the Piazza called Via Maggio, for Enrico lived off this steep incline on top of which stood the baroque Basilica of Monte di Berico. It, too, had a dome, a belvedere–a clock. It was one minute to four when we pulled before Enrico's villa, a white modern structure with red tiled veranda and roof. To Californians it looked like Beverley Hills, not the Berici Hills.

Enrico was waiting on the veranda. Seeing our bus, he hurried down the drive, with arms extended, and in lightly accented English welcomed us warmly.

"How nice to see you, and you, too! I am Enrico Della Pace, and I have been looking forward to your visit." And then, turning to me, he dropped his arms, smiled happily, and planted a quick kiss on each cheek. "And of course, I am happy to see you, my lovely friend, Candida. Of course, you. So happy."

Wes winced. Rob look dour, but there was nothing sexual in these hugs and kisses. Italians were not as reserved as Americans. All this time, our host was beckoning us up onto his veranda, waving us on through the broad, dark red tiled hall, past the sunken living room with Persian carpets and a massive fireplace. To the right, bedrooms stood open, each bedspread snowy white. No one appeared to inhabit them. Our destination was the large rear balcony, just beyond a small kitchen in copper with blue tiles. From the balcony we overlooked the pre-Alpine range of mountains that seemed nearer because of the clear air.

Several tables with white cloths had been set up with silver wine buckets. Bottles of various *liquore* (liqueurs) stood around them; platters of cheese, including gorgonzola, *fondant*, as the French call anything half melted, and my favorite Italian delicacies unobtainable in Alviso. The black olives in oil were from Enrico's groves. There were country breads in various shapes, with sharp bread knives stuck into each; cookies, (*biscotti*) fruit, ceramic pots of condiments, platters of pickles, and several kinds of olives; fresh vegetable sticks, cheese filled, and arrangements of cold cuts (*salumerià*) on ceramic plates; black grapes lay on the table. I thought of Caravaggio's portrait of Bacchus.

The short wine glasses of Italy here were cut crystal. Daintier ones with silver stems surrounded the liqueur bottles. Tall crystal glasses beside bottles of mineral water, still and *gassata*, (carbonated) for those just thirsty.

Enrico made most of the liqueurs or *liquore* himself. He was proudest of his *Grappa Giulia*, brandy distilled from fermented grape pomace. I knew how powerful it was. His *sidro* (fermented cider) put Normandy's to shame. His cherry liqeuer (*aquavit di ciliege)*, seemed milder than German cherry liqueur (*kirschwasser)*, until a few minutes after you downed it.

The hill below was planted in apples and olives. A larger farm near Vipiteno in Alto Adige to the north had more acres. I asked if he knew Teresa's nephew, Arturo? Enrico said, "Yes, he is quite the playboy. Where did you meet him?" I told him about Theresa, my visit to her Florentine villa. Enrico, shrugging his shoulders, emitted but one sound: "Eh." in English.

His tenants brought him more produce than the family needed. While he lived alone most of the time, his sister, Elena, and brother-in-law, Mauro, lived downstairs in their own apartment; his parents next door. Italians often built that way; so several generations and their offspring grew up under one roof, or on one parcel. In semi-rural areas like this, the mentality lingered. The house next door, barely visible through the trees, was the one in which Enrico had been born. His elderly parents now had two caretakers. I had not met them, but I might well have had I stayed in Vicenza longer than two days, in a hotel on the town's main square.

I had been instantly attracted to Enrico, and he to me. A businessman, he yet pondered the humanistic verities. I met him just walking down from Mount Berico after visiting the church. Passing him digging in his front garden—I thought he *was* the gardener. After a long chat, he invited me in for a drink. We went to dinner together that evening, a rustic place with superb steak. I entertained his sister once in Berkeley, after she had visited a friend in San Francisco. I drove her to the Oakland airport.

"I'm not made of wood," (*Io non sono fatto in legno*) he had said when we were sitting together after a lovely meal in a rural restaurant on his orange sofa together, drinking Grappa Giulia. I was twenty-six then, and the night was balmy. But then, *I* was "made of wood." I had a dissertation to research in Florence. I returned to Florence; to Cal. We exchanged letters–a dozen times in six years. Friends. We were meant to be friends. Our fate was not in our own hands.

Enrico wanted to know everything the tour had seen and done, and asked those he approached, while opening more bottles, or refilling glasses: "And what did you see in my country that interested you most? What art struck you as most moving? Have you come to any conclusions about American life compared to Italian life you might share with me?"

He digested their answers as they his *antipasti*, with which his refrigerator was well stocked. Whenever a platter emptied, he ran indoors and brought out more. We were ravenous guests (*ospiti*), unfed since leaving Venice.

Anita told him she "loved Assisi especially," not mentioning her misadventure there.

Ellen said, "My favorite experience was the five star Hotel Principi in Rome." Enrico did not laugh, though his eyes, also hazel, seemed to.

Agatha and Ian told him that "The highpoint for us was our wedding in Fiesole." Agatha added, "Our marriage will surprise a lot of people we know back home. Some with ill feelings."

Enrico told them to remain devoted. "Prove them wrong," he advised. He had had some experience with marriages. Divorce. Later, I whispered to him that they were, respectively, a nun and priest, "Anglicans, not Catholics," I added.

When I caught Wes eyeing me skeptically, with one raised eyebrow, I sauntered over to ask if he had tried the meat balls (*polpette di manzo*). He hadn't, so I brought him a dish and a fork–a propitiatory offering. Men are as jealous as women, but women take the rap for jealousy more often.

If you asked Enrico about his faith, he would have told you "believing, but not practicing" (*credente, ma non praticante*). He had struggled for years with the Church to obtain his first divorce and it looked to me as if he were heading for a second. Two divorces in Italy made you a social pariah—unless, of course, you happened to be a rock star. When I introduced Enrico to Allison, he said, "If I ever have a daughter, I would want her to be as beautiful as you." Allison kissed his cheek. I told Enrico she had been a postulant nun when we started.

"I never kissed a nun before," he said, thoughtfully. I said she was an Anglican. He looked relieved.

Wes and Rob came over together (this togetherness could get on my nerves) and talked with Enrico about Italian films. Enrico enjoyed movies, and could recount scene by scene Fellini's greatest: who starred in which roles, and what each character said. They talked about *Divorce Italian Style*, where only murdering your wife gave one the freedom to marry your mistress. But that was back in 1961, not in the 70s. Enrico laughed, but his laughter must certainly have been mixed with somber memories. Wes and Rob had also experienced a divorce. I knew from my parents's case there was always some lasting bitterness.

Enrico talked with Reed of cars. Reed asked what car he drove, and Enrico took him into his garage a—fifteen year old Fiat. Reed was shocked. But, seeing Enrico laughing, he laughed, too. In Italy it wasn't considered the best taste to flaunt your wealth by buying luxury cars. We had entered an age where some people—liberals and independent thinkers—were beginning to decry needless luxury. Europeans had personally experienced World Wars I and II. *The world's future well—being depended upon reducing our wants,* I thought.

Then Elena and Mauro arrived from downstairs. Mauro carried a heavy baking dish of *Polenta e Fontina in Torta* (polenta with Fontina cheese pudding), Elena's contribution to the festivities. He put the dish down carefully on tiles. Both of them came over to give me a hug. Elena asked how my research was going. It had been five years since her visit to me in the States, before I moved to Alviso, with its aging Bohemians, Mexican workers and cheaper rent.

I asked about her parents, and she said her mother was not feeling well today. She thought she was coming down with something. Her father no longer left the house. Matilda, whose ancestors had once owned all Vicenza, indeed, the very ground this house stood on, and so much else in northern Italy, opened her purse and took out a very old silver crucifix on a chain. She spoke to Elena in fair Italian.

"Please give this cross to your mother," Matilda instructed. "It was my grandmother's. She always said: 'Say ten Hail Mary's wearing this cross and you will get better immediately.'"

Enrico wanted Elena to refuse it, as the cross was obviously dear to Matilda. But Matilda insisted, so Elena put it into her pocket thanking this Visconti descendant for her kindness. Matilda looked happy. What ancient Visconti injustice had she just neutralized?

"Would anyone like to see where I make and store my grappa?" Enrico asked. It's in my wine cellar, very deep down. Since we had been enjoying his grappa very much, especially the men, they instantly formed a line and followed him down to the cellar. I took a few moments to admire the way the sun was beginning to light up the upper reaches of the high hills of the Berici ridge, which, in this light, looked closer and higher than when we arrived. The hum of the females of the group, all of whom had eaten and drunk a glass or two of grappa, were laughing and talking in a more relaxed manner, now that only the female contingent was present. When they laughed, some reached a high pitch indeed. Which is why ladies always seemed noisier without a masculine cohort, but sweeter.

When the men returned from Enrico's cellar, I suspected they had sampled a bit more grappa, all but Carlo, who had to drive us onto Verona safely. It was time to say our goodbye's.

"Thank you so much, Enrico, for your wonderful hospitality, cooed Ellen. Bill, looking rather out of it, echoed her gratitude. Everyone said the party had been wonderful, and a few who went off to use the bathrooms before we left.

I deposited a platter of *polenta* squares on the kitchen counter, and Enrico, who followed me in, said, "Ah, Candida, Candida! If only I had met you before I remarried. If my second wife decides to divorce me, and you are still single, think about Italy as your permanent home. Surely we could find a position for you at the University of Padua. And I could surely find one for you here, in this house and in my heart. Think of this if you find yourself alone for long. You know, we are only five days apart in age." That was true. I had forgotten. He was five days older.

I could only reply, "Thanks for everything you have done. Our friendship runs narrow, but deep, and it is possible it could run deeper under other circumstances. I won't forget. Never, Enrico." He kissed my forehead, then kicked the door to the kitchen shut, and planted a long, firm kiss on my lips. The rest of the group passed down the hall and out onto the veranda. Rather unsteadily, I hurried to join them. Enrico followed, smiling, but with a sad look in his eyes. No one's life was perfect. All of us had some regrets.

When we were all back on the bus, we waved at our host, who stood beside Elena, and both waved back until we were out of sight. I couldn't help it, but I was crying.

Mindy said, "Don't cry, Candida! It was a wonderful party. Thank you for letting us see a real Italian home."

Wes leaned toward me. "Enrico is wonderful. I can tell he thinks you are, too. Who wouldn't? I do." I dried my tears with his handkerchief. My tears were not for what was, but what might have been. What was to be was hidden in shadows, now chasing us down the A4 to Verona.

Verona, near Lake Garda, (*Lago di Garda*), overflowed with Germans in summer. They had threatened Italy under the Romans; threatened the Franks, Pepin and Charlemagne. By 1404 Verona had won Venetian protection against the Empire. The Lion of San Marco was as prominent here as the ladder of the Scaligeri, the dynasty who'd ruled Verona (thirteenth century) for decades.

Our Hotel Victoria was behind the *Piazza Erbe* (square of plants). I refused to take that as a sign. We were not vegetating, just vacationing. Our stay was nearing its finale, yes. To love, sex? What would happen to Wes and me when he flew off from Malpensa Milan's airport? Like Scarlett *O'Hara,* I would "think about that tomorrow."

The Victoria's plushy lobby screamed "money" and "privilege," so naturally, we were all delighted.

"Take three hours," Rob told us as we got our keys from the desk. "We've just dined at Enrico's, but by ten, I suspect, we'll be ready for a light supper."

A bank of elevators sped us to our rooms, and it was impossible to carry one's own luggage. Even Gianfranco let a bell boy grab his, saying, "Well, I am on vacation, too." He wasn't, but this was probably the best one he'd have in his whole life.

Rob was on second floor, Wes on third, and I was on fourth. I had a living room and a refrigerator. I took out a lemon soda, added ice, and had wriggled out of my slacks–was my waistband tighter–? when the phone rang.

"Room service." I paused. It was Wes.

"What kind of service?" I asked.

"Not the usual. What's your number? I'm coming up."

In three minutes he was up, drained my lemon soda, and pressed his body against me. He was "up" indeed.

"Do you realize," he asked, as he removed my blouse and bra, "that we have two and a half hours before we have to move a muscle?"

"And if we don't," I quipped, "you'll never forgive yourself?" He grinned, and toppled me gently onto the bed. There was nothing to forgive.

Dinner was in a restaurant above the rushing Adige. I know there were shrimp on skewers for starters. It was sometimes the starters that were the real dessert. That was what Wes and I found, anyway, before we even left the hotel.

CHAPTER XXII

VERILY VERONA; MERRY MILAN

Walking to the Victoria, I felt glad. Sad. Milan next. Tour's end. Would my relationship with Wes end, too? We spent the night together in my room.

At breakfast, everyone seemed happy. Back home, our group would renew relationships, including those with doctors, dentists, etc. Wes had attended to my body. But I was young and needed no mending. Unless, my heart broke. And he? Did he need repairs? I never asked. Odd how one can love deeply and remain shallow.

In the morning, Rob showed us two gates through which German barbarians had broke in upon Rome. The *Porta dei Leoni* (Gate of Lions) was just a few steps from the *Piazza Erbe*, both first century A.D. landmarks.

"Why Lion Gate?" Matt asked. "Were the Romans bragging of leonine strength?"

Rob squinted. "Romans were masters of the personal attack. If Romans were lions, their enemies had to be rabbits."

"Far out," enthused Matt. As a literary major from Reed College and a debater he understood *ad hominem* attacks.

Rob grunted. "One undermined an opponent's confidence by bragging of one's own strength. So Rome bragged, but relied on fortifications."

Wes mulled. "I remember Augustus's (d. fourteen A.D.) lost legions. Varus, his general, lost three in the forest at Teutoburg five years earlier. Before that, Julius Caesar, his great uncle, totted up German defeats in his *Gallic Commentaries*."

"Octavian was a boy then," Rob averred.

"Later" Wes went on, "when he was Princeps, (First Citizen), he banged his head on his wall and cried, 'Give me back my legions.'"

"Too bad his great uncle Julius wasn't at Teutoburg instead of Varus," said Ralph. "He would have barbecued those barbarians." Betty winced.

Legions, I thought, are lost by us all, youth, health, power. Returned home, how much would these tourists, *our* legionaries, have gained? lost?

The treasury, (*Porta dei Borsari)* was Verona's first entrance. The Arch of the Gavians (*Arco dei Gavia)* was built to honor the Gavia family. Both were first century A.D. buildings. Andrea Palladio had strolled beneath these passages to architectural fame.

We visited the Roman theater across the Adige. Roman stone cutters had cut an open air auditorium from its banks. Theater goers still sat steeped in starlight.

We entered the arena (thirty A.D.) that seated 16,000, visible from Piazza Bra, a square where old men had sat at sidewalk cafés drinking *caffè lattes* since the sixteenth century; when coffee from Yemen passed through Egypt into Italy, long before it became trendy in San Francisco in the 1950s. Here on the piazza, old men looked up from newspapers furtively, eyeing attractive women. Coffee was their excuse; their only pleasure was eying attractive women.

The arena, Italy's third largest, required advanced reservations. Foreigners reserved seats a year ahead. Verona's operas were held there.

"Did the Veronese throw Christians to the lions?" Allison asked. "No record of it," Rob told them. "But poor athletes were killed by their opponents."

"Oh, poor souls," Agatha sighed. "Pray they got baptized before they met their death."

"Sand soaked up their blood," Rob said. Sandy grimaced. Being lesbian did not mean she was insensitive to suffering. She wore many beads. It was not apparent that she *was* lesbian. The beads advertised the jewelry shop. Proximity to Lake Garda advertised Verona. Woe betide tourists who arrived thinking they'd grab a hotel near the station. Many had to sleep outdoors, or continue on to Malcesine on the lake for lack of reservations. Not all those caught without a reservation wore beads. Some wore silk suits.

When Rob asked the group its pleasure, the ladies chose Romeo and Juliet's balcony. Andrea Smithwitch said, "I majored in the English Renaissance and must make the pilgrimage." As long as she felt obligated to Shakespeare–not Wes–it was fine by me.

At no. 23 Via Capelo, Romeo had climbed up to Juliet's balcony– to steal a kiss. Must have used a ladder. Their romance, doomed by feuding families, featured this stolen kiss; a purloined bride; a drawn sword; fallen friends and foes; a secret marriage, a fatal mistake, eternal separation. Juliet took something like Valium, given her by Friar Lawrence to avoid being married to another man. Her sleep mirrored death. When Romeo found her, he drank poison. Juliet, awakening, and seeing him lifeless, plunged his sword through her heart.

"I didn't mind Romeo's taking poison," Allison observed. "But I loathed Juliet's using his dagger. So phallic."

"A man's ending," nodded Sandy.

"Lucretia did the same thing when Tuscans ruled Rome," Ralph said. "Read Shakespeare's *The Rape of Lucrece.*"

"Hollywood 50s endings concerned love and hope," Joan stated. "Now women are not even given meaningful parts." Joan was herself hopeless. She had become emotionally involved again with Rob, another meaningless role.

"I saw three Peter Sellers movies before leaving," Peg said. *Where Does it Hurt?* (1972) about a corrupt doctor; *The Blockhouse,* (1973) about men trapped on D-Day in Normandy; and *The Optimists (1973),* about street entertainers surviving tough times." I thought of this tour in each connection.

"Women are missing from all those films," said Lynette. "The public doesn't expect much of women, so directors kill them off or leave them out."

Anita said, "Romeo does neglect Juliet–but Shakespeare didn't do much for Romeo, either."

"Friar Lawrence meant well," said Meg, "which was more than could be said for a friar in Assisi." She jerked her head toward Anita.

From this romantic house we moved on to the Scaligeri tombs flanking a tiny church (Santa Maria Antica) of the Scaligeri, fourteenth century rulers of Verona. Above the doorway was an equestrian statue of

Cangrande I (d.1329). By 1387, Matilda's Visconti relatives had arrived, conquering the Scaligeri. Walking beside me, her ruby ring made blood red splotches on Scaligeri tombs. History was full of irony. Like life.

We crossed the Piazza dei Signori. The Palazzo dei Capitanio (Military Headquarters) and Palazzo della Ragione (Court of Law), (fourteenth century). Dante's statue in the Piazza (nineteenth century), was covered by pigeons. I wondered if he ever contemplated shoving Verona's public works administrators into the *Inferno*? No. He had too many classical and Florentine sinners to house.

Read the newspapers. People are brutes. They starved children; enslaved them for sex. Didn't send them to Head Start. Abused old folks and cashed their social security checks. Factory farms eliminated family farms by the early 1960s; strip mining left gashes in the Appalachians. Rivers "bloomed" from fertilizer and the Great Lakes were not clean. African girls were mutilated so they could not enjoy intercourse. Muslim women were enshrouded so they could not enjoy a breeze. Power companies turned off heat in Maine and Minnesota for unpaid bills. A modern Dante could fill many infernos.

Passing Dante's statue, I patted his hand. A Verona cop said, "Don't touch," (*Non toccare*). Only the pigeons could. Art existed so that we might not only handle it, but get a handle on it. Touch and be touched. Poor Dante. He could still touch me if I couldn't him.

"Shall we cross the *Ponte dei Scaligeri*?" (Scaligeri Bridge). It was built by Cangrande II (1354-76); rebuilt from material dredged from the Adige River after the Germans blew it up (1945).

Matt remarked dryly, "How nice of the Austrians to build an arsenal for Italy's new King and Parliament in the nineteenth century. You couldn't ask for nicer dictators." The Germans and Austrians were not among Matt's favorite Europeans, being Jewish. I understood. We returned to our hotel off Piazza Erbe. The market, in full swing, hid the ancient fountain in its midst; a Roman statue that spat laterally into Renaissance faces.

Our bags were stowed. We stopped at San Zeno Maggiore (1120-38), near the Milan exit. "Fifteen minutes!" Ferrell shouted. We piled off the bus, grumbling.

"Mantegna's altarpiece," he explained, honored St. Zeno, Verona's patron saint.

"Not the Stoic philosopher?" Arnold queried.

"Not that Zeno, no," Rob affirmed. "A local boy made good. He was called 'The Laughing Zeno,' because of his Romanesque grin. A saint of perpetual amusement; a rarity."

San Zeno was one of Italy's most famous Romanesque churches, (fifth century). Mantegna's altarpiece (1457-59) was a tryptych of Madonna and Child. The Virgin's halo had spokes, wagon wheel style. She was on the church's Rose Window, with images depicting man's fortunes, rising, falling. Medieval Life was a gamble, not a gambol. Everybody took risks. I had taken one myself; a lover Dad's age.

We left, ignoring the eleventh through twelfth century bronze doors, the Saxon and Veronese saints. None but Zeno was laughing. Being a saint was usually serious business.

Milan *(Milano)* was seventy miles due west of Verona on the A 4. Goodbye, Verona!

In Milan we checked into our last hotel, the *Principe di Savoia*. I thought of the princes of Savoy, Teresa's relatives. Tony's, too. I hoped he was happy.

Charles Clark had conquered parsimony. A five star from the late nineteenth century. The bathrooms, artistry in hygiene. Two pools. The top one resembled a marble theater, with a proscenium, torchère lamps, and frescoed ceilings. Two tiled dolphins swam beneath, waiting for naiads of antiquity, the sirens of Ulysses, Europa on her bull. I was tempted to take the plunge, but opted for lunch instead.

The hotel plunged me into "The Ambassador's Suite." I had to give permission—again—for Wes to come up here, since this level excluded the unprivileged. Rob wasn't up here, either. I, Candida Darroway, was Rapunzel, a Grimms' heroine. Originally a Persian story, Rapunzel influenced the story of Saint Barbara, whom now the Church claimed never existed. Still, Barbara's father had locked her in a tower. Barbara was depicted with that tower in one hand, a sheaf of wheat in the other. Just a legend, she was still a woman of substance.

Rapunzel was in a tower, too. "Rapunzel, Rapunzel, let down your long hair...." I recalled reading as a child. I didn't get who was asking or why.

Well, Wes didn't have to climb my hair. He could take the elevator–with my permission. The plaque on the door warned that this suite cost 359 U.S. dollars. Per person. It had three rooms, a spare bedroom, two full bathrooms, one half of one for guests. There was furniture everywhere. A fireplace. A balcony overlooking Milan. I was ambassadress to Lombardy!

Besides language, history, and bits of literature, I offered advice, help. I phoned the Director of the Sforza Castle on Matilda's behalf as soon as we arrived to discuss her ring. I rang the desk. "*Pronto.* Candida Darroway here. The Director of the Sforza Castle Museum, please? (*Per piacere*). No, I don't know the his name. Could you find it for me?"

"One moment, please" (*Momento, per piacere*). A pause. "Signor Franco Gabriele. Shall I place the call?"

"*Sì, grazie.*" When *Signor* Gabriele answered, I explained that I was a professor of Italian, representing an American tourist in my care, one Matilda Visconti. There was a pause, followed by "*Sì?*"

"*Sì, Signore.* She owns a ring of Byzantine provenance. A ruby, inscribed "Gian Galeazzo." I paused. "Twelve carats."

Heavy breathing on Gabriele's end. "Really?" (*Daverro?*)

"*Già,*" (*Yes indeed*). "The ring is beautiful. Professor Balestreri of Florence proclaimed it a fifth century masterpiece."

Signor Gabriele asked, "Prof. *Emiliano* Balestreri of the University of Florence?"

"Yes, *certo,*"(certainly) I told him. "*Signora* Visconti wishes to show you this ring. Interested?"

"Yes, Indeed. I'm free at 10:30 this morning."(Sì, *senz'altro. Sono libero alle dieci e mezza*). Before hanging up, I mentioned bringing two advisors. The Director said that was fine. He would send *his* escort to wait for us at the second door to the right of the entrance, inside the Piazza delle Armi, (Square of Armed Men). Clear? (*Una Scorta sera alla seconda porta a destra sulla Piazza delle Armi, l'entrata al Museo. Claro?*)

"*Claro,*" I confirmed, enjoying a review of the many ways to say "yes" in Italian.

"Until later, Miss Darroway,"(*Fino a più tardi, Signorina Darroway*).

At breakfast, I told Wes that Matilda and I would not be going to the Brera this morning. I asked Rob, "Can you take the group to the Brera (*Museo Pinocoteca di Brera*) alone this morning? Matilda, Andrea Pellatierra, Jonah and I are going to the Sforza Castle to talk with the Director about her ring. We'll see you back here at one o'clock for lunch."

Ferrell looked at the ceiling. "Ah, it's the *Pinacoteca* for us peasants, then. Nice of you to plan our morning, Candida." An act. He would have gone there anyway. The *Pinacoteca* held Milan's greatest Renaissance-Baroque collections. Rob would be in his element. His acolytes would cluster adoringly. Our task would be political, difficult; but helpful to Matilda.

I had a suggestion that all approved. "About 5:00 P.M., let's walk *to La Scala* (Theater at the Staircase), Milan's opera house. It's a shady walk at that hour. Then to the *Galleria Vittorio Emmanuele (1877)* close by (glass-domed, iron work indoor shopping center). We'll have coffee; watch Milan go by." The group approved; Ferrell too. I knew he could be placated.

The Sforza Castle (*Castello Sforezesco*) may hold within it a portion of the old Visconti one. Then again, maybe not. (*Forsé che sì, forsé che non*). Francesco Sforza may have built his curvilinear fortress *around* the Visconti's; or over its foundations. Nobody is certain. Red brick, like the Visconti's, the Sforza was now a museum of Italy's history.

The group left. Mindy hugged me goodbye. Anita would miss my thoughts on great art. "Men can't see through a woman's eyes," she lamented. Sam would miss my "interpretations of oddities," which we two found compelling. Sam. Beneath a rough exterior, I sensed a curious, sensitive intellect.

We took a cab to the Castle. Our escort met us. Signor Gabriele had an impressive office overlooking the park. Rising to greet us, so, too, did a small man in gray, Professor Alfredo Faziani, who had once studied gems under Prof. Balestreri in Florence. Faziani knew we had already gotten Balestreri's opinion. Signor Gabriele could have played the lead in Donizetti's *Don Pasquale*, Rossini's *Figaro,* Verdi's *Rigoletto*. He had a habit of smoothing his hair with his left hand. To make a good appearance? I introduced Andrea and Jonah to him to a chorus of "Pleasure" (Piaceri), all 'round. Signor Faziano and Andrea had once met at one of Balestreri's lectures. They renewed old (if shallow) acquaintance.

Matilda spoke first. "I know little of my heritage, *Signor* Gabriele." To Professor Faziani, the gemologist present, she handed her ruby ring. He gasped when he took his loupe out of its case and, turning toward the light streaming through the windows, caught its details. "It's the real thing, no doubt of it." *(La vera cosa, senza dubbio)*. "Probably end of the fifth century."

Signor Gabriele looked out the window. "We must consult with our trustees." Then, turning back: "The ring will, I'm sure, be judged to be part of Italy's national heritage. Our lawyers will be consulted, but they will doubtless recommend its return to Italy. And where better to keep it, but in our Museo del Castello vault?"

Matilda gasped. "You cannot take what is not yours! The ring is all that remains to me of my Visconti forebears. Taking it from me would be stealing."

"Dear lady," said Gabriele, "We won't steal it, though theft *is* a growing problem in Milan these days. So many Albanians; Middle Easterners. Drug lords. East European Mafiosi." He didn't mention Italy's own. "Instead, we will offer you something of equal value to this token of your illustrious ancestors." He called "illustrious" the Visconti thugs and thieves who conquered northern Italy. *How tactful*, I thought, but the Sforzas who replaced them were no less "illustrious." Both dynasties grew by thievery.

"For example," Gabriele proposed, "we could grant Signora Visconti lifelong tenancy in an apartment of, say, twelve rooms, remodeled to her specifications. We could provide a maid and a cook." Matilda gasped, nodding agreement.

"Just one moment Mr. Gabriele." This from Jonah. "What about wearing her ring when she wants? She is very attached to it."

"That, no," the Director replied. The dangers of her getting mugged in this neighborhood are fairly high. She could be followed by someone in a car while out for a walk. Or, she stops for the streetlight *(semaforo)*. A thief on a scooter passes close to her; separates the ring finger from her hand—with a knife!" We all shivered. He continued. "But, we would make a duplicate, and no one, not even *Signora* Visconti, could tell them apart."

Jonah thought for a moment. "And the thugs on scooters? Could *they*? You must provide her a chauffeur and car for protection."

Signor Gabriele agreed, but reiterated, "The real ring, though, stays in our collection once the papers are drawn up and signed."

I thought that reasonable. Jonah upped the ante: "All right. You give her this apartment, but include a stipend, annually deposited into her account. Let's say 400, 000 lire. After all, she is Italian royalty, related to most of Europe's royals! She cannot serve as Italy's representative to those courts on her U.S. retirement income as a secretary?"

Mr. Gabriele stroked his chin. "You Americans don't do pensions very well, that's true." He played with the corner of his frayed desk blotter. "Okay." A stipend of 300,000 thousand per annum."

"Four hundred thousand Mr. Gabriele," Jonah insisted. "We aren't going to take a lire less. It would be demeaning." Gabriele smoothed his hair with one elegant hand.

"Va bene." (O.K.) The sum you last mentioned every year for the rest of her life." He eyed Matilda appraisingly. She was in her early seventies, a little woman. She might pop off in a few years. Or live to be one hundred. You couldn't tell. *(Non si sappeva.)* Milan had polluted air. Lousy drivers. Thugs.

We shook hands. For now. Gabriele, pressed a button under his desk. A young man with several cameras appeared a minute later.

"Giovanni, photograph this ring, please. Fifteen shots." Giovanni set to work. The ring, against dark blue velvet, was photographed in various positions. Giovanni gave it back to Signore Gabriele. Their touch lingered.

"Dear Giovanni. You've done well (*Caro* Giovanni, *hai fatto bene*). I noted the "dear," and the familiar "tu" form of address. A relative? a lover? Matilda put her ring back on. Giovanni, bowing, left.

"I understand you leave in two days," Mr. Gabriele said to Matilda. "Our staff will put together a contract, with pictures of the apartment and a guarantee that it will belong to you (renovated, furnished, well maintained, rent free. This proposal will be ready in ten days. Respond to any detail that does not suit, *Signora*. When we can agree, sign it and have it notarized. Here is my card. Call me personally. Fly back to Milan, at our expense, and order furnishings, carpets, draperies, whatever. When we ask for your ring, sign a consent form. You will get the title to the apartment immediately after. The real ring will remain with us then. Meanwhile, an expert craftsman will prepare an identical facsimile using 14 ct. gold, but a semiprecious red stone. Garnet, perhaps. Which the Signora may keep." We shook hands.

The escort walked us down the hall to an elevator. On ground level, he unlocked a door, and we entered a room filled with odds and ends of art and ruined furniture. There were twelve more such with storage "closets" the size of an average American bedroom, the whole with a pleasant garden view. The kitchen was the size of a reception room.

Matilda said it was much too large for a kitchen, and asked if it could be divided into a family room, an office, a smaller kitchen? a half-bath? The escort jotted these suggestions down in a spiral notebook. "We can do that." Matilda's eyes lit up, and we left "her" apartment.

I asked, "Is her apartment close to the *Salla delle Asse* (Room of Planks) where Leonardo da Vinci painted willow branches, representing himself and Ferrara's d'Estes?"

"No, *Signorina*, that work–badly deteriorated–is being restored. I hope your group will visit *The Last Supper*. That da Vinci work is also slated for restoration, but not until 1979."

With this, the official bowed, and gave us his card. "*The esteemed Counsel and former Head of the Milanese division of Legal Justice, Il Signore Armando Di Fassulio.*" Di Fassulio was head of a council of ten lawyers who would work out the final details of this arrangement. Fassulio. Was his family related to the owners of the original Altamonte farm?

"Were your family Neapolitans?" I asked.

"Why yes," he said. "Before the late nineteeth century we lived in Naples. Later, family members moved to Milan, or San Francisco. There my relatives farmed a terraced mountain overlooking San Francisco Bay. In the 1930s or 40s, they sold it to a school called Altamonte College."

"Yes," I said enthusiastically. "I teach there." Mr. Di Fassulio's face was wreathed in a big smile. "Imagine that!" he said. "*Piccolo mondo.*"

(Small world). I put out my hand and shook his. It was like shaking hands with the owners of Alta Monte farm. At the door, he bowed again.

"Goodbye, *Signor* Di Fassulio. Matilda said, "Pleasure to have met you." (*Piacere di fare la sua conoscenza*). Jonah said, "Goodbye, Sir, Have a nice day." Mr. Di Fassulio's family had contributed to California's heritage. In a way, we owed our tour to their labor with vines, to selling produce by the Bay.

Back at the hotel, the group straggled in. "Some museum!" Reed nodded, wanly. Ellen and Bill were white with exhaustion, as were the Harkers and Huntsmans. Museums were workouts, even for the young and middle aged. Rob suggested we stay in our rooms until five to rest. We would have a light snack at the hotel before attempting to find La Scala, the Gallerie, and the Duomo.

"By then," he proclaimed, "the heat will have dissipated, and we'll have more energy."

"Good idea, Rob." Wes had gone to his room. Rob stopped me. "What happened with Matilda?" he asked.

I told him. "Well, Candida, you've done her a great turn." He patted me on my back, a singularly unusual gesture for Rob, who normally (except at Sienna on our balcony) did not touch me. But his big hand lingered there a moment, and I felt uneasy, ducking awkwardly the hint of male domination. Rob smirked. I stepped into an elevator car that opened just then and took me to my suite. Sweet to be an and ambassadress (*ambasciatrice*). Not sweet to see Rob's smirk cloud up as the door closed. I couldn't be ambassadress of goodwill to everyone, especially not to Rob, whose concept of boundaries was dim. I recalled playing the role of Miranda in *The Tempest*. Rob was too cultured for Caliban, but reminiscent of him in temperament. Was Wes an older Ferdinand? Or Prospero? Either way, I loved him.

For once, Wes did not scale my tower, I wanted rest more than lovemaking.

"You're growing old," grumbled my id.

"You're growing wiser," purred my superego.

"Thanks," I said. My id had gotten enough attention. I'd neglected my superego of late.

The Po Valley was as hot as Rome. The group reassembled at quarter past five. We snacked lightly in the hotel bar on salads, or stuffed croissants (tuna, chopped egg with capers) or cold cuts. Matt and Reed had beer and big pretzels with a side of French fries. Young men. Then Carlo gave us a lift up Via Manzone to Via Verdi, our resolve to walk it having withered.

La Scala Opera House (1776-8), a splendid colonial building (designed by Giuseppe Piermarini), seated 2,800 people. We walked under the central of three equally sized arches to the ticket window. We were scheduled for a late afternoon visit. Charles had not forgotten! The entrance had columns of white and gray marble, pale yellow walls above a white marble floor. Inside the theater, seven tiered, golden *loggias* swept in concentric rings toward the domed roof, flanking the stage on both sides. From over the stage, you could count the hairs on the heads of the orchestral players, or examine the ribbons on *Lucia di Lammermoor*'s shoes, the mole on Carmen's shoulder.

The gold fringed curtains were three quarters lowered, making a great backdrop for a shiny Steinway, opened, as if someone had just finished playing. Ferrell's eyes narrowed seeing it open. We were down by the orchestra pit, when suddenly, he sprang up the steps to the stage like a large, lithe cat. He seated himself at the piano bench, left shoulder toward the rear of the stage. This provided a dramatic three quarter view of his handsome face, auburn hair; longer, since we had been traveling three weeks. He raised his hands. The familiar first movement of Opus 27, no. #2: Beethoven's *"Moonlight Sonata."* So sonorous, melting, tender. In the middle of his performance, two La Scala guards came running down the aisle. I envisioned Rob's bodily removal. But removing Ferrell's muscular, six four, two hundred thirty pound corpus wouldn't be easy. These guards were small men. Still, they wore clubs! I did not want to lose Ferrell, who, if not my friend or lover, hinted at both—when not stirring up resentment against me.

The guards folded their arms over their chests. When we clapped, they shouted "Bravo!"

Then they announced, "You're under house arrest! Come with us."

Ferrell replied, *"Buon giorno. Vi amo."* (Good morning. I love you.) It wasn't morning. He didn't love them. They marched him to the entrance, using their walkie-talkies as cattle prods. They stopped at the office of the Directress of Tours, i.e, an administrative post. Only Rob and the guards were admitted. His having "ripped off" the *"Moonlight Sonata"* prompted a stern faced lady–mustachioed–to phone the *Guardia Civile* (National Guard) and local *Polizia* (Milan police) to see if Rob had any prior arrest record in Italy. He didn't. So they let him go, but banned him from returning to *La Scala* for a year.

Playing a sonata was a lesser offense than ripping off a T–shirt at the Sistine Chapel's souvenir shop. Who in the world wouldn't be better off for having heard the *Moonlight Sonata*? He hadn't harmed the Steinway. He even closed the lid. Hippies felt "ripping things off" was akin to re-distributing the wealth, like Robin had in Sherwood Forest. This Robin was more like the king than a hippy.

We waited in the foyer. Barry spoke up. "Will this make the newspapers?" A banker, Barry was leery of getting his name in the papers. Not all of his transactions, unlike Arnold's, also a banker, were strictly honest. He wanted no publicity.

"What could the papers say?" Sam asked. *American Art Professor Arrested for Playing the Moonlight Sonata in Broad Daylight at La Scala?*

Matt grinned. "How about this: *'With-it Leader of Renaissance Tour Impersonates Beethoven at La Scala'"?*

Jonah regretted we hadn't defended Rob, "not being allowed into the bearded lady's den."

"Mustachioed," Mindy corrected her husband. "People beard lions, not ladies, in dens. That's from Sir Walter Scott's *Lochinvar.*" Jonah was beginning to think this little blonde Seventh Day Adventist convert to Judaism was worth educating. He might send her to Altamonte College.

"Who wrote The lady or the Lion?" Anita queried, forehead creased. No one spoke. Wes corrected her. "It's *The Lady or the Tiger*, and I forgot the author's name, but it has to do with giving an accused man a choice of opening one of two doors. One contains a ravenous tiger, who will devour him. Behind the other waits a ravishing lady who will wed him. No one of us could think how these fates might apply to Rob, unless he was forced to marry the mustachioed lady. The thought made me giggle, but the alternative, the tiger, might represent being booked at the police station. There the only "bite" would be a fine. Fortunately, it hadn't come to that. Rob was released after being cleared of criminal activity. I kept mum about his stealing the T-shirt. We trooped out of La Scala relieved.

I asked, passing by a statue in a traffic circle, "Is that Giuseppe Verdi?" The Verdis were an old Milanese family, and Verdi's operas– *Aida, Rigoletto, La Traviata, Il Trovatore, La Forza del Destino, Otello, Falstaff,* etc., were the culmination of Italian style opera.

Ahead, Rob raised Altamonte's flag going toward the Galleria. It was not a white flag of surrender. Its red lilies, Donatello's Marzocco bear, and the *Porcellino* of Florence hinted we were from the University for Foreigners at Florence (*Università per Straniere*). Of course, that was a red herring. Who knew where Altamonte College was? The Milanese would know we were Americans. Who else would advertise their college's location being "On the Peninsula?" when Italy's dwarfed ours? Businessmen in silk suits smirked in passing.

We entered the *Galleria Vittorio Emanuele* reveling in its dome of glass and steel, a spider web of ineffable industrial beauty. Wasn't "ineffable" the adjective Rob had applied to me in Rome? It meant "incapable of being expressed." Whenever something is incapable of it, people hesitate. Better to be "de facto" than "ineffable."

Seven P.M. Happy Germans were eating cake and whipped cream. (*Kuchen mit Schlagsahne*). These large blonde invaders ate cake whenever tired, depressed, happy. The spoils of Italy were now cake, coffee, sports cars and designer sunglasses. German blood ran deep in Italian veins. Neither Pepin the Short; his son, Charlemagne; the Saxon Ottos; the Valois; nor the Habsburgs, including Franz Joseph, who defeated Victor Emmanuel II in 1859, ever gave up their desire for Italy. It had attracted Germans since the third century B.C.

Belinda shrugged. "My feeling is Italians and Germans fought until they became co-dependents."

Jonah remarked, "When Germans could no longer make the big sale to Italy, they went to war (1914) and fought the Italians. When they did make the sale, they allied with Mussolini. Defeated by the Allies in 1945, no more sales *could* be made, because each national economy lay in ruins. Millions of workers were dead. Recovery took decades—not to mention aid from Uncle Sam."

Milan's Duomo had begun as a small Roman church (335A.D.) St. Ambrose (fifth century) baptized St. Augustine (d. 530) in a baptistery still open to visitors. The Lombards added a new basilica (836). A fire damaged it (1075). The present Duomo was begun (1386) by Lucchino Visconti (1291-1349). When he died, his brother, Giovanni, ruled until 1354. It was then that Milanese possessions were distributed among three nephews; one, Gian Galeazzo, put his name on Matilda's ring.

"Hey, Look!" Sam exclaimed as we entered the Piazza del Duomo. "A killer church!" Odd expression, considering that churches were about eternal life. The Church does not *readily* admit to killing anybody. But Sam was Sam. Enthusiastic. Sensitive. Intuitive. In fact, the Church had killed its enemies as readily as the states around it, fighting for territory.

The Basilica was an ice palace burning in the sun's last oblique rays. Ian, who had studied French at Princeton commented on it.

"*Style Rayonnant*" (Fr., radiating style) Ferrell explained, recovered from his interrogation at La Scala and a double Irish coffee in the Galleries, explained.

"Two fourteenth century Frenchmen designed it. The first, Bonaventure (Fr., Good outcome), brought his love for the French Gothic south. The second, Mignot, criticized Bonaventure's work as lacking 'science' and predicted its imminent collapse. Gian Galezzo had his engineers check it out. It never collapsed."

Now Wes squinted up at the Duomo, saying, "Science and art are complimentary, like love and marriage." Could that be true? Wes was a romantic. But his comment revealed a recognition of the need for more than inspiration to hold a solid structure together. Was this remark about a building or an apology for closing down a loving relationship? Did our love lack a strong inner structure, built on the shifting sands of three weeks? Would a sane woman compare a cathedral with a love affair? The Duomo took over six centuries to complete. But people weren't Duomos!

Matilda wanted to see her family's monuments. The dynasty's founder and heirs, including Gian Galeazzo (d.1402) and two Visconti Archbishops should be buried here. Lodovico Sforza finished the octagonal cupola that shelters them. He decorated it with sixty statues of saints, biblical figures and pagan sibyls, too. He was following the example set by his father, Francesco, who by 1452 had finished the nave and aisles to the sixth bay.

We searched with Matilda for any Viscontis. Finally, a sacristan asked if he could "be of any service?" Matilda explained what she was looking for. The sacristan smiled unctuously.

"Oh, *Signora*. The great northern Italian Reformer, blessed Archbishop Carlo Borromeo (d.1584) removed all *laymen's* monuments from this Basilica. The Borromeos wanted only holy men, not politicians, to rest under this cupola."

"Where were laymen's remains buried?" Matilda asked.

The sacristan shrugged. "Only the good Lord knows" (*Solo il buon Dio lo sa*). Then he left us, laughing quietly. Diabolical fellow. If I were the archbishop here, I'd fire him. To the left of the altar, as he surely knew, were the ostentatiously marked sarcophagi of Ottone and Giovanni Visconti (fourteenth century), two of Matilda's archiepiscopal ancestors. Not laymen. Borromeo couldn't banish *them*, and Matilda knelt beside each to say a prayer. She wasn't the churchgoer Anita was, but piety runs through Italian veins. It was a shared legacy from the Romans who got it from the Jews who got it from tribal gods who copied the ancient goddesses.

"The Duomo changed from Gothic to Roman and back to Gothic," Rob mused.

Anne was intrigued by such stylistic transformation. "I'd like the characters in my travel novel to grow up and out due to actions that reflect, not just changed circumstances and attitudes, but interactions between fellow tourists and other folks. Some might turn their motivation slowly inside out until their character was largely changed, while refusing to tolerate changes in others." Some might revise themselves entirely."

Allison thought all change internal. "We change ourselves if we are able," she said authoritatively. "We don't change because styles pressure us." Anne looked amused. Did her own twenty-odd year advantage over this heiress, recently a postulant nun, give Anne insight into manipulating characters in ways that may have seemed to Allison too structural? How *were* characters constructed, anyway, if not to some extent like buildings? Surely the "builders" who wielded the keenest tools made the deepest impressions–on monuments –and on characters?

Rob looked reflective. He told us that "stylistic change–the character of buildings"–could work backwards and forwards. "As I recall, Federico Borromeo created a non-Gothic, Roman style Basilica around 1649. In that year a Frenchman named Buzzi decided the Basilica should resume its original Gothic form. And gradually, over more than three centuries, it did," he mused.

It seemed easier to me to transform buildings than hearts. Ellen's, for example.

The cathedral's changes were interesting. Men had done marvelous things in large numbers over time with the proper tools. But authors were not only without tools stronger than ink, paper, memory and invention, but without supervision by experts working from blueprints showing the final outcome. What in human lives was measurable? A cathedral was a great artistic achievement. But how many people realized that a great novel was as complex a work, more difficult in that it dealt with thoughts, feelings, and malleable destinies, not the permanent placement of stone? A good novel mirrored life. A cathedral did not. Cathedrals stood on tradition and preconceived notions. Novels not.

Anita said the façade was "finished" in the 1960s. "Recently, she added, "debris turned up that no one knew how to re-position." A novel was more organic. Just try changing one action, one motive, one false move on the part of a character. Where would one put the rest? No one could put life's "debris" back in its rightful place, either. I should check this out with Anne, especially if she intended to publish her novel of our tour.

On our way out, Rob said, "Napoleon had himself crowned King of Italy here, a romantic in a Romantic setting."

"Ruskin, the art critic," Wes reminded Rob, "called this cathedral 'peculiarly barbarous,' 'not pure;' though Henry James thought it 'if not supremely interesting...nor logical... 'commandingly beautiful' and 'superbly rich.'"

Arnold, fond of Mark Twain's Innocents Abroad, recalled that Samuel Clemens had devoted a chapter to Milan and described the cathedral as impressive. Well, who wouldn't?

We left the piazza and returned to our hotel two hours before dinner. Wes scaled my "tower" having been resourceful enough to find a service staircase leading from the kitchen to the fifth floor. He knocked and I peeked out the peep hole to see him, distorted and miniaturized. How privileged was this Rapunzel! His ascent was romantic. He kissed my hair, neck, eyes, lips. He insisted on my sticking out my tongue. He sucked it before perpetrating a really deep French kiss down my throat, symbolic penetration. He removed all my clothing to the waist. *The Overture.*

A short First Act. Love on a *chaise longue.* I seated myself on Wes, facing him. Followed by a brief *Intermezzo* or *Entr'acte* during which I lost my bra and blouse and we smudged the velvet chaise with bodily fluids–his. I removed the whitish matter with a damp towel. Then, placed on top of the quilted satin bedspread, I was stroked, Wes choosing parts of my body that appeared most worthy of stroking, at a tempo achingly slow.

Second Act. I initiated the action by throwing the quilted blue spread onto the twin settees serving as a footboard to a king-sized stage. Wes jumped onto stage. I jumped on top of Wes and stuck my tongue down *his* throat. He rolled me over and there followed the rest of this act, ending in thunderous applause from the audience of one (me).

Second Intermission. It was during this portion of our performance that Wes and I rehearsed the reasons why this couldn't be an extended run.

"You know we've talked over all the possibilities that our love offers. It doesn't seem likely that marriage is one of them," (Wes's Probalistic Version).

"It isn't your fault–it's just Time. You've had a marriage, a divorce and two children on their way to independence. I haven't." (Candida's Plodding Plot Version).

"If I were not dependent on my goddamned teaching salary, I'd kick it in and marry you in California. I've never loved like this before." (Wes as Besotted Economist).

"I cannot risk the North Pole (Madison). I have chronic bronchitis that would lead to *Respiratory Hell.*" (Candida as Licensed Pulmonologist).

Now I knew the curtain would rise on the *Last Act* of this operatic hell tomorrow, when Wes boarded the plane for San Francisco at

Malpensa airport. Meanwhile, we dressed for dinner, in our separate cells. I chose the lavender dress from Trieste, the jeweled ballerinas. The Concierge recommended an intimate restaurant two blocks away. We walked to *Livia's Trattoria Ecco!*

Tables for six glowed with candlelight, were strewn with flower petals. The menu was extensive, but our table ordered the same dinner being gastronomically compatible. Wes, me, Anne, Arnold, Jonah, Mindy. Our soup was *minestrone alla Milanese*, a mild bacon, plus all kinds of vegetables, and rice, flavored with chopped basil, served with Parmigiano. Delicious. Our first course, veal chops *milanese*, breaded, served with lemon wedges. (*Costolette alla Milanese al limone*). They arrived with mushroom *risotto*, Loddigiano cheese and arborio rice in beef stock and white wine. The ravioli had pumpkin stuffing (*Tortelli di Zucco*). How can Italians consume so many carbohydrates and stay thin? Our dessert was *Crema al Mascarpone* (cream cheese with sugar and rum). I tasted some of everything, but couldn't finish anything. Lombards were once Germans! Italy's snows receded; Italian appetites never.

Anne and Arnold discussed November wedding plans.

She said, "I told Arnold we might wed before Thanksgiving and honeymoon in the Caribbean, escaping Thanksgiving altogether." Arnold had a house on Martinique.

He asked, "Could you and Candida make it out East for our wedding?"

"No, I'm sorry," Wes said. I cannot swing it." I couldn't either. "Dear friends, we both have to teach," I said.

"We'd love to come," Mindy told them. "Jonah has business in Boston then. Thank you for the invitation."

Academics are serfs compared to insurance company CEO's. We stay on the manor, hooked to the plow.

Afterwards, I went straight to bed and didn't see Wes until morning. I saw Rob, though, getting into the other elevator with Joan. I heard her say, "Why not? Why in hell not?" The door closed. I keyed myself up to my tower where they imprison women who have no hope of marriage. Rapunzel. Saint Barbara. None of us had much.

CHAPTER XXIII

THE LAST SUPPERS

I, Goddess Candida, awoke to Phoebus Apollo's kiss. God of sunlight, music et. al. His first rays woke me from a dream in which I was being borne in my lover's arms earthwards. Then, Apollo took off, leaving me in total darkness, plummeting down, down to utter darkness where I missed him. No other lover about. I called for help, but none came. I was done for. Dead. Water lapped on a nearby river bank. The Styx? I could hardly breathe from fear, until the phone ringing on the nightstand beside me awakened me and thus I emerged from the shores of Hell.

"*Pronto?*"

"It's Wes, Candida. Cut out the pronto thing." I told him that he had awakened me from a terrible nightmare, part Greek, with Phoebus and the River Styx and just a smidgeon of Dante. A real Inferno. Hell. "You had dropped me, Wes, and then deserted me, and I died, and Phoebus took off..."

"Candida, I'll never drop you. That wouldn't, that won't, ever happen, even if I do go back to Wisconsin. I promise I'll always be here for you. Or, rather, there for you. What Phoebus?"

"Phoebus Apollo."

"Oh. I thought it might have been a nickname for Ferrell."

"Wes, you can't be jealous of him. He's sometimes rather thoughtful, though often, thoughtless. Occasionally cruel. Like Caliban in the *Tempest* at times. But not always. He and Joan are getting it on, just now, you know."

"I don't, and don't want to. Besides, do you *know* that? You're in the Ambassador's Suite. Were you there under the bed? Waiting your turn?" I couldn't think of an answer that was not more impertinent than that. So I didn't. Answer, that is.

"I apologize, sweetie. That was a really stupid attempt at humor. Totally uncalled for. Candida?" I waited a moment before resuming the conversation.

"Yes?"

"Candida, please forgive me. And let me come up? I've had to get all dressed just to come down and appeal in person to the desk clerk, who was not simpatico. At least, not to me. He would be to you. Your elevator is only accessible by your personal permission."

I was tempted to ask, "And what is the purpose of this call?" but I was still frightened from the dream, and longing to be picked up from the nether regions. Oh. I'm glad I didn't use that phrase. It would make Wes guffaw. *Do* people still guffaw? To laugh loudly was what guffaw meant in the eighteenth century.

I called the desk and Wes was allowed up. He arrived in shirt, tie, and suit, but made wonderful to me love in his white T-shirt. The rest of his outfit he placed carelessly on an armchair, along with dress pants and striped shorts. His T-shirt smelled faintly like laundry detergent, Tide, with a hint of laundry bleach. But I didn't protest. I really couldn't have said a thing. And after, when I could have, I didn't. We lay panting, staring at the ceiling. Today was our last together in Milan, perhaps our last time together. The sibyls could read the future. Which of us mortals could?

Wes, intuitively: "If you think this will be our last day together, you're very much mistaken."

Candida, admiringly: "You have something of the seer in you, Wes, a hint of Signor Beppo."

Wes, cynically: "Beppo my ass. An old man with repressed hots for you tried to impress you for his own purposes and you think he's a prophet."

Candida, the Judeo-Christian: "None of the two or three Isaiahs, certainly. But resembling Elijah, who made prophetic statements before disappearing in a fiery chariot. In Beppo's case, walking into his restaurant office; no chariot. And you shouldn't deride the love of older men for younger women, darling," I said playfully. He threw a pillow at my head, but I ducked, leaving him to mumble something about atheists being the real true believers, the worst critics.

He dressed, preparing to go back down and shower before breakfast. Shirt half buttoned, he grabbed me and kissed me long and tenderly. I thought I might cry. But kissing and crying at the same time is difficult.

I held back until he threw on his jacket, grabbed his tie, stuffed it into his pocket, and left. Thank goodness he was wearing loafers. His socks, no. Those he left on my dressing table. There was a faint onion-like odor to them, and I was reminded of the fact, known to all women, that men are really secret slobs. When he was gone, I had a good cry.

I dressed in basic khaki and tan, tying a camouflage print scarf around my waist for that guide in deepest Africa look, though only Leonardo da Vinci's *The Last Supper (Il Cenacolo)* was on our morning's menu.

Breakfast over, Carlo drove us to see it, a painting made for the artist's patrons, Ludovico Sforza and Beatrice d'Este, based on the verse from *John* 13:112, "One of you will betray me." Jesus had announced that one of the twelve Apostles would turn him over to the Romans for execution. This was supposed to be a wedding present to Beatrice? It was a terrible choice, for the betrayal of one's Lord, in this case, husband, was a serious offense, never mentioned at weddings.

"The painting was ultimately given to the convent of Santa Maria della Grazia in central Milan to decorate its dining hall," Rob told us.

"Why all these churches dedicated to a graceful Mary?" Sam asked, waiting for my response. Sam was increasingly involved in the viewing of art. No one answered immediately, because from the theological point of view, this was not an easy question.

Wes tried. "Sam, Mary is full of God's Grace, call it love, different from our word graceful though related to the Italian word for 'Thank You' (*Grazie*). And of course, we should be thankful for a God who loves us. All those meanings are interwoven, because medieval Catholics were thankful that by God's Grace or love a Savior was born, through the vessel of a virgin. A willing vessel," Wes added, "though a perpetual virgin. Beginning in the late eleventh century, and more ardently in the next one, there was a rush to name new churches in Mary's honor. She became the tender mother of us all, the *mediatrix* (fifteenth century) with her Son on our behalf. She was so tenderly loved that Annunciations abound in museums."

And in all this, I thought, *her real husband, Joseph, was not involved at all, just left to marvel at God's using his wife, Mary, for this holy purpose.* The angels were just as pleased as punch, as now woman would see that her choices didn't count for much, and that man would be saved; providing he behaved like an angel. Sam blinked. He now had much to mull over, as I knew he would.

Even Rob, listening to Wes's simplified, yet satisfying account, nodded. As for me, I thought that medieval men seemed after the twelfth century "Renaissance" gradually to have realized that life as they knew it was needlessly cruel. All the more reason for turning to Mary, provided expressly for their comfort. Comforting was a woman's job.

Wes went on. "At her highest, Mary was depicted in majesty, enthroned, with angels, saints, and of course, her child." I remembered that the most exalted image I'd ever seen of her was an early fifteenth century Massacio, in which she was depicted beneath the Holy Trinity, but with her head at the level of the crucified Christ's knees. That was in Santa Maria Novella in Florence. I used to stop in often after doing research.

"Mary," Wes was finishing up, "stood in a line of anthropological earth mothers. She was graceful because she kept her place, not on the level with the Trinity; below it." I thought, *kept it by accepting a lower rank, yes.* Sam was thinking all this over.

Rob added to Wes's lesson on Mariology. "She, as Mother of God, aided men and women in this realm of suffering by her prayers, as her Son did by providing a way out of it all, Eternal Life with Him in Heaven. But only for contrite, baptized believers. There was a competition for heavenly goods just as there was for material ones." Rob paused. No Muslims, atheists, heretics or Jews made it into Heaven. *Only Christ and his mother,* I thought. I forgot about Joseph, because his role was minimal.

Wes added, "Only those Catholic believers who did as they were told got into Heaven." Wes, being Lutheran, was not big on Mary's role in salvation. "It has become the fashion recently for feminist historians to see in Mary a reflection of ancient goddess cultures, where women ruled men," Wes explained, adding, "but religious belief demands further elaboration."

After that, I couldn't help but rehearse the feminist views that had been blooming recently. "The very notion of women's prophetic power was anathema to traditional scholarship. Controversy has raged around the notion of Neolithic earth mothers. Women and some pro-feminist male scholars, too, have increasingly identified with the vanished Earth Mother/Goddess thing. Traditional scholars regard them as wishful dreamers. Faith in a male deity alone was the Christian thing.

"Everything, as usual in scholarship," I told the group, "was subject to debate. Without evidence. None that would be accepted in a court of law, anyway." Unless the court was corrupt.

Wes presented the high medieval view well. "Mary was so spiritual," he said to Sam, "so full of Grace, that she became a role model for all women, and even, all men." I must have looked detached, considering that I defended no theory of divine power at all.

Ferrell whispered to me: "You cunning little atheist, you. If I could only read your mind just now." If he could have, he would have known I was hoping to find a ladies' room. Not a psychic, I ignored him.

My co–leader whispered again. "You didn't believe a word of what Wes told Sam."

"Entirely beside the point," I replied. "Wes did a fine job explaining grace, gratitude and salvation." Rob was jealous.

Sam was digesting Wes's interpretation. Samantha asked, "Do you need an antacid tablet, Sam?" He shook his head, no.

We proceeded to *The Last Supper*. It was scheduled to be restored a few years from now, using a copy made by one Giovanni Pietro Rizzoli, during the first half of the sixteenth century. Thanks to his meticulous, full scale reproduction, details of the badly faded original would emerge. Giampietrino had probably worked closely with Leonardo in Milan between 1495 and 1498, when the master drew what would become a masterpiece on the walls of a monastery's refectory. Art historians predicted, once it was restored, viewers would be able to see more details in the tablecloth, and the feet of the diners under the table.

Clearing his throat, Rob told us, "According to some sources, Ludovico had intended this as a celebration not of his wedding, but of his death. The fresco you are about to view was supposed to be part of the remodeled church that Ludovico intended to serve as a Sforza family mausoleum."

Betrayal of a marriage vow was so common in the Renaissance (and ever after), that it would have been superfluous to warn Beatrice that a Renaissance duchess was at "particular risk" (to quote Beppo) if she should have an affair after the marriage contract was signed. Husbands were not to blame if they strayed; just wives.

We descended the bus steps. They were high, and I did it, not easily, but by myself. I had made steady recovery from that fall in Florence, though still scarred, still experiencing pain.

"One of the surprises of this work," Rob explained when we entered the refectory, "is that the 'room' is merely insinuated. One must remember that there *are* no three windows in the background behind the thirteen diners, and that Jesus does not sit with a semicircular lunette overhead. The lunette was drawn to make a show place for the signature of Ludovico Sforza."

"I think Leonardo should have signed instead," Allison said. Rob objected. "The purpose of Renaissance art was not to glorify the artist, but the patron," he told her. "Without patrons, no great paintings."

"And without great artists, those who could afford to patronize art, would not have been remembered. At least, not as men who had taste, aesthetic values and culture," Mindy pointed out. "Money isn't all that promotes civilization. Talent counts for more."

"But poverty doesn't produce works of enduring beauty," Barry argued. "Money is what the Renaissance was all about. That and power."

"The power of spiritual truth and classical wisdom were crucial," Ian volunteered. He had not studied the humanities at Princeton for nothing, even if he took a theological degree. He had a point. I thought of the cave paintings at Altamira and Lascaux. Great art. When those paintings were begun, nearly forty thousand years ago, there were no art patrons. The artist himself was powerful due to insight. Raw talent. Invention. How unlike the tradition of the Renaissance where power and wealth were midwives to splendor. Yet, there had once been other ways to be artistic. Art was in us all, though few of us suspected it. Fewer still ever got in touch with their inner artist.

Looking at *The Last Supper*, the viewer saw Christ at the table's center, eyes downcast, arms resting palms up on it. Pieces of the bread for Passover dotted the table. Plates were empty on a white table cloth. There were no glasses on the table. Just bread. The scene was a group of four triads–three men in four groups simultaneously expressing their emotions at the dreadful announcement of Christ's imminent betrayal. Betrayal undermined our confidence. Destroyed our faith in friends. Our well–being. Our political and economic life. By betrayal, I included lying, hypocrisy, and greed (which betrayed the communal interest).

Ferrell suggested we "Look to the left and see Bartholomew in blue; James, son of Alpaeas, in red, and Andrew, bearded, in tan; a group surprised at Christ's announcement." He was peering closely at this triad while describing it.

Rob stepped back, noting, "A second triad portrayed Judas Iscariot, whom Peter had accidentally bumped into. Judas's head is lower than anyone else's. Peter looks angry and holds a sharp bread knife pointed away from Jesus on his left. The third member, John, the youngest, seems in a dead faint, his whole body under his brown cape tipped to the right, away from Jesus' red-clad right arm and toward Peter. The latter's curly white hair contrasts nicely with John's long, blonde curls."

Judas was in green, my favorite color, but one artists used to indicate envy. Some critics think Judas stares at Christ wondering who leaked his plans.The traitor's hair was blacker than anyone else's, black meaning filth. His right hand clasps a purse. He has just tipped over a salt shaker.

Anita, who recalled from parochial school Jusas's duplicity announced, "That purse he holds already contains the twenty-one pieces of silver for which he sold Christ."

Myrna didn't understand the sparsely prepared table. "At our house the Passover meal was rather elaborately supplied after the part with the bitter herbs, matzos and Mogen David wine."

"Imagine," Barry said, "there aren't even wine glasses on this table. If Judas threw over the salt, it wasn't because he was drunk. And Maneshevitz is better wine than Mogen David, Myrna. We always used Maneshevitz in my house." Myrna didn't say anything after her husband's admonition.

Ferrell spoke quietly, "Salt had a deep meaning. An old Hebrew saying about 'betraying the salt' meant betraying the salt of the earth, one's master."

Jim Harker said, "Most moderns wouldn't consider their boss the salt of the earth. They regard management the enemy, out to weaken unions and keep the middle class down by hiring part-time labor."

Sam, whose failed career as a stockbroker had exposed him to cheating money men, nodded. Their shenanigans had driven him to drink. "We need better managers," he said glumly. "If there were more regulators with clout, we'd have fewer people on welfare, fewer attending Alcoholics Anonymous."

Rob continued. "To Jesus's left, Thomas, James the Great, arms raised, and Philip, who just wanted an answer to the question Jesus hadn't asked, but everybody else was asking: 'Who will betray our Lord?'"

Andrea grimaced. "The question goes unanswered, like most of society's pressing questions," she said. Sometimes Andrea surprised me with her acuteness. It was usually when she wasn't zeroing in on Wes.

Sam said, "The question might be put like this: 'What did Jesus ever do to you, Judas, you ass-hole?'" Samantha blushed and immediately shushed him.

Then Allison spoke. "I would think Philip was asking, 'Don't you realize what Jesus *could* do for you? For everyone?'" Allison hadn't forgotten what she had learned in theology class from Mother Superior as a postulant. I thought of Philip Roth's old novel, *When She was Good*. But Allison wasn't still "good." Or rather, she was infinitely better, in my opinion, because she had become a skeptic and an acute observer of reality.

The last triad included Matthew, Jude Thaddeus, and Simon the Zealot. Matthew had more allusions to the *Old Testament* in his gospel than any other gospel writer. He gave a long discourse on the end of the age. This topic should interest modern polluters, so fond of flying to Europe, of owning gas guzzling Buick Roadmasters and Cadillac Sevilles with V-8 engines, despite the past year's gas shortages. The end *might be* near. Matthew had written for Jewish Christians, and Christ's Sermon on the Mount was the ultimate lesson (rarely followed) on how to treat our fellow man ethically. We could stop indulging our every whim and reduce carbon consumption.

"Jude Thaddeus," Rob intoned, "whom some have thought the brother of Jesus, but who called himself the brother of James, wrote the *Epistle of Jude*. In it, he warned against false belief in the letter of the Law, and urged ethical relationships between all. Like Matthew, he turned to the last man seated at the end of the table to Jesus' right, Simon the Zealot."

The Zealots, I knew well, had been associated with the Canaanites and were an exigent lot. Simon, though, seated next to Christ, seemed the calmest of all and thoughtful. Was he really a Zealot? They usually have all the answers. Matthew and Philip get no answer from Simon. So *was* he a zealot? '*Forse che si, forse che non...*' Maybe yes, maybe no. How do we determine the zeal of those who sit quietly, trying to solve life's conundrums?

Anne asked, "Why were Judas and Jesus both reaching for the same piece of bread?"

Ian, an Anglican priest, knew his *New Testament*. "According to *Matt.* 26:23, 'The one who has dipped his hand into the bowl with me will betray me.' This is a clue that da Vinci provided."

Ian clued Anne in, but a clue is just an insinuation; a suggestion; not definitive proof. Perhaps all of Christ's insinuations were true because he was scripted by the Author. Generally, I don't trust authors. They may write in tongues we cannot decipher; they may be barely fluent in it even if it is their own. I thought of my students at Altamonte and how they struggled.

Sandy Craigie, no churchgoer, said, "Maybe they were short on bowls in the kitchen," and Belinda, her partner in life and business, reminded her, "I bought extra bowls in San Gimignano for our shop. You can't have too many for beads."

"Let's not forget that great art was not cheap," Rob insisted, but a gift from wealthy autocrats to plowmen and porters, chamber-maids, and later, to liberal democrats, socialists and modern artists less able to market their own works."

Jonah asked how we could forget that when the Sforza name was right over Christ's head? Himself a plutocrat, and Jewish, he thought that signature constituted unnecessary boasting. Though rich, Jonah was democratic. He never boasted, but patronized art in his temple, in San Francisco. He was a major contributor to San Francisco's new symphony hall. He was a good man, even if his first wife had failed to hold his affection. No one was perfect. Not even his first wife.

On the way out, some of us stopped to buy post-cards. We piled back into the bus and Rob grabbed the microphone. "Are we all here? Ellen, too? Now, ladies and gentlemen, the art portion of this tour has just ended. Should you care to see more paintings, the Brera Museum is close to our hotel. If you'd rather just rest up, that is another option. Shoppers can do their own thing. Remember, today lunch is *not* included, so make plans accordingly. And tonight is, of course our last banquet, marking the end of our tour, except for breakfast tomorrow. The banquet is to be held in our beautiful hotel dining room. Remember, our flight from Malpensa Airport leaves at 9:30 A.M. We must leave the hotel no later than quarter to seven. Breakfast will be served between 5:45 and 6:30 tomorrow and bags must be in the hotel corridors before you come down, ready to be stowed in the bus. Accordingly, we will dine at eight o'clock tonight, so everyone can be in bed before eleven. On behalf of Altamonte College, I have been honored to be your tour guide for Renaissance art."

"*Bravo!*" "*Grazie!*" "Great work, Rob," filled the bus, amid much clapping. Having let him bask in the applause a minute or two, I took the mike.

"And as your co–leader and guide to Italian culture, language, and literature, I have been pleased to accompany you on your Renaissance adventure. In exploring this era, I feel we explored our own better angels, and saw revealed before us some of the demons that so tortured our European forbears, some of their joys we also have shared. Thanks for you attention and kindness." (*Tante grazie per la vostra attenzione e compiacènza*).

"Hear, Hear!" Matt shouted.

Wes bellowed, "*Dieci con lodi!*" an Italian soccer expression I didn't dream he knew, meaning something like "Congrats on a perfect performance." There were some "thank-you's" from Anita, Mindy, Meg, and Reed, Allison. Jonah clapped loudest and blew me a kiss. I heard murmurs from some of the others. These didn't last as long as Rob's acclamation, but then, I wasn't Rob.

Back at the Hotel Savoia, the group split up. Belinda, Lynette, Allison and Sandy went shopping; Sam wandered around the *Pinocoteca Brera* with Matilda for she had missed out going yesterday. I had also missed the *Brera*, but I suddenly felt finished. Finished with tourists. Finished with art. Finished with Milano.

I rode my special 'charger' up to my tower and climbed into the freshly made bed, stripping to just my panties. Immediately at rest, I was soon back in Florence with Teresa and the *Principessa*, who kept trying to interest me in her sons, the Counts (really no accounts), or grandsons, so the family's name would continue through my womb. While I dozed, Signor Beppo from Piazza Navona appeared, floating over the *Principessa*'s head, predicting danger if I accepted one of the dynasty as a suitor. And while all this was going on, Teresa's sister Silvia in a floral silk nightgown slit up to her thigh was tugging my panties down!

I escaped Silvia and the dynastic males. I headed for the Piazzale Michelangelo, arriving totally nude. Everyone else was similarly unclad, except for the statues, which were all clothed. I dined like the princess I was before becoming–in my dream–*Ambasciatrice* to the Kingdom of Italy. The phone rang.

Wes. Without doing more than rolling over, I picked up the receiver and said "Hi, darling." It was the desk clerk asking if it were all right to send him up. Certainly, go ahead." *(Certo. Faccia pure.)* I answered the knock on the door, opening it without bothering to look out the peep hole, hearing the voice of Signor Beppo muttering that I was "at particular risk." I opened the door and in strode Ferrell. I stepped back, reminding myself of Masaccio's Eve, covering her chest with her hand, as I now covered did mine. I still wore my panties, while Eve had none to wear.

Without a word, Rob grabbed me and hurled me onto the bed, removing his pants, while climbing on top of me. His powerful body pinned me to the mattress. He was tugging at my panties the way Silvia had just done.

"Don't," I screamed. "Please, Rob, No!"

"I've taken all I can from you and your ostentatious sexuality. You deserve to be raped for your whorish behavior. Some advertise it, but you flaunt it." I screamed.

The phone rang. This time I was *really* awake. It was Wes, asking if he could come up to my 'tower.' I resolved to use the peep hole before opening the door to him, just in case. The tour, Rob, my imagination, the summer heat, the summer itself had finally got to me.

Wes came in only after I carefully scrutinized his face. In the peep hole he seemed very large in the middle (he wasn't) and short legged, while his head seemed micro cephalic, like one of those distorting mirrors they used to have at the Santa Cruz boardwalk. Life had enough distortions without mirror tricks.

"We've got the afternoon to ourselves, my girl, and you *are* my girl. Only don't expect much. I'm just knocked out from the thought of leaving you tomorrow." I nodded, feeling miserable.

"Also, I've developed a nagging but fairly intense pain in my back and hip, from an old football injury. Still, I wanted to climb in beside you and hug you before I fell asleep." Then, "Ouch" Wes yelped as he cautiously maneuvered himself onto the bed and under the covers.

"Ouch?" You really are in pain," I expostulated. "You've never complained before!" He hadn't. *Just like a man*, I thought. I found some codeine pills left over from Florence. He took one–grumbling– with a glass of water and slept for three hours. I got up and started to pack. The phone rang.

"Hi, Candida. It's Jonah. Hope I didn't disturb your rest or anything else important?" In his way Jonah, like Signor Beppo, was, if not a visionary, intuitive. Perhaps just experienced.

"No, not. What can I do for you, Jonah?"

"I want to know what's going on around here. Before I speak to the hotel's Director."

I was totally in the dark. "*Is* something going on here, Jonah?"

"Candida, I've been wandering around the hotel. First the work-out room, where I found Jim and Belinda in shorts–you haven't seen anything until you've seen that woman in shorts–loading lockers with liquor and wine, chips and caviar, peanuts, crackers, cheese and I don't know what else."

"Oh, how strange," I murmured.

"That's not all, Candida. On the hotel terrace, I saw Barry, Sam and Matilda entering through the bushes. The men were carrying sacks with bottles; Matilda just bread sticks and a cake. They didn't see me, hidden behind a fountain surrounded by tall bushes. But I heard them talking about a 'party' later this afternoon. Matilda asked if they had plastic cups and knives to spread the pâté and caviar on the crackers, the bread."

"Obviously, Jonah, the group is having a party to which we have not been invited; of which we have been kept in the dark. I wonder where it will be held?" I had the biggest spread in the group—three rooms and large entrance way. "Had I known, Jonah, I would have volunteered to have it here."

"Candida, our contract with the hotel states explicitly that all parties must be hotel catered, and that private room parties are contrary to safety regulations as well as to the privacy of other guests. We would be obliged to pay a stiff penalty if this party got started. I must stop it now. Any idea of who might be hosting it?"

"No, Jonah, none."

"All right. I'll talk to the Director and get back to you as soon as I have anything to report."

Meanwhile, Wes was waking up. "What's up, sweetheart? Anything wrong?" His voice, though concerned, sounded miles away. I explained the situation.

"Gee," he exclaimed, now wide awake. "We must be the only ones besides Jonah and Mindy who were not invited. Rather insulting, don't you think?"

I had to agree. "It seems intentional, yes."

"I bet it's Rob's party," Wes mused. "I think this is his backhand at you directly, and indirectly—at me. Jonah was left out because he alone could override the plan, as Altamonte's insurer." Was Wes overly sensitive to the understated rivalry between himself and Ferrell, two men of the same status and acumen but of such different temperaments? Was I responsible? Was Rob's on again, off again play for me, something I had largely (but not as firmly as I might have) resisted, the thing that had made my relation to him so poisonous?" The phone rang again.

"Candida? Jonah. I've talked to the Director. He reiterated that this party will be shut down, if necessary, by the hotel police. He said that while the hotel would be glad to provide us with a large room in which to hold such a party, at a 'nominal' charge of two hundred dollars, he would place an additional tax on all the group's purchases—the hotel's usual markup. You'd be surprised how much vodka and gin—not to mention caviar–cost in Milan, with an additional twenty-five percent markup."

"No, Jonah, I wouldn't be."

"Then, there's a minimum charge per person, which is twenty-five bucks! That would take care of service, napery, flowers, utensils, cleaning costs, the works. Call Charles and explain what has happened. See how much he would pay for this shindig."

I called. Charles snorted into the phone after I explained the situation. His answer? "Nothing." He pointed out that we had contracted for a banquet, not a cocktail party, too. Then he hung up.

I phoned Jonah back. "Charles said 'nothing.'"

Jonah muttered, "For once, he's right. I wouldn't want Altamonte to be sued by this hotel for breach of contract, nor pay these charges myself. After all, neither Mindy, nor I, nor you, nor Wes were invited. I don't know who else was left out. Maybe Anne and Arnold? Probably, because we've been so close. I will tell the Director to shut it down. And I will tell him to tell Rob that it is now so shut." With that, he hung up.

As it turned out, the party *was* Rob's idea. The accidentally-on-purpose omission of any mention of it to six tour members including his co–leader was, Rob insisted, when I called to ask, "Nothing personal. I just forgot to tell you six about the party. An unintentional oversight."

Oversight is one of my least favorite words. It could mean something forgotten about, accidentally neglected. It could also mean the very opposite, something carefully controlled. Its meaning is purely contextual.

Wes thought the whole plot "rotten" of Rob. I urged him to take a hot bath in my tub to alleviate his back pain. I gave him a massage, but ended up getting into the tub to do it properly. The rest followed naturally–and very gently–once we had toweled off. An aching back is no party even if you have a party with whom to share it.

The *Principe di Savoia's* dining room was green and white marble, green velvet, and crystal chandeliers with white marble floors, white coffered ceiling, and small gold lamps on every table for four. Intimate. Nevertheless, I felt in some ways it was a kind of chessboard where Jonah was king, Wes the knight, I the queen, and Ferrell the pawn. He was visibly crestfallen, his secret bash quashed. As for this banquet–it was lavish. Many of us had not gone out for lunch after viewing da Vinci's masterpiece, counting on the cocktail party to tide them over. Maybe some of the peanuts and crackers did. Maybe Matilda ate her bread and cake alone or with a friend or two. And some could make a meal on vodka, gin, and bourbon and still show up to banquet in good spirits, no pun intended.

Our soup course arrived. Creamed lobster (*Zuppa di gambero di mare alla crema*). Followed by the first course (*il primo*)–cannelloni stuffed with seafood, crab meat and artichoke hearts in a pale green sauce of *pesto* and cream *(cannelloni marinara del chef)*. Our second course (*il secondo*), was veal chops scaloppini, Milanese style (*scaloppini Milanese di vitello)* with fried polenta cakes. A peach sherbet *(sorbetto di pesca)* cleared our palates for the third course (*il terzo)*: petrale sole with toasted almonds (*sogliole in crema di Mandorla tosta*), accompanied by beet root salad and endive. Dessert was a Milanese specialty, pudding made from a cake rich with butter, eggs, candied fruit, raisins, sliced and soaked in rum and Marsala wine, milk, egg yolks, sugar, before folded into it and stiff, beaten egg whites (*budino di panatone)*. That pudding was served cold and it was rich beyond belief. Coffee followed. At the very end, the waiters brought small boxes of rich candied figs to each table, a sweet remembrance of a banquet fit for kings, queens, knights, and pawns. Us.

While we ate our dessert, a man with an accordion played two songs everyone could recognize: "Old Lang Syne" and "I Left My Heart in San Francisco." I was leaving mine, not in San Francisco, but in Milano. Jonah tipped the accordionist handsomely, and he bowed as we rose to leave. He might have been Signor Beppo's twin brother in looks, only happier of demeanor.

On the way out of the dining room, Sam said, "That was a great last supper." Agatha winced.

I defended Sam. "Even if we aren't apostles of anything special, we deserved it."

"We're apostles of good will," said Samantha. And we were. Sometimes. Ian thought we were striving, like the original Apostles, to understand our situation, but like all but Judas, not always able to grasp the whole situation. Fortunately, there was nothing much at stake if we sometimes failed. There was for the Apostles.

Ferrell came up to Wes and me as we were making our way through the lobby.

"So sorry about the mix-up over the damn room party. I was sure I'd mentioned it to you, Candida. Must have slipped my mind. Hope you'll forgive me, and you, Wes, and of course, Jonah and Mindy, Anne and Arnold. Embarrassing. Wish it hadn't happened."

I was quiet for a split second, then I said: "Rob, I'm sure that Jesus felt the same way. Nothing hurts like betrayal." With that we got into our respective elevators and went on up to bed. Each to his own, for a change.

The flight on Alitalia left at half past nine, so the group rose by 5:30 A.M., breakfasted by 6:30; and left with Carlo for Malpensa, thirty-one miles away. We made good time. I hugged Carlo and Gianfranco goodbye. Dad had called last night, unexpectedly. He approved of my taking an extra week in Rome.

"Fly down, business class. Stay in the *Hotel Principi* because you were happy there. Don't worry about money, he told me." He deposited four thousand dollars in an account for me in the Bank of Italy (*Banco d'Italia*) near the Spanish Steps to cover my luxurious stay at the Principi. He added that he would pay the difference between my old ticket home and business class to San Francisco. Sometimes, Dad really surprises me by remembering that I am his first born. Mostly, he forgets. True, I can barely tolerate his second wife, Chérie, a dyed blonde, perpetually harassed. Their kids, ages ten and twelve, both boys, drive her crazy. Dad is proud of them, but he doesn't raise them. Nobody does. The maid tries. They are too old for a nanny. Chérie shops and does lunch.

I saw Wes off. I stood by him with my bag until his was checked through. He proceeded to Gate 16A; me after a bit to 15 B. For a half hour I sat next to him at his gate and cried, while he stroked my hair, patted my hand, and swore never to desert me in his heart. A group of Hare Krishna followers passed by, chanting, but rather blank of face, as if they were not really passing by at all, but rather bypassing a reality they had overcome. After that, we just held hands and said nothing.

I stopped snuffling. His flight was called. I watched him leave. He didn't see me wave after giving his boarding pass to the lady in the blue suit. I walked on to gate 15 B.

My flight was called twenty minutes later. I handed the ticket taker my boarding pass. I found myself running down the steep incline to the airplane's front door. Leaving Milan was like getting out of jail where all the bars were memories, not all bad, just memories. I stuffed my carry–on bag up overhead. I'd already sent the large bag ahead to San Francisco, where Dad promised to pick it up for me. No one was around to wave at. I appreciated the Scotch and soda I ordered gaining my business class seat to Rome, a short flight. And the cashews. Nice. They gave you peanuts and soda pop in cattle class.

CHAPTER XXIV

ROME, MOSTLY ALONE

Leonardo da Vinci airport, (Fiumicino), bag in hand. "Parco dei Principi," I told the cabbie.

"Heavy traffic, Miss. *Pazienza.*" I was patient. He was an adept driver. I tipped him well. A bellboy took my bag. When the *Direttore* saw me, he hugged me.

"So happy to see you, Miss Darroway. Without the group."

"They flew home today," I said.

"Much better," (*Molto meglio*). My fifth floor room–blue, with jolly red and yellow Chinese lamps, ebony tables–held no lilies. No one kissed the nape of my neck or unhooked my bra.

The cashews wore off. Lunch after a brief stop at the bank. On the way, I'd window shop on Via Veneto. I passed a mailman pushing a rusty bike, scarred leather bag on its handlebars. He fell into step beside me, talking. I exchanged pleasantries. Middle-aged. Bad teeth.

"You stay at the Principi?" he asked. "Rich lady. Married?" (*Sposata?*) I shook my head no, and wished him a nice day. I'd never see him again.

I was wearing jeans–bell bottoms–yellow scooped neck Tee, the gold necklace. Designer shops dotted Via Veneto. Prada. Dior. Ferragamo. They could make your head spin; bank balance plummet.

I wore my Timex. I stopped before the Philippe Patek shop to guess which watch Dad would have bought. Among the watch faces, one human one was familiar. Duane Becker's, eighteenth century studies, French; Italian. Columbus, Ohio, as in University of. I did not turn. He tapped my shoulder.

"Candida Darroway! Heard you speak on Boccaccio. Fabulous. What's with Rome? Got a post-doc?"

"Duane Becker! What a surprise!" What else could I have said? *Goodbye, Columbus*? Tall, late thirties (?), blonde, a hunk in designer blue jeans, explorer's jacket.

Duane worked on Condorcet. He taught the first two Italian language courses, but French was his specialty.

"You look wonderful, Candida," he said, his glance lingering on my décolleté. "I'm here doing research." No briefcase, I noted.

"Not me," I said. "I was co–leading an art-history tour, but they left this morning. I'm leaving Saturday."

"I had a Fulbright in Paris," he said. "Studied the poetics of peace and war." I blinked. Poetry in war? Forget Homer. The poetic impulse was never at peace with war. Generals used poetry to whip up enthusiasm for killing. But is death beauty? Beauty death? Was I plagiarizing Keats? No. Paraphrasing George Keats' notes on John's lost MS., *Ode on a Grecian Urn* (1819). "Beauty is truth, truth beauty..." Hardly "all ye need to know."

"Can I hang with you?" he asked.

"Sure. My first stop is a bank. Near the Spanish Steps." (*Scala di Spagna*).

"My hotel's above them," Duane said. "The Hassler."

"Nice." The Hassler was a huge five star.

"We'll take Via Veneto to *Ludovisi*, then *Condotti*. There's a Bank of Italy there," I said. "After that, the *Corso* to *Piazza de' Fiori*, full of cafés, produce stands. Bric-a-brac. We'll coffee up on Fiori, then lunch, if you care to join me, on Piazza Navona." Duane was agreeable. From a flower vendor he bought me a gardenia. The vendor clipped it to my hair. I traveled thence forward under clouds of perfume.

Teenagers jammed Rome's narrow sidewalks. Twice I was jostled into the gutter.

"Take my arm" Duane urged. Except for his earlier tap on my shoulder, this was our first mutual physical contact. We were both wearing thin clothing. His unlined explorer's jacket let me feel his muscles. He probably lived more in gyms than archives. Nice. I withdrew two hundred dollars at the bank.

"*Grazie, mille*" (Many thanks), I said to a blank-eyed clerk. I might have emptied the Prime Minister's account. She wouldn't have blinked. Some day, I bet, they'll have machines from which you could draw your cash– as blank of expression as this teller.

The *Piazza de' Fiori*. Rome's oldest market. The name was ironic, since executions had been held here. Giordano Bruno, the philosopher (1546-1600), a Dominican friar, was burned here for heresy. In Venice (1591) the Inquisition nabbed him. Imprisoned in Rome, they burned him over there—where two Irish Jesuits sat drinking cappuccinos under his statue. Bruno's torture wasn't on their conscience, as the assassination of Socialist presidents wasn't on the CIA's.

Duane asked me about the next Modern Language Association's October convention. "Coming, Candida?" I was a bit startled at the *double entendre*.

"No. Sorry. I attend several a year, but this year not the MLA." Those meetings gave randy scholars a stimulus not exclusively intellectual. More unwound at conventions than manuscripts. A large hotel with thousands of scholars and grad students offered all a chance to list towards lust. Professors no longer in the lists located their lust. List. Lust. Any linguistic connection? Was a master's thesis lurking there? Ahead, Piazza Navona.

Duane's good looks and downward glances provided sexual tension. I knew about research. He was researching *me*—my scooped Tee and plunging bra. He checked out my cleavage crossing the piazza. Though it was now very hot, I hoped he would keep his cool.

Ah, Bernini's Four Rivers Fountain. Three weeks ago, I was here with Wes. Duane's eyes spotted *da Beppo's*.

"Candida, that's a perfect lunch spot. Shaded, close to a fountain."

I nodded. Our table was on the spot where Wes, Rob and I had lunched. Only now, it was a table for two. We sat facing the 'Danube,' the statue representing Europe. Once a Roman circus grounds, the piazza was also a medieval jousting field; in the seventeenth century used for carnivals. Power and entertainment yield civilization, war, peace. Poetry? not so often.

"I want *lasagne verde*," (pasta with spinach) Duane said." I had it yesterday. With beer."

"Why not experiment? Try *cannelloni. Spaghetti con vongole* (with clams)? A seafood platter (*frutti di mare)* on lettuce and radicchio with marinated artichokes (*Carciòfi sotto olio marinara*)?"

Duane ordered *lasagne verde* again and a large beer. I ordered *canneloni*, and a small beer (*una birra piccola*); then a large one, having quickly drained the small. It was hot under the awning. While eating, we spoke of people from conventions.

"Let's have ice cream for dessert," Duane pleaded. We ordered mixed flavors (*gelati misti*), each bowl had four different ones. We shared and shared alike. It wasn't until I saw him looking more intently at me than the *pistacchio noccìola* (pistachio nut) that sharing dessert hit me as an intimate sweet. Suddenly, something colder than *gelato* passed overhead–Signor Beppo, smiling. "Good afternoon (*Buona sera*), Signorina Darroway e Signore." He bowed.

"Buona Sera, Signor Beppo. Nice to see you again." (*Piacere di rivederla*).

"No group," he said complacently.

"Yes, Sir, I'm alone" (*Sì, Signore. Sono sola*). This was manifestly ridiculous. He let it pass. But Beppo wasn't interested in Duane.

"You are safe now." (*Lei e sicura, adesso*). So much for Becker.

I thought Beppo was being ironic. He probably regarded himself a fortuneteller. Mine. When we had finished, Duane tipped our waiter frugally. We left.

In the square Duane asked, "Who's the geezer?" We were now behind the fountain, hidden from view.

"The owner. Mr. Beppo. I think *he* thinks he has unearthly powers. It's possible," I joked. Duane frowned.

"Where are you staying, Candida? Which hotel?"

"The Parco dei Principi on Via Veneto," I said. "Near where we met today."

He looked at me sideways saying, "You don't do things by halves, do you?" I didn't answer. Duane repeated, "*Do* you?"

I looked up at him with an innocent smile "Actually, I sometimes do." He laughed and hailed a cab.

"I don't." The cab swung alongside. "Albergo Hassler, Piazza Trinità Dei Monti, #6, Spagna," Duane said in Italian. Excellent accent, I noted. I must have done him good–linguistically. He was using the Italian he *said* he taught reluctantly.

The cab dropped us above the steps on which Byron, Shelley and Keats once lived. We stopped before the Hassler. Far below one saw the *Fontana delle Barcaccia,* a boat-shaped fountain.

"You're well lodged," I observed. The Hassler was huge.

"I thought we'd have a drink on our terrace," Duane said. The hotel was dark inside. Its terrace occupied the fifth floor's rooftop.

"Vegetation is better than that dark bar downstairs," Duane pronounced. We stepped out of an elevator onto a terraced paradise, revealing all Rome. I breathed in the scent of lemons, tropical flowers.

"Duane, are you married?" I hadn't thought to ask.

"Divorced. Four times. Four kids."

"And yet you seem easy to get on with," *and probably to get it on with,* I thought. Heat, perfume, a handsome man, a luxury hotel and, shortly, a mixed drink, maybe that one with a parasol stuck into a lime wedge. Several ladies nearby were drinking those.

"I *am* easy to get on with—unless one pushes the wrong buttons." I didn't respond.

Oh, Wes, I thought, *you must have felt how empty your house in Madison was re-entering it* yesterday.

"Are *you* married, Candida? Engaged?"

"Neither. But I fell in love this summer. Older man. It may not work out." *That was dumb,* I thought. Dumber still: "How old are you, Duane?" The question was so gauche that Duane laughed before answering.

"Thirty-five," he replied. "Good answer?"

We were only three years apart!

"Four divorces?" I changed the subject in my favor, not his.

"Really, three. One annulment. Just out of high school."

The waiter appeared. Duane ordered bourbon on the rocks. The waiter looked at me.

"I'll have that parasol thing with the lime wedge." (*Quella lì, colla parasole*). I have had few mixed drinks in my life and those ladies seemed contented.

"Is it a screwdriver I just ordered?" I asked Duane, not thinking it could be interpreted as a Freudian slip. He shook his head. No.

I knew less about mixed drinks than mixed company. I'd only had three lovers in my life, and as many mixed drinks. I had my first (lover, not mixed drink) at Berkeley. One time only–a terrible mistake. After that, I put myself on the Pill. Thank goodness for them. I remembered a 1960s film with David Niven and Deborah Kerr – *Prudence and the Pill*. Prudence made it possible for me to consider a normal love life, not to marry the first man with whom I slept. Mom didn't have that chance. Molly did, but didn't take it.

Our drinks arrived. We tried more tactfully then to find out about one another. We were both Associate Professors, which, in a large university like Duane's, was excellent at thirty-five. Altamonte, was not so great, even at thirty-two. We mentioned places we'd been or hadn't. People we knew or didn't. Favorite novels. Mine was Saul Bellow's *The Adventures of Auggie March*. His? A series called *Forward the Foundation*, by Isaac Asimov. "Did he garden?" "No." "Did he have a cat?" "An Irish setter." "Woman-friend?"

"Not now. Women hear you've got four kids and had three divorces, and don't rush to get involved." This, soberly.

Was he honest about no women friends? *"Forse che sì, forse che no."* Maybe yes, maybe no.

We drank sedately. Our interests included writing fiction, but lit departments discouraged it and wouldn't give credit toward promotion, unless you wrote a best seller that became a movie. When all safe topics seemed exhausted, Duane proposed dinner.

"Oh, delightful." *Really.* I hated dining alone. The waiters turned flirtatious. Couples stared with pity, as if you were too weird to attract a man.

"Well, look. It's 5:30. Come to my room and rest before we go out to dine." I considered it. Briefly.

"Not a good idea, Duane"

"You're right. Sorry. I'll call a cab for you and pick you up at your hotel at nine?"

"Better," I affirmed. He signaled the waiter *("Cameriere!")* and paid our tab. Then he asked for a cab. Soon the waiter returned. A taxi awaited. We passed outside under the portico. Duane opened the taxi's rear door for me. He gave the driver instructions– "Hotel Parco dei Principi," then climbed in, too, his hand over mine.

Arrived, he paid the driver and walked with me to the entrance. Under the same palm trees I'd walked under with Wes. The lobby. The elevator, where I realized suddenly, I felt dizzy. I don't tolerate alcohol well. Two beers and a mixed drink. Whew.

Duane said, "Not to worry. I'm a steadying influence."

The elevator opened. I pushed five. When it opened, I had twenty feet to walk to reach my room. Duane took my key, unlocked my door, and stepped aside so I could enter.

"See you at what? Nine?" I asked. But he was already hanging his jacket in my armoire. His jeans. Kicking off his loafers, he entered my bath, ran my shower. Two minutes later, damp, with a white towel encircling his torso, he stood before me, blonde chest hair slightly bronzed.

"Voilà," he said tossing the towel over the desk chair. I could see he was up and running. Erica Jong would have cheered. Perfectly "zipless." He climbed into bed on top of me, and slowly, kissed every protuberance before entering me. It was not love with a perfect stranger, but with a perfect physique. The strange thing? When the "spirit" moved him, he whooped like a cowboy on a bucking bronco. I wasn't bucking, but the f-word rhymed. Duane was the fourth man I'd had sex with. I couldn't remember the name of the Berkeley boy. Tony. Wes. Duane. Suppose I'd had eight instead of four? Or sixteen? Would I recall their names–techniques–now?

Our dinner was in my hotel. A lovely meal. I don't remember a thing we ate. The wine was *St. Émilion*. Its label? *"Pavie-Decesse."* *Décès* meant death or bereavement in French. What would Beppo say? Teresa's mother? She was rather witchy in appearance. Paired with Beppo? A power couple. Dark power, perhaps, but power. Duane phoned next morning. He had to go to Naples, returning Thursday. Today was Tuesday. He'd call when he got back. He had "enjoyed my company." I should think so.

I entered the imperial breakfast room, Roman Emperors waiting. Augustus gave me a dirty look; he had given his own daughter and granddaughter death sentences, his daughter's for adultery. I sat as far away from him as possible.

Tiberius, his successor, looked patient, withdrawn. Hating Rome, he ruled from Capri after 26 A.D. Nero smirked. *His* morals weren't much. Titus seemed sympathetic. He had loved Berenice, a Jewish princess. Rome conquered Jerusalem (70 A.D.) Their liaison was politically impossible. Romans disliked Jews. Titus gave up Berenice, keeping Judea.

Marcus Aurelius, a Stoic, had seen it all before. My fling with Duane? Part of the universal plan. Stoics, like political candidates, never gave detailed explanations. They expected you to stick to the "universal plan." Didn't say why.

After breakfast, in plaid seersucker pants, a tight pink cotton Tee and feeling twenty-three, I dipped into the Via Condotti, coming upon the same mailman. He walked me to the crossing. He had to turn left there.

Before turning, he said, "I have been thinking about you, lady from Principi. When you getta back to hotel?"

"Very late," I lied. "I'm visiting a sick friend in the Alban Hills. There's your light. 'Bye," (*Ciao*).

On the Corso, I bought a straw hat, wide brim, pink band. Everything matched, proving that though I could act like a hippie, I wasn't one. Hippies didn't match. Near the Capitoline hill, I paused. To my right, St. Peter's. Not up to it. The crowds, the treeless avenue. Too hot.

A beachwear boutique beckoned across the street. Its large signs advertised seasonal discounts, (*Sconti*). A bell tinkled. A middle-aged woman, worn down by life or its lack, stood up to greet me. I bought a red and white polka dot bikini; rubber beach sandals; sun lotion; a beach towel. Everything was discounted. The saleswoman put the lot into a plastic bag inscribed *"Prada."* I wondered what had been in this bag when it left that designer shop? I couldn't have afforded whatever it was.

I walked to the train stop near the Coliseum, heading for Rome's ancient port, Ostia Antica, now an archeological attraction five miles from the sea. My train was boarding. Its last stop? The Lido (beach) on the Tyrrhenian Sea.

I sat on the right, not to miss the stop for Ostia Antica, fifteen miles southwest of Rome. Ostia (B.C. fourth century), came from *ostrium* (Lat., mouth). The port once sat at the Tiber's mouth. Time changed everything. Would it change my love for Wes? I was embarrassed about Duane. "Forget him" said my superego sternly.

Ostia Antica's sights included the Baths of the Seven Wise Men and Neptune, plus the Forum. Romans loved bathing. There was a Nymph of Eroticism, far from the entrance. No trees. It must have been 100 degrees F. There was an isle of painted faces; a school of Trajan; Pavone's Tavern; more. Best not to stray far from the *Cardo Maximus*, a street with shops behind Ostia's capitol, linking its Forum to the Tiber, and close to the gate. I could leave fast if I got overheated. There were no cafés here, no drink stands, even.

On the *Cardo* fish, grain, vegetables had been sold. Mosaics of those items graced floors, counter tops. Eye appeal, order, convenience. The Romans were a tidy lot. Dictators often were. Augustus transformed a republic into a dictatorship with minimal mess. Mussolini made trains run on time, some to concentration camps, perhaps my relatives in them. Hitler had efficient gas chambers. Americans had more liberties, but made bigger messes. They had inadvertently obliged socialists to join with communists; students to occupy administration buildings to defend their rights. The Equal Rights Amendment (ERA) passed both Houses of Congress last year. States were unlikely to ratify it. What should have been a mere tidying up, would probably make still messier our imperfect democracy.

We supported dictators, the Duvaliers in Haiti; the Shah of Iran. But popular leaders–e.g., Fidel Castro, who replaced the dictator Batista, a crook we labeled a bulwark against Communism–we kept trying to overthrow. Would ERA signal the beginning of a higher morality, or just underline inequality between the sexes?

Nixon tried to overthrow our democracy. He resigned after Watergate became public. Ford pardoned him for undermining democracy itself. Dad got upset when I talked like this. And *he* was a *lawyer*.

I had spotted two American soldiers rambling about the ruins. Now I heard a deep voice ask, "I wonder if the shopkeepers' names are visible?"

"Beats me," came the reply. Maybe that girl knows." They came sauntering up.

That "girl" was me. One of the soldiers, about forty, was an Army Master Sergeant named Charlie. His young friend, Bobby, was a Private. They were stationed in Vicenza, Enrico's town.

"I'm a lifer," Charlie said, meaning in the army until retirement. Stocky, wire glasses, balding, broad-shouldered, forty-ish, he was not very tall. The boy, Bobby, six two and coltish, looked like someone you watched trade his trike for a two wheeler with training wheels; that for a bike and the bike for a motor scooter, until at sixteen, he drove off in his dad's truck.

"You know Latin?" Bobby asked, pointing to a mosaic floor. "You look like a teacher."

"I am one," I replied. "But not of Latin. Of Italian." While we stood trying to figure out certain symbols—I could read Latin—but not fragmentary inscriptions—I thought about Duane. I blamed the sex on that parasol thing; on missing Wes, but not on my morals. No man would blame his own, and these days, no woman needed to. I was my own woman.

Still, I'd be careful. These were soldiers. *Be friendly, not flirtatious,* I thought.

They stayed close. They valued what I knew about antiquity, which was considerable. I thought I spotted a shopkeeper's name. "Sextus." Bobby laughed. "It means six," I told him. Was the owner the sixth of his line? Was Sextus his family name? Or was this just the sixth shop on the Cardo? I didn't know. When thirst struck, we left. We were all beach bound.

"There'll be bars I hope," Bobby panted. "And girls?"

"Should be both," I answered, maternally.

Bobby: "Hot dogs and hamburgers?"

Charlie: "We'll have lunch. With cold beer."

Fortunately, another white train marked "Ostia Antica to Lido" was waiting for us.

We boarded. The sign in the bathroom said "No drinking water" (*Aqua non potabile*). To make sure their former allies from the last war, now Italy's biggest group of visitors, didn't poison themselves, they spelled it in German, too. (*Kein trinkwasser.*) A skull and crossbones beneath the warning was plastered by a red 'X.'

Fifteen minutes later, the sea. The boardwalk had more cafés than Santa Cruz, Ca. We stopped at a take–out counter. We ordered, paid, and waited for our number to be called. Charlie and Bobby carried our trays to an outdoor table. The sausage rolls (no American hot dogs) were delicious. The beer frosty.

After I used the café's primitive rest room to don my new bikini and rubber sandals, I put my street clothes back on. My regular shoes and undies went into the "Prada" bag, towel on top. The soldiers were sitting on a pier with their feet in the water, waiting for me.

Beside them, in the water, I noted something striped among the pier's pilings. Fabric. Red and white stripes. I made out part of a word … "rezzo"? It appeared to be an awning.

"Look, Charlie. Down there. An awning's come loose. Could you guys fish it up and spread it on the beach? We only have small towels." Charlie peered down. They were wearing theirs around their necks now. To soak up sweat. Hand towels.

Charlie grinned. "Orders received; orders executed." They shucked off pants and shoes. They had worn swim trunks under their outer wear. Down into the water they went, and dislodged the metal frame stuck between pilings, wrestling it onto the sand. It read, "Beer of Arezzo" (*Birra d'Arezzo*), lower edge fringed. Untorn, its metal parts were just bent. The soldiers pounded the bends out on stones. The awning, flattened, became a beach "blanket." They placed stones on the corners, for a breeze had sprung up. I put on sun screen, and shared it. We left our stuff beside the wet awning, and, joining hands, dashed into the surf, where we whooped and hollered like kids. Our swimming styles were as diverse as our lives' journeys. I side stroked. Charlie did a great breast stroke. Bobby, a classic crawl. Forty minutes later, we climbed out, tired, arms linked, walking back to "*d'Arezzo's*" on the beach, the awning half dry.

"Anyone for more sun screen?" I asked. Bobby put some on his face–already red, and Charlie slathered it on Bobby's shoulders. I applied more to my front and shoulders. Charlie slopped some on my back. I thanked him, as I couldn't reach and burned easily. Bobby did Charlie's back.

Finally, the sun weakened. The breeze dried our bodies. Only the side of us facing the awning remained damp. Since I had the biggest towel, I used it first, and gave it to the men after their small ones proved inadequate. They used those to whisk sand out from between their toes before putting on their socks, shoes. Then they combed their hair. My bikini bottom pants had dried completely. The top, with padded front, hadn't.

"Turn around, fellas. I want to take this wet top off." They did so, and I slipped back into my dry bra. Soon, hair combed, lipstick reapplied, I was ready to go.

"How do I look?" I asked, when we left "*d'Arezzo's.*"

"Beautiful," said Charlie, so solemnly I laughed.

"Like the teacher of your seventh grade dreams," Bobby answered. He had just shared a piece of his early adolescence with me. I was touched.

We left *d'Arezzo's* as an offering, a sacrifice to Apollo.

Chugging past Ostia, we shared memories. Near the Coliseum, Charlie spied a pizzeria with tables, umbrellas. Pizza smells filled the car.

"Let's have dinner there. Swimming makes you hungry." It was nearly eight o'clock. The last rays of August's sun dipped behind all but the tallest monuments. This pizzeria was popular with families. Kids (*bambini*) ran around the tables. Babies wailed dolefully. We ordered *Pizza di San Vito* (sardines, tomatoes, onions and *Caciocavallo* cheese, a specialty of Palermo). Charlie's choice. *Pizza Rustica Leccese* (Lecce, a city in Apulia, on Italy's "heel," famous for onion pie, tomatoes, chopped anchovy fillets and black olives). Bobby's. For me, *Pizza Calabrese*, like Bobby's, with tuna as well as anchovies. We shared slices, drank more beer, ate a salad for three. Charlie insisted we toast each other with *spumante,* his treat.

It was our dessert, our goodbye. We exchanged names and addresses, and, after hugs all 'round, the soldiers walked backed toward the Trevi fountain, near their *pensione.* Suddenly spent, I hailed a cab. It was the

427

best day I ever spent in Rome. In my room, the telephone was flashing. Two messages. One from Wes:

"Hi, sweet Candida. Don't forget to have a good time in Rome. Or how much love there is for you in my heart in Madison. I thought I'd die when I buckled my seat belt in Milano. Wanted to undo all the seat buckles. All yours, too. Love, kisses, Wes."

My eyes watered. A lump formed in my chest. Then Duane:

"Uh, Candida. I have to go to Naples and speak with an Italian Condorcet expert. I'd rather be dining with you tonight. Really. I'll phone around 8:00 A.M. Thursday. Let's do it over again. Duane." Maybe I wasn't ready for a man as determinedly in my corner as Wes. But clearly, a man like Duane wasn't in my corner, nor on the phone at eight. I left the hotel Thursday at nine to explore a museum.

I would do the Palazzo Doria Pamphili, an immense private "home," embassy, and museum off the Via del Corso near the Palazzo Bonaparte. I put on seersucker clam diggers. I put on a new blue Tee. Cap sleeves. A bit on the small side, it made my breasts look larger, waist smaller. At the end of the Via Veneto, my bus stop, the mailman rode his rusty bike up to me, face suffused with joy.

"Signorina, I want to marry," (*Signorina, voglio sposare*).

"How nice. Who?" (*Che bello. Chi?*).

"You. You are the perfect brida for me." (*Lei e la sposa perfetta per me.*) Incredible.

"Only," he said, "because you are already a grown woman" ("*una donna già fatta*"), I would not want all that Roman girls wanted. I told him I was engaged. I wished him luck in his search for a girl who would not want much. My bus arrived, opening with a hiss.

"Goodbye," (*Ciao*). I watched his shoulders slump as he walked slowly from the bus stop. How could he possibly know how very much in life I had, let alone wanted? Or what price tag was attached? A big house, for one, not an apartment in a squalid Roman neighborhood. Several kids in private nursery schools and (after a short interval) their education at Harvard. Yale. Research in Europe. A vacation cottage in Camden, Maine. Two cars, as America did not believe in public transportation, and sixteen year olds drove themselves to high school, when we'd need three. This mail carrier had to fit into the universal plan. Not likely on his own terms.

I arrived at the *Doria Pamphili*, no group, no guide, many choices. Rooms rented by Brazil's Embassy were out of bounds. Ditto the owner's apartments, for a Pamphili still lived here. The present one opened parts of this pile as a museum with a stiff ticket price. Collected rent from Brazil. Probably got his house cleaning state-paid.

His fifteenth century palace had a Poussin Room, a Velvets Room, Gallery of Mirrors, first wing, third, fourth. I supposed the second was where Brazil and the Pamphilis hung out. There was a Byzantine room, private chapel, an Aldobrandini Room. Several Aldobrandinis who lived here became popes.

The first pope in residence was Innocent VIII (1484-1492), and he had to pawn his papal tiara. He raised more cash by holding the Sultan's brother for ransom. He died just as Spain discovered the New World with all Bolivia's silver, Mexico's gold. Had he lived longer, Innocent could have retrieved his tiara.

The best known pope, Innocent X (1574-1655), was a great nepotist. Popes took care of their nephews, sons. They had both. Four of Innocent X's nephews became cardinals, though the first resigned to marry Paolo Borghese's widow, Paolina Borghese. Innocent X, born Giambattista Pamfili, sat for Vélasquez, Phillip II of Spain's court painter. Shown at an angle in a large arm chair with ball–not Medici balls–the chair's, Innocent opposed the Peace of Westphalia (1648). It was signed anyway, ending the Thirty Years War. Rome's privileges were reduced.

Innocent had enemies, the Barberinis. He confiscated their property after they fled to Paris. He condemned five propositions on Grace (Bishop Jansen's) thinking them Protestant. They were really Augustinian. St. Augustine was a great saint, keen on God's Grace. Grace was hard to pin down. Most popes–and saints–lacked it. Being full of Grace was Mary's thing. Being full of greed was more papal.

Innocent wore a red skull cap. His satin cape buttoned over the white pointed collar of his silk gauze dress. Both arms rested on the oak chair's arm rests. His long fingers, with pointed, polished nails, looked as if he never personally signed, let alone wrote, a papal Bull. His right hand sported a square ring, a dark ruby, with a white seal. In his left he held a letter, refolded, as if he did not care for its contents. Not even Velasquez could reveal what those restless eyes saw.

Innocent was dominated by his sister-in-law, Olimpia Maidalchini, his chief advisor; years younger than he. Some contemporaries thought them lovers; modern historians do not. Innocent's corpse festered in St. Peter's for three days, presumably because Olimpia was loathe to pay for Innocent's burial. She was probably one of several of his entourage who stole the gold he kept in chests under his deathbed. She pleaded that she was a poor widow (both her deceased husbands were very wealthy), and could scarcely afford the pittance she paid for his burial. Some claim an ordinary parishioner paid for it.

The second painting I pondered was Caravaggio's *Penitent Magdalen*. This special friend of Christ, an ex-whore, was beautiful. She wore a full sleeved white peasant blouse trimmed with silver and lace under a damask jumper in gold, with red threads. Today it would be sofa fabric. Even weeping, Mary was gorgeous. Most women crying are not. Her red hair matched both her jumper and the chair covering.

Caravaggio made the Magdalen match her "vanities," too–luxuries severely criticized by Savonarola a century earlier. A glass vase may have held unguent or perfume. Pearls with matching earrings; amber beads lay nearby. And though today one might never associate her with the life style of a hippy, in a certain sense, she epitomized a passionate hippie woman who defied convention and ran after someone she knew loved her soul, a man with whom she was falling in love. Jesus once reproved her for spending too much money on oil to rub on him, instead of on food for the poor.

I looked up now at the bare room in which Caravaggio placed her. An unseen window poured light down on her. God's forgiveness? A blessing for being so loyal a follower of Jesus, who cherished her? *Weep No More My Lady*, your sins are forgiven. You will go directly to Heaven, without passing through Purgatory.

In a way, this portrait was an annunciation, though not like Filippo Lippi's (1406-1469). Caravaggio saw that the Magdalen was forgiven for her pure heart. To the Church, sex defiled bodies, and celibacy was preferable to marriage. Faith, good works and God's Grace would save a good person. Marriage wasn't even a sacrament then.

Unlike Caravaggio's Magdalen, Lippi's Virgin Mary was one hundred per cent pure. An angel announced her approaching motherhood. This angel held a lily in his left arm. I thought of Ferrell's lilies. Symbols of purity? Or of impure desire? Could the purity of lilies be spoiled by impure motives?

Lippi's angel was all pink, white, blonde, winged. No dark feathers for her wings. Or were they *his*? Weren't angels androgynous? Above this angelic head, God's hand from the upper margin of the canvas loosed a dove. The Holy Spirit poured forth rays. Mary was full of divine life, pregnant in a church pew. Her white cap–she was a blonde– set off a navy cloak. Her right hand was raised; eyes lowered. Her mouth turned down at both corners accepting her fate, her infant's to be. Woman's lot was to accept. Unlike Magdalen, Mary was the perfect woman, not the forgiven one. If she were so unhappy at this announcement, how must Joseph have felt?

My fourth painting was another Caravaggio. He had been my favorite ever since Sam and I saw his *Dying Bacchus* in the Borghese Museum. Here, in *Rest on the Flight to Egypt*, Joseph, Mary and baby Jesus have sought shelter in Egypt. They rest. Mary held Jesus, asleep, on her lap. Her red hair was done up in a bouffant "do," with a braid and top knot. Where did she find a beauty parlor in this wilderness? She slept too, her head drooping over her baby's. Her outer garment was red. An under blouse, white. A black skirt enveloped her extremities. She frowned while asleep. Joseph, an old graybeard (proving he couldn't have been Jesus's father) was seated on the left, wide awake, holding up a book of musical notation for a female angel, a violinist in an age when violins did not yet exist, invented only in 1510. A special lullaby for baby Jesus and his mom.

This angel was one curvaceous babe, with long gold curls. She reminded me of Janis Joplin, though I never did go to the Fillmore concerts in San Francisco to see her in person. Molly told me about her impressions of Janis, not conventionally beautiful yet attractive. Men set norms for female beauty; women slavishly followed them. Janis had bad skin, but was otherwise nice looking.

This angel, nearly nude, wore a silk scarf draped over parts of her backside, dipping down over her left rump. Only her instrument, a violin, covered her front. Joseph stared in wide-eyed wonder. But he was less interested in the violin than the angel's breasts.

The angel was spectacular, except for her wings. They were bird-like. Black and gray feathers like those of crows and sparrows stood in ludicrous contrast to her creamy skin. She needed new wing-wear. One wondered if Lippi's lady friends couldn't have provided a fetching cape to hide them. Mindy's white satin one would have been perfect.

Mary had wed an older man. I loved Wes, an older man. Mary got stuck with all the baby sitting. And she was *Mary*, not a scholar dashing around libraries to document obscure points of literature to earn a promotion, like I had to do. Mary's narrative was written for her. Literary scholars wrote their own. I remembered skimming through a book in Kepler's Book Store in Menlo Park in which Mary was called a woman stripped of autonomy. Her very pregnancy was announced by an angel. All Mary did was nod.

Could I do motherhood, scholarship, teaching and child care nodding, while Wes concentrated solely on scholarship? Pursued his inner angels? In any case, women could now do more than nod. Thanks to Roe v. Wade, they had a choice. They could shake their head "no" as well.

I was hungry. I looked for exit signs. On the Corso, I marveled at how well I had pursued *my own Renaissance*! Without Ferrell. I taught the subject at Altamonte, and wrote about it, but now it was my own. I was not constrained by anyone else's narrative, not in museums, not in bed.

I stopped at an ice cream shop and ordered raspberry and peach frozen yoghurt, the colors of Caravaggio's Magdalen portrait. I thought of the mailman's impertinent remark about my age. The Virgin Mary and Mary Magdalen weren't bothered by aging. They were covered under a different kind of Universal Plan than that of the Stoics: great art and the Church kept them forever young.

On Via Condotti, I noticed a long white convertible keeping pace with me by the curb. I turned away. When it continued to follow me, I turned curb-wise. The driver, Marcello Maistroiani's double, guided a white Lamborghini convertible while looking intently at me.

"Miss," he said in accented English. "You are so pretty. Come sit beside me. I have a villa in the Alban Hills. My pool is heated. My heart, too. Where's your hotel? Throw a few things into a bag and come away with me."

"Thanks, but I'm married," I gasped. I spun my college ring around quickly so that only the band showed. "My husband and children are waiting. In the Hassler." He held up his own left hand with a glittering diamond and gold marriage band.

"I'm married, too. Let them wait!" (*Lasciali stare*). Then, head thrown back, he accelerated and drove off laughing.

Safe in my hotel, I dreamt Wes and I were marrying. When I awoke the phone was ringing. Wes! Finding me in a mood of dreamy wakefulness, he asked if we could have "sex" over the telephone. I would *never* tell anyone what was said. It was more intimate than sex itself. When he hung up, I was orgasmic. Describing lovemaking was as efficient as making it. Actually, words spoke louder than actions. And lasted longer. Physical contact melted with the fleeting orgasm produced. When he hung up, I dropped into a post coital sleep.

I dreamt again, this time of Italian 2a, where my students struggled with Vittorini's *Women of Messina*. We cover half the novel each semester. Irregular verbs. Realism. Plot analysis. Grading. I woke suddenly. Still on vacation, thank goodness.

I dined at the Principi, waiters buzzing like bees around me. Thursday. The phone rang at 7:00 A.M. Duane.

"Hi, love. I'm stuck in Naples for another day. Off to Amalfi tomorrow, unfortunately, to see a private collection of Condorcet's letters. I met a scholar whose ancestress was getting it on with Condorcet. Can't miss out on this."

"Then it's goodbye, Duane. I leave on Saturday."

"But we can still meet when we have conventions, no? I'm looking forward to it." I hung up without a word. Bright young man, Duane. Going places. Just not with me.

Okay. My day for St. Peter's. I dressed accordingly. Mid-length sleeves. Long skirt. I took a cab. Once inside, I marveled at the drop in tourists since early August. People were actually praying. For luck, I kissed Peter's toe, knowing Wes had as well. It made me feel closer to him. Wes, not Peter. I took an elevator that whisked me up to a broad corridor leading to the dome where views of Rome could stop weak hearts. Dad had asked me to take pictures of Rome from the cupola. Keeping my back to the wall, I held my Olympus II up high and snapped. I was too frightened to frame my shots. Having done the circuit, I went back inside. I guided my feet in a straight path…and fell to the floor. Guards came and put me on a stretcher. They ran me to their office. Several tucked my skirt around my legs. This was St. Peter's, after all. They got out a stethoscope.

"Is the girl all right?" (*Va bene la ragazza?*) someone asked. I felt a blood pressure cuff on my left arm. Someone peered into my eyeballs with a small light. "*Sì, sì*. Another Kim Novak as in *Vertigo*; remember," (*Ricordi*)?

The last two days in Rome I visited Paolina Borghese. She winked at me. I winked back. I walked about the Forum, like a real tourist. Wes called to wish me a good flight home. I couldn't stop crying. My real home was in Wes's heart, as his was in mine.

"I want to see you, I wailed. I miss you."

They upgraded me to first class at Leonardo da Vinci airport. I ate roast beef and crab. If anyone asked, I'd be a buyer for Saks. I was wearing my gold necklace. I matched. They'd believe me. Nobody asked, though. The men in first class were either gay or old, and the only other woman was reading John Updike's novel *Couples*. I bet she was single. Updike's a great read for the sexually needy.

CHAPTER XXV

FINDERS, LOSERS

S.F. airport. Hare Krishnas doing their thing. I reached Alviso at 10:00 P.M. and fell into bed, after eating one of two wizened apples.

This wasn't the Principi. No Egyptian cotton sheets; armoire, chaise longue, view. Under my faded bedspread, curled, a dead honey bee. Having tossed it, I slept. Not soundly.

I was looking for something. Couldn't remember what. Out back, a dreamscape of elephants. One pachyderm stuck her trunk through the opened window over the kitchen sink. I was co–leader of Altamonte's African tour. I gave her the last apple. She thanked me, and headed out for a mudbath in Alviso's sloughs.

Three A.M. I almost wakened, calling Wes to bed, scolding Duane for hogging its sagging center. We were at the Hassler. Their mattresses didn't sag. Mine did. I awoke in Alviso. Alone. Seven A.M. I had to shop; do laundry. People *had* made love here while I was away. They entered through the kitchen window. I'd go to Altamonte for my check, new text books. I needed to cut my hair. I pulled the linen from its moorings, stuffing the machine. The sound of it working so hard on two sheets and two pillowcases reminded me to ask my landlord for a new washer. He hadn't done anything but paint the porch steps in 1970. They were already peeling.

I would breakfast at Peet's and raid Safeway up the Peninsula–later. I donned a striped Tee, blue jeans, deck shoes. A lace broke. I tied the ends together. I grabbed a cardigan because the Bay Area had myriad micro-climates. They had prepared me to deal with the tourists. Rob. Weather and people–so changeable.

I filled my tank at a cheapie station. Gas was nearly a dollar a gallon. I ate a prune Danish at Peet's. American coffee. How I missed Italy's. I drove to the college up highway 101, having turning off at 237. I drove at fifty-five m.p.h. I'd save gas. People honked. They were doing sixty-five; seventy. Wasteful. Illegal. After San Bruno, all uphill. Was my engine pinging? It had to hold out for two more years.

Once in the faculty lot, I ran to the pay office, noting how dry the redwoods looked. California was in drought mode again. My check was waiting. Good old Roger! He hadn't deducted for Trieste.

I ran to Buzby Hall. Dashed up the creaky stairs and unlocked my office door. Biblical devastation! The pipes over my desk were bare. Strips of wall board and paint flakes sifted "snow" onto all surfaces. *Moonlight in Vermont*. Thankfully, my books were in the closet. Praise be to the Goddess! A dank smell pervaded the air from dripping water pipes. The floor was soaked. My office had escaped the drought! My desk had been moved doorward. I dialed Administration. Cathy Steele, secretary, picked up.

"Cathy Steele, Assistant to the Assistant, speaking."

"Hi, Cathy. Candida Darroway. I'm standing in Hell–my office–hoping I have another and help moving there."

"Welcome back, Professor. Your pipes began to leak soon after you left. They've moved you to the part–timers' offices. The part–timers were eliminated. Pick up a new key. Your textbooks are in the mail room. I'll try to find a janitor to help, but if not, start moving yourself." I ran to Administration.

My rule for running at Altamonte is to look down. Pavers were missing. Students pried them up from the paths. Building and Grounds were supposed to make concrete paths. Probably the concrete would go to the new skating rink instead. Sudden impact.

"Rob! I didn't see you coming."

"You were looking at your feet." Ferrell stared at my sneaks. His shoes were fine Italian loafers.

"I stayed in Rome another week," I said. "My office is an archaeological dig. Leaky pipes. I'm moving to the part–timers' room." Was that a signal?

"Spacious digs, those. We unloaded part–timers in languages. That O'Connor guy was just the first." Rob's eyes gleamed. Was he insinuating that I was next? Nonsense. I was tenured.

"I have to pick up a new key, so excuse me, Rob." Surprisingly, he fell into step, a slower one that obliged me to walk.

"You'll need help moving. I'll lend a hand." I felt uneasy with the old, charming Ferrell. Helpful. Concerned. Why? I got my new key. The move, short, was a diagonal across the hall–next to Molly's office.

In Buzby, Rob hung his jacket in my new closet. He moved fifteen boxes of books. He filled four bookcases near my new desk, chosen for its view of the quad–tall trees, green lawns, a fountain for a centerpiece.

At one o'clock–he put on his jacket. "Sorry to leave, Candy, but I have a meeting. I'll be here at nine tomorrow so you'll be in good shape for opening day." Was this the Ferrell who hadn't invited me and my friends to his Milan "party?" And why the "Candy" again? What mixed messages Rob sent!

I started transferring items into my desk's top drawer–scissors, note paper, envelopes, scotch tape–all you need for teaching except knowledge. I put my Smith Corona on a small table near the desk. How had Renaissance authors written books? Feather pens and lamp black was how.

Finished, I felt the same satisfaction I had when six, rearranging my pencil box. I breathed in the heady scent newly varnished floors! I found colored folders "lost" in my old cupboard. Into a file cabinet they went to be filled with whatever teachers receive besides disappointment.

I opened the lower drawer, (an oak desk, navy surplus) dropping more folders between wooden slats. The drawer above was empty, but I couldn't get my binder paper to slide in. I reached back and drew out a notebook, bound in purple taffeta, on whose glowing cover was an embossed gold cross with IHS in raised letters; below, S.J., Society of Jesus. This must have been Father O'Connor's. Ian said he'd disappeared. I checked inside for an address. Finding none, I tossed it into my briefcase. The binder paper slid in easily now.

Heading for Safeway, O'Connor's first name popped into my head: Sean. Father Sean O'Connor. I could see his face, reddish hair, green eyes; arched eyebrows, and beautifully shaped mouth that I had once, to my shame, wondered if any woman but his mother had ever kissed?

We never talked. Our schedules differed. He had his first class in classics at eight A.M. I rarely arrived before 9:30. Sometimes, I watched him walk swiftly across campus, where he seldom appeared. I saw him once in the hall and think I said "Good Morning, Father." Did he nod?

He arrived before his first class and left immediately after, which was the same hour as my first, and in a different building. Molly told me he taught in a parochial school and studied at Cal. Dr. Moss, our Chairman, told me his General recalled him for teaching bawdy literature–Ovid, Petronius. Juvenal, Terence. Lost to us, then. His notebook got buried under my handouts, books.

School started. I decorated my huge office. I found armchairs in campus storage, a hassock. A floor lamp. I could read away from the windows. Views made me dream of Italy. Wes. I put a small table beside my reading chair; a used Indian rug under the coffee table Mom had never liked. Now, I could invite Molly for tea. I had an old electric kettle; four cups and saucers from Mom's old set, with matching sugar bowl, creamer. Plastic spoons. Troubled students could bend my ear and sip tea. *Tea and Sympathy.*

I hoped Prof. Moravia was right about my Cal prospects. I recalled our Pisa conversation and waited. I waited for Wes's calls, very frequent. I put the phone down wet. We were both so lonely.

On Friday, Ferrell "knocked me up" as the Brits say, "Just to see how your office looks. You've done wonders here." Then, he left. The second week, on Thursday, he strode in without knocking. Since I was pouring myself tea, I poured him a cup, which he swiftly drained. I poured him another, waiting for him to speak. He stirred his sugar swiftly.

"I–ah–wondered... if we might–you and me– have dinner, Candida? You don't have to say yes or no now."

I said nothing. He fled then, mumbling how well I looked in yellow. My new used cashmere cardigan was yellow. A good color on me? Not really. Was a dinner date with Rob a good idea? Not really. He never referred to this subject again.

A month later a call came from the new Chairman of Romance Languages at Cal, Dr. R. Murtree. I had never met him before. He had called to confirm that the search committee for an Associate Professor of Italian Literature was considering my candidacy. Could I come for an interview? My latest articles raised "provocative questions of rhetorical style," influenced by little known writers. I was one of three candidates. I asked for a Wednesday date, so that I need skip only one class, French I. When so informed, that class cheered.

The next Wednesday, I dressed for fall. It was still warm out, but I could not wear a limp summer outfit. I got a professional haircut in Palo Alto. Fifty dollars. I wore a navy suit–wool– and a white blouse. Since I had no class, I stayed home until eleven, then left on highway 237 for highway 17 which took me into Berkeley. I parked on Haste, and strolled along Telegraph Ave. Crossing Bancroft, I passed under Sather Gate, the University's main entrance. Its shadow cooled my sweating body, a coolness that recalled Signor Beppo, for some reason.

The interview was set for Wheeler hall, third floor. Still over an hour away. I bought milk and a tuna sandwich at the Student Union, and ate outside. I wanted to clear my mind as I filled my stomach. Suddenly, a handsome fellow in a striped shirt, blue jeans and sneakers stopped at my table.

"Professor Darroway! You here! You don't remember me, do you? I'm Sean O'Connor. I taught..."

"Classics at Altamonte," I finished. Your name has come up. No one knows how to find you. Are you enrolled at Cal? Your clothes. They're–different." He laughed. His green eyes sparkled. Two emeralds under long, dark eyelashes.

"I left the Order. Wasn't cut out for the Society. The faith. I converted to Rome at Princeton; baptized Episcopalian. Celibacy wears. Obedience ossifies. I'm teaching in a Lutheran prep school in the city. Working on my doctorate in classics here. Passed my orals in June. My dissertation's on Petronius, *"arbiter elegantiae"* in Nero's court. That's what Tacitus called him."

Hmmm. An arbiter of elegance might not approve of Good–Will outfits like mine. "Arbiter of elegant language?" I asked, still thinking about my suit.

"Of everything," O'Connor laughed. "Petronius loved luxury; criticized the poor for loving it, and wrote satires to differentiate between pleasure lovers. He knew about luxury, once proconsul, then governor of Bithynia. If I finish by next year, they'll hire me. Meanwhile, I moved back into my parents' little place on Nob Hill. And you? Still at Altamonte?"

"Yes, but I have a job interview at 1:30 in Wheeler Hall. I have a crack at an associate professorship. I couldn't be more surprised."

"I'm not. I've read your articles. All of them." How odd. While trying to think how my work related to his–and too nervous to think straight–O'Connor continued.

"I read your book on Boccaccio, too. Awful cover. Great material." I explained that the editor, Don Hicks, would have annoyed his *arbiter elegantiae*. We both laughed.

"I think he was after my bod," I added reflectively.

"Why on earth *wouldn't* he be? You've a great..um.. presence, Candida. And mind. I'm sure he noticed. I did. Could I have your phone number?" Well. This ex-Jesuit was no shrinking violet. Molly would call him a "stud."

"Look," I said, "It would be a good idea if you would write *your* phone number and address down. Dr. Moss is clueless. Ian MacDonald, a Princeton classmate, mentioned you this summer. He'd like to keep in touch. He recently married a nun from Grace Cathedral, and he's local; lives off of Fell Street."

"Old Ian? Kind of a stuffed shirt. But good for him. And her. Oh, dash it. I don't have a shred of paper on me."

"Wait," I said, diving into my brief case. I felt the raised cross and drew out the notebook. O'Connor stared.

"Where did you get that?"

"Found it in my desk in the part-timers' room. My old office fell apart. They gave me the whole room, having let all part–timers go. Kept their desks, though."

We laughed.

"You chose the one overlooking the fountain," he stated.

"Yours?"

"Yep. Best view. We're both aesthetes." How would *he* know?

"Find anything in it?" Both his dark eyebrows raised slightly. I stared. Wes would have raised just one.

"Just this notebook." I held it out to him. Want it? He shook his head.

"Standard Army issue, I mean, the Order's. You've read St. Ignatius's quotations?" I had read a couple.

"Read the last page," he suggested.

"The last page?" I looked. "It's empty."

"The *very* last page," he prompted. It was a gold end-paper. Not to be written on. But something *was* written on its reverse, at the bottom.

"I am falling in love with Candida Abigail Darroway." My God! I hadn't *seen* this. I looked up, flustered.

"How could you have fallen in love with her? I mean, with me?" Stammering now. "We didn't..we never.. did we? ..spoke.. "You meant.. symbolically?"

"No, the way a man usually falls for a woman. I felt I was cut out for *you*, not the priesthood. But the few times I lingered in the hall outside your office, I ran off instead. A Catholic girl at Princeton wouldn't date me because I wasn't Catholic. I showed her. I converted. Then I snookered her. I got ordained." I've built up more nerve since leaving Altamonte, the Order." I could tell.

"I'm not Catholic or Episcopalian now; just a humanist, or a scamp–like Petronius." I looked again at the inscription. It continued in tiny print: "Candida would never be attracted to me. Mortal sin? Mortal longing." I felt dizzy. Speechless. O'Connor pulled up a chair next to mine.

"Here." He grabbed the notebook, tore out a jagged half page and wrote his phone number and his parents' address on it, the small place on Nob Hill. *Sean Lester O'Connor*. Born San Francisco, April, 29, 1939." I noted that he was two years older than me.

"Now yours, please." I scribbled my own information on the remainder of the page. "Candida Abigail Darroway. Born San Jose, *O'Connor* Hospital, San Jose, Dec. 6, 1941." I added my office number at Altamonte and for some reason, my home phone number. Both pieces fit like a jigsaw puzzle. When he saw the name of the hospital, his eyes widened. Emerald pools.

"No kidding? *O'Connor*? Gee! Linked since your birth."

"Yes, Along with ten thousand other babies and a notebook," I joked. "Who keeps it?"

"Finders keepers!" he grinned. "It's yours with my blessing. Sorry. An old habit, giving my blessing." He blushed.

"I have to run, Sean. My interview is in fifteen minutes." He ran with me. We charged up the path and veered left. At Wheeler's entrance, he blew me a kiss.

"For luck– and love," he yelled, running down toward Sather Gate as if it were his ultimate destination.

My interview went well. There were four members of the department, from only one of whom I had taken courses, Prof. Moravia–Romance linguistics. Antonio gave me a hug before I sat down before them, a bit embarrassing. The Chair, Prof. Roswell Murtree, I'd not met before. His specialty was twentieth century novels. Two other members of the Italian faculty were also new hires. Antonio was the only prof I still knew, and he was about to retire. One of the new scholars, Gianni something, was interested in early modern poetry, eighteenth, and the other, Roberto DiMarco was in nineteenth century drama. They really needed a person for the late medieval period to the seventeenth century. They had read all my articles, and admired my dissertation, now book on Boccaccio's platitudes. Murtree asked if I could handle twentieth century novels should the need arise, and, he assured me glumly, it would.

"Could you?" I nodded.

"I know many works by modern novelists," I announced, not immodestly.

"Which authors?" asked Murtree, suspiciously.

"Oh, Moravia, Antonio's cousin. Plus Calvino, Sciascia, Levi, Chiara, Fenoglio, Soldati, Ginsberg, Tomizza, Pratolini, Pasolini, Vegevano, Fallaci, Bacchelli, Silone, Ortega, Verde…..a few others. But these are the ones I read most often. I teach my language students the rhetoric and modern vocabulary of today's Italian. My mother and grandmother were Italian. I've spoken Italian all my life." A small lie (*una piccola bugia*), since there *had* been a gap after my parents' divorce. They didn't need to know that. "We wouldn't want beginning Italian students to speak like Boccaccio, would we?" I asked.

They laughed, impressed that I was a native speaker. Or if not, damn close.There were few questions I later remembered them asking.

"We have your 'oeuvre,'" Dr. Murtree said, after little more than forty minutes. "We'll get in touch."

We shook hands. I ducked into the ladies' room and watched them leave through a small window. They looked like toy soldiers, from this third floor level as they headed toward the library. I opened my purse to find Sean's name and phone number. Was this interview or that one more significant?

Sean phoned fifteen minutes after I got home.

"Candida? I play for keeps. If you consent to go out with me, it's fair to warn you that I will propose marriage. I have given this a lot of thought."

"O'Connor, did you give as much to turning Catholic? Becoming a Jesuit? You left me two hours ago. How much thought *could* you have given this? Are you as thoughtful writing your dissertation?" I was ribbing him. He laughed.

"Have dinner with me tomorrow in the City. You'll see." I took his meaning. Late night out in the city, but my habitation in Alviso? That meant staying overnight in the city, and that meant—well, I wasn't ready for what it meant. Rob had tried that one last year. And I was in love already. With Wes.

"O'Connor, let's not rush in where angels, etc. We might dine in San Mateo, out on Coyote point? We'll have a Bay view, a city view. Then you to Nob Hill; me to Alviso. We'll get to know each other better—but not yet as well as I think you're thinking."

Cautious Candida. I could hardly even think of dating this classicist without Wes's face before me—hazel eyes, *one* raised eyebrow. I saw him across the miles. I knew I must tell him about this.

We dined that Saturday night on Coyote Point, across 101 from San Mateo. The restaurant, a lodge with a grotto pool at its entrance was dramatic; its Bay view, more so. The sun was setting when I arrived. He was waiting in the parking lot, in a new dark green Cadillac Seville. He pulled me inside and kissed me.

I pulled away. "That's dessert; not the main course," I told him, suddenly breathless. We admired the grotto on our way to the entrance.

From our table we watched young men on wind sails swooping toward shore, their backs lit by the last rays of light, nylon suits iridescent. City lights came on. Broiled salmon swam across our table. Our wine glasses sparkled. Finally, dessert. *Tira missù* and espresso. And something else. Sean was pushing a small blue velvet box toward me with a teaspoon. Very slowly. When it neared my wine glass, I opened it. A large sapphire sparkled on a platinum band. I raised it to the candles. It radiated light. I put it back in the box without trying it on.

"Maybe one day; not now," I said gently. "Your feelings seem genuine. But we're total strangers. Remember how you fell in love with a spiritual ideal that did not fit your needs? It's as easy to mistake a physical ideal for an ideal reality." He was amused.

"You think that if I made one error, I'm error prone? That last girl did not find me suitable. I've tasted love before, though. Still, I will wait for *your* taste to change. You like things that match, I've noticed. Well, you and I match. You don't see it yet. But you will." We left the restaurant with spinning heads and hearts.

Two lunches in San Francisco. Ghirardelli Square. Union Square. I asked about his parents; told him about mine.

"My parents are great," Sean enthused. "Mom will love you. Dad will see my sister in you. She died of leukemia. I've already talked to them of you."

Two lunches in Half Moon Bay; two in Sausalito. Then, an invitation to dine in his parents' home; to stay overnight. My bedroom on the second floor was across from his parents.' Sean had a small apartment on the third floor, under the eaves, a former maids' quarters. His parents were wealthy. They were staking us to our revels, paying for his tuition, his dinners out.

The "little place" on Nob Hill had sixteen rooms and a finished basement. Sean's three rooms on the third floor were cozy. His sitting room had a converted gas log fireplace. His kitchen was big enough for two on a do–si–do basis. His tub was circa 1915, re-porcelainized, claw legs. From his balcony, views of Sausalito, the Golden Gate.

"Candida," he said, "My parents want grandchildren. They only have me, now. Be prepared. Dad whispered how beautiful you were; Mom was impressed by your new position at Cal. All this while you were stowing your gear in the guest room—which I swore not to enter. But don't let them make up your mind for you. Make it up for yourself. And when you do, choose me! Marry me!" Heady wine.

I turned to descend his staircase. Sean caught my arm and turned me toward him. He kissed me long and ardently, one arm traveling from down my back to my rear end, which he squeezed–softly.

I shivered. "Choose me for your Valentine?" Easy. But "Choose me for Life?" Hard. In the library his parents were waiting. His mother, Sybil, was a talented water colorist. Sean Sr., an older version of Sean, white haired, handsome. Sybil walked me down the corridor, one arm around my shoulder, to show me her watercolors. She exhibited in two galleries. She knew Rob, Maria Pellatierra.

We returned to the library and toasted "Happiness." Sean added, "With Candida Abigail Darroway O'Connor." I spilled champagne on my 'new' dress then. His parents asked about my work; what in Italy pleased me most; the group. They couldn't ask what I thought of Sean. They asked about my family, instead. I gave a hasty outline. Sean Sr. knew my Dad professionally. They'd been on opposite sides of two court cases. They watched Sean straighten a lock of my hair that kept falling over my eye; watched as I reached up to touch his hand when he did.

Sybil reminded me of Teresa, without Teresa's wild enthusiasm. Sean Senior had a determined quality. Lawyers were determined. He listened carefully, asked follow-up questions, weighed my answers about Renaissance art, literature, the tour group. Was he thinking, "Had you a lover on that tour?" Lawyers are usually steps ahead of witnesses.

Seated at the dining room table, Sean's father asked, "Are you French, Candida? You look it."

"My father's ancestor was Voltaire: *de Arouet* became Darroway. On the maternal side, Jewish: Goldsmith. In Italian, Orefice. "My maternal grandparents were refugees from Lucca before World War II. In the sixteenth century they had to leave Castile. Before that, who knows? Morocco? Syracuse? Canaan? Ur? Arabia?"

"Eden!" Sybil interjected. "Home of the only perfect woman before the Fall."

"Mom, there *was* only one then. And she was *almost* perfect, like you." Sean said. Sybil knew Sean handled her well.

"In love, certainly?" asserted Sean Sr. "Adam and Eve *were* lovers."

"Adam wasn't perfect, but lovable, Sean. I know, being your wife." Sybil had a dry sense of humor.

Her son quipped, "Adam and Eve were *made* for each other, Mom." He gave me a meaningful look.

"Your forebears, Candida, were surely brave, sensitive, sensible. Look how you turned out," said Sean Senior. Gallant. I suddenly saw him at Sean's age, a young lawyer, becoming rich, a man of parts, less impetuous than his son, but as determined. Sean had his dad's good looks; not his lawyerly calculation.

The dinner, shrimp cocktails; leg of lamb with Franconia potatoes baked in butter; baby green beans; salad; lemon meringue pie. Everything was superb. Sybil made it all herself.

Afterwards, while Sean helped his mother clear, his father walked me into the living room, a noble room, in yellow wall paper with a tiny print. A huge fireplace. On the mantel, lovely glass objects. Above, a portrait in oils of Sean's sister, who, except for her hair color, looked less like Sean, and remarkably like me. The painting, by a famous local artist, pulled together everything of beauty in the room.

"This was Anne's favorite room," Mr. O'Connor said quietly. "She was something like Sean, but more restrained. Rather like you in temperament, looks. And a gifted pianist." I gazed at the giant Steinway at the room's end. I could only play "chopsticks."

"She died at twenty-five, four years ago. Leukemia. Engaged, not yet married. A beautiful young woman, like you." How flattering to be compared with her. Then, abruptly, "Well, do you think you can love my son?" I was taken aback by a question so ...roundly put.

"I don't know yet, Mr. O'Connor. I have things to sort out."

"Well, sort away. Sean is not the most patient man, but the most persistent. He will give you time; his notion of it, anyway."

Sean and Sybil entered the living room. I was about to sit by the fire. "Not there. By me," said Sean, and before I could sit, added:

"That's Mom's chair. We'll do the love seat. It's only right." When I went for one end of it, he pulled me toward the center tucking his arm around my waist. And so we sat in the middle, hip to hip, as last summer I had sat in the Hotel Principi beside Wes.

"I must say, you two look handsome together," said Sybil, smiling. "You match, somehow. Candida, the next time you come to dinner, we might have my parents in. They've heard so much about you from Sean. Now, as for your mattress. We have several guest rooms. I chose the medium firm one for you. But there's one that quite firm, and a pillow top that Sean's dad thought too soft. We want you to get to know us and our guest room mattresses very well."

Sean said, "Mom, my mattress would be perfect for her. You know you put her across the hall to keep me away."

Sybil, said humorously, "No, dear, to keep you safe from Candida." We all laughed, though I knew I was blushing.

I looked at Sean questioningly. "You told your parents you want to marry me, did you?"

"I did; I do, I will. Like Caesar. 'I came, I saw, I conquered.' But take your time. You'll come around."

We adjourned to the library, for liqueurs. They were educated people, and we talked of many different things. I liked them very much. At half past eleven, Sybil hugged me, and took me up the stairs. I could hear Sean's Dad say, "She's so like Anne." I slept deeply, dreaming that Wes was stroking my forehead, before he tiptoed from the room.

After breakfast, I thanked my hosts for their warm hospitality. I said, "I know Sean is very special, very solid and tender, too."

"He is all that, my dear," said Sybil, hugging me." I think you are quite alike." Sean's dad kissed both my cheeks.

"After all, you are French and Italian," he joked. "It's only right."

Wes had left a message on my phone. "Candida, call me. I'm lonesome for you." I washed my face and hands, loathe to contaminate Wes, the phone, my conscience. I called and blurted out the Sean part. I'd already told him of my Cal hire. I cried. I sniffed. I said,"I love *you*. I don't know what to do."

"I'll tell you, then. Marry Sean. He will make you happy. Pregnant. He is your age. Has a great family. Don't regret our three weeks of love. We will cherish our memories. Just don't talk of them to Sean. He's too young. Be happy. And, Candida, darling, whatever happens, I will always love you. Should anything go wrong, which it won't, I'm here." Then he hung up.

Molly called. Matt had proposed. A November wedding. November. Next month. Would I be Maid of Honor? Of course. I was so happy for her.

"What color dress?" I asked.

447

"Lavender or blue. You choose. Stop by my office tomorrow. I'll show you." I chose pale blue, a separate top, a separate skirt–a re-usable outfit in *crepe de chine* and satin that would see me through parties, dances, dinners out.

Several days later at Cal, where I would start to teach in January–Altamonte had been nice about letting me out of my contract–police swarmed the campus. There had been rumors of a radical student demonstration at Sproul Hall. Shades of the 60s. Now, all was quiet. Sean and I were to meet at the Union. Barely seated, I spotted Allison Rollins, walking by, with a backpack of books. She appeared out of shape.

"Allison! Come join me. I'm glad to see you." She stopped, hurried over, breathing hard. She shucked off the heavy backpack, and hugged me. Her lovely skin was mottled. She had gained much weight since August.

"What are you studying?" I asked.

"Psychology," she said in answer to my first question. And to the unasked second, "I'm nearly five months pregnant." I told her about my new job. Then I asked.

"Who is the baby's father?"

"Ian, who else? Remember that night in Trastevere when Ian and I dressed in civies and danced in the restaurant's garden? Well, we wound up in bed. Just once. At the Principi. Our first and only night of love."

"Your first night," I echoed mindlessly. "But how will you manage studies and child-rearing? Ian married Agatha, after all."

"Oh, I'm going on for a doctorate. I'm not for traditional marriage. I'm giving the baby to Aunt Agatha, and 'Uncle' Ian to adopt. They're mad for a child, and my aunt is pushing fifty. This kid is related to the three of us. But I'll be its 'aunt.'" She had to run to a class, but thanked me for the chat.

"Let's do lunch some day, I called out." But she was too far ahead now to hear. Sean arrived. "Who was that girl?" he asked.

"One of our tourists. She was a postulant at Grace Cathedral," I added. Sean needn't feel that he was the only one who had fallen from a spiritual niche.

"Sorry I'm late. The police wanted everyone in Dwinelle Hall to talk to them about any suspicious students. I didn't have any suspicions, so I didn't take long to question. The students I know aren't protesting anything but the cost of pot."

Sean was a T.A., teaching two classes for a pittance while writing his dissertation; cheap labor. His Teaching Assistantship slowed his dissertation. But he was so smart. It was half done. He would finish and be hired, I was certain. We talked about how nice it might be to have a house, two jobs, a baby. I had not committed myself, though. Still considering. We ate pecan pie. At four o'clock, I hit highway 17 with scads of essays to correct.

Two days later, Anita called. She and Reed were marrying in January. Would I be her bridesmaid? She had chosen maroon and blue velvet for the bridesmaids, five of each. Which color would suit me better?

"Maroon for me, Anita. Thank you for asking me." Anita was on cloud 9. She said that Officer Bianco had informed her that the monk who had tried to rape her had been sent to a clerical rehabilitation facility and was no longer at Assisi. She felt vindicated.

What with Molly's wedding and Anita's, and Anne and Arnold's in Boston, which I couldn't attend, I had present shopping to do. Perhaps Sean would help. Even if men were poor shoppers, they were good at carrying stuff. We could do lunch later. I started counting up the couples from the trip who had or would soon marry–Agatha and Ian; done deal. Molly and Matt; Anita and Reed; Anne and Arnold next week. I thought of Wes and felt sad. But he had advised me to marry Sean. Even if I had not agreed to it yet. Four weddings resulting from our tour to Italy.

I did all my shopping before Molly's wedding. I mailed my gift to Anne and Arnold; a plug-in food warmer. Sean was good at shopping. He scooped me up with the other presents; that is, he proposed–again. I accepted. The blue sapphire sparkled on my second left finger. It was so big everybody thought it was costume jewelry. Like Matilda's ruby. Five weddings then. Just not with Wes.

We were married in a Unitarian Church in San Francisco on Valentine's Day, 1974. The guests included the two most recently married couples, plus Agatha and Ian. Molly hoped no one could tell she was expecting. She was just past her second month, and no one could. Matt treated her like a glass *object d'art*. Mindy and Jonah, Myrna and Barry, the Pellatierras, who knew Sean's parents. Meg and Peg came, each dressed differently. Teresa was my Matron of Honor. Arnold and Anne flew in from Boston bearing an an eighteenth century coffee service: a pot, eight cups and saucers, and eight spoons. Arnold said it was one of his family's sets, an authenticated Paul Revere. Priceless. I hoped they hadn't been offended at my food warming tray, but Anne said they used it every night, the only gift she had found useful.

Sean's best man was his first cousin, Brian O'Connor, and Brian's five year old son, Dickey, our ring bearer. Dickey's twin sisters, age seven, wore blue tulle and pink rose crowns; our flower girls. My bridesmaids were Anita, Molly, Myrna, Mindy and Allison, now at the end of her seventh month.

When they objected that they couldn't be, being married or pregnant, I said "Nonsense." If one waited to marry until thirty-three (I turned 33 in November), bridesmaids wouldn't be virgins. By the time I had graduated high school, virginity was a rare commodity, of which I had cornered the market. The Pill became popular when I was in my late twenties. I'd been on it for six years, but stopped taking it the night I accepted Sean's proposal. Ian kept a proud eye on Allison's belly. I wanted a baby, too.

Dad gave me away, although in some ways, before marriage. My Mother and Jim and my step-siblings, sat next to Sybil and Sean's Father on the family side of the aisle. Dad and Chérie sat behind Mom and Jim.

I invited Ferrell, after some soul-searching, but he declined. He knew Andrea and Maria Pellatierra, even Sybil, and Sean Sr. through their art connections. He knew the the tour group members who attended. But he refused the invitation. I was relieved.

The Unitarian Minister, who knew nobody, was perfectly scripted to do a wedding for strangers. He waxed philosophical about marriage, life, love. He was pleased that Sean and I were humanists, for humanism, "fostered the life principle." He spoke of the "perilous state of our Republic," our "abhorrence of wars"—the last Viet Nam soldiers pulled out last March. He spoke of the "need for community organization" and "giving up carbon burning engines." There were gas lines everywhere, people filling up according to the last digit on their license plate. He urged us to "communicate" with each other, to "write to friends regularly." He pondered how "art and literature created stronger marital bonds, a nurturing community." He was a regular Ralph Waldo Emerson, I thought. No mention of God; just peace, art, brotherhood.

My wedding veil made my nose itch. Would I sneeze? I didn't. Weddings provided the means for fighting: *boy babies became soldiers*, I thought. At last, "Emerson" said:

"If you are tempted by lust for others, a 'Lust for Life' can strengthen marriage. In the name of the one Universal Principle, I now pronounce you man and wife. "You may kiss the bride." Sean lifting my veil, found me laughing, so ours was a French kiss. I hoped no one noticed.

Dinner for one hundred people at the Fairmont; the Lawrence Welk band played. Sean's Dad insisted on paying for it while mine, less wealthy, paid for the bridal party clothing, church hall, flowers and gifts for the wedding party members. Dad bought a wooden fire truck for Dickey, and the flower girls got ballet outfits, for they were beginning lessons.

We honeymooned in nearby Carmel. We had taken but three days off and the week-end and so made do with five days. I think much of the time we spent in bed at a lovely inn. We ate, walked along the ocean, and stared at the seals just long enough to give the maid a chance to change the bed linen. We promised ourselves a longer honeymoon when Sean's dissertation was completed–perhaps by July.

Both fathers paid the down payment on our house near the Berkeley School for the deaf. A large, clapboard structure, built in 1915. It needed work. Over the next four years we replaced sinks, flooring, wallboard, hot water heaters, a furnace, roof, windows, the porch. I kept the kitchen cupboards–so quaint–and clawed bathtub. Sybil came often and painted pastoral scenes on bedroom walls, in bathrooms, on wooden chests. She hung swags of lovely fabric over windows, and made heavy drapes on her sewing machine–set up in our dining room for convenience–for windows we needed to close.

Sean finished his doctorate in June and was hired as Assistant Professor in Classics. But what kept us busiest, was Lester. Lester, conceived on our honeymoon, made his eight and one half pound, twenty-three inch appearance in early November, 1974. His hair was red, eyes green–a true O'Connor. He was impetuous in his love for my breast (like his father), and entranced by everyone who dangled a toy before him. He was smarter than other babies, and much was expected of him. His diapers proved how much. Lester was an old O'Connor name. I knew it would turn into Les, which rhymed with…Oh, well. His second name, David, was Dad's name.

Little Les grew stronger and longer. When he turned three, Sean was promoted to Associate Professor, for publishing his first book. It got excellent reviews. We taught, gave speeches at conventions. Sybil and Mom proved willing babysitters, though on an every day basis, Les entered a nursery school at two and a half. A year later, he was attending one of Berkeley's premier pre-schools. The weekends were devoted to him. Hardly had we consumed his third birthday cake, when Sean said to me: "Don't you think we should start working on a new research project? A sibling for Les?"

I was wary, since we were already so busy. But wasn't that why I'd married this lothario of the linen? I was nearly thirty-seven. It was now or never. Why not push the envelope–my uterus?

I took the old bug (new transmission) to school each morning after dropping Les off at pre-school. Sean preferred biking to work. He always wore his helmet, because I insisted. We lived on Claremont, up over College, where it stops at Derby. To get to school Sean pedaled down Derby; turned right on Piedmont, left on Bancroft and down to Sather Gate. The tenth of February, 1978, dawned wet and cold. The fog was heavy.

"Sean, you'd better ride with us in the car. It's opaque out there," I called down the stairwell. But he had eaten a bagel, had his coffee, and left. He liked to review his notes in his quiet office before his first class at 9 A.M. It was 7:45 now. I gave Les his breakfast–apple juice, cocoa puffs with skim milk and a banana. He loved "banas," the only word he pronounced incorrectly. I think he did it to prove how normal he was. His teachers loved him. I had oatmeal, coffee, and orange juice. I threw two yogurts and an apple into a paper bag for lunch. I rarely lunched out. A bag lunch saved time for home life. By eight o'clock I reached my office. Dr. Murtree and my two colleagues from the Italian department were huddled outside my door.

"Oh, don't tell me I have a plumbing leak." A leak had brought Sean into my life. Funny, never thought of it like that before. I had my key in my hand. Murtree took it and opened my door for me. My colleagues followed us in. Odd.

"Candida, sit down," Murtree, said. Roberto DiMarco and Gianni Signorelli stood one on each side of me one hand on each shoulder. Then Gianni, who was six feet five, squatted down to look straight into my eyes.

"Candida, there's been an accident." I stared.

"What? A shooting on campus? Campanile jumper? What?"

"Sean. He was struck by a pick-up truck opposite Sather Gate. The truck swung through the corner red light. Sean flew over the handle bars and hit his head on the curb near the Gate. He died instantly, in all probability. A male nurse heading for Hearst Gym to teach a course in life saving tried artificial respiration for thirty minutes. They called 911. It was too late."

Sean's funeral was held in the Unitarian church where we were married almost five years ago. The minister, grown fond of Sean, gave a touching eulogy. I left Les with a neighbor. I could not bring him to his Dad's funeral. Sybil, Dad O'Connor, my parents, friends–came to give support, but when you lose a young husband, best friend, lover and young son's daddy, there's not much to give.

An in ground burial is ghastly, but Sean, preferring cremation, said that if something happened, his parents would need a place to lay flowers. The site was next to his sister's. When I reached home, the baby sitter was playing with Les in the family room. Sybil and Dad O'Connor moved in the next day, with suitcases. They stayed for two weeks, Sean's dad commuting to San Francisco work each day, returning each night. Sybil never left my side. We cried, spoke of Sean, hugged Les. At the end of two weeks, I sent them home. I had "to do it for myself," as Pete Seeger sang.

Those first weeks Les asked about Daddy every hour. Since the "research project" didn't happen, Less would be a fatherless, only child. But when he saw Sean's favorite chair, he patted and kissed it, saying "I love you, big Daddy."

CHAPTER XXVI

LOSERS KEEPERS

Sean's death and Les's life were for months my only realities. I found research and writing, teaching, seminars, grad students–surreal. I was excused from committee work. Dr. Murtree thought being an Associate Prof. and a widowed mother sufficed.

I lost weight; worked spasmodically on *Mandragola*. I ate out of jars, cans, "cooking" mostly for Les–hamburgers, macaroni and cheese, drumsticks, scrambled eggs, Campbell's tomato soup laced with frozen vegetables for vitamins. I stopped drinking wine, unless Sean's folks invited me to dinner; Mom and Jim took me out; Dad and Chérie brought a bottle over. I visited Teresa for Easter. Sybil took Les.

Teresa, shocked when she saw me, said "Eat. (*Mangia*). You're *Waiting for Godot*, and he isn't coming." I sobbed.

"Candida, honey, you'll get sick. Sybil cannot raise Les, much as she might like to. You're his mom." Teresa. A surgeon, excising a malignancy, supervising recovery. Her prescription?

"Start dating. Start. You're thirty-seven. Beautiful. Les needs a father. Plenty of bachelors long for someone like you, and would adore Les. Get with it."

"How's Tony?" I asked.

"His Cajun girl friend dropped him for a trucker. I told him the same. 'Start dating' you handsome engineer." Just promoted manager of his oil rig. He has lots to offer. But not to you. Pity, being Irish-Italian. Like little Les." We looked at each other a longish moment.

"Damn, Candida. I'd call him now if he *were* right for you. But Tony's no scholar." We cooked Sicilian; Teresa, a countess whose mother was a princess, and had urged me to join the dynasty.

"Sweetie, titles don't matter when you have to let four ranch hands go because foreign garlic is selling cheaper than Gilroy's. Cheap labor. Oh. how I hate it. Oh, how I need it." We laughed. Ate. I gained three pounds.

Sybil had Les all week. She took him to an egg-roll, a bunny ballet; the Cathedral's tot center. He dyed eggs. She bought him a female rabbit in a huge cage, placed in our back hall. Les fed his pet carrots. Jelly beans. He named her "Sean." I wept.

"Her name is Shana, Les. This rabbit's a girl." Les called her "Shana" when I was around; otherwise, "Sean."

The Midwest Language Association met in Cincinnati after Easter. Murtree left a phone message. "Candida. I gave your next week's classes to Gianni and Roberto. I'm sending you to Cincinnati, business class. You leave Sunday, 16 April, 10:30 A.M. Oakland, via Dallas. You arrive 6:00 P.M. Cincinnati. Back home Thursday. I had a call from Prof. Ike Jansen, Marquette. One of his presenters had a nervous breakdown. I volunteered you to speak on *Mandragola*. Call me a.s.a.p."

I wouldn't go. He couldn't send me off in three days without a speech. I had a book in progress, not a speech, for crying out loud. Midterms neared. I had obligations to students. They needed me. No. I needed them. I phoned "Murt."

"Dr. Murtree? Candida. I will not be given this…this bum's rush to speak before a convention I hadn't planned on. Am I a sack of grain to toss to the winds?" Murtree grew up on an Iowa hog farm.

"No," he said. "A woman grieving; on the edge of a breakdown. Can't be more diagnostic. Gianni and Roberto will take your classes. Get out in front of the lit crowd again. You're wasting away. Literally, literarily. Ike pledged to take you to great Italian restaurants. Cincinnati's the Rome of the Midwest. They'll fatten you up." Murtree, the hog farmer.

"Candida, you need to do this." In the background, his teenage daughter yelled, exasperatedly, "Daddy. Get off the phone already."

Hurriedly, Murtree added, "Be brilliant. Have a good trip."

Sybil picked Les up three days early so that I could write a speech. I sat up late two nights slapping it up; trying to reach conclusions consistent with *The Prince,* where corrupt practices were accepted, providing public safety was preserved. If corruption caused suffering, but saved the state, then no law, God's or man's, mattered. The prince, however brutal, was an o.k. guy. I couldn't work in Machiavelli's *Discourses* since in that work the people legislated, not the prince. In *Mandragola*, a popular comedy (1518), the clergy were particularly corrupt. How to explain such dark comedy to an audience who might not have read it? Or worse, might have?

Sybil returned with Les and drove me to Oakland airport Sunday morning. She managed him well, as she had his daddy. He was dead. Les lived. Me too, partly. Sybil knew everything about Les now. How to cook for and read to him. She looked ten years younger. I, ten older. Soon we'd look the same age.

I kissed Les, hugged Sybil, left weeping. No one goes to Cincinnati. In the business class lounge I ate a bran muffin with milk. I was ravenous on board. I re-read my speech eating cashew chicken with rice. My paper looked okay, even if plastered together from half of an unfinished study.

I'd never visited Cincinnati, but had heard about the Netherlands Plaza, a famous *Art Déco* landmark, near city center. I thought of Italy, Wes. Travel stimulates memory. Four years ago? More. I had repressed memories of him since Sean. I never wore his necklace. It was with me now, though. Hidden in my purse. How much freer female sexuality was today, in 1978, than in 1973. My female students filled me in. They shopped in S.F.; drank espresso on Columbus Ave.; went disco dancing at night clubs. Smoked pot. Drank Chianti. Talked of 'freaking-out' like crazed hippies. Which they were *not*. They adored progressive jazz. Had I *ever* been progressive? On the Italian tour, yes. I had found love then. And soon afterward, yet again! Now, my heart was in ashes. I *had* progressed to… despair.

The Netherlands Plaza jarred. Metallic bric-a-brac everywhere. Purple, green and fuchsia furniture. A poster advertised a disco band in the ballroom tonight. Not for me. I registered and went to my room on the twenty-ninth floor. Vertigo notwithstanding. There were no lower rooms since I had not registered early.

The elevators were all wood paneled. Fine. Watching myself in a mirrored car for 29 floors would have been humiliating. I had aged eight years in eight months.

My smallish room had just a double bed, a desk, and one easy chair. No *chaise longue*. No lilies. I got vertigo looking out the window. I remembered St. Peter's cupola and fainting from fear. I closed the drapes and looked inward. It was becoming a habit.

Flinging myself on the bed, I slept fully clothed. When I awoke, it was 8:00 P.M. I was wrinkled. Ravenous. The phone flashed three messages. One, Ike Jansen's, Chair of the Machiavelli panel. "Call back upon arrival." I called. No answer. I assured his message taker that I would be there tomorrow.

Sybil, next. "Having fun with Les," she said. Then, "Hi, Mommy. I love you so-o-o much." Sybil ended with "Enjoy yourself, honey." Last, a panel member. I vaguely remembered reading her article on a citizen army. Her name was Something (the recorder crackled) MacIntyre. Her room was no. #710. I dialed. No answer. I left my number, saying I'd meet her for breakfast at 8 A.M. wearing a navy blazer and blue plaid skirt, a reasonable facsimile of my old school uniform.

Going down to dinner, my stomach growled. My slacks were black bell bottoms. Over them, I wore a satin big shirt, pink and lavender. Perhaps I'd be mistaken for the décor. I wore the gold necklace, too—token of a former life. I was more sure of the past then of the future now. The necklace gave me courage, a reminder that my life had not begun with Sean and would not end with him.

I hoped the main lounge would look better at night, but the pink and purple carpet; steel elevator doors; columns holding up nothing– struck me as grotesque. I longed for a softer décor; Rome's *Parco dei Principi*.

Art Déco. An ode to 1920s modernism, machine-made planarity. It featured plastic, chrome, metals; ethnic art, ivory. I thought of Hemingway shooting elephants in Africa amid tropical flora, elephants just targets for "Papa." Art Déco mashed *Art Nouveau* and *Bauhaus* with Cubism. Sun rays morphed into steel beams that could pry up the flooring. *Ouch!*

In a crowded lounge, I felt abandoned. Even Duane Becker would have been welcome. Sean made me forget how to be alone. I wished this were New York. I loved the Empire State Building where Deborah Kerr and Cary Grant failed to meet–and Cary discovered years later an auto accident had incapacitated her. Oh Sean. *Our* incapacity was total, not for endurable time but for all time. *If only you were here*, I thought. But he wouldn't be.

Art Déco, born in 1925 at an international exposition, hyped substances I disliked–Bakelite, forerunner of plastic; *vita-glass*, that lacked the life its Sanskrit name promised. It denigrated classical, neo-classical and nineteenth century materials. It was a kind of modern "statement" that said nothing important or romantic. Well, romance had faded by the 1970s. People were into egocentric passion, not romance. A sexual revolution was in full swing. A convention was palpably erotic. My Italian venture, by contrast, had put a premium on mystery, tenderness, growth.

In the Palm Court's restaurant, I recovered. Greeted by the *maître d'* (headwaiter), I sat under a subdued pastel inlay of artichoke blooms. I liked them, until I noted the same motif repeated at intervals down the whole wall. Silhouetted against this design, I "heard" myself shouting, "Look at me. I'm all alone." I felt a total outcast when my petite filet arrived. I had ordered tomato juice to drink. The salad had a cloying raspberry dressing. *Faux gourmet,* I thought grimly.

The next morning, I met Polly McIntyre, who taught at North Carolina State. She was in her late-twenties, and wore owlish horn–rims. She had a Master's degree, but was working on a doctorate summers–at Duke. I had once done a Montaigne seminar there, taught by a Montaigne scholar, who had accepted a few historians as participants. They never heard of Deconstruction and rejected it as a-historical. Duke was big on Deconstruction.

I read Montaigne's *Essays* there and decided that Deconstruction devalued social, historical, and linguistic backgrounds. Authors, too. Some theories, I thought, could not be proved. Others should not be. Later, I published an essay on the pedagogy of Erasmus and Montaigne, both skeptical humanists. Both scholars aimed at readers' hearts and minds. In that they were positivistic, not skeptical.

Miss MacIntyre left before I finished my coffee, requesting I be at the lecture room early to meet the panel. I noticed her stockings, deep brown, had pale "ladders" down the backs. Would anyone climb them? I hoped so, for her sake. Sartorially, romantically, she needed help.

Once arrived, Polly introduced me to Ike Jansen, panel Chair.

"Hello. I'm Prof. Darroway and will be speaking on *Mandragola.*" Just then I noted a blackboard nearby with my name and the title of my speech chalked on it. By Polly, probably. She was efficient. Was efficiency a substitute for romance?

"Prof. Darroway. So pleased you could join us." Prof. Jansen introduced me around. I was the last of four speakers. Their subjects? War, politics, manufacture. I myself felt unfortified. I had skimmed *The Prince* and the *Discourses*, but wasn't solid on the dynastic and political history of the era. Only the play really appealed to me. Scholarship was piecemeal if one were honest. The point about *Mandragola* is that no one ever was. Honest, not piecemeal.

Jansen mispronounced my first name, saying "Candee' da," not "Can'di da" and called me an Assistant, not an Associate, Professor. At least the board behind him got my rank right. *"Thanks, Polly,"* I thought.

"Mandragola," I began, "is a comedy still performed. It's about longing–for children, sex, money, honors earned and unearned. Its premise is that people know the right thing to do, but do it only when forced, willing, or profitable." Tittering. "In short, this play makes everyone vulnerable to sin, bribery and deceit, while hiding sins too enjoyable to forego." Laughter. Like the tour group when Ferrell lectured.

"Machiavelli concluded: "If one knew how to change one's character as times and circumstances changed, one's luck would never change." Chuckles. My audience interested, I powered on.

"In this play everybody has good luck because they change their character to suit circumstances." Snorts from a man with heavy eyelids. A short haired women in a pin striped suit chortled. A Professor in gray tweeds guffawed.

"Luck often enabled Machiavelli's characters to succeed," I said. "I once saw Strauss's opera *Die Fledermaus,* a nineteenth century opera. It embodied Machiavelli's principles of doing good if enjoyable, but abandoning it when tedious." Laughter. "Timeless human foibles and hypocrisy kept audiences amused because they recognized those characters as themselves. Erasmus's *Praise of Folly* sensitized readers to their hypocrisy. The Renaissance deplored hypocrisy. Moderns make it a virtue." Everyone roared.

I finished by comparing human foibles from the fifteenth century with those of our era. My last remarks were: "People who are happiest, change with circumstances. If they do, good for them. Even if feigning change, they're better off in the long run. Dramatic rebellion against circumstances creates conflict. By avoiding it, people learn what's worth fighting for; who they really are." Had I? I would be hypocritical *not* to. The audience gave me a standing ovation.

"What a delightful presentation from Prof. Darroway," said Prof. Jansen, grinning as he retook the podium. Any questions for her?"

A woman asked, "Was Machiavelli correct to suggest that a malleable spine helped to secure happiness in our greedy world?"

I gave a glib reply. "No. But many others beside Machiavelli, obviously, have. Politicians, for example. The Machiavellians, so-called."

A man up front, with a bristling mustache, asked, "Do you think this a veiled critique of the church, represented by the friar?"

"Well, I think Machiavelli was a more objective critic than Boccaccio, whom he often imitated. But then, he was objective about everyone. So, 'veiled?' No." An appreciative eruption. I added, "And Cardinal Giulio de' Medici, later Pope Clement VII, supported Machiavelli's historical research. While there was a general criticism of the clergy, it was not pointed. Or, if it were, some Medici popes didn't care." Laughter.

"Last question," Ike Jansen said.

"Do you think, Prof. Darroway, that the end justifies the means?"

"If the end is just, the means must of necessity be as well. So, yes."

The session over, people came up to thank me. One man handed me a reference he thought I should check out. The room emptied, but for one figure who strolled up the center aisle with one raised eyebrow and a slightly crooked smile. Oh my God! Wes.

"Hello, Candida. Wonderful to see you. This will be a great book." He hesitated, then hugged me.

"Wes. It's wonderful to see *you*," I repeated lamely. Thank you for your compliments."

"Appraisals, rather. I heard about your promotion. Congratulations. Your wedding, son. Thank you for sending announcements. That was thoughtful. How is it being married? a mother? An Associate Prof? You must be happy, and deserve to be. But you look so thin, Candida. Are you eating? A husband, toddler, a job at Cal might wear anyone down. Do look after yourself."

"I...I try. To look after myself, my boy. But you haven't heard..." I couldn't finish. By now everyone was either off to another lecture or the bar. Camaraderie. Gossip about mutual acquaintances. Criticism of a dreadful speech one of your critics gave. The fun part? Staying on top. Looking impressive. Making contacts. Conquests. Academics were often conquistadors. Duane crossed my mind again.

"Candida. What's wrong?" My head on the podium, I cried as if tears could wash away the pain.

"Wes," I said, taking his handkerchief, "Sean died last year. Killed, on a bike, at Sather Gate. Kid ran a red light. Sean went flying. They couldn't resuscitate him. My father-in-law helps me make house payments. Dad pays the taxes. But life is miserable now. So I look terrible." I was weeping. Wes was shaken.

"You couldn't look terrible." He stroked my hair and lifted my chin gently upward. "Tears later. A drink at the bar now. Everyone else is. Why shouldn't we? I can't think of two people more in need. Could we dine afterward?"

I was free. Ike Jansen forgot to invite me to dine with the panel. A drink would do me good. My eyes must have been red like Shana's; my make-up smeared. The bar would be dark.

"Give me a minute." Powder helped hide my red nose, dark circled eyes. Lipstick needed reapplying; hair fluffing. The necklace stayed in my purse.

"You look your old self, Candida. Magic in make-up." He had always been so encouraging.

Wes explained his presence. "Didn't come for the convention, Candida. Got the program, but you were not on it. I'm here because my first cousin, Randolph Spotswood, lives here; though not for much longer. He's in hospice. Pancreatic cancer. We were close as boys, a year apart. I came to pay a last visit. I'm feeling rather mortal myself. Your loss is worse. I am so sorry."

We went down to the bar, silent in the elevator. It was dark there. Hidden in a booth, I ordered a Black Russian, Wes, a Manhattan. We talked of our lives, not love. Of the group. Of cards received from friends made that summer. Wes had sent a gift to Arnold and Anne, too. He had a letter from them after they returned to Brookline, Mass. Their Caribbean honeymoon lasted three months. Ralph was writing an article on Etruscan burial rites for *National Geographic*. Jonah had invited Wes to visit in San Francisco–whenever. And Mindy was half-way through a master's degree at Cal.

"I know. She's a psychology major," I said. I see her on campus occasionally. Did you know Allison Collins had a little boy? Ian's, conceived after Trastevere in the Principi. Agatha and Ian have adopted him."

"A precious wedding gift," Wes said, smiling.

"Jonah told me," I confided, "that Barry Schwartz got rid of his Peruvian nanny–Myrna followed him up those outer stairs and found out. Their twins are in second grade now. Barry takes them to school; Myrna picks them up. Maria is now Barry's father's "nurse" in Palm Springs. So now Mrs. Schwartz gets her beautician's full attention." Wes laughed.

"Time to change partners again," he quipped. Then, realizing how that sounded, looked stricken.

"Forget it. Slip of the tongue."

He told me about Sam and Matilda. Andrea Smithwitch sent the news. I believed it.

"Andrea said Sam is living with Matilda in the Sforza Castle. He's her driver, protector, like her son. He's given up drinking and taken up painting; sold some in a gallery near the Duomo. He takes Matilda to La Scala and has learned Italian. Andrea ran into Samantha at a charity ball. Samantha's got a new lover in her cottage."

"I, too, heard from Matilda," I told him. "Did you know that after she signed the contract for her apartment the museum got the two rings confused? They gave her back the original. She didn't suspect a thing until Prof. Balestreri asked if he might examine it again. He discovered that the museum had returned her heirloom." Wes laughed so hard I thought he might tip his glass over, and moved it out of harm's way.

"Now the fake one's in the castle vault. Jonah advised Matilda not to tell a soul." Wes tossed back the last of his Manhattan and praised Jonah's business acumen.

"If the museum's experts couldn't tell the difference, tourists at a show won't, either. I assume Sam wasn't told. Matilda can keep a secret. She's a Visconti. Her granddaughter Elisabeth should get the 'copy,' i.e., the original, if anybody does. After all, the Sforza were as predatory as the Visconti. It cannot *be* returned to its rightful owner. Jonah gave her good advice." He ordered a second Manhattan and gave me the cherry, as he always had in Italy.

I was nursing my Black Russian. Half empty. I had a home. A son. Grand in–laws. Closer relations with my parents. Friends. A great job. And two or three more hours of Wes Spotswood. My glass was filling.

"Wes, did you know that Matt and Molly are the parents of a two year old girl and Molly's expecting again? They're having this one by C–section when the time comes." He hadn't heard.

"Arnold and Anne came to my wedding, Wes."

"Yes, I knew that. Anne gave up trying to write that novel about our tour. She found the characters either too predictable or too unpredictable. She was, uh, … shocked that we hadn't….married. Each other, I mean. She was disturbed by Ferrell's games and thought he might have been the reason. That we didn't marry."

"Oh, we know better," I replied. "We were flung together. Like characters in *Mandragola*. We did what served at the time. Even if it wasn't for always." A long pause.

I broke it. "By the way, Roger Garvey's Secretary, Alice Harvey, was Charles Clark's lover. She shared whatever extra profits he raked off when he gave us cheaper digs. Garvey fired her. But he and Jonah decided not to press charges. Still, you should know that we were being gamed." Wes was dumbfounded.

"Imagine," he murmured.

"Neither Rob not Jonah figured it out," I responded. "We expected honesty."

Wes looked steadily at me. "Your name means naïve. But most good people *are* naïve–unprepared for dishonesty."

I told him how Rob had never mentioned the Milan party, but had helped set up my new office. I didn't mention how that led to finding Sean. Our lives, mine and Wes's, stopped in Milan, and never started again until this afternoon. Though this could hardly be a start. A re-capitulation, merely, like the third movement of a sonata. A restatement of a minor theme in the sonata of our two lives.

We met in the lobby for dinner. Under a purple parrot I wore a black dinner suit, its long skirt slit up to one knee. A white satin halter blouse was tucked into the narrow belt. I wore Wes's necklace. Was it wrong? Too suggestive of our sensuous past? I hated to leave it in my room. It looked smashing with my outfit. My jacket, black velvet with a flaring satin collar, rested on the arm of my chair. People stared at me as I sat there. One professor came up to me, someone who had heard my lecture, and told me how much he enjoyed my speech.

"Thank you," I said. Then Wes stepped toward me from out the elevator doors.

"The necklace," he said simply. He held a yellow rose corsage. Carefully, he pinned it to the my jacket lapel, then held it up for me to slip into."

"Oh, Wes. You never gave me flowers before," I said involuntarily.

"Nope, I left that to Ferrell. Gold necklaces were more me." We laughed. My heart felt lighter.

The Two Lovers (*Les Deux Amants*) was a small restaurant, with vases of blue iris on each table. We ordered snails (*escargots*). Wes thought I should conquer my inner gardener. A cream of lobster soup (*crème de potage aux homards*) followed. I could have stopped there. Our entree was *entrecôte* of beef, rib steak served in a cognac sauce that was truly unbelievable. A simple green salad (*une salade simple*) next. Pear tarte (*tarte aux poires*) and filtered coffee (*café filtre*) for dessert.

"Wes, why did you agree to a French restaurant? You never were a Francophile."

"I did it on purpose. So we wouldn't have to relive nineteen Italian dinners that could only harrow already harrowed feelings." I could parse that statement. Wes left nothing to chance, despite a casual manner. Walking back to the hotel, we were silent. Upon entering the foyer, Prof. Jansen came over to apologize for forgetting to invite me to dinner.

"Tomorrow night? You are staying a few more days, aren't you? The panel wants to make your acquaintance. Bring your friend." He looked up at Wes."Ike Jansen, here, Marquette. Romance Languages."

"Wes Spotswood, Professor of Italian Renaissance history, University of Wisconsin. Thanks for the invitation, but I am not yet sure of my plans. Candida is, of course, free to do as she wishes."

"How about lunch, instead?" I asked Prof. Jansen. I'm not certain I can make dinner tomorrow." We agreed on lunch, and then Wes saw me up to floor twenty-nine.

"I'd like to see your view. It must be spectacular." His presence, not the view this time, made me giddy. I sat down in the armchair, and he walked over to the windows. The Ohio River. The Art Deco train station. Suburbs in three states (Ohio, Kentucky, Indiana), and the hills where as a boy, he had lived for several years, with the cousin now dying of cancer.

"I'd forgotten how bountiful nature was to this city, that river, those hills," he said simply. Then he sat down opposite me on the other side of a tiny cocktail table, pulling up the desk chair.

"Will you dine with me tomorrow?" he asked. "My ticket home is for Wednesday morning. How about one more dinner together? Or not. What do you prefer, Candida?"

"Let's," I agreed. *The second would probably be our last*, I thought.

"But—nothing more." We locked glances. Looking at him there, he seemed a ghost from a happy past. Handsome, sympathetic, not quite real. Or, rather, *too* real.

"Wonderful. Dinner tomorrow. I will leave you to your convention until then. I need to go back to see Randy. Shall we meet again at 5:30 in the bar? You choose the restaurant this time. I assure you, Candida, this has been the happiest evening I've had in five years." He rose, came up to my chair. Took my hand and kissed it. Then he left, leaving my heart skipping, and for the second time in eight months, nearly happy.

I attended two partial sessions next day. I entered one posted "Ariosto in Mantova"—a city I knew well—but a session I left after the first speech. I went shopping. I bought a necklace for Sybil, a scarf for Teresa, and a lapel pin for my mother. For Les, ten hand puppets.

Back at the hotel, a poster read, "Laura, the Real Woman, not Petrarch's Paragon." Petrarch was Boccaccio's friend. The lectures were amusing, but not scholarly. The speakers were graduate students, and like my own students, they felt that imagination and flippancy could cloak a myriad of research omissions, undocumented conclusions.

I took the elevator to the twenty-ninth floor, showered, changed. Conventions give some ersatz glamour to professors' lives. The less fusty ones. I wore a black and rose wool dress with a short flared skirt, appliqued flowers on top, three-quarter sleeves, black skirt. With it, a double strand of pink pearls. The effect was arresting. I had never worn this dress. Sean did not like the top. Sybil bought it for me in a fashionable designer's shop off Union Square. Her son thought it garish. Men.

The bar was crowded. But Wes and I found the same booth as before, and ordered the same drinks. He reached over to outline one of the appliqués with a fingertip.

"Wonderful handicraft," he said. "Lovely dress, Candida. You are a living portrait." My heart skipped a beat. Wes discussed our tour—our whole relationship was one trip, plus phone calls when we returned.

"Last night we analyzed our fellow tourists. Now I want to hear about the places in Italy you preferred." I thought a moment.

"Orvieto. Todi. Urbino. San Gimignano. Siena. Florence."

"Not Rome? Not Venice?"

"Oh, well. In Rome I was so unsure that I could get us into a central five star. And Ferrell was playing me false; and then, he brought me lilies. It caught me off base."

"And Venice?" Wes pressed.

"I knew it too well. Charles stuck us on the Lido; the group ganged up. I had to escape. You were peeved."

"Yes. Not because you went to Trieste. Rather, that you did not trust me enough to tell me your destination. I was worried sick about your safety."

"You feared I would have an accident?" I queried.

"I was unable to say what I feared, some sort of injury, yes. The unknown terrifies those left behind."

"And you, Wes?" I changed the subject. I didn't dare ask him about his love life. "How are you managing in Madison? Any adventures?

"Oh, yes. I was Acting Dean for three years. I quit. My adventures with faculty were grotesque; many self–promoters wanting to best their adversaries. I got no research done. I sat through endless meetings. Alienated two dear friends. After I quit, I finished a book on the end of the Medici dynasty. It has had good reviews."

That night I chose an Italian place around the corner from our French one. We ordered some favorite dishes, including potato dumplings (*gnòchi,*) and liver (*fegato veneziano*), with caramel cream pudding (*crema caramele*) and espresso to finish. I spoke Italian with the waiter.

Years dropped from my shoulders. I felt almost hopeful. Wes had to leave by ten to get enough sleep to make a nine A.M. plane to Madison. That morning we breakfasted early, but barely spoke. Every time I looked up to say something, he looked down to avoid my gaze. The reverse was also true.

"Who tied our tongues last night?" he asked. "The waiter, the liver or the pudding?"

"Wes, we have gone through this before. A plane takes you away. Probably, forever."

"Nonsense. Not this time. I'll catch *all* your speeches. I'd catch *you* if it were practical."

"But it isn't," I said without emphasis. He got up and carried his small suitcase to the lobby. I stood outside with him until his taxi arrived. "At least we won't have another ghoulish airport scene like that in Milan," I said, my voice cracking.

"I'll phone, Candida. I have your new number. You have mine. You need strength for Les, so keep eating." He paused. "Call me if anything, and I mean *anything*, troubles you. Call if you just need a friendly ear to bend." The taxi came and swallowed him.

I attended several sessions on Wednesday. I kept rhyming 'Wes' with 'Les.' It sounded so cheery. I lunched with three members of the Machiavelli group. Polly had left. Ike Jansen paid for my lunch.

"I promised "Murt" to treat you well, and so far, I haven't," he lamented. I protested that he had been very kind. I did not tell him why.

I left on Thursday, arriving at Oakland Airport at 5:00 P.M. Dad O'Connor picked me up.

"Welcome home, daughter," he said. We sped across the Bay Bridge in his Mercedes. Les was delirious with joy when I arrived. He was several months past four. His little arms clutching my legs made me lose my balance. "Easy, superman," I yelled. I picked him up, all warm and wiggly, full of life. My life. Sean's. He was the heir apparent to it and to this mansion.

I gave Sybil the necklace I'd bought for her in Cincinnati. It was so right for her—onyx and pearls, with little gold beads in between. She put it right on, hugging me. "I love it," she burbled. "It's so me." Les tore into his hand puppets. "Thanks, Mommy," he yelled, and went off wiggling his fingers, wearing Pinocchio and Mickey Mouse on his left hand, the big bad wolf and Red Riding Hood on the other.

I got back to teaching and taking care of my big house and little son. Wes called Thursday night. He called Friday and Saturday, too. When he missed Sunday, I called him. He was sad. His cousin had just passed away.

"But happier for your having visited him, Wes. You made his passing easier."

Now Wes was making my life easier. These days when I came home from work there was the certainty of his calling. Usually after I had put Les to bed with a story. Then Wes. I went to bed smiling.

Six weeks later he phoned on Saturday, at 8:00 A.M. I knew something had happened. What?

"Candida? I have some news to share." My heart wobbled. Had he met a woman? A grad student? Did he have an incurable disease?

"What?" I yelled into the receiver.

"Something good, dear girl. I have been offered the Chair of Renaissance History–at Cal. Shall I accept?" I began shaking and dropped the phone.

"Candida? Are you there? Have you dropped something?"

"The phone. I was shaking so it fell. Yes. Take it, Wes. Oh, take it."

Early the next day Sunday, I was still in my housecoat and Les was playing on the kitchen floor with his plastic trains. The doorbell rang.

I ran down the hall to the door. There stood Wes, his smile crooked, his eyebrow raised.

"Hello, Wes. I hoped it would be you. I felt it would be. You took the red-eye, didn't you?"

"Yep. Think of the money I saved. The sleep. Sorry I didn't warn you first. I just had to see you, Candida."

Les, missing me, and sensing something important was up, came running down the hall in his sleeper with the rabbit feet, carrying his engine in one hand and his little raggedy blanket in the other. Spotting Wes, he looked up. His green eyes blinked, and his red curls cascaded over his forehead.

"And who are you?" Wes asked, bending down to look at my boy from near his own height.

"Lester. I'm Lester David O'Connor."

"And what do they call you at pre-school?" Wes asked.

"Les. They call me Les." Then, thinking a moment, my son asked this stranger, "Are you going to stay around for a while?" Wes looked at the boy and picked him up, train, blanket and all. Then he looked at me, with one eyebrow arched. I nodded.

"Les, I'm Wes Spotswood. And yes, I am going to stay around a long while. I'm thinking, forever."

Wes and I were married at B'nai Israel, Molly's ultra Reformed Berkeley synagogue. We didn't use the Unitarian church where I had married Sean. Too unnerving. A judge? We weren't criminals. Molly took charge.

"Our Rabbi Flexner was once a beatnik in New York's Soho district. He got his rabbinical training in a Conservative rabbinical school, but grew more and more Reformed after ordination. He moved west. B'nai Israel is a soulful admixture of religious drop-outs, drop-ins, singles, families. Our Outreach Program is to all who have saved remnants of former faiths, but wish to participate in Jewish life, too–for whatever reason. You and Wes could find a home there, Candida. I'm sure Rabbi Flexner would marry you, your mother being Jewish. Atheism doesn't count here. We have plenty of doubters. A lot of ex-Unitarians, some cool ex-Presbyterians. Shall I ask?"

Wes and I had an appointment with the rabbi that very afternoon. He lived next door to the Temple, once a Baptist church, now bearing a blue and white Jewish star over the door where once had been a cross. We walked into the temple with him to get a feel for the sanctuary. The original altar was gone, but a large organ, a choir loft, and a painted blue domed roof with little windows all 'round remained. Blue carpet. Byzantine. Except for the lack of a cross. Instead, the Star of David, and the bimah with the Torah.

Flexner was about Wes's age, gray haired, wiry. I explained my parentage. Wes volunteered that he was a *pro forma* Lutheran. He told Flexner his father's family had had one Jewish relative who entered his family from Alsace in the seventeenth century, and his mother's side had had two Jewish converts, one Rhenish, from Rudesheim, and one from Lausanne, Switzerland, both in the eighteenth. Wes told Flexner that he had mastered Hebrew in his seminary days, and had on several occasions participated in Madison's Reformed Friday night services.

Whereupon the two men started a lively discussion in Hebrew about spirituality and our purpose on earth. I didn't know Hebrew. I didn't know about our purpose on earth. Wasn't it to be happy?

Later, in Flexner's study, an untidy space off his living room, they talked of ethics and politics, in English. The rabbi was fascinated to learn that Sean had been raised an Episcopalian, became a Jesuit and had married me in a Unitarian church, to which we had belonged for over four years. He was glad I had a son. He hoped I would have more, and cocked his head at Wes. Wes smiled, but didn't say anything. Flexner asked if we wanted a huppa (wedding arch). Danceable music and a huppa, yes.

An April wedding, my bridesmaids all lavender and yellow. They included Molly, Anita, Mindy, Myrna and Allison, plus Wes's daughter, Gillian, twenty-one. Both Anita, expecting her second child, and Molly, her third, were large and thought they ought not be bridesmaids. But I argued that "Virginity is where the heart is,"–my own contribution to cardiology, gynecology. A maternity shop on Shattuck stocked maternity bridesmaids' gowns, in both yellow and lavender.

As it turned out, B'nai Israel's congregation was as musically adept as it was culturally diverse. The choir practiced weekly tambourines, bagpipes, cymbals and clappers (the latter two ancient Jewish instruments). Molly got Uncle Izzy to come sing. Rabbi Flexner played guitar. We had prayers chanted in Hebrew. Flexner told us the earliest Hebrew chants were related to the earliest Christian ones–and part of the congregation were Christians anyway–as were Dad's relatives; Sean's. This congregation had two families of Indian Jews who used clappers in chanting, and a Chinese Jewish couple who did chants in Chinese and Hebrew, using gongs.

"Will the huppa have flowers?" I had asked Rabbi Flexner.

"Of course. Flowers were signs of God's beneficence to man."

We chose a Sunday in April, 1978, so that Easter vacation (which fell very near Passover that year) could provide a short space for our honeymoon before school started up again.

Our wedding day arrived. My long sleeved gown was elegant, ivory satin, with sweeping train, a perfect size six. I chose a fingertip veil with a chaplet of fake pearls. Everyone said I was a beautiful bride. I felt beautiful. Wes assured me I was, as did Mom, Teresa, Sybil and Dad O'Connor. Even my own father, formerly distant, said I looked "grand" before escorting me down the aisle for the second time.

The huppa was decorated with lilies of the valley, not the kind Rob had sent me in Italy. Their little white bells filled the sanctuary with a divine scent. Les was our ring-bearer. Rabbi Flexner finished his service. Wes and I were pronounced "man and wife," and then we both stepped on the wine glass we had sipped from during the ceremony— red Mogen David wine.

From Temple B'nai Israel we shot up the hills to the Claremont Hotel, where, after some wonderful waltzing, everyone formed a circle and danced the hora. I had to kick off my high heels to do it without killing myself, but Molly and Anita sat this dance out, the hora being no exercise for ladies nearing their due date.

Reed accompanied Rabbi Flexner on his clarinet. Wes insisted we invite Rob, who, to my surprise, Rob accepted, and even did a cornet solo that lasted fifteen bars, delighting everyone with its clear tones, jazzy beat. Wes was as good at the hora as Rob was on the cornet. After that, we waltzed, and the younger set moved on to such disco dances as the Hustle, the Click Clack, the Bus Stop and The Skate. I didn't know the steps to these, nor did Wes. But we managed to dance to "Night Fever" by the Bee Gees; followed by a last waltz "The Anniversary Song" (Al Jolson) which always made older folks cry. Dad O'Connor cut in on us; then my own father cut in on him. I knew they were going to be paternal rivals for my affection and Les's. It was a nice feeling, with Wes and Les's two granddads the same age. Some ambivalence. But much in common. The human condition was itself ambivalent. Machiavelli and Montaigne were experts on that.

There were Yemenite chants from cantor Abraham Zevi Idelsohn's ten vol. work, *Thesauraus of Hebrew Oriental Melodies*. His most famous piece, "Come, Let's Rejoice" (*Hava Nagila*) put broad smiles on all faces, because it was so familiar. I noticed Mom, wearing the pin

I had bought her in Cincinnati, sang with tears running down her face. Bubbie Brondel had taught her that song as a child, and she, me.

Ferrell seemed peculiarly happy to see Wes again, and vice versa. Men are strange. Who would have guessed it? Rob informed us that he was engaged to be married to an old colleague from Kansas and had never been so happy. He had taken a professorship at Kansas City at the University there, and was looking forward to returning to his birth state in summer for his wedding, his new teaching post. We were happy for him and told him so. He beamed at us and kissed me on the cheek.

Sybil and Dad O'Connor sat with their friends the Pelatierras, and later, Rob. Teresa, Matron of Honor, sat with Wes's son, David, an usher, and daughter Gillian, and Wes's Best Man, David Seagram, a handsome man nearly Teresa's age. The last two were having an animated discussion. Mr. Seagram asked if he might write to Teresa, and she drew her ranch card out of her evening purse. She never let on that she was an Italian countess, so I knew he had one surprise in store at least. I guessed flights between Milwaukee and San Jose would rise over time.

EPILOGUE

Wes adopted Les after our weeklong honeymoon in Vancouver. It had to be a short one because school started the day after our return. To spare the O'Connors pain, Les's adoption papers read, "Lester David Spotswood–O'Connor." Two years later, I stunned Wes with a little girl, whom we named Pandora Grace; hazel eyes, brown hair, and one eyebrow that went up when she was startled. When asked about her name, part pagan, part Christian, Wes answered:

"Pandora, Candida's choice, is classical, referring to the trouble she let loose from a box. I added Grace, which is Christian. Through Grace troubles are diminished by hope, or if you prefer, faith. Salvation from troubles is sometimes closer than you imagine." When asked to explain, he answered, "Sometimes troubles fly out into the world before chance, Grace, or just plain luck arrive to make everything right again. That's what happened to Candida and me."

"I, Candida Darroway O'Connor Spotswood, could not have put it better myself."

The End

CPSIA information can be obtained
at www.lCGtesting.com
Printed in the USA
FFOW03n2240091215
19508FF